BOOKS BY TERRY C. JOHNSTON

Cry of the Hawk
Winter Rain
Dream Catcher

Carry the Wind
BorderLords
One-Eyed Dream

Dance on the Wind
Buffalo Palace
Crack in the Sky
Ride the Moon Down
Death Rattle

SONS OF THE PLAINS NOVELS
Long Winter Gone
Seize the Sky
Whisper of the Wolf

THE PLAINSMEN NOVELS
Sioux Dawn
Red Cloud's Revenge
The Stalkers
Black Sun
Devil's Backbone
Shadow Riders
Dying Thunder
Blood Song
Reap the Whirlwind
Trumpet on the Land
A Cold Day in Hell
Wolf Mountain Moon
Ashes of Heaven
Cries From the Earth

BANTAM BOOKS

New York
Toronto
London
Sydney
Auckland

Praise for the novels

RIDE THE MOON DOWN

"Bass is a near-mythic Davy Crockett-like character, but author Johnston imbues him with Everyman emotions. . . . Readers of past Bass adventures will not be disappointed."

—*Booklist*

DANCE ON THE WIND

"A good book . . . not only gives readers a wonderful story, but also provides vivid slices of history that surround the colorful characters."

—Dee Brown, author of
Bury My Heart at Wounded Knee

"Packed with people, action, and emotion . . . makes you wish it would never end."

—Clive Cussler

BUFFALO PALACE

"Rich in historical lore and dramatic description, this is a first-rate addition to a solid series, a rousing tale of one man's search for independence in the unspoiled beauty of the old West."

—*Publishers Weekly*

"Terry C. Johnston has redefined the concept of the Western hero. . . . The author's attention to detail and authenticity, coupled with his ability to spin a darned good yarn, makes it easy to see why Johnston is today's best-selling frontier novelist. He's one of a handful that truly knows the territory."

—*Chicago Tribune*

CRACK IN THE SKY

"No one does it better than Terry Johnston. He has emerged as one of the great frontier historical novelists of our generation."

—*Tulsa World*

DEATH RATTLE

TERRY C. JOHNSTON

DEATH RATTLE

A Bantam Book

PUBLISHING HISTORY
Bantam hardcover published December 1999
Bantam mass market edition / June 2000

Map by Jeffrey L. Ward.

Library of Congress Catalog Card Number: 99-15684.

ISBN 0-553-57286-5

Published simultaneously in the United States and Canada

Bantam Books are published by Bantam Books, a division of Random
House, Inc. Its trademark, consisting of the words "Bantam Books"
and the portrayal of a rooster, is Registered in U.S. Patent and Trademark Office and in other countries. Marca Registrada. Bantam
Books, 1540 Broadway, New York, New York 10036.

PRINTED IN THE UNITED STATES OF AMERICA

OPM   10   9   8   7   6   5   4   3   2   1

*For all the trails
he has guided me down,
I dedicate this story
to my old Bantam friend,
Charlie Newland—
you've always been there
to lead the way!*

Let us live o'er those deeds again
Of trap-line, camp and desperate fray;
Where roved the long-haired mountainmen
Who broke the trails and led the way.

—EDWIN L. SABIN, *"Old" Jim
Bridger on the Moccasin Trail*

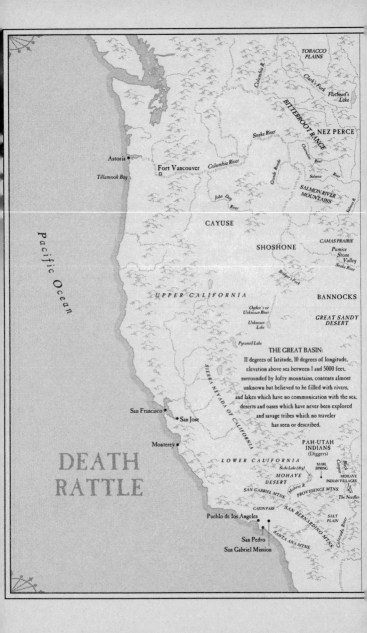

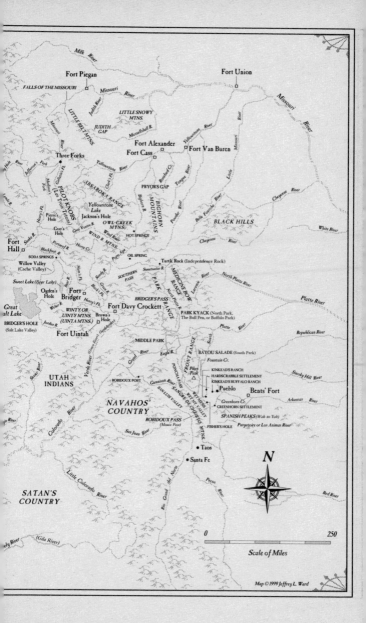

Map © 1999 Jeffrey L. Ward

DEATH RATTLE

1

Damn, if this dead mule didn't smell like a month-old grizzly-gutted badger!

Titus Bass swiped the back of his black, powder-grimed hand under his nose and snorted with that first faint hint of a stench strong enough to make his eyes water. Without lingering, he spilled enough grains of the fine four-F priming powder into the pan, then carefully raised his head over the dead mule's still-warm rib cage.

The sonsabitches were gathering off to the left, over there by big Shad Sweete's side of the ring. Really more of a crude oval the two dozen of them had quickly formed around this collection of ancient tree stumps when they started dropping every last one of their saddle stock and pack animals with a lead ball in the brain.

"Dun' shoot till you're sure!" Henry Fraeb was bellowing again.

He'd repeated it over and over so many times it was beginning to nettle the gray-haired Bass. "We ain't none of us lop-eared pilgrims, Frapp!" he growled back at the trapping brigade leader.

The man they called Ol' Frapp twisted round on that

one leg he was kneeling on, spitting a ball out of his gopher-stuffed cheek into his sweaty palm. "Gottammit! Don't you tink I know ebbery wund of you niggurs?"

"We'll make 'em come, Frapp!" Elias Kersey shouted from the east side of their horse-and-mule breastworks, shoving a sprig of long, dusty-blond hair out of his eyes.

"Don't you worry none 'bout us!" another man growled down Bass's right.

"Here they come again!" arose the alarm.

Titus twisted, rolling on his hip so he could peer behind him at the far side of the narrow oval, where some of the defenders hunkered behind a stump here or there. Then his eyes slowly climbed over the heads of those other beaver trappers as they all sat entranced, every eye fixed on the half-a-thousand. Sure was a pretty sight the way those horsemen had been forming themselves up over yonder after every charge, gathering upon that wide breast of bottom ground where the warriors knew they were just out of range of the white man's long-barreled flinters.

About as savvy as Blackfoot, Bass ruminated as he watched the naked riders start to spill out in two directions, like a mountain torrent tumbling past a huge boulder plopped squarely in the middle of a creek. Foaming and roiling, building up force as it was hurtled into that narrow space between the boulder and the grassy banks itself, huge drops and narrow sheets of mist rising from the torrent into shafts of shimmering sunlight—

"Shoot when you're sure!" Jake Corn reminded them, the expression on his dark face gone cloudy.

"One nigger at a time!" Reuben Purcell cried out as the hoofbeats threatened to drown out every other sound in this river valley. "One red nigger at a time, my Mamma Purcell allays said!"

Sure as spit, these Indians had grown smart about the white man's guns, maybe hankering to have a white-man gun for their own.

From the hairstyle, the way they made themselves up, Bass figured them to be Sioux. He knowed Sioux. A bunch of them had jumped him and Sweete, Waits-by-the-Water, and the young'uns too, couple summers back when they were returning down the Vermillion, making for Fort Davy Crockett on the Green. In that scrap Titus had been close enough to see the smeared, dust-furred colors of their paint, close enough to smell the old grease on their braids and forehead roaches. Not till then—no, he'd never seen a Sioux before.

But he and Shad had hacked their way out of that war party and made a desperate run for the fort.

Sioux.

If that didn't mean things was changing in the mountains, nothing else did. Why—to think of Sioux on this side of the divide. Damn, if that hoss didn't take the circle—

Titus picked one out. Made a fist of his left hand and rested the bottom of the fullstock flintlock on it as he nestled his cheekbone down in place and dragged the hammer back to full cock.

Down the barrel now that rider somehow didn't look to be Sioux. Most of them on this end of their grand, fronted charge didn't appear to be similar to the warriors who had jumped him and Shad two years back. He guessed Cheyenne.

The way they started to stream past, peeling away like the layers of a wild onion Waits gathered in the damps of the river bottoms, he'd have to lead the son of a bitch a little. The warrior took the outside of the procession, screaming and shaking his bow after each arrow he fired.

Titus held a half breath on that bare, glistening chest—finding no showy hair-pipe breast ornament suspended from that horseman's neck. Instead, the warrior had circled several places on his flesh with bright red vermillion paint. Likely his white, puckered, hanging scars, directly above each nipple where he'd strung himself up to a sun-dance tree. And a couple more, long ones though, down low along his ribs. Wounds from battle he proudly exhibited for all to see. Let his enemies know he was invincible.

Bass held a little longer, then raised the front blade of his sights to the Indian's head and eased off to the right a good yard. What with the way the whole bunch was tearing toward the white men's corral at an angle, there was still a drop in the slope—

He was surprised when the gun roared, feeling the familiar slam of the Derringer's iron butt plate against the pocket of his right shoulder.

What with the muzzle smoke hanging close in the still, summer air, Bass was unable to see if his shot went home. But as the parade of screaming horsemen thundered past his side of the breastworks, he did notice that a handful of ponies raced by without riders. One of those animals had likely carried the big fella with the painted scars.

Farther back in the stream, other horsemen were slowing now, reining this way and that to avoid a horse that had plunged headlong and flipped, pitching its rider into the air. Some of the warriors slowed even more; two-by-two they leaned off their ponies to scoop up a wounded or dead comrade, dragging his limp body back across the coarse, sun-seared grass that crackled and snapped, hooves clawing at the powdery dust that rose in tiny puffs with each hoofbeat, the dead man's legs flying and flopping over every clump of sage, feet crazily bouncing, wildly sailing against the pale, summer-burnt-blue sky.

Few of their arrows made it all the way to the breastworks they had formed out of those sixty or more animals. The half-a-thousand clearly figured to make this a fight of bravery runs while the waterless white men slowly ran out of powder and lead.

At first some of the trappers had hesitated dropping all the horses and mules. They bunched their nervous animals together, tying them off nose-to-nose, two-by-two. But with those first frantic, wholesale charges, the Sioux and Cheyenne managed to hit enough of the animals in the outer ring that the saddle horses and pack mules grew unmanageable, threatening to drag off the few men who were struggling to hold on to them. Arrows quivered from withers and ribs, from bellies and flanks.

Then the first lead balls whistled in among Fraeb's men. Damn if those red bastards didn't have some smoothbore trade guns, fusils, old muskets—English to be sure. Maybe even some captured rifles too—taken off

the body of a free man killed here or there in the mountains. One less free trapper to fret himself over the death
of the beaver trade.

Arrows were one thing, but those smoothbore fusils
were a matter altogether different. While such weapons
didn't have the range of the trappers' rifles, the muskets
could nonetheless hurl enough lead through their remuda
that those Indians could start whittling the white
men down.

There were a half dozen horses and mules thrashing
and squealing on the ground already by the time the St.
Louis–born German growled his thick, guttural command.

"Drob de hurses!" Fraeb shouted. "Drob dem,
ebbery one!"

Many of those two dozen mountain men grumbled as
they shoved and shouldered the frightened animals apart
in a flurry. But every one of them did what they knew
needed doing. Down the big brutes started to fall in a
spray of phlegm and piss as the muzzles of pistols were
pressed against ears and the triggers pulled. A stinking
mess of hot horse urine splashing everyone for yards
around, bowels spewing the fragrant, steamy dung from
that good grass the horses pastured on two days back.

In those first moments of sheer deafening terror, Bass
even smelled the recognizable, telltale odor of gut. Glancing over his shoulder, he had watched as the long coil of
purple-white intestine snaked out of the bullet hole in
that mule's belly so that the animal itself and other horses
tromped and tromped and tromped in nervous fear and
pain, yanking every last foot of gut out of the dying pack
animal's belly.

He had quickly poured some powder into the pan of
his belt pistol, lunged over a horse already thrashing its
way into eternity, and skidded to a halt beside the very
mule that had been his companion ever since that momentous birthday in Taos.

Stuffing his left hand under the horsehair halter, his
fingers went white as he jerked back on the mule's head,
shouting in what he hoped would be a familiar voice, a

calming voice. As a horse went down behind Titus, one of its slashing hooves clipped the trapper across the back of his calf and he crumpled to his knees. Gritting his teeth with the pain as he struggled back onto his feet, Bass yanked on the mule's halter again and shouted as he pressed the muzzle of the short-barreled .54 just in front of the mare's ear.

"Steady, girl," he whimpered now. Tears streaming. Some of anger. Some of regret too. Lots of regret. Then pulled the trigger.

He had gripped the halter as she pitched onto her forelegs, her back legs kicking some, struggling to rise, until she rolled onto her side. Nestled now in the shadow of her body lay that dirty, grass-crusted rumple of her gut.

Titus knelt quickly at the head, staring a moment at the eyes that would quickly glaze, watching the last flexing of the wide, gummy nostrils as the head slowly relaxed, easing away from him.

"Good-bye, girl," he whispered, the words sour on his tongue.

Bass patted the mule between the eyes, then quickly vaulted to his feet and wheeled around to reload. Prepared to continue the slaughter that was their only hope of living out this day.

He remembered another mule, the old farm animal that had grown old as Titus had grown up on that little farm back near Rabbit Hash, Boone County, Kentucky, beside the Ohio River. And then he sensed a cold stab of pain remembering Hannah. The best damned four-legged friend a free man could ever have in these here mountains. Hannah—

The trappers dropped them all. Fraeb and some others still hollered orders above the tumult. Every man jack of them knew what was at stake. The resistant, dying animals must have smelled the dung and the piss, must have winded the blood of their companions already soaking into the dust and sun-stiffened grass of this late-summer morning. They dropped them one-by-one, and in twos as well. Until there was a crude oval of carcasses and what baggage the men could tear off the pack animals and get shoved down in those gaps between the big, sweaty bodies that would begin stinking before this day was done and night had settled upon them all like a benediction.

Twenty-four of them pitted against half a thousand Sioux and Cheyenne. Not to mention a hundred or more Arapaho who had showed up not long after the whole shebang got kicked off with that first noisy, hoof-rattling charge. Damned Arapaho must have been camped somewhere close and come running with all the hurraw and the gunfire.

Titus grinned humorlessly and pushed aside the one narrow braid that hung at his temple. The rest of his long, graying hair spilled over his shoulders like a curly shawl. All of it tied down with a faded black silk bandanna that also held a scrap of Indian hair over that round patch of naked skull left him so long ago. He thought on that bunch of Arapaho who had caught him alone many, many summers before—and stole his hair. Remembering how he eventually ran across the bastard who had taken his topknot . . . how he had lifted this small circle of hair from the crown of the scalper's head. Recalling how glorious it had been to take his revenge.

So Titus grinned: maybeso some of the bastard's relatives were in that bunch watching the Sioux and Cheyenne have at the white man's corral. Wouldn't be long now before those Arapaho would figure it was time to grab some fun of their own.

Glancing at the sky, Bass found the blazing sun over his shoulder. Long as they'd been fighting already, and it wasn't yet midmorning. That meant they were staring at a double handful of dead-slow hours behind these packs and stinking carcasses. And with the way the first of the women were starting to bristle along the crest of that hilltop yonder, the warriors weren't about to ride off anytime soon, not with the whole village showing up to chant and sing their men on to victory, on to daring feats of bravery, on to suicidal charges that would leave the bodies of one warrior after another sprawled in the grass and dust of that no-man's-land all around the trappers' corral. Bodies fallen too close to the rotting breastworks for other riders to dare reclaim.

Titus blinked and wiped the sweat out of his eyes with the sleeve of his faded, grease-stained calico shirt. And saw the flecks of blood already dried among the pattern of tiny flowers. The mule's blood. Bass glanced quickly at the sun once more, wondering if this was the last he would ever lay eyes on.

Would he ever see the coming sunset as he had promised himself summers and summers ago when he managed to ride away from that scalping, a half-dead shell of a man clinging to Hannah's back? Would he ever see another black mountain night with its brilliant dusting of stars as he lay by the fire, staring up at the endlessness of it all, Waits-by-the-Water's head nestled into his shoulder just after they had coupled flesh to flesh? Would he ever again see their children when they awoke each morning, clambering out of their blankets and tottering toward him as he fed the fire and started the coffee—eager to fling their little brown arms around his neck, squeezing him with what he always took as their utter joy in having another day to share together.

Together.

Oh, he wished he was with the three of them now.

How thankful he was that he had compelled Waits to remain behind with the little ones. If the three of them were here among these twenty-four ill-fated men now . . .

With the breakup of that last pitiful rendezvous shared by a few holdouts in the valley of the Green River, Bass had watched old friends disperse on the winds. Some gave up on the mountains and pointed their noses back east to what they had been. Others like Meek and Newell set a new course for Oregon country where the land was fertile and free.

But a hardy few had determined they would hang on, clinging to the last vestige of what had been their finest days. What had been their glory.

Never again would the big companies dispatch their

trapping brigades into the high country. There was no money to be made in trading supplies for beaver pelts at a summer rendezvous on the Wind, the Popo Agie, or some fork of the legendary Green. Bridger and Fraeb formed a new partnership and brought out that last, undersized pack train from St. Louis in '40. Afterward, while Bridger led a small band of trappers north, Fraeb and Joe Walker started for California with a few men of their own.

Bass marched his family north with Gabe's under-manned bunch. And when Bridger turned off for Black-foot country, Titus had steered east for Absaroka and the home of the Crow, his wife's people. There would always be beaver in that country—even if he had to climb higher, plunge deeper into the shadowy recesses than he had ever gone before. And, besides—traders like Tullock were handy enough with his post over at the mouth of the Tongue. He'd continue to trap close to the home of his wife's folk; trade when he needed resupply; and wait for beaver to rise.

The way beaver had before. The way it would again.

They had a fair enough winter that year—cold as the maw of hell for sure, but that only meant what beaver he brought to bait were furred up, seal-fat, and sleek. When the hardest of the weather broke, he took a small pack of his furs down to Fort Van Buren on the Yellowstone, only to find that Tullock couldn't offer him much at all in trade. So Titus bought what powder and lead he needed, an array of new hair ribbons for his woman, a pewter turtle for Magpie to suspend around her neck, and a tiny penny whistle for Flea.

How Bass marveled at the way that boy of his grew every time he returned to the village from his trapline or a trading venture. At least an inch or more every week Titus rode off to the hills. Even more so when he returned from a long journey to the Tongue. Flea was four winters old now, his beautiful sister to turn seven next spring, looking more and more like her mother with every season.

Where it used to break his heart at how Waits-by-the-

Water first hid her pox-ravaged face,* it now gave him comfort that she had made peace with what the terrible disease had cost her: not only the marred and pocked flesh but the loss of her brother. Every time Bass returned from the hills, come back from the wilderness to the bosom of his family, he quietly thanked the Grandfather for sparing this woman, the mother of his children, from the cursed disease that had decimated the northern mountains. And, he never neglected to thank the All-Maker for the days the two of them had yet to share.

With the arrival of spring following that last rendezvous, he decided to mosey south, taking a little time to trap if the country looked good—but intending above all else to be in the country of the upper Green come midsummer when Bridger planned to reunite with Fraeb. On the Green last year before going their separate ways, there had been serious talk of erecting a post of their own.

Damn, if that news didn't stir up a nest of hornets among the old holdouts! Hivernants the likes of Gabe and Frapp ready to give up on trapping beaver? The two of 'em turning trader?

Such black notions he had done his best to push out of his thoughts over that winter. No sense in his tying his mind in knots around something that was nothing more than talk. Why, Frapp and Gabe had been out in these here mountains pretty near from the beginning. If anyone else but himself knew beaver was bound to rise again—it was them two! But . . . when Gabe or Frapp gave up trapping and settled down to trade fixin's for furs, why— it meant nothing less than the old days was over for certain.

By the time Bass reached Black's Fork of the Green, he was nonetheless startled to discover that Bridger and his men had started laying down cottonwood logs, chinking them with clay from the riverbank. They had the walls and some of the roof done six weeks later when Fraeb

---

* *Ride the Moon Down*

and his outfit rode in from their exploratory expedition
to California, not one of their pack animals swaybacked
under furs. Not much of anything to show for all those
months and miles. Out west to the land of the Mexicans
Fraeb's outfit sold off all their beaver for some beans,
soap, tobacco, coffee, and sugar, along with seventeen
mules and a hundred mares. Not to mention trading for
the head-hammering *aquardiente* those Mexicans brewed
out there beyond the mountains.

After a little celebrating at their reunion, wetted down
with some whiskey Bridger traded off a small train of
emigrants bound for Oregon who had tarried at Gabe's
half-completed post long enough to recuperate their
stock, Fraeb proposed a short journey south by east
where the men might trap and make meat. Bridger stayed
behind with a handful to continue work on their post
before winter slammed its fist down on the valley of the
Green.

Bass chose trapping and hunting over the mindless
chores of a cabin-raising sodbuster. He figured he'd
pounded enough nails and shingled enough roofs back
east to last him the rest of his days.* So when Henry
Fraeb's twenty-two rode out for the Little Snake, Titus
went along. He reckoned on sniffing around some country he hadn't seen much of since he lost hair to the Arapaho. Might just be a man could find a few beaver curious
enough to come to bait.

Besides . . . among the old German's outfit were
some of the finest veterans still clinging to the old life in
the mountains. Yessirree! This hunt that would take them
into the coming fall might well be the last great hurrah
for them all.

Those long days of late summer seeped slowly past.
None of them ran across much beaver sign to speak of,
and where the men did tarry long enough to lay their
traps, they didn't have much success. Not like the old
days when a man could damn well club the flat-tails, they

---

* *Dance on the Wind*

were thick as porky quills! The hunting wasn't all that fair either. Game was pushed high into the hills. Bass and others figured the critters had been chivvied by the migrations of the Ute and Shoshone.

Turned out the game was driven off by the hunting forays of this huge village of wandering Sioux and Cheyenne, not to mention that band of tagalong Arapaho.

The sun had been up a good three hours that morning when one of Fraeb's outriders spotted a half dozen horsemen on the crest of the hill across the Little Snake.

"If'n they was Yuta, them riders be running down here first whack," Jake Corn snorted. His black beard extended right on down his neck and into his chest hair in one continuous mat. "Begging for tobaccy or red paint."

"Snakes too," Rube Purcell added. His greasy, matted, deerhide-brown hair was already flecked with snows of age. "Poor diggers them Snakes be."

"Those ain't either of 'em," Elias Kersey growled. "An' that's a yank on the devil's short-hairs!"

"Lookit 'em," Bass remarked. "Just watching us, easy as you please. Ain't friendly-like to stare so—is it, Frapp?"

The old German hawked up the last of the night-gather in his throat and spat. "Trouble is vhat dem niggurs lookin' at."

Fraeb picked four men to cross the river ahead of the rest, making for the far slope and those unfriendly horsemen. Stop a ways off and make some sign. See how the winds blew and the stick floats. Then the rest started their animals into the shallow river just up the Little Snake from the mouth of a narrow creek. The trappers had the last of the pack animals and spare horses across right about the time the first muffled gunshot reached them.

Every man jack jerked up in surprise, finding their four companions wheeling round and returning lickety-split, like Ol' Beelzebub himself was right on their tails, one of their number clinging the best he could to his horse's withers as they lumbered down the long slope. Behind them came the six strangers. And just behind that half dozen . . . it seemed the whole damned hillside suddenly sprouted redskins.

"Fort up! Fort up!" came the cry from nearly every throat as the four trappers sprinted their way.

Fraeb's twenty spun about, studying things this way, then that—when most decided they would have to make a stand of it right there with the river at their back.

"Pull off them packs for cover!" one of them bellowed.

But Bass knew right off there weren't enough packs to make barricades for them all. Not near enough supplies lashed to those pack saddles to hide behind, and sure as hell not any beaver bundles to speak of. One last-ditch thing to do.

"Put the horses down!" One of the bold ones gave voice to their predicament.

"Shoot the goddamned horses!" another voice trumpeted as the four scouts reined up in a swirl of dust and hit the ground running, reins in their hands.

That's when Titus could make out the yips and yells, the taunts and the cries—all those hundreds of voices rising above the dull booming thunder of thousands of hooves.

A tall redheaded youngster next to him came out of the saddle and was nearly jerked off his feet when his frightened mount reared. From the look on the man's pasty face Bass could tell this might well be the most brownskins the youngster had ever seen.

"Snub 'im up quick and shoot him!" Bass grumbled as he lunged over to help the redhead.

"Pistol?"

"Goddamned right." Then Titus turned his back and double-looped his own mule's lead rope around his left hand as he dragged the .54-caliber flinter from his belt with his right.

"Drob de goddamned hurses. Ebbery one!" Fraeb repeatedly roared as the first few animals started falling.

From the corner of his eye, Bass watched the redhead obey. As the mount's legs went out from under it, the horse nearly toppled the trapper. But redhead scrambled backward in time, spilling in a heap atop Titus's thrashing horse.

"You got a pack animal?" Bass demanded.

The redhead lunged onto his feet, craning his neck this way, and that, then shrugged. "Not no more."

"Get down and make ready to use that rifle of your'n," Titus ordered, then turned to bid farewell to the mule just a breath or two before the screeching horsemen dared to break across the flat into range of their powerful, far-reaching weapons.

He laid a hand on the mare's neck as she breathed her last, stroking the hide until she no longer quivered. Gazing out over the slopes where the warriors gathered just beneath the ranks of their women, children, and old men . . . when he saw her.

Clearly a woman. Dressed in the short fringed skirt that exposed her bare copper legs draped on either side of her brown-spotted pony. A short, sleeveless, fringed top hung from her shoulders where her unbound hair tossed on every hot gust of wind. Make no mistake: that was a woman. While the warriors were stripped to their breechclouts and moccasins, wearing medicine ornaments and power-inducing headdresses, the one intently watching the action from the hillside was clearly a woman—and probably a powerful one to boot.

Around her stood more than a double handful of attendants, young women and boys, all on foot. Together they joined in her high-pitched chants. She must be imploring the warriors to fight even harder, dare even more with each renewed assault.

"You see dat she-bitch?" the gruff voice asked in a masked whisper.

Bass turned to see Fraeb settling in beside him, joining him between the horse's fore and hind legs.

"Who she be, Frapp?"

The old German stared at the hillside, reflecting for a moment before answering. "She der princess."

"Princess?"

"Ya. Der princess dey fight for."

Titus couldn't quite believe how preposterous it

sounded. "A woman's giving the orders to all them bucks?"

Elias Kersey nodded. "That bitch makes medicine for them bucks to rub us out."

Now Titus had to grudgingly agree, as an idea dawned on him. "Yeah, medicine. I'll bet if one of us knocked that damn princess down—them brownskins see their own medicine shrivel up like salt on your ol' pecker, Frapp."

"She come close your side, Titass—you knock her down, ya?" Fraeb asked as he rocked back onto his hands and knees to crawl off.

Licking his dirty thumb and brushing it over the front blade at the end of his rifle barrel, Bass vowed, "See if I can do just that."

Back over at the far end of the oval after the horsemen made their twelfth deafening rush on the corral, Henry Fraeb once more was squealing out orders, ordering more of the men to hold off firing—thereby making sure they would have at least half the guns loaded at all times. No more than a dozen were to fire at once, he noisily reminded them again and again after every smoky volley. No less than a dozen must be ready should the whole hillside erupt in an avalanche of hooves and bows, flooding in a great rush for the white man's corral.

But charge after charge, the five hundred never thundered down the long slope and across the river bottom at once, never dared press close to that maze of deadfall and tree stumps, rushing en masse against that corral of buffalo robes, blankets, and bloating carcasses. As the morning wore on, the ground in front of the dead, stinking horses and mules reminded Bass of an autumn field of barren, windblown cornstalks. Almost as many arrow shafts bristled from those huge animals the mountain men had sacrificed to make this last stand.

Well before the sun climbed to mid-sky, two of the trappers lay dead, and the rest were grumbling with thirst. The river lay all too seductively close at their backs. Its faint, late-summer gurgle almost loud enough to hear—were it not for the grunts of the sweating men as they reloaded their rifles, or hurriedly refilled their powder horns from the small kegs pulled from among the scattered baggage. A peaceful, bucolic gurgle as the creek trickled over its gravel bed, to be sure . . . were it not for the rising swell of war cries and the soul-puckering power of the coming thunder of those hooves.

"Dey comin' again!" Fraeb would announce what every last one of the twenty-one others could see with their own eyes while the summer sun beat down on that corral of rotting horseflesh and desperate, cornered men.

"Remember," Bass turned to whisper at the redhead nearby. "Wait till you got a target."

"What's it matter?"

He turned and looked at the youngster's face. "It'll matter. Each of us gotta take one of the bastards out with every run they make at us . . . it'll soon enough matter to *them*."

Titus watched the redhead swallow hard and turn away without comment to stare at the oncoming horsemen. Sweat droplets stung Bass's eyes. Grinding the sleeve of his calico shirt across his forehead, he calmly announced, "They call me Scratch."

"Scratch?" the redhead repeated. "No shit. I heard of you." His eyes went to the black bandanna covering Bass's head. "Word has it you lost hair."

Grinning, Bass nestled his cheek along the stock of his rifle, squinting at the front rank of horsemen. "That was a long time ago, friend."

He found another likely target: tall; a muscular youth brandishing what appeared to be an English trade gun in one hand as his spotted pony raced toward their corner of the corral. The Sioux and Cheyenne were clearly going to make another long sweep across a broad front again, hooves tearing up grassy dirt clods as they streaked past the long axis of the barricades where most of the trappers lay or knelt behind the bloating carcasses.

The redhead's rifle boomed. Then it was Scratch's turn to topple his target.

"Name's Jim. Jim Baker," the redhead turned to declare. "I'd like to say I'm glad to meet you," he explained as he rolled onto his back to yank up his powder horn and started to reload. "But I don't figger none of us gonna get outta here anyways."

"You listen here, young fella," Bass snapped. "I been through more'n any one man's share of scraps with red niggers—from Apach' on the Heely, to Comanch' over in greaser country, clear up to the goddamned belly of Blackfoot land itself. We ain't beat yet—"

"How the hell you figure we gonna get outta here?" Baker demanded as he jammed a ball down his powder-choked barrel. "We ain't got no horses left to ride—"

"We'll get out, Jim Baker. You keep shooting center like you done so far . . . these brownskins gonna get tired of this game come dark."

"G-game?"

"Damn straight, it's a game to them," Bass explained, then tongued a ball from among those he had nestled inside his cheek. As he pulled his ramrod free of the thimbles pinned beneath the octagonal barrel, he laid another greased linen patch over the muzzle and shoved the wiping stick down for another swab. Only when he had dragged out the patch fouled with oily, black powder residue did he spit the large round ball into his palm and place it in the yawning muzzle.

Baker glanced at the body nearby—a hapless trapper who had poked his head up just a little too far at the wrong moment and gotten an arrow straight through the eye socket for his carelessness. Penetrating into the brain, the shaft had brought a quick, merciful death. The redhead grumbled, "This damn well don't appear to be no game to me."

"No two ways to it, Jim: this here's big medicine to these brownskins," Bass explained as he reprimed the pan. "White men ain't been hoo-rooed by Sioux and Cheyenne much afore this, you see. Lookit their women up on that hill, singing and hollering their medicine for 'em, screaming billy-be-hell for their men to rub us out, all and every last one."

"They can do it," Baker groaned with resignation. "Damn well 'nough of 'em out there."

"But they won't," Titus argued. "Ain't their way to ride over us all at once. Sure they could all come down here an' tromp us under their hooves. They'd loose a few in rubbing us out but they'd make quick work of it."

"W-why ain't they?"

"There ain't no glory in it, Jim." And Bass grinned, his yellowed teeth like pin acorns aglow in the early-afternoon light. "Them are warriors. The gen-yu-wine article. And the only way a warrior gets his honors is in war. This here's war—a young buck's whole reason for livin'. Wiping us out quick . . . why, that ain't war. That's just killing."

Baker wagged his head and rolled onto his knees again to make a rest for his left elbow on the ribs of his dead horse. "I don't rightly care what sort of game them Injuns is having with us. I figger to do my share of killing."

Bass rocked onto his rump and settled the long barrel atop the fist he made of his left hand, which rested on the horse's broad, fly-crusted front shoulder. Green and black bottleflies already busy laying their eggs in the ooze and the gore.

Gazing up the slope, he was surprised to find the woman had moved. Damn, if she wasn't coming down toward the bottom close enough that he might just have a chance to knock down Fraeb's warrior princess.

Closer, closer . . . come on now, he heard himself think in his head as she and her unmounted courtiers inched down the hillside, their shrill voices all the more clear now in the late-afternoon air. If he held high, and waited for that next gust of hot wind to die . . . he might just hit her. If not the warrior princess, then drop her horse. And if not her pretty spotted pony, then one of them others what stood around her like she was gut-sucking royalty.

He let out half a breath and waited for the breeze to cease tugging on that thin braid of gray-brown hair that brushed against his right cheek. Bass quickly set the back trigger, then carefully slipped his fingertip over the front trigger, waiting, waiting—

When the rifle went off he bolted onto his knees to

have himself a look, not patient to wait for the pan flash
and muzzle smoke to drift off on the next gust of wind.

Her brown-spotted pony was rocking back onto its
haunches, suddenly twisting its head and neck as the
double handful of courtiers scattered—diving and scrambling off in every direction. As if plucked into the sky, the
warrior princess herself sprung off the rearing pony the
moment its forelegs pawed in the air a heartbeat, then
careened onto its side.

A few of the more daring attendants immediately surrounded the princess and started dragging her up the
slope, away from the fighting, out of range of the white
man's far-reaching weapons.

Scratch watched how reluctant she was to back away,
amused at how she continued to stare over her shoulder
in utter disbelief as she was yanked up that hillside, her
eyes transfixed on the tiny corral where the trappers were
somehow holding out. Perhaps she even wondered just
which one of the cursed, doomed whiteskins had killed
her beautiful, invincible pony. Likely heaping her vilest
curses on the man who had gone and soured her powerful medicine she had been using to spur the naked horsemen to perform their death-defying charges.

"And well you should do your share of the damned
killing, Jim Baker," Bass replied to the redhead as he
rocked backward and dragged the long barrel off the
horse's front shoulder.

Scratch swatted at a dozen flies hovering around his
sweaty face and tugged the stopper from the powder
horn between his teeth. "Because killin' ever' last one of
these bastards we can drop afore sundown comes is the
only way this bunch of half-dead hide hunters is gonna
slip outta here when it gets slap-dark."

2

But there wasn't a man among them willing to attempt slipping off before moonrise lit up this high desert.

Good men these were, but . . . Scratch realized most of them were followers. Not that they lacked in courage, just that they weren't eager to strike out on their own in the dark without Henry Fraeb leading them back to the Green River.

"He's for sure dead?" Bass asked some of the first to crawl up to meet him near the tree stumps.

"*Enfant de garce!*" Basil Clement swore. "I see lot of dead, and that Frapp ees ver' dead!"

Jim Baker sat staring at how Fraeb's corpse leaned back against one of the stumps, his jaw hanging open in a horrifying grin, rivulets of blood dried over most of his face as it spilled from the bullet wound that had nearly blown off the top of his head. Baker shuddered and turned back to the council. "He sure does make a damn ugly dead man."

"Remind me to say some kind words over your worthless, fly-blowed carcass when you go under," Bass chided, jabbing an elbow into Baker's ribs.

"Didn't mean no disrespect by it," the redhead grumbled apologetically.

Scratch turned from Baker and asked the group, "So how many of you gonna come with me?"

Not a one spoke up. The silence of that twilight council was almost suffocating to him. Bass slowly eyed most of the twenty others who huddled nearby in an arch around the dead booshway.

"Ain't none of you got the eggs to make a break for it with me?"

"They'll have scouts prowling," Jake Corn finally put an argument to it.

"But they're like to come at us again in the morning," Bass grumbled to those men who first started to cluster near the center of their corral back when twilight began to erase the last of the day's shadows. "How long any of you figger our powder to hold out?"

No one had an answer to that.

"I'm gonna stay," Jake Corn volunteered bravely.

At least give the man credit for speaking up and spitting out his mind.

A lot of the half-breeds and Frenchmen nodded without saying a thing. Good, spineless followers they were. Almost made Scratch want to puke.

But he knew when he was beat. Knew how fruitless it would be to try to convert noisy cowards into quiet heroes. "Maybeso you're right," Bass relented, his shoulders sagging.

"I'll go with you, Scratch," Baker offered immediately.

He weighed it a moment, then decided. "Thankee, Jim. But, maybeso we all ought'n go . . . or we all ought'n stay. Best we'll hang together or we'll fall separate."

"Leastways, we got us some cover here," Elias Kersey offered.

Then Rube Purcell added, "And we know they ain't likely to run us over tomorrow if'n they couldn't today."

Several of the faceless men grunted their assent.

"It gets dark enough," Bass suggested, "some of us

oughtta belly down to the river and bring back some water."

Five men volunteered. He could tell that handful really were brave men. They just needed to be told what to do.

When the cloaking darkness finally came and the first faint stars were just beginning to twinkle in full radiance, the five crawled from the far side of the corral with what oaken and gourd canteens the whole bunch could find among the scattered baggage or tied to those saddles still strapped on the bloating horses.

Bass watched them go, then turned to catch one of Fraeb's half-breed, no-brained Frenchmen loading his pipe bowl with shreds of tobacco.

"That spark you'll strike gonna make for a good target of your poor self," he growled as he closed a bony claw on the man's shoulder, another hand around the pipe itself. "No telling how close them brownskins could try crawling up on us to put a big hole in one of you."

"The man's right," Jake Corn agreed. "No pipes."

Then Titus went on to remind them all they must stay close to the ground when they felt the need to move about the corral so the evening sky would not backlight them. No sense in learning the hard way if those Sioux and Cheyenne had any true marksmen lying out there in the night.

Later, after the water carriers returned and the men scrounged through possibles sacks for some dried meat or a little pemmican, feeding their wounded first, Scratch could no longer put off the chore. Crabbing over toward the far corner, he rocked up onto his knees and toes to quickly yank aside the front of his breechclout. Here and there in the corral, others were doing the same—every last one of them finding it all but impossible to make water crouching on his knees. Not a one of them dared to stand in doing their business. Too risky, what with the warriors who might well be slipping up in the night.

When finished, Titus shuddered, sensing how quickly this high prairie cooled off once the sun had been sucked from the sky. Dragging his rifle beside him, he did his best to hold his breath while he crabbed back over to the mule's carcass where he struggled to free one of the thick, wool blankets. It would have to do: his other blanket and the buffalo robe were hopelessly pinned beneath the mule, its hide, the blanket, and the robe all bristling with more than half a hundred arrows. Draping the lone horse blanket across his shoulders, he left the stinking gut pile and the mule's riven belly behind. Reaching his saddle horse, he sank back against its backbone and let out a sigh.

He pulled off his wide-brimmed, low-crowned hat and flopped it on his belly as he allowed his head to collapse back among a few of the arrow shafts prickling the carcass. He was weary but doubted he could really sleep. Instead he lay watching the stars crawl overhead, inch by inch, listening to the muted sounds of the others, listening for any suspicion of the enemy.

He wondered if she would be watching this same sky too, way up there in Crow country. As she stared up through the smoke hole at that triangle of sky near the top of her mother's lodge. While Waits-by-the-Water rocked their children to sleep in her arms . . . singing softly to them, making up those hero stories about their father.

Scratch didn't realize he had fallen asleep until the quiet whispers of those nearby stabbed through his dreamy reverie. It really had turned cold. He shuddered and ground the heels of both hands into his eyes. Blinking them open, he found that false dawn would arrive momentarily. But for now the skyline behind them was no more than a sliver of gray suspended between a blackened sky and an even darker horizon.

" 'Bout time you woke up."

Bass rolled to find Baker sliding up on his haunches, dragging half a buffalo robe with him.

"You been up all night?"

"When I woke up a bit ago, I seen you was asleep," the redhead explained. "So I decided to stay awake till you got done."

Looking around at the dim forms taking shape in the first filtered gray of predawn, Bass said, "I figger nothing much happened."

"One of the wounded fellas died," Baker declared. "But he went quiet."

An icy drop of cold snaked its way down his spine. He shuddered in the half-light. "Goddamn, but I hate when a man dies noisy."

Better that they go like Jack Hatcher. Now, there was a man what knew how to die. Go out singing his favorite song. Mad—Jack—Hatcher. For as noisy a life as the coon lived . . . he sure went quiet.

Titus asked in a whisper, "No one heard nothing from out there?"

Baker admitted, "Not that I know of."

"I better see the others is ready when first light comes," Scratch said, dragging the blanket off and reaching for his brown, weathered hat. He tugged it down over the black bandanna. "Maybeso you try for some shut-eye while you can, Jim Baker."

"Uhn-uhn. I'll come with you," the redhead volunteered. "Make sure every man's up and fixed for powder."

He knelt there, staring at the youngster a moment more, feeling the grin starting to crease his leathery, oak-brown face. "Just like a pup, ain'cha?"

"What you mean by that?"

Wagging his head, Titus set off with Baker at his elbow. "I 'member when I was young and fool-headed like you—back when I could go days 'thout any sleep."

"I'll be fine," the tall one protested.

Finally Bass stopped, grinning as he slapped a hand on Baker's shoulder. "I'll bet you will at that."

One by one the others who had been dozing amid the carcasses were coming awake. The two who were badly wounded soon began to ask for more water. Bass and Baker looked over what remained in the canteens, then asked for volunteers to crawl down to the creek with them before the sky got any brighter. No small wonder the men in that corral had already drained nearly every drop they had brought back from the stream at twilight, what with the way the sun had leached so damn much moisture from them throughout that long, long day beneath the cruel, late-summer sun. Come nightfall and their first chance to slip down to the creek, the men were nigh as parched as a green hide dusted with canning salt and a dose of alum.

As the light slowly ballooned around them, Scratch could see that someone had laid a greasy leather shirt over Fraeb's head. The old German's mortifying remains still sat on the ground, leaning back against that hundred-year-old fire-charred stump. But it was clear one of the men simply couldn't stand looking at that ugly, gap-toothed, death grin of Henry Fraeb's any longer. Maybe one of the half-superstitious Frenchies, he figured. They were Papists, to be sure.

This bunch would have to decide what to do about their dead when it came time to skeedaddle out of there.

"Them's the only ones I see," a man whispered huskily.

"Where? Where?"

There was a lot of muffled shuffling when most of the sixteen who could still move on their own crawled over to the near side of the corral. Every last one of them staring quiet as deer mice at the slope while the coming light continued to give a changing texture to the hillside where the warriors had gathered throughout the previous day. At first, Scratch was not sure what he was seeing—not until enough gray seeped sidelong through the mouth of the valley to their right, exposing more of the slope.

Nothing there but some sage and stunted cedar, along with a scattering of jack pine. No horsemen, as far as he could tell.

"I see 'em!" one of the others called out a little too loud.

"There—on top of the hill!"

"That all there is?"

Plain as the coming sun that six or seven of them, no, at least eight, had stood watch atop that crest through the short summer night.

"I don't see no more of 'em."

Hopeful, Titus strained his eyes to be as sure as the rest. If the breast of the hill was no longer blanketed by the horsemen, if those chanting women and old men no longer bristled against the skyline, perhaps this coming sunrise would not be their last.

"Could be they're only guards," Baker offered as he stopped at Bass's hip.

Scratch nodded while many of the others murmured in wonder of just what this meant. "Maybeso they hung back to see if these white men would slip off during the night. To wait up there till first light to be sure we was still here."

He wanted to laugh a little, perhaps cry too—quickly glancing around their prison, that corral of stinking, putrefying horses and mules.

"Their magic is broken," Bass explained barely above a whisper.

"What was that?" one of the men asked, edging closer on a knee.

"I said their medicine's broke."

"Let's get," came the first suggestion.

"On what?" another shrieked in indignation. "We ain't got a horse one!"

"I'll walk, goddammit."

"That's for sure," Baker growled, then turned to Bass. "But where we going?"

Scratch sighed, staring down at his mule and the saddle horse, the animals he had sacrificed to save his life. "Anywhere but here."

"Maybe north—"

"Yeah," Bass agreed. "Back to the Green."

"I say we light out west for Davy Crockett."

Titus considered that a moment, then told those men all younger than he, "You fellas take off where you want to go. I can't stop you from heading out. Only thing I'm sure of here and now . . . we split up, it's just gonna make us easy pickin's for them brownskins."

The one with deep-set, anxious eyes stepped up to ask,

"So what's your all-fired mighty idea? Ain't Davy Crockett just 'bout as close as the Green?"

"May well be," he answered. "But that fort lays yonder where I had me my first scrap with them Sioux. So I figger this country's thick with 'em."

Another man stepped up close. "We can get us horses at the fort."

"How you figure they'll have enough horses for all of us?" Baker bellowed.

"Maybe the Snakes have some ponies for us—"

Titus wagged his head dolefully. "If the Sioux are chasing through this country," he argued, "it's for certain the Snake aren't anywhere this far south."

"That means we gotta go north for horses," Baker explained.

"Makes the most sense to me," Bass replied, turning to look back at the hilltop where the eight horsemen waited out the coming dawn.

"How long afore we go?" one of the younger ones asked.

"Soon as we're ready—we'll move out," Titus assured them.

"What about my outfit?" grumbled one.

"I'm fixing to take my truck with me," Bass explained. "I figger you can bury what you don't want to carry. Or you can just leave it behind for them bastards up on that hill when they come down to dig through what's left. Red niggers left me poor more'n I care to count . . . so, for me, I'm walking away with my hide, hair, an' everything I can carry—"

"Man can't carry much!" one of them scoffed with a gust of mirthless laughter.

Pointing at a copse of cottonwood saplings at the water's edge, Scratch said, "I figger to make me a travois."

"You ain't got no horse to carry your goddamned travois!" another snorted.

"I'll drag it my own self," Titus growled as he turned away for the carcass of his pack mule. Over his shoulder he said, "Maybeso, the rest of you figger on doing the same."

Behind him some of the voices continued to argue among themselves. He didn't care. Digging one of the small axes from his packs, Titus went directly for the cottonwoods. By the time he felled the first sapling, others were joining him. Three young trees was all he needed, Bass figured. Two with large, sturdy bases—and a third he could use to lash the two together in a narrow vee. After hacking the branches off the three saplings, he dragged them back up the rise to the corral.

He had done this before, he told himself.* Sure, he had been younger, stronger too. But that had been winter, by damned. And he had been forced to cross the Yellowstone—wading through the icy floes on foot. He could do this. It was a matter of have to.

Don't give no mind to the sage and cactus, the sharp stones and numerous dead-end canyons they'd bump into between here and the valley of the Green. If only he could get there, he knew in the pit of him that he'd find some Ute or Snake, trade some horses from them, and get back to Waits-by-the-Water. He'd done this before . . . way back when he didn't have near this much to lose.

Man gets older, maybeso he finds he needs certain things, certain people, a little more than he ever had before. Man gets older, he's damn lucky he's learned what's most important.

Dropping the three saplings, he collapsed to the ground and dragged one foot around so he could inspect the bottom of his moccasin. Then the other. They wouldn't last long, thin as they were rubbed.

Good thing Waits had stuffed a dozen pair in his possibles before he kissed her good-bye. Already he had used at least half of them through the rest of the spring and into the summer. Moccasins wore out. Some men made repairs if they could. Bass stuffed the old ones away in his plunder. Now he'd pull them out to wear double if he could. Maybe even cut them up into strips he could tie

---

* *Crack in the Sky*

around his moccasins, protecting those places that suffered the most wear.

He wondered if these other men would make it across all the sage and cactus and rocks on foot. He wondered, because he knew none of them had near as much spurring them on. Because none of them had near as much to lose.

After notching the two large saplings where the crosspiece would lay atop them, he used short lengths of the half-inch rope he unknotted and yanked off the mule's pack. The sun was emerging over the horizon by the time he started dragging everything off the elkhorn pack saddle that he had strapped onto the backs of two mules over a lot of years. Both of them dead now. Scratch vowed he would drag it along too—if he could pull it off the carcass.

Already the air was warming. It would be another scorcher of a day. And the animals would smell even worse. Beginning to rot, their juices bubbling and boiling inside, meat turned to soup in time.

"Baker," he called out to the redhead, "cut you some meat from your horse. Back there on the rump where the muscle's deep."

"Meat?"

"Rest of you do the same," he instructed the circle. "Make sure you got some meat to carry off with you. We're gonna need something to eat 'long the way," he explained as he dragged his knife from its scabbard.

"Shit—I aim to shoot what I need," one of the men protested.

Another man roared with laughter, "Eat this goddamned putrefied horse when I can bag me some fresh meat?"

With a shake of his head, Titus stood and said, "What if we don't run onto no game slow enough for a man on foot?"

A long-faced young man wagged his head. "I can allays find something to eat what's better'n ol' rotten horse!"

"You fellas do what you wanna," he replied with a

shrug, turning back to the cold haunch. "I ain't your booshway."

Baker watched the old trapper wag his head in disgust. "Don't pay 'em any mind, Bass."

Scratch stopped to look at the redhead. "I ain't got the time to fret myself over such stupid idjits." Then leaned atop the horse carcass. "Don't know how Frapp ever did cotton to taking along such a bunch as this to nurse."

"Maybe Fraeb wasn't the smartest fella himself," Baker said as he came up to Bass's side.

"The German had savvy," Titus snapped angrily. "And more grit in him than you and this hull bunch all together."

Baker was cowed. He waited several minutes, then to the old man's back he asked, "What about them wounded?"

"If'n they can walk, they'll walk," Titus explained. "If they can't, we'll have to drag 'em on travois." He got up slowly, working kinks out of his back. "I'll go see how many can get along on their own."

"You want me to help you?"

"No—start on the animals," Scratch declared, sensing the young man was apologizing for his ill-considered remark about the dead. "We'll wrap up the meat best we can, bury it deep in our plunder. Be sure you cut deep to take out your steaks—down where it ain't started to go bad and turn to soup in the sun yesterday."

Three of the five wounded told him they'd try to walk. Another with a bad shoulder wound didn't figure he was strong enough to pull his own plunder. And the last one was so bad off he would have to lay in a travois, a strip of folded rawhide between his teeth to clench down on every time he was moved. He wouldn't be long; but a gut wound was a nasty, slow way for a man to go. Bass divided that handful's meager goods among the rest.

By late morning Fraeb's ragtag bunch was ready to pull out. He had gotten the German's men to agree that they would all take a turn at pulling the wounded man as they plodded north. His would be the heaviest travois.

"If you was bad off like him, I know you'd want the others to drag you outta here."

There had been no dissent.

Kneeling within the narrow end of the vee he had constructed of the saplings, Bass stood, raising his travois to start forward. He took the head of the march, turning to look over his shoulder at the skyline where the warriors had dismounted now, watching the white men. Where the creek valley took a bend, Bass looked back at the hilltop one last time. The Sioux were gone.

Now this bunch could really start to worry.

Likely, those scouts had gone off to tell the rest of the village that the white men had abandoned their fort. From here on out, when the Sioux attacked, the horsemen would have an easier time of it riding over the trappers. With every step Bass worked to convince himself that they'd corral up quickly within what baggage and packs they had strung out on the many travois, doing their best to hold the warriors off any way they could. For as long as they could.

The sun seemed to hang in the sky that long afternoon, unmoving like a stubborn mule. That comparison made him remember. Step by painful step, damn—if it didn't make him remember. Try as he might to squeeze out the hurt that first part of the day, Bass finally gave in and let the tortured remembrance of Hannah course through him like the burning sting of a poison coursing through his veins.

Even when he called for a halt and the bunch dropped their travois, every man collapsing into the dust and the sage, huffing and pulling at their canteens of tepid, alkali-laced water. The first few times he reminded them only to wet their lips, to wash their tongues and the insides of their mouths with one swish of water rather than guzzling at their dwindling supply of moisture. Especially since they had no idea where they would end up come sundown. Near a creek or not. Soon enough he gave up trying to convince them to conserve their water.

A mountain man wasn't supposed to worry about

water. But . . . a man didn't have to if he had a horse to cover ground. However, the going was slow on foot.

No telling how far they had come by the time the sun had sunk and the long shadows were no more. That's when they started searching in earnest for a place to wait out the night.

Scouring every crease lying between the hills, the trappers still came up dry—every creekbed nothing more than a sandy strip of dust. Then as twilight was sucking the last of the light from the sky, they spotted a dark hollow in the rolling tableland ahead. Dotting the hollow was a sprinkling of brush, vegetation barely bigger than the sparse sagebrush that struggled to survive in this high desert. Spread out in a wide vee behind him, the trappers lunged step-by-step toward the dark, beckoning green.

Reaching the coarse grass and stunted willow, Bass dropped the travois from his weary hands turned to numb, stonelike claws. Then he went to his knees in weary exhaustion as the first of the others stumbled to a halt around him.

Crawling out of the vee, he stayed on hands and knees, searching for the source of the seep by sound, feeling along for the growing moisture beneath his fingertips. There it was, at last. No more than an oozy seep, and a little warm at that, but it was water.

Rocking forward, Bass put his face down into the shallow pan-sized spring and lapped at the wetness. It was bitter with salts, but it was water. And damn if it weren't cool.

"Gimme your canteen," he demanded of a half-breed Frenchman, the first to come up at his shoulder.

Once it was filled, he scrambled out of the way and let the others at the seep while he lurched over to the travois where the dying man lay groaning. His parched lips were swollen and cracked. His leathery face sunburnt and coated with a fine layer of alkali dust.

"I brung you some water."

But the man didn't open his eyes. Didn't respond. Nothing more than the quiver of those lips as he mumbled unintelligible sounds. Kneeling over him, Bass pressed the narrow end of the gourd against the swollen lips and slowly poured the springwater into the man's slack mouth. More than half of it dribbled down his bearded cheek, and he sputtered so badly on the rest that Bass gave up.

Poor fella wouldn't be long now. Gut shot the worst way to go under. Man took a long, long time to die. Could be this one wouldn't make it through another day of the bouncing, jarring ride as they pressed north by west for the Green River come morning.

He died quiet and merciful, sometime late on the afternoon of the second day's march. That night at their waterless camp, the men took turns scraping out a shallow trough from the hard, flinty soil. The moon had risen by the time they rolled the body into its resting place, then covered the dusting of earth with what rocks they managed to find across the side of a barren hill.

Over low fires they broiled thin strips of the stringy horsemeat that was beginning to take on a sharp tang. What they had left wouldn't spoil if they jerked it. Titus figured they'd be down to chewing on parfleche and eating their spare moccasins in another three or four days if they didn't ration what little meat they had left among them.

In the cool air that third morning, they had themselves a bad scare.

"Shit," one of the men grumbled as the whole bunch jolted awake in their blankets, "only see three of 'em."

"Where there's three watching—might well be three hundred waiting," Bass declared.

Baker inquired, "What you figger 'em to be?"

For a moment longer he studied the gray hillside, then wagged his head. "Ain't got no idea. But I don't make 'em for Sioux still keeping an eye on us. They'd follered us, caught us in the open, and been done with us quick."

"So who they be?" Elias Kersey asked.

They all watched as the trio slipped out of sight behind the far hilltop. "Don't matter now," Titus sighed. "They for certain ain't the friendly kind."

"Maybe Snake?"

"Maybeso," Bass answered. "Or Yuta. Either way, what they see'd of us down here 'thout no horses, I reckon they figger us to be slim pickin's. Ain't worth stealing from, or worth killing."

One of the younger trappers crawled over to ask, "That mean there's a village close?"

"Likely it does."

"Maybe we can find it today," Rube Purcell said, enthused.

"Don't set your sights that high," he warned the angular man. "Best we can hope for is to find a trail and see if it might do to follow those tracks toward the Green."

A pair of the Americans immediately set off for the distant hill in the predawn light. The rest waited in that waterless camp for them to return with their disappointing news that the riders had circled out of the southeast, and their trail led off to the southwest, a jumble of rolling hills.

Some of the men instantly began to grumble that they should have started for Fort Davy Crockett in Brown's Hole, since that was likely the trio's destination.

"Could be they were the last of the Sioux scouts keeping watch on us too," Bass declared. "I'm making for the Green. There's a lot I don't mind gambling over—but walking right into that Sioux village again sure seems like short odds to me."

When it came time to start out again a few minutes later, about half of the others didn't immediately follow. He wasn't going to let it matter to him if they had decided to take off on their own. Bass vowed to focus his efforts on cutting a fresh trail that might well mean finding a friendly village of Shoshone or Ute. At least Baker, Kersey, Corn, and Purcell were behind him—they were a steady lot.

A little later when he glanced over his shoulder, Titus discovered the rest of the bunch strung out behind him in a ragged procession, their moccasins and travois poles scuffing up small puffs of the yellowish dust. If the Sioux decided to hit the white men now, they'd be easy to roll on over.

It didn't matter, he told himself. Just keep walking—every bone-jarring step was one more step closer to Waits-by-the-Water and the youngsters.

What the hell was he doing down here anyway? Had he come out of Crow country to trap beaver in the Wind River Range and the valley of the Green? Or, had he really moseyed south in hopes of holding on to a past that was dead and all but buried?

Maybeso, he had ventured down this way hoping to run into some of the old faces, to talk over the shinin' times, share something of a bygone life. But Bridger had stayed behind to oversee the construction of his small post, and now even Fraeb was dead. As dead as the partnership between those two old hands.

Dead as the beaver trade.

Truth was, there weren't enough trappers left in the mountains to make it worthwhile for Bridger to hunker down in one spot and become a trader. So who was it Gabe hoped to turn a profit on at the new post he was raising? The Yuta and Snake in that country?

The way of things now dictated a squaw got more for a buffalo robe than a man did for trapping beaver. No matter which way Titus looked at it, seemed his whole world had gone belly-up.

What was a man to do?

3

◆

Spring came early, wet and muddy that next year.

Winter had been mild enough up north in Absaroka country, the sort of weather that made his feet itch to be up and on the move rather than lying around camp the way the Crow men would.

A fella could well grow soft and lazy between the last autumn hunt and first of spring trapping. So Bass had done his best to keep himself busy. All through that winter when he could no longer fight off the restlessness, he kissed his family of a morning and rode off alone for a few days at a time, haunting the icy streams and creeks where the beaver waited out the winter in their icy lodges. What beaver were left.

There were stretches of country where a man wouldn't run onto any fresh sign—no newly felled saplings, no slides, no dammed-up meadows, and certainly none of the huge, domed lodges where the beaver and their kits spent the winter dry and warm. But if he persisted, if he pushed on into the seldom-tracked creek valleys, if he dared climb higher into the icy hills, he did find a few of the flat-tails that had survived that onslaught of the last twenty years.

It was in such remote valleys that Titus Bass was rewarded with something more than a few sleek pelts. Gazing down upon those white slopes crisscrossed with the pale flesh of the skeletal aspen and furred with the verdant emerald of pine and spruce, he found himself renewed again and again. Listening to the sough of the wind in the snow-crusted evergreen as it fled to distant places, many times hearing nothing more than the quiet breathing of his three horses. Sometimes only the beating of his heart.

That deep, abiding cold, and a silence like no other.

On occasions at his solitary fire as winter's darkness sank in around him early of an afternoon, he would look back upon those nine days of dragging his travois and the followers behind him, marching away from the country of the Little Snake, steadfastly pointing his nose for the country of the Green. Heat and dust, the sting of the alkali making his nose bleed, dust caking his mouth, burning his slitted eyes as they bore into the distance beneath that high, relentless sun. Eyes vigilantly searching the wavering, shimmering skyline for landmarks, for horsemen, for friends or foes.

Each day he found the others strung out behind him a little more. Some were just slow working up the wherewithal to start out in the morning, to kneel, pick up their travois load, and put that first step behind them. So a few were slow in making it in to their pitiful camp each evening as the light came down. They straggled in for hours after dark. And the following morning, they would straggle out—always following the deep tracks his drag scored in the flaky, wind-scoured topsoil.

He would look back over his shoulder at times, watching them coming, strung out like a few uneven beads on a thong grown too long, most of them wavering, lunging ahead a step at a time as the dust stived up from their moccasins, from the ends of every pole . . . and he would think how strange was the appearance of this dark, staggering creature—like some long, disjointed, many-legged centipede dragging itself through the pale, yellow sand . . . body parts irrevocably following its head.

Dragged along by the sheer power of his will alone.

Persistent he became, if nothing else. One step at a time. One morning, one midday, and one afternoon at a time. Eat the dried horsemeat and promptly fall into the sleep of a man beyond weary, his mind grown too numb from the heat and the thirst to think on little else but to dread the coming dawn when he would have to scoop down inside himself once more and determine if he could push on this one more morning, this one more midday, and finally this one more afternoon as the sun burned itself a red track across the western sky.

It was afternoon when he thought he recognized the river valley from the low butte he had climbed, hopeful after these nine nights of fitful sleep, awakening at every cough, with every rustle of a man in his blankets—worrying if he should post a night guard . . . and in the end finding himself so hungry, so parched, so goddamned weary that he only worried in his dreams.

But there it was on that flat above the cutbank where the stream flowed into the Green. On that patch of bottom ground stood the dark shadow of those cottonwood logs piled one atop the other to form a small square . . . so reminding him of Bonneville's post squatting far to the north along this same Green River.

"L-lookee there," he croaked as Jake Corn and Jim Baker stuttered to a halt with their dust-caked travois.

"D-don't see it too good," Corn confessed, licking his cracked lips and squinting his red-rimmed, alkali-burned eyes. "Can't see no roof."

"That's 'cause there ain't no roof, Jake."

Baker's face went gray with disappointment. "Where's Bridger, them others stayed back with him—"

"Way I lay my sights, they give up and pulled out sometime back," he explained as two more trappers lunged to a halt nearby and took to gazing at the scene below. "But lookee there: that smoke low off again' the hills—"

"Don't see no smoke," a Frenchman interrupted.

"There, miles up the valley." And Titus pointed.
"Look in the trees and you'll see it."

"S-so far away . . . still," another man grumbled.

"What you take 'em for, Scratch?"

He looked at Baker, then grinned weakly. "Likely
Snake. S'pose we keep on till we can pay our respects on
their camp."

It was nearly dark, with the last shreds of the longest
shadows of the day clinging to the low places, when he
heard the first dog bark. It so reminded him of coming home from a long day of squirreling in the thick
woods, hearing ol' Tink start to bark and bay as the old
hound burst ahead, smelling home before he even
reached the clearing and spotted the cabin and barn
amongst the clutter of elm and oak.

A second dog had taken up the warning, and soon a
dozen or more of the half-wild curs were yipping, their
cries echoing off the low bluffs framing the valley where
the last copper light was disappearing from a ragged
string of clouds to the west. He shuddered to a halt between Baker and Corn the moment they heard the hoofbeats. Out of the tall willow and cottonwood more than
ten of them streamed, spreading out in a broad front,
bristling with weapons as they confronted the strangers
staggering up one by one behind Bass.

First whack, those Snake had to see just how bad off
these white men were. White men on foot? Glor-eee!
That had to be something for them warriors to witness.
Bass recalled a smattering of their tongue, inched through
enough of his clumsy sign language too, to explain how
they'd been jumped by the Sioux, forted up behind the
horses and mules they were forced to sacrifice, then how
they had dropped the pony being ridden by that warrior
princess who surely had to be directing the battle. All of
that before the trappers made beasts of themselves and
started dragging their burdens back north.

How many days?

In response to the warrior's question, Titus pulled the
short twig from where he had it safely stuffed inside his

wide belt, and quickly brushed the pad of his thumb over the notches he had carved each night before he fell into a stupor of sleep, gazing up at the sky he hoped she was watching too.

Ten . . . this will be ten since we sent the Sioux packing.

There are more of you?

Bass had nodded. Then twice he flicked up the fingers on both hands as he held them out before him.

The horseman signaled the others on both sides of him, and most of the riders nudged their ponies away, streaming past on either side of the trio, hurrying on down the river valley to gather up the rest of the stragglers.

Turned out it was Rain's camp. The old man who came to Fort Davy Crockett two years ago reporting that white men he had taken in for the night, fed, and given his finest hospitality had shown him their appreciation by stealing some of his horses.* Two women helped the crippled, slow-moving old man out of his lodge to stand before the first dozen of the trappers who limped into that camp, trailed by a parade of children and barking dogs.

"I have seen your face," Rain said as he studied Titus Bass up close with his rheumy eyes. "Two winters ago: did you ever steal my ponies?"

"No, I was not one of those who stole your horses," Bass said in his halting Shoshone tongue, emphasizing it with his sign. "But, I went with the men who took your horses back from the white men who stole them from you."

"I knew I had seen your face," Rain replied, clutching the arms of the two women unsteadily. "It was a good thing you took those ponies back. Because the others dishonored themselves by stealing my ponies—*no* white man could ever again come into this country with his own horses and ride back out. I would make his ponies mine."

---

* *Ride the Moon Down*

"You see, it is plain we need horses."

"You walked a long way from this fight against the Lakota?"

"La . . . kota?" Titus echoed the word.

"That is what they call themselves," Rain answered. "We made a prisoner of one of them two summers ago. He explained, this Sioux word is the white-man name for his warrior bands. But, the Creator gave his people the name of Lakota. He died bravely at the hands of my people. I fear they will be a strong enemy if they come into this country to try taking it from us."

"Do you have horses to trade?"

Rain grinned, all but toothless in that wrinkled walnut of a face. "So if the Lakota did not ride off with your trade goods, I think we could find enough horses for you to call your own."

It was not a big village, but neither was it small. That night the Shoshone ignited a big fire at the edge of camp where they heated some antelope stew, broiled some buffalo steaks, and welcomed the white men back from the maw of the desert. Stuffed beyond belief, Titus watched as some old men brought out their drum, plopped it down near the fire, then began to play, drawing the young men and women of the band to the hypnotic music. Some of the more energetic, younger trappers got up to stomp and gyrate with the Shoshone, but Scratch eventually dragged his blanket and buffalo robe off down the creek to the far side of camp where things weren't near so noisy.

When he awoke later to the throb of the drum, every bit as thirsty as he had been on their ten-day walk, Bass knelt beside the stream and drank until his belly ached. The second time he awoke, he found himself ravenous and ready to put away another three pounds of buffalo flank steak. At the trappers' fire, he discovered that most of the old drummers had retired, but at the drum sat an enthusiastic ring of white men, both French and American, hammering out a rhythm for the sweating, enthusiastic Shoshone youngsters who had every intention of making a night of it.

After stuffing himself a second time to the point of a bellyache, Scratch trudged back through camp to sprawl on his buffalo robe and blanket, asleep almost as soon as he hit the ground. He did not awaken until the sun had fully risen and a troublesome fly would simply not leave him be.

For the white men that next day was given over to more eating and sleeping, and not until the second morning did they began negotiating in trade for some of the Shoshone horses. The first item of business was to mutually determine what value the animals would have in the pending trade talk. That agreed upon, the trappers and the Shoshone leaders had next to settle on the value each individual trade item would have. These two long discussions lasted into the evening of that second day, so it was decided they would begin the actual barter on the following morning.

Bass figured Rain had seen to it he came out on the better end of the bargain, getting a lot more horse than most of the other white trappers. And three of the finest animals to replace the mule and saddle horse he had sacrificed at the Little Snake.

Needing to make some meat for his journey north, Bass went hunting with two young warriors before dawn on the fourth day. They had five antelope down and gutted, strapped across the backs of their horses, and were on their way back to camp when Titus asked, "Ever hear of a Snake warrior by the name of Slays in the Night?"

The older of the pair nodded. "He was my uncle."

"W-was?" Titus inquired. "He is dead?"

With a shrug, the warrior answered, "As good as dead. He left his band many summers ago, taking some young men with him who wanted to plunder the white men wherever your people could be found."

The other youngster spoke up. "He has never returned, none of those who went with him either. So we think they are all dead."

It was some time before Scratch declared, "I knew your uncle. Knew him long, long ago. His woman made good pemmican."

"You have not seen my uncle in a long time?"

He studied the young man's face as they led their horses down the long slope toward the brown, fire-smoked lodges of the Shoshone camp. "I don't remember for sure, but I think I saw him eight summers ago."*

"We were just boys then," the youngest said. "That was about the time he left to go steal from the white men."

Clearing his throat, Bass halted. "I must tell you: your uncle and his warriors tried to steal from me."

"Did he get away with your horses and trade goods?" the nephew asked quietly.

"No. I had to kill some of the young men who rode with him," Bass explained. "At the time they took my horses, I did not know the raiding party was led by my old friend Slays in the Night. There were two of us. We killed some of the warriors with him. But when I found out it was my old friend . . . I left him afoot to live or die by his own hand."

The young nephew was long before he replied, "It was right." When the three of them had continued toward the village, he added, "A man must not steal from his friends."

To Bass, that was the worst sort of theft. Many times after seeing Slays in the Night for the last time, Scratch had brooded on it—wondering if the warrior hadn't known just whose animals he was stealing. Was he sure who his victim was? Or, had it only been coincidence?

Several times in the last two years, he had brooded on how those white trappers had preyed on Rain and the old man's hospitality. The worst sort of treachery, committed against those who were trusting. So good of heart they fall prey to those who say one thing and do another. Let such thieves steal from enemies or strangers—not from friends.

Chances were Slays in the Night had come through his ordeal of being put afoot by Bass that summer so long

---

* *One-Eyed Dream*

ago. Even still, it had been so many years since their confrontation that the odds weren't very good the Indian could have survived long in his newfound lust for booty and plunder.

What was it that made men change from good to bad? Was it simply because the world around them was no longer the same and some men believed they must change too? Of a time he would have put his life in the Shoshone warrior's hands. But Slays in the Night had become another person, the way Asa McAfferty had changed seasons before.

So why was it that Bass looked at everything, looked at everybody, around him and wondered why he was the only one not grown different over the years? Did the changing nature of the fur business, did its decline and utter ruin, mean that those men in the fur trade *had* to change? Did events that were bigger than any one man always have to alter the lives, the very character of puny humans?

Or could one man hold out against the rest of the world, at least his world of these western mountains? Sure he could, Bass decided. But he would have to figure out something else to do if beaver plews were never again to make a man and his family a decent living. What else was a man to do, when no one wanted to buy the beaver he trapped?

A trapper was what he had been for more than seventeen winters now. How could he expect himself to pack up and return east when it felt as if these mountains were all he ever knew? Or how could he abandon the Rockies and migrate to Oregon country with Doc Newell and Joe Meek? He didn't know where to go to find the answers . . . but he did know someone who might help him sort through the knots that had his thoughts so tangled.

Late that winter after returning to Absaroka, he had taken the family with him when he tramped east from the Crow camp near the foot of the Bighorns, striking out for the mouth of the Tongue where Samuel Tullock squatted inside Fort Van Buren, waiting on the Indian trade to recommence come spring.

"I wanted to see a white face, listen to some white talk," Scratch explained as he blew smoke from that first, deep pull at the pipestem. "Maybeso, to hear just what news there lays on the upper rivers, to hear it from the lips of the company its own self."

The trader snorted as he sipped his hot coffee there at the fireplace with Titus. "I sure as hell ain't the company, Scratch!"

"You're the by-god American Fur Company to this here country, to these here Injuns." He stared into the bowl of his old clay pipe a moment before he finished. "You're the bone and sinew to the beaver business."

"Beaver's down," Tullock admitted gravely. "Ain't likely to ever come back, Scratch."

Titus had looked around the small trading room and asked, "Buffler?"

"Just as many as the Crow and others have to trade."

After sipping at his scalding coffee, Titus asked, "What happens when you've forced the Indians to kill all the buffler for their skins? What then?"

But Tullock had snorted with a wide smile. "Ain't no way that can happen. Too damned many of the big shaggies—"

"But it happened to beaver, Sam'l. Time was, you 'member we never thought we could trap ourselves out the flat-tails."

"Damned sad thing it is too," Tullock commiserated. "There ain't all that many beaver left nowdays . . . and what beaver there is don't bring much of a price no more."

The American Fur Company set a depressingly low value on his beaver—despite how Tullock might want to help—but Scratch needed supplies.

"Give me the best dollar you can on these here plews, Sam'l," he pleaded. "I need fixin's afore I head south to trap this spring."

"Where you figure to go?"

"Down the Bighorn to the Wind River."

As Tullock began separating the furs from those two small packs Bass had packed to Van Buren, the trader asked, "You ever think of trying Blackfoot country?"

"Smallpox didn't kill 'em all, did it?"

"No, not all," the trader admitted.

"I value what I got left for hair," Bass declared. "Blackfoot country will have to get a lot more peaceful afore I go gamble my hide up there."

The easy beaver was a thing of the past. It was clear that a man would have to work all the harder if he was going to trap the prime grade of fur the traders were still wanting. Any plews that didn't measure up, the company men simply refused to take off a trapper's hands.

But he ended up with enough credit that he could purchase what he needed for his outfit that spring, as well as have enough left over to spoil Waits, Magpie, and Flea with a few small presents like ribbon, finger rings, tiny mirrors, some brass bracelets, and a pair of small penny whistles for his children. That and a new white blanket for his wife, the one with narrow red stripes across the entire length of it, just the blanket Waits-by-the-Water had been wanting for some winters now.

When they put Fort Van Buren behind them three days later, Scratch had his fixings for a brand-new season in the mountains, along with a few geegaws and some pretty foofaraw for his woman and young'uns, not to mention a good-sized pack of beaver pelts trader Tullock didn't put much store in. Titus decided that he would take them and the rest he still had back in the Crow camp with him when he headed south. Maybe another trader would put more value on the days in the freezing streams, the nights in those solitary camps, the stretches of lonely country he had traveled to find those beaver.

Maybe some other trader waiting in some other post on some other river somewhere south of here . . . maybe a man like Jim Bridger at his Black's Fork post. Only a man who'd trapped his own self would know the proper worth of a pelt.

Taking leave of her and the children early that spring was every bit as miserable as his homecoming last au-

tumn had been a rejoicing with his resurrection from the
near-dead. All but eight summers old, his daughter
clamped one arm around her father's waist and another
around her mother's as the parents embraced for that last
time. And with only five winters behind him, Scratch's
tiny son clung to one of his father's legs, his arms and
ankles locked for good measure as he gazed up in unbridled bewilderment to watch the tears stream down the
grown-ups' faces.

She began to whisper, "I can go with you—"

But he laid two fingers upon her lips. "We talked of
this last night. It's better you remain here with the children, to live among your people while I go search place to
place."

"We lived those seasons together years ago, never separated."

He nodded, then pulled her cheek against his chest.
"That was before we became parents. Before you . . .
you were almost taken from me. I promise you we will
travel together again."

"You said you would take me back to Ta-house."

"Yes, and I will keep that promise."

"We will see our old friends again after all these winters," she said. "When can we go?"

He had realized she was trying in her own roundabout
way to convince him to take her and the children along
with all her talk of a far-off trip to see long-ago friends.
So he said as gently as he could, "I don't know."

"When you return? We go then?"

"No, not then," he answered quietly, but firmly. "But,
we will go there someday. For now, I have to find a
trader who will take my beaver. So I will work my way
south, trapping as I go, always looking for a trader who
will realize how hard I work."

"You could stay here with us," she begged. "Hunt and
ride off on pony raids like Apsaluuke men do with their
days. You don't need to hunt the flat-tails—"

"I don't think I can live a life like that." He explained
what she must surely know already. "I cannot give up
and become Indian like the men of your tribe. Nor can I

give in and become one of the many who go back east to scratch at the ground or own a store . . . don't you see that I am a man in between who doesn't belong in either world?"

"Man in between," she repeated thoughtfully, as if giving it careful consideration. "No, you are not meant to be a warrior who lives only for the battle or the ponies he might steal. And I agree that you could never go live among the white people again."

Gently wagging his head as he grasped her face between his hands, raising it so he could stare down into her eyes, Titus said, "I must go in search of a place for myself. Everything is changing around me. I am not of your world, but I am no more a part of the white world. I can only pray that I can find a new place now that everything has gone crazy around me."

"When will I see your face again?" she asked.

"I hope to return before the coming winter," he admitted, believing it would be so and that nothing could prevent him from keeping his vow to her.

"When the leaves on the aspen and the cottonwood begin to turn yellow, every day I will look for you on the horizon, every day," she choked out the words.

He smothered her mouth with his, unable to speak for the hot ball stuck in his throat. Then he knelt there right in front of her and flung his arms around the children, embracing them fiercely. After kissing their cheeks, their foreheads, and their eyes, he stood again and pressed his lips against her mouth one last time.

"Be-before winter." His voice was raspy with regret as he quickly turned away, took up the horse's rein, and climbed into the saddle.

Ever since that morning, it had tortured him to think of just how many lonely nights he would have to endure until the coming winter turned the earth hard as iron. Until he lay against her damp skin all night through—

The wind was not right, so those riders could not smell the smoke of the small fire Bass had left behind in his camp. Titus squinted in the late-afternoon light and did his best to study the distant horsemen picking their way

in and out of the tall willow down there along the Popo
Agie. From the way the heat waves danced up from the
valley floor, it looked as if there could be three riders,
maybe four. He couldn't be sure.

Black, swirling figures lost then spotted once more
against the meandering braid of vegetation . . . until he
realized there were only three animals. And only one of
the horses carried a rider. The two others were strung out
behind the man—

The horseman had his knees folded high along the
front flanks, his bony knees almost rubbing the horse's
withers. Only one man Scratch had ever known rode in
such a way, his stirrups lashed so short he had the appearance of a too-large man riding an undersized pony
and saddle. Bass almost wished he had taken the long
spyglass with him when he stepped away from camp to
hunt the wet places for greens and shoots. With it he
could make sure . . .

But, in his marrow, Scratch was already sure. It had
to be.

He stood there in those trees bristling upon the gentle
slope above his camp, letting his eyes draw a line away
from the horseman, scribing what had to be the rider's
path he would take down to the mouth of the next creek.
Bass could easily reach the post on foot before the rider
appeared out of the cottonwood there on the other side
of the stream.

Scratch heard one of the rider's horses snort as he
clambered to a halt and emerged into the open, crossing
his arms and standing just so, casual though a little
winded.

"Howdy, Bill!" he called out as the rider came into
sight of the creek crossing. "Har' you now?"

William S. Williams yanked back on his reins in surprise, his rifle raised up with lightning speed. "Goddamned you, nigger! Been a Injun, I could've gut-shot
you for pulling such a prank!"

"I'd been a Injun, Bill," Bass roared, slapping both
thighs with mirth, "*you'd* been gut-shot awready!"

"Blazes, but you give a man a start: poppin' up there

right outta the ground." And the skinny man slid his rifle back across the front of his saddle.

"Didn't do no such thing, Bill," he replied with mock solemnity. "I see'd you from way back up the slope. You was making your way for my camp. Seems you just didn't know it. C'mon across the crick an' leg down off your horse."

Ol' Bill Williams urged his horse into the fast-running stream, pulling the two packhorses behind him. Onto the south bank the animals clattered to a halt on the rocky cutbank. "Where you bedding down, Bass?"

"Yonder in the trees," he answered. "Your belly ready for some fodder?"

"No coon in his right mind ever passes up a meal," Williams admitted. "Never know when he'll next have a chance to strap on the bag."

The late spring sun had settled behind the Wind River Mountains, and the cool air was sinking off the high places by the time they both sighed and pushed themselves back from the slabs of meat Titus had suspended over the coals on sharp sticks he had stabbed into the ground around his small fire pit.

"I got coffee," Bill declared.

"Tobaccy too?"

Williams nodded, slowly inching to his feet on crackling knees.

Scratch inquired, "You been to a trader lately, have you?"

"Not since last autumn it was. Laramie. I ain't got much, but running onto ol' friends is sure as hell good cause to break out the last of what I do have."

That had always been the mark of those hivernants, seasoned veterans of the mountains. They were willing to share the last of what powder and lead, coffee and tobacco they had with a compatriot. A man never knew when he might be the one who would be short of fixin's one day.

"Where you been since Laramie?" Titus asked as he came back from the creek, having filled the coffeepot with clear, freezing water racing down from those snow-fields high above them in the mountains.

"Here and there," Williams offered. "Spent time on the Rosebud, tarried some on the Tongue. Wintered the longest on the Tongue."

Titus set the pot on the fire and pulled off the lid. "You get up to Tullock's post?"

"Never did." Then Williams stood and walked around the fire to one of his rawhide parfleches where he pulled free a large skin bag. He tossed it to Bass across the low flames.

Pulling the drawstring loose, Titus smelled the aroma of coffee. He knelt at the fire near the pot and poured three heaping handsful into the pot before replacing the lid and yanking on the drawstring. "Where you away to now, Bill?"

"West a ways."

They were quiet a long time, listening to the last calls of the tiny birds at the crossing, hearing the lick of the water coming to a boil, the tumbling of the coffee as the lid began its delicate dance. Bass grabbed a short twig and pulled the pot to the edge of the coals, then relaxed back against his saddle.

"Last I see'd of you, Bill—was down to Taos," Scratch remarked. "Become a trader your own self—growed wearisome of standing in freezin' water up to your cock-bag."

Williams snorted with that. "Blazes, if nothin' come of that endeavor! Packed up my plunder and hightailed it for the hills." He sighed, stared at Bass a long time, then asked, "You ever run across that nigger what took your hair?"

"I did, few years back," he answered. "Fact be, I run onto him later on that spring after I first run onto you."*

Williams dug a louse out of his beard. "What ever come of it."

He turned and looked at Bill, a rueful smile coming

---

* *Crack in the Sky*

across his face. "You soft-brained idjit! Here I sit right afore you. What you think happed?"

"Just callated there'd well be a dandy of a tale behin't you cutting that red nigger's trail," Williams explained.

Titus had settled the grounds, poured them each a cup, and settled back against his saddle with his feet to the fire when he next spoke, "I . . . set things right."

Williams studied him a moment, then seemed to realized he would get little else for the time being. "A good thing, when a man sets things right."

He sipped his coffee, then asked Williams, "You're laying your sights west to find better trapping?"

"Ain't going west for beaver, Scratch."

For a moment Bass gazed at the small packs of beaver pelts William had pulled off the pack animals and flung to the ground earlier.

"Gonna take your plews to John Bull at Fort Hall?"

Bill shook his head emphatically. "I don't figger to go nowhere near Hall."

"Maybeso you do your best to keep your goddamned meat-hole closed 'bout where you're going and what you aim to do when you get there, because I didn't up an' tell you how I killed the nigger what scalped me, left him gutted for the magpies and crows to pick over?"

With a shrug, Bill said, "Naw, I was just sitting here reckoning on if you'd be one to come with me."

"Come with? Where, goddammit?"

"Down to Fort Winty,"* Williams explained. "Got plans to meet some fellas there."

"Who?"

"Peg-Leg, Dick Owens, Silas Adair, and others."

"What you fixin' to do, if I throw in with you?"

"Beaver's all but dead, Scratch. I don't plan to curl up an' die with it," Williams growled sour as green rhubarb.

"Where you lay your sights?"

"I hear there's money to be had in California."

"That's a long ride just to find you some Mexicans.

---

* Fort Uintah, in present-day northeastern Utah.

What can you do in California you can't do down to Taos or Santy Fee?"

Williams's eyes shimmered bright as Mexican tinwork in the flickering firelight. "Ain't what we're gonna do, Titus Bass . . . it's what we're gonna bring back." Then his whole face lit up with a merry smile. "Horses."

Taking a long sip at his coffee, Bass was surprised to sense a surge of unexpected excitement ignite within him. He had to admit it had been a long, long time since he had felt this particular tingle of unbounded adventure. Since he had felt this sort of keen, sharp-edged tang stirring deep in his very soul, sensed this craving to be gone to far valleys and new dangers.

"You want me to go steal horses in California with your bunch?"

Bill Williams nodded eagerly, rocking up on his knobby knees so he could lean close. "I'd ride anywhere if I had a man like you at my back, Titus Bass."

For a long moment Scratch stared at those flames licking along the split limbs in the fire pit, realizing the anticipation was licking its way through him in much the same way with its own undeniable passion.

"Awright," Bass finally relented with a rasp to his voice, his throat constricting with unbridled eagerness. "I'll be at your back when we ride into California to steal a few Mexican horses."

"I 'spect I better tell you it ain't gonna be stealing them horses that's the mean trick, Scratch," Williams confessed, both his face and tone of voice gone solemn of a sudden. "It's getting back out of California with them horses . . . an' our hides too."

4

───────◆───────

What Ol' Bill Williams had in mind wasn't to merely ride into California and ride back out with a few Mexican horses and mules.

No . . . he was instead consumed with a burning vision of leading the biggest, grandest raid ever: returning to the Rockies with a herd that would number in the thousands.

South by west from the Popo Agie the two of them pushed hard across the next six days, starting when it grew light enough to pick their way into the dawn, remaining in the saddle until they grew so weary they no longer dared to grope through the darkness, sinking to the cold ground to spend another fireless night.

Dried meat and creek water was all the fare this pair allowed themselves as they plodded across the great saddle of the Southern Pass, dropped over to the Sandy, continuing down to the Green. South from there to the narrow valley trappers had christened Brown's Hole where they reined up outside the walled stockade of Fort Davy Crockett. Near the mouth of Vermillion Creek the two picketed their horses and lashed a wide strip of oiled canvas between three old cottonwoods to protect their pelts and supplies before moseying over to the post to see who might be about.

The first peal of thunder leaped from a bank of dark, distant clouds rumbling out of the west. Already the dry, crackling air smelled heavy with the portent of rain. The breeze had picked up and the clouds were lowering by the time Bass and Williams approached the front wall. Titus pulled back on the thick strap of rawhide that had been nailed to the cottonwood logs, dragging open the narrow gate on its squeaky iron hinges. More than a dozen men, women, and children gathered in the courtyard turned with the noise.

"That really you, Bill Williams?" one of the men cried out as he stood.

"Gloree, if it ain't Jack Robinson!" Williams answered the call. "Heard you was off with Carson."

"Didn't neither of us do no good," Robinson replied as the two stepped up. "So Kit's sashayed on down to Taos to see 'bout some *aquardiente* and Mexican gals."

"A dangerous mix that'll be for li'l Kit," Williams replied. "I didn't figger he'd stay a hunter for the Bents very long."

"I 'member you too," Robinson said as he turned to Bass. "You're the one they call Scratch."

With a wide grin Titus replied, "I'm sure as sin folks call me a lot of things!"

"In that time we spent together," Robinson explained, "Kit told me how you helped him in his duel with that parley-voo bastard named Shunar."

"That does take me back a ways," Titus remarked a bit wistfully as many of the others were drawing close. "Seven—no, eight—summers it's been."

"Don't none of you coons go getting down in the face since there ain't no more ronnyvooz," Williams growled, slapping Bass on the back. "I figger we're 'bout to raise some serious hell and put a chunk under it our own selves!"

"Bill Williams!" A voice rose from the far side of the

small compound. "An' I'll be go to the devil if it ain't Titus Bass with him!"

Scratch shouted, "Billy Craig, get your skinny pins on over here!"

The group of strangers parted slightly as Craig stepped through, extending his hand to the newcomers. Quickly glancing over the group, Williams laid his bony paw on Craig's shoulder and said, "You've gathered a good bunch, from what I see, Billy. All old hands, that's for sure."

"Wish't I had more for to go with you, Bill," Craig declared.

"Any more fellers still to come in?"

Craig wagged his head. "No one else who wants in on our ride."

"That be a shame," Williams answered. "They'll miss out on the best summer since the ronnyvoo of thirty-seven when we shot up that bunch of murderin' Bannocks!"

"Some of the rest who turned me down say they don't wanna come because it's a crazy idea of yours and Smith's," Robinson explained.

Williams glared at him in disbelief. Then turned to another trapper as he said, "Didn't you and Mitchell here tell 'em what we found in California that first time we went?"

With an eager nod, Levin Mitchell said, "Horses and mules for the taking!"

"After we get done having us a doe-see-doe with them see-nor-reetas!" snorted Jack Robinson.

"I was hoping for to have at least twenty men, Billy," Williams admitted.

"Maybe Peg-Leg's gonna find some down at Fort Winty for us," Craig observed.

"That where the one-legged nigger's gone?"

His head bobbing, Craig said, "Smith's gone on ahead to see to getting the broodmares."

"There some Snake camps about?"

Robinson explained, "Not a sign nearby. That's why

Peg-Leg put out for Robidoux's post. Word was, there's Yutas camped down there."

"What you want from the Yutas?" Titus asked. "Figger to get a few of them bucks to come along on your trip to Californy?"

"What we need to buy or trade off them Yutas is a half dozen or so wet mares."

"W-wet mares?" Scratch responded. "I thought you'd get all the horses you wanted from the Mexicans."

"Told you we was going back for some big doin's this time, didn't I?" Williams said. "We callated the best way we can strip that many head of horses off them Mexican ranchos and back across the desert to these here mountains was to take us some wet mares along."

"Mare what are nursing foals?" Bass still could not comprehend. "Them li'l' foals only gonna slow you down."

"We ain't taking the foals," Williams announced. "Gonna leave 'em behind."

He started to glimpse the masterful plan of it slowly materializing, just the way he would gently adjust the sections of his telescope to bring a distant object into focus.

"So you'll take them wet mares along to hurry the stole horses back from Californy," Scratch said, slapping Williams on the back exuberantly. "I'll be damned if that ain't some!"

"I come up with that plan my own self," Williams boasted, his chest swelling. "Ever since we come back from California, I been waiting to put all the other pieces to it. Now I wish't we had more riders."

"Bet Peg-Leg's signing up a few more down at Robidoux's post right now," Craig advised.

"Where's Sinclair?" Bass inquired.

Craig pointed at the mud-and-log hut at the back of the three-sided stockade. The river served as the fourth wall of the enclosure. "He's inside, dusting and combing out some robes he traded off a band of Yutas last week."

"So tell me, niggers—is there any whiskey in this pisshole of a post?" Titus asked, grabbing Williams by the back of his neck. "I don't know about you boys, but Bill and me here are near half froze for a hard drink after all our cold camps and too goddamned many saddle sores."

"Let's go swab our gullets, Scratch!" Williams roared. "And have us a drink to Peg-Leg signing on some more riders."

One of those problems with getting older was that the hangovers hurt more than they used to.

That next day when he awoke pasty-mouthed, cuddled within his buffalo robe and blanket, curled up back to back with Bill Williams beneath that sheet of oiled canvas, Bass hurt all over—just the way he would if he had been pummeled in a St. Louis riverfront brawl. He wasn't even certain how they'd ended up back at their camp outside the stockade. Under their own power? Maybe not.

He sat up slowly, pulling the robe back from his face, greeted with a bright dawn, the cottonwoods still dripping rain from last night's storm, the air cool and vibrant with a tang of moisture to it. The bright light hurt his head more than it should until he found his wide-brimmed hat and pulled it down low over his eyes. But it was the side of his face that hurt more than anything.

Perhaps he'd fallen and didn't remember. Maybe one of the other trappers had flailed his fists around when he got into the cups—with one of the blows slamming against his cheek.

"Bill," he whispered. Even the sound of it hurt between his temples. So when Williams did not respond to some gentle nudging, Titus decided not to awaken the trapper.

Gingerly laying his fingers against the side of his own face, Titus found his cheek swollen. Nothing more than that gentle touch made him wince: in an instant his jaw was in utter torment, so extreme a poker-hot pain exploded in his head, taking his breath away.

Slowly the heat subsided in his jaw and he could open his eyes again. Careful to hold his head just so, Titus dragged back the blanket and robe from his legs. He had to pee in the worst way.

Standing in the brush a few yards away from their shelter, Bass wondered how much he owed Prewett Sinclair for all they drank the night before.

"You wasn't the hard punisher, Scratch," the fort proprietor explained later that day when Bass plodded back through the post's gate and found Sinclair at work unfolding, then refolding, a few bolts of calicos and other coarse cloth on a narrow counter set up in the trade room.

Billy Craig sat in the corner on his pallet, scratching his belly with one hand, his wild hair with the other. "Ol' Solitaire was the punisher."

"He get me back to camp?" Titus asked, eyeing one of the small kegs on the counter.

"Looked to be that way." Levin Mitchell stirred in his bedroll. "Bill was shining on till it come time he figgered he should get you back to your bedroll."

"But that's when Solitaire went soft at the knees and spilled right down on his face," Craig snorted with a giggle. "He was out and there was no raising the dead!"

"I need me a cup of that barleycorn, Sinclair," Bass mumbled huskily, doing his best to talk without moving his jaw.

"Couldn't understand you too good. Something wrong with your mouth, Scratch?" asked the trader as he noisily slid a tin cup down the counter to the small keg where he began to pour out the cheap whiskey.

"Ain't anywhere I don't hurt," he confessed, rubbing a gritty eye. "My head thunders like a herd of loose ponies with ever' little noise. But I just crawled out with my jaw on fire this morning."

Sinclair pushed the cup at him across the narrow counter. "Lemme look."

In a moment the trader nodded to the others. "He's swolled up." Then he tapped the trapper's cheek as gently as he could. Again Bass winced and jerked his head away. "It's hot, Scratch."

"Bet it's a tooth," Mitchell advised. "Had me a bad one last year."

"Tooth?" Titus echoed.

"C'mere," Sinclair said and gestured him over. When Bass wasn't quick about leaning over the counter, the trader promised, "Listen, I won't touch you again. Just wanna look. C'mere now and open your mouth. Have me a look inside."

Titus looked down his nose as Prewett Sinclair leaned close, holding a candle between their faces as he peered into the trapper's open mouth.

"Wider," the trader demanded.

"Aggggg," Bass growled, his mouth opening as wide as he dared, the hot pain flaring as he did.

Sinclair leaned back and rubbed his nose. "Smells to me like you got a rotten tooth in there, Bass."

"Sm-smells?"

"Like meat going bad," Craig added, with a nod of his head.

"M-meat goin'—"

"You look all swolled up in there, what I can see," Sinclair continued. "There"—and he pushed the cup a little closer to the trapper—"you g'won ahead and drink your whiskey."

"Sinclair's rotgut hooch gonna take the edge off your hurt," Mitchell explained.

With an unsure, reluctant nod, Titus took up the cup and sipped. Slowly at first to see how the whiskey would burn his inflamed jaw. If he kept the potent liquid off to the left side of his mouth, it wasn't near so bad. But his head hurt so damned much that he had trouble swallowing. Nevertheless, Scratch succeeded in getting some of the whiskey down, eventually warming a stomach that had wanted to revolt at the first swallow.

"Maybeso this is gonna help some," he told the others as two more of the trappers pushed through the door to join them in the low-roofed trader's cabin.

"Go on and drink up," Craig said as he stepped to the counter to have himself a look at Bass's jaw. "You're gonna want to drown as much of that pain as you can afore we yank that tooth outta there—"

"Y-yank?" Scratch sputtered, some whiskey dribbling off his lower lip.

"Gotta come out," Mitchell agreed. "Just like I pulled my own tooth last year."

"P-pulled your own tooth?" Titus echoed, his eyes growing larger.

"Drink up, Bass," Sinclair declared. "It's on the prairie."

Both of the trappers who had just arrived lunged toward the counter, as one of them hooted and slapped a flat hand onto the wood planks. "On the prerra! Hur-raw! Let's drink, Sinclair!"

"Not for the likes of you," Sinclair snarled as the trap-per jerked back in surprise. "We're gonna get Bass drunk here, then pull a tooth out of his head."

The entire room watched as Scratch slowly poured the stinging whiskey past his lips, letting it slide down his tongue, past the back of his throat and on to his warming belly. In their eyes was a look of unabashed envy. A free drunk, compliments of the Fort Davy Crockett trader.

When he pulled the cup away from his mouth and licked some drops hanging from his shaggy mustache, Sinclair took the cup from him. When it was refilled, Bass took another long sip of the whiskey that tasted even smoother than that first cup.

"Awright," Titus mumbled, feeling his tongue thickening, "so if Ol' Bill fell on his face and wasn't moving a muscle . . . I figger you boys joined in to help get him and me back to our trees?"

"None of us figgered you needed any damn help," Mitchell explained. "Because you started dragging him out the door."

Craig sniggered some now. "You wasn't pulling him out into the rain and mud by his collar like this!" And he pantomimed by seizing the back of his own shirt and raising it until his arm flapped.

"H-how?" Bass stammered.

Sinclair explained, "It was a pretty sight. Watching

you weaving back and forth, leaning over to grab Bill by his ankles, dragging him around right over where Mitchell's standing now, you good as falling yourself while you're fighting to get Ol' Solitaire out the door and into storm."

Titus wiped the back of his hand across his wet lips. Then he licked the back of his hand, tasting the faint sting of the peppers, the all-but-hidden sweet molasses. "I dragged him by his leg all the way back to our camp?"

Mitchell shrugged. "Dunno, Scratch. We throwed the door shut after you got him dragged out the gate!"

Already his head was growing a little fuzzy, that whole strip of skin above his eyes gone numb. Doing his best to concentrate, Scratch said, "Bill was beside me while ago when I come awake."

"Did you check to see he was breathing?" Craig roared, stirring up a storm of renewed laughter.

"Maybeso Scratch drowned Ol' Bill in a rain puddle on the way back to camp!" Mitchell hoo-hooed.

"Yeah!" Sinclair jumped in. "Can't you just see poor Scratch dragging Solitaire back to his robes—so drunk Bill can't close his own mouth so he drowns?" The trader threw back his head and flopped his upper body back onto the counter, his arms flung akimbo as his mouth went slack, jaw dropped open.

"Shit, Prewett!" Craig hollered. "With his mouth open like that, only natural that Ol' Bill drownded out there in the rain!"

"Poor Scratch." Mitchell pounded a hand on Titus's back. "You was so drunk you didn't know any better—drownding our friend the way you done."

They had him worried. Especially now that his head had grown so fuzzy. "M-maybe I ought'n go see to him just so I can be—"

Bass had taken a handful of steps before Craig snagged Scratch's arm and spun him around. "Hold on there. Way you're walking—you ain't fit to go off to check on no one."

"Someone ought'n go see—"

"Maybe you're right," Sinclair agreed. "Mitchell, you

or one of the others—go see to Ol' Bill. See if he's breathing yet."

Mitchell turned and nodded to one of the other trappers, a half-breed Frenchie named Toussaint Marechal, and together they stepped through the low doorway into the bright sun, disappearing across the fort compound.

Suddenly Craig leaped to the open door and shouted after them, "If'n you wake Solitaire—be sure you tell him we're fixing to pull Scratch's tooth. I'll bet that ol' preacher'd wanna be here to see this!"

"Ain't none of you gonna pull my tooth!" Bass protested. "Gonna do just fine by my own self."

"Maybeso," Craig replied. "We'll see how steady your own hands are . . . 'cause it's for sure you're ol' legs ain't!"

"What you figger'm I gonna use to pull it?" Scratch asked, giving Craig a playful shove as he turned back to Sinclair.

"Dunno for sure. Mitchell's the one said he pulled his own tooth," the trader declared, then looked at Craig. "What'd he use?"

"Had him some pinchers in his shooting pouch," Craig explained helping steady Bass. "What he uses to pull his ramrod out when he's pulling a dry ball or an old load."

"M-makes sense." And Scratch nodded, inching away from Craig. "I got me my own ball puller I can go get."

A suspicious Craig quickly scooted over to block his way. "You wasn't thinking of running off, was you?"

Bass leaned back against the counter noisily, sensing for the first time just how thick his tongue had grown. "Naw. Need to get my ball puller so I can be a tooth puller, s'all."

"Thought you was sneaking off—"

Lunging out, Bass seized Craig by the front of his greasy cloth shirt with his right hand. "You figger me for being feared of pulling my own tooth, don'cha?"

"Dunno if you are or not—"

Shaking the younger trapper, Bass growled, "How

'bout we let you start this here fandango by yanking out one of your own goddamn teeth."

Seizing Bass's wrist in both his hands, Craig attempted to wrench the older man's grip from his shirt. "Y-you gone stupid on whiskey!"

"Don't you ever again let me hear you say to my face or behind my back that you think I'm feared of something," Scratch bellowed inches from Craig's face. "Maybeso, you was a braver man than me a few years ago when we was cornered inside Robidoux's post by Thompson's bunch."

The trapper ruminated on that a moment, then released his hold on Bass's wrist. "Yeah, I remember. You talked down them Yutas had us surrounded." With a sigh, Craig grudgingly admitted, "Likely you saved our hair that day."

Dropping his hand from Craig's shirt, Titus mumbled, "You really ain't a bad sort, Billy. Only want you to stay away from my damn mouth."

Mitchell and Marechal shuffled back in the door, the cool of the rain-cleansed morning wafting into the trading room with them.

"Bill's gonna be sleeping for some time to come," Mitchell announced.

Pulling the cup of whiskey from his lips, Bass slurred, "He ain't drowned, is he?"

"Not by rain, he ain't," Mitchell replied. "But he's been damn near drowned with whiskey that he ain't gonna be here to watch you pull your tooth neither." The younger man yanked up the flap to his shooting pouch and pulled out the small tool. "Here you go, Scratch. Have at your tooth."

"When you're ready," Sinclair prodded, sliding a round mirror in a heavy oak frame across the top of the counter planks.

Scratch reached up and pulled off his hat, flopping it on the counter. "Gimme that ball puller."

"What 'bout the blood, Prewett?" Mitchell asked as he handed Bass the tool.

Titus swallowed hard. "W-what blood?"

Craig said, "You're gonna have a big hole in your jaw where that tooth come out. Maybe 'bout the size of a lead ball."

Nodding, Mitchell assured, "I bit down on a piece of leather till the bleeding stopped. Your jaw looks more swolled up than mine was—so I reckon you're gonna bleed some—"

"Nawww, I heal fast," Bass boasted, then turned to gaze into the mirror Sinclair was raising to eye level.

For a moment he stopped and did nothing more than stare at his image, unmoving. Gazing first at the swollen jaw, then at all the gray in his beard and mustache, amazed at just how gray had become all that hair emerging from the bottom of the faded black bandanna. Even his eyebrows were turning a stark white against the oak-brown of his skin. Since the last time he had looked in a mirror, Bass had seen his reflection only in the placid surface of a high-country pond, maybe the dark, shimmering reflection staring back at him from a cup of coffee. Nothing as clear as this . . . inspecting all the little lines and tiny wrinkles, the deep furrows between his eyes and those carved from the outside of his nose down to the corners of his mouth. A face that was damn well marked with most everything in his life, for good or for bad.

"Awright," he relented. "Let's pull this goddamned tooth."

Slowly opening his jaw, wider and wider still, Titus was surprised at how little that stretching of his hide and muscles hurt now. Maybe this wouldn't be so bad after all. No matter how tender that whole jaw was. Yet it continued to throb, despite the whiskey that had effectively numbed everything else from the shoulders up.

Prying apart the handles of the small tool so that he widened the two small jaws just so, Titus turned his head to the side slightly and inserted the ball puller inside his mouth. Sliding it back across his tongue toward the tooth that had a blackened crown, he took a slow, deep breath . . . then let it out.

While he positioned the tool's jaws on either side of

the offending tooth. He had no more than gently closed the jaws on it than it immediately felt as if the tooth had become his whole head—completely empty and hollow, filled only with an unbelievably hot pain.

Yanking the tool from his mouth, he gasped and gasped again, struggling to catch his breath, hoping to somehow put an end to the throbbing heat in his head. His hand trembling, he dropped the tool and swept up the whiskey cup between both of them, bringing it unsteadily to his lips. Slowly he guzzled everything left in the cup, then let out a moist sigh as the pain slowly became bearable once more.

"God-*damn*," he murmured with his thick tongue. "I got bullet holes in me, and scars where red niggers poked me with arrers. But never have I hurt like that afore!"

"Ever you broke a bone?" Craig asked.

"Nary a one, this child ain't," Bass confided.

"You gonna try again?" Mitchell inquired, staring at Scratch's mouth.

He brooded on it, then said, "Maybeso that last drink of whiskey has done it, boys."

Clanking the tin cup onto the narrow counter, Scratch swept up the ball puller as Sinclair repositioned the mirror. Again he slowly opened the tender jaw and once more he inched the tool toward the rotten tooth. Sucking in a breath, Bass opened the metal jaws and did his best to position them on either side of the inflamed tooth. The instant the tool brushed its surface, with no more than a whisper of contact—it was as if a small charge of powder went off in that jaw.

He flung the tool down. As it skidded across the counter and tumbled onto the clay floor, Scratch spun round and round trying his best to cup that excruciating side of his face, an elbow knocking the mirror out of Sinclair's hands. It clattered onto the counter where the trader managed to keep it from tumbling to the floor.

"C-can't do it," Scratch rasped in the midst of the fading pain.

"Lemme have a look," Mitchell requested.

He shrunk back from the trapper, hollering, "No!"

"I ain't gonna touch your goddamned tooth," Mitchell protested. "Lookee here, I'll keep my hands down, see? Just open your mouth so I can look at it."

His eyes widening with suspicion, Scratch slowly opened his jaws as Mitchell rocked up on his toes and peered closely into the older man's mouth.

"Damn," Levin Mitchell muttered as he rocked back again. "That tooth looks wuss'n mine did."

"Wager it hurts wuss'n yours did too!" Bass grumbled.

Mitchell turned to Sinclair and Craig. "That jaw of his—the whole thing is swolled up. He's got it bad."

"What could happen if'n that tooth don't come out?" Craig asked the others.

With a shrug, Sinclair declared, "Maybe the poison in his jaw crawl up to his brain and kill 'im."

All of them turned as one and gazed at the older trapper. By now there were more than a half dozen of them crowding into the trading cabin.

"You think we oughtta?" Mitchell asked the others with a devilish look in his eye.

"Oughtta wha?" Bass echoed, his eyes squinting in alarm.

"No other way," Craig said with a shrug of his shoulders.

The trader nodded, "Best thing we can do for the man."

At that moment, Scratch had a foggy notion of what they were fixing to do to him. Whirling on his heel clumsily, he almost went down as he attempted to throw a shoulder into one of the younger men, spilling him backward.

"Grab 'im, boys!" Sinclair bellowed behind the counter.

Suddenly the others converged on him, grabbing arms and legs as Bass let out a high-pitched, unearthly howl.

"Grab his head! Grab his head!" Mitchell ordered.

One of the strongest of the young men clamped his beefy arm squarely around Bass's forehead and pinned the older trapper into the crook of his shoulder.

The pressure on his face, indeed his whole head, was

suddenly unbearable. Lashing out with both feet, Titus slammed into two of the others, catching one of them dead center in the groin, sending the young man hobbling backward for the doorway, doubled over and yipping in breathless pain like a scalded coyote pup.

His hands stiffened into claws, his arms flailing like the wings of some doomed bird of prey, Titus struggled against his young attackers, now unmindful of the pain in his jaw as he twisted this way and that to free his head.

Within moments they collapsed to the floor together. Sinclair was shouting orders, Craig and Mitchell too. In seconds they had seven men on him, with the trader commanding the others to raise Bass to the counter. With a heave they hoisted him into the air, his arms and legs flailing again, then plopped the older trapper onto the planks with a hollow thud. They had him pinned and helpless again.

Sinclair's face appeared right above Bass's, inches away. "We're doing this for your own good, Scratch. You don't get that tooth out, you'll likely die of poison gone to your brain. Leastways, you won't be worth a tinker's dam for the horse raid."

"G-god-d-damn you," he muttered between his teeth clenched shut with all the strength he could muster so they couldn't get to his tooth.

"Go to work, Mitchell," Sinclair growled, rocking up on his toes to get better leverage, bracing the heels of both hands against Bass's hairy, whiskey-soaked chin to slowly force the mouth open.

Already the waves of pain were making his eyes water, so hot, stinging. He started gasping for air as he watched Mitchell approach from the corner of his eye.

"Turn his head this way some," Mitchell ordered the big youth who imprisoned Scratch's head.

Fight as he did, Bass realized he was powerless to stop what was about to happen. So he went limp, his head pounding, his hot, empty belly rumbling with the sloshing whiskey, wondering if he was about to be sick. Most of all he tried to tell himself it wasn't going to hurt near as bad as leaving the tooth in . . . that he'd get through the pain and to the other side of this agony . . . that the pain was something small compared to all he'd been through—

Then those metal jaws clamped onto his tooth and it felt as if Mitchell was trying to tear his jaw right out of his mouth. When the tool started rocking back and forth, Scratch began screaming in the back of his throat—a sickly, feral sound—no more than a despairing gurgle now that his jaws were pried open and only his tongue was free to move.

An explosion of black powder ignited inside his head, blowing off the top of his skull. Icy-hot shards of pain splintered out from his mouth, slashing into his brain, down his throat, making it difficult to swallow, impossible to breathe.

"I got it!" a voice roared in victory.

Of a sudden the cool blessedness of a black syrup poured over him, releasing him from the heat. Causing him to tumble down, down, down—

5

◆

He snaked the tip of his tongue through that gap between his back teeth. There at the bottom of the left side of his jaw a second tooth was gone now.

In the week since Mitchell pried out the first, its gaping hole had knitted up quite nicely, what with the way Scratch swished whiskey or salt water around in his mouth several times a day. But this second hole hadn't closed yet, being fairly new the way it was.

For a few days there, his swollen, inflamed jaw began to feel better. Then the whole packed up and lit out from Sinclair's Fort Davy Crockett. By that second morning on the tramp, Scratch woke up in almost as much pain as he had suffered before. This time he understood what had to be done, especially when Levin Mitchell came over to inspect his jaw in the gray light of that miserable, rainy dawn. The trapper tapped his finger against the side of another tooth in Bass's head, and Titus groaned in agony. Not only with the heat of that immediate pain, but grumpy with the anticipation of what was to come. The only thing that had ever come close to that sort of torture had been when the Arapaho ripped off his topknot.

Bill Williams headed off to his packs to dig out a small canteen of whiskey while Bass dug for his ball puller in a gray-tinged resignation.

"Hol' me down, fellas," he begged the rest. "I know what's coming and I'm gonna be kicking like a three-legged mule here when Mitchell grabs hol't of that tooth."

He did, for sure too.

But for some reason, that extraction didn't hurt quite as much as the first had. And although he continued to bleed throughout the rest of that day on the trail, his jaw nonetheless felt better than it had for a long time. Maybe two of them, side by side, had gone bad together, he thought. Better to be shet of them both and start healing the poison that had swollen the whole side of his head.

Titus swatted at the tiny buffalo gnats swirling around his sweaty face now and pulled the hat brim down lower to shade his eyes from the midday sun as they plodded southwest down the Green River for Robidoux's post. Five days gone from Brown's Hole and Sinclair's fort already, which by his reckoning should put them close to rendezvousing with Peg-Leg Smith, what with the way this bunch had been licking over the ground.

He and Bill Williams ended up riding off for Fort Uintah with thirteen men in tow. To march right into California with Bill's brazen plan of sweeping up two thousand or more Mexican horses, Scratch knew they would need more than twenty riders. For the time being, the success of their California expedition rested in the lap of Thomas L. Smith, that fiery redheaded, hot-tempered veteran of both the Rocky Mountain beaver trade and more than one lucrative journey to the land of long-horned ranchos. If Peg-Leg ended up drafting another ten or more recruits, then their foray against the land of the missions would make each of the riders a wealthy man no more than weeks from now.

But if they attempted to punch their way into and out of California with too weak a force—hurled up against not only the vaqueros tending the ranchos but small squads of Mexican *soldados* as well—then this daring ride west into that foreign land lapped by the western ocean could well be their last hurraw. And he would never see his family again.

The days had not only been growing longer but hotter too, each night not nearly so cool as they had been. Summer was ready to bloom. The knitting of the stars overhead had taken a definite northward shift, along with that tilt to the path the sun scoured across the sky each day. It glowed hotter every morning, and hung up there longer every afternoon.

Then today they had run across these mists of troublesome buffalo gnats—disgusting little creatures so tiny a man might miss them if it weren't for the fact that they traveled in clouds that swarmed and swirled around the heads of their horses and pack animals, hovered around every square inch of bare flesh the men had exposed to the galling heat. It was as if the creatures' very feet were on fire when they alighted on his flesh, even before the gnats began to bite and burrow.

No wonder the shaggy buffalo had long, coarse, matted hair shrouding its eyes. An admirable protection from these annoying insects that zealously followed the herds, or any other warm-blooded, breathing creature who happened to pass close enough that the cloudy swarms sensed the body heat of those other unsuspecting mammals.

By midafternoon when they stopped to let the horses drink, the swarms surprisingly drifted off, theirs a dark mist weaving up the cooler bottom of a coulee as the sun finally appeared committed to falling toward the western horizon that day. Bass knelt on the creekbank, leaned over, and drank alongside the men and animals. Then he freed a second black-silk kerchief where he had knotted it around the strap to his shooting pouch and soaked the cloth in the cold water. After wringing it out, he rubbed it over his face, pulling his long hair aside so he could swab the back of his clammy neck. That done, he crudely knotted it around his long, coarse hair, allowing the damp handkerchief to drip, drip, drip down his backbone as he stood and stepped over to Williams.

"Was just cogitating on somethin', Bill," he began.

Williams looked up at Bass. "The heat can damn well swell up a man's head like that. It's a fact."

"I figger you got yourself a damned good reason why you're heading southwest across the wastes to California this time of year."

"I do." And Williams bent over for one last noisy slurp at the creek. Then he stood and explained. "Any other time of the year, this right here would be a problem."

The leader gestured at the gurgling creek.

"Water," Titus observed.

"Water," Williams repeated. "Come late summer, them creeks and springs and seeps down in that country we're gonna have to ride through will all be drying up—disappearing into dust."

A few of the other riders were stepping closer as Scratch remarked, "Weather'd be cooler come autumn."

"But with nary a drop of rain or a flake of snow to refill them waterholes," Williams declared. "Naw, my friend—you'll see for your own self that there's but one time of the year to make this crossing. 'Specially when we're pushing thousands of horses ahead of us, and every last one of 'em needs a lot of water to make it back to these here mountains."

"Only gonna get hotter from here on out," Scratch stated. "South where we're headed."

"We ain't see hot yet," Williams warned. "Ain't seen nothing of dry either. I wouldn't dare try what we're about to do any other time of the year but here at the end of spring. Turning back by midsummer. Any later'n that—why, our bones might just rot out there in them wastes with the bones of all them Mexican horses we couldn't get back to the mountains without water."

With a grin, Bass snorted, "So you claim we ain't on a fool's errand?"

"Could be, ol' friend," Bill replied, smiling.

"That's good," Titus said as he slapped a hand on the older trapper's shoulder. "I was beginning to wonder if you wasn't making it sound like this was serious business. Sure as hell glad to hear we're out on some great lark you dreamed up, Bill! Beaver's gone to hell and the mountain trade is disappeared like winter breath smoke—why, no better reason we ought'n just have ourselves some fun!"

"Especially if it's the last thing any of us do in this here life," Williams said, his grin slowly fading. "Awright, you *ciboleros*!" he shouted at the others, calling them buffalo hunters. "Let's get back in the saddle—by my reckoning, we'll be pounding on Robidoux's back door by sundown!"

The sun had turned every butte and mesa a startling red, so bloodily surreal it seemed as if the entire earth around them were the same burnished copper as were those trinkets and religious objects hammered out by a Mexican craftsman. Then down in that wide bottom he recognized from three years past, Scratch spotted the stockade and the small herds of horses grazing here and there on the low hillsides farther downriver.

They could hear distant voices hallooing and begin to make out telltale shadows of men emerging at the top of the near wall, a few coming out of the stockade on foot to have themselves a look. Across the river from the post stood a scattering of lodges, low and squat. Ute, he suspected.

"That you, Bill?" a voice cried as they approached.

"Peg-Leg?"

One of the figures hobbled away from the rest of those on foot and waved his hat. "You brung a good bunch with you?"

Williams reined to a halt beside Smith, held down his hand, and they clasped wrists. "Not near enough to bring out all them horses I planned on, Peg-Leg." He straightened in the saddle and sighed. "I'm hoping you done us some good here."

"Got a few hands, Bill," Smith admitted. "But I didn't come up with near as many as we'd hoped would come west with us to the Mexican diggings."

"Let's go have us some victuals," Bass said as he brought his roan to a halt on the other side of Smith.

"Lordee tells. That really Scratch?" Peg-Leg asked as he pivoted on the wooden limb.

"How-do, Thomas," Titus cheered as more of their bunch came to a halt around them.

For a moment Smith glared hard-eyed at Bass, then suddenly grinned as he held up his hand to the horseman. "Been a long time, Scratch. I see no gol-durned Blackfoot's knocked you in the head and stole what you got left for a mangy skelp."

"You was hoping my hair would get raised after we stole them horses back from you?"

Smith laughed easy and genuine. "I ain't never carried me no hard feelings for nothing, Scratch. Less of all, for you and them others coming here to take back them Snake horses."

"It's all water gone downhill long ago," Titus mused.

"Damn sure is," Smith agreed. "Why—when me an' Bill left here after that ruckus we had with you an' Walker, we ended up stealin' a lot more horses from the Mexicans that year!"

"More horses'n we could've stole round here!" Bill roared.

Williams and Smith had their chuckle before Peg-Leg turned and hobbled off with a wave, starting the procession toward the stockade as shadows quickly deepened. More hallooing greeted the new arrivals as they neared the walls, men streaming out that lone open gate as lanterns began to glow behind the tiny, rawhide-covered windows pocking the walls of those few miserable cabins inside the fort.

"Robidoux here?" Bill asked.

"He's here," Smith declared as they halted before the gate. "But he'll be leaving for Taos soon to fetch up more trade goods. Leave off your horses to graze over yonder with ours and bring your gear inside the walls. We been sleeping inside under the stars nights waiting for you."

"We? Who else you got gonna be a good gun to have along?" Williams inquired.

"Two of them went with us that first year, Bill."

"Who?"

"Dick . . . Dick Owens," Smith declared guardedly, his voice lowering. "And, Thompson too."

"*Philip* Thompson?" Bass echoed in alarm.

Smith pursed his lips, narrowing his eyes knowingly, and nodded. "You two fellers just stay outta each other's way, and we won't have us no trouble on this ride."

Just how in blue blazes could two men keep from stepping on one another's tails when both of them were going to be following Bill Williams and Thomas L. Smith out to California and back again with several thousand horses?

Maybe he just ought to pack up come morning and light out for the Bent brothers' Arkansas fort, or one of those posts farther north on the South Platte. Perhaps he could dig up his cache near the mouth of the Popo Agie and trade off a few peltries, managing to end up with what geegaws he wanted for his woman, those things he wanted to give his children. Not everything to be sure. Only a soft-brained idiot wouldn't admit that the bottom had gone out of beaver and it was going to be some time before the business rehabilitated itself. But in the meantime, Scratch figured he could get a little of this and a little of that, enough to show his family just how much he cared. If a man didn't bust his ass to make it so his family could have a few good things—what in hell did a man bust his ass for anyway?

Time was, when there were no strings on his heart, Titus worked those freezing months in the high-country streams so he could reward himself with a good time once a year or so at summer rendezvous, maybe afford a new shirt or a pair of those fancy black-silk handkerchiefs, besides his necessaries. But a man didn't work just to make a living . . . that made him nothing more than a slave to those who bought the fruits of his labor.

Now there weren't that many buyers left. And what those few buyers were paying for plew wasn't near enough to make a good living for any man daring to

wade around in icy streams. Beaver was gone belly-up.
Buffalo hides brought a squaw far more than the labors
of any trapper. Buffalo better'n beaver? These mountains
sure as hell had gone crazy!

Any man with a tin cup full of beads, a few hanks of
silk ribbon, or a dozen packets of vermillion could talk a
back-broke squaw out of a buffalo robe . . . when a
man had to work hardscrabble in finding a likely stream
with good sign, choose where to make his set, wade out
crotch deep to pound in his trap stake, then wait before
he would return to learn if his efforts had been rewarded
or not.

But with buffalo, all a nigger had to do was trade off a
few cheap geegaws for a winter-kill't robe!

Maybe there was a chance the Bents or other traders
on east of the mountains would give him a fair enough
price on his beaver that he would not have to return
home to Crow country empty-handed come autumn. He
sure enough had time to pull out in the morning, tramp
south to avoid those low passes still clogged with snow,
then swing back north again along the Front Range—
getting back home to her in good time before she'd start
to fret and worry.

Perhaps when he got back home, he might even trade
away some of that foofaraw he bartered off the traders
for a few robes from the Crow women up in Absaroka.
He could carry those robes over east to Tullock near the
mouth of the Tongue—

What a chuckleheaded fool he was! Caught himself
scheming how to become a robe trader on his own hook.
No sense in sinking that low. A man had his pride and
self-respect. A man had to earn himself a living . . . not
live off the sweat of others.

But, this raid on California might well be the last shining chance to rear its head up in the middle of the twisting path that was his life. In dimly remembered years
gone before he had recognized that first great opportunity
when it stared him in the face near Rabbit Hash, Kentucky. Eagerly he seized that chance to escape the life of a

farmer, to float down the great rivers all the way to New Orleans—to grapple with life on his terms.

But once in St. Louis he had all but smothered that fire in his breast out of fear or not knowing, worse yet—out of self-doubt. Another opportunity beckoned, standing squarely athwart his path, seductively beckoning him to the Rocky Mountains if only he dared to stare Lady Fate in the eye.

When he lost hair and was left for dead in those shining mountains, lesser men would wisely have chosen a different path from there on out. And when he learned that three former friends had stolen everything from him, lesser men would never have set out to put things right, or die trying. Later when an old friend killed a chief's wife and Bass was handed the task of bringing back the hair—most men, lesser men to be sure, would have ridden off and never come back. . . .

Over and over life had laid obstacles and opportunities in his path, to do with either as he saw fit. And here at Fort Uintah as the raiders gathered before setting off for the California missions and ranchos, Lady Fate was beckoning to him once again. Luring, enticing, seductive in her sloe-eyed, half-lidded come-hither of an unflinching invitation. Ride to California and bring back his share of the horses he could then sell to the highest bidder. Just as things had been with beaver in the heyday of the fur trade.

He could turn his back on what might be this one last chance before these mountains changed forever . . . turn his back, ride away come morning, and wonder for all the rest of his days what might have been for him and those he loved.

But, Titus Bass had never shirked opportunity, or flinched in the face of challenge. As one of the last hardy holdouts, he had ridden down the moon on the beaver trade. What more was he expected to do, after all? This raid could bring him the wealth that had eluded him for all these seasons. But to make it, he had to put up with Philip Thompson.

"That who I think it is, Peg-Leg?" the tall, rawboned

Thompson asked as Bill Williams's newcomers stepped into the post square.

"Who?" Smith asked.

"That one." And Thompson pointed arrogantly at Bass.

Most of the other trappers eased aside, left and right, so that no one stood between them now.

"Shit, Phil," Dick Owens replied dumbly. "You know 'im. That's Bass. He was with Walker, Meek, and the rest when they come to steal back your horses an' kill you few winters back."

"I 'member that!" Thompson snapped as he came to a halt about four paces from Titus. "I remember saying I figgered the whole shebang weren't worth killing a white man over . . . but this here nigger said he'd gut me if he had the chance."

Williams stepped into that dangerous ground between them. "There was a fire lit under all of us that cold day. No use bringing it up again—"

"There's only one other nigger I wanted to get my hands on as bad as I wanted to get my hands on Joe Walker," Thompson admitted with a grumble. "The white nigger who made them Yutas turn away."

Titus said, "Ol' Bill never told me you was carrying a turrible grudge for me after all this time, Thompson."

"Only against Walker for calling me out," Thompson confessed.

"But you allays talked 'bout Bass in the same breath as Walker," Dick Owens disclosed.

"That's right," Thompson said. "I carried a sour belly for saying you'd gut me if'n you had the chance."

"We all had bad feelings back then," Smith explained. "But now we're going to California together so we're peaceful—"

Williams interrupted, "Out in California both of you can shoot your share of bean-bellies to get it out of your craws. Just don't cause me no problems or I'll leave both of you hanging from a low tree so the buzzards can pick out your eyeballs."

Smith turned on Thompson. "You wanna back out of our plan, Phil?"

"No," Thompson replied grudgingly. "I wanna go to California, an' steal enough horses to make myself a rich man."

Then Smith turned to Bass. "Awright, Scratch. Do you wanna back out of Bill's plan?"

Wordlessly, he glared at Thompson a long moment before answering. "I'm riding to California with this outfit."

"If you're both coming along, then hear me out," Smith warned. "You two can either have it out right here and now—get it over and done with so's one of you is dead on this spot . . . or, you can swear to me an' Bill there ain't gonna be no problems here on out."

"Why—sure, Peg-Leg," Thompson vowed. "I figger I can let bygones be bygones with this nigger said he'd gut me first chance he got. I'll make peace with Titus Bass." And he held out his hand as he took two steps forward across that open space.

The rest of them waited around Scratch as he stared at that hand Thompson offered. Finally he said, "I s'pose if we're gonna be fighting Injuns and Mexicans, we don't need be fighting each other."

He seized Thompson's big paw and shook it, looking briefly into those eyes where there really was no warmth. Although Thompson's handshake was firm, although there was a smile on the man's face, Titus Bass didn't believe Thompson meant any of it.

Williams turned to Smith. "Now we got that settled, you come up with some broodmares, Peg-Leg?"

Smith nodded eagerly. "I traded for eight of 'em."

"Where you get 'em?" Mitchell inquired.

Peg-Leg jabbed a thumb in the direction of the nearby village. "Them Yutas are keeping an eye on 'em till we're ready to ride off."

"They'll keep the foals with them?" Williams asked.

"Yep, just the way we planned, Bill. I promised 'em some horses for the use of their mares."

The bony, angular old trapper turned back to the

entire crowd and roared, "Looks like we've got a reason
to let the wolf out to howl tonight, boys! In two days
we're on our way to California . . . an' that means
there won't be no whiskey after we ride outta here!"

It was downright boneheaded of him to expect that no
trouble would ignite there inside Robidoux's stockade after they started mixing liquor with the bold talk of men
about to ride off on a daring journey, uncertain of their
return.

"Maybeso out to California, we'll all get a chance to
see just how big your *huevos* are, Titus Bass," growled
Philip Thompson, his tongue thickened by whiskey.

Williams laid a hand on Bass's forearm without saying
a word. After a moment, Titus slid the arm out from
underneath the hand.

"You wanna know how big my eggs are, you don't
have to wait till Californy," Scratch shot back. "S'pose
you come find out right now."

Thompson took a swig of his whiskey, then dragged
the back of his hand across his lips. "I don't figger neither
of us is in any shape to have at each other right now, ol'
man. Better we square off when we ain't been drinking."

"In the cups or not, you're a yellow-backed polecat,
Thompson."

The taller man bolted upright, wavered unsteadily a
moment as he rocked on the balls of his feet, preparing to
lunge across the circle for Bass, when two others caught
him by the arms.

"Lemme go!" Thompson snarled as he flailed at those
who held him prisoner. "I'm gonna tear out his gullet
with my own hands!"

"You heard 'im. Let 'im go," Bass echoed as he stood
and adjusted his belt, his left hand brushing the handles
on both knives where they lay tucked at the small of his
back. "Man wants me to kill 'im here and now—I'll
oblige the nigger."

Thompson's face grew red with more than the flush of
whiskey. "Y-you're the one's gonna d-die tonight!"

Smith came up to stand in front of Thompson, who danced from side to side as far as he could to keep his eyes on Bass.

Peg-Leg said, "You've had more'n your fill of whiskey this night, Philip. G'won to blankets and sleep it off—"

"I ain't goin' nowhere till I get my hands on that ol' nigger!" Thompson roared, trying to shove Smith aside.

"I said go to your blankets," Smith repeated, seizing Thompson's shoulders in his hands. "Either you go on your own, or your friends can drag you off."

"No one's gonna drag me off!"

Scratch hollered, "I said let 'im go so we get this done here and now!"

That's when Williams stepped in front of Bass. "The son of a bitch gets heavy in the horn when he's in the cups, Scratch," Bill explained in a sharp whisper. "He goes and sleeps it off, he won't even remember any of this."

"Trouble is—I'll remember," Titus warned.

"You ain't nowhere near as drunk as him," Williams declared. "Man with as much savvy as you oughtta know he should play out a little more rope for a horse gone wild."

Bass wagged his head, saying, "One of us gonna get kill't—"

"First off I'll kill you, Bass!" Thompson screamed. "Then I'll go find Joe Walker, Meek, and them others!"

With a sigh, Williams said, "Tell you what, Scratch. You swear to me you'll lay back and not pull on Thompson's short-hairs . . . and I'll promise you I'll watch your back till we get out of California and back across the desert."

"Then what?" Titus asked in a harsh whisper, his eyes glaring at the howling Thompson, who was wildly flailing his arms around.

"Come then . . . I'll let you do what you want with the bastard," Williams vowed.

"Why don't I save us a lot of time and trouble," Scratch snorted, "and just let him take me on right now."

Williams clamped onto Bass's upper arm and squeezed down hard. "I need Thompson. He's been to California with Peg-Leg and me before. 'Sides, if'n I throw Thompson out, he'll take near all the rest of these fellas Peg-Leg had waiting for us here. We can't do California 'thout Thompson."

On the far side of the circle Titus watched an increasingly angry Smith suddenly swing an arm back and backhand Thompson. But that only made the drunk madder, lashing out with a foot at the wooden peg leg. Smith pivoted swiftly, then stepped close as he yanked out a belt pistol and cracked Thompson on the temple. The drunk sank between the two men struggling to hold him on his feet.

"Get him back to his blankets!" Smith grumbled. "I don't wanna see any more of him till morning."

"His time's coming, Bill," Titus reminded the older man.

Williams nodded. "Just say you'll wait till we get to California and back across that goddamned desert."

"Maybeso I should just leave off and go my own way." Bass whimpered with regret that he'd even come this far. Staring in the eye what lay ahead from here on out.

"You didn't ride all this way with me just to turn back now," Williams argued. "You gonna try to find beaver this time o' year? It's the goddamned high summer, coon! Naw—you come this far with me because you knowed you wanted to do it. Maybe do it for your woman. Maybe do it for your own self. I don't figger you for one to pull out now."

He wanted to tell Williams he was wrong, wanted to shout it into his face . . . but the old trapper could likely see right through him—and already knew why Titus Bass had come this far.

"Awright," Scratch finally said, some of the tension seeping out of his muscles. "I'll walk wide around him . . . for now."

"That's all I ask, Scratch. Comes to Thompson and his

friends, I promise you I'll watch your back till it's time for you to settle this between the two of you."

"I'll get my robe and blanket, leave the stockade," Bass said quietly before he started away. "Better I go bed down somewhere else for the night."

6

———————— ◆ ————————

With Bill Williams and Thomas Smith at the head of the column, the twenty-four men put Fort Uintah behind them. Titus Bass rode with those who brought up the rear with those eight broodmares, hanging off to the left where he and his own animals wouldn't have to eat so much of the dust kicked up by all those hooves.

The stars twinkled faintly in the sky, and the moon would still be some time in setting as they took off down the west bank of the Green River. At their backs rose the Uinta Mountains, their peaks mantled with white as summer had yet to begin. Ahead stood a broad plateau* that took on wondrous colors with the coming of the sun— smeared yellow, red-orange, and vibrant crimson too. The Green twisted and screwed its way through that barren escarpment, a land of stunted cedar and piñon joining the ever present sage. Until they began to ascend the heights into that plateau's canyonland, the raiders would run across small herds of buffalo. But once on the other

———————————

* Present-day Tavaputs Plateau, in east-central Utah.

side and dropping to the Colorado River, the shaggy beasts would be no more. This would be their last chance to make meat.

Williams had them put into camp early that first afternoon. Their animals had yet to be hardened to the sort of trail that would become commonplace in the weeks ahead. And they needed to kill, butcher, and dry some meat for the lean times that were sure to come.

Three of the others who had been recruited by Peg-Leg were more than willing to mess in with Scratch. After making camp, they remounted with Bass to ride west into that short-grass country slashed by a maze of shallow washes and flash-flood erosion scars. Far ahead of them to the west lay the snowy heights of the Wasatch Range. All three of these companions had served the last years of the beaver trade with American Fur brigades, ofttimes with Jim Bridger leading the way. But this trio shared something much more indelibly in common with Titus that convinced him the three were good men to stand at his back no matter what might rear its ugly head on the coming adventure in California: They were counted among those who had managed to walk away from Henry Fraeb's fight against the Sioux and Cheyenne on the Little Snake the year before.

They hadn't covered many miles under a graying sky before running across a small herd of less than a hundred beasts nestled down in the cleft at the foot of the plateau. The bulls hung together in three bunches, grazing at the outskirts of the scattered herd. The cows and yearlings dotted the center of the lopsided bowl where the first of the red calves were dropping to new, lush, emerald grass watered every afternoon with the arrival of a brief, harsh thunderstorm.

Since trading his roan off the Shoshone late last summer, Scratch had discovered his saddle horse was not trained as a buffalo pony. No matter, he had reflected several times since. Here in his forty-eighth summer, he damn well didn't relish running meat anyway. Besides, the wind was favorable. Coming out of the west. In their faces. They could do with a stand.

"Better we hobble the horses yonder in that brush and make our creep up that draw," Bass suggested.

Elias Kersey nodded, his now faded top hat wagging, and all three dismounted with Titus, leading their saddle horses and pack animals into the shadows of the coulee. Quickly tying them off nose-to-nose, two-by-two, the four trappers emerged from the mouth of the draw in a crouch.

Scratch stopped them with a signal, then whispered, "Maybeso, we'll only get one shot apiece when the guns go off—if'n they set to a run. Best you boys make your one shot count."

"Just like shooting them Sioux," Jake Corn whispered with a grin that warmed his whole face. His cheekbones were so high they gave his eyes such an Oriental slant that upon meeting last summer Scratch had first believed Corn was a half-breed, Canadian-born Frenchman. He was instead a river-bred Cajun with a dusky drop of Creole blood in his veins.

Without another word the four fanned out, waddling away in a crouch from one clump of brush to the next, slowly working their way into killing range on the cows and yearlings. If nothing else was handy, a bull would do. But the cows made far better eating, especially when they would be drying wide strips of their tender meat for the trail ahead.

Crouching right beside a clump of cedar, Scratch withdrew the wiping stick from the thimbles pinned at the bottom of his fullstock, .54-caliber flintlock that he had carried west that spring of 1825. For a moment as he settled on his rump, Bass let his eyes run over the scratches, nicks, and gouges, every one of those wounds to the reddish-hued curly-maple stock a story of survival against all that these mountains had thrown against him, survival against all that the warrior tribes had failed attempting to rub him out. "Make 'Em Come," he had named this beloved rifle many winters ago. Through all the terrors and the joys of his seasons in the Rockies, this weapon had remained at his side like a steadfast friend, whether Bass was making meat or saving his hair.

Like him, the fullstock rifle carried its own scars—a silent testament to the many seasons the two of them had endured when lesser men had given up, or gone under. Come a day he figured he would run onto a good gunsmith at one of the trading posts and have the weapon rebored, the worn rifling freshened after so many years of hard use. Just running his hand down the forestock as he brought it to his shoulder now, allowing his fingers to brush over the buttstock as he nestled his cheek into place . . . it was as if he were caressing the hard-written story of his life, even to touching the scars and wrinkles that had turned his own leathery, lined face into a veritable war map of his years spent crossing and recrossing the high lonesome.

That long and angular man, Reuben Purcell, was the first to get off a shot, not far away to Bass's left. One of the big females shuddered, took no more than a half dozen faltering steps, then eased onto her knees and keeled over.

Titus took a few breaths to survey the nearby cows, quickly deciding on one as the buffalo grew nervous. Another rifle thundered, and he didn't even glance over to see which man it was or what animal he had hit. Some of the cows were starting to inch toward the first buffalo Purcell had dropped. A few others were moseying over to sniff at the second cow dropped.

Bracing one end of the ramrod on the ground as the wind picked up, Bass made a fist at the top of the wiping stick, laying the bottom of the forestock atop the fist as he eased back the hammer to full cock. Nesting the frizzen down upon the pan where the priming powder lay waiting next to the touchhole, he pressed against the back trigger, thereby setting the front hair trigger to trip the sear and spring in the lock with his slightest touch. With his cheek pressed against the stock, he laid the front blade down between the curved antlers of the buckhorn rear sight, with a tilt just so that put the blade into the tiny notch at the bottom of the buckhorn.

Only then did he let out half a breath as his finger slipped over the front trigger, barely inching the rifle to

the side so the front blade held on that wide girth just
behind the beast's front flank. The rest of the breath
seeped out as he held, waiting for his squeeze on the trigger to—

The rifle bellowed, a whisper of smoke spewing from
pan and a spray erupting from the muzzle. The breeze
had picked up enough that the gunsmoke disappeared
quickly enough for Titus to watch the low-velocity round
ball strike the cow's hide where a puff of dust exploded.
She sidestepped once, then again, and with the third time
shook her great head, slinging blood from her nostrils
and lolling her red tongue from her open mouth where
more blood dripped into the dirt and grass.

Across the bowl, a streak of lightning tore the darken-
ing sky asunder as he started to reload. Beyond the hunters, the buffalo grew all the more restless with a sudden,
sharp crack of thunder. Although they milled around, no
longer content to graze, the buffalo hadn't stampeded
away. Within seconds the sky started to pelt him with
tiny drops of rain. He quickly dropped a second cow. No
doubt about it now: They'd be skinning and butchering
at the height of the coming storm.

He hunched over his rifle, carefully sprinkling more
priming powder into the pan, then dropped the frizzen
protectively before standing to start back for the animals.
In the cold, blowing rain the four managed to butcher out
the boss, tongue, humpribs, and rear flanks from every
one of their kills, besides some length of intestine they
planned to prepare that night around the fire. In the distance, both north and south they overheard faint gunfire
as others made meat and the thunderstorm passed on by.
Each stiff gust of breeze made the blood-smeared men
shudder in their rain-soaked clothing, then the sun sank
low enough that it popped from the bottom of the clouds,
painting the plateau country with vivid shades of yellow,
red, and a dark, bruised purple.

With their pack animals unable to carry any more of a
burden, the four bloodied trappers mounted up, ready to
turn their noses back for camp when Jake Corn pointed.

"Lookee yonder, boys."

Bass's eyes narrowed at the high ground in the mid-distance. "Sure 'nough don't look to be any of our fellas, does it?"

"I make out more'n thirty of 'em," Elias Kersey announced.

"They ain't the friendly sort, we'll have to leave off the horses and meat to make a run for it," Rube Purcell said gravely. "That be the preacher's truth."

"Don't go fretting yourself just yet," Scratch chided, recalling how that previous summer the four of them had watched as half-a-thousand enemy horsemen rode down on Fraeb's two dozen.

"Bass is right," the squarish Kersey agreed. "They ain't movin' much. Just watching."

"Who you reckon they are?" Purcell asked, standing beside his saddle horse. Everything about the man was long, rail-thin, or ran at right angles.

"They meant us trouble," Titus confided, "that bunch'd already be tearing down here for our hair."

Kersey declared, "That's 'sactly why I figger 'em for Yutas."

"Sure they ain't some of them Sioux or Cheyennes run onto us last summer?" worried Corn.

Scratch shook his head, "We're too damn far west, south too, of the raiding ground for those niggers. Could be Bannock, but—I think Elias got it right. We'll know more when we get up close."

"Get up close?" Purcell repeated, his eyes suddenly growing large in that overly long face, with a jaw that reminded Bass of the bottom of a coal-oil lantern.

"We got meat to haul back to camp," Bass explained.

Purcell climbed into the saddle saying, "W-what if there's trouble from 'em?"

"Then . . . there'll be trouble," Scratch asserted flatly.

"Let's cover some ground, fellers," Kersey ordered.

The four hadn't yet reached the base of the hill they would skirt to reach camp, leading their slow-paced pack animals, when the Indians disappeared from the ridgetop on their right.

"That ain't a good sign," Jake Corn groaned.

"No two ways about it," Bass echoed. "Man needs to worry when he can't no longer see them brownskins."

By the time the four brought their plodding pack-horses around the base of the hill and camp was in sight, they spotted the warriors a ways ahead, making straight for the columns of smoke, coming on at an angle that cut across the dusty plain. Strange thing was, the horsemen were spread out in a broad line instead of riding single file the way Indians normally traveled. That was a bit worrisome. Right about then he wished he was back in that camp already—at least he'd have the extra rifles and pistols he packed along everywhere.

In the distance he watched a tall, skinny figure emerge from the brush. Beside him hobbled the other, one-legged, booshway of this horse raid. They stopped and each held up an arm in greeting as the horsemen halted some fifty feet from the two white men. Those warriors on either end of the broad front turned to watch the approach of several hunting groups returning from different compass directions.

As Bill Williams and Peg-Leg carried on a conversation by sign with the Indians, Bass led the other three and their animals around one end of the warrior line. A few of these strangers turned on the damp, bare backs of their ponies to glower at the four of them and their supply of butchered meat.

Coming to a halt behind their two leaders, Bass leaned down and asked of Williams, "You make 'em for Yutas?"

"They is. But faraway southern cousins to the ones we know up north," Bill declared as Smith continued slowly motioning with his hands. "Hunters from a bunch we run onto three years back on our trip out to California. They remember the one they call the Tree-Leg."

"Tree-Leg, they call him," Kersey repeated. "Mebbeso it's good news to have them figger our booshway for a friend."

Williams wagged his head. "Ain't necessarily so. They're mad as spit-on hens that they was out hunting and our bunch's gone and run off some of their buffler—killed some buff they say is rightfully theirs."

"To hell with 'em," Bass growled with indignation. "Wasn't a feather or a braid nowhere near where we four dropped our buffler!"

"Tell 'em we left the hides," Purcell announced. "Ain't any use to us, so they can have 'em."

"Rest of the meat too," Corn offered.

Smith turned to talk to Williams as more of the trappers drew close, making some of the warriors who carried only bows anxious at their approach. "Their feelings been stomped on, Bill. This head nigger won't take any hides, or what's left of meat—"

"We'll make the son of a bitch a few presents," Williams explained, "then maybe him and his bucks'll move on." He turned back to the warriors, and his bony hands began to gesture.

Scratch watched Bill tell the Ute horsemen that he would not speak to any man who would come riding up to his camp shouting that the white men were thieves for killing a few buffalo. But, he continued with his hands, Williams told the Ute leader that he would make presents to a friend who visited the white man's camp to smoke in peace.

"And drink some coffee," Smith reminded.

Williams whirled on him. "Don't you 'member the way these niggers drink coffee! We damn well don't have near enough to be brewin' up a batch for ever' bunch of scalawags we bump into down the road!"

But in the end, coffee would be a suitable peacemaker. While some of the trappers set coffeepots on to boil at three of the fires, the Ute horsemen dismounted and hobbled their ponies nearby before entering the camp and settling on their haunches around the flames as twilight continued to swallow the land.

"What say, Elias—you make us some o' your dumplings outta the gut we brung back?" Rube Purcell suggested after they had a fire crackling and were starting to slice their fresh meat into thin strips for quick drying.

"Dumplings?" Bass echoed. "You mean boudins?"

"Naw. Rube's had my dumplin's before," Kersey offered, pushing some of his long, blond hair out of his eyes. "I do have me a li'l flour."

"Real dumplin's?" Titus marveled, his mouth watering. He winked at Purcell and said, "Figgered you was just pulling on my leg."

While the water in the coffeepots started to roll, Jake Corn and Rube Purcell diced the liver into small pieces, along with short sections of the greasy intestine, as well as some of the lean backstrap, combining it all with a bit of the fleecy fat trimmed right off the boss, or humpribs, of the buffalo. At the same time Elias Kersey was mixing up his flour and water, along with a dash or two of their precious salt, forming a dough he rolled into palm-sized balls.

On the other side of the fire Scratch had been busy scraping all the rich, thick marrow from heavy bones he cracked open with a small camp axe. Each greasy clump of yellow marrow Titus scraped out with the tip of his knife quickly melted once he dropped it into the cast-iron skillet at Kersey's knee. The well-seasoned skillet began to spit and spew at the edge of the flames the moment Kersey plopped more than a dozen of his dumplings into the hot grease. The fragrance of their frying was almost more than Titus could bear, making his mouth water as it hadn't in a long, long time.

As a veteran of their first raid into California, Philip Thompson hung near the fires where Smith and Williams had seated their brown-skinned guests. While two of the Ute leaders parleyed with the white men, the rest of the warriors spoke quietly among themselves. From time to time some of them even peered curiously over their shoulders at the fire where Kersey and his bunch were tending to their supper.

"You don't figger 'em for pulling some shenanigans, do you?" Jake Corn asked as he tied up the ends of those last sections of gut they had filled with diced meat and fleece before they would be stuffed under the coals of their fire.

Bass shrugged. "Never know, but this here bunch

don't number much more'n us. If they figgered to get the jump on us, they'd made a rush on our camp a while back." Then he pointed to the dumplings, "Ain't they ready yet, Elias?"

"Yeee-awww! If that man ain't hungry for my vittles!" Kersey howled. "I'll be skinned if they ain't. C'mon and help yourselves, fellas."

The rail-thin Reuben Purcell was the first to begin stabbing at those dumplings, pulling them from their frying pan, spearing them into his tin cup, then settling onto his haunches across the fire as two other trappers moseyed up to the fire, plainly sniffing the air.

The shorter one's eyes twinkled as he peered at the skillet where Kersey set the last of the dumplings to fry in the popping grease. But he nonetheless remained silent as his wide-shouldered, bandy-legged partner spoke up.

"Merciful a'mighty—that smells good! Wha'chu made, fellas?"

"Dumplin's," Jake Corn said, grease dripping off his lips, spilling into his chin whiskers.

"I'm Silas. Silas Adair," the talkative one explained, then licked his lips as his eyes never left Kersey's frying dumplings. "If that smell don't get a man's hungers up."

"Tell you what, boys—have you something to add to the pot," Bass offered, "you're more'n welcome to sit and share what we got cooked for ourselves."

With his tree-stump-thick arm, Adair nudged the stocky trapper on the shoulder. "Roscoe, go fetch us some gut and a few ribs too."

The quiet one nodded and quickly turned away.

Purcell said, "He don't talk?"

"Coltrane ain't a mute," Adair replied. "But, he ain't ever been one to talk much at all."

"Sometimes, that's a good thing," Bass observed as he watched Coltrane scooping up a length he cut from the coil of buffalo intestine, dropping the gut into a small kettle at a nearby fire where Philip Thompson and his bunch were entertaining a number of the warriors.

"Any one of them fellas'd cut your throat if that

Thompson so much as asked 'em to," Corn declared right out of the blue.

Bass turned suddenly to look at the man seated to his right. "That's a strange thing to say to me."

"Jake is right," Kersey agreed. "That bunch of hard cases sticks with Thompson like ticks gone fat on an ol' bull. They're gonna jump you when that sumbitch says to jump you."

Scratch put a bite of dumpling in his mouth and sucked the grease from his fingers before he said, "Don't matter what those bastards try, or when they do it. I'll be ready."

"Yeee-awww!" snorted Kersey. "That's what I liked about you right from the start over there in the fight we had when Fraeb was rubbed out. There ain't no shuffle-footing about you, Titus Bass. You're a man what sees things for what they are. This is this, and that is that. I tell you, I much admire that in a man."

Bass glowed at the compliment, feeling his cheeks grow hot with the blush that spread beneath his gray beard. "Most all my friends, they call me Scratch."

"Scratch, is it?" Silas Adair asked. "Why, I didn't know you was the one I heerd of called Scratch."

"What'd you hear 'bout him?" Purcell asked, his mouth stuffed with dumpling as the quiet Roscoe Coltrane returned, setting down his kettle filled with intestine and humpribs.

Pushing an unruly sprig of copper-red hair out of his eyes, Adair grinned at Bass and winked. "Heerd how you died, two or three times. That's what I heerd tell."

"Only three times, they say?" Scratch echoed. "Hell, I've riz up from the dead more'n that!"

"Help yourselves, fellas," Kersey suggested, gesturing at the sizzling skillet.

They watched Adair and Coltrane greedily dig in, scooping dumplings from the grease. Around the fire the six of them ate and ate till they belched, making room for more of the greasy dumplings, their lips, indeed the entire lower half of their faces, shiny in the firelight. About the time the last of Kersey's dumplings had been speared

from the skillet, Jake Corn was kneeling at the far side of
the pit, using a long twig to scoop his boudins out of the
coals. As he speared each one with the tip of his knife,
picking it up to plop the footlong section of broiled intestine onto a man's plate, steam hissed from the tiny punc-
ture wound Corn had poked in the stiffened, crackling
tube of gut.

It was well after dark when Smith and Williams finished their parley with the leaders of the Ute hunting
party. Illuminated by the low flames of a half dozen small
fires, the white men got to their feet with the warriors
who rose and moved off for their ponies. Bill Williams
called three of his men close, then momentarily watched
them step away into the dark before he shambled over to
the fire where Titus and the five others sat smoking their
pipes in the afterglow of their hearty repast.

"Need three of you to take the next watch," Bill ordered. "After a couple hours go by, those three I sent off
gonna come back here and get the next watch. That
bunch'll come wake me when their time's done."

Bass nodded to Kersey.

Elias looked up at Williams. "Me and Scratch here
will go."

As Kersey was glancing over the rest of the men, Williams said, "You need one more."

"How 'bout you, Roscoe?" Bass inquired, staring at
the solemn one.

Without any change in his expression, even looking up
from the fire where he knelt with a twig to relight his
pipe, Coltrane nodded.

"That makes three of us, Bill."

Just before he turned away, Williams said, "See you in
the morning."

"You 'spectin' trouble?" Purcell asked as the leader
turned his back on them.

Bill contemplated the flames a moment before he answered. "We're bringing our stock in close, 'specially
them broodmares we need. Those Injuns figger on riding
off with our horses, I don't aim to make it easy for 'em."

"We'll sleep light, Bill," Titus said.

The bunch at the fire remained quiet in their own thoughts for some time until Silas Adair stood and stretched. He tugged down on the brim of his battered, black-felt hat. In the fire's light it appeared the hat had been singed at the back where it caught on fire when he used it to fan some flames of a time. "C'mon, Roscoe—we best go get our blankets."

Bass watched the two men trudge away to the nearby fire. Then he turned to the trio left with him. "You fellas promise me something."

"What's that, Scratch?" asked Jake Corn.

"Trouble ever comes—no matter when, no matter where . . . you fellas promise me you'll watch my back."

"A fight starts," Kersey began, "there ain't no Injun gonna get close enough—"

"I ain't talking 'bout Injuns, Elias," Titus interrupted. "I need you to watch out for Thompson and his weasels."

"That's just what we aim to do," Corn vowed. " 'Cause I figger you for a man what'd do the same for any of us."

Likely, those warriors were sitting out there in the dark, watching every precaution the trappers took to bring their stock in close to camp and post guards around those animals. More than once Bass chuckled to himself how that must irritate the piss right out of those Ute who had plainly come into camp with no better purpose than to eat the trappers' food, drink the trappers' coffee, and count the trappers' guns. Something about the redskins had convinced him they were a thieving lot, right off . . . and if they coveted anything the white men had along for their journey to California, it was the guns. In the constant warfare waged against their Apache neighbors, those rifles and pistols and smoothbores would more than tip the scales in the Utes' favor.

How it must gall the hunting party to watch the white men prepare for trickery even though the double-tongued Ute leaders had professed only the strongest of affections for those trappers who passed through their land!

Twice during his watch that night, Titus was certain at least one of the warriors was making a crawl for the horses. A sound out of place, maybe an odor brought him on the shifting breeze. Both times he would bring the rifle's hammer back to full cock and noisily stride toward that side of the remuda. That second time he was sure enough of what he'd heard that he dropped to his knees, lowered his head, and peered at that strip of horizon where the pale, starlit sky met the darker earth. There he spotted three of them lying among the sage, really nothing more than shadows humped upon the ground.

The temptation to shoot and wound one of them, even kill one of the slippery bastards, was almost more than he could endure. But Bass was sure they saw him too, had to hear him approach before his moccasins ground to a halt on the flinty hardpan, sure that's what brought the trio to a stop in their crawl toward the animals. Maybe just fire a warning shot somewhere between them . . .

"You two-tongued sonsabitches!" he bellowed instead. "You don't get and stay gone, I'll wear your hair my own self afore morning!"

From either side of him he heard running feet as Kersey and Coltrane sprinted out of the dark to join him.

Huffing, Elias asked breathlessly, "You see something?"

"Three of 'em," Bass replied, kneeling and motioning the others down close to the ground with him. "Lookee there."

"If that ain't a yank on the short-hairs!" Kersey exclaimed.

Scratch asked the other two, "What you figger we oughtta do with 'em?"

"Run 'em off," Kersey declared loudly as he stood in the dark, punching a wide hole out of the starry sky as Bass peered up at the man. Elias stomped toward the warriors as voices grew sharp in camp behind them.

"You sneaky bastards," Kersey was grumbling out loud, his s's whistling past a broken front tooth.

Scratch was just turning, drawn to look over his shoulder with the approach of footsteps coming out from

camp, when he heard the telltale *thwung* of a twisted
rawhide bowstring. On instinct he flung himself to the
ground beside Coltrane. In that same instant he heard
Kersey yelp.

Bass watched the trapper collapse to the ground, lost
from sight along the skyline. But he could hear Elias
groan, twisting, his body grinding noisily in the sage and
dirt out there in the dark.

Coltrane was already moving, lunging off the ground
into the night. A second bowstring snapped in the dark.

Scratch started to rise, crying, "I'll kill ever' one of you
bust-ass red-bellies!"

Of a sudden the night glowed for an instant as the pan
on Roscoe Coltrane's rifle ignited and the muzzle spat a
long tongue of bright yellow flame. The roar of his
weapon was immediately answered with a loud screech.

As he started toward the noises, Titus watched Coltrane take form out of the dark as the wide barrel of a
man went to his knee over a clump of sage. Skidding to a
halt, Bass saw that it wasn't brush at all, but Elias Kersey
balled up on the ground, clutching at his hip.

Coltrane's eyes flicked up.

"I took an arrow," Kersey grumbled between clenched
teeth.

Scratch was already bringing the flintlock Derringer
up—

—as Kersey added, "Don't know how bad I'm hurt."

At first he only heard them as he inched cautiously
away into the dark. Then he saw one materialize, and
suddenly another. They were doing their best to drag the
third one off but were making a noisy rescue of it. In that
next heartbeat they must have heard him slipping up behind them because they stopped, both of them dropping
their wounded comrade and reaching for their weapons
as they spun into a crouch. On their knees the small warriors were no taller than the scrub oak and bristly
sage. . . .

But Titus thought he knew one of those shadows out
there was more than some leafy brush. He brought the
rifle to his shoulder.

Without taking time to think, Titus laid the front sight on the dark clump, clenched his eyes against the coming glare, and pulled the trigger in one fluid motion. The moment the gun boomed and shoved against the crook of his shoulder Scratch opened his eyes, watching one of the shadows tumble backward with a loud gust of air slammed from the warrior's lungs.

In an instant all became pandemonium behind him in the direction of camp. For a fleeting moment he had just started to turn to look back over his shoulder. That's when another sliver of the night peeled away from the ground with a hair-raising shriek. An arm held high and brandishing a stone club, the Ute bolted toward the trapper, bounding over the sage and brush with ease.

Taking one step back, Scratch shifted his empty rifle to his left hand and with his right yanked out that short belt pistol. Dragging back the hammer with his thumb, he held . . . watching how the shadow raced closer and closer, dodging side to side, screaming his vengeance.

Wait, wait till he gets close enough to make a sure shot of it. Closer . . . wait—

Extending his arm he followed the target through the next heartbeat . . . until the emerging shadow suddenly became bare chest and naked legs. Holding on a spot midway between breechclout and that screaming mouth—he squinted his eyes shut to the coming glare and pulled the trigger.

Immediately opening his eyes, Scratch could almost make out the man's face, and the look of utter surprise on it, as the Ute's legs went out from under him and he toppled backward in a sprawl, kicking at a clump of sage.

"Bass!"

It was Peg-Leg's voice.

"Over here!"

Out of the dim glow emanating from the flickering light of their campfires appeared the wooden-legged booshway and four others, all of them huffing as they followed their ungainly leader through the maze of scrub brush to reach the scene.

"They get any horses?"

Bass recognized the voice of Philip Thompson. He answered, "Not a goddamned one."

Smith teetered to a halt beside Titus to say, "Did they get any of the men?"

"One for sure—Kersey." And he pointed back off to the left.

Thompson stepped up to Smith's elbow, leaning in so his taut face was lit with starshine. "And how many of them Yutas you let get away, Bass?"

His eyes narrowing, Titus looked away from Thompson and gazed evenly at Smith. "We saw three of 'em. Coltrane dropped the first one—"

"Afore, or after, Kersey was hit?" Thompson interrupted.

"Elias was awready down afore Roscoe pulled down on 'em," Bass explained to Peg-Leg, doing his damnedest to ignore the proximity, the very sneer of the other man.

"How'd you come to fire your gun?" Smith inquired.

"They was dragging off the one Coltrane shot," Titus explained. "I figgered to teach 'em some manners when it comes to jumpin' fellas like us."

"How many of 'em get away?" Thompson demanded.

Now Bass gazed back at the man. "Can't rightly say 'bout your side of camp, Thompson. But speaking for my watch on horse guard, not a one of them thievin' brown-skins is still breathing."

"I damn well didn't realize just how handy you was to have around, Titus Bass," Thompson replied, dripping with sarcasm. Then he started to snigger as he turned on his heel and started back for camp, followed by the others who had raced up with Smith.

Peg-Leg hobbled past Scratch. "Let's go see for ourselves what you've dropped out here."

They found his second kill no more than a few yards away, the first warrior out farther in the cold and the dark.

Smith sighed as he stared down at the body. "You want the skelp?"

"What the hell'm I going to do with this wuthless nigger's hair?"

Shrugging, Peg-Leg said, "Don't matter what we do now, I s'pose. The rest of them Yutas gonna dog our back trail here on out."

"An' if we bring them California horses back through this same country," Titus grumped, "likely them Yutas gonna make things even harder on us . . . all over again."

7

———————◆———————

They had laid in camp that dawn, particularly watchful with the coming light for any attack from the Ute.

But while they could hear the dim, distant chant of the off-key and mournful death songs, the trappers didn't see a thing of the unsuccessful horse thieves.

Even before the sun rose, booshway Williams had made a decision. "Keep cutting up your meat, boys," Bill told the edgy, sleepless men. "Lay it out to dry and keep your guns primed. I figger us to stay here. Our flints are fixed just dandy right where we are."

The old trapper had that right. Here the Americans had water, shade from the early-summer sun, enough to eat, with a little grazing for their animals too. Damn foolish for the men to risk abandoning this place if they hadn't finished jerking the buffalo for their long journey . . . especially if those Ute were still out there, waiting to spring an ambush somewhere on down the trail.

Throughout that day the twenty-four of them took their rotation at horse guard while the rest continued the monotony of their butchering. Thin slices of the lean buffalo were suspended on a framework of green limbs erected over smoky fires. Even more of the meat lay out in the sun, exposed to arid westerly wind. Near sundown one of the men hollered out, warning that he sighted a handful of horsemen appear on the crest of a nearby hill. The camp fell quiet while the two dozen came to stand and watch. As twilight faded, the distant horsemen disappeared from view, dropping out of sight behind the knoll.

"Keeping an eye on us," Smith advised. "Sleep if you can tonight, fellas—but we're making a running guard till first light when we can move out."

After the Ute had slipped in so close the night before, it was natural that some of the trappers were outright jumpy their second night of guard duty. The slightest sound emanating out of the dark, even a sudden shift in the cool, desert breeze, snapped a man alert—aware of just how loud his own heart was pounding. It finally grew light enough that Smith and Williams awakened all the men to prepare themselves for a possible attack. But as the hills brightened around them, no warriors appeared. Near or far.

It was time to push on.

The men bundled their meat, kicked dirt on their fire pits, then saddled up before the sun made its call on the day. Twenty-four of them prodded their horses and pack animals into the high plateau country, keeping the Green River in sight on their left as they continued south, every step taking them farther and farther from the cool, beckoning mountains.

While the remainder of the remuda would loyally follow, the men put their efforts into keeping the broodmares out front. They were the animals ready to bolt away, turn around, and race for home to reunite with their colts. From time to time one of the mares would get it in her head that she was going to peel away from the rest and start back at a lope for the familiar, quickly tearing away at a wild gallop through the sage once the trappers attempted to turn her nose back to the south. It was dusty, exhausting work for the saddle horses pressed into this terrible duty of tearing mares away from their colts. All for the sake of stealing more of their four-legged breed from California masters.

Six more mornings, middays, and long afternoons spent picking their way through the deeply scarred plateau before they were able to drop onto the bottom of what had the appearance of being a great three-sided bowl. Far to the east lay a few faint and jagged heights along the horizon. To the west stood the last great peaks of the snow-blanketed Wasatch Range. And ahead of them waited more of the low buttes and ridges as they pressed on down the Green through a land sunburnt anew, searching for a grand and muddy river.

Near evening two days later they struck the Colorado, camping near that junction where the Green willingly gives itself to a greater torrent rushing for the sea.

"You ever been on the Heely* far south of here?" asked Jake Corn that night.

In that heartbeat he remembered an old friend, and a long-ago journey into the land of the Apache.†

"Yeah," Titus said quietly, his gaze climbing to the myriad of stars overhead. Wondering just which one of them might belong to Asa McAfferty. "I trapped on the Heely of a time with a good man. We run traps together for a few seasons."

Corn leaped up so he could stride over and squat right beside Titus. "Ever you two see a Munchie?"

"M-munchie?" Scratch snorted. "Some kind of furred critter—"

"Injuns," Kersey corrected with a matter-of-fact air.

Now Scratch was bewildered. Wagging his head in consternation, he said, "Never heard of no Munchies."

"Was hoping you'd see'd 'em," Corn admitted.

Purcell nodded. "Me too."

"Hell, I see the way your stick floats now," Bass said. Tapping a finger against his temple, he continued, "These here Munchies are hoo-doos and such—"

---

* Gila River
† Crack in the Sky

"They're real!" Purcell snapped, shaking the stem of his blackened clay pipe at Bass.

Titus peered at the nonplussed look on Reuben's face, then quickly glanced at Kersey, and Corn. Finally, his eyes came to a rest on Adair. "You ever run across any M-munchies, Silas?"

"I ain't see'd 'em neither," Adair confessed, straight-faced, his copper-red hair gleaming in the fire's light. "But—merciful a'mighty—I have knowed a half dozen coons said they seen the Munchies for their own selves."

"Munchies," Bass repeated the word again. "If they're Injun . . . what sort of brownskin they be?"

"Well now," Kersey sighed, looking around the group. "Rest of you boys tell me if I get any of this here story wrong." He wagged his head as he studied Bass's face. "Can't rightly believe that here sits a man what trapped down on the Heely and didn't ever see him a Munchie."

Titus suddenly felt a compulsion to defend himself before this council of true believers. "Maybe I did, an' just didn't know it."

Adair snorted. "From what I've heard: if'n you had see'd a Munchie, you'd damn sure know it!"

The others chuckled as darkness came down on that desert country quickly cooling with the disappearance of the sun.

"J-just how would I know a Munchie to see one?"

Corn cleared his throat, "Elias—*you* go right on and tell the man."

Quickly rubbing a dirt-crusted finger beneath his nose, Kersey began to tell Titus Bass about that tribe of highly civilized, white-skinned Indians reputed to live in a deep canyon just beyond the valley of the Gila.

"I hear they eat off plates made of solid gold!" Purcell interrupted. Above his square-set jaw sat a mouth little more than a tiny crease in that expanse of chin. Even when he smiled—as he did right now—his mouth did not turn up at its corners. Instead, the narrow crease merely widened.

"And with forks of gold too!" Corn insisted, shoving back from his forehead some of his coal-black hair just becoming dusted with a little gray at the temples, but most remarkable for the narrow white streak that emanated from the center of his brow.

Kersey waved a hand for quiet, then leaned toward Bass. "Every one of 'em wears gold earrings, bracelets, armbands, and anklets. Gold belts tied around themselves too."

And Elias went on to explain that the Munchies were a peace-loving people who had somehow miraculously survived for centuries in the midst of the cruel Apache.

"Centuries?" Bass echoed. "How long's that?"

Elias continued, describing how the Munchies were not Indians at all but descendants of a band of Roman adventurers who claimed they had sailed to North America fifteen hundred years before Columbus bumped into the eastern shores of the Americas. Rather than return home, they had intermarried with southwestern Indians. A peace-loving people, the Munchies didn't even have a word in their tongue for "enemy." And they no longer possessed any weapons.

Shaking his head, bewildered, Scratch observed, "Don't know how the 'Pache ain't wiped 'em out afore now. Them 'Pache stayed on my trail for days till they caught up and jumped us."

"The Munchies too savvy for 'em," Corn disputed.

Scratch's eyes flicked from one man to the next, still a little skeptical. "After all this time, ain't none of you ever seen a Munchie?"

"Can't speak for Silas or Roscoe," Kersey said, "but the three of us never been down in the Heely country like you was, Titus."

"I ain't ever trapped on the Heely either," Adair admitted.

"So how you fellas so all-fired sure of these here Mun—"

"I know three fellers see'd Munchies," Corn protested. "Three different times too!"

On around the fire it went, with each of them explaining how they might not ever have seen a Munchie with their own eyes—but they all knew at least one person who had run onto the mysterious tribe of explorers sometime in the past, even to providing vivid and detailed descriptions that corroborated previous accounts given by other witnesses.

"Do tell," Bass finally relented. "Maybeso we'll get ourselves a look at one of these here Munchies on our way to Californy."

Kersey shook his head emphatically. "No, we ain't gonna be nowhere close to Munchie country, Scratch. Nowhere close."

They turned southwest the next morning, following the north side of the Colorado the best they could, yet hour by hour that path grew all the harder as they found themselves climbing and descending, climbing and descending through a canyon country without relief for horse or horseman. As the days stretched longer, the sun grew hotter, their ride becoming all the dustier the farther south Smith, Williams, and Thompson led them toward distant ridges draped with green, a most seductive color to men choking on alkali dust and gagging on the salts in tainted water. Oh, how that green beckoned them more every day.

The raiders had gone through most of their dried meat by the time they had crossed two narrow rivers and made it to those luring heights covered in piñon, cedar, and dwarf pine. A few antelope, an occasional mountain sheep or lion, and those ever present black-tailed hares that flourished in this country were the simple fodder brought into camp each night as the raiders threaded their way across a convoluted maze of canyons. When they could, the horsemen stuck with the high ground, gazing down upon those bewildering wrinkles that explained what shrinking and drying the earth's crust had undergone eons ago.*

Out of that labyrinth they steadily climbed, emerging atop a high and desolate plateau country. Off to their left the Colorado had begun to carve itself into a torturous,

---

* Bryce Canyon, present-day southern Utah.

twisting canyon of unbelievable depths. The days grew longer, hotter still, the air so dry that the breeze itself sucked the moisture right out of a man. Bass hadn't been across this sort of barren, timberless territory since that flight from the Apache along the Gila River. All around them rose the mesas and buttes long ago carved by wind and water, now brushed with vibrant tints of crimson, ocher, and a violet hue that deepened as the sun sank each evening.

"You fellas cross any sign of Injuns today?" Bass asked the others at their fire that night.

"Lots of sign," Corn replied. "Ain't see'd no Injuns howsoever."

Kersey peered at Bass, asking, "You ain't getting spooked, are you?"

"Maybeso I didn't see what I thought I saw," he confessed.

But that night as he lay in his blankets, holding at bay the memory of her touch, the feel of her mouth on his, Titus could not convince himself that he *hadn't* seen that squat, naked, deeply brown Indian duck from sight as Bass rode along the far right flank of the raiders. By the time he reined away from the rest and loped over to the rocks where he had seen that brief flicker of movement, the Indian was gone. So he lay in the dark now, trying to tell himself that what he had seen could only have been some four-legged critter.

The next evening, however, the Indians showed themselves.

Panic gripped the whole outfit as they were going into camp for the night. On foot both booshways scrambled through the horses to reach the post where one of the guards stood pointing.

"Well, damn-me!" Reuben Purcell exclaimed in a gush. "There must be a hunnert of 'em!"

But these were not the Ute who had dogged their trail weeks ago. No, these Indians did not carry weapons of war—nothing more than crude spears with a sprinkling of small bows among them. Besides, these short, stocky

Indians did not own any horses. All hundred or more of them showed up on foot.

Their leaders stepped out from the center of that broad line of squat, brown bodies, calling out from a safe distance, hailing the white men. Smith, Williams, and Thompson waved in a friendly enough manner, then moved forward on foot. Both small groups stopped some twenty yards from the other and immediately went to making sign.

When the booshways returned to their men, Williams announced, "This here bunch called the Sampatch.* They was a real skittish sort last time we come through here a few years back—'bout as shy as deer mice with a red-tailed hawk circling overhead. But yestiddy they sure 'nough recognized ol' Peg-Leg here with that wood pin tied under his knee!"

The Sanpet headmen had invited the white men into their camp located several miles off. The trappers rode among the tiny brush huts, staring down at the wide-eyed children and the bare-breasted women dressed in short grass or rabbitskin skirts. As the sun began to set and the temperature moderated, many of the Indians tied cloaks of rabbit fur over their shoulders for warmth while a supper ritual began. As open, welcoming, and warm as the Ute had been treacherous and deceitful, the Sanpet offered their very finest to their guests from the north.

"Can't remember the last time I et rabbit," Scratch admitted. "Likely it was back in Kentucky, when I was a younger lad."

"How long's that been?" Jake Corn inquired.

"Left home at sixteen," he sighed wistfully. "Thought a time or two of going back. But it's been, what—more'n thirty winters now I been gone. Likely there ain't no one left anyways."

"Hell," Kersey retorted. "I'll bet you've got kin back there still."

With a wag of his head, Bass confessed, "Only kin I

---

* More properly, the Sanpet, distant members of the Ute family.

got now is them folks I left back in Crow country . . . and what good men I ride with too."

"I thank you proudly," Reuben Purcell replied.

Squatting on the ground with their brown hosts, the trappers picked the rabbit bones clean and tossed them into the fires. They were also served a pulpy root the Indians mixed with water, then scooped off bark platters with their fingers. After dinner the headmen presented the booshways with a generous basket of those roots to take along on their journey. Well after dark that night Philip Thompson led a handful of the white men back into the village, claiming there were enough of the half-naked women to go around because the Sanpet were more than anxious to have an infusion of some white blood into their tribe.

Scratch watched the men go, then rolled over and closed his eyes, thinking hard on that yearning in his loins, remembering how Waits-by-the-Water was the one to satisfy his every longing, turning and tossing uncomfortably in his hunger for her until sleep finally came.

On they plodded the following days, piercing a desolate valley surrounded by hills all but barren of any life. Each hoof, every moccasin too, stirred up choking billows and lingering cascades of the acrid alkali dust. Two nights later they killed and butchered one of the weakening horses—a tough, stringy meat that blackened quickly over the fires. From the carcass they butchered enough to feed the bunch for the next two days, if they conserved all they managed to carve from the bones.

A little south by west, Smith and Williams continued their march all the deeper into a dry, flaky land. Their eyes burned with the constant sting of the alkali dust, seared by the relentless sun, the trappers nonetheless persisted in their search for game. Anything. Even those poor, frightened rabbits. They saw nothing else—no antelope or deer, nothing to hunt but those tiny rabbits. Over time, the men were growing glum, quieter and quieter each night as they went into camp.

"Don't you worry boys." Peg-Leg did his best to cheer them around their greasewood fires. "This country won't last for much longer. We're bound to strike that river I 'member joins down to the Colorado."

Three endless days and one more give-out horse later they struck that very river,* narrow and tumbling with silt, near its mouth. At sundown that evening Bass joined the others to sit right up to his chin in the turgid water—letting his body soak up all the moisture that this hellish country had done its best to suck right out of him.

Jake Corn slipped into the water with the handful of companions. "We're going down the Colorado from here," he explained what he had heard Smith telling some of the others in camp. "It's gonna be a ways afore we hit the Ammuchabas.† From there on, Peg-Leg says we got us a dry crossing."

"D-dry crossing?" Bass nearly choked in disgust. "What the hell we been doing, if it ain't been a dry crossing awready?"

"Ol' Bill says there's a stretch of some real bad desert coming up," Corn continued. "A real water-scrape of it. Just a few days of dry lakes and disappearing rivers, though . . . then we're in California—land of free horses."

Sitting here soaking in the river, Titus had figured they had come through the worst of it: those trackless wastes, nothing but timberless buttes and mesas, plateaus and canyons meandering back to nowhere. So if they still had the worst ahead of them, why didn't he just turn around here and start back for a more hospitable country come morning? No matter those Ute he would have to slip his way around . . .

It couldn't be. There was no way possible on his own. By any reckoning, he was likely a thousand miles from her now. Where he lay on his blankets later that night looking up into the desert sky might as well have been on

---

* Today's Virgin River in far northwestern Arizona, named for fur trapper Thomas Virgin, who served on Jedediah Smith's ill-fated second "Southwest Expedition" to the Pacific coast in 1827.

† The mountain man's distinctive and phonetic name for the Mojave Indians.

the other side of the moon from Absaroka. Cool, green, snow-drenched Crow country. He swore he'd take a blizzard on the Mussellshell rather than another long day in this hell, simmering in his own juices. Absaroka, a land where even on these summer nights a man had to pull on a blanket to keep from shivering. How he yearned for the cool touch of her skin, yearned for just how fevered she made him.

Smith, Williams, and Thompson led out with the mares the next morning, guiding the raiders due south down the Colorado now, piercing a rainbow-hued land barren of much vegetation. No more than the scrub sage, stunted jack pine, cedar, and fragrant juniper. At times the trail was a tangle of brush and a litter of blackened volcanic rock—everything that drove Scratch to believe they had to be approaching the maw of hell itself.

They stumbled across a salt cave the Sanpet had spoken of as if it were a mythical place. Stepping inside the narrow, fifteen-foot-high entrance, no more than a crack in a canyon wall, Titus could not help but regard this as a most magical place. Less than ten paces from the narrow cave opening, a small chamber opened up, expanding to more than forty feet across. Here in the glow of their sputtering torches the walls, the ceiling, the cave's very floor glittered with the most brilliant, snowy-white rock salt Scratch had ever seen.

No more would the raiders have to rely on gunpowder to season their stringy, tasteless horsemeat. With their butcher knives and axes, the trappers chipped hunks of it from the walls, packing all they dared load upon the failing horses as they pushed on down the red-brown torrents of the Colorado—a temperamental, impetuous pariah of a river.

But day after day they were forced to weave their way back from the Colorado, detouring around this branch or that of the river's most tortured recesses.* On through this kaleidoscopic wilderness, for as far as the eye could

---

* Black Canyon of the Colorado.

make out in the shimmering heat and swirling cones of the dust devils that dogged their march, they persevered. Day after day they pushed on, their horses weakening from want of proper fodder, the men growing more and more sullen and quarrelsome at the night fires. But Bass had made his vow to Bill Williams, avoiding any track that would cross the path of Philip Thompson.

They were more than halfway to California now. Which meant they were finally drawing closer and closer to their goal with every night's camp. Come a day, Scratch promised himself, Thompson would cross him and he would no longer be bound by his promise to Solitaire.

For days now it had been a red, raw, inhospitable land not fit for habitation. They had been almost a week without spotting game of any kind, even the tiny black-tailed hares. Hardly any wood worth a man troubling himself with for their fires either. Only the stunted wash willow, the pungent creosote bush, mesquite, and the infrequent Joshua tree. Those, and the first of the barrel cactus, replete with long spines at the end of which was a tiny barb that made it torturous to pull out of moccasins, hands, and the thick, sweaty hide of their weakened horses that clumsily brushed by the barrels.

Every day saw one or more of the animals die off— simply unable to go on, perhaps unable to even stand come morning. So they put a lead ball into each poor creature's brain and set to butchering what meat still remained on its bony carcass by the time the horse dropped, literally walked to its death.

Then, of a sudden one afternoon while the men were walking those horses too weak to carry them any longer, the raiders emerged from the canyon through the mouth of a valley that grew from five to fifteen miles in width. As every one of them drew up and halted, gazing about at the wondrous scene, Bass was struck with the feeling that what they were witnessing could not be real. He must surely be dreaming this, his brains cooked so severely that the mirages actually looked believable. He convinced himself that he was looking upon a mirage, since the

banks of the muddy Colorado now appeared fertile—
bordered with grass and brush. Even some scanty timber
stood here and there.

And nestled there in that wide bend of the beautiful
valley sat the first of the Mojave villages.*

Green. A deep, luscious, vibrant green for as far as
their tired, reddened, sunburnt, and alkali-seared eyes
could see. Mesquite trees gave shade to long stands of
wash willow. And everywhere a short, coarse grass beckoned their trail-weary horses.

Already the warning had been given, carried to the
villages the very moment the white men had emerged
from the mouth of the canyon.

Out of their shabby houses constructed of branches
and mud, the Mojave bristled noisily, far outnumbering
those strangers who had just appeared out of nowhere—
these pale-skinned, dust-coated, emaciated scarecrows
wearing the skins of animals hanging off their bones.
More quickly than it took for a man to gulp down a tin
of whiskey, the Mojave surged to the fore—seventy,
eighty, no . . . even more than that confronted the
white men. Perhaps more than even the trappers' guns
could handle. Each one of the short, dark warriors yelled
at the top of his voice, clutching his bow at the ready,
arrows pointing at the interlopers.

It was clear the Mojave did not hold the same soft
place in their hearts for these white men as did the Sanpet
to the north. From their belligerent actions there was no
mistaking that they were a truly frightened people, a tribe
somehow convinced that these pale strangers could mean
no good.

Just when Titus was wondering what the booshways
would do to push past this armed blockade ready to rub
out the white men, Smith and Williams trudged wearily
back to one of their pack animals and dug out some trade
items. A pair of shiny tin cups Bill clanked together, some
small, paper-backed mirrors Smith flashed in the sun,

---

* Near the pinnacles now called "The Needles."

along with coils of copper wire for bracelets and arm-bands. As Peg-Leg unfurled a long strand of red ribbon and allowed it to spill across the stunted grass, the faces of women and children suddenly appeared between the hips and legs of their men. All that angry talk hushed to a whisper, and now the Mojave began to mutter among themselves.

In moments the Indians parted slightly and four of their number stepped forward, cautiously to be sure, speaking in their indecipherable language. When the white leaders persisted in shaking their heads, unable to make sense of the sounds, they urged one of their number to move forward—a young man in his early twenties. Unsure and anxious, he spoke a few words.

"Louder!" Williams demanded across the open ground.

The youth started again, louder this time.

"By gad, Bill!" Smith exclaimed. "That's Mex' talk!"

Williams asked his partner, "Think you know 'nough to palaver with him?"

"We shall soon see, coon."

"*Buenas dias, amigo,*" Peg-Leg began, scooping out of a waxed-paper bundle a handful of small hawk's bells. These he shook gently in his palm as he slowly started forward, speaking more Spanish.

"Peg-Leg knows his Mex' talk pretty good, eh?" Titus asked as he came up to stand at the elbow of Bill Williams.

"I wouldn't know if'n you put your skinnin' knife to my windpipe, Scratch," he admitted. "Never learn't much of it."

"But you was trading down in Taos years ago!"

Williams shrugged. "Knowed me a li'l back when, I s'pose. 'Nough to get me by 's'all. But—I don't recollect much of their talk now."

It wasn't long before Smith returned to the trappers, bringing the youth and the three older men with him. "Bill—this here young feller run away from the missions."

"Run away?"

"Them padres named him Frederico. He told me how them Mex' padres whipped their Injuns and made life hard on 'em," Peg-Leg explained. "He run off by hisself one night a few months back. Somehow made it across the desert and dry sinks on his lonesome."

"By damn," Williams whispered low, his eyes twinkling. "This here boy and them others come with him is what we need to lead us right back to that valley where the Mex padres got their missions and ranchos. He'll damn well take us right to the horses, Peg-Leg."

The same light flickered in Smith's eyes. "I'm gonna ask these here chiefs 'bout us layin' to in their valley for a few days—graze our horses to get 'em stronger afore we leave, put some meat back on the bones of our men, Bill. Just a few days to rest while you and me do some jawin' with our young Frederico here about what desert lays atween us and them California ranchos."

8

———————◆———————

Their hosts actually lived on both sides of the Colorado. Three other villages stood across the muddy river. No sooner had the pale-skinned visitors shown up than the inhabitants of the other towns began to noisily cross the roiling current on flimsy rafts constructed of reeds lashed together with a fibrous rope. These white strangers were nothing less than a curious spectacle. Never before had the Mojave seen many outsiders pass through their country.

These were a strong, athletic people. Part of the Yuman family, they had a reputation for being fierce and aggressive warriors. For generations beyond count, the Mojave men had practiced extensive body tattooing using strong plant dyes—red, blue, and even white, to adorn their swarthy skins with potent symbols. Most of the men wore only a short, reed breechclout, and all went barefoot, using no moccasins of any description. When off on a rare hunt that would keep them away from their village for several days, most men wore nothing at all.

It was the custom of the women to wear nothing more than a short reed skirt around their hips. All that exposed flesh of breast and leg only served to entice the Americans into offering a handful of buttons or a yard of simple cotton ribbon in exchange for a few minutes of heated coupling behind one of the squat huts.

From the way the headmen instructed their most alluring young women to post themselves around the periphery of the trappers' camp that afternoon, Titus figured the Mojave were not only eager to trade for some of the strangers' goods but also exceedingly anxious to have white bloodlines mingle with theirs for generations to come.

These simple people lived in small, four-sided log-and-mud shelters, a crude roof of thatched brush over which the Mojave tossed sand for added insulation from the heat. For a tribe not prone to do much hunting that would have to take them far from this canyon of the Colorado, it was an uncomplicated life. Instead, the staple of their diet was the salmon they speared or caught in fibrous nets. Too, the Mojave cultivated extensive gardens of beans and corn, water- and muskmelon, and even some cotton. A mainstay was their wheat, which they stored in tall, upright, cylindrical granaries with flat tops, until they were ready to grind their wheat into flour.

While the men did not often hunt, the Mojave did nonetheless relish horsemeat. Rather than using equine animals for transport from place to place, these Colorado River Indians instead caught, raised, and even stole horses simply to eat. Much easier, Bass thought, than walking out of this valley to search the surrounding desert for a few scrawny rabbits or tortoises.

Here after their long, torturous ride through a barren, desolate canyon country devoid of game or good water, a trackless desert waste fit only for the likes of lizards, cactus, and spiny toads . . . why, to Titus Bass this fertile, green valley where these dark-skinned people raised their horses and cultivated a variety of crops seemed like a veritable Eden.

Late in the afternoon while the trappers were stoking their supper fires, eight of the Mojave men left their village, heading for the white man's camp. But just short of the trappers, those eight stopped and dropped armloads of wood onto the grass. While a half dozen of the men turned on their heels and made for the village once again, two of them began to sort through the wood, selecting a few lengths of timber. For the next few hours Bass watched the men erect a small scaffold from the wood those six others continued to deposit near the white man's camp, lashing the timber together with a fibrous rope the Mojave women braided from rushes and reeds. Beneath the low, upright braces, the men piled smaller brush and limbs. But it wasn't until long after supper that he learned the purpose of that empty scaffold.

As soon as the sun had passed behind the far western wall of the canyon, the entire valley was thrown into shadow. With supper finished and the air cooling, most of the trappers sallied off from the fires, headed for the village and those young women who waited just close enough to the white men to make their willingness known. Everyone from their mess had departed for the village and a long-overdue coupling except for Bass and Roscoe Coltrane. They sat smoking their clay pipes, staring at the flames or the newly emerging stars. Twilight was already smearing the shadows into night when they heard the approach of many feet.

Both trappers turned to find more than fifty of the Mojave headed their way. At the van of their march, four men carried a long form on their shoulders. Behind the quartet walked two women holding torches that sputtered, licking at the evening breeze. Stopping beside the scaffold, the four hoisted the body atop the low platform. As they stepped back, the two women came forward, accompanied by a lone man who now recited a long, mournful dissertation.

"I s'pose they're praying," Bass whispered to Coltrane.

Roscoe nodded, but uttered not a word.

With a wave of his hand, the Mojave shaman inched back, gestured, and gave the order to the two women. They leaned forward on either side of the scaffold and jammed their torches into the thick nest of driftwood and dried grass stuffed beneath the body. A quiet, eerie chant began as the flames caught hold, an off-key dirge that grew in volume as the fire grew hotter, leaped higher, licking all around the deceased, beginning to consume him.

"Ever you know any folks what burn their dead?" Bass asked of Coltrane.

Captivated, Roscoe never took his eyes off the ceremony, his face illuminated with the dancing light from those flickering flames as he shook his head.

"Me neither," Bass replied.

He watched as one Mojave after another stepped from the crowd, carrying a few meager items in their hands. A woman carried a bow. Another female had some crude fibrous clothing draped over her arm. A young man raised aloft a club for all to see, while a young girl moved forward carrying a short spear in both hands.

Titus said, "I figger they're gonna burn ever'thing that man had to his name. Like some of the Injuns in the mountains give away all a man has after he's dead."

The shaman continued to reel off more of his foreign and mystical words, then paused before he gave the order. The individuals who held those few meager belongings now tossed them atop the body being consumed by flame, then every one of them quickly shrank back from the great heat the funeral pyre generated. Its growing light reflected off the striated orange and reddish-brown canyon walls as exploding fireflies of sparks spiraled skyward from the river valley.

As the scaffold collapsed and the flames began to recede, members of the dead man's family retrieved a few burning limbs from the fire and set off behind the shaman when he started the crowd back for the village. The group stopped at one of the huts, where the family came forward together, setting the dry walls aflame with those faggots carried from the funeral pyre.

"Almost like he never lived," Bass whispered morosely. He saw Coltrane wag his head sadly, then turned again to watch the flames greedily lick away at the brush and log shelter. "Rubbing out ever' sign he ever was.

Ever'thing he ever had is gone in less'n a goddamned night. Not a single trace that fella was ever around . . . 'cept for his kin still breathin'."

As the bonfire died and many of the village finished obliterating almost every clue of a man's existence among them, night deepened in the valley of the Colorado while most of the white men cavorted with the willing young women of the Mojave.

After brooding on it there in the fire-lit darkness beside that silent man, Scratch finally admitted, "I s'pose that's just about all there'll be for any of us, Roscoe. Things come an' things go, and when we die we don't need 'em no more. Maybe burning all his plunder's a fair notion of things. Older a man gets, he finds out such foofaraw wasn't important anyway. Maybeso these here Injuns got a good notion when all's said an' done . . . for what's truly important still remains long after any of us is gone."

Coltrane turned and gazed at Bass's face, then the once-mute man spoke for the first time in many weeks. "What's important to you?"

Initially startled by the reticent man's sudden speech, Titus finally declared, "Kin, Roscoe. Kinfolk, and what few friends I can count on."

Three more days passed while the white men languished in this unexpected Eden.

During those long, early-summer days most of the men ate or slept or frolicked in the river with some of their newfound female friends. And when night came down, the exuberant trappers stomped and jigged and sang, until they could wait no longer and slipped back into the shadows to couple with one of the Mojave women.

At the fires each evening, Frederico stammered through his poor Spanish, explaining his childhood in California, while Peg-Leg translated haltingly for the others. The young Indian described how in his youth he chose to become a novitiate working in the fields among hundreds of other Indians, all of them living under the

rigid strictures of the padres' church. But the lessons he
learned were not the sort that would save his heathen
soul from an eternity of damnation. Instead, Frederico,
like the hundreds of primitive California Indians living in
the hills and vales surrounding every Catholic mission,
soon discovered they were nothing more than slaves who
toiled in the vineyards, sweated over the extensive fields,
tending to virtually every need or whim of the Mexican
friars and those soldiers posted nearby.

Growing more and more disillusioned with the cruelty
of his religious taskmasters, Frederico determined he
would run away to those mountains lying far to the east
of the mission. With two companions he escaped during
the return of a work detail, the trio managing to hide
until nightfall when the three young men started for the
distant foothills. But they soon learned that even the foothills and high slopes covered in their evergreens were no
sanctuary. Mounted Mexican soldiers caught up to them.

Rather than return to the mission and the torment he
would have to suffer, one of the young men threw himself
off a rocky ledge, his broken body tumbling into the
chasm below. Frederico and his friend were promptly
clamped in shackles and turned around for the mission.

When the pair hobbled along too slowly to keep up
with the soldiers' horses, the boys were lashed with
braided horsehair quirts. Stumbling and falling constantly, they finally reached the mission, where both collapsed at the feet of the friars—who immediately ordered
their most trusted Indian servants to bind the runaways
to a pair of posts erected a few yards outside the walls.
There a stern, steel-eyed, and militant padre took a rawhide cat-o'-nine-tails from his rope belt and turned the
runaways' backs to ribbons of blood and tattered strips
of flesh.

With pooling eyes now, Frederico related how he had
passed out with the severity of the flogging, unable to
endure the pain or loss of blood any longer. The last
sounds he heard were the unearthly cries of his young
friend. Later, when he awoke in a cell where his feet were
shackled, Frederico asked a friar when he could see his

friend. The priest declared that his friend had gone away mysteriously . . . and would never be coming back.

Yet in his bones, Frederico knew that last part was nothing less than the ugly truth. Few of the escaped slaves ever survived their recapture. Their deaths simply served as a vivid example to the other Indians forced to witness the brutal public flogging of those who attempted to flee their cruel bondage to these self-righteous and most holy Mexican taskmasters.

Not long after Frederico's recapture, his two young sisters were transferred from the mission, taken away to join a group of women who were consigned to the nearby soldier barracks where they served as concubines for the Mexican cavalry. Overwhelmed with a sense of helplessness, eaten up with utter hopelessness, Frederico realized he alone could do nothing to free his sisters from their fate. All he could do was to attempt another escape. That, or die trying.

This time when he made his dash east to the foothills of those beckoning mountains, he did not tarry to hide among the timber and the boulders. Instead, Frederico scaled the slopes, pushing all the way to the top of a narrow pass, where he gazed down upon that impenetrable desert below him. One last time he peered over his shoulder to the west where lay nothing but a legacy of misery and pain. There wasn't a thing left for him but torture and death at the hands of his Mexican conquerors if the soldiers ever recaptured him. The young Indian crossed over, pitching himself into the desert.

Discovered near death where he lay huddled in the skimpy shade of a patch of cactus, parched with thirst and unable to move, Frederico was rescued by a few young Mojave warriors who had ventured onto the wastes in search of wild horses, hunting for any branded animals that might have escaped the California missions and extensive ranchos. Taking the half-dead slave to their villages on the Colorado, the Mojave hissed and snarled when Frederico explained why he had such a patchwork of terrible scars across his back and shoulders.

From that day, his rescuers never asked again of the

pale-skinned strangers far to the west. The Mojave had saved his life and given him a home.

"Will you guide us back through that pass in the mountain?" Peg-Leg Smith asked Frederico when the young Indian had finished his dramatic tale that third night at the fire.

"You will not be lost," Frederico replied, wagging of his head with reluctance.

"What do you want to lead us?" Smith inquired. "Tell me what I can give you in trade. We need you to show us the pass through the mountains that will take us to the ranchos."

This time Frederico shook his head more emphatically. "There is nothing you can give me that would make me take another step across that desert. Nothing in this world that will make me return to the land of my murderous captors."

In the cool, shadowy dawn that next morning, the booshways had their grumbling men rolling out early, ordered to bring their horses and pack animals into camp. Onto the pack saddles they tied skins filled with horsemeat they had traded from the Mojave. Every man went to the river one last time to fill his gourd or oaken canteen, along with those skin bladders the booshways had purchased from the Indians.

A large group of the Mojave followed their headmen to the visitors' camp, bearing some last gifts of melons for their guests at this parting. From the front of the crowd stepped young Frederico. Over one shoulder he had tied a rabbit-skin blanket rolled into a cylinder. Over the other was suspended a four-foot section of grayish, greasy horse intestine now swollen with river water and tied off at both ends with a loop of braided twine.

"Wood-Leg," he called in his imperfect Spanish as he stopped a yard in front of the white leader. "If I show you across the desert and on your way into the mountains . . . I have thought of one thing you can do to repay me."

"Tell me," Smith replied eagerly. "Tell *us* and it will be so."

"I will take your men there—all the way to the ranchos," Frederico vowed before the stunned white men as the sun just then struck the top of the canyon above them. "If you and your men will help me free my sisters from the Mexican soldiers."

They put that oasis at their backs.

Frederico led them onto the desert near a grouping of tall, sandstone obelisks,* gigantic, mute monoliths left behind after eons of erosion by wind and water. They reminded Bass of other eerie rock formations he had encountered across the seasons, giants that took shape and somehow grew animated in the last light of the day. Hoodoos, for sure.

Their horses carried them northwest around the base of some dry, forbidding high ground. Stopping among the late-afternoon shadows in the lee of those low mountains, the raiders spent their first night upon what Frederico told them might be the last good grass their horses would have until they reached the far mountains of California.

"The Injun said to save your water here on out," Bill Williams warned the trappers. "He can't rightly remember if'n there's waterholes or not out there. Only come through part of it on his own. The rest of the way the Ammuchabas brung him in."

The next morning's march found the horses plodding slower and slower with the rising temperature. But as hard as they were working, the animals didn't break into a lather. Titus figured the arid, superheated air was relentlessly sucking the moisture right out of the critters the way it was leaching it right out of him.

At midday when the sun sulled overhead like a stubborn mule refusing to budge, Frederico located a small patch of shady Joshua trees.

---

* The Needles, near present-day Needles, California.

"We'll rest the horses here," Smith declared, his face coated with a thin layer of whitish dust.

"Sleep if you can, boys," Williams suggested as the men slid from their mounts much the same way they would after a thirty-six-hour ride in the saddle. "I figger we ought'n wait out the rest of the day and move on come dark."

With the setting of the sun, they put out again, their horses still slow, especially those wet mares they had to harness and picket at every stop to prevent them from bolting and turning for home back in the Rockies. Although the light had drained from the sky, the first part of the night remained remarkably warm. But by moonrise, the air began to cool. There was little vegetation growing upon the surface of the desert that would serve to hold in the day's heat. And once the heat of the day evaporated a few hours into the night, these wastes turned downright cold. They sweated out the day, and now shivered in the saddle at night.

By the following morning as the sun came flaming off the horizon behind them, the raiders had their first real opportunity to behold what awaited them now in striking out from the Mojave villages. Far, far, far away along the western rim of the earth lay a ragged, broken skyline of distant mountains. Between here and there, in every compass direction, lay the almost colorless, lifeless, unmarked desolation of an unimaginable desert. Supporting no game to speak of, allowing no vegetation but an occasional and spiny species, this flat wasteland was interrupted by nothing more than patches of low, pale gray rock forms that served as the only landmarks to give the men their bearings on the bottom of this dry, trackless, inland sea.

For men who had penetrated the deepest recesses of the forests along this continent's spine, for these hardy adventurers who had squandered their youth threading back and forth through the high Rockies, these bare, stony heights were simply not deserving of the appellation *mountains*. Such barren, rock-strewn, sun-baked iron heights as these only served to taunt a man, reminding him of what incomprehensible beauty he had left behind. . . .

Again and again Scratch reminded himself that he had seen desert before. Not only when he and Asa McAfferty had attempted to trap the Gila River and were forced to flee an Apache war party across a stretch of desert, but he believed they had surely been through the worst country ever in those two weeks just before stumbling into the Eden of those Mojave villages. But . . . Titus Bass had never seen desert anywhere as bleak and barren as what stared them in the face at that moment.

Even on the high plains east of Crow country, truly an arid land where little rain ever fell, where late in the summer a man's brains boiled out in the sun—nothing he had ever encountered could have prepared him for this descent into the maw of this fire-baked brimstone hardened beneath a merciless, unrelenting one-eyed sky. Scratch thought it was as if nature itself had shut off Mexican California, protecting it by setting an ocean on one side, then stretching this intractable desert on the other—both of them barriers few men would ever dare cross.

But, he constantly reminded himself, Peg-Leg and Ol' Bill, along with Thompson and a few of their companions—they had crossed to California a few years back. Little matter that they had penetrated to the coastal country farther north, Bass convinced himself that those horse-stealing veterans could see the rest of them through.

Yet with the next morning's sunrise as they limped into a parched, mud-baked cluster of skimpy vegetation* and came out of the saddle to wait out the day, it didn't feel as if they had covered much ground at all in that night just behind them. In the growing light, he couldn't swear those distant mountains were any closer than they had been days ago when the Indian led them away from the Colorado and onto this bleak and empty desert.

"Maybeso, this is a easy way for them Ammuchabas

---

* Today's Marl Springs.

to kill us all off an' steal our horses," Silas Adair grumbled in resignation as he curled up in a narrow patch of shade thrown down by a scrawny, half-dead mesquite tree.

"Kill us how?" Reuben Purcell asked.

"This Frederico nigger we got for a guide," Adair complained. "He leads us out here till we all die. Then the rest of 'em come out to rob our packs, take our guns, an' pick over our bones!"

"That's crazy talk," Bass grumped at Silas as a wispy dust devil skipped past their shady shelter. "The sun's boiling your brains to soup."

"I'd give most anything to ride back to them Ammuchabas right now," Jake Corn confessed. "This here country's ugly as a dried-up tit."

Every morning a breeze always came up like this, kicking dust and sand at them for a while, creating the little wisps of those dust devils every sunrise and sunset when the desert and the air above it were either warming up or cooling off. Blasted by sand: just one more torture man and beast had to endure in their interminable crossing.

Scratch shifted his big-brimmed felt hat down over the side of his face and laid his cheek on his elbow again as he did in attempting to sleep out every one of these lengthening days.

Their Indian guide didn't know how long the journey would take, how many more days until they reached the western foothills and entered those green and beckoning heights. But when Titus turned to look over his shoulder at where they had come, those bluffs and mesas where the Colorado River cut itself through didn't appear to be shrinking much at all.

From one muddy, dying waterhole to the next they plodded on, making camps around little seeps if need be, marking hours and miles and days until they could wearily collapse from their horses and fall into a light, restless sleep. Then the raiders reached a dry lake bed,* where

---

* Present-day Soda Lake.

they sank to their knees in disappointment, finding little to drink at a tiny spring they located among a patch of blackened, volcanic rock. Little of the parched grass to feed the horses.

And no more of their own horsemeat.

That morning they selected the weakest of their animals and slit its throat, catching most of the blood in kettles and cups for those men desirous to drink what many believed was truly a life-giving elixir, especially if a man suffered from want of the lean, rich meat of buffalo and elk, mountain lion or antelope. Too damn long with mountain fare. But here, so far from the Rockies, these refugees had only a poor, half-skeletal, dried-out old horse to choke down, its flesh turned gritty with an endless swirl of dust and sand.

Most days they simply couldn't scare up any wood to speak of where they ended their night's march. Which meant there was no cooking for the lean, stringy sections of meat they butchered from the weakest of the animals the raiders began to sacrifice every other day or so. Nothing more than the drying properties of the hot, ever present wind or the heat put out from a broiling sun to jerk those strips of black, stringy muscle the trappers draped upon the spiny cactus or laid upon the eons-old volcanic rocks that dotted the landscape where they rested out their days upon this floor of an ancient inland sea.

After those first three nights, time began to run together. When the sun eventually fell and no longer tortured the men and their beasts, the booshways stirred, moving slowly, deliberately among the raiders, goading the trappers onto their feet as the shadows lengthened. They would then take account of their horses, resaddle, and move out.

If they found an animal unable to make that night's march, or if the trappers required more meat, the men sacrificed the poorest of the poor to the knife here in the coming of twilight when the raiders were more rested. At first the men had enjoyed a quaff of the hot blood as it squirted dark, thick, and sticky from the horse's neck. But by the fourth day few were anxious to dip his head or his cup down into that gaping wound. Something so hot, so syrupy, held little allure for these men slowly being sucked dry by the desert below and the sun above.

Lo, beyond the searing heat of the sun, they suffered another torture from that endless sky stretched above them. At least once a day blackening clouds appeared on the far horizon, quickly tumbling their way. In such dry, pristine air, the men could discern the thick streamers of rain advancing with that thunderstorm hurtling toward them. Instead of raising alarm, the sight brought cheer to these parched emigrants. Chattering like schoolboys playing hooky at a forest pond, the horse thieves stripped naked as a borning day hoping the rain would pelt man and beast alike.

But the storms never failed to hurry on past, every cloudburst sweeping by without a single drop ever touching the naked riders and the thirsty earth. Although the thick, swollen, storm clouds released a torrent of moisture from their undergut, every last bead of rain dried before it came anywhere close to the ground. As the sun reappeared and the air rewarmed, the horsemen pulled on their clothes once more, grown all the gloomier with that agony of expectation, the self-deluding torture of misplaced hope.

And every step of the way was accompanied by an incomprehensibly deafening silence.

Back home in his mountains the slightest sound would echo back to a man, reverberated off a granite escarpment or the thick forests themselves. Why, even the high plains rolled and pitched enough, truly a country so crisscrossed with coulee and watercourse that he could count on some echo to accompany most every sound.

But here in this endless desert, every utterance, each small scratch or cough or sneeze, was immediately swallowed up by the land's utter immensity.

Be it the whicker of a horse too weak to make any more of a sound, or the groans of discomfited men as they lunged to a stop in their tattered moccasins and pitched onto their knees, immediately rolling into a ball in the only shade they could find . . . maybe no sound louder than the steamy splatter of a man's piss as it struck the iron-clad hardpan of the desert floor. This was a land violently jealous of its silence.

There were times Scratch chewed on a little of his dwindling reserves of plug tobacco, hoping to stimulate a little saliva. And when that would not work, he dug out a .54-caliber lead ball and slipped it under his swollen tongue. Five days after stumbling past Soda Lake, some of the men opened a vein on their wrists or the backs of their hands, sucking at some semblance of moisture retained by their bodies. A few even tried to drink their own hot, pungent urine. Although Titus understood it was more pure than any water they might stumble across in this hostile country, he could almost puke at the thought of gagging down something so warm from his tin cup. . . .

Hell, everything was damned hot in this desert.

"Here," Bill Williams announced as he settled beside Scratch in the skimpy shade of a Joshua tree as the sun slipped off midsky.

Elias Kersey leaned forward on an elbow, peering at what Williams revealed in the upturned crown of his hat. "What's that?"

"Leaves of a weed* the Injun just give me to pass around."

"What we s'posed to do with it?" Titus asked as he plucked out a leaf. "Chew on 'em to make our mouths water?"

Williams shook his head. "Lookee there what the Injun's doing? He told Peg-Leg we was to smoke it."

"What for?" Scratch inquired.

"Frederico says it helps take away the pain."

Purcell crabbed over, the first to reach in and pull out enough of the weed to stuff down the bowl of his clay pipe. "Been a long time since I had a smoke anyways."

It wasn't long before the two dozen shared a few com-

---

* Jimsonweed, smoked by the Mojave, as well as their neighbors: the Paiute, Cocopah, and Yuma.

mon sparks that flint and steel ignited on smoldering char until all were sucking at the dried leaves that stung their tongues. Within minutes the men grew more quiet than usual, every one of them soon absorbed with a dreamy reverie brought about by the narcotic effects of the bitter leaves.

Scratch drifted, half dozing as he recalled the gentle rattle of the mountain breeze coursing its way through the cottonwood and quakie, the unmistakable soughing of that first wind of winter fingering its way through the branches of fir or pine, stabbing its way through the thick overcoat of the blue spruce.

For the longest time Titus had the unmistakable impression he was sleeping—despite the fact that he had his eyes open. And those eyes were no longer squinting but growing wider and wider instead as the sun gradually went down, marking the passage of time as twilight loomed around them. Looking to his left, Scratch found their guide loading some more of the dry leaves into his simple Indian pipe crafted from the hollowed-out legbone of a horse. Maybe that red nigger did have something here with smoking these crumbled leaves: how it eased a man's pain. At least no one was complaining of the nagging, persistent discomfort they suffered from both the thirst and a belly-gnawing hunger.

Time passed and he couldn't reckon on just how much. While the air cooled, Bass noticed the nearby horses lazily shifting from one exhausted leg to another, observed men rolling from hip to hip seeking to make themselves more comfortable in the windblown sand, or watched nothing more than the changing properties of the light as a shadowy band slid ever so slowly across the grease-hardened wrinkles and fading bloodstains smeared across the tops of his leggings. The last of the day's light crept over him as if it were an animated creature of the desert itself.

Then he thought of them back in Absaroka. And found himself dwelling on her—on the way she laughed so uncontrollably with how easily he poked fun at himself. Remembering the way her eyes took on a deep intensity when she hungered for him. So he naturally thought of pretty little Magpie and his bright, inquisitive Flea. He yearned to be back for their birthdays . . . but first he had to get out of this life-robbing desert.

Directly overhead sailed more than a dozen wrinkled-necked buzzards keeping an eye on the trappers and their animals, following their march, picking over the bones of the horse carcasses the raiders left in their wake. Eegod, but it hurt to stare at the sky too long, so he shut his eyes and waited for the pain to pass.

Sometime later he was awakened by a man's heavy, labored breathing—and realized it was his own. Not daring to breathe deeply of the hot air because it burned his lungs like a blast from a blacksmith's bellow. Reminding himself to suck it in shallow, shallow.

Upon opening his eyes he discovered the sun had leaked out of that last quarter of the sky, which meant even more time had passed. Quickly glancing at the heavens above them, he found it nearly black with wings. A few buzzards, yes—but even more of some bigger species, their immense wingspans circling overhead in that hot yellow sky.

Floating up there on the rising thermals, patiently waiting for the men to pick up and move on, so they could descend from the sky and pick over the remains of what the men left behind. Any strips of horseflesh clinging to the bones. Squawking and wing-flapping over the putrid gut piles. Sharp, curved beaks fighting off the others so they could peck at the dead, glazed eyes of the horses, feasting on the rotting carrion until there was nothing left but bone to bleach under the sun and course-less winds.

Come dark, they'd have to get out of here, Scratch decided. If they didn't, those damned birds might well grow bold enough to attack the weaker horses and mules, maybe unto challenging the most defenseless of the men.

Titus closed his eyes again for a few minutes and tried desperately to think of how hell might feel. Could it be any worse than this?

Down in hell did the buzzards and other carrion eaters tear flesh from a man's body, pick at his eyes . . . even before he was dead?

In hell did a man simply give up hope of ever seeing her again?

9

———————◆———————

The condors and vultures had landed around them as the sun sank. Something more than a hundred of the birds had gathered—first blackening the sky over this daylong bivouac, eventually landing to encircle the parched men and their near-dead animals.

A few of the other raiders were just starting to stir as the shadows lengthened. Titus felt woozy, sick to his stomach, but as soon as he sipped at some of the warm water in his gourd canteen, the feeling started to pass.

"Bill," he said when his eyes landed on Williams, "we gotta get this bunch moving soon as the sun's gone."

The old trapper nodded, slowly rocking onto his knees with a sigh. "The Injun says we should reach water afore morning."

Just over Williams's shoulder one of the buzzards fluttered across the sand to nab a sidewinder, its sharp beak striking out to clamp down on the snake, violently tossing its head side to side, then pitching the sidewinder into the air to break the snake's back in a second place.

"Damn, if that sight don't give me the willies," Bill grumbled as he struggled to stand.

"C'mon, fellas," Titus urged as he crouched over Kersey and Purcell. "Up, boys—up."

One by one the two dozen were slowly coming back to life as the temperature dropped degree by degree. They sipped at the last of their mineral-laced water, bathing their cracked, swollen lips and their bloated, black-tinged tongues. Most of them had long ago learned to hold a small gulp of the water in their mouths, letting the moisture fully soak into the membranes before swallowing what little was left of the warm liquid that hadn't been absorbed.

That first sip after a daylong drought always hammered the inside of a man's skull almost as bad as some of Willie Workman's raw-brewed Taos lightning going down on an empty belly. It made his eyes swim and burn. It set a man's teeth and gums to aching after all those tissues had grown severely parched. And the longer these men went without clean water, the worse this torture would become.

"Save the last you can for the critters," Bass reminded them.

Adair grumped a bit, but once their tongues were wet and a silk handkerchief dampened to tie around their heads or knot at their throats, most of the men set about carefully pouring what little they had left into their hats and offering that final measure to their horses or mules. Titus's saddle horse licked the inside of his old felt hat with such gusto he was afraid the animal might well gnaw right on through the damp crown.

As it turned out three of the pack animals refused to get up. With some struggle, the men were able to strip the baggage off the horses. Then the booshways set about redistributing the loads carried by the rest of the animals. Weak as they were, Bass figured, the horses and mules really couldn't be asked to carry much more weight.

While the sun continued to sink behind the far horizon, Bill Williams ordered the men to tear through their packs, paring what was needed from what they could leave behind. Powder and lead, heavy by any reckoning, was given primary consideration. The rest of their possibles would go into smaller, lighter packs they went about lashing on the backs of those horses and mules still able to bear up under the burdens . . . if for only one more night, just until they reached a damp stretch of the Mojave River.

Everything else they would leave behind.

"Shouldn't we cache it?" Reuben Purcell wondered, gazing over his shoulder at the mounds of supplies they were about to abandon in the lee of that stand of Joshua trees.

Kersey added, "Maybeso them Ammuchabas come steal all this from us—"

"Take it along if you can damn well carry it," Titus grumbled, sunburned and short of temper.

A wounded look crossed Purcell's face when he said, "Just figgering we should bury it."

"If'n you got the strength to dig down into this here ground," Scratch advised, "go right ahead and do it."

"You don't figger we're coming back for it?" Kersey asked.

Bass shook his head. "I callate we oughtta find us a differ'nt road home—a ways north of here."

No one disagreed with that.

"How far you reckon till we get to them hills?" Jake Corn asked as they started away from their stand of the spindly cactus trees.

Bass trudged beside him on foot, all two dozen men leading their weary horses now, including the eight reluctant broodmares they held on halters at the front of the ragged column. "Four days, maybeso five."

Later that night, the trail grew a little easier on the men and animals. Until now they had been forced to fix their gaze on a distant landmark, then march directly for it, whereupon they would locate another landmark lying at the right compass heading. Over and over through the night. But now they struck the gently meandering bed of a river* that appeared to steer them right into that distant

_____
* Mojave River

line of hills.* For the most part, they found the riverbed dry. Here and there a little damp sand, just enough that they stopped from time to time in the middle of the night, got down on their knees, then scooped, dug, and tore at the sand in hopes of uncovering enough of the soapy water to give their suffering animals a drink.

A man could always cut off the flat ears of the pancakelike cactus, pluck out the spines, and slice through the armorlike protective skin so he could suck at the acrid-tasting pulp. But the horses and mules needed water, real water.

Finding nothing more than damp sand in those holes they clawed in the riverbed, the men lunged back onto their feet and stumbled away again beneath a sky so black it seemed to reflect the brilliance of a million stars. All Scratch could discern of the horizon in any direction was that the dusting of those twinkling stars abruptly ended somewhere far out there at the edge of the earth. That had to be the horizon, he reminded himself as they slowly plodded along in a world of dark velvet: a blackened sky above and this desert floor below them, the ground grown just as black as the heavens.

When the moon came up, it gave an eerie, silver glow to the pale desert hardpan. And with that light the land seemed to take on a renewed life. Tiny mice appeared, only to be hunted by the saucer-eyed elf owls streaking out of the darkness. Pin-legged, long-necked roadrunners darted in and out of the cactus, chasing string-tailed rodents and lizards alike. Mile after mile the invaders were kept company by those soft sounds rising along the dry riverbed as the night took on a life of its own: the incessant rattle of ground crickets, the flurry of wings, the hiss of scurrying feet scratching claws across the millennia-baked sand.

It was still dark when those in the vanguard spotted something shining in the meandering riverbed far, far ahead.

---

* San Bernardino Mountains

"I figger it for water," Smith confided.

As the word bounced back along their ragged line of march, the men spread out in a broad front, every last one of them eager to see this revelation for themselves. Titus raised his nose, concentrated, then sensed what faint breeze was coming at his back. It would have been an entirely different matter if the air had been coming into their faces—

That's when the first of the horses snorted. Then a few others whickered. And Scratch's saddle mount tugged on its lead rope.

"They smell it!" Williams croaked with a dry, flaky throat. "Give 'em their head!"

Of a sudden the animals at the center of the march bolted. Weak as they were, and burdened too, none of them took off like uncorked lightening. A number of the men stood in among the horses, vainly trying to control the beasts now that the odor of moisture was faint—but certain—upon the shifting desert breeze. Two men collapsed as horses lumbered past them, their ungainly packs swaying side to side, knocking the trappers down.

After not speaking for so long, the first time Scratch attempted to yell he found his swollen tongue stuck to the roof of his mouth. "L-let 'em go!"

This was no wild, picturesque stampede, this clumsy, lumbering dash for the water by those weak, emaciated, overburdened animals. Then men were right behind them, loping toward the shallow black pool.

Struck with wonder, Bass shuffled to a stop, staring at the distance and realizing for the first time exactly what he was seeing. A half mile to the west he spotted another shiny, narrow pool dimly reflecting the black of the night sky just the way a freshly-oiled gun barrel shimmered in firelight. Beyond it another quarter of a mile lay a pair of pools huddling strung end to end. And so on from there as his eyes crawled away to the western horizon.

Those spotty pools were all there was of the river. Here and there it disappeared beneath the sand, slipping back beneath the dried-up riverbed sand and flat-out disappeared. But unlike pools and ponds and small lakes of water that would eventually evaporate under a relentless summer sun, this river continued to flow—sometimes above ground, more often just beneath the desert floor.

He shambled to a stop among the rest of the men who were sitting or lying right in the shallow, inky waters, splashing themselves as the horses and mules stood all about them, noisily slurping their fill.

"These critters gonna get loggy," Scratch warned.

"W-what the hell differ'nce it to you?" Thompson snarled as he pulled his face out of the pool, water sluicing down his brown beard in rivulets.

Bass turned away from Thompson, telling Williams, "We let these critters drink too much, Bill—they'll be loggy."

"Will you listen to that?" Thompson roared as he slapped the surface of the water in derision. Behind his own galling laughter arose that of his friends. "Bass wants us to quit our drinking and pull the horses off!"

"I'll bet he wants to have the water all for his own self!" John Bowers sniped at Thompson's elbow.

"You're hobble-headed, you stupid son of a bitch," Bass snapped back as Bowers got to his feet.

Williams grabbed hold of Bowers's arm. "Hol't on, boy."

Bowers tried to shake his arm free. "Maybeso he'd like to have me hold 'im under till he drinks his fill!"

"There's more water ahead, Bill," Titus explained. "The animals don't gotta drink till their bellies swolled up right here."

Williams and most of the others turned slowly to peer in the direction Bass pointed. Some more of them got to their feet, water streaming off them in waves as they peered west.

"T-this cain't be the last of it," Peg-Leg Smith agreed softly, its sound a question as he dragged the Indian guide out of the pool and onto his feet beside him. In a staccato drumbeat of harsh Spanish, Smith growled at the escapee. Then slowed down the second time he repeated his demands.

Back and forth they chattered a minute more until Smith freed his grip on the Indian's shoulder.

Peg-Leg turned to the others and explained, "Says this here river's gonna lead us all the way to the mountains now. On the other side lays them California ranchos."

"Ho-o-o-o-e-e-e!" Williams cackled as he hopped a jig in the shallow water, sending up rooster combs of spray.

Bass stomped up, splashing. "Tol't you, I did. We'll have us water all the way to the mountains now!"

He immediately looped his right arm into Bill Williams's right elbow, and they proceeded to slog and splash around and around in the utter joy of their deliverance.

"Better we stay here rest of the night," Smith said as he slogged over to the pair coming to a breathless halt.

Williams peered behind them, recognizing the narrow gray band that lay at the curve of the flattened horizon. "Day's coming soon enough, true enough, Peg-Leg."

Bass grudgingly agreed. "These animals got too much water in their bellies awready—ain't gonna be fit to go on now."

Thompson roared, "There the bastard goes again—telling us the wisdom of his mind!"

"For this he's right!" Williams snapped. "Me an' Peg-Leg say we stay put right here. Maybeso we'll find something for the critters to eat when it get light."

Smith nodded. "And push on come evening."

Later, as the gray streamers of dawn gradually crept over the horizon, it was plain enough for Scratch to recognize that the horses and mules had been too long without enough water, too long at this little pool that they weren't gonna be worth a damn. A man or beast gone too long without sufficient water had the stomach shrink so profoundly that on their first ingestion of large amounts of water they would grow painfully sick. Within minutes of their reaching the pool, the first of the horse thieves began to crawl to the riverbank on their hands and knees, retching, puking up the salty, gritty, mineral-laced water their bellies simply refused to hold down.

Those strongest among them began to strip the ani-

mals of their packs and saddles, dropping the baggage
onto the sand. Later, as the light began to balloon around
them, the trappers for the first time saw the extent of the
grass that surrounded the pool here in the midst of the
desert's austere severity. And as dawn approached, their
eyes made sense out of the shapes in the mid-distance.
Vegetation. Not just barrel and cholla and ocotilla cactus.
Not just the stunted, half-dead mesquite and Joshua
trees . . . but vegetation that might actually shade
a man.

With the coming of day, they gazed into the westward,
recognizing how each short pocket of the narrow river
coursed through a fertile vale watered by the river in
those patches where it remained above ground. Where it
disappeared, the vegetation ended. On and on, above
ground and under, all the way to that far string of low
hills, each tiny oasis was strung together on a narrow
ribbon of moisture that, come late summer, would disap-
pear entirely. A time when every last one of these oases
would wither and shrivel like a cluster of overripe fruit,
dying for another year.

Instead of that monotonous gray and volcanic black of
their endless days on the desert, this sunrise greeted them
with a surprising palette of colors: the whites of mariposa
lilies and tiny primroses, violet lupine, and the fleshy-pink
verbena, not to mention the untold hues of every nearby
cactus now blooming in their abbreviated cycle of life.

For the moment it reminded him how Waits-by-the-
Water harvested mountain and prairie wildflowers in the
spring, drying them before she crushed the petals and
crowns, then dumped them into large rawhide bags. For
weeks and weeks thereafter, she would rub the petals on
her skin or into the thick folds of her hair, the very air
around her a heady aura with their gentle scent.

How he wished she were there to see this with him, the
children to frolic upon the short, matted grasses and
splash at the riverbank where the water had turned a
brief, rosy hue as the sun burst over the edge of the earth.
Small wrens and cactus sparrows once quiet and still,
hidden among the branches of the trees and brush,

suddenly began to trill and call as the light came up. As the air began to warm over time, even the flies came out. Not tiny, shriveled creatures, but those huge, cruel, bloodthirsty horseflies that so troubled man and beast alike in the mountains.

There must be enough life abounding in each small oasis for these brutal, biting creatures to feed upon.

As he laid there in the shade, occasionally swatting at those huge, hot-footed tormentors, Bass saw the desert as a land where every species fed off something else. Even the simplest part of the equation—like these damnable horseflies—might appear sleepy, perhaps slothful throughout most of the day as the sun's fiery intensity grew. Still, every creature was both predator or prey in a most inelegant food chain. Every creature bred to be swift in attack or fleet in escape. Both traits necessary for survival in this hostile land.

It had always been that way. Knowing when to attack, when to retreat.

With this desert dawn Scratch came to realize that in this knowing lay the utter heart, the very secret, to his survival.

Those in the lead had dismounted and stood, men and animals filling a small clearing at the skyline. Riderless horses came to a halt and began to crop at the grass with the broodmares, taking advantage of this midday stop.

Bass came up behind them, sliding out of the saddle before he threaded his way on foot through the grazing horses to reach the broad flank of two dozen men staring west from the saddle of the mountain pass.* Below their feet lay the land of the *Californios*.

Through eyes long blasted by desert sands, baked by an incomprehensible heat, reddened with days upon days of tortured sleep—they peered down upon the land of the Mexicans. Ranchos and missions, horses and mules, se-

---

* Cajon Pass, aptly given the Spanish word for "box."

ñoritas and squaws, mild ocean breezes and sweet Spanish wine.

"Damn, if that don't look good to this child, Peg-Leg!" Bill Williams squealed with delight, slapping a bony hand on his partner's back.

Smith turned and looked over his shoulder at the twenty-two riders they had brought across the desert to reach this mountain portal to California. "How long you figger it'll take for us to get the boys and our animals ready for some raids?"

"Better part of a week," Williams admitted. "Maybe more."

"Way I remember it," Thompson boasted as he came up to stop nearby, "them Mex soldiers didn't put up no fight a't'all, and sure as hell didn't follow us for far neither. I don't figger we oughtta worry 'bout wasting our good time resting up—"

"You wanna go off on your own now," Williams interrupted him, "you just go ahead, Thompson. Take the men what wanna ride with you and go. I don't want no man—not even you—giving me no trouble on anything I say from here on out."

"I wasn't meaning no—"

"G'won and leave, Thompson," Williams snapped.

Thompson glanced a moment at Smith, as if to implore his old friend's support. But while Peg-Leg might have been his friend, it was immediately plain that Smith was not about to go against Williams merely to support Thompson's foolhardy eagerness. The chagrined trapper admitted, "I don't wanna go off on my own hook."

"There's only one way we're gonna grab for the biggest herd of horses ever was stole from California," Williams declared sternly, louder now as he began to address the whole group, "and that's for all of us to hang together, cover each other's backs all the way in, and all the way back out."

"Bill's right on that track," Smith confirmed. "We don't hang together when the gunsmoke starts flying—ain't many of us gonna make it out of California alive."

"So let me ask this here and now, one time and one

time only," Williams growled at them. "Any man here what figgers he can lead this bunch better'n Peg-Leg and me . . . let that man step right up."

Most of the men twisted this way and that, glancing quickly at one another to spot any movement. But no one stepped forward.

"Looks like it's just you an' me gonna booshway this bunch, Bill," Smith said.

Williams pointed down the slope. "Yonder I see a meadow where two of them li'l cricks run through. Plenty water, and there's more'n 'nuff timber down there too. Good grass for the horses while they fatten up again."

"Let's go make camp, boys," Smith suggested. "We'll stay put till we put some meat back on our own bones, an' it comes time for us to shine on them Mex ranchos."

Across the next eight days the horses grazed, sticking close to those eight wet mares the trappers kept picketed close at hand. After only five days of rest, Frederico argued with Smith that he wanted to move on—if not with the white men, then by himself. Smith protested that such an unwise move would put the guide in danger, might well get him caught by the soldiers and put to death by the priests . . . then where would the horse raiders be?

Without their damn-fool guide, that's where!

Ultimately, Peg-Leg convinced the Indian that he was better off not going anywhere near the mission or the soldier fort either because of the chance of getting caught. The bitter truth of it, he explained to Frederico, was that should the Indian be seized by the Mexicans, then there was nothing stopping the white men from going right on with their plans to steal horses and mules. Without Frederico, there was no reason for the Americans to go through with their plan to rescue his sisters. The two of them would remain prisoner concubines of the *soldados*.

The Indian's only chance to free his sisters lay in doing exactly as the Americans told him.

Behind them stretched hundreds of miles of desert wilderness, a land with little to offer beyond waste and want. But below their mountainside camp lay rolling green plains, cold streams tumbling toward the valley, slopes dotted with more vegetation than they had seen since abandoning the Rockies: willow bordering the creekbanks, shady groves of sycamore and elder dotting the hillside.

On that eighth night of recouping their horses and their strength in the hills, Williams announced, "Be ready to ride at sunup."

That momentous morning they kept the broodmares on short tethers as they rode into the dimly lit dawn emerging over California. The men closely ringed the rest of the horses, with riders hugging both flanks, their best horsemen riding drag to keep the stragglers caught up now that they were dropping into the unknown—a foreign country where most of these invaders had, until eight days before, never watched a single sunrise. A land where these *Norteamericanos* would not be welcome because they had come to steal what belonged to the *ricos,* those wealthy landowners.

The twenty-four were trespassers in this green, fertile land captured between that low range of mountains the Americans were putting at their backs and the coast where the great salt ocean began. Strangers. Interlopers. Trespassers. And thieves.

Down they curved through the pass that took them on a southern route, down the timbered slopes into the foothills where the native grasses grew even taller still, nourished by the moist breezes and what rain the mountains trapped. As much as he strained and squinted into the west as the sun came over the range at their backs, lighting up everything before them, Bass could still not see anything blue in the distance. When, he wondered, would they lay eyes on the ocean?

They camped that night in the foothills and moved on at first light, following their Indian guide as he swept them around to the west once they left the rolling hills and emerged into an endless, grassy valley broken only by the myriad of narrow streams tumbling off the slopes, each one lined with an emerald border as it hurried to the seacoast. This valley was nowhere near as lush and green as his home in the wilds of the Rocky Mountains—its rounded, carpeted hills covered with little more than grass. Only the deep clefts between the knolls where the waters gurgled possessed any brush and trees. Mostly . . . grass.

But—he realized—that was exactly what nourished the horses of these *Californios*. The grass made this a horseman's paradise.

Even though it was no later than midafternoon, Smith and Williams pulled them up behind a pair of low hills and gave orders to make camp for the night.

"The Injun—he say we're close to his mission?" Philip Thompson asked Smith eagerly, rubbing his hands together.

"Not far," Peg-Leg responded. "We don't want none of them soldiers spotting our smoke so keep the fires small, back under the trees."

Williams walked over, dragging a bundle he had just taken from the back of his pack animal. As the others leaned in to watch, the old trapper tore at the knots in the rope, then flung back the oiled canvas to expose some well-weathered Navajo blankets, their colors faded from seasons of use. He stood with two of them hung over his arms.

"Here," Williams said, tossing the first to Frank Curnutt, one of Thompson's allies. "You look dark enough to be a Mex, Frank." Then he pitched the second to Bass. "An' I damn well know you 'member some of the Mex tongue, Scratch. Want you come along with me and the Injun."

"How come he's going and I ain't?" Thompson bawled. "I been here before!"

"But you damn well don't speak no Mex," Smith challenged. "If'n any of 'em get spotted, they're gonna have to talk Mex."

"Bass don't need to go," Thompson argued with a sly grin. "You talk better'n most Mexicans I know, Peg-Leg."

"I ain't going," Smith admitted. "I'm staying here with

you, if'n any bunch of *soldados* wander by and find us camped here."

By this time Williams had knelt and picked up his last two heavy Navajo blankets. "Felix—how 'bout you coming too?"

Warren caught the blanket and smiled at his friend Thompson. "Me and Frank keep a eye on Bass for you, Phil."

Unfurling the last blanket for himself, Williams removed his hat with one hand and located the slit at the center of its fold with the other. After pulling the blanket over his head he replaced his floppy hat and held out his arms expressively. "What you think, boys?"

"Look the Mex to me," Silas Adair said with approval.

"C'mon, Frederico," Williams commanded as he turned back to his saddle horse. "Let's go have us a look at where them padres sent off your sisters to live with them *soldados*."

Hanging in the lee of the hills, the five horsemen picked their way northwest along the rim of the valley. Every now and then Bill would signal for them to dismount and leave their horses behind. Then the quartet would follow the Indian up the back slope of a knoll where they dropped to their bellies to break the skyline. From each prominence the trappers gazed across a new stretch of the valley, wary of any vaqueros tending their great herds of horses, mentally plotting the location of the few ranch buildings they came across.

On the last of those stops, the sun was about to drop below the brims of their hats as they peered down upon a cluster of adobe structures behind a mud wall. Frederico tapped Williams on the arm.

"Can't make out all he's saying," Bill grumbled disgustedly. "Goddamn red nigger with his Mex talk—"

"Something about the soldiers," Bass broke in.

"I damn well know that," Williams snapped. "*Soldados* this and that. What he sayin' about the god-blame-ed *soldados*?"

"His sisters," Titus explained. "He says that's where they are."

That bit of news quieted Ol' Bill's muttering like a slap of thunder. "*Si, si,* Frederico," he whispered.

Clearly the Indian had become excited, pointing out the adobe buildings ringed by a high wall of mud and wattle. "*Soldados . . . y mis hermanas—*"

"Your sisters, yeah," Scratch repeated.

In the late-afternoon light he studied the big compound, those backlit buildings erected inside the low wall. Although there were no tall parapets, there was no mistaking this for a fortress of sorts. Nothing remained outside. Even the stables ran along the full length of one wall. Some of the Mexicans had their horses out in a corner of the compound, soaping the animals down. At another corner a blacksmith worked to reshoe a glossy, majestic black. Across the yard stood what appeared to be a low, one-story barracks. The roofs of a pair of buildings rested at either side of the double-wide gates, which stood open. Titus had no clue what those rooms were.

All the way at the rear of the huge compound stood a two-story building, a wide porch running across the full width of the structure, with a balcony across the width of the second floor. Several windows and two doors broke up the expanse of adobe on both floors.

Felix Warren let go a low whistle. "That's a heap of Mexicans down there."

Bass quickly turned to Frederico, "*Cuánto es?*"

At first the Indian shrugged, then his face went serious and he began flipping his fingers into his palms.

"What's he doin'?" Frank Curnutt demanded.

"I think he's ciphering how many's the lodge," Titus replied.

"It don't really matter, does it, Scratch?" Williams asked.

Bass said, "Sorry, Bill—I don't catch the drift."

"If'n there's twenty of 'em, or if there's eighty of 'em down there . . . we still know what we gotta do."

"Y-you can't be serious 'bout our outfit fighting all them Mex soldiers!" Frank Curnutt scoffed. "Why don't we just ride right on around 'em and they won't be none the wiser."

Williams argued, "But Smith give his word to the Injun here."

"Shit!" Warren snorted. "What's your damn word to a Injun? That's like shoveling fleas in a barnyard!"

"The Injun brung us here just like he said he would," Williams said heatedly, his eyes narrowing on the trapper.

"Let the Injun go raise hell with the soldiers if he wants," Curnutt argued. "It ain't gonna chap my hide to leave this red nigger to go his own way."

"You ain't listening to Bill," Titus growled. "He told you the way it's gonna be."

Curnutt's eyes closed into dangerous slits as he squinted over Williams's shoulder at Bass. "A white man's word to a Injun ain't but a piss in the wind."

"Bill and Peg-Leg both told the Injun what we'd do if he got us through that desert—"

Interrupting, Curnutt snarled, "Don't mean we gotta fight them soldiers. Hell, them two sisters of his nothin' better'n Mex whores now anyway—"

Springing onto his knees, Bass vaulted past Williams and snagged hold of the front of Curnutt's colorful serape before the other two could react. Jerking his leg up, Titus pressed a knee down on the right hand that Curnutt was attempting to wrap around his knife. "You heard Bill. We give our word to the—"

"I didn't give *my* word!" Curnutt spat, arching his back as Scratch pinned his left arm with one of his hands. "Sure as hell Thompson didn't give his word to no red nigger either!"

"Get off him," a voice warned at his back.

Williams tensed, rolling onto his hip to peer behind Titus and said, "Put the knife down, Warren."

Bass immediately twisted to look over his shoulder, finding Felix Warren rocking onto his knees, his big skinning knife out before him. Slowly and out of sight beneath his serape, Titus inched his fingers toward one of the two knives at the back of his belt.

"You figger on doing something stupid with your sticker," Scratch warned, "Curnutt here gonna be a dead man for it."

"Tol'cha: Get off 'im, Bass."

Williams tucked his legs under him into a crouch now, slowly pulling his belt pistol into view. Although he did not raise it enough to point its muzzle directly at Warren, it would have been apparent to a blind man that this was no veiled threat. "You're goin' again' my word, Warren."

"Just tell 'im get off Frank."

"Maybe I will," Williams said. "But not till you put that skinner away."

Bass shook his head emphatically. "I ain't gonna get off this son of a bitch till he shuts his meat hole 'bout helping the Injun."

Felix Warren just started to inch forward, saying, "Then you're a dead man—"

Then Williams brought the pistol up, raked his arm forward, and jammed the muzzle against Warren's ribs. "This here's gonna make a damn big hole in you by the time the ball comes out your back."

Warren's eyes widened, nearly crossing when he peered down at the pistol and the brown hand holding it.

"It's your play, Felix," Bill explained.

Bringing his eyes up to glare into Williams's, Warren started pulling the knife back toward his belt, saying, "I'll put it away . . . then you get that bastard off Frank."

"Get off him, Scratch," Bill ordered as Warren's knife slid into the scabbard.

"Not till the bastard tells you he won't go running against your grain, Bill."

Williams dragged the pistol away from Warren's rib cage and said, "I think Curnutt understands who's booshway of this here horse raid—don't you, Frank?"

"You are, Bill."

"I s'pose you can crawl off him now, Scratch."

The instant Bass took his weight off the man's arms, Curnutt spun out from under him, rubbing the wrist where Titus's bony knee had pinned it against the ground. He shrugged his shoulders to settle the serape back into place, glowering at Bass.

"I want you boys stay away from each other," Williams ordered. "We got horses to steal. You understand, Scratch?"

"Soon as the horses is stole," Bass said low, the words rattling at the back of his throat, "I got some business to see to, soon as the horses is stole."

"Your time's coming," Curnutt warned with a sneer.

Titus wagged his head as he slid backward off the skyline and got to his feet. "Won't be by the likes of you two."

"That's right, Frank," Warren snorted with a wide grin. "We wouldn't wanna go an' spoil Thompson's li'l fandango with this son of a bitch."

10

───────◆───────

When did the mountains roll over on themselves? Who was the first to pit white man against white man?

Oh, sure—there'd always been John Bull's boys working for Hudson's Bay Company, poking around over in Snake River country where they didn't belong. And there'd been those years while Rocky Mountain Fur Company did everything it could to hold the high country against Astor's mighty American Fur Company brigades probing the mountains from forts along the Missouri River. But . . . how did it ever come to pass that when the beaver business went to hell it became every man for himself?

Or, had things always been that way and Titus Bass was just one stupid nigger who failed to read the sign?

Maybe while he hadn't been looking, that unspoken code between men had broken down. Time was, a man came into the mountain West, he accepted the certainty of a few immutable laws. You took care of those who stood at your back. You didn't steal what furs another man busted his hump to earn. And you stood by those Indians who had taken you in . . . God knows there were already enough red niggers out here willing to part a child from his hair at the blink of an eye.

It all had to do with knowing who your friends were, and who weren't. So, when did Scratch's whole world heave over on itself? When did these mountains start filling up with men who couldn't give a good goddamn for the way things used to be?

That next morning after the ruckus with Curnutt and Warren, Smith took Thompson with him and rode south through the hills to have a good look at what herds might await them on the ranchos in that direction. And Williams took Bass to scout the look of things on west of the Mission San Gabriel along the foot of those loftier mountains timbered with yellow pine and fragrant cedar.

Not very far beyond the soldiers' post, Titus had his first gander at the strangest cattle he had ever laid eyes on.

"Longhorns," Bill explained. "Leastways, that's what such critters ought'n be called."

Like nothing else, these Mexican cattle were. Unlike the full-bodied, short-horned breeds raised by those farmers back in the States, these were rangy and far leaner animals, head-heavy with a pair of saberlike horns that curved and swirled gracefully out from their bony skulls.

"You s'pose you here longhorns are a Mex breed?"

Williams shrugged. "Maybeso the Spanyards brung 'em over to Mexico like they is."

"Longhorns," Bass repeated, almost under his breath, trying hard to imagine more than a handful of the creatures crowded together, stuffed down in the belly of those huge, tall-masted oceangoing ships he had seen so long, long ago in New Orleans. "I'll be go to hell."

Could be they were the perfect breed for such arid country as this, a land where it didn't rain all that much, despite the proximity of damp ocean winds. Farmers back east in the States did well with cattle that required a lot of the lush grasses that grew in a country where a lot of rain fell. But out west . . . well, now—maybe those

Spanish did have something right when they brought those longhorns to Mexico a few centuries ago.

Near midafternoon Williams and Bass spotted a confused cluster of buildings in the distance and pulled up on the side of a hill that overlooked the extensive settlement.

"You make that for a rancho?" Bill asked.

"Naw, I don't," he squinted in the light. "Too many folks."

There were. Many of them coming or going, some moving in or out of the settlement on horseback, in wagons or carriages. Besides, there simply wasn't any sign of those sorts of structures a man assumed he'd find on a Mexican ranch. No corrals or barns or outlying huts where the servants lived, no rows of those low-roofed barracks where the vaqueros slept when not in the saddle.

"Lookee there, Scratch," Williams said. "See them sails in the harbor there? By blazes, that's a town!"

When Bass turned his head he found Bill grinning at him. "What you up to, Solitaire?"

"I figger the boys are due a grand spree afore we go round up the biggest cavvyard ever took from California and get high behind for the mountains again," Williams declared with a matter-of-factness. "A li'l likker, and some wimmens too."

Titus sighed, recalling the heady numbness of Workman's corn whiskey down Taos way. "Maybe some popskull and a spree could take the edge off things for all of us afore we gotta leave Californy in a hurry."

"Let's circle to the south for to get back to camp," Williams advised, eager to be on the way again. "See what horses there are for the taking."

It was well past dark and the moon had risen when they found their way back to the others. Already Smith and Thompson had come in to report there had to be more than two thousand head of Mexican horses. The Americans and Frenchmen were growing anxious to get on with their raids.

From their springtime camps in the central Rockies, these men had ridden something on the order of a thousand miles or more to reach Mexican California, the land of the horse. They had suffered hardship the likes of which few men would ever choose to endure. Besides being forced to drink their own urine and blood to cross the southern desert that early summer, these twenty-four had subsisted on skinny, played-out horseflesh and bitter-tasting cactus pulp. Not hard to understand that these trappers had grown restless, anxious to be gathering up horses and turning them east for the Bent brothers' post on the Arkansas . . . eager to be doing just about anything instead of cooling their heels in these California hills.

"Peg-Leg, I figger it's 'bout time for me to dust off the bad news and tell the boys what I got in mind," Williams announced around a chunk of Mexican beef Silas Adair had managed to cut out of a nearby herd early that afternoon.

Smith nearly choked on his coffee as he sputtered at Bill's surprise. "I found a lot of horses for the takin', Solitaire. There ain't no bad news in that!"

"Couple thousand ain't near enough," Williams grumbled dramatically, then quickly winked at Bass as the other men around them began to groan and grumble in disappointment. "I figger it still ain't the right time to steal horses."

Smith bolted to his feet, some coffee sloshing out of his tin. "Your brains run out your ears back there in all that desert, Bill? I tol't you: We found us plenty horses south of here."

"Ain't yet the time, boys," Williams repeated. "Not yet, sorry."

"Dammit to hell!" Philip Thompson flung his whetstone down at his feet. "So when does the high-an'-mighty Bill Williams figger on it bein' time to gather up the horses we come across the desert to steal?"

Williams slowly dragged the back of his hand across his mouth and chin, then licked the shiny grease from his hand and fingers. "We'll go steal horses soon enough, boys. But not till me and Scratch lead you all down to a li'l California town to have ourselves a spree."

"A sp-spree?" Peg-Leg sputtered.

"You mean likker?" Reuben Purcell asked.

"Mexican likker," Titus confirmed with a smack of his lips.

With a bob of his head, Williams said, "Likely that means some lightnin' for those of you wanna smash your faces on the floor just once afore we head back home. And for the rest, some sweet California wine or pass brandy—"

"Women too?" Jake Corn interrupted. "They got women down there?"

Titus gaped at Corn a moment, then said, "How the hell you figger California gone and filled up with Mexicans, if'n there wasn't no women to pleasure all them damned *pelados*?"

They whooped, and hollered, and hurrooed. Several of them took to swinging around in pairs, arm-in-arm or grandly doe-see-doeing there in the fire's light.

Smith leaped around the fire and pounded Williams on the back. "We go find this village of yours in the morning, Bill?"

"Damn, if we won't!"

Peg-Leg flicked his eyes up at Bass. They twinkled with devilment. "So tell me, Scratch—what's the name of this here village you boys found?"

The *Californios* called it Pueblo de los Angeles.

A sprawling, no-account coastal village by some standards. Hardly worth remembering, and of little redeeming value . . . but for the fact that it lay a long stone's throw off the bay where the high-masted seafaring ships anchored to supply the ranchos and that mission of San Gabriel.

None of that international trade mattered to those twenty-four thirsty interlopers invading a foreign land. Soon enough would come the work. Soon enough would come the trials and the gunfire, then enduring another desert crossing they had to survive. So for now, these *Norteamericanos* would drink their fill and rub up against every willing woman they might find in the watering holes and stinking cantinas dotting the Pueblo de los Angeles.

That many horsemen, every one crudely dressed in buckskin, calico, and wool, were certain to attract notice. By their unkempt beards, trail-leathered skin, each rider bristling with weaponry, there could be no mistaking the two dozen for strangers come calling on this coastal village. Just as apparent too was that these twenty-four were not seamen who had just jumped off a Boston merchant ship anchored in the nearby harbor. No, these men and their distinctively jug-headed Indian ponies and mules had come a long, long way to reach this little village nestled between the hills and that green ocean.

Streetside conversations stopped as the Mexicans turned to study the strangers. Shopkeepers and customers crowded in doorways or peered from windows as the horsemen moved slowly down the rutted lanes littered with refuse, dung, and the occasional body of a dead cat or dog. As the horsemen passed one knot of the curious after another, Bass caught snatches of words the villagers mumbled among themselves.

Extranjeros.

Long road.

Come for the furs.

No, perhaps . . . come for horses.

"As likely a place as any," Williams announced as he reined aside at the front of a long, low-roofed adobe hutch, its front walls marred by none of the small windows pocking other buildings, windows filled with panes of selenite or slates of mica.

No window here. Nothing but the low-beamed, narrow doorway that stood open in the morning sun. Beneath the tiled roof protruded *vigas*, those pared and peeled logs that poked out beyond the walls, from which hung long *ristras* of peppers and cloves of garlic. Embedded in the side wall were but a half dozen hitching rings, and room for no more than a few of their horses at what was left of a broken-down hitching rail out front.

"Tie 'em off two-by-two," Peg-Leg ordered.

That would at least keep their animals from wandering, hitching them nose-to-nose on the open ground at the side of the cantina. And with as many of them as there were, none of the trappers figured any Mexican would dare attempt slipping away with their loose stock.

"Welcome, Yankees!"

At the corner of the building in a patch of shadow stood a tall Mexican, his sunken cheeks deeply pitted with the ravages of some long-ago disease. He was grinning widely, half bowing graciously as he eagerly wiped his hands on the long tail of his coarse, linen shirt he had not cared to tuck inside the waist of his stained leather breeches. Sweeping a long hank of black hair out of his eyes, this older man swept an arm toward the door in a graceful arc.

"Yankees, come!" he repeated.

"*Gracias,*" Williams replied as he stepped past the Mexican, the first to enter the cantina's shadowy, cool interior.

As they threaded past the bartender, Elias Kersey whispered to Bass, "He think we're sailin' Yankees off one of them ships, eh?"

Before Titus could say a thing, the Mexican suddenly leaped in front of Kersey, smiling warmly and nodding as he gestured toward the open door. "Yankees, *si*! Come, come—Yankees welcome!"

They flooded in behind Bill Williams, most pausing to soak in, and grow accustomed to, the change from bright light to dimmest shadow. As his eyes adjusted, Titus quickly glanced over the interior, measuring the patrons huddled around their rough-hewn tables. It was plain there weren't enough chairs or tables to seat all two dozen newcomers. But the cantina owner had already recognized this shortcoming and was clapping his hands together, sending two of his men to bring out several thick blankets they unfurled onto the hard, clay floor.

"*Sientense ustedes, por favor!*" all three of the cantinamen repeated, indicating the blankets they spread at the foot of two walls of the long, low room.

While some of the trappers settled in the last of the

chairs at the few open tables, most collapsed onto the
floor, filling the offered blankets, where they leaned back
against the wall, eyeing the jugs and jars on the double
shelf resting behind the long, open-faced bar. Every wall
had been painted with *jaspe,* that whitewash the Mexicans concocted from a selenite compound they burned in
their *hornos,* or beehive ovens, then mixed with water.
The thick paste was then spread by hand on the walls and
finished off by brushing the *jaspe* with a patch of sheep-
skin. To keep the brittle whitewash from rubbing off on
customers, the Mexicans had draped *mantas,* or printed
muslins, about halfway up the walls. The crude but un-
pretentious decor so reminded Titus of his visits to Ger-
trude Barcelos's brothel in long-ago and faraway Taos.

With the strained, too-quiet atmosphere that morning
as the Americans settled, Bass was drawn to the owner's
nervous stutter as the older man leaned on the table
where Smith and Williams sat with Thompson and their
Indian guide.

"What's he telling you?" Bill demanded of his partner.

Peg-Leg explained, "He says the Injun gotta go—says
he don't serve Injuns here."

Thompson immediately hissed, "This damned Mex
don't have no right to tell us he won't serve our friend,
Peg-Leg. You let this son of a bitch know we could tear
his place to the ground with our hands—"

"Such hooligan actions wouldn't be a good idea,
fellas."

Turning as one, all two dozen watched a large,
roundish man with fleshy jowls bristling with thick, graying sideburns get to his feet back in the shadows, then
stride in their direction as the cantina owner nodded to
the man and pivoted and shuffled back to the bar.

Thompson shot to his feet, growling, "Who the hell
are you to be telling—"

"Cap'n Janus C. Smathers," the stranger announced
as he came to a stop at Smith's table. His thumbs were
hung in the armpits of his ample vest sewn from a dark
blue wool, at least twenty tiny brass buttons straining in
their holes strung down the flap.

"You're 'Merican?" Peg-Leg asked in disbelief.

With a nod, Smathers swept his arm toward two tables of men tucked back in a shadowy corner. "All of us. American, like you. Adventurers, to be sure."

Williams held out his hand and introduced himself. "Bill Williams, M.T."

Smathers cocked his head, asking, "What's an M.T.?"

"Master trapper," Bill answered proudly.

"You're fur hunters, I take it," Smathers replied. "Here to search the coastline for otter?"

"Maybeso," Williams answered.

"Listen, fellas," Smathers began. "The governor down at San Diego frowns on Americans coming into California to harvest California furs then haul them right back out of here to parts unknown."

"You an' the governor don't need to fret none. We won't be going down near this here San Diego," Thompson snipped.

"Best advice I could give you is don't say a thing about coming to California for furs," Smathers advised, turning away from the antagonism of Thompson. "And be wary of causing any trouble that would bring attention to yourselves." He glanced quickly at Frederico. "In that respect, it will be best if you take the Indian outside. These *Californios* don't like any wild Indians from across the mountains taking liberties that the Indians around here don't have out of hand."

"Oh, he ain't a wild Injun from across the mountains," Smith snorted. "Frederico here's a mission Injun."

Smathers's eyes grew big, and he flicked a look at the Mexicans nearby as they were placing clay cups on several small wooden platters atop the bar. "Good God— he's a mission slave?"

"Runaway—"

"Don't say another word about him!" Smathers warned with a snap. "If you want to keep him and you value his life, take him out of here and hide him where you can. An Indian spotted here in the village is something that will soon draw the wrong kind of attention."

Smith asked, "They ain't 'llowed to come to town? Can't have a drink?"

"Right on both counts," Smathers explained. "They're slaves. I've been coming to California for eleven years already, make a trip around the cape every year. In all that time, I've still to make peace with most of how these people live here. But me and my seafarers are visitors, so we haven't any say."

"Thanks, Cap'n," Williams said as he stood and stepped around the table to prop his hand on the Indian's shoulder. "Tell 'im why he's gotta leave, Peg-Leg. Tell 'im he has to stay outside to watch the horses. We'll bring him some likker later on."

Once Smith finished his explanation, Frederico glanced up at Williams, then the ship's captain, and eventually stood. He started for the door beside Williams without a word of protest.

"These *Californios* ain't like us," Smathers declared as the old trapper led the young Indian outside. "There's one church here—they're all Papists you know. And that one church rules those who run the government with an iron fist. It's a closed society, gentlemen—and a culture where Americans are welcome only if they toe the line and don't commit any act against their religion or their laws."

"A lot like Taos and Santy Fee," Bass said as he stopped near the table.

Smathers regarded Titus a moment, then said, "I don't doubt that, mister. Never been either place myself, but I have no reason not to believe one part of Mexico would be any different from another part."

Bill was coming back inside as the two Mexicans brought over the first of the small trays holding those short, clay cups to distribute them among the tables and those men squatting on the floor. Behind the pair came the owner, pouring a liberal amount of a pale liquid into those cups eagerly held up by twenty-four thirsty trappers.

"Should you require anything, need my assistance with the local authorities," the captain explained, "my

ship is anchored in the bay. The *Windward,* out of Port-
land. That's nor'east up on the coast of Maine. You fellas
just ask anyone down near the wharf for the *Windward,*
and you'll find someone to row you out to fetch me."

Holding out his hand, Williams said, "Thank you,
Cap'n."

"You've chosen a good day to celebrate," Smathers
declared. "A Saint's Day this be."

"Which of their damned saints are they celebrating?"
Smith demanded, licking drops of whiskey off his lips.

Smathers tugged down on the tails of his vest. "San
Juan's Day. The twenty-fourth of June."

"Any day's as good as this'un for whiskey and wom-
ens!" Williams cheered.

"Captain Janus C. Smathers," the man repeated his
name to the group. "Remember it if you need my help.
While I'm anchored in the harbor of this foreign land, I
remain at my countrymen's service."

"What's the C stand for," Bass inquired.

Smathers turned to Titus, saying, "Cautious. The C
stands for cautious, fellas. Remember my advice: keep
your heads down and don't stir up any waves. A good
day, and pleasant journey, to you, fellow pilgrims."

"Fill your chair, Scratch," Smith offered as he scooted
the simple chair back from the table.

Titus glanced at it, then at Thompson's hardened
glare, and finally to Smith. "Thanks anyway, Peg-Leg. I'll
drink over by the wall with them boys."

In a flash, Frank Curnutt roughly shoved his way past
Titus and plopped down in the chair the moment Scratch
turned away from the table.

That first wash of the harsh corn liquor over his
tongue made Bass's eyes water. It had been a long, long
time since he had tasted such raw, head-thumping spirits.
Likely not since those final days in Taos. None of those
finer brandies the company traders secreted in their river-
side fur posts, or the smoother grain alcohol the traders
hauled out to rendezvous every summer could compare
with the teeth-jarring power of this Mexican hooch.

"Whooo!" he rasped, blinking his eyes. "Wonder if

they strained this here likker through a ol' Comanche's breechclout."

"Don't smell like it!" Reuben Purcell argued with a grin, holding his clay cup under his nose.

"But it damn well tastes awful suspicious," Elias Kersey said, wrinkling up his face.

"I've had me plenty of worse," Bass announced. "This here ain't bad for what it is—Mexican whiskey."

By the time an hour had galloped past, the talk had grown loud and merry. Smathers and his men had abandoned the cantina just before the owner and his help brought out platters of tortillas and steamy bowls of beans. The hungry Americans greedily scooped up the beans using the soft tortillas as spoons or ladles, and devoured everything set before them.

"Lookee here now," Jake Corn said, jabbing an elbow into Titus's ribs as Scratch was loading a little tobacco into his clay pipe.

Bass turned as most of the trappers noticed the nine women stepping out of the bright sun, entering the open doorway. The cantina owner hurried over, speaking quickly to one of the women, who wore large brass wires suspended from her ears. He pointed out the table where Smith and Williams sat. Half of the women dressed in the loose-fitting, off-the-shoulder *camisetas* and the short, full skirts called *enaguas* followed their fleshy leader, who had generously smeared crimson *alegria* juice on her pasty, powdered cheeks. She had clearly seen her better days, yet walked over to the Americans with an unmistakable air of supreme confidence.

In hushed tones she and Smith chattered for a moment until Peg-Leg stood.

He announced, "These here gal's come to have some fun with us!"

"Bang-tails?"

Smith turned toward the questioner. "You damn bet they're whores, you stupid nigger."

"If that don't take the circle!" Purcell leaped to his feet, lunging for the closest as the women fanned out across the room. "I ain't humped since we left off them Mojave gals."

Corn stood, nudging Bass with the toe of his moccasin. "Ain't you coming to poke you one of these, Bass?"

"Had me Mex gals before," he answered. "Besides, I got me a woman of my own."

"But she ain't here," Purcell argued, dragging the woman onto his lap. "An' it's been a long time since you rid atween your woman's legs, ain't it?"

"Don't reckon I need to go," Titus explained with a shrug. "You boys go on and have your fun with them whores. I'll be sitting right here when you get your humping done. 'Pears I'll be the one leading you fellas on back to camp so you can sleep off your sore heads."

"Don't want no honey on your stinger, eh?" Kersey spouted. "Then I'll poke one of 'em center just for you, Titus Bass!"

"Thankee kindly, Elias," Scratch replied. "Can't claim I didn't have my own share of Mex whores back in my rowdy days."

Corn prodded, "Any man can still get rowdy, Scratch."

"Nowadays I got a lot more rings 'round my trunk," he declared with a grin. "But you fellas go grab hold of those gals and don't let 'em buck you off, boys!"

"Don't gotta ask me more'n once!" Adair roared as he started for one of the women who had moved over to join other Americans at the bar.

It made for a good business proposition, Titus figured. The women could drink for free of the cantina's liquor because they were assuring that the Americans were consuming all the more, spending most of their hard American money. At the far end of the long bar a greasy blanket hung across a low doorway. One by one, three of the women headed past that blanket with three of the trappers, arm-in-arm and laughing at some joke no one understood.

Another three of the women perched on one lap after another, generously rubbing their hands, bellies, and rumps against prospective customers while two of the whores leaped onto the edge of the bar where they hiked up their skirts so they could wrap their legs around the ribs of a pair of trappers as they all drank and flirted despite their foreign languages, laughing crazily and getting all the drunker as they waited their turn at the tiny cribs in the back of the cantina.

Three-by-three the Americans lurched past the greasy blanket, back to finish what they had started out front, turning over their women to other trappers who drank and ate as they waited their few minutes in the cribs. By the time the last men were emerging from the rooms behind the bar, some of the first were boasting that they were ready for another go-round with the whores, which meant Smith was having to ante up more of his dwindling supply of gold coin.

From where he sat leaning against a side wall, Bass could peer out the open doorway when a trio of horsemen reined up in front of the cantina. He hadn't seen uniforms like theirs since Jack Hatcher's bunch had chased into the winter mountains hoping to wrestle back some hostages from marauding Comanche.

"You expectin' company, Bill?" he called out to Williams.

He started walking toward Titus and the door. "Who?"

"Soldiers."

"How many?"

"Only three," Scratch answered.

Stopping in his tracks, Williams harrumped and turned back for the bar, saying, "I ain't worried till they send a whole shitteree of Mex soldiers for us."

Instead of coming right inside after tying their horses off to a single ring out front, the trio walked past the doorway for the corner of the cantina. A little slowed and deliberate in his movements due to the heady whiskey, Titus struggled to his feet against the *manta* draped on the wall and stepped outside, finding the three soldiers moving among some of the horses and mules. From what he could tell, they were inspecting the rear flanks for brands.

He snorted with the humor in that. Indian ponies simply didn't have a brand.

"Help you with something, fellas?"

All three turned at his call, two of them flicking their eyes to the third as they came over to stop before the trapper. When that man in the middle spoke, his Spanish spilled out far too fast for Bass to grasp more than a handful—hardly enough to go on.

"Ho-hold on," Titus suggested. "*No comprendo.*"

"*Norteamericanos?*"

"*Si,*" Scratch answered.

"Ahhh," the middle one with the goatee replied. "*Extranjeros.*" Then he started speaking rapidly again, gesturing back at the horses.

"Yes, they are mine," Bass started to explain. "Something wrong?"

The soldier shrugged one shoulder and motioned to the others as all three stepped around Bass for the darkened doorway.

Inside, the bartender noisily greeted the soldiers, waving them over to the bar where two of the whores each had a pair of trappers at their sides. The trio fixed their malevolent gaze on the Americans until the owner clattered some cups in front of them and began pouring them drinks.

The three toasted, then turned to gaze over the cantina patrons as if comfortable with the foreigners. But the moment a woman pushed past the curtain from the back rooms holding the arm of Roscoe Coltrane, one of the soldiers cried out her name. After flicking him a glance, she steered the trapper in the opposite direction, toward the last of the empty chairs.

"Shit," Bass muttered. Sure as rain, trouble was coming.

The soldier slammed his clay cup down on the bar, then tugged at the bottom of his short-waisted leather jacket, its stiffened epaulets extending off the man's shoulders. He had all the appearances of being a man on a mission.

As the soldier stomped across the earthen floor, he

loudly berated the whore, finally seizing her upper arm in his big, brown hand, yanking her up and whirling her around just as she settled on Coltrane's lap.

"Leave 'er be," Silas Adair growled at the soldier, appearing at the table so quickly he knocked a chair aside.

By that moment the soldier with the goatee was shouting at his companion, gesturing him back to the bar. The angry soldier stood frozen a moment longer, glaring down at Coltrane's hand on his knife, at Adair's fist locked around the butt of his pistol still stuffed in the front of his belt, then smiled wanly as he tapped the hilt of the saber short-chained over his left hip. The soldier released his grip on the whore and turned on his heel, slowly.

Scratch finally took a breath and bent over, picking his empty cup off the blanket where he had been sitting, starting for the bar as the whore cursed the soldier and spat at his heels.

In a blur the Mexican turned and slapped her across the jaw, making her reel to the side, pitching into Coltrane's arms. Lunging forward, the soldier grabbed the screaming woman's arm and yanked her away from Roscoe as Coltrane snagged her other wrist. By now the other whores set up a caterwauling and shrieking so loud it would have raised the dead back in Santa Fe.

Reaching across his waist, the soldier pulled free his short saber with a loud, metallic scrape. The moment Roscoe stopped yanking on the woman and let her go, the Mexican spat into the whore's face. Coltrane's face flushed with anger as he rocked onto the balls of his feet, ready to pounce . . . but in a flash of candlelight, the soldier held that glittering saber out before him.

Adair grumbled, "You want I should shoot 'im, Roscoe?"

"No!" Smith answered for him. "That's more trouble'n we bargained for right now."

"Maybe 'nother time," Williams suggested. "Don't make nothing of this, Coltrane. She's just a soldier's whore an' this *pelado* greaser's jealous 'cause she humped with a gringo."

That brought a wry smile to Roscoe's face as the tension started to drain out of his shoulders. He rocked back onto his heels. As his smile broadened, Coltrane extended the index finger on his right hand and held it under his left ear. Then with a loud, guttural sound, he slowly dragged the finger around the front of his neck, across his windpipe, until he reached the right earlobe.

That done, Roscoe turned his skinny back on the soldier and settled in a chair at Adair's table. Which seemed to prompt the woman to begin thrashing and kicking, attempting to free herself from the soldier's grip. Infuriated at her attempts, he hurled her against the bar, watching the whore crumple to the floor. Coltrane flew out of his chair and shrank into a crouch at the instant the soldier brought up his saber and started inching forward—barely wiggling the tip of the weapon in that narrowing distance between himself and the American.

He jabbed. Roscoe backed a step. Another feint, and Roscoe retreated another step, staring down at that short saber. Inch by inch by inch—

Until he had Coltrane backed against the wall.

Bass motioned Kersey, Purcell, and Corn up behind the other two soldiers as he cocked back his arm. Hurling the arm forward, he threw his clay cup against the back of the swordsman's head. It shattered as the soldier stumbled, got watery in the knees. Coltrane swung his arm in an arc, knocking the saber from the Mexican's grip.

In that moment the other two soldiers started away from the bar, Kersey and Corn lunged forward with their pistols and cracked the Mexicans on the back of their skulls.

"That ain't messy at all, now is it, Peg-Leg?" Corn asked.

"Just as long as we don't kill any stupid hard-dicked Mexican *soldado*," Williams groused. "That'd be damp powder an' no way to dry it."

"That's right—we showed these greasers not to trouble us no more," Peg-Leg added. "G'won now, boys— throw all three of 'em outside so we can go on an' have ourselves li'l more fun."

11

But trouble came calling them by name.

While a half dozen of the trappers were dragging the trio of unconscious soldiers out the door into the summer sun, the cantina owner was hopping animatedly among the Americans: cursing, shrieking, tugging at the celebrants to stop them in their tracks. Trying to convince the gringos they were about to make a terrible mistake.

While some of the whores whimpered, most inched away from their American customers to huddle together in a corner of the cantina. It was clear they were frightened of what had just happened. And even more apprehensive of what might well now take place.

There was no talking any of those women into the cribs behind the bar now. The last trio of trappers flung back the blanket curtain and burst into the room, their fornication rudely interrupted. Those three appeared all the more pitiable as they implored their women at the same time they were scrambling back into their clothing.

When the cantina's barmen indicated in no uncertain terms that they wouldn't serve another drink to these unwanted guests, four of the trappers either leaped over the bar or swept around the end of it to snatch up glass and clay bottles for themselves. The moment the bartenders attempted to intervene and save the liquor, both were soundly pummeled by the four drunk Americans.

Seeing that these unwanted customers were beating his hired men, the cantina owner dashed back to the bar, where he tried his best to drag the trappers off the bartenders, shrieking at the Americans.

"What's he shouting, Peg-Leg?" Williams demanded.

"Says the soldiers're coming back."

"Let 'em," Thompson snorted. "We'll thump their heads again!"

"No." And Smith shook his head. "He ain't talking about them three niggers we throwed out in the street. This'un's saying that bunch went to fetch up more soldiers. He wants us long gone by the time they get back here with more hands."

"We ain't leaving here without something for the trail, are we, boys?" Thompson roared at his compatriots as they crowded against the bar.

"What you got in mind, Phil?" Frank Curnutt asked when he let one of the hired men drop from his grip so he could lumber back up to the bar.

"I don't figger we should leave a drop of whiskey in this damn rathole," Thompson bellowed.

Felix Warren squeaked in disbelief, "Y-you ain't gonna break ever' bottle, are you, Phil?"

"Stupid idjut! We're gonna take their likker with us!"

It reminded Bass of a swarm of single-minded wasps, how the white men turned and swept through the place. They ended up finding several big baskets in the cribs behind the bar, along with a pair of the dingy tick mattresses. These they set down on the bar itself and proceeded to load up what glass bottles and clay jugs were left on the shelves. Between the bottles and jugs they stuffed handsful of old, musty straw they yanked from the dirty mattresses hastily split open with their knives.

Bass was the first to spot the furtive shadow peek in at the doorway, gesturing to the Americans. He hurried to the guide, who began talking in his native language, eyes like milk saucers.

"Slow, slow down, Frederico," he begged, grabbing the Indian by the shoulders. "*Habla español*, dammit!"

Taking a gulp, Frederico started very, very slow, sorting through the vocabulary in the foreign language. Every now and then Titus grasped a word.

"Where did you go when the soldiers rode up?" Scratch asked.

"Hide," he said, and pointed around the corner of the cantina.

They both looked up suddenly, gazing down the long lane at the distant thunder of approaching hoofbeats.

Frederico cried, "We hide now! *Vamos! Vamos!*"

Far down the wide, rutted lane Titus could see how the villagers were backing against the adobe walls of their huts and shops, dragging children into the folds of their skirts or hoisting them onto those simple *carretas* they rushed to wheel out of the way. Stubborn mules brayed and confused sheep bleated as herders whipped the animals out of the avenue and up alleyways as the pack of oncoming horses drew nearer and nearer.

Then Bass saw them, realizing he didn't have much time.

"Bill! Peg-Leg!" He hurtled his call in the doorway. "We're in the soup now! A whole heap o' *soldados* coming!"

By the moment he reached his own animals and began untying them, the rest of the Americans were bursting out the door, a half dozen of them lugging the heavy woven baskets by their handles, the necks of bottles and sprigs of musty grass bristling from the top of each basket.

"Tie that on the back of my horse," Adair demanded as he and Reuben Purcell lunged up with a basket of their own. Together they hoisted it atop the packs on the horse as Bass stepped up to quickly diamond-hitch it down atop the rest of the load and tied it off.

"You wastin' time to steal this here whiskey might well make it the last drink you'll ever have!" he growled at them.

Adair's eyes flashed at Scratch, then flicked down the narrow avenue, squinting in the sun. "We get our asses out of this fight, I'll damn well buy *you* a drink, Titus Bass."

Over the noisy chuffing of their horses, the clatter of bits, and squeak of leather, the trappers could suddenly hear the panic-ridden screams of those villagers leaping out of the way as the soldiers pressed on, shouting as they first came in sight of the *Norteamericanos*. For now, all sound was focused, funneled, trapped entirely between the adobe walls on either side of that narrow, dusty street.

Snagging hold of the big round saddlehorn the size of a Mexican orange, Titus swung into his saddle without using the big cottonwood stirrup. He took up the lead rope to his packhorse and pranced it to the cantina door as Williams burst into the light. "You the last one, Bill?"

"Wasn't no one else in the back," Williams declared as he skidded to a halt with that sight down the lane. "Shit!" he grumbled as he got his first look at the soldiers.

"We gotta slow 'em down with lead!" Peg-Leg hollered from atop his horse.

"Aim low," Bass advised.

"Low?" Smith roared.

"We kill a bunch of these *soldados*," he huffed, adrenaline firing his veins, "ain't a one of us ever gonna get out of Californy alive—they'll bring in soldiers from all around to track us down to the last man!"

Williams demanded, "You really think we can get outta this scrap 'thout killin' a passel of them soldiers?"

"Scratch's right!" Smith shouted as his partner clambered into his saddle and pulled up his long rifle. "Drop their horses first. Bass, you and Coltrane, Curnutt and Kersey—you niggers're our best shots! Get up there and blow some holes in that first rank!"

With a lot of jostling those four trappers arrayed themselves across the wide, rutted street. In seconds they found their horses too fractious to work from the saddle, so all dropped to the ground and threw their rifles to their shoulders.

"When I give the word!" Smith bellowed behind them as he leaned over to sweep up some loose reins.

"I want four more of you boys to bring your guns up here—have 'em for these shooters," Williams ordered behind Peg-Leg. Then he stared down the street at the onrushing enemy, shaking his head while he asked, "How the hell many of them bastards is there?"

"More'n we care to get tied down scrapping with, Bill!" Smith roared as he peered up the street. "Now, boys! Fire! *Fire!*"

Those four long rifles belched gray smoke, their staccato echoes reverberating off the adobe walls of the homes and shops lining the dusty street. Huge lead balls, each one more than a half inch in diameter, slammed into the chests or necks or heads of those onrushing horses at the front of the charge.

Pitching forward or rearing backward in a skid, whinnying in pain and shrieking in terror, the small Spanish barb horses collided at the front of the formation, hurling their riders this way and that. One cavalryman landed under the hooves of the oncoming horses. Another smacked against a wall with his horse as it crumpled in front of three other mounts close on its tail. And the third was flung into the side of a wooden display of fruit, while the fourth slammed into a wagon stacked with crates stuffed with live chickens. Bloodcurdling squawks and white feathers both exploded into the late-afternoon sky.

Williams ordered, "Get up here with them loaded guns!"

Warren, Corn, Adair, and Samuel Gibbon all passed off their rifles to one of the quartet of marksmen, taking the empty weapons before they dropped back four or five paces to reload.

Throwing back the frizzen, Scratch assured himself the pan on the strange gun was primed. Dragging the big hammer back to full cock he snapped the frizzen into place over the pan and brought the butt to his shoulder. Different feel, this cheekpiece, different too how the front blade nestled down in the base of this rear sight—wondering how the rifle was sighted, just how far away the ball would strike center. Were these iron sights set for eighty yards? Maybe a hundred?

The next rank of soldiers had regrouped and forced their way through the clutter of downed horses and spilled riders. Close enough now that Titus figured it didn't much matter by the time he set the rear set trigger and lightly nestled his finger against the front trigger. He'd hold midway between the bottom jaw and that cleft between the horse's legs.

It went off with a surprise.

"Get back here to your horses!" Smith hollered as the roar of those four guns was still rattling down the adobe channel of that village street.

Horses were rearing, falling, spinning, cavalry soldiers pitching off under hoof.

"Load 'em on the run, boys!" Williams commanded. "Let's get gone while we can!"

Titus took one last look over his shoulder, back down the lane as he brought the packhorse around behind him and leaped into the saddle. A few of the big Mexican animals were thrashing, bleeding in the dirt. Others already lay still, humped against one another where they had fallen. Two of the motionless animals had pinned their riders beneath them, still in the saddle. Soldiers swore, screamed, shrieked for their comrades to help free them from under their dead or dying animals. Echoes bouncing and rebounding from the mud walls of that bloody street in Pueblo de los Angeles.

Behind the fallen carcasses and soldiers a few men bellowed orders . . . but most of the trapped soldiers were cursing, some vaulting out of their saddles with their rifles, attempting to shove through the clutter of men and wounded horses so they could get a shot off at the fleeing gringos. At the same time the rest at the extreme rear of the formation were clumsily getting their mounts wheeled around and started down a side street or alleyway.

"There'll be some comin'!" Bass warned as he and the

mutelike Roscoe Coltrane brought up the rear. "A few of 'em still on our back trail!"

At the eastern outskirts of the village the trappers began to gradually fan out as their straining horses rolled into a gallop and were given their heads. Titus wondered how long the animals could take a bruising chase, considering what the horses had been through in crossing that desert. These bigger horses still might not stand a chance against the smaller Mexican animals because the Spanish barbs weren't handicapped, save for the weight of the soldiers.

Jehoshaphat! How his head thumped painfully, screaming with every hoofbeat as his horse licked it down the hardpan road between the coastal pueblo and Mission San Gabriel. He had come to hate hangovers, especially the sort of hangover that buried its vicious talons into his head even before he'd had the chance to enjoy his whiskey at all.

California hooch. The prickly squeezin's were nowhere near as smooth as Willy Workman's Taos lightning had been. No, this California popskull tasted like the greasers'd strained it through some poor field peon's longhandles!

Riding at his left knee was Roscoe Coltrane. On Bass's right rode Elias Kersey. Just ahead of him Rube Purcell stood partway in the stirrups, his knees flexing, so he could twist around a bit and have himself a look at the back trail.

Bass took a look too.

Purcell saw Titus turn behind him. He hollered into the wind, "How many of 'em you see coming, Scratch?"

"Fifteen, maybeso twenty," Titus yelled when he had faced front again. "Not near enough to give us any trouble if it comes to a fight."

"They'll give up, don't you think?" Kersey asked.

With a nod, Scratch said, "Ain't a one of them soldiers wanna bite off more of us'n they can chew."

Kersey asked, "They just gonna make a show of it?"

"Yeah," Scratch hollered. "So them folks back in that village can see their *soldados* running off the Americans."

"Then they'll pull off," Purcell hollered.

But only when the trappers and the soldiers both were well out of sight by anyone in the village—several miles on up the valley road to San Gabriel and well-hidden behind several intervening hills. And not before Scratch's belly started crawling with apprehension that the pack animals were about to go bust and give in. He could see it in their wide, rheumy eyes, read it in the thickening phlegm around the nostrils of every animal straining around him. One thing especially telling was Scratch remembered they hadn't watered the horses since early that morning. Hardly any bottom left in them by now.

This chase couldn't have lasted much longer before the Americans had to pull back, fort up, and force a showdown of it. But from all his years of experience with them, Titus Bass hadn't been a bit impressed with the bottom, fortitude, or fight in the Mexican soldier. Not those around San Fernando de Taos who had left it up to the trappers to track and trap a large band of Comanche raiders. Not those drunk, jealous soldiers who had busted into the tiny cribs at the back end of a Taos bordello either. And surely not this crop of Mexicans who cuffed their whores around as if that brutality would make them big, brave men in front of the foreigners.

"Tell 'em to pull up!" Bass cried at those fanned out in front of him the moment he watched one of their pursuers wave his arm and signal the others to rein back and pull around.

He watched over his shoulder as the soldiers slowed to a halt, got their horses circled up, then lined out into two short columns to start back down the road winding through the tall hills, returning for the village after making a good show of it. They'd run off the infidel *extrajanos*. Showing the invaders who was boss in California.

Titus thought of Captain Janus C. Smathers and his seafarers—hoping nothing the trappers had done at the cantina would make things hard on those few Americans who had come a long way under sail to do some business with the *Californios*. Here and there, up and down the coast, he figured there were plenty of Mexicans who didn't mind having some foreign visitors—even if the Mexican government did not want to tolerate the strangers. And chances were good there were even more Mexican citizens who, even if they did not particularly want to rub elbows with any Americans, at least coveted those American goods brought to their coastal towns.

Odds were, nothing untoward would rub off on Smathers and his crew because they had been long gone from the watering hole before any of the trouble raised its ugly head. Fact be, only one who could make things tough for the captain would be that cantina man. But then, any Americans who entered a foreign land had to figure that the chances were good someone, somewhere, wouldn't be real happy seeing such well-armed strangers show up uninvited. That sort of thing lay in the cards. Americans coming in ships off the ocean. Or Americans crossing that great moat of an impenetrable desert, come all the way from the Rockies.

Trouble was, these trappers were about to give the Mexicans one more reason to hate gringos.

Not since the days of that great '33 rendezvous had he seen near so many horses as this!

None of those warrior bands of Shoshone, Crow, Assiniboine, or Ute he had ever run across could boast anywhere near this many animals in their individual herds. As he stared at the sight, Titus couldn't reckon on how they would manage to get this many horses back across all that desert, and over the mountains too. But he was getting ahead of himself. First, they had to get the herds—and their own necks—out of California.

Not to mention that little business about busting into the soldier outpost to free Frederico's sisters.

Scratch figured he'd just worry about one thing at a time. No sense in fretting himself over that homebound journey when they hadn't even put California behind them.

After escaping Pueblo de los Angeles by the skin of their teeth yesterday afternoon, the raiders hurried east into the foothills, at sundown circling south a little until they ran across a canyon where Williams and Smith determined they'd spend the night. It was a cold camp. No fires. Only some dried longhorn beef to chew on as they nursed their hangovers. Twenty-four men with pounding heads that made them grumpy, even a little belligerent, especially when six of them were awakened at a time to take their rotation on night guard, ordered to watch the valley and listen for the approach of any soldier patrols.

But the self-assured Mexicans hadn't pressed their pursuit. No one followed the infidels into the hills. So the trappers laughed at the cowardly soldiers who had given up the chase far too easily—and congratulated one another on this expedition that was turning out to be far easier than any of them had expected.

In the cold, predawn darkness, Thomas Smith and Bill Williams, along with the four others on their watch, moved through the brush and those eighteen forms wrapped in their blankets and robes on the cold, bare ground. In minutes the raiders had gathered up their animals, slipped halters over noses or slid bits into the horses' jaws, cinched down saddles, and relashed diamond hitches over the bundles on the backs of the pack animals. The shivering Americans moved out in the starlit darkness, the breath of man and horse alike spewing with the consistency of a puffy, silver gauze in the last shimmer of a sinking half-moon.

Peg-Leg had them on a hillside overlooking a broad, oval valley before the sun tore itself off the hill at their backs. The meadows were thick with grazing horses. Williams and Smith quickly talked things over.

Then Bill reined his horse around and announced to their twenty-two. "This here's where we get on with what we come to this here Mex country for. Drive them horses north till we strike that valley where the mission stands. Just short of there we're gonna turn east for the pass."

"You all drove horses afore," Peg-Leg reminded them. "So you know what to do."

"A horse here or there gonna get fractious and take off

on you," Williams warned. "Let 'em go. Keep the herd together and let a few rambunctious ones go."

Titus snorted, "Didn't think you was aimin' to leave any horses behind in California, Bill!"

As the men chuckled nervously, Williams grinned apishly and replied, "Only ones I plan to leave these greasers is the gentled horses they got tied up to some *rico*'s porch rail this mornin'!"

Smith waited until the restless raiders got quiet. "Your bunch ready to leave off when the time comes, Titus Bass?"

Scratch quickly glanced over the five who had elected to join him on their own quest for adventure. And Frederico's eyes were on Bass too when Titus turned back to the leader. "I don't figger any of us knows what we're biting off, Peg-Leg. As for me, I callate my li'l ride's gonna be lot more of a hurraw than get forced to suck down the dust of all those horses you're gonna start toward the pass."

Williams brought his horse up beside Scratch's, reached over, and the two of them grabbed each other's wrists, squeezing tightly. Bill said, "You'll watch that poor, half-skinned topknot of your'n now?"

"I allays do my best," Bass replied. "Don't let your horse go step in no prerradog hole."

Tugging his hat down on his forehead, Bill eased his horse back, sawing the reins to the left. "Awright, you niggers! Let's go run us some California horses!"

None of them whooped and hollered as they started down the slopes, spreading out in a broad front nearly a quarter mile wide as the valley brightened below them, sunrise coming moment by moment. Soon enough there would be noise from the hooves to muffle any man's exuberant revelry. But for now they swallowed down the urge to holler and shout. There'd be time enough once they got a few thousand head of horses up to the pass and started over for the desert.

Jehoshaphat! More horses grazing down there than he had seen in many a season. And from what he could tell in the early light, the herds blanketed this meandering valley all the way to the horizon. Bass and Frederico, joined by the five others, angled off to the left away from the others, racing toward the west side of the grassy oval to sweep clean those slopes and turn the Mexican horses north. Ahead of them and off to the right a half mile or more rode the first two of the raiders. Appeared to be Smith and Williams, driving those six broodmares still alive after the desert crossing right in through the midst of the first herds, threading their way up the middle of the valley.

It almost took his breath away for a moment to watch that amazing sight from where he was perched up here on the gentle slopes, seeing how the California horses initially parted in fear as the trappers drove their six wet mares through their numbers, those herds regathering behind the two trappers and their mares to start loping north. Just like a man would take a lone strand of fringe, soak it in blood, and drag it through the sand . . . picking up more and more grains the farther he dragged it along the surface of the ground. Hundreds now, even more, streaming together in that one direction. North for the valley of Mission San Gabriel.

For the first few hours they didn't spy any sign of a Mexican, not until late morning when Bass spotted a small band of vaqueros appear on a knoll northeast of the swelling herd. Bill and Peg-Leg were intent on keeping the pace of the march slow enough that the horses wouldn't tire before they faced the hardest work of their escape. Best to leave some strength for that climb into the hills, making for the pass. And by pushing the leaders no faster than a lope, there was less of a chance that the horses would tire of this run and drop out. Scratch decided this slower, more deliberate, pace of the march made a lot of sense . . . but the pace might well make it easier for any pursuers to catch up to the raiders.

Pursuers like any band of angry vaqueros who would ride down off the hills to prevent the *Norteamericanos* from stealing this unbelievable bounty of Mexican horses.

Scratch kept his eye on those horsemen kicking into a

lope for the right side of the herd where Thompson and three others were strung out to keep the stragglers bunched. Ten vaqueros, maybe less. Two-to-one odds against the Mexicans wasn't anything to worry about. The greasers were far better horsemen than they were with their weapons.

The first puff of smoke appeared above one of the vaqueros. A moment later the faint boom of that gunshot rolled across the valley. None of the Americans fell, and the horses didn't appear to shy. Then one of the Mexicans galloped in too close, and gunsmoke appeared above the far edge of the herd. A louder, deeper boom reverberated from those hills to the east now.

"Bass!"

Adair's fearful cry yanked Scratch's attention back to his west side of the valley. Just as Scratch was turning to his left, another gunshot rang out, just up the hillside.

"*Rifleros! Rifleros!*"

He twisted in the saddle at the cry, spotting the onrushing horsemen who were warning one another that the Americans were accomplished riflemen. Titus spotted at least another ten, maybe a dozen, vaqueros starting down the slope toward the trappers. Another puff of smoke blossomed just above them and a shot rang out.

Suddenly the small of his back burned, causing Bass to flinch so violently he almost pitched forward out of the saddle.

Immediately shoving his reins into his right hand that clutched the rifle, Titus put the fingers of his left hand to the small of his back. More than tender, that shallow furrow along the muscles was on fire. Blood not only tinged his fingertips but was soaking the edges of that long rip made through his faded calico shirt.

"Goddamn these greasers!" he roared as he stuffed the reins into that left hand again.

"Gonna be just like Blackfoot!" Jake Corn bellowed, kneeing his horse to the left on a course that would carry him for the vaqueros.

" 'Cept there ain't no damn greaser's scalp wuth

takin'," Titus hissed, wincing with the pain the flesh wound caused him as the wind whipped past them.

"The sonsabitches figger they can get the horses back from us?" Rube Purcell hollered.

"They want 'em back bad enough," Elias Kersey warned, "we better see to it they don't get in close enough to the herd!"

"Empty your gun only when you can empty a saddle!" Bass ordered, sensing the wounded muscles starting to cramp, hot and tight.

"*Chaguanosos!*" one of the vaqueros shrieked in fury at the raiders.

So, they call us desperados, Scratch brooded, wishing he were close enough to the man who shot him, within reach so he could rip out the Mexican's eyes, his tongue, maybe his windpipe too.

Another Mexican smoothbore popped as the horsemen approached within fifty yards, then angled away from a collision with the Americans. To Scratch's rear, Frederico cried out. Bass turned in time to watch the Indian waver in the saddle, clutching at the horse's mane as he struggled to reach down for the dangling reins. Easy to see from the way the guide bounced on the horse's back that the Indian was not doing well. And by the time Titus slowed his own horse to match the speed of Frederico's mount, he could see the dark smear of blood on the youth's left arm, just above the elbow. The arm hung, but it did not flop around as if the bone had been broken.

Snagging the reins into his right hand again, Bass shouted, "Do this!" He curled up his left arm tightly, pressing the elbow against his ribs, clamping the fist in the pocket of his shoulder.

"*Si,*" Frederico obeyed.

"Get down there with the horses!" Scratch ordered in his poor Spanish.

The guide would be safer in among the stolen animals than he would out here on the left flank, with these Mexicans popping shots at them.

By the time Bass turned his attention back to the vaqueros, about half of them were peeling off to sprint along the slope against the direction the herd was taking. The rest, however, were still headed for the trappers, prepared to strike the edge of the herd at a sharp angle.

"You can shoot 'em now—or wrassle 'em later!" Scratch bellowed.

Three of the trappers' guns roared simultaneously. The fourth an instant later. A vaquero pitched backward off the rump of his horse into the onrushing herd. Another wobbled in the saddle, clutching his belly. A third rider's horse skidded to a halt, fought the bit, slashing its head side to side, then collapsed to its knees and keeled to the side, tumbling downhill, crushing its rider the moment it smacked the ground and rolled through the grass atop the screaming vaquero. The last rider spun out of his saddle, landing spraddle-legged on the slope, and didn't move.

From the looks of things, only he and Elias Kersey had their guns still loaded. Corn, Purcell, Coltrane, and Adair were about the business of reloading on the run: bringing up those long rifles, pressing muzzles against their lips to blow down the barrels in snuffing out any errant spark that might still linger from the last charge, or some tiny fragment of a smoldering patch. Up came the curved, carved powder horns, black grains flying like crushed peppercorns as the trappers attempted to pour what they could down the barrel, struggling to match their efforts to the rolling gaits of their horses. After spitting a lead ball from their cheek into the muzzle of the gun, most of the men yanked out their wiping sticks to ram the ball down against the breech. But Roscoe Coltrane seized his barrel near the muzzle, then swung the rifle butt against the ground as his horse continued its uninterrupted lope. More of the powder spilled and flew as the four scattered the fine, black grains into the pan before snapping down the frizzen.

"They'll be comin' up behin't us!" Kersey warned after a glance over his shoulder.

Twisting round in the saddle where the trappers galloped at the back of the herd, Titus watched those vaqueros still atop their mounts turn away from their wounded and dead, regrouping as they stabbed their horses with those huge, cruel rowels on their spurs and bolted into a gallop. This time it was clear they were no longer attempting to match the easy lope of the herd and the American thieves. The Mexicans intended to strike back for the hurt just inflicted upon them.

"Merciful a'mighty!" Adair cursed. "I don't like havin' them niggers ahint us!"

"Keep a eye on 'em, boys!" Bass said. "They come close enough again: we'll rein about and throw down on the bastards!"

"Spread out now!" Kersey ordered. "Don't bunch up!"

Titus could hear the vaqueros hollering among themselves now. Only voices—nothing he could discern as words. Just the noises of men working themselves into a fighting lather. A shot rang out. At this range, and one of the damn fools was trying to shoot the Americans in the back with their smoothbores, on the run too!

"Here come more of 'em!" Purcell screamed his warning into the thunder of the hooves.

Far off to their right the vaqueros who had initially attacked Thompson's flank side of the herd were angling sharply across the valley now as the stolen horses streaked on by them.

"Be-gawd! They're groupin' up!" Corn shouted.

Sure enough, there were more than ten of the Mexicans now arrayed in a wide front directly behind the stolen horses. Step by leaping step, moment by fleeting moment, the vaqueros were angling to the left on a dead run, racing ever closer to the half dozen Americans on Bass's corner of the herd.

For the moment, Scratch scolded himself—wondering what had ever come over him that made him decide on this journey to steal some California horses with Bill Williams. He'd never stolen a horse in his life, but here he was about to get shot in the back and left for dead by some greasers in a faraway foreign land where his wife and his young'uns could never mourn over his bones. How stupid an idjit was he?

"W-we gonna turn and fight 'em?" Adair prodded, his voice pulsing, rising and falling with the horse's gait.

"No! We don't stand us a chance like that!" Bass cried loudly. "Get everyone in there atween the horses!"

"What?" Corn demanded.

"Geddap in there!" Scratch ordered. "They can't shoot us so good if'n we got all them horses around us!"

Jabbing heels into his mount's flanks, Titus spurred the animal into a gallop, weaving it a little left, then a little right, leading the way while he plunged into the back of the herd. His pace a little faster than that of the stolen horses, he led the others deeper and deeper still, putting more and more of the animals between them and their pursuers. Glancing over his shoulder again, Scratch saw how the five others were spread out right behind him—stabbing their way into the thick of the herd.

"Keep your heads down!" he ordered, tucking himself as much as he could over the round Santa Fe pommel.

Instead of pursuing the thieves into the herd, the Mexicans warily hung back at the rear of the stolen horses. Not daring to enter the surging mass of animals on the run.

"C'mon, boys!" Bass rallied. "We best put some more room atween them and us!"

He kicked his horse in the ribs again and sprinted away, faster still. Running much slower, the stolen horses gradually streamed to the rear as the Americans put a hundred yards, then a hundred fifty, between them and the vaqueros.

"They stealing anything back?" Scratch asked the moment he turned to look over his shoulder.

"A few," Kersey answered as they watched the Mexicans wave rope coils overhead and snap long, silken whips in the air, wrangling about three dozen of the horses away from the rest of the herd.

"No matter," Titus grumped. "Them at the back wasn't good runners no how."

"You still figger to go after them two Injun gals?" Corn shouted as he edged up on Bass's right heel.

"You gettin' cold feet, Jake?"

"Just a bad feeling's all," Corn confessed.

"Why?" Titus asked. "We ain't seen a soldier. Only a few vaqueros what tried to get their horses back."

"What happens when they don't send all them soldiers out to stop the others boys the way you said they would for Bill's plan?" Corn asked.

Scratch brooded on that a moment, squinting into the sunlit distance as the horses at the front of the herd swept up more and more loose animals the farther north they raced down the valley for the San Gabriel Mission.

"Way I see it—every one of us gonna ride outta that soldier fort with Frederico's sisters," Scratch vowed. "Or, ain't none of us coming back out at all."

12

It was down to the nut-cuttin' now.

Bill Williams and Thomas Smith signaled Philip Thompson on by with the stolen horses, wave after wave of the animals streaming north into the valley where stood the San Gabriel Mission. The two booshways reined over to the side of the hill and halted, waiting for Bass and his bunch to cut their way out of the side of the herd. The seven of them came to a halt near Bill and Peg-Leg.

"Sure you don't want me to come 'long with you?" Williams asked, his eyes focused on the bloody tear in Titus's shirt.

"Don't worry—just a scratch, s'all." Bass looked over his men, then shook his head. "The Injun got hit, but it ain't bad. 'Sides, you're gonna need ever' man you got, Solitaire. The seven of us can see to what we gotta do for Frederico's sisters and catch on up to you."

"How long you figger that'll take?" Smith inquired.

"If'n we can steal a couple soldier horses for them women afore we ride outta there, we'll cover some ground," he suggested. "But, if them *soldados* take all their horses when they ride out to follow you boys . . . then a couple of us gonna be riding double. An' that'll slow us down some."

Williams's eyes narrowed once more on Scratch's bloodied shirt. "You need anything more?"

"Can't think of what it'd be," Titus replied with a sigh, turning away to watch the last of the horses lope past. He whistled low and said, "Them Bent brothers gonna shit in their britches to see so many horses."

Smith grinned hugely. "What them two don't take, I'll drive right on back to Missouri to sell my own self!"

Bass held out his hand to him. "See you soon, Peg-Leg."

"Don't go make a bull's-eye out of yourself, Titus Bass."

Williams held out his hand now and they shook.

Scratch reminded, "We ain't caught up with you in three days—"

" 'Bout the time we should reach the desert on the other side," Bill interrupted.

"Then you oughtta just reckon on us not catching up to you boys at all," Scratch admitted, then suddenly cracked a lopsided grin.

"You'll come out fine on the other side," Williams offered, wearing his own hopeful smile.

"If'n I don't, Bill," Titus sighed as the grin disappeared, "do for me like you promised you would. Trade off my share of the horses and buy a passel of plunder with 'em. Take all that foofaraw on up there to Absaroka an' find my woman. Give 'er what I got comin' from my share of them horses."

"Least I can do for you, friend," Bill admitted. "You're the man seeing we keep our promise to the Injun got us 'cross the desert."

Titus reared back, stretching the muscles in his old back already tired from the morning's ride. "Take good care of our packhorses, won'cha fellas?" He tugged down the front of his brim there in the hot afternoon sun and reined hard to the left. "Let's ride, fellas!"

With Frederico wearing a bandanna around the

wounded arm at his side, Titus led the other five directly across the valley stripped bare of all horseflesh. The sprawling mission itself was less than a mile away; and the soldier fortress not all that far beyond it. They planned to slip up behind a knoll that lay to the east of the post and tie off their horses. Bellying up to the top, they'd lie patiently in the brush and watch the small fort below, hoping that the Mexicans would do what the trappers expected.

Together with Williams and Smith, Scratch had cobbled out this plan that sent most of the raiders with the two booshways, driving the stolen horses right on past the mission walls, near enough to the soldier post that the gringo thieves would make themselves a taunting challenge. And when the *soldados* rose to the bait—every last one of them saddling up and riding out to sweep down on the Americans and make a sure, quick fight of it—then Bass's small outfit could slip right into the soldier post and hurry the two women right back out again.

Not that the fortress would be totally abandoned. They figured they could expect to encounter a modest resistance from no more than a handful of soldiers left to watch over the place—maybe a blacksmith, some stable hands, and a cook or two as well, perhaps even a guard at the gate—but not enough of a force that would prevent the *Norteamericanos* from riding away with Frederico's sisters.

"This here brush is good," Scratch told them as they came to a halt at the bottom of the low knoll. "Leave the horses here. You follow me and the Injun to the top. Get on your bellies afore you break the skyline."

He gestured Frederico to join him on the climb, but just shy of the crest he reached out and tapped on the Indian's bare arm. Pointing at the ground, Bass went to his belly. When their guide dropped to his stomach too, the seven crawled in and out of the brush to the grassy top. As they came up on both sides behind him, Bass could hear the others scritching over the gravel and dirt, rustling the stunted cedar and brush.

Titus rolled onto his left hip, pulled up the flap to his

shooting pouch, and dug at the bottom for the spyglass. Flat on his belly again, Bass extended the three sections, then swiveled the tiny brass protective plate back from the glass in the eyepiece.

Training the spyglass on the post below them, Bass slowly retracted one of the leather-covered sections to bring the scene into focus. And felt the hair prickle on the back of his neck. The post was a beehive of activity. Cavalry horses were everywhere. A few of them were already saddled and stood outside the stockade wall with their riders. Other soldiers were engaged inside the compound, throwing saddles onto their mounts. And still more Mexicans were leading their horses out of the narrow barns and into the central square. Titus could almost imagine the racket made as horses snorted, stomped, and whinnied. As the men shouted orders, hammered across the hard ground in their boots, their stubby muskets and short sabers clinking . . . this half-baked army could never creep up on an enemy by surprise.

But, the Mexican Army never would have to do that out here in California, he decided. Or in northern Mexico either. They were merely an army of occupation, able to subjugate a weak and peaceable Indian population. Nothing like the warrior bands of the mountains and plains: intractable, bellicose, and intensely jealous of their territory. No, Titus figured, these Mexican soldiers had all grown soft and lazy because they had never been summoned into battle with a real enemy. Not the way soldiers near Taos and Santa Fe constantly had to deal with both Apache and Comanche.

This bunch charged with guarding the San Gabriel Mission and the nearby valleys were such predictable fools. They formed up outside their adobe walls and rode off as the gates were dragged shut. More than fifty soldiers loped past the base of the knoll where the seven lay in hiding, headed right to left as they pushed on down the road that would carry them east for the foothills and up toward the pass in pursuit of the *chaguanosos*. Titus realized some of those soldiers knew the route well enough—from time to time they had pursued fleeing slaves, tracked runaway Indians into the low mountains—attempting to capture their prey before they reached the desert moat on the far side of California.

As he lay there watching them go, Titus was struck with the remembrance of slaves running off from their masters in the southern region of the States. For the first time in many, many years recalling Hezekiah: the bareheaded former field hand who had worked for a Mississippi gunboat brothel madam named Annie Christmas, the slave owner he had wronged in a brawl against Ebenezer Zane's riverboatmen. Annie Christmas, an angry, spiteful shrew of a woman who promptly sold Hezekiah to the highest bidder, shipping him off north to the Muscle Shoals.

With that small band of Kentucky flatboatmen looking on outside of Kings Tavern, a Natchez tippling house, sixteen-year-old Titus Bass had freed Hezekiah from his cage, releasing the slave from what cruel fate might await him at the hand of his new taskmaster. At Owensboro on the Ohio River, the Negro prepared to push on west—giving Titus his farewell and announcing that he was taking his former boss-lady's surname as he embarked on his new life as a freedman.

Hezekiah Christmas.

Scratch pulled the spyglass from his eye and turned slightly to peer at the guide. He'd never thought to ask what the youngster's Indian name was. Frederico was merely the name the Catholic fathers had branded on the Indian—just as the friars gave all their slaves Spanish names, since they were baptizing these former heathens into the holy Spanish church, thereby saving their immortal souls from a life everlasting in the lake of endless fire—

"How many you make out?" Kersey interrupted his reverie.

Again he squinted through the eyepiece and attempted to count what men he could see. "I figger there's at least one on the gate I can't see a't'all, maybe two what closed it."

"What of the others?" Purcell demanded.

Bass counted a moment. "I see three others. That could mean there's at least three I don't see."

Corn was visibly tallying his fingers, staring at both hands. "All right. We can take care of them."

Adair asked, "You see them women? Any sign of his sisters?"

For some time he studied every visible corner of the compound, gazing into every narrow window or doorway for some hint of movement that might betray a woman. But, he didn't sight a hint of Frederico's sisters.

"You are certain your sisters are at the soldier post?" Titus asked in his faltering Spanish.

"*Si*," the guide responded. "They were taken from the mission—"

"But," Scratch interrupted, "how long ago?" He knew Frederico had been gone from California for some time, escaped to the Mojave villages.

"Not for long—"

"This past winter?" he inquired. "Tell me how long it has been since you saw your sisters carried off to the soldier post?"

The youth's face sagged along with his shoulders. "Almost all the seasons. Come autumn, I ran away to the desert."

Bass sighed. "Just shy of a year," he said in English.

Corn was the first to capture the meaning of that. "Been a whole year since he knowed his sisters was down there?"

"Almost." Titus reluctantly nodded. "Maybeso this ain't but a fool's errand we're on, fellas."

"*Por favor*," Frederico pleaded with his dark eyes as well as his tongue. "Help me save my sisters."

For himself, Bass nodded, but turned to the others to declare, "I can't make you others ride down there with the Injun to find two women who likely ain't still alive no more."

Adair's eyes squinted as he turned his head to stare down into the valley at the post. "I figger them soldiers used up both of them squaws pretty hard, then killed 'em when they wasn't no use no more."

"What're you asking, Scratch?" Kersey prodded.

"Me and the Injun, we'll slip down there—"

"Just the two of you?" Purcell inquired.

"I figger to show him his sisters ain't . . . around no more," Titus explained. "Then we can come on your back trail and catch up to the herd together."

"There's too many of them lop-eared greasers for one man to handle down there," Corn declared, tugging down on a low-crowned hat that had been at one time of a cream color. "I'm going with you."

Kersey nodded, rubbing a hand across his dusty leggings cut from a red wool blanket. "Count me in too, Scratch. You'll need some men at your back, even with them fat Mex soldiers."

"Awright," Adair relented. "Me and Roscoe gonna throw in too."

"We all go down there an' kill ourselves," Purcell groaned, wagging his head.

"Maybe not," Kersey suggested in a whisper, rubbing the end of his sharp, aquiline nose, a most prominent feature on his face: tracked with tiny blood vessels as if someone had crisscrossed it with an inked nib filled with indigo. "Scratch, I got a notion for you an' the Injun here."

"Dust it off and spill your idee."

"We have the Injun go round to that post—on foot it's gotta be. Act like he's just a dumb, lost Injun, needing to find his way back to his mission."

Bass smiled, a light coming across his whole brown face. "I'll wager them soldiers gonna let the Injun in—"

"And he can have a look at things on the inside," Corn interrupted to finish the plan.

"So he's got inside to see if his sisters are still around," Titus said, nodding with approval.

He rolled onto his hip and quickly stammered through his skimpy Spanish vocabulary, wishing the California Indians understood sign language as well as those tribes of the high plains savvied it.

Sliding backward on their bellies until they were no longer in danger of breaking the skyline, Scratch and

Frederico started down to the animals. There he stopped, grabbed the youth by the shoulders, and studied the youth up and down.

He retightened the black bandanna around the bloody arm, then—without a word of warning—Titus bent to scoop up a handful of dirt. Spitting into his palm, Scratch mixed the mud with a couple of fingers. When he went to smear the mud on Frederico's face, the Indian flinched, pulling aside.

"No," Bass said in a soothing manner. "We make you look dirty. You have been lost. You were hungry for days. You must fool the soldiers to free your sisters."

A light went on behind Frederico's eyes, and he nodded his permission. Titus smeared a little of the mud on his face, some across his chest, and the rest on his knees. Then he took another handful of dust and powdered it on the mud before stepping back to look at his handiwork.

Suddenly he pulled his knife and snatched up the long flap of the Indian's breechclout, nearly ripping off a long corner of the cloth, leaving the fragment hanging.

"See? You do not wear the Mexican pantaloons the other Indian slaves wear at the mission," Titus explained as he stepped back and gave Frederico another appraisal. "You are a wild Indian. The soldiers must believe you are a wild Indian to let you inside that fort."

"*Si*, this will work," Frederico said quietly as he held out his right arm to Bass. They clasped wrists.

"We'll be watching from up there," Titus declared. "Get away as quick as you can."

The Indian nodded and turned away, trotting around the bottom of the wide knoll.

"Frederico!" Bass called. "Don't cause any trouble by yourself. And don't let your sisters know you have come to rescue them."

With a fading grin, the youth took off on foot.

Titus and the others scrambled back up to the top of the rise and bellied down among the brush. He took out his spyglass and waited for Frederico to appear on the plain below them, zigzagging through the undergrowth, making for the stockade at a lope.

After long minutes of peering through the lens, watching almost breathless until the gates finally opened, Scratch announced in a whisper, "He's in."

Frederico disappeared, and the gate was closed once more.

"We wait?" Purcell asked impatiently.

"We wait," Elias Kersey told him.

But even Titus itched to know what was going on by the time Jake Corn revealed in a rasp, "Gate's opening!"

"Is he coming?" Purcell inquired, squinting in the harsh sunlight. "The Injun coming?"

The gate swung clear, and two horsemen left the compound.

"Nawww," Adair responded, disappointment heavy in his voice. "It's just a couple of soldiers—"

"Be-gawd!" Corn said little too loudly. "Them soldiers're draggin' the Injun off somewhere!"

Behind those two Mexicans a third horse emerged from the gate. Frederico sat astride its bare back, his arms held out straight, lashed to a narrow tent pole laid across the top of his shoulders, wrists tied to either end. His brown ankles were lashed to another tent pole that hung underneath the belly of the horse. Trussed up like a hog for the slaughter.

"T-they gonna kill the Injun?" Kersey asked.

"Could've done that in their fort," Bass said, wagging his head in angry consternation. "He must've done something wrong—said something wrong, for them soldiers to be cartin' him off."

"Where they taking him?" Corn inquired. "Back to the mission where they near killed 'im last time?"

Titus nodded as another pair of soldiers brought up the rear of the short procession behind their prisoner. "I think they're taking the Injun to them holy padres as a gift. A wild Injun for them padres to make a slave."

Kersey wondered, "They can't have no way of knowing he's their whores' brother?"

"Hope not," Scratch said with a long sigh. "C'mon, fellas. We gotta bust that Injun free."

"Shit," Purcell grumped as he crawled off his knees. "I just knowed you was gonna say that."

They had no choice but to make a race out of it.

Mission San Bernardino wasn't all that far away, through a short string of tree-lined hills. No time to gallop ahead and set up an ambush.

When the soldiers came in sight ahead of them, the adobe walls and flying buttresses of the mission off in the distance beyond the Mexicans, Scratch kicked his heels into the horse and roared, "It's a stand-up ride-through, boys!"

As he shot away, the five others yipped or grunted as they jabbed their horses into a hard gallop. Now and then across those last moments as they raced up on the Mexicans, the soldiers disappeared around a bend in the wagon road, or were momentarily hidden by a stand of leafy trees. They were taking a leisurely pace with their prisoner and their march.

With less than sixty yards separating the trappers from the enemy, one of the soldiers suddenly turned and peered over his shoulder. He nearly spilled off his horse when he twitched in surprise and fear, whirling back around in the saddle so quickly that one of his boots slipped out of its stirrup. He called out—the man next to him jerked around to look back down the trail.

Then they both started yelling to the pair in front. Frederico did his best to turn at the waist, unable to accomplish much with his legs tied under the horse's belly. When the two guards in the lead slowed up, the Indian's horse nearly collided with them. With a struggle Frederico managed to keep himself upright as the animal lurched to the side of the road. All four of the soldiers reined their horses around, putting themselves between their prisoner and the Americans.

Bass figgered the soldiers had to be surprised to see the Americans show up. They must have believed all the trappers were wrangling the stolen herd right about then, on their way up to the mountain pass. Besides, the guards could have no idea why the *Norteamericanos* were bearing down on them, yip-yipping like coyotes on the prowl. But when the Mexicans brought up their firearms, Titus decided it didn't matter if they knew he had come to rescue the Indian or not. The six of them had the upper hand, and it was time to throw down their call.

"Empty their saddles, boys!" he bellowed as he brought up the long flintlock.

Tugging on the back trigger to set the front, Titus attempted to match the bob and surge of the horse beneath him. Finding a target—

But the Mexicans fired first. A ball whirred past Scratch's shoulder like an angry hornet. One of the horses behind him cried out. Then came the loud clatter as the animal went down. In a fury again at the scorching, weepy flesh wound on his side, Scratch squeezed down on the front trigger, felt the rifle's sharp-edged butt plate slam back against his chest.

Passing through the billow of gray gunsmoke at a gallop, he watched the lead ball knock the soldier heels over head, spilling the man backward out of the saddle onto the hot, dusty road. Weapons were popping around him. Gunsmoke and dust turned yellow, hazing the slanted afternoon light.

Another soldier clutched a red blossom on his chest, slowly keeling to the side of the road into some brush. A third cried out and sagged forward across his horse's withers, arms akimbo.

That was enough for the last Mexican. He yanked the reins aside and brutally jabbed his big rowels into the animal's ribs. Turning tail and running.

"Who's got a loaded gun?" Kersey shouted.

"I'll take 'im!" Adair vowed and hammered his moccasins into the horse's flanks, bursting away from the others.

As the fourth guard dashed past Frederico's mount, the Indian's horse shied backward, twisting in fear, its eyes as big as bean platters.

Swaying clumsily, unable to maintain his balance any longer, Frederico spilled to the side, the end of the long,

smooth tent pole striking the ground, his legs yanked upward, twisted by the other pillory lashing them together.
The prisoner's horse needed no more reason to bolt than
that. As the frightened animal brought its hind hooves up
to attempt to gallop away, the legs and hooves clattered
against Frederico and the pole where his bare arms were
slashed. He was about to be dragged down the rutted
mission road—

Bass closed the distance in two heartbeats. Gathering
his reins into his left hand with his rifle, he attempted to
lean out of the saddle and seize the halter knotted around
the horse's head. But the terrified animal wouldn't allow
Titus close enough to grab the halter as Frederico grunted
with every bump, cried out in agony, the horse skidding
to a sudden halt, prancing round and round in a tight
circle to stay away from the trapper.

In angry frustration, Scratch jerked up straight in the
saddle, pulled out his pistol, and fired a ball into the animal's head.

As the air gushed from its lungs, the horse wheezed in
death, settling immediately onto its forelegs, the rear half
of its body slowly twisting to the side as the dying animal
came to rest in the short grass at the side of the road—
pinning Frederico's leg and hip beneath its ribs.

The Indian was shrieking in pain, terror too, as
Scratch pitched himself out of the saddle. The instant his
feet hit the ground he was stuffing the pistol into his belt
and throwing a shoulder into his own horse. As it sidestepped out of his way, Titus dropped his empty rifle to
the road and bolted over the dead animal, pulling a knife
from its scabbard at the back of his belt.

Slashing at the ropes binding Frederico's ankles, he
first freed the leg that lay twisted atop the dead horse's
ribs. Once he slid back over the animal, Bass sawed
through the ropes binding one wrist, then the other as the
Indian slowly quieted. The moment his arms were freed
from the pillory staff, Frederico attempted to sit up, only
to cry in pain.

"This here's gonna hurt," Titus growled at him in English as he stopped at the Indian's back, stuffed his hands

under Frederico's armpits. Then he clamped his eyes closed—and pulled. Leaning back with all his might, he tried to shut the Indian's screams out of his ears as he dragged the youth from beneath the dead horse.

The air went out of Frederico in a whimper. Opening his eyes, Scratch found he had freed the leg. Letting go of the Indian, he crouched beside the leg and gently palpated along the bones.

"Don't feel nothing broke," he said to the guide, then looked up at Kersey, who sat atop his horse just behind Frederico.

Elias asked, "That Injun ride?"

Bass asked Frederico, then looked up at Elias. "Yeah. Says he can ride."

"We better get back to that fort if'n we're gonna free them women," Corn said.

Adair came to a halt by Elias. "The longer we take, the behinder we're gonna be from the rest of the fellas and that herd."

Titus helped Frederico stand, then said, "Rube—get one of the soldier horses for the Injun."

"Let's get going," Corn prodded.

"Wait," Scratch suddenly declared.

"Wait?" Purcell whined as he yanked a soldier horse over.

"Get the clothes off these here soldiers," Titus ordered.

Adair repeated, "Their clothes?"

Scratch started to explain, "Four of us gonna be soldiers when we go riding in there proud as prairie cocks—"

"What about the other two of us?" Corn asked. "How we gonna get all of us in there?"

"A couple of gringos got caught by the *soldados*— that's how we're all gonna get in there."

Elias Kersey's face lit up like a full winter moon illuminating a fresh snow in the northern Rockies. "Four soldiers guardin' their two prisoners! Yee-awww! If that won't be a yank on the devil's short-hairs!"

•   •   •

Scratch was the first to spot the lone sentry posted atop the adobe wall as the seven horsemen approached the soldier post.

"They're watching us now," he warned the others in a low voice.

"Hope them Mex buy this," Kersey growled.

Dressed in the stolen uniforms, Elias and Coltrane were riding just in front of Frederico, who was flanked by Jake Corn and Reuben Purcell, both of whom still wore their buckskin leggings and poor cloth shirts. All three had short sections of rope looped, but unknotted, around their wrists, making it appear they were bound prisoners. Behind these three rode the last pair of impostors: Titus Bass and Silas Adair.

Back at the scene of the fight, the trappers discovered that neither the round-bellied Corn or the gangly-limbed Purcell could fit into any of the bloodied uniforms. As it was, the four who did strip out of their buckskins to pull on pantaloons and soldier jackets found the Mexicans' clothing a trifle snug. But, Scratch reminded them, they would be undertaking their ruse for no more than a short ride: only until the gate was open and they were inside the compound.

It wasn't until they were within the shadow of the front wall when Corn suddenly asked, "What if they got 'em a password?"

Shit—why hadn't he thought of that? Why hadn't Jake asked about it before. Bass was angry with himself.

But that lone sentry stationed atop the wall's interior banquette did not call out. All he did was slowly walk along the top of the wall, staying right above the horsemen, moving toward the gate, holding that musket and bayonet across his chest. When he stopped directly over the gate, he called out to those inside.

"What'd he say?" Adair demanded in a harsh whisper.

"Told 'em open up," Bass growled, the hair at the back of his neck prickling with warning.

Wood scraped against wood as the huge bolt was

withdrawn, then massive iron hinges creaked as one side of the gate in the wall swung open.

"This is it, boys," Titus whispered to them.

Kersey and Coltrane started their horses forward together, but that sentry on the ground shouldered back the gate only far enough to admit one horse at a time. Titus felt himself sweating. This precaution wasn't a good sign of an open-armed welcome. Next through was Frederico, followed by the two white prisoners.

A voice called out in Spanish. Another voice hollered in reply. He damn well knew it wasn't any of the trappers. Hurry, hurry, his mind raced—wanting to get inside to hear what was being asked of the first impostors.

Scratch was the last to slip through the narrow opening, finding the others strung out in the compound. He turned quickly in the saddle—a guard behind him at the gate. The only other guard in sight on the low, narrow banquette above them. As the gate swung closed with a thunk and the guard leaned his rifle against the wall so he could manhandle the log bolt into place, Scratch told himself his wariness was getting far too old. It had played him for a fool this time. From the looks of things, this was going to be prime pickin's.

At the exact moment the guard at the gate picked up his rifle again, the sentry atop the banquette leveled his weapon on the horsemen and cried out in a shrill voice.

Eight soldiers suddenly appeared in doorways on three sides of them. In that blink of an eye, ten old Spanish muskets were pointed at them.

"What'd he say! What'd he say!" Purcell demanded with a shriek.

"They want us to drop our guns," Bass translated.

"We're rawhide if we do," Corn grumbled from the corner of his mouth.

"These greasers damn sure gonna hang us later," Scratch said boldly. "Or we can die here and now like men."

Kersey said, "You heard 'im, fellas—"

One of the soldiers interrupted with a shrill shout: demanding the Americans drop their weapons.

"On three, fellas," Bass ordered in a calm voice that would give no warning to the soldiers, "we'll make our play. One. Two . . . three!"

Up came all their weapons as the trappers ducked aside. The Mexicans had an advantage in the brief stand-off: their muskets were already aimed at the Americans. Like parched corn rattling in a frying pan, the guns popped on all four sides of them—the trappers' weapons booming as Bass watched smoke and flame and shredded patches jet from the muzzles of the enemies' smooth-bores. The horses cried out, lead landing among them—wheeling, rearing, shoving against another.

One of the men in front of Titus grunted; the breath was driven from the lungs of another. They still had an advantage, he told himself as he slapped the rifle into his left hand and the horse started backing up, bumping into another. He and his friends were loaded for bear. While the soldiers only carried those muskets, the trappers all had more than one weapon.

Pistols came out of belts and sashes, held at the end of their arms as those soldiers still alive disappeared back into darkened doorways. All of them yelling at one another. The sentry on the banquette and the guard at the gate did not fare so well.

"We'll have to hunt 'em down one at a time!" Corn cried out.

Whirling in the saddle, Scratch aimed his pistol at the sentry and fired. As the ball struck him, the soldier was slammed back against the adobe wall, then bounced forward, pitching off the low banquette to strike the ground flat, unmoving.

Purcell was hit, clutching his side as he slumped against the withers of his horse. Adair was sprawled on the ground, the fingers of both hands interlaced over a nasty wound in his thigh.

"Don't give 'em time to reload!" Titus warned, sprinting for one of the doors.

Instinct told him and the others that they needn't race for those doorways where a soldier lay blocking the entrance, or sat crumpled against the doorjamb. The empty doorways meant the trappers would have to go in after the others.

In the lamp-lit, shadowy interiors, a fleeting drama was played out as metal and wood collided, men grunted in exertion, groaned in pain, boots and moccasins scuffing the hard-packed clay floors.

Mule-eyed, the soldier caught reloading in the corner of the room looked up as Bass rushed him, raising up his musket to parry the long skinning knife Scratch waved in front of him. The musket knocked the knife hand aside and the ball of a fist slammed low into the trapper's gut.

More than mere pain, the fist drove the air out of his lungs. Gasping, Scratch stumbled back two steps, blinking against the flash of shooting stars. He saw the soldier turn and pitch the musket aside, scrambling for the wall where a long scabbard hung from a peg. The saber grated free of its sheath at the moment Bass lunged forward, arm high overhead, bringing the skinning knife down in a blur.

The blade caught the Mexican in the top of the shoulder. He buried it to the hilt as the soldier struggled to get the other arm raised, to bring the saber into action. Just when the saber reached chest level, Titus seized the man's wrist in his left hand.

Using the buried knife for leverage, Scratch drove his left knee into the enemy's groin. As the Mexican stumbled back a step, whimpering in pain, Scratch shoved the enemy's arm up, up with that saber until it lay across the soldier's neck.

Then brutally ripped it sideways.

Hot blood splattered over them both as the air in the man's lungs wheezed from the gaping, bubbling wound.

Letting go of the soldier, he watched the Mexican fall, the eyes growing glassy and lifeless. Bass placed his foot on the man's shoulder and pulled his knife free. Wiped it on the soldier's jacket, turned, and crouched at the doorway, peering into the afternoon sunlight.

With the next heartbeat he was astonished to see a shabby, disheveled woman appear at a nearby doorway.

"Celita!" cried Frederico.

The woman took one step, then a second into the courtyard, wearing a loose-fitting, smudged, sooty dress that many times had been ripped and torn.

With that second step she suddenly stopped and peered over her shoulder furtively. Out of the shadowy rectangle behind her emerged Celita's sister.

"Mayanez!" the Indian sobbed and started toward the two women. Then immediately halted in his tracks.

Right behind the small female stood a large, bare-chested man, his muscular arm locked around Mayanez's throat. In that hand pressed against her ear he clutched a knife, while at the end of the other outstretched arm, he held a pistol pointed at the back of Celita's head.

Frederico growled something in Spanish as he rocked onto the balls of his feet, both hands flexing into fists and claws, fists and claws.

"What'd he say?" Kersey demanded.

"The Injun says that's the blacksmith," Bass translated.

Corn demanded, "How's he know that?"

"When Frederico come here a while back," Scratch declared, "that bastard was dragging one of the sisters off by herself for a little fun."

13

---◆---

"This big son of a bitch figgered to dip his stinger in one'r both of these gals while them soldiers was away chasing horse stealers?" Kersey asked as he inched closer to Bass.

"Easy to see he's a hard user, Elias," Bass sighed, his mind working, squeezing down on their predicament with the two women.

Corn started, "This messes things up real good—"

But Frederico interrupted, sputtering something in his worked-up, incomplete Spanish.

Nonetheless, Titus caught enough words. In his own halting Spanish, he told the Indian, "Stay put now."

"This *genizaro** speaks my language too, *chaguanoso*?" the blacksmith growled.

"*Si*, he does—"

"Like you, gringo," the Mexican said.

"*Chaguanoso*," Titus repeated the word the blacksmith had used. "What's it mean?"

---

* The Mexican term for the "wild" or "gentile" Indians who had been acquired by the Franciscans or the ranchos through capture or purchase.

"You're a horse stealer," said the blacksmith. "A low form of life, horse stealer."

"Better than a big-talking man who hides behind women."

The big Mexican grinned. "You want these women, eh?"

"Yes, we came for the women."

The blacksmith's eyes narrowed in confusion. "Aren't there enough Indian women where you come from, gringo? Can't you get some for your own fun?"

For an agonizing few moments Bass translated that in his mind, turning it over and over to make sure he got it right. Then he said, "We came to take the women away with us—"

"Get your own women, *chaguanosos!*"

"No," Bass shot back, twisting the knife in his right hand. "We come to take these two women back to their people."

Slowly the blacksmith's eyes crawled to the Indian. From there he glanced at Purcell and Adair both crumpled on the ground, bleeding. Then his eyes quickly danced over some of the soldier bodies scattered across the compound. Those black, forbidding eyes that so reminded him of Emile Sharpe's glare eventually came back to rest on the old trapper.

"That nigger's gotta go down afore we leave here," Kersey observed as he peered at Adair and Purcell.

"I give you one of the women," the blacksmith offered with a shrug. "Go, whore!" and he shoved the muzzle of his pistol against the back of her head.

She stumbled forward a step and froze, her eyes wide with terror as she turned slightly to gaze at the Mexican.

"We are leaving with both of them," Bass warned, just as he spotted the Indian guide going into a crouch. "Frederico—don't move! This one, he is mean. If you do anything stupid, he will kill your sister."

"S-sister?" the blacksmith echoed.

Titus's gut sank with the realization he'd made a terrible mistake.

The Mexican asked again, "This one I will keep is the Indian's sister?"

Titus shook his head. "We're taking both—"

"No, gringo. I give you the sister and we keep the other whore."

"Both."

"Maybe . . . they are both sisters, eh?" The big Mexican's eyes squinted cruelly.

"You give us both, or we kill you," Titus said. "There's many more whores at the mission. You can have them to keep—"

"*Si*, there are so many Indian whores at the mission," the blacksmith interrupted. "Why don't you gringos get some whores from the padres there—just the way the holy friars give us women for our beds. And when we need more women, the friars give us all we need, the ones do not work hard enough in the vineyards."

Scratch took a tentative step forward. "Why do you need other women when you already have—"

With a loud, harsh gush of laughter, the blacksmith rocked his head back quickly, then said, "Women do not always last. Some get hurt very bad when our play with them is too rough. Then we can no longer use whores who are hurt so bad. And," he shrugged, "some of the whores, they kill themselves if they get the chance—grab a gun or knife to hurt themselves badly. Ah, the holy fathers know not to ask any questions when we go to them to ask for more Indian whores from the mission!"

Sure as hell those men of God didn't ask, Titus brooded. This was nothing short of a deal made between the devil and his evil minions themselves. At every California mission the soldiers kept hundreds of Indian slaves terrorized and docile for those self-righteous Franciscan friars, while the padres repeatedly turned over an array of the youngest, prettiest Indian girls to the army posts. Appeared that the friars and the soldiers both had something the other needed badly. And with their most unholy bargain, a peaceful colonial order was struck in this new world.

"When the soldiers come back," Titus said, "go get

some others. Can't you see how you've used these women up?"

"What?" roared the blacksmith. "They are not dead yet! Go away before I have to kill them just for fun while I have myself poked inside one. A *geniazo* whore is bound to die sooner or later anyway!"

In a frightening blur, Frederico dove forward, tackling Celita, both of them spilling to the side at the Mexican's feet. At this moment Mayanez twisted in the blacksmith's grip and planted the fingers of both hands into his face, unmindful of the slashing he did along her forearms with his knife. She screamed in pain—but dug her claws into his face even more fiercely as she kicked and thrashed with her tiny bare feet. The Mexican shrieked in his own torment.

Backwards he stumbled as Kersey and Bass lunged forward.

"Stay down!" Titus yelled at Frederico as he rushed toward the blacksmith. "Get her out of here!"

Another step backward the blacksmith stumbled, desperately attempting to hack the shrieking woman from his flesh. Up and down his face, neck, and across his chest she scratched, ripping ribbons of crimson on his brown skin. With the two Americans closing in the big Mexican roared in pain and desperation, seizing a handful of Mayanez's black hair. He yanked her head back and shoved the pistol into her face.

"NO!"

But just as Titus reached the blacksmith, the Mexican pulled the trigger.

The back of the woman's head exploded, bright blood splattering the Mexican, Titus, and even Elias Kersey too.

With a shriek of horror, Celita tried to grab for her brother, but an enraged Frederico sprang to his feet and flung himself on the blacksmith at the moment Bass was diving under that huge hand gripping the knife. Together they thrust the Mexican back against the adobe wall with a loud grunt.

Back and forth Titus raked his skinning knife across the soldier's gut, slicing deeper and deeper with each heave of the bone-handled weapon. Gut spilled at their feet, the two trappers slipping, stumbling in the blood and greasy coil as the Mexican slowly, slowly slid downward, his back pressed against the wall.

The stench was heavy and foul, nothing new to Bass. Both trappers inched back. Kersey knelt to pull Mayanez's body away from the blacksmith as the Mexican's half-lidded eyes gazed up at Titus.

For a moment he stared down at his riven belly, the pile of dirty intestine between his legs, blood flooding his uniform breeches; then his glazing eyes fought to focus on Scratch.

"*Chaguanoso,* eh—I think women only bring the trouble for a man. See how it is with me? The women, they only bring big, big trouble for a man. . . ."

With a rush the air escaped the Mexican's chest, making that distinct and unmistakable rattle Titus had heard more times than he dared count. Years and years, surrounded by sudden, capricious death.

Behind him, Frederico and Celita crouched over Mayanez's body.

Scratch turned to Kersey. "Get me a blanket, Elias."

With the gray soldier blanket, Frederico and Celita wrapped up their dead sister while Bass and Kersey went over to join Corn and Coltrane by the wounded Adair and Purcell.

"Gonna use your belt, Silas," Scratch said as his fingers worked at the buckle.

When Roscoe had his friend Adair propped up, Titus dragged the scabbard and a small pouch from the belt, then stuffed the wide strap under Silas's thigh, a few inches above the dark smear of blood. Once the end of the belt was back through the round buckle, Titus tugged it tight, then half-hitched the strap under itself to secure the tourniquet.

"I lost lotta blood," Adair groaned in a weakened whisper, his head sinking back against Coltrane's chest.

"You ain't gonna die here," Scratch said. "Less'n you want me to leave you."

"Silas? Die here? With a bunch of dead Mex'can

soldiers?" Kersey chortled, his *s*'s whistling as he clearly did what he could to cheer up Adair. "Now that'd be a yank on the devil's short-hairs!"

Bass turned to give his attention to Purcell. "How's Rube?"

With Jake Corn's help, the skinny man pulled the tail of his shirt up even farther so Titus could see for himself. "Well, damn-me, Scratch, if that ball didn't go right on through. An' that's the preacher's truth."

"The man's nothing but bone and sinew-strap anyway," Corn declared. "If a ball don't hit him in a bone, you ain't gonna hurt this nigger none."

"That's the narrow truth of it," Purcell said.

Scratch nodded. When he stood, Titus flexed his back, suddenly aware of his own raw flesh wound once more. "Wrap him up, Jake. Me and Roscoe gonna boost Silas into the saddle. We best be making tracks for the hills."

On his own, Elias cleared out the long, low-roofed stables, driving what few horses and mules remained in their stalls out to the central *placita*. Celita and Frederico tied their sister over one of the soldier horses while Bass and Coltrane got Adair hoisted into his saddle and settled with a startled grunt of agony. Titus studied the thigh one last time, not finding any new blood dampening the crusty buckskin around the bullet hole.

"Damn," he said quietly as he gazed up at Adair.

"W-what?"

He grinned. "Looks like you're gonna live, nigger."

"I'd kick you with that bum leg if'n I could, Titus Bass," Silas grumbled as Scratch turned away.

Jake Corn handed Titus his reins, and Bass rose to the saddle as the late-afternoon light was stretching shadows to their fullest.

"Rube!" he called. "You start out the gate, make tracks for the hills. We'll start these animals moving behind you."

Corn asked, "Taking 'em all?"

"What critters don't run off from us between here and that big herd the others is driving up to the pass," Scratch replied. "Like Bill Williams said, we aren't gonna leave any of these here *Californios* a way to come ridin' after us. Not if I can help it."

Damn if just about sundown they didn't run into a herd of wild horses. A large band of them, roaming the hills, free as you please.

Bass decided that if the fourteen riderless soldier horses were going to drift off and mix in with those rangy mustangs, then he'd let them wander. No sense in the trappers laboring their own saddle mounts so hard just to keep the army horses together. They already had their work carved out for them in just getting up to the pass itself. But to Scratch's surprise, rather than enticing the soldier horses away from the raiders, the curious leader of the wild herd instead loped along beside the trappers' procession as it wound into the foothills.

"Looks to be we're dragging even more horses outta California," Kersey observed with a wry smile. His mark of distinction was a once shiny, now worn, black beaver-felt top hat, its stylish ash-gray ribbon and bow greasy from much handling. Although much tattered, the top hat gave Elias a very proper air at times.

"I'll wager this bunch don't stick around with us for long," Titus countered.

But for a second time that day Scratch was proved wrong. It was almost enough to make a man take stock of his hunches! Time was, he was pretty damn trail savvy about most anything he came across. Oh, there were occasions when he'd get things wrong—like with a drunk or especially when it came to women. Never could callate what either of those would do when they put their minds to something. But guessing wrong on what those horses would do was a matter quite unsettling to him.

For many years now, Titus Bass had believed he understood horses and mules better than he understood a lot of folks. But maybe he had gotten old and a little soft in the brain. Or, maybe times had changed everything around him. That might account for the strange behavior of these wild, four-legged critters. Or . . . maybe everything had been turned cattywhampus out here in California—nothing the way it was back in his mountain world.

At least now his nose was pointed for home. But that only made him yearn for her all the stronger.

Jake Corn rode drag, bringing up the rear of their small cavvyard. Roscoe Coltrane stayed even farther back from the rest, riding just out of sight of the others, training his constant attention down their back trail. He was to fire a warning shot if he spotted any *soldados* or vaqueros chasing their tail roots. The plan was to put the wounded Adair and Purcell, along with the two Indians, ahead on the trail with as many horses as would join the four to provide them some cover, while the other four turned and waited for Coltrane to come up.

Plan was, if they ended up being tailed by a small bunch of Mexicans, then the trappers could spring an ambush along the way. But if it turned out to be a large force of soldiers, like that outfit they had watched ride away from the fort earlier that day—then there would be no waiting around. They'd whip and lather their horses, climbing hard for the pass, hoping to catch up to the others driving the herd they had just yanked out from under the noses of the *Californios*. They could slip over the mountains and down to the desert—on their way back home without any more trouble . . . if the vaqueros and the *soldados* didn't end up joining forces in the pursuit.

In his own way, Titus prayed he wouldn't have to hear Roscoe Coltrane's warning shot. Then all they'd have to worry about was the possibility that big swarm of soldiers they'd watched ride out of the fort earlier in the day was somewhere between them and Peg-Leg's bunch.

Twilight lingered long enough for them to wrangle their horses through that last patch of low, wind-stunted scrub timber nestled across the pass. While the west slope behind them remained sunny, night was already seeping over the hillside before them. The way the shadows had disappeared and twilight hovered around them, Bass wasn't certain when he called a halt to wait for Coltrane to catch up. At first he thought his eye might be playing tricks with him; he decided he had to trust in his ears. That dark mass far down the slopes below them had to be the noisiest gathering for several hundred square miles.

Inching his small herd forward at a walk now, he watched a pair of riders take shape at the tail end of the crawling procession, heard their voices too as those human sounds mingled with thousands of snorting weary animals having started their way down the eastern slopes.

Elias Kersey whooped and whistled, causing the pair to turn in their saddles, spotting the small band of horses approaching from behind, down out of the wide, rolling saddle. Both of them called out to the raiders ahead in the march.

In minutes Bill Williams and Tom Smith were loping back along the edges of that huge herd.

"You lose anyone?" Peg-Leg asked as he pulled up.

Kersey waited till Bass came to a halt beside him. Elias explained, "No dead. But we got shot up at the fort."

Williams asked, "Them bastards was laying for you?"

Shrugging, Bass replied, "Maybeso. Purcell's gonna pull through. Ball passed right through him. Adair an' his leg ain't doing near so good."

"Silas gonna make it?" Smith asked.

"Next day or two gonna tell," Kersey responded.

Titus looked at Williams. "You gonna put some more country between us and them Mexicans afore we rest, Bill? Maybe drive the herd all night?"

With a shake of his head, Williams said, "We recollect a spring down below a ways—saw it back when we was coming up. Me and Tom figgered to take the herd on down there for to camp a few hours."

Smith agreed. "These horses likely to smell that water anyway and go on down there on their own. We'll bed 'em down there for the night and push on when there's enough light to see."

Williams sighed, "They're tired, and so are we."

Frederico and his sister passed by the four trappers at that moment. Smith waited till they were disappearing into the gloom, then asked, "Where's the other gal? Wasn't we busting two women out?"

"One of them Mex' kill't her," Bass said. "But them two brung her body along other'n leaving it with the *Californios.*"

With a low whistle of approval as the end of the small herd approached, Williams asked, "Where the hell you get all them horses, Scratch?"

"Didn't wanna leave the soldiers nothing to ride, so we drove out with ever'thing in the stables," Kersey explained.

"Most of 'em is wild," Scratch declared. "I kept thinking them wild ones gonna drag off the soldier horses—but they didn't. Stayed with us all the way up to the pass, so we brung 'em all over together."

"Damn, Bill," Smith exclaimed, then turned to Kersey and Bass. "You fellas got any idee how many horses we come outta California with?"

"More'n I ever see'd with a white man!" Titus roared.

"I ain't at all for sure," Peg-Leg said. "But we'll get us some count come morning."

Williams quickly added, "We was callating we got more'n four thousand awready!"

"F-four thousand!" Kersey echoed in astonishment. "Yee-awww!"

"How the hell we gonna divide up all them?" Bass inquired.

"Maybeso we don't have to," Bill responded. "What we sell 'em for, we'll divide. But the herd gets sold together."

"That's more'n the Bents can buy," Kersey stated.

Scratching at his chin thoughtfully, Williams said, "What they don't buy, we'll shoo on back to Missouri and sell the rest of 'em to the corncrackers in the East."

The last of the soldier horses and wild mustangs were easing past. "C'mon, fellas," Smith prodded. "Let's get these animals on down to water and fort up for the night."

Silas Adair was a grumpy sort who might be given to complaining a little about this or that, but he had not

groused once during that painful, jarring ride up and
through the pass. When a patch of ground got too rough,
Adair jammed a short stick wrapped with antelope skin
between his teeth and suffered on through. By the time
the rest had the herd pulled off by the spring and the
thousands of horses were milling about, waiting to water,
Bass joined Kersey and Coltrane, who were seeing to Silas. His face with that big bulbous nose glistened in the
first flames at that small fire they built back against the
rocks to radiate the heat. Beneath that copper-red hair,
he was drenched with sweat.

"I've had me better days'n this, boys," Adair confessed
a little breathless.

Coltrane knelt over Silas with a bandanna he had
soaked in the spring. With it he bathed his friend's face.

"The bleeding stopped," Kersey announced after inspecting the thigh wound. "I'll fetch you something to
eat, soon's it ready, Silas."

Night came down quickly, tucked here as they were on
the east slope while the sun slid on past that narrow strip
of Mexican California. The Americans quickly sorted out
a rotation of nighthawks as the able-bodied would all
take their turn at riding the fringes of the herd until
enough light oozed out of the eastern sky for them to
move on. Scratch's watch would be the last before dawn.

As weary as he was, sleep was still slow in coming.
The ground was either too rocky, or his thick blanket
wasn't warm enough, or the throb of too many hooves
on the ground where he rested his ear too loud . . . it all
made sleep hard to come by for him, his blankets close to
where they had settled Purcell and Adair for the night.

Titus Bass lay staring at the stars here on the high
ground between California and the desert where they
would once again be tested. This time across, however,
they could push as hard as they wanted. With all these
horses, the raiders would have no worry for fresh
mounts, no reason to concern themselves over a steady
food supply, even a source of moisture between springs
and water holes as they navigated the wastes for that land
of the Ammuchabas. Enough stringy horsemeat to fill

their bellies until they reached buffalo country; and enough of the thick, hot horse blood to see them all the way back to the cold, clear streams of the Rocky Mountains.

Just as he felt himself drifting off on that hard ground, Titus heard the soft, stifled sobs of the two Indians weeping for their dead sister. He listened for some time, wondering what Frederico and Celita would do with the body. What was the custom of their people? Did they scoop holes out of the ground as the white man did, or did they leave the departed in the limbs of tall trees for the winds to reclaim them? Or as some claimed the Cheyenne did, would they wedge the body back into the rocks, seated upright and facing the rising sun?

What would the two do now with Mayanez? They were leaving behind their home, those hills and valleys of California where their people had been enslaved by the indolent Franciscan friars and forced to labor in the mission vineyards and fields or be brutalized by the Mexican soldiers. Where would the two of them go now? Did it make sense for Frederico to return to his new life in the Ammuchaba villages?

Where did one go when there was nowhere else to turn?

It was a question Titus Bass prayed he would never have to face.

Lying there in the dark, Bass pulled the thick blanket over the side of his head, pressing it against his ear, doing his best to blot out that quiet sobbing. It served only to make him sense a gnawing emptiness of his own. Titus realized he knew something of how the two Indians felt, had some experience with mourning. As the beaver trade died, as the annual summer rendezvous slipped farther and farther into the past, as more and more of his fellow white men fled the Shining Mountains—Titus Bass had pondered just where he was to go. Where was he to point his nose when there no longer was any direction for him to take?

Wallowing in that confusion, her face swam before the dark of his eyes—her cheeks smooth as the day she had first spoken to him beside the icy river. Cheeks yet untouched by the smallpox scourge that had ravenously devoured the northern plains, sated its appetite on the Blackfeet and others, in the process nearly robbing him of his wife. The swimming vision smiled and held out her arms to him, pulling him down upon her, welcoming him into her wet, waiting warmth. He sensed how she reached out to seize his hardened manhood insistently, to guide it inside her, her own breathing coming quick and shallow as she thrust her hips upward, seating him hungrily to his full length—

Suddenly he was aware of the Indians crying—no longer sobbing softly. Their wails immediately dispelled the heat of that too-real vision he was desperately reaching for here on the low divide between Mexican California and that no-man's-land of desert wilderness. Now they were wailing, supplicating their own god.

Would his own god answer his private prayer, Titus wondered? Would he make it back to Absaroka alive and whole to caress her soft flesh, to have Magpie press her head into the crook of his neck and to bounce Flea upon his knee?

He rolled onto his other hip and did his best to conjure her up again, thinking how good it felt to sleep curled against her bare back, one of his hands nestled between her soft breasts . . . how she often reached back and took hold of him in his sleep, arousing him with her fingers, awakening him—knowing he could never refuse her.

"Bass!"

Yanking the edge of the blanket from his face, Titus blinked into the black of night—realizing he had finally fallen asleep. After rubbing the heels of his hands into both eyes, Bass recognized Pete Harris kneeling above him.

"Get up, goddammit," insisted this friend of Philip Thompson's. "You're taking over my watch."

"Where?" he asked as he kicked his blanket off.

Harris pointed east before he trudged off without a word.

Scratch pulled on his capote, belted it, then stuffed two pistols into the belt. Finally he grabbed his rifle and pouch and started for the edge of the herd. Carefully feeling his way along in his moccasins, Titus toed atop some of the tall boulders scattered around the watering hole, settled onto his haunches, and stared out over the extent of the herd. The sheer size of the remuda dwarfed their little camp—the horses filling the narrow, grassy meadow that stretched farther than he could see here in the cold, dry air of these last hours before dawn. They'd be pushing the animals on when it grew light enough. On down to the sands where they would begin their crossing.

This high desert darkness had a dreamlike quality all its own: cold enough to keep him wide awake although he was never really sure what was real and what was not in this world of darkness that had closed in around him. Over time the sky lightened below them, along the horizon at first, slowly grinding his way, yard by yard. Shapes took form in the coming of day. He began to recognize brush from horse, boulder from man. Animals snorted. Someone threw some kindling on a dying fire.

He could see it was Peg-Leg, kneeling there on his good leg, that wooden pin shoved out from him at an angle, shoving the old coffeepot closer to the flames with a grating scrape across the rocks—

Erupting in a hundred directions at once, the big, black pot exploded. Smith tumbled backward as embers from the fire shot upward in spirals like a thousand fireflies suddenly hurled up, freed from a clay jar. Many of the raiders were yelling, one of them crouching over Smith, helping Peg-Leg up when a second gunshot echoed in this rocky hollow where they found water for their stolen horses.

A third, then fourth, gunshot reverberated off the rocky walls now. One of the trappers went down in the half-light, noisily screaming. Bass was already off the rock and on his belly, staying low, watching the wounded trapper slide backward as Adair rolled sideways off his improvised travois, painfully pulling himself out of the firelight the moment the rocky defile came alive with the roar of confident voices. Mexicans.

"They ambushed us, goddammit!" Williams was growling.

Smith peered from behind a low boulder, his eyes sweeping the rocky ledges above him. "Came up on us while we was camped."

"How'd they follow our trail in the dark?" a voice called out.

"It wasn't no big secret where we was headed," Williams grumbled as he shoved his rifle against his shoulder.

"Silas!" Scratch hissed as he slid in beside Adair. He started to rock the wounded man off his bad leg.

"Can't get up!"

Titus shoved his rifle into Adair's hands, then hoisted the man back onto the crude travois. Stepping into the vee, Titus grabbed the cradle's support and heaved forward as the air around them was rent with bullets. *A damn good thing those soldiers never weren't any good with their poor smoothbores, or they'd likely have more of us already cut down.*

Above the Americans reverberated the commands of the Mexican officers, echoes ordering the soldiers down from the timber and rocky cliffs, goading them to close quickly on the outnumbered and surprised Americans. Those horses grazing nearest the camp grew restless, stirring this way, then that, like a flock of wild wrens as stray balls landed among them, gunfire drawing closer and closer, voices growing strident and desperate. Shots ricocheted off the rocks with shrill cries of warning.

The wild horses were the very first to break, lunging past Titus, sweeping some of the California horses with them as the nervous animals blocked him from reaching the boulders where the rest of the Americans were retreating one by one by one.

"They got knives on their guns!" Adair screeched.

Huffing wearily, Scratch whirled, glancing over his shoulder—finding that the Mexicans did have long knives pinned beneath the muzzles of their rifles. Four of those bayonets glittered in the remnants of the fire's light that gray morning as the *soldados* slowly advanced over the rocky ground toward Bass and his travois.

"Titus Bass!"

He whipped back around to find two of the trappers standing atop the rocks, making conspicuous targets of themselves as they leveled their weapons on those four soldiers closing in on Scratch. He and Adair were trapped—frightened horses milling between him and the boulders where the others had taken cover.

One of the Americans fired. Scratch watched the bullet graze the forestock of a soldier's musket before it slammed into the man's chest, shoving him backward off his feet as his own weapon discharged into the air.

Dropping Adair's travois, Titus reached down and yanked his rifle out of the wounded man's hands. He dragged the hammer back as the weapon reached his hipbone. Set the back trigger and leveled the muzzle at the closest Mexican.

He felt a ball rake his upper arm with fire as brilliant flame jetted from his own barrel. Not far past the shreds of burning patch that had exploded from the flintlock's muzzle, he watched the soldier spin around on his boot heel, screwing himself into the grass with a grunt of surprise and pain.

Another gun roared on those rocks behind him. A third soldier pitched backward off his feet, landing flat on his back in the grass. Only one more of them to keep off Adair, one more Mexican who instantly stopped, eyes wide with terror as he gazed around him at his three dead companions.

"Get over here, Titus Bass!" another voice boomed from the rocks.

Turning on his heel he found only a few horses blocking his retreat now. Laying the rifle alongside Adair's hip, he yanked one of the pistols from his belt, then slapped it into Silas's waiting hand.

"Use it when they get close," he huffed. "Only when they're close enough you're sure to kill one of the bastards!"

His lungs were screaming with hot tongues of breathless fire by the time he lunged to the bottom of the boulders and dropped the travois. Quickly kneeling beside Adair, Scratch raised one of the trapper's arms. He ducked under that thick blacksmith's arm and rolled Silas across the back of his shoulders. Dragging his own legs beneath him, Titus rose slowly, unsteadily, with the heavy man's bulk centered atop his spine.

"Merciful a'mighty!" Adair gasped in pain as his wounded leg dragged off the ground and slammed into the back of Scratch's hip. Silas clutched desperately at the front of Titus's shirt with one of those broad-beamed blacksmith's hands.

"Help him!" Williams was roaring as Bass stumbled uncertainly around the base of the rocks.

Coltrane was at Titus's side in the next heartbeat. Short and stocky, but built like a whiskey barrel—Roscoe slipped under Adair's other arm and dragged Silas crosswise onto his own shoulders. With his two thick arms looped under Adair's armpit and one of his legs, Coltrane sidestepped into a narrow crevice between the jumble of boulders as lead smacked the rocks around them.

One of the Mexican's bullets grazed the boulder just above the spot where Scratch knelt to retrieve his rifle. With a shrill scream of its own, a tiny fragment of granite was shaved off near his ear. The long cut it opened along his left cheek burned with a tongue of icy fire.

Looking up, he found Tom Smith holding his hand down for him. Grasping Peg-Leg's wrist, Scratch dragged himself through the crevice behind Coltrane and Adair.

"You're the last," Smith growled.

"The bastards're chivvying the herd!" someone roared above them.

"Kill as many of 'em as you can!" Bill Williams ordered. "We'll drive 'em back, then go round up them horses again!"

But there were too many Mexicans.

That was plain enough for Titus to see. They were all over the rocks, bristling at the edge of the cliff to their left, more shoving their way through the frightened horses. Vaqueros and soldiers both. Yelling at one another now that they knew they had the horse thieves surrounded and whipped. Yelling at the Americans to surrender or be killed.

"S-surrender?" Williams screeched as Smith translated.

Two more balls of lead smacked the rocks behind them.

"Don't fret none, Bill," Peg-Leg said. "Ain't none of us goin' to no California hoosegow for a hanging now."

"They'd sooner kill us all as put us behind their bars," Scratch explained. "If we surrender, we'll be helpless. That's when them bean-bellies gonna cut us down."

"That's right," Kersey snorted. "They won't waste no trouble hog-tying us back to California."

"Maybeso we're gonna go down here and now," Scratch told them all as he rammed a ball home against the breech of his rifle. "But leastways, fellas . . . we can show these *pelados* how to die like men."

14

◆

He wondered if the Mexicans hung horse thieves. Maybe they wouldn't waste time with a rope—just stand them up in front of a firing squad, their backs against the fort wall, blindfolded or not, and let these bad-shooters bang away at them.

Right then Bass didn't know which way he preferred to die. Hanging seemed like such a terrifying, prolonged way to go, especially if his neck did not break at the bottom of the drop: suspended, swinging there until he choked to death, legs kicking while he soiled himself.

Any time these greasers hit something with their muskets, it was more idiot's luck than it was skill. Chances were a firing squad would botch the job but good, wounding him badly rather than killing him outright with a clean bullet through the heart. Then he'd be no better off than swinging from a noose, forced to endure the agony of his wounds until he bled enough to pass out, no longer in misery.

"How many goddamned greasers they bring after us?" Thomas Smith shrieked as he whirled with those two big horse pistols in hand: .62-caliber smoothbores they were.

Their attackers weren't all soldiers. Not all wore those short blue jackets draped with braid and the flat-brimmed hats. The rest must damn well be vaqueros come after the thieves—maybe to even a personal score for all the killing done yesterday morning in the valley.

"We need powder!" one of the trappers yelled.

"What's in my horn s'all I got," another explained.

Kersey's voice bellowed, "How you fixed for balls? Anything less'n fifty-four'll work. Who can spare me some balls?"

"Here, Elias," Scratch called out, digging into his pouch as he crabbed over. "I got a handful for you."

Appreciation lay deep in Kersey's eyes as he scooped out more than a dozen from Titus's palm. "Ain't this a yank on the devil's short-hairs, Scratch?"

"Never thort I'd die in California," Jake Corn grumbled. "Allays thort it'd be Blackfoot."

"Maybeso a griz," Titus said as he wheeled back around at the growing noise from their attackers. "I figgered to go out wrasslin' with a griz . . . but not till I'd bounced me some grandpups on my knee."

Reuben Purcell groaned, "We cain't shoot 'em all! Too dang many!"

"Don't none of you give up!" Bass snapped at Purcell the moment after he fired and was throwing his rifle butt to the ground to begin reloading.

"Just shoot ever' living one you can," Corn declared.

"Jake's right," Bass said, glancing a moment at the fear tightening Purcell's face. He felt bad for Rube, sorry that he'd snapped at the man, maybe even made Purcell feel cowardly—when he was for sure Reuben wasn't a coward. He'd held his own without complaint back when Ol' Frapp went under. "Knock 'em down one at a time. They ain't gonna rush us 'cause they know that's certain death, boys. We can hold 'em off—"

"Robiseau's down!" came the cry.

Williams growled, "Blazes! That makes four more out of the fight!"

Titus spit one of the round lead balls into the palm of his hand, rolled it between his thumb and forefinger, then pressed it into the muzzle. Dragging the wiping stick from its thimbles at the bottom of the forestock, he rammed the ball down against the powder charge without a patch. No time to mess with such things. He'd use a greased patch on that gummy, unburnt powder fouling the barrel after another shot or two. But for now—they had to hold the Mexicans back, keep them at bay . . . maybe they'd even give up and pull off their attack.

The sun was coming. It had grown light enough that Titus had no trouble making out the dip and sway of the mountainside as it fell away to the desert far below. Why'd he ever crossed that godforsaken piece of sandy ground? He had no business in such inhospitable country. Not that he hadn't crossed some water scrapes in his time, like that trail running from Santa Fe and Taos clear back to the settlements of Missouri. But, this was something different. They'd come here to ride off with every last Mexican horse they could lay their hands on.

The sun was coming. Might well be his last.

Just that Titus could smell death hovering nearby. Hell knew he had experienced enough of it: killed plenty men himself, or been there as men died . . . so he could for certain smell death's fetid stench strong in his nostrils right now.

Bass made the next shot, dropped one of the vaqueros, all of whom were more daring than most of the overcautious soldiers.

He set about reloading—and wondered how many of the others would die before the Mexicans finally got him. There wasn't going to be any firing squad for them. No hangman's noose thrown over the branch of a tree. Bass snorted at that image—there wasn't a tree tall enough in these parts to hang a man from the back of a horse! These soldiers were going to rub them all out and not take a one of them back to California.

As he grabbed for his priming horn, Titus looked about for Frederico or his sister.

Maybe the two of them had been killed early on in the fight and he couldn't spot their bodies. Better chance that they'd run off at the first sound of trouble and were hiding back in the rocks somewhere. Titus couldn't figure out how, but by doing something bold and amazing those Indians must have slipped on through the noose of Mexicans that was tightening around the trappers. Likely the soldiers allowed them through because they had come here for the horse thieves.

Cradling the forestock in his left palm, Bass quickly looked for the closest target.

Not that he begrudged Frederico and Celita at all. God knew they'd suffered plenty at the hands of their enslavers. He didn't begrudge them getting away, escaping and fleeing and making what life they could beyond the reach of those Franciscan friars and cruel soldiers. He imagined them crossing the desert on foot, making for the land of the Ammuchabas.

"How many of us left?" Smith demanded.

Williams shouted, "I ain't keeping count no more, you idjit son of a bitch!"

The moment he had pulled the trigger, Bass looked around right and left, saw for the first time those men who were wounded—some lying in the grassy dirt, others sitting as they slowly bled all over themselves, a man here and a man there—scattered throughout their rocky fortress. So few of them left standing now with the Mexicans popping up—a dozen at a time—all the soldiers shooting by volley, then sinking back down to reload their old muskets.

"But for the grace of God," Coltrane muttered.

The sudden sound of it stopped Bass cold. "R-roscoe? That you talked?"

Coltrane turned, half grinned sheepishly. He only nodded.

"Told you he talked, didn't I?" Adair said from his travois.

Silas sat with his back propped against a boulder, those two horse pistols filling his hands, his horn and pouch tucked in his lap. Ready for the moment the Mexicans charged.

"It's been good knowing you boys," Titus said before

he gave it a second thought. "All of you. 'Specially you, Roscoe. Even though we ain't ever talked."

"Good knowing you too, Titus Bass."

He could instantly tell by the looks on the faces of those other men around them that they felt the same way. Good comrades these. They would stand at his back when the last moment arrived, when he would be thrust on to whatever lay on the other side. Much as he had worried himself about hoo-doos and malevolent spirits crossing through from their world to this through a crack in the sky . . . he was surprised to find he felt strangely at peace right then. Assuring to be in the company of good men who weren't about to give up even with death's odor strong on the wind.

The soft light in every set of those bloodshot eyes that met his told Titus Bass these men sensed the same indescribable bond they had forged through adversity, want, and sheer fortitude. Around him now were men who had suffered together, nearly died together, but had seen each other through. There was no greater camaraderie men could share than this: to stand together, shoulder to shoulder, and stare death back in the eye.

Ebenezer Zane. Isaac Washburn. Jack Hatcher. Asa McAfferty. Bird In Ground. Rotten Belly. His father-in-law, Whistler. Jarrell Thornbrugh. And finally Strikes In Camp, his wife's brother. Those good men who had passed on before him, their very souls now the stars twinkling upon the dark firmament of the night sky.

Even those who he prayed still lived, men like Josiah Paddock and Shadrach Sweete. Big Throat Gabe Bridger, little Kit Carson, and Broken Hand Fitzpatrick.

The sort of man who did not strut and crow like some puffed-up prairie cock. Instead, the sort of friends who quietly stood their ground and weren't noisy braggarts who would crumple and fall when the last raise was made and that last hand of the game was called.

Kersey brushed some of his long, dusty-blond hair out of his eyes and held out his grimy hand. "You got a few more for a friend, Titus Bass?"

The instant Scratch looked down to pull up the flap

and stuff his hand into his pouch, he heard the shrill whine as lead ricocheted off the boulder behind them— heard the air burst from Elias's lungs as he spilled there at Scratch's feet.

"My back! My back!" Kersey screamed, digging at the wound immediately blackening his greasy calico shirt with a slick that reminded Titus of the blackstrap molasses his mam would pour over johnnycakes back when he was a boy in Rabbit Hash, Boone County, Kentucky. There on the southern bank of the Ohio.

Although wounded in the arm, Jake Corn quickly crabbed across the trampled grass, hovered over Kersey, and pressed his hand upon the deep furrow.

"Lay still, Elias," Bass cooed as he knelt, glancing into Corn's eyes.

"Don't move," Corn reminded, then looked again into Bass's eyes, his face gone a pasty white with uncertainty for his best friend.

Titus could tell how the deep furrow must hurt, watching Kersey grind his teeth in pain. "Better you don't move till . . ."—and he scrambled to find what more to say—"till we drive these greasers off."

"You ain't . . . gonna drive 'em . . . off," Kersey gasped against the agony of that ugly wound that continued to seep around Corn's best efforts. "They aim to rub us . . . all out—"

Of a sudden lead zinged and splatted all round them, making the Americans duck as one. Then a few, like Bass, dared peer up to discover the Mexicans had gained a superior position on the edge of an outcrop above them. In those seconds as he watched, more and more uniforms joined the first, one after another plopping onto their bellies, aiming their muskets down at the boulders where the horse thieves had taken refuge. Right where the Americans found themselves trapped like fish in a rain barrel.

"Bring the wounded over here!" Williams ordered.

"You heard him!" Bass cried, starting to crab toward Adair on his knees. "Drag the wounded over to Bill afore they're shot up some more!"

The trappers no sooner had started pulling their

bloody companions toward a shadowy hollow in the rocks when they whirled around together—all of them instantly aware of the clatter of metal scabbards on the rocks, the scrape of boot soles clambering up the boulders, the grunts and cursing of the Mexicans who suddenly appeared behind them. The soldiers had broken through the gap in the boulders and were preparing to finish the slaughter.

"Gimme a gun, goddammit!" Kersey rasped, seizing Corn's wrist in desperation. "I'm gonna kill one more of them sonsabitches before I go down!"

Corn tenderly wrapped Elias's fingers around a pistol he pulled from his belt. Jake twisted about on his knee, crouching at Kersey's shoulder with Bass, every able-bodied man leveling his weapons at the soldiers.

There were too many of the Mexicans. This would be their last hurrah. No time to reload after the next shot—

"Fire!"

Someone hollered that order. Maybe Smith, perhaps Williams. It didn't matter. The trappers' guns exploded into those first soldiers to penetrate the rocky fortress. Shrieking in surprise and pain, the soldiers and vaqueros fell back, the front rank dead or seriously wounded. Behind them others were yelling, pressing forward—their leaders furiously waving sabers as they resumed their all-out assault.

Even more of the dusty blue jackets appeared on the rocks as the gunsmoke cleared. Already so close the Americans had no time to reload. If the soldiers did not reload and shoot their smoothbore muskets, if they kept on coming with their long, glittering bayonets, they would close on the raiders, so close each man could look into his enemy's eye . . . to see there the fear or dread, even hatred, as the Mexicans lunged near enough to jab and slash with their bayonets—

Where there had been only cheers of impending victory and lusty battle oaths among the soldiers an instant before, suddenly there were cries of surprise and shrieks of panic. At the very moment the Mexicans were about to plunge in among the trappers and those empty guns, the soldiers and vaqueros wheeled about—trapped between the Americans and a new adversary.

Behind and above, on all sides of the trappers, the dull, gray boulders sprouted naked brown bodies. Warriors wearing nothing more than short breechclouts and moccasins, firing one short hunting arrow after another from their small, powerful bows.

Frozen in that moment of utter disbelief, Bass blinked—unable to fathom the sudden appearance of these short Indians. Like the Ammuchabas, very much like Frederico himself. None of them tall, in any way like the statuesque Crow, Shoshone, even Blackfoot. Much smaller in stature as they bounded across the rocks, surrounding and overwhelming the startled and quickly demoralized soldiers.

The Mexicans still able to stand found themselves surrounded and began to slowly back from the field. From one moment to the next, a brown warrior fell to a soldier bullet—but even more brownskins stepped into the gap, pressing their vicious attack. Screaming, u-looing, and . . . from somewhere nearby came the constant, heartbeat thunder of a huge drum, a sound swelling all the larger as it reverberated within this rocky defile. Almost deafening as it pounded in the ear with the shouts, screams, warnings, and death rattles of Mexican and Indian alike; those shrill whistles of frightened horses; the scrape of soldier gun and scabbard dragged over the rocks as terrified men made a frantic escape; a steady *thung-thung-thung* of those short horn bows.

Without mercy, the naked attackers fell upon those too slow, those who fell behind the rest in this mad flight. Every wounded soldier or vaquero was descended upon, his head yanked up—throat slit brutally before a last gasp could be taken, dark blood seeping into the green of the short grass, splattering the yellow of the trampled dust. But these warriors did not stop to take the black hair of their victims. Instead the Indians leaped to their feet once more, shouting anew, their hands and arms and stubby knives drenched with the crimson that glistened in the first rays of the coming day.

On both sides of the Americans, even through the startled trappers themselves, the Indians sprinted after the terror-filled Mexicans. Passing right on by the horse thieves without so much as a blink of acknowledgment. Without the slightest attempt to harm the stunned Americans in any way.

Almost as suddenly as the warriors had appeared, they were driving the soldiers before them—dropping every laggard, quickly finishing off the wounded, then pressing their advantage of swift and total surprise. Then they were shadows, for the sun had risen far enough to paint these death moments with the first filaments of light, creating the first, flitting specters of smudge and stain at the same instant.

A single voice gradually arose above the others—this one booming, low and reverberant as the black belly of thunder itself. Very much unlike the higher, shrill cries of the warriors whipping their way after the retreating soldiers. A voice that echoed and rattled from the boulders.

Bass turned immediately as the shadow crossed Corn and Kersey, squinting up at the low cliff above and behind them. Peering over his shoulder, he could see only the glare of sudden rays of the rising sun backlighting the shadowy figure. A form so dark he appeared to be a piece of the night itself, no more than a fragment of the night now gone with the coming of this day.

Behind this figure the sun of that new dawn made the man's form all the blacker, all the more shadow than he was of substance. Titus tried to shield his eyes, squinting up as the leader shouted orders to his warriors.

Tall. Was it only that Scratch crouched down here and the strange figure stood up there that gave this man the appearance of such great height?

As the leader bounded off the cliff and started hand over hand down the rocks, dropping out of those first rays of the sun, many of the trappers stood and turned in disbelief. This Indian was nothing like his warriors. The hundreds who had swarmed after the Mexicans all had their black, coarse hair cropped at the shoulder, bangs cut straight across the forehead, just above the eyebrows.

But their leader was bald—his black head as naked as Titus had ever seen a man's skull.

Still, he dressed no different than his warriors. Around his waist hung the same skimpy skin breechclout the others wore, and on his feet the same crude moccasins tied at the ankle.

While the warriors were dark brown in color, their leader's skin was instead a deep, rich black that glistened with sweat. He approached the white men with all but the color and sheen of a glistening vein of coal tucked into the side of those hills bordering the upper Tongue and Powder river basins. And when he dropped to the ground within the boulders themselves, turning now to face the Americans, Titus realized there was even more to the difference between this leader and his fighting men.

Besides the fact that he stood a full head taller than even the tallest warrior, the only hair remaining on the leader's head were those bushy eyebrows—each one like a furry gray caterpillar above eyes narrowed, half lidded in the brand-new light. Singing out in his people's tongue, this war chief joyously welcomed back the first of the returning warriors, flush with victory.

All around the Americans now more than fifty of the short, brown fighting men pressed close, at least a hundred more shoving up behind them—every last one smiling at the whites they had just dragged back from the precipice of death—grinning as if nothing could be more fun than killing Mexicans. Soldiers or vaqueros—it did not seem to matter. These short-haired, laughing Indians were splattered with the blood of their enemies—for that nothing could bring them any more joy.

Scratch looked around as some of the trappers began muttering among themselves. He turned with the others who watched the tall, black-skinned leader slowly step through the ranks of the white men, carefully peering at each hairy, pale face, studying it intently, before moving on to stop and study the next.

Something about the leader's broad nose, those expressive, almond-shaped eyes . . .

To everyone's surprise this leader put his hands on his hips and shouted to his warriors—immediately silencing them. As the last of their number obeyed, Bass realized he could almost hear the thud of his own heart, the faint cry of a nearby bird, and the scrape of the tall man's moccasins on the gravel under his feet.

Then the leader spoke, clearing his voice before he said, "Ti . . . tuss? Ti . . . tuss Bass here?"

Unsure he had actually heard what he thought the tall one just said, not completely certain with the strange accented inflection to the words that had emerged from the chief's lips, Bass glanced about, seeing how some of the trappers stood staring slack-jawed at the chief, the rest of the white men turning to peer at Titus in disbelief.

"He say B-bass?" Williams repeated, astonishment carved on his lined and wrinkled face.

"Tituss," the leader repeated as he turned to stare at Williams inquisitively, breaking the word into a pair of distinct syllables once again, a long and pronounced *s* on the end. "You Tituss Bass . . . yes?"

"H-him," Tom Smith said, pointing.

The leader turned slightly, took three steps toward Scratch, halting within an arm's length of Bass where he cocked his head, studying the white man's face, his eyes squinting as if mentally reckoning on something of great breadth and weight.

Bill Williams slid up to stand close, not quite between them. He asked the tall leader, "You k-know him?"

"Tituss?"

Stunned into speechlessness for so long, Scratch could finally admit, "Yes."

"Tituss Bass!" the tall one repeated, the name sounding more clear with repetition. "Excuse, please. No English for long, long time. You—Tituss Bass? Tituss from Ohio River?"

Scratch's brow furrowed, his head swam in confusion. "I . . . I come from the Ohio—yeah. Long, long ago."

For a long moment the leader closed his eyes, raising

his face to the sky as his lips moved silently. Then he lowered his chin and stared into Bass's eyes once more. "Long ago. Been a long time I don't speak the white words, long time now. You—me . . . at the Owens . . . Owensboro—farewell a long, long ago."

Swallowing hard, struggling to make sense, examining those eyes that did not belong to this time and place, knowing those black eyes belonged instead to somewhere in the past—

Holding out his big, rawboned hand, the tall man said, "Thirty-two years now we come here. In your world, it is thirty-two years."

Bass stared down at the offered hand in utter disbelief. Where was he thirty-two years ago? So he asked, "On the Ohio?"

Again the tall leader struggled for the words, then he said, "It so long ago—I remember the place and the time . . . better than I remember English. But English coming back now. Forgive, but I trouble with the words to say."

"You're too damn dark for any of these here Injuns," Tom Smith demanded as he hobbled up. "Just who the hell are you?"

"He know me," the warrior leader said, looking again at Titus.

"I-I know you?"

"You knowed me long ago, Titus Bass," the tall man explained. "I am the man you set free from a slaver's cage. The man you set free at Owensboro on Ohio River."

Scratch's eyes widened.

A huge, warm smile cracked that black face as he continued, "I am the man Annie Christmas called Hezekiah."

It was the Negro he had busted from the barred cage on the back of that wagon outside a Natchez tippling house as the Kentucky-bound boatmen were doing their best to slip through that riverbank settlement without being recognized. Back then sixteen-year-old Titus Bass had looked into that cage behind the Kings Tavern, recognizing the tall, bald-headed Negro who had tended bar in Annie Christmas's gunboat brothel tied against the riverbank as Ebenezer Zane's men were floating down the Mississippi for the ocean port of New Orleans.*

Because Hezekiah had failed to stop the brawl that had killed one of her prized whores and a couple of her bodyguards, Annie promptly sold off her bartender to a wealthy landowner who would squeeze his money's worth out of the big, muscular slave. But before they pushed north from Natchez, the slavers had to stop for that autumn night, have themselves some supper and a few drinks, then perhaps a fleshy whore to wrap her legs around them until dawn when they would venture out to the wagon yard to discover one of their slaves busted free.

Much to the misgivings of the other boatmen, Titus Bass brought Hezekiah Christmas with him on that long walk back along the Natchez Trace, eventually reaching the country of the Muscle Shoals as they pushed north for French Lick, the end of that wilderness road. It was just past a travelers' stand and a rainy river crossing that the slavers caught up with the boatmen. In a quick and bloody scrap, young Titus Bass hung his life out for the Negro.

Scratch explained the story in detail, down to their parting at Owensboro on the Ohio, weeks later.

"Y-you give this here Neegra a paper what said he was a freedman?" Philip Thompson asked in scorn and disbelief.

"He was a man, and I freed him," Bass replied. "I figgered he ought'n go west where a man might stand on his own legs 'stead of being accounted for by the color of his skin."

"You sure as hell are one chuckle-headed fool!" Thompson roared. "Lookit him! Cain't you figger how

---

* *Dance on the Wind*

much this Neegra would bring one of us on the slave block?"

Hezekiah glared down at the white trapper. "You wanna take me back to your slave market, white man?" He held up his hands, wrists pressed together. "Go right ahead on—put me in your irons."

For a moment Thompson's eyes flicked about anxiously, then he smiled. "Maybeso we can take you on back with us to Missouri with these here horses. Sell your black ass to some slaver. It's for damn certain I'll get more for you'n I'd get for a dozen Mexican horses!"

A handful of Thompson's compatriots guffawed at that.

"If'n you try taking Hezekiah," Bass warned, "you're more soft-brained than I ever give you credit for."

Thompson's jaw jutted and his brow knitted in fury as he demanded, "What the hell you mean I'm soft-brained?"

"Shit," Titus scoffed. "You'd be one dumb idjit to lay a hand on Hezekiah here."

"W-why?" the white man blustered with a roar of laughter. "You gonna stop me?"

"Me," he answered, then dramatically swept his arm in a wide arc, " 'long with all Hezekiah's Injuns. You make a play for him, you wouldn't last no more time'n it'd take you to eat horsemeat for breakfast."

That instantly drowned all of Thompson's plans in very cold water, and the man sheepishly shrank to the back of the Americans as Williams and Smith stepped forward to discuss their immediate fortunes with Hezekiah Christmas.

Within minutes the warriors went about burying their own dead in the rocks while the white men buried their two dead comrades in the dry, flinty ground. By midmorning they constructed travois for what wounded could not continue east on horseback.

And just before midday, the trappers and Hezekiah's Indians finally started the day's march, gradually gathering up small bunches of stray horses as they pushed the herd on down the slopes for the desert wastes. On that journey, the travel-weary Negro and the young Kentucky boy now grown old rode knee to knee while they both attempted to hack their way through so many intervening years.

"I got me gran'chirrun now," Hezekiah explained, more and more of his English returning to his nimble tongue. "Me—a gran'pap, Titus Bass! Gloreee be! To think of it: never would've had me no wife hadn't been for you."

"You'd got yourself a gal somewhere, I'm sure. Two of you raised up some young'uns—"

"Nawww, them slavers'd kill't me first," Hezekiah growled, the muscles in his jaws tensing. "That'd been fine by me too. No life for this here Neegra, being no slave."

Titus cleared his throat, trying out a smile to foster a grin on his long-ago friend's face. "I can't believe you're a gran'pap. How old a man are you?"

"I never learn't much ciphering, Titus Bass. But I do know Miss Christmas tol't me my last summer with her I was twenty-four years. And I kept me a count ever since, from that time I was made a freedman by you. Thirty-two winters it's been."

Slowly he calculated it himself. "Damn if that makes you fifty-six, Hezekiah."

"How ol't are you now, Titus Bass?"

Scratch wagged his head, figuring. "Why, I'll be forty-nine come this winter. Back when we run onto one another—how could anyone ever figger we'd ever get this old?"

"I'd never'd been old at all, wasn't for you."

Bass felt his eyes brimming, his heart seized with a sharp stab of warm sentiment. "Then we're even, Hezekiah Christmas."

"Even?"

"Less'n you brung your Injuns down on them Mexicans," Scratch declared, "me and the rest of these here horse stealers all be dead right now."

Christmas's eyes narrowed in a serpentine fashion.

"My people hate Mexicans. Kill all them Mexicans we can kill ever' time they ride into our mountains."

The impact of just how close he had come to going under was hitting Titus. He declared, "You didn't come along with your Injuns when you did, I'd be hash right about now. So how'd you know to come save me?"

With a gust of soft, contagious laughter, Christmas said, "Didn't know it was you, Titus Bass! Didn't really matter it was you neither. Like I said, all we was gonna do was kill ever' Mexican we could get in our hands. But you being there was just something meant to be, Titus Bass."

"Maybeso us crossing paths again after all these years was meant to be, Hezekiah," Scratch declared with a toothy smile. "Way things was lookin' with them Mexican soldiers 'bout to rub us out—your ol' bare head was the sweetest sight I see'd in a long, long time!"

"Many's the night I laid on my blanket, trying to fall asleep," Christmas admitted, the look in his eyes gone soft again, "doing my best to figger out a way I'd ever thank you for setting me free from them slavers. An' the farther I come—sailin' way out to California—the harder it was gonna be to find me a way to square things between us. After while, I got to figgerin' I'd live out the last of my days owing you for my life—"

"Great Jehoshaphat! If you didn't square things back there in a big way, Hezekiah!" he interrupted as he laid his hand on the Negro's bare, muscular forearm. "No more talk 'bout it, ever again . . . what I wanna know is when the devil you gonna tell me how you come to be out here so far away from where I last saw you on the banks of the Ohio?"

15

◆

"Just like you said for me to do, I gone west, down the Ohio," Hezekiah Christmas explained. "But that country didn't suit me so much. Folks there . . . they didn't take to no freedman so good."

"What'd you do?" Scratch asked. "Where'd you go when you found things weren't so hospitable for you west of Owensboro?"

Hezekiah told how he crossed the Ohio, turning his nose east, pushing farther and farther north. He made a few pennies when and where people would pay him for his work. And when he no longer had any money to pay for his keep, or no white man would offer him his keep in exchange for a little work, Hezekiah slept out in the forest, or here and there stole a chicken and other victuals to fill his gnawing belly as he kept on searching for that place where folks would no longer regard him as nothing more than an ex-slave, not even so much as a freedman . . . a land where they would regard him only as a man.

"Never heard of New London," Bass said after Hezekiah had explained how he made his way all the way to that seaside town in Connecticut. "What's a man with a strong back like yours to do in such a place?"

"I went to sea," Christmas said with a chest-swelling pride. "Cap'n Philbert. A good man, that one."

On the *Lady Jane,* Philbert's sleek, low-slung coastal packet, the crew made swift runs up and down the Atlantic seaboard. With their hold crammed full of goods from New England, they plied the coastal waters to those southern ports where they off-loaded, then filled up the belly of the *Lady Jane* once more with bales of cotton, tobacco, and even rum from the West Indies.

"For six years I learned every bump and dimple on the seaboard," Hezekiah stated. "Then Cap'n Philbert, he was give the chance to sail a big, big ship out on the ocean."

Philbert was offered more pay to command a massive, three-masted schooner that would make regular runs around the Cape Horn to California, beginning with that first season of 1819.

Titus watched the way a wistful look came over Hezekiah's face as he talked about that maiden voyage of the *Yankee Pride,* plying the coast of South America and eventually tacking into the bay at San Diego, then sailing north to their next port where they put in at Pueblo de los Angeles. It was in that coastal village that Hezekiah fell in love with the Spanish ladies, and they with him.

"*Valgame Dios!* Way them wimmens stared at me with their big eyes, why—I don't figger any of 'em ever see'd a Neegra afore!" Hezekiah confessed with a grin. "Truth be, I had eyes for one of them ladies my own self. But she was the wife of a soldier. He bought her fancy clothes and drove her around in a big carriage all the time. I'm sure he didn't think much of his wife making eyes at no poor seafarin' Neegra from America faraway. *Malditos Americanos.*"

He had decided California had to be the land of milk and honey—brimming with women, wine, and all manner of earthly pleasures. The freedman set his sights on putting down roots in California.

"I asked Cap'n Philbert for my leave—an' he let me

stay behind when the *Yankee Pride* turned south for the Cape and her home port. Even spoke for me at the Mission San Gabriel where one of them padres spoke a little American talk. They was to give me a home there, an' a place to work for my keep too. The good father tol't me how I'd have to work in the fields with the Injuns, sleep with 'em too. None of us got much food neither."

Less than a year later, life in Spanish California changed forever. No longer were they a colony. Now they were part of an independent country. And nothing in Mexico would ever be the same again.

"After 'while, things wasn't so good no more. I didn't know where to turn for help," Hezekiah continued. "A stranger in that land—no better off'n I was back in the South."

The new Mexican governor heard of this strange black American and came to visit Christmas at the mission. From the very start it was plain that the governor was suspicious of the stranger. Here in the first days following their revolution, the Mexicans were afraid of their own shadows.

"But he said I could stay on at the mission for one year with the *mansitos*."

"*Mansitos?*"

"These here." And Hezekiah gestured at the young men around him. "It's what the Mexicans called the tame Indians."

"After the year, what were you s'pose to do?"

Christmas wagged his head. "I was s'posed to be gone on a ship to America afore my year was up."

Until the next ship arrived in the bay, the governor and the Franciscan friars declared the American would have to find gainful employment in the mission fields and vineyards with the rest of the poor *mansos*. But that ultimately meant he was slaving from dawn till dusk for two meager meals each day and a roof over his head in the Indian quarters every night.

"They was bound to do their best to turn me into a slave again," he declared with a fury boiling just beneath the surface. "*Un Americano, pero de mas cristiano de la santa fe católica.* I was American, but they was gonna do all they could to make me a good Catholic, like they was making all the *mansitos* into good Christians too."

Then the first of the slaves decided to run off.

"But they was brung back the next day," Christmas said. "And beat to an inch of their lives for it."

The cruel whippings delivered by the army officers in collusion with the padres did not deter those Indians brave enough to attempt escape again.

"That second time they paid with their lives, and most of the rest got a bad beating just to show 'em who was the boss."

Christmas tried his best to explain how he was coming to see these short, brown-skinned Indians as no different than his own people back in America. How the sadistic Mexican officers and those self-righteous Catholic friars were no different than the brutal slave masters back in the southern states. A bond had been formed.

Over time, Hezekiah helped one after another of the slaves escape for the hills. Some were caught and brought back alive. Others were returned to the mission tied over the back of a horse.

"The dead ones was hung up on posts to rot, have the birds peck at their eyes—to be a lesson for the rest of 'em," Hezekiah explained.

Ultimately, a very cruel priest and an ambitious army officer formed a powerful alliance, and the beatings at the mission increased. Still, when he could in the weeks that followed, Christmas did what he could to help the Indian slaves escape . . . until one night he was rousted from his bed and dragged from the cramped room where he slept with more than two dozen Indian men, carried off to confront the padre and the colonel. There in the friar's office a pair of soldiers emerged from the shadows, a severely beaten Indian slung unconscious between them.

"The Injun was one you helped run off?"

Christmas nodded. "*Válgame purísima María*—dear Virgin Mary . . . I didn't blame the fella for telling 'em who it was helped him and others get away."

Now the priests and the Mexican soldiers knew who

was to blame for inciting their peace-loving slaves into revolt. Come morning, he would be tied to a post in front of the mission's Indian population and beaten, not only until he bled—but, explained the friar, until he died. A lesson to cower all the Indians at Mission San Gabriel.

"How'd you come to get away, Hezekiah?"

The freedman told how he had immediately flung his handlers from him, seizing a knife from a soldier's belt, then grabbing the closest man—the friar himself. With his sacred hostage, Christmas backed from the mission, making for the soldiers' horses they had tied outside the walls. It was there a scuffle took place, with the Mexican colonel giving his soldiers orders to shoot at Hezekiah despite his clutching the priest against him.

"*Dios mio!* More'n one bullet hit that mean ol' padre," Christmas admitted. "Many's the time I thort about it since, but I figger that soldier chief meant to kill the padre. *Malditos sean!* Curse them."

Hezekiah wheeled and leaped atop one of the horses, dragging away a second one to ride when the first grew too tired to push on into the mountains.

Three days later, he encountered a handful of runaways he helped to survive on nuts and rabbit meat until they could begin hunting larger game. And ever since Hezekiah had been in the mountains—getting word to the California missions that if the slaves would only try to escape, most could make it to freedom. Up here, far from the soldiers, he and the others had provided a refuge for runaway slaves, living out what he felt were the finest years of his life with his Indian wife and their children.

"Time to time, we watched white men come out of the east, climb out of the desert and cross over to the California missions—*y caballos quieren, por es vienen tan legitos*—for the horses they wanted they come all this way," Hezekiah explained. "Later on it was when one of the runaways told us these was Americans, come to steal Mexican horses and mules, take them Mexican animals—*quizás muchas*—many horses, back toward the States."

But Hezekiah Christmas never had any desire to make

himself known to the Americans. No urge to return east himself. As he explained it to Titus, he did not see himself as an American. Back there in the States, he would either be a slave in the South, or nothing more than a poor, second-class citizen in the North.

"An' back there to the west," Hezekiah said as he pointed over their shoulders at Mexican California, "I'd be no better off than the rest of these here poor *mansos* the Mexicans made their slaves."

"You been up here a long, long time," Bass said, "and never wanted to go back east?"

With a shrug, Christmas said, "I can't 'spect you to unnerstand."

"You're wrong, Hezekiah. I figger I know just how you feel."

"Y-you do unnerstand why I won't ever go back?" the Negro asked.

"Maybe I know 'cause I got me the same feelings as you at times." And Titus nodded. "Better you stay a man in between, here in this no-man's-land between California and them proper white folks in the states of America. Right here you're as free a man as any fella ever there was. Able to look any man in the eye."

"*Qui milagro es este!* What a miracle this is!" and Hezekiah grinned. "You unnerstand—just like you unnerstood when you busted me out'n that cage on the Mississap."

"*Si*, my friend. Man finds himself a place his heart's at peace, like you done," Bass finally admitted softly, "that man best be about putting down some roots."

"We watched your bunch ride through the pass for to steal the horses," Hezekiah declared late the next night when Williams and Smith finally stopped the herd to give them and the men a few hours of rest. "An' we watched you coming back again with all them horses. Figgered we might as well pick off a few of those Mexican horses from you ourselves."

"You and your red niggers was gonna steal some of our horses?" demanded Henry Daws.

The white men gathered at the two fires fell quiet while the Negro slowly turned toward Philip Thompson's group.

"Ain't that just like a Neegra!" Thompson himself cawed, made bold in the company of so many friends. "Go an' steal what another man's got by his own sweat!"

The others cackled with Thompson.

"You had plenty 'nough," Christmas said, easing round to the fire once more.

"Don't turn your back on me, you wuthless black son of a bitch!" Thompson growled. "I'll teach you to—"

"Stay where you are," Bass warned as he lunged to his feet, swallowed hard, and inched his hand toward the butt of that pistol stuffed in his belt.

"What? The ol' man's gonna stick up for this black-assed bastard!" Thompson roared, half bent with laughter.

"No, he ain't," Christmas claimed, his back still turned on Thompson. "No man's gotta stick up for me."

That dashed cold water on Thompson's raw laughter. "What'd you say to me, you black bastard?"

Now Hezekiah turned to peer over his shoulder. "Afore I come to California—I run onto lots of stupid white men like you. Whorin' and drinkin' up an' down the Mississap."

Bass watched how the firelight played off the growing red of Thompson's face.

"Black nigger or red nigger," Thompson growled, his hand tightening around the handle of his knife. "Neither one wuth the trouble it takes to kill 'em."

Titus turned toward the man, his pistol in plain view now, warning, "You aim to get to Hezekiah, gonna have to come through me first."

Easing his knife out of its rawhide scabbard, Thompson said to the men on either side of him, "If Bass yanks on that belt gun, you fellas shoot 'im dead."

John Bowers and Samuel Gibbon both grinned,

leveling their rifles at Scratch. Bowers said, "Be glad to 'blige him, Phil. Be glad to."

With that crooked smile widening, Thompson took another step toward Hezekiah—

"You gonna get yourself killed," Bill Williams warned him as he stood suddenly at the edge of the fire.

Tom Smith put his hand on Williams's arm. "You damn well better stay out of it, Bill. Phil's been wanting to cut his way into Bass for some time now."

"Ever since Bass stole back them horses from us at Robidoux's fort," Thompson confessed.

Williams protested, "I recollect there was a hull bunch of others took 'em back from us 'sides Bass—"

"But none of them bastards ever been standing so close to me as Titus Bass is right now."

Scratch asked, "That's et on you ever since, ain't it? What me and Meek and Joe Walker all done to you."

"Too damn long." Thompson's crooked smile grew cruel. "So I'll cut this black bastard's throat . . . then I'll open you up like a gutted hog."

"The man's good with a knife," Williams warned out of the corner of his mouth. "Damn, damn good, Scratch."

For a moment, Bass glanced at the eyes of the others as they pointed their rifles his way. Then he stared at Thompson while he told Williams, "I ain't never been partial to knives myself, Bill. But I allays hold my own in a fight. The rest of you,"—and he waved both arms to the other white men who were still gathered close—"just back off now. Give us some room for this li'l fandango Thompson wants to dance with me."

"Watch that Neegra!" Felix Warren bawled as Hezekiah rose to his feet.

"I'll kill the black nigger myself, Phil," Pete Harris offered.

"Just keep Bass out of it till I've cut this black-assed bastard into li'l red pieces."

As he slowly withdrew his own knife from his belt, Christmas asked, "He really good with a knife, Titus Bass?"

"Dunno, Hezekiah. Never see'd much fight in the man," Bass goaded, hoping his words might well prod Thompson into a blind lather. "He's always give up when it's come down to real fighting."

"G-give up?" Thompson squealed like a stuck pig, twisting his big knife this way and that in the firelight.

"Always let others do your fighting for you, ain'cha, Thompson!" Titus needled.

"Gonna kill you my own self here an' now—"

As the tall white man started toward Bass standing at the left side of the fire pit, Christmas surprised everyone by suddenly shoving Titus aside. That muscular heave sent Scratch sprawling into the legs of some bystanders as Hezekiah sprang into what open ground lay between the two white men—landing in a crouch, his skinning knife out before him. A weapon only half the size of Thompson's huge butcher's blade.

The trapper stopped, then a wicked smile slowly came across his face as he lumbered forward, feinting first this way, then that, side to side as he slowly advanced.

"Hezekiah—no!" Bass cried out in desperation as more of the California Indians appeared at the edge of the light.

Dick Owens bellowed, "Kill 'im, Phil!"

With a wild lunge, Thompson made a wide swipe with the butcher knife. Christmas vaulted backward as the white man's arm shot past in a blur, angling up the tip of his smaller knife so that it raked the underside of Thompson's forearm. With an anguished gasp, the trapper turned the wound over to inspect it there by the firelight, his eyes narrowing less in pain than in growing fury.

"Awright, you black sack of assholes," he grumbled. "You want me kill you first so bad—"

But Thompson was interrupted and kept from moving from that spot when Bill Williams bolted forward, pistol in hand. The instant the muzzle was jammed against Thompson's ribs, the trapper's mouth stopped moving. Nothing more than a round, wide hole in Thompson's face as his eyes glared down at the pistol and the hand that held that weapon.

"Leave 'im go, Solitaire!" Smith demanded. "This ain't none of our goddamn business."

"Drop the knife, Phil," Williams ordered, ignoring his partner.

Smith stepped closer in the next heartbeat. With his hand on his own pistol and a harsh edge to his voice, he said, "Maybeso I didn't make it so clear, Bill. I said this weren't none of our business."

That's when Williams finally turned to glare at Smith. "I'm making it my business, Peg-Leg. You got a problem with that, then you can take it up with me soon as I blow a goddamn hole in Thompson's lights."

"Y-you taking sides in something ain't your affair," Thompson hissed at Williams.

"He's right, Solitaire," Smith warned. "You're coming down on the wrong side of things here. I ain't gonna let you take the Neegra's side on this."

Pulling a pistol from his belt, Scratch declared, "Peg-Leg, it's Thompson on the wrong side all the way 'round. I won't stand for no man—Thompson or *you*—bringing harm to the fella what pulled our hash out of the fire yesterday morning."

"You think hard on that, Peg-Leg," Williams advised. "You an' Thompson 'bout to pull some soft-brained stunt. A damn fine way to thank the man what brung all these Injuns to help us throw back the greasers."

"They even saved your miserable life, Thompson," Bass growled.

"I wanna see your blood soaking into the dirt under my feet, Titus Bass," the trapper growled, twisting his big knife this way and that in the air.

"G'won back to your fire," Williams ordered.

"Now, dammit! I told you, Solitaire," Smith snarled. "I'm leading this outfit too an' I say Thompson don't have to go nowhere—"

Ignoring his partner, Williams interrupted by saying, "Told you go back to your fire, Thompson. Now get!"

For a moment, Thompson glared down at the pistol pressed into his ribs, then into Williams's face. Finally . . ."Awright."

As he turned on his heel, Thompson roughly shoved Bill's pistol aside, then slid the butcher knife back into its rawhide sheath.

Williams peered over at Smith. "Spit it on out, Peg-Leg. Like a mouthful of hornets—'pears you got some trouble with me."

"Wasn't none of yours to—"

"I made it mine."

Titus took a step closer to Smith. "Sounds to me you don't figger we owe our lives to Hezekiah Christmas?"

The one-legged trapper peered at the tall Negro with growing disdain. "Don't owe nothing to none of these red niggers," he grumbled. " 'Specially don't owe a thing to no black-assed renegade run off to live in the blanket with these Digger Injuns."

Bass watched Smith pivot away on his wooden pin. "Don't understand you, Peg-Leg." He waited until the redheaded trapper stopped and looked over his shoulder at him before he said, "We just come out of Californy with the biggest herd anyone ever stole . . . so we should be having us a hurraw right about now 'stead of fixin' to kill a friend what came to—"

"That black son of a bitch ain't no friend of mine!" Thompson roared from the nearby fire.

"Last I'll say is that son of a bitch and his red niggers better be turning back where they come from afore first light when we push on," Smith warned.

Just as Titus was opening his mouth to speak, Christmas beat him to it by saying, "We turning back, that's for sure. That desert down there ain't fit for the likes of man or horse, neither one. I ain't gonna waste the life of one of my men to help your sorry white asses from here on out. Come morning—you won't have to worry none 'bout Hezekiah Christmas and his *mansos.*"

Smith dragged the back of a hand beneath his nose in a gesture of real disdain. "Make sure you ain't here come sunrise." With that said, he returned to the other fire where he stood with his back to Williams and the rest.

"I go bed down out there with my men," Christmas quietly told Titus.

"You're welcome to sleep here with us—"

"No, we ain't welcome here with any of you," Hezekiah interrupted, beginning to step away.

Bass caught his bare, brown arm. "Promise me you won't leave afore we said our farewells."

Christmas's eyes flicked aside to stare over Bass's shoulder at the distant fire where Smith and Thompson stood among like-minded men. He finally gazed at Scratch. "Come morning, we'll say our good-byes . . . one more time, Titus Bass."

Scratch awoke with a start, twitching as the long arm locked around his neck. Sensing the pressure of the butcher's knife's sharp edge press against the bottom of his windpipe there just below the muscular arm that imprisoned his head.

"How's it feel to know this gonna be the last breath you ever take on earth, Titus Bass?"

He stared up into the dimly lit face of Philip Thompson, watching the firelight and shadow flicker across the cheekbones, the cruel curve of the lips as the man gleefully sneered down at Bass.

"You're a cockless woman, Thompson," he cursed, raspy with the sharp pressure against his throat. "Sneaking up on a sleepin' man so it can't be no fair fight."

"Gonna cut your throat," Thompson promised. "Like shooting a mad wolf. Don't have to be no fair fight to kill a mad wolf."

When Scratch slowly started to raise his right hand, he felt Thompson shove down on his throat with the knife, sensed the sharp edge press into the skin.

"I'll cut you afore you get that damned hand in the air," Thompson vowed. "Just want you be lookin' into my face when I split you open . . . so I can watch you die—"

A sudden gasp burst from Thompson's lungs, his eyes grown as big as Mexican dollars. On instinct alone, Scratch instantly twisted into Thompson's arm, raking the butcher knife across his throat as the big trapper went taut above him. A second, putty-wet slap made Thompson jerk a second time, his mouth dropping open as his eyes started to roll back in their sockets.

Shoving his elbow into Thompson's ribs, Bass felt the man's rigid muscles suddenly sag. He shoved himself out from under the trapper and rolled onto his hip, gasping for breath and putting his fingertips against the damp flesh wound gaping across his throat.

Two short arrows protruded from Thompson's back, halfway above midline, both buried deep.

The trapper sank to the side as his eyes went white.

Bass glanced at the fingers he took away from his neck wound, finding his flesh smeared with blood. Then in disbelief he looked over his shoulder, finding Hezekiah standing at the edge of that corona of firelight, a third arrow nocked in the bowstring, held at ready. Behind him stood an arch of more than a dozen of his warriors, the strings of their bows pulled taut to their cheekbones.

He finally sucked in a deep breath of air, shocked at how good it felt. How could he have been so foolish to sleep so hard that Thompson got the jump on him? Was it that he believed he was among friends—safe enough here, far from Blackfoot country? With Thompson ready to make good on his threats, how could he have allowed himself to drop his guard?

For what seemed like a long, long time, the only sound besides his own ragged breathing was the crackle of the two fires, dry cedar popping sparks into the black of that desert night beneath a milky quarter-moon. Bass peered up at Hezekiah, the deepest of unspoken gratitude for the bowman in his eyes.

Then his attention was drawn away to the far side of their encampment—finding Felix Warren and Frank Curnutt standing stock still there at the edge of the flickering light. Warren had a pistol in his right hand, a tomahawk in his left. Curnutt held only his round-barreled smoothbore.

Titus swallowed hard, then growled, "You niggers keeping watch to make sure Thompson kill't me?"

The two didn't say a thing. Didn't move a muscle

either. Instead, they kept staring at Bass, looking to the Indians, and glaring at the big, baldheaded Negro.

"Speak up, fellas," Bill Williams ordered as he emerged into the firelight. "Answer the man's question."

Curnutt started to wag his head, not as if he were denying a thing. Only a gesture of futility.

"You was in deep with Thompson, wasn't you?" Titus demanded, clambering to his feet. "Fixing to murder me together."

"N-no," said Warren. "Only Thompson. We knowed he was gonna kill Bass but we was only—"

"But that Neegra kill't Thompson!" Curnutt squealed with anguish. "Kill't a white man!"

"Sounds to me like what Thompson was fixin' to do was murder," Williams growled, watching Smith hobble into the light. "How 'bout you, Peg-Leg?"

Smith wagged his head with reluctance. "Ain't really murder when it's atween two fellas, Bill."

"Wasn't no fair fight—that Neegra shootin' Thompson!" Warren protested.

"You fellas almost had you a hand in this bastard killing me," Bass grumbled as he started around the fire for Felix Warren.

Both Curnutt and Warren started to move, but immediately realized Williams had his two pistols pointed at them. They stared at the muzzles while Bill said, "When a nigger jumps a man in his sleep—'thout it being a fair fight . . . that's a murder, any way you lay your sights, Peg-Leg."

"Tell you what, you sonsabitches." Bass stopped some twelve feet from Warren and Curnutt. "I'll give you a better chance'n you and Thompson was gonna give me."

"I'll kill you, you come any closer," Curnutt warned with a high, feral pitch in his voice.

Titus snorted with a raw gust of laughter, saying, "I ain't gonna kill you like you niggers was gonna do me."

"You want me take their guns?" asked Jake Corn as he stepped up.

Curnutt's and Warren's eyes flicked here and there

around them as they watched the other Americans gather close, imploring Thompson's other comrades.

"Maybeso we better, Jake," Williams decided. "Don't let us have no trouble outta you two."

At first both men refused to let go of their weapons when Corn and Coltrane hurried in to grab hold of the firearms and that tomahawk.

"I'd as soon kill you both right now my own self," Williams warned.

Smith lunged into the compact group, shoving Jake and Roscoe away as he protested, "These two ain't done nothing to Bass, nothing to any one of you!"

"Get outta the way, Peg-Leg," Williams demanded. "They don't drop them guns—you're likely to get hurt too when I start shootin'."

Peg-Leg whirled on Williams. "M-me? Y-you 'pear to be forgetting just who the hell's the brains in this here outfit—"

"Shuddup, Peg-Leg. I ain't got no more stomach for you," Williams snapped. "Clear outta the way."

Smith took a long moment to stare into the muzzles of those two pistols Williams held before him, then back into the old trapper's face. "Got no more stomach for me? W-what's that mean? Why, you'd been nothin' weren't it for me asking you to ride along to California with me!"

"That tears the blanket, Peg-Leg. You go your way and the rest of us go ours."

"Go my own way? You're talking crazy, Solitaire! You can't mean . . . dammit, most of them horses belong to me!"

"Fair is fair, Bill," Titus said as he came up to stand beside Williams. "Let him have his rightful share afore you send him off."

"Send me off?" Smith's eyes narrowed into slits. "Send me off, is it? You low-down back-stabbin' Diggers! None of you have any of them horses weren't for my hand in leadin' you all to California!"

"Just be satisfied I don't do to you what Thompson was gonna do to me or Hezekiah . . . all because you been covering his back ever' step of the way," Bass stated.

Silas Adair asked, "What you figger's fair for the three of 'em, Bill?"

"These here two can go with Peg-Leg in the morning, I s'pose."

Bass watched their shoulders sag with something akin to relief. "You figger to cut 'em loose short of fixin's?"

"W-what's that mean?" Felix Warren demanded.

"Take their guns from 'em," Williams instructed. "We'll give 'em back come morning. Leave you a dozen balls and enough powder for those shots. Give each of you something to ride, along with a ol' horse or two for vittles to get across the desert."

"What you fixin' to do with me, Solitaire?" Peg-Leg demanded haughtily.

"You get the same," Williams stated flatly. "No more. No less."

"We're partners, Bill!" Smith roared. "I led this hull bunch out to California—"

"You been doing your damnedest to get sideways with me near ever' step of the way back, Peg-Leg. None of these fellas know much of what you been cookin' up in your head," Williams menacingly said to his longtime friend.

"These here are my friends, Bill!" Smith roared. "I can't let you—"

"You can't let me?" Williams interrupted quietly. "Tell you what you can do. You can take what horses I'll give you, and it's yours to decide if'n you take these two bastards along with you or not." Williams glanced over at Warren and Curnutt, then returned his steady gaze to Smith. "If'n it were me, I'd leave these snake bellies to make things out on their own. Them an' Thompson put you in a real fix, now didn't they?"

Smith's hands clenched into balls of fury in front of him. "Sounds like you're stealing all my horses from me, Solitaire."

Before Williams had a chance to utter a word, Bass

stepped up and stuck his face right up close to Smith's, saying, "Way I see it, Bill's making it more'n fair to give you and these two back-killers a fighting chance at that desert out there. If'n I was you—come mornin', I'd take him up on it . . . and get."

16

———— ◆ ————

Soon as it was light enough for a man to see, Bill Williams and the others watched as Thomas L. Smith cut out a small part of the herd for himself. Peg-Leg had elected to take Curnutt and Warren with him, if not for companionship in that lonely expanse of desert they were staring in the face, then for their help in wrangling the three hundred horses that the other raiders felt Smith was due for seeing them through to the valleys of southern California.

"I reckon you know the way if any man does, Tom," Williams said when the horses had been divided off and the sky was graying hundreds of miles away to the east. "You go on back by way of the Ammuchabas, you'll fare good."

Smith's eyes narrowed as he glared down on his old partner from horseback. "You make it sound like you ain't coming back through the Ammuchaba villages."

Taking a step back, the lanky old trapper said, "We ain't."

Startled, Smith asked, "H-how you going back, Bill?"

"This here's your chance, Peg-Leg," Williams repeated

mysteriously. "I'm doin' this 'stead of killing you an' them others outright—"

"*Why* you treating me this way?" Peg-Leg demanded, clearly unrepentant.

"You come down on the side of murdering a friend of mine in his sleep. I got nothin' more to say to you. Use this chance, Tom."

For a moment Smith pressed his lips tightly together as if about to spew some venom, then he vowed, "I'll see you back to the mountains, Solitaire." His dark, dangerous eyes snapped over to glare at Scratch. "See you back in the mountains too, Titus Bass."

They watched the trio pull away into the murky, predawn light as another two dozen of the horses ambled off from the herd to join Smith's animals. Bass, Williams, and the others had seen to it that the three men were equipped with a horn of powder, enough lead to see them to one of the southern posts, and only enough fixings to keep them alive in the deadly crossing that lay ahead.

That seemed fitting to Scratch, really seemed more than fair, considering they all had a hand, one way or another, in scheming to murder a man in what was clearly less than a fair fight. Maybeso Peg-Leg didn't have a direct role in plotting or carrying out Thompson's scheme to cut Bass's throat . . . but Smith had made no bones about siding with Thompson and his kind ever since the day all twenty-four of the raiders set off from Robidoux's Fort Uintah.

Even now on this red, raw, desert-summer morning as the thousands of horses grew restless—it made Bass wonder what he himself had ever done to Tom Smith that would cause Peg-Leg to throw his weight on the side of Phil Thompson and his compatriots. It simply couldn't be Scratch's hand in taking back those horses Smith, Thompson, and the others stole from Fort Hall and the Shoshone chief named Rain early in that winter of '39.

Something far deeper, something down under the skin had gnawed away at Thompson across the intervening seasons. Something Bass was coming to realize that he himself had kept from his conscious thoughts, a matter that had come to trouble him so deeply over the last few years it went to the core of everything he was as a man.

With the death of the beaver trade, the summer rendezvous had withered right along with it. And with that demise of everything these beaver men had placed all stock in—their world was shattered, destroyed, gone forever. With nothing at all to replace it.

Not that the beaver men didn't have anything to do in the mountains. They could choose to live with the tribes moving slowly with the seasons, or they could stay busy hunting meat for the fur posts, perhaps even ride into California for some horses. But . . . any of that was nothing more than a vain attempt to fill the real, gaping void of what had torn apart their lives.

Never again would they be what they had been. Beaver men. A rare breed with an unwritten code between them. They endured shoulder to shoulder against all enemies, and stood at one another's backs when death loomed near. Never again could they be what once had given their lives worth.

But now . . . now that they were no longer beaver men, cracks opened up in that code. White men stole from white men, and from the friendlies too. And finally . . . white men had turned on white men.

If outright, cold-blooded murder had come to the mountains, Titus knew the West would never again be the same. The West he had come to know was as good as gone, good as dead and all but buried.

As Bass watched those three men and their horses fade beyond the distant curve of the earth, disappearing into the desert dawn, he was suddenly struck with a remembrance like clabbered milk. Silas Cooper, Bud and Billy too, had stolen his beaver before fleeing the mountains with their booty, land pirates who preyed on the labors of other men. The remembrance lay inside him like meat gone bad.

While they had lied, cheated, and stolen from him— Silas, Bud, and Billy had never murdered. Rotten as they were, especially Cooper, none of the three had never committed any evil worse than thievery. Leastways, what Scratch knowed of.

There had always been men Titus would just as soon not ride or camp with in these mountains. Except for those three thieves who ran off with his furs back in the spring of 1827, there had never been a question of him trusting the partners he hooked up with. Even those company men and booshways he stayed as far away from as possible because they simply were not his sort of men, he knew the chances were good he could even count on them when the stakes were high and the last raise of the night was called.

That's just the way things were in the mountains. *Were*. The way things *had been* in the wild, raw yonder he had come to call home. The unspoken code of these first, hardy few was no more. Right now he found himself more sure than he had ever been that his was not just a dying breed, but a breed that had already been rubbed out.

"Let's get them pack mules loaded!" Williams cried as he turned around to face the half circle of Americans. "We're riding out in less time it takes you niggers to piss in the sand!"

They scattered as Hezekiah's Indians shook out their coarse straw mats and thick Navajo blankets, then rolled them together and tied them over their shoulders beside those quivers of short, deadly arrows. Quivers almost empty after that furious battle with the Mexicans.

Titus quickly looked over the shorter, brown men until he spotted the tall one. "Hezekiah!"

Christmas turned, finding Scratch coming, and smiled in that ebony face. "Titus Bass. These white men you come here with, they ain't going back by the Ammoochabees?"

"The booshway figgers on us tracking farther north. It's high summer now. Water's drying up even more this far south. We're gonna lose a bunch of these horses no matter—"

"We can tell you where you'll find the springs,"

Hezekiah interrupted, extending his arm to point off to the northeast.

"S-springs," Scratch echoed. "You can tell us?"

Bass hurried Hezekiah over to Williams and announced what information the freedman could provide.

"Why don't you come and show us?" Titus asked, hopeful.

Peering over the other trappers for a moment, the tall Negro could not help but see how that invitation nettled some of the white men. He wagged his head and sighed, "I belong with my men—"

"Bring them too." Titus interrupted. "The Bent brothers got 'em a Negress for a cook over to their fort. Her husband's the blacksmith—a Neegra too. You damn well ain't the only black-skinned son of a bitch in the mountains—"

"No, it's better I show you where you'll find them springs are—let you go on with your own kind, Titus Bass."

And before Scratch could protest any further, Hezekiah dropped to one knee there before them, motioning Williams and Bass to crouch with him. A handful of others came up to stand over the three. First, Christmas shoved some sandy dirt into a footlong mound. Here and there he placed some pebbles, other places he used the tip of one index finger to burrow some tiny, shallow indentions in his crude map.

"Watch the rocks, Titus. Count the rocks," Hezekiah instructed gravely. "Here. Here. And here too—no matter how hot it gets, you'll still find water. But less'n you count the rocks, I fear you'll miss the springs. Water comes out up again' the rocks. But mind you—not all them rocks got water by 'em. Count the rocks as you go an' you'll be sure which ones."

The white men closely studied the map the Negro scratched on the ground. Then one by one Williams, then Bass stood and dusted the knees of their leggings.

"Why'n't you come 'long with me?" Titus pleaded.

"My people are back there." And Christmas pointed. "In those mountains."

"Go fetch your family, catch up to us. We'll damn well go slow with this herd so you can find us. We get over the mountains we figger to sell the horses and you'll get your share of them wild ones—"

"Better I stay where there ain't no question that I'm a free man," Christmas cut off Bass's argument, looking into the faces of the other white men not all ready to turn over any of their horses to a Neegra gone to the blanket. "Right here's where I found some li'l peace for the first time in my life, Titus Bass. It's plain on the faces of these others that back in that land where you're headed with your horses . . . they won't never look at me like a free man."

"Things don't have to be that way up high enough, back far enough you won't likely see 'nother white face but mine for a long time to come," Scratch explained, hopelessness starting to sink in. "Why, there's even a ol' friend of mine—a Neegra named Beckwith—was a war chief for the Crow, my wife's people. This Beckwith was—"

"After what you done to help me all them years ago— it's enough for Hezekiah Christmas that my friends helped save your life, Titus Bass," he interrupted. " 'Long with the lives of your friends too."

Titus looked his old friend in the eye. "Damn if you ain't as good a man as ever come to the mountains, Hezekiah Christmas. Which way your stick float now?"

He sighed thoughtfully, then said, "We'll go back by way of the ground where we kill't the Mexicans. Gather our arrows out of the dirt, pull 'em from the dead bodies too, afore goin' on back to our wives and chirrun."

"Your grandchildren too, Hezekiah." He had felt this same sentiment welling up in him before. Nonetheless, after all those last and final farewells he had endured, the partings never got any easier. "Damn if you ain't gone and discombobulated things all over for me."

"Why you say that?"

"I set you free back on the Natchez Trace long ago . . . and here you gone and not just saved my ol' hide once, but twice't in two days!"

"We're square, Titus Bass. Never you make no mistake of that."

"But you pulled my hash outta the fire twice—"

"Don't you see," Hezekiah snorted, "if'n you'd never set me free from that slaver's cage, never pertected me when them slavers come after us, I'd never been out here to save your poor white hide two times for good measure!"

Scratch stepped close to the Negro, held out his hand, and they clasped as Bass said, "You give me back my life, twice, Hezekiah."

"An' I'd save your worthless white ass again if'n it come down to it, Titus," Christmas promised as he gripped Scratch's wrist in his big, black hand, the veins prominent on its back like an oiled, knotted Kentucky riverboatman's rope. "No matter how many times God His own self puts it in my hands to save you . . . I'll do it again without question—'cause I'd never had this life with these good Injun people less'n you set me free and took me north to the Ohio."

Scratch felt the instant sting of tears burn his eyes. "You're as good a man as ever there was, Hezekiah Christmas."

The Negro grinned as daylight limned across the desert spread at their feet. "You give me back my life years ago. 'Bout time I done something to repay you. Now we are square."

"Just 'bout as square as any two men could ever be."

All around him the others were mounting up and Williams was barking orders for the march, sending men out to sweep in the sides of their monstrous herd of California horses. Titus finally released his old friend's forearm.

"You ever come to the northern mountains, you best ask for me, hear?"

Hezekiah nodded with a smile. "Count on that. I ask for Titus Bass."

"It's for damn sure most folks gonna point you the right way you ask for me."

"If ever I turn my back on this world here, I find you, Titus Bass. I find you no matter what."

• • •

He had watched the Negro turn without another word
and gesture for his men to mount upon their half-wild
California horses, shooing a small herd before them as
they wheeled about and started back up the long, grassy
slopes dotted with scrub cedar and the last of the lean
Joshua trees, heading for their homeland and their families.

Once the others were on their way, Hezekiah stopped
his horse and reined around to have himself a look down
the slope, long black legs dangling down from the
rounded belly of his short, California pony. Bass held his
arm high, outstretched, with his big-brimmed hat in his
hand. Side to side he waved it in one long arc, and when
he saw Hezekiah hold his bow aloft, Bass swallowed
down the bitter clog of regret that lay thick in his throat.
He turned his horse around and pulled his hat down over
the sweat-stained bandanna.

All he had to do now was get back to the mountain
country, cross over, and sell off his share of those horses
that would survive the deadly crossing. Spring to spring.
From one clump of rocks to another . . . until he could
gaze into her eyes again. Just to see her and the little ones
again, he would cross this fiery furnace of a desert, he
would crawl all the way over those high and terrible
places. To hold them once again, and promise never,
never to ride away to California again.

Family. The feelings he had for his own kin often
made him think back on those two gentile Indians the
Franciscan friars had baptized with names symbolizing
their new Catholic status. It made perfect sense for Frederico and Celita to turn back to the mountains with
Hezekiah's fighting men now. They belonged to that
growing band of runaways more than they would ever
belong to any cluster of cowed and brutalized neophyte
slaves at the Mission San Gabriel. They were free again,
just as Christmas had been given his freedom near the
banks of the Mississippi three decades before.

Many times across the next weeks Scratch had vowed

he'd drink that whole muddy river by himself . . . if only they could find more water.

They found that first spring—right where Hezekiah said it would be. Nestled in among the rocks where the horses fought to get at the pools formed as the warm, underground water bubbled to the surface. Williams had them lay over a long day and night at the spring before continuing the next leg of their crossing.

That hot, dry, late-summer air sucked every drop of moisture right out of the men and the animals with a relentless brutality as they moved east-northeast, transcribing a path between each intervening landmark until they reached the second spring three days later. There they found a little less of the warm water bubbling out of the ground. Summer was torturing the desert, drying up what narrow ribbons of rivers had briefly flowed weeks ago, relentlessly sucking the seasonal life out of the underground springs a drop at a time as their subterranean moisture evaporated into air heated by a long-riding, merciless sun that refused to go down while it baked a man's skin the way a narrow strip of gristle would sizzle in an iron skillet.

By then they had begun to lose horses—a few at first—the weakest, the youngest perhaps. Williams and the others made sure the six Ute broodmares they had driven all the way to and back out of California were the first to drink at every stop, and the first to be allowed what skimpy grass they came across when it came time to rest the herd. The mares were vital to them all—man and beast alike—dragging the herd and the raiders all back to the mountains by a primal lure compelling them to return to their young.

Titus was beginning to think he knew how both life and death now clung to those mares.

Every time Titus would shade his eyes and turn in the sweaty saddle to gaze upon their back trail, he would spot those dark forms wavering with a waterlike quality out there on the pale horizon. Poor, played-out horses that could no longer go on—both those that somehow still managed to stand weaving with their heads hung in defeat, and those that had already accepted defeat, their legs crumpling in sheer exhaustion and dehydration, lying sprawled, heaving on the sunbaked hardpan of the desert to breathe their last: waiting, waiting, waiting as the skies above them slowly filled with the patient, high-soaring, black-winged birds of death sinking lower and lower toward their exhausted prey.

Never before had the buzzards and vultures had it so good in this land void of most everything but a slow, agonizing death. An emptiness filled with little more than arid heat, a limitless expanse that not only sucked the moisture right out of a man but also leached his hope and will to go on, drop by relentless drop.

He dreamed of Absaroka through those days on the precipice of hell—his mind's eye yearning on the high, lofty snowfields mantling the mountains, the green of grasses tall enough to brush a horse's belly, the blues and teals of streams or ponds lying beneath a never-ending sky. He dreamed of her still as the bottom went out from under him and his horse sank beneath him, tumbling into the sand.

Bass lay there exhausted, totally unmoving too, aware only on some nonmobile plane of urgency—listening to the horse grunting helpless as it attempted to get up, whimpering low in its throat because the animal realized in its own primitive way that it would never get back on its legs.

He closed his eyes, feeling how the sun stabbed right on through his thin cloth shirt, pierced the buckskin leggings—wondering if he would ever get back up. Titus tried to dream of the cool of Absaroka again one last time before it would be too late and he could remember no more.

"Bass."

He blinked, looking up, finding the outline of a face hovering right over his—totally in shadow because the man's head completely blocked out the sun. Squinting, he blinked again as the man's salty, stinging sweat trickled into his eyes. The sweat in his own made everything swim, but Titus finally made sense out of the features, that pale, blond hair turning gray.

"Ros . . . Roscoe."

"Brung a horse for you," Coltrane said sparingly as he pulled on Scratch's arms, slowly dragging Bass to his feet.

His mouth pasty, tongue thick and slow, Titus asked, "How come you—"

"Ain't leaving a one of us to die," Coltrane explained, likely stringing more words together than he had in a month of Sundays. "You're steady enough here, I'll get your outfit."

Roscoe dragged Bass's saddle from beneath the dying horse, then cinched it onto another of the spare animals he brought over, its legs plodding, big hooves scuffing furrows in the hard sand.

Without a word, Coltrane made a stirrup by weaving his fingers together and hoisted Titus into the saddle.

Just staring down at the short, squat man made him feel more clearheaded, less woozy, despite the compelling heat. As he watched the hundreds of horses continue to plod by, recognizing one lone trapper after another strung out there at the edge of the dwindling herd, Titus was suddenly struck with the realization that Roscoe had just spoken more words than the man had ever uttered to him before.

"W-why?" he asked when Coltrane remounted and their horses lumbered into a shuffling gait once more.

"I know you'd do the same for me."

Then Roscoe Coltrane reined away, saying no more.

For the rest of that long, sizzling afternoon, Scratch's thoughts dwelled on those few words spoken by a man not given much to speech at all. "Ain't leaving a one of us to die." Then he would think again of, "I know you'd do the same for me."

It gave him enough hope that there might be a few still left who remembered the glory days, remembered the old ways. Men who still fervently clung to the code.

Spring by spring, with long stretches of relentless heat in between the warm seeps when they did their level best to rest the horses, short nights when they traveled in the

starlit darkness, feeling their way along past the landmarks Hezekiah Christmas noted for them. Spring by
spring, the summer aged on them—days grown so old
and parched they began to find less and less water. The
land was drying up about the time they reached a country
more rumpled. If nothing else, a stunted and scrawny
vegetation prickled the surface of a changing panorama.
And then—there in the distance one sunrise as they
slowly brought the herd to a halt for the day near a dry
lake bed—Bass believed he sighted a ragged skyline
where the orange of a new day was brushing itself clear
across the uneven horizon. From one end of the earth to
the other.

"Elias—lookee there and tell me what you see," he
prodded as they came out of their saddles that late-summer morning.

"Them hills?"

"More'n hills," Silas Adair ventured as he came down
on his good leg, still favoring the other with its wound so
long in healing.

Titus nodded. "Maybeso the mountains."

"Which'uns?" Jake Corn asked.

"Dunno what they're called," Bass said. "If'n they be
the ones I'm figgering on."

"Where they rise?" Silas inquired.

"Far south of the Salty Lake. We crossed below 'em
coming down the Green."

Excitement brightened Corn's parched face. "W-we
come that far? You mean we're back in the Rocky Mountains?"

"A'most," Adair declared wistfully.

It was a remarkable moment as the Americans stripped
the damp saddles and soggy blankets off their horses,
picketing the riding animals in the scrub vegetation before
they rolled out their dusty bedrolls and lay down to wrap
themselves around a few hours' sleep while the sun came
up behind that distant, saw-toothed skyline. Hope crept
back into their parched souls, hope itself beckoning from
the very edge of the earth.

• • •

Bass slowly rolled over there atop his sweaty blanket in the late-afternoon heat and peered from underneath the wide brim of his felt hat. He hadn't been sure what he saw flitting in and out of the nearby rocks—not sure at all even why he had awakened to sight the merest hint of motion. Whatever it was . . . *who*ever it was, hadn't made a sound yet. Nothing that alarmed any of the dozing men, not a noise to spook any of their horses.

That jumble of rocks lay at one side of what they had left of the herd after those weeks of dry, desert crossing—something on the order of half the horses they had driven east over Cajon Pass. The rest had perished mile after grueling mile back there in the wastes before the trappers reached this rocky, canyon country where rattlesnakes and jackrabbits abounded.

For a good part of this day those huge boulders had provided little shelter for the weary men, but now that the sun was in its final quadrant of the sky, the glare was threading its way through a scattering of wispy clouds, no longer scorching the skin-clad figures curled atop their dust-caked, threadbare blankets.

In the shadow of those iron-red rocks, more of the forms showed themselves, then were gone with a wolf spider's quickness. Titus wasn't sure if they were human or just some overcurious critter. There—a flicker of hair. Next, a flitting glimpse of skin tanned so brown their hides blended right into the sere-colored boulders. So quick the movement could have been that of an antelope fleeing a predator . . . or maybe the movement of the predator itself circling in on its prey.

Slowly he extended his left arm as if stretching, his fingers tapping Kersey's elbow. "Elias!" he whispered under his breath. "Lookit the rocks. Tell me them ain't red niggers."

Cracking one eye and slowly shifting his head, Kersey peered at the rocks warily. "Diggers."

"I was 'fraid of that," Bass grumbled. "Trouble be—they don't seem scare't of us."

"Only one reason for that, I'd wager," Jake Corn whispered under the floppy hat he had laying on his face. "They likely got us outnumbered four or five to one."

Kersey shifted his rifle slowly. "Maybe they just got their curiosities up an' don't really mean no harm—"

"Don't be chuckleheaded, Jake. Them brownskins wouldn't be skulking around if'n they didn't mean us no harm," Bass snorted as he sat up suddenly, wrenching up the rifle where he had it pinned between his legs. "Bill!"

Scratch had no sooner spit out that alarm than the Indians took form, bolting up from the boulders. Shrieking, they boiled out of their hiding places in the nearby rocks. Almost as one, the groggy trappers snapped awake, snatching up weapons and bellowing commands or curses in their surprise.

Quickly his eyes raked left, then right across the rocks, looking for which one might prove to be the squat enemy's leader. But Titus could not tell which of the poor, naked brown men might be commanding the rest. Even more of them washed over the rocks in waves.

"Make your first shot count, boys!" Scratch bellowed at those around him as the trappers threw themselves down behind what skimpy baggage they were dragging back to the mountains. "We might not get us a second one."

"Blazes!" Williams thundered over his shoulder as he plopped on his belly and slid the barrel of his rifle atop a small pack of furs. "Bring up them other guns!"

Rising onto one knee, Titus took aim offhand at the flitting forms charging in a zigzag toward the trappers' camp across a wide front. He was the first to fire. An instant later a half dozen guns exploded. A heartbeat behind them even more. Beyond the pall of gray gunsmoke, brown bodies flopped onto the pale, sandy soil. Writhing, screaming, clutching at glistening red wounds penetrating their sun-blackened bodies.

That sudden, unremitting horror knocking holes in their ranks brought the rest skidding to a dusty halt. Some knelt to grab their wounded and their dead, turning in their tracks to drag bodies back to the rocks as more than a hundred voices cried out for retribution in a frightening cacophony.

"Merciful a'mighty!" Silas Adair cried. "How the hell many of 'em are there?"

"*What* the hell are they is what I wanna know!" Charles Swift asked.

"Diggers!" Scratch yelled as he dug out a lead ball from his pouch and thumbed it into the muzzle of his rifle without taking the time for a patch. He could tell the lands and grooves of the bore were already fouling with powder.

"Usual' they're more nuisance than trouble," Williams growled. "But this arternoon I s'pose they figger we're easy pickings—"

He and the rest were suddenly interrupted, falling quiet the instant they became aware of the herd: hundreds of horses neighed and whinnied, growing nervous, frightened by the unexpected gunfire. In a matter of moments, the horses would be heeling about, thundering away across the broken canyonland.

"They come for the horses?" Reuben Purcell asked. "Let the li'l bastards have some of our goddamned horses!"

Bass angrily rammed the ball home, eyeing the Diggers as they appeared to be forming up for another charge. "They want our plunder too, Rube."

"Shit!" Williams muttered, rolling close with his rifle. "An' we was almost back to the Rocky Mountings with them horses too."

Answering the cry from one throat, the enemy swarmed out of the rocks for another assault. Midway to the white men, most of the Indians stopped to fire their short bows—some standing, others dropping to their knees—then yanked more of their short, deadly arrows from rabbitskin quivers looped over their walnut-brown shoulders.

Here in the desert of the Great Basin, these impoverished, barefooted people subsisted on tiny animals, insects, and even an occasional wild or stray horse they managed to capture. With such a capricious and precarious existence, Bass realized, it was no surprise that these Diggers were emboldened by the wealth of the white men—compelled to attack for no loftier reason than survival itself.

The white man's plunder, not to mention those hundreds upon hundreds of enticing horses, together represented a continued existence to these primitive, feral, distrustful Indians.

Polette Labrosse grunted next to Scratch.

Bass immediately spun on his knee, catching the half-breed Frenchman as the man collapsed, clutching one of those tiny arrows where it was lodged in the muscles of his neck. Labrosse laced his fingers around the shaft, tugging frantically as he crumpled onto the wind-polished hardpan desert sand. The blood was dark, so dark it appeared to be about as black as a glistening Popo Agie tar as it oozed through the half-breed's fingers.

"C-cain't get it out!" he gurgled, bright gushes pouring from his tongue, spilling down his chin.

"Leave it!" Scratch ordered, enfolding the man in his arms, squeezing him against his chest as Labrosse began to gag his life away. He knew the man was good as dead where they sat.

Polette Labrosse pulled his head away from Bass's chest, sighed a little as he gasped, "Kill dem for me, Scratch. Kill dem all, would you?"

Without another noisy gurgle, the half-breed's eyes rolled back and he went limp in Scratch's arms, surrendering to that blessed unconsciousness come as he lost a gush of blood from his mouth. Titus let the man sink gently to the sand, then whirled around on his knee, dragging out his priming horn.

Sprinkling a hurried spray of fine priming powder, he dragged the frizzen back over the pan and yanked back on the rear trigger as he jerked the rifle into position against his shoulder. Once more, the enemy was everywhere around them. So many of them rushing in that they became a blur.

But in gazing down his barrel, it wasn't the charge that snagged Scratch's attention. It was some two dozen short,

brown warriors turning away from the charge unexpect-
edly, wheeling aside to make a wide loop around the
trappers' camp where they reached the outskirts of the
herd.

Waving their arms and screaming like demons, the
Diggers succeeded in spooking the nervous horses. Bolting off, their tails held high and their eyes as big as Mexican dollars, the animals scattered this way and that,
racing north in a leaderless stampede.

"Ah, shit!" Williams bellered like a buffalo bull with
its bangers caught in catclaw brush.

"There go our goddamned horses!" Purcell screeched
in pain.

Not only were the trappers under attack by an overwhelming number of daring bowmen . . . but in one fell
swoop the white men had just lost all their hard-won
California horses.

17

───────────── ◆ ─────────────

Somehow they managed to hold the Diggers back that third furious charge, then a fourth, but less concerted, rush too.

Between each wave of brown raiders, in those nerve-racking interludes while the trappers prepared for the next assault, the arrows never stopped falling out of the sky or whispering through the brush—most of the missiles falling harmlessly among the stunted cedar and sage. But a few of the deadly stone points randomly struck close to some of the men, causing no more than a nuisance.

But what proved even worse was that, over time, more than two dozen of the arrows—their small, stone tips meant for bringing down rabbits—did manage to strike much bigger targets: tormenting the last of the riding horses individual trappers had picketed close at hand, in camp. What with all the gunfire, screaming warriors, and a steady rain of stone-tipped arrows, these few frightened animals were being driven even more mad, becoming even more noisy as they fought their pins and handlers.

Then one of the riding mules collapsed with a brassy

breee-hawwwww, spraying piss over two nearby trappers as it went down in a spraddle-legged heap. Two of the men promptly plopped down on the damp ground between the dying animal's legs, employing its heaving rib cage as a breastwork.

"Lookit them li'l brown niggers!" Dick Owens cried, pointing at the two dozen or so warriors who had raced in a wide loop around the trappers' camp and were scampering away after the fleeing herd.

"They'll run from now clear to Judgment Day," John Bowers declared. "Never gonna catch them California horses!"

But it was only a matter of minutes before those Diggers appeared to realize the futility of their footrace, grinding to a halt and turning around out there against the distant horizon. Failing to herd those frightened, stolen horses, the warriors sprinted back to rejoin the fight.

Moment by moment now, the brown noose formed by those Digger warriors perceptibly drew tighter and tighter around the white men. And as it did, the Indians were sure to grow more bold, certain to inch all the closer with their deadly bows. With the sheer number of arrows landing among them, the first of those terrible little stone-tipped missiles pierced Toussaint Marechal's thigh. Then another arrow clipped Francois Deromme in the arm. The damned things came floating down at an arch, falling out of the late-afternoon sun, finding a man here or there. No matter where the arrows struck—in the arm, or the leg—they managed to leave a nasty and oozy wound, even where a tiny flint point slashed along Joseph Lapointe's skull, scraping a bloody furrow just beneath that skin from the outer edge of his eye clear back to where it protruded from his ear, dripping crimson on his shoulder.

With a sudden grunt of surprise, Bass sensed the stone tip pierce the thick ham of his left buttock.

"Damn you, sonsabitches!" he roared while collapsing onto his opposite hip, seizing the arrow's shaft in his free right hand.

Only meat, he brooded as he gave the shaft a tentative

tug. The torment was white hot, making him clamp his eyes shut with the diminishing waves of sharp, piercing pain—but he kept tugging nonetheless. No bone—nothing but meat—for that tip to bury itself into. Nothing at all like ol' Bridger's arrowpoint, left to calcify in his back for more than three years.* So he managed to pluck the damned thing out of his ass with an agonizing, teeth-clenching struggle.

The sheer oozy tenderness of the wound, not to mention the ignominy of where he'd been shot this time, only served to make him all the madder at these exasperating enemies. Doing his best to shift his weight onto the opposite knee, Titus hurried through the ritual of reloading without wasting time digging for a greased patch to nestle the huge lead ball he shoved against the grains of powder he already had poured down the long barrel.

Aim, fire . . . then reload again—while the Diggers screamed at every charge and sang their death songs with every retreat. Aim, fire . . . then reload—while the trappers around him cried out when they were struck with an arrow, all of them cursing their little brown enemies, or shouting a fading encouragement to one another.

Damn, Scratch sulked angrily, chewing on the inside of his cheek, realizing just how thirsty he had become as their fight ground on and on. Just to think of it: here they were now, caught out in this godforsaken wilderness fit only for frightened ground rats, emaciated jackrabbits, and hairy spiders the size of a man's tin cup—finding themselves with all but a handful of their horses run off. Put afoot here after all they'd gone through to steal those California horses, to rub the Mexicans' noses in their theft. Stranded now in this blazing desert with no way out but to walk.

And to top things off, Bass knew with that jagged, seepy wound soaking the back of his breechclout, he wouldn't be sitting a horse for days to come!

As much as the Diggers tried their damnedest to inch

---

* *Ride the Moon Down*

in close enough to attempt one final, deadly rush—they never worked up the courage to see it through. Wounded as some of the trappers were, they stoically, quietly, steadfastly went about their business tugging out the tiny stone arrowpoints, wrapping black silk bandannas around their bloody wounds, then went back to reloading, firing again, reloading and firing over and over as the shadows lengthened.

The sun settled to the far edge of the earth, and shadows faded there in the lee of those red-hued, iron-tinged rocks.

With that gradual, but most dramatic, change in the light playing off the huge boulders, all the fire gradually seemed to slowly seep out of the Diggers' attack. One by one, and in small clusters, the warriors retreated behind the jagged rocks, slipping out of sight before they disappeared out of range—not only refusing to charge the thunderous guns anymore, but every last one of them choosing instead to race barefoot after those scattering horses.

"They got what they wanted," Bass grumbled as the trappers watched the last of their attackers pull off and the desert fell quiet.

He tried to get up on one knee again, but that buttock still cried out in pain. The muscles had stiffened, cramping around the wound. Titus barely caught himself from falling to the side, then propped the rifle under his shoulder, pushing his way up on the good leg, refusing to think about what poison the goddamned red niggers had used to turn their annoying little arrowpoints into weapons that would bring a slow death.

"Daws, get a fire started," Bill Williams ordered, more angry than a spit-on hen. "A big goddamned fire!"

"We gonna use that fire to light the night, Bill? Keep them Diggers off us?" Henry Daws asked.

"Yeah?" Pete Harris chimed in. "So's we can see 'em coming after dark?"

"No, the fire I'm telling you to stoke ain't for us," Williams explained, his jaw muscles flexing in harsh ribbons.

Right then Scratch could read something in the older man's eye that most of the younger men never would. Uncertainly, he hobbled up beside Williams and stopped to ask, "You fixing to roast some of this here meat, Bill?"

Williams nodded, a wild look to his bloodshot eyes. "Digger meat."

In utter disbelief, Adair stuttered, "B-burn these here Injuns, Bill?"

"Damn right he is," Titus confirmed.

"Y-you ain't fixin' to make meat outta these damn Diggers, are you!" Dick Owens shrieked.

"Meat's meat," Bill explained angrily; then turned to Scratch with a malevolent glint to his eyes. "You hear these whining squaws, Titus Bass? Men like you an' me we ain't never been so squampshus 'bout what we put down our feed bags!"

When Williams stomped away angrily, headed for the closest of the dead warriors, Rube Purcell stepped up and nervously asked Titus, "You two ain't serious 'bout cooking them Injuns for us to eat?"

Bass stared at Bill's back a moment more, then looked Purcell in the eye, declaring, "Maybeso we go an' burn them dead niggers—it's gonna teach the rest of 'em a lesson so they won't follow us outta here."

"That mean we ain't gonna cook 'em to eat, right?" John Bowers prodded, wanting some real reassurance.

"Solitaire can eat Digger if he wants," Titus grumbled. "As for me—I ain't about to eat nothin' or no *one* what shot me in the ass."

Samuel Gibbon asked, "Sounds like we're gonna burn 'em?"

"Ever' last hell-dog of 'em," Scratch declared defiantly. "You heard Bill! Now build a fire! A goddamned *big* fire!"

"We . . . we leaving, Scratch?" Reuben Purcell inquired as he came up to Bass's elbow.

Titus pivoted around on his heel. "Damn right we're leaving. We'll count heads and what horses we got left. Bury them men we have to, drag the rest best we can. Once't we get that fire blazing and them dead niggers throwed on the flames—we're gone from here under them stars."

Adair inquired, "Where you figger you and Williams gonna lead out tonight?"

Titus dragged the back of his hand across his parched, cracked lips. "Where, you're asking me, Silas? Why—to see what horses we can still round up afore we push on for the Uncompawgray."

Titus Bass elected to walk, leading his horse. It was that or suffer the agony of a saddle-pounding. That snare saddle with a thick leather mochilla draped over its frame simply wasn't going to give his poorly placed wound the slightest comfort. Even with the furry padding of a small section of buffalo hide Scratch sliced from his sleeping robe, he found himself flinching with discomfort, if not wincing in downright pain when he tried to nestle down atop the saddle.

Unsteadily, he dropped to the hardpan desert floor, where he began to trudge the canyon ridges among the handful of their winged and wounded—those not able to move on their own. The rest hurried on into the dark with Bill Williams, following the wide, moonlit trail of the fleeing horses, their hoofprints dotted with the clutter of small moccasin tracks. Ol' Solitaire had vowed he would make the Diggers pay for the trouble they had visited the trappers, even if Bill and the others didn't get back but a dozen of those hard-won Spanish barb horses.

From time to time that evening, and on into the blackening of the desert night, Scratch turned to peer over his shoulder at that fading cone of flickering yellow light. A good thing the wind blew out of the west as evening came on, he pondered. The unearthly stench of those burning bodies was more than a right-minded man could stand. Not that Titus was squeamish—not in the least. Across all those seasons he'd spent west of the Big Muddy, after all, he'd killed enough of those who had attempted to kill him.

The Diggers could have sneaked up and cut out a

small portion of the herd to feed their miserable selves, instead of attacking the white men settled down for some hard-won sleep, instead of greedily running off all those hundreds of California horses. Had the brownskins been satisfied at slipping off with just a few, chances were Scratch could have talked Williams and the others out of wasting any time or effort pursuing a paltry number of the scrawny animals.

But when those red niggers made it plain as sun they were out to kill white men, those red niggers deserved no quarter.

A man often made some allowance for simple-minded savages what didn't know any better—but when the Diggers descended upon the trappers with their full intention of killing Williams's raiders so they could steal everything of any glittering value . . . then the red-bellies sealed their own death warrants.

Out here in this hostile environment, just like the predator and the preyed upon—life had never been anything more than cheap.

"Once't I hear dem Diggers eat their own chirrun when they get hungry 'nough!" Francois Deromme declared as he rode along, perched in his saddle above Titus, his left arm in a sling improvised from a black kerchief.

"Man'd have to be a animal to eat his own young'uns," Joseph Lapointe grumbled.

"That's what the hell they are," Deromme argued. "I neber see'd it with my own eyes—but I hear more'n one man tell me dem Diggers get hungry 'nough, they eat their young."

"Maybeso you're right," Lapointe agreed. "We all know them Mexicans ride up to this here country, for to steal women and young'uns, drag 'em back to Santee Fee and Touse for slaves in the fields. The Comanch' and the Yutas do it, too—they're always stealing Digger women and young'uns."

"So you figgair dese here Diggers don't give a damn 'bout their chirrun?" Deromme prodded.

"Look around you, fellas," Scratch interrupted their

discussion. "A empty belly in this here country gonna cry out for food only so long afore one of these red niggers gonna fill it any way he can."

"You figgair they do eat their young, Bass?" Lapointe inquired.

With a halfhearted shrug, Titus said, "I figger these here Diggers gonna eat most anything they can put in their mouths just to stay alive."

Rumors did indeed abound among the American fur men, not to mention those tales told down in the Mexican provinces, concerning the Diggers' sacrificing their children to fend off starvation. Although no white man had ever actually witnessed such barbarity with his own eyes, many a trapper had seen how these pitiful wretches shamelessly abandoned their blind, lame, and young to die alone in the desert when fleeing from powerful attackers.

Another certainty that lent a weighty probability to such legendary cannibalism in the minds of these trappers was what this austere country did *not* provide in the way of sustenance. Rarely had a fur man ever sighted any real game in the form of deer or antelope. Most of the time, even the bony jackrabbits were hard to spot. In certain seasons, these Diggers somehow sustained themselves on a diet of crickets and grasshoppers, even ants and spiders too. Word had it the Indians dried these insects beneath the blazing sun, then pounded the bodies into a fine meal that, when mixed with a little water or the moisture squeezed from a cactus frond, would form a paste they could bake on flat rocks at the edge of their fires.

Bright as the stars were that night, not to mention the illumination from a three-quarter moon, the wide and scoured trail wasn't all that hard to follow through those blessed hours of darkness. And in those final moments before the sky began to gray off the east as they trudged along, it even grew outright chilly. Feeling a little weak from the loss of blood and not having a thing to eat in the better part of a whole day, Scratch damn well didn't want to let the desert's cold sink in clear to his marrow. He stopped to rest for a few minutes while he untied his trail-worn capote from behind the saddle and pulled it onto his arms, knotting the sash around his waist.

Then he continued into what remained of the yawning, black desert night.

"You hear that?" Henry Daws asked.

The few came to a halt around Bass, quieting their animals as all of them fell silent. Listening.

There it was, for certain. The sound of gunfire. Not a rip-roaring battle of it—but a few shots echoing now and then. Of a sudden, they heard the low, rumbling thunder too.

"Dem's horses!" Francois Deromme cried.

Jack Robinson cheered, "An' it sounds like they're coming our way!"

"Damn if they ain't," Bass cursed, his eyes flicking left and right, frantically searching for cover. "We better be finding us somewhere to get outta their way."

"You figgair dem others find the horses?" Lapointe inquired.

"Sure as hell did find 'em!" Deromme declared. "Dey bringing the herd back for us."

"Hold on—I callate you've got things all twisted up," Bass argued, knowing full well there wasn't a good reason the herd had turned around in its tracks and was headed for them. "Them horses is on the run."

Robinson asked, "Bill and the rest got 'em all back from the Diggers, didn't they?"

That thunder of the hoofbeats seemed to swell noisily in the next few heartbeats as Titus grappled with what to do. In moments the horses would be all but on top of the handful of white men.

"Head for them rocks, fellas!" Bass shouted, lunging away despite the agony in that ham. "Diggers or Californy horses—this here desert's dead set on killin' me afore I can get back to the mountains!"

At the very moment the eastern horizon turned a blood-tinged gray, the front ranks of the herd took shape out of that arid dawn. A dark, bobbing wave thundered toward the wounded and halt as they scampered for a

low cluster of volcanic rock. The trappers reached their
shelter just before the flying manes and fluttering tails
took form out of the slanting gray clouds of dust. Intermingled with the pounding hooves arose off-key yips and
coyote calls of excited men.

Titus held on to hope that it would be Bill and the
others, bellowing on the fringes of the herd.

But when some three dozen of the stolen animals
loped past the rocks, the cries and hoots came right behind them, more distinct. And something clearly wasn't
right about those calls.

"It's the Diggers!" Lapointe shouted.

"Get down!" Bass ordered as he realized the horizon
wasn't darkened with horses. It was clotted with the warriors. "Get down outta sight!"

It was plain that these Indians who had attacked them
were, at least for the moment, consumed with chasing
after a few dozen of the horses on foot. They were
screeching and screaming at the horses, driving them
south by west back in the direction where the trappers
had been camped. One of the Diggers appeared to spot
Bass as the warriors loped past on foot, yelling at the
horses, keeping the animals on the run. But none of the
Indians stopped. As Titus waited to be discovered and
overwhelmed, his heart pounding, more than a hundred
of the short brown Indians streaked by, their knees
pumping like steam pistons as they raced after their four-
legged quarry.

Their shrill, intermittent cries and the hoof thunder
quickly died, swallowed by the utter emptiness of that
desert morning.

"They didn't spot us!" Toussaint Marechal called out.

"Shit—they saw us," Bass protested, relieved that so
many of the enemy was now heading away from their
line of march. "Had to see us when we ducked in here.
They just wanted them horses more'n they wanted our
sorry asses."

"We better get moving," Joseph Lapointe said as he
stood and adjusted the bloody bandanna that covered

one of his eyes. "Them brownskins might just turn on around and come back for us."

"Let's hope we can catch up to the rest of dem horses," Marechal said as he hobbled out of the rocks behind the rest.

"Better you pray we catch up to Bill Williams and the rest of our boys," Scratch argued. "To hell with them Mexican horses while there's red niggers out to raise our scalps in this here desert!"

It wasn't until midmorning, with the late-summer sun starting to do its evil work, when Francois Deromme first spotted the faint scum of a dust cloud hugging the horizon to the north. Minute by minute, the cloud grew, advancing on that band of wounded trappers.

"You don't figger it's 'nother bunch of them Diggers, do you?" Joseph Lapointe asked.

Bass shook his head. "Naw. Nothing gonna raise dust like that but a whole passel of hooves."

But just to be sure they didn't get burned, the trappers quickly looked about, spotting a likely outcrop of rocks where they might find enough room to conceal themselves and their horses.

On and on, minute by minute, the shimmering gold cloud gobbled its way across the desert toward them. From time to time, sunlight glanced like streaks of mercury, rays glittering from the density of the cloud. Then the first of the volving legs emerged from the base of the dust.

"It's them horses!" Jack Robinson screamed with glee. "See? It's our horses!"

In the next heartbeat, not only did the front ranks of the horses emerge out of the billowing dust, but also two riders—both of them whooping and yipping like coyote pups on the prowl.

"I'll be go to hell and et for the devil's tater!" Scratch cheered as he started hobbling into the open.

He ripped his wide-brimmed felt halt off his head and started waving it at the horses and that daring pair of riders out in the van of the herd. With all those animals racing directly at him—from where he stood right then it seemed as if the desert was belching free every horse that had ever come out of California.

At the head of the herd, those two riders pointed and waved their big hats, one of the horsemen angling off to his left. Once those animals in the front flanks were following him, the other horseman turned aside as the herd pushed on.

"Jehoshaphat! If that don't look to be Ol' Solitaire hisself!" Bass roared, wagging his hat once more at the end of his arm.

Williams came up at a lope, his horse skidding on the flinty ground. Every inch of the man was coated with a thick layering of fine talc that shook loose, forming a gauzy cloud that billowed into a bright halo around him as his animal shuddered to a halt.

"Titus Bass! That really you?"

Scratch spat out some of the sand that was settling around them all, a choking, blinding cloud of it kicked up by those hundreds of horses. " 'Onery as ever, Bill," he coughed.

"Damn, if you ain't covered ground on your own shanks! Walked all this way with that arrer hole in your ass?"

"He did, Bill!" Deromme said with a cheer.

"That our horses?" Titus inquired, glancing at the herd as it peeled aside, headed west.

"What we could get wrangled back together," Williams confided. "The rest we'll let the desert have. Maybe them Diggers run across some of 'em one of these days."

"Roast a haunch or two of Mexican horse, eh?" Bass said. "Where was you headed with 'em?"

"The horses? Why—we was comin' back for you boys."

"See?" Robinson said. "I told you all along Bill wouldn't light out of the desert without us!"

Bass scooted closer to Williams's bony knee, gazing up at the old trapper coated with that layer of brown dust. "Who's leading 'em now?"

"Kersey," he replied. "We figgered to find water for 'em afore night over yonder at them hills." He pointed. Then looked down at Bass. "You coming with us?"

"Damn right I am," Scratch growled. "A whole passel of them horses are mine, Bill. To get 'em this far, I near died of thirst, got my head shot off by Californy greasers, and a'most had my throat cut by a white man. I ain't about to let any of you side-talking varmints run off with what critters are mine!"

Williams rocked his head back and laughed so hard some more fine dust shook off him in a mist. "I figger that means you're coming with us! You sit a saddle yet?"

"Ain't tried—but I'll keep covering ground on foot any way you care to lay your sights."

"That's what I like in this man, boys!" Williams cheered. "You just can't beat a good man what puts his head down and keeps on coming!"

"You heard, Solitaire," Titus said to the others as he turned around to face them. "There's a herd to wrangle. All you fellas what are fit to help them others with the horses, saddle up and catch them horses. The rest of you what're ailin' too bad can lay back and come along with me."

Only Toussaint Marechal and Joseph Lapointe ended up staying behind with him, watching the others wave their farewells, then ease away toward the tail end of that massive herd.

Titus suddenly looked up and asked, "Ain't you going on with the rest, Bill?"

Patting his dust-crusted, lathered horse on the withers, Williams said, "I'll lay off running them animals for a while, Scratch. Maybeso, you boys could use some company on your leetle walk."

"Much 'preciated, Bill."

The four of them had covered several miles in the blazing sun before Williams, right out of the blue, confessed, "We got less'n half what we drove outta California, fellas."

Bass glanced over at the skinny man walking beside

him, leading his own horse. "You figgered you'd make it back to the mountains with more, did you?"

Williams was slow to grin, but smile he did, his brown teeth a shade or two darker than the pale dust coating his severely tanned face. "Shit, Scratch—you got me there! Never in all my days could I have figgered to get this many horses out of California and 'cross that killer desert."

"But we done it, Bill."

"By damn, if we didn't!" Williams exclaimed. "But just think of all them horses what left their bones behind us."

"No reason for you to feel sad for gettin' only half of 'em to the mountains. Lookit us—we're standing here, still alive!" Titus snorted some dust out of his nose onto the desert hardpan. Then he looked squarely at Bill. "We had us some shining times out to Californy, didn't we, ol' friend?"

Williams smiled hugely, no longer grave, and slapped Titus on the back. "We did have us some fun, didn't we, Scratch? By blazes, if we didn't have us a whole damn lotta fun!"

It took them the better part of a week, but they finally put the Green River at their backs, escaping the worst of that broken canyonland where it took all they had to keep any more of the stolen horses from slipping away in that rugged country.

Throughout the days the trappers kept the animals under a rotation of wranglers while the rest of the men slept. At dusk they saddled up and *ki-yiiied,* waving hats and coils of buffalo-hair rope to start the last three broodmares they still had alive. No longer were they pushing the rangy animals, not the way they had run the herd out of California, goaded them over the mountains and into those first stretches of desert. None of the survivors wanted to lose any more of their horses. So the cautious men inched forward each night, searching out the water holes and springs.

For nights on end, Bass had been forced to follow the slow-moving caravan on foot. But by the time they had begun their climb into the first low foothills, Titus was tying on his last pair of moccasins, deciding it was time to give that ham a try before he was forced to walk barefoot. That evening he settled back into the saddle, tenderly doing what he could to keep his weight off that wounded buttock. Trying his best to ignore the painful hammer of the horse's gait as it made its way over the uneven ground.

Far off in the distance, the verdant green of the Rocky Mountains beckoned seductively to these men who had outlasted months of desert sand, scorching sun, and their own limits.

It set Scratch to wondering how could a man live in such warm places as these, especially the sort of man who settled in valleys where other men congregated—building their shacks and huts and barns, forced to breathe each other's air, where they had no seasons of winter, spring, or fall to their lives? How did folks live like that?

But he realized there were lots of men who did live out their lives perfectly content to do without the harsh edges any wilderness scraped away on a man, settlers who were absolutely content to live a life untested. His father had been one. One of the many.

It was Titus Bass himself who was too damned different to get along with the steady sort what came to fill up these open, feral, unforgiving spaces.

Crossing a wind-scoured country of cedar, juniper, and stunted yellow pine, the raiders were forced to angle north along the base of a great plateau. Once around the end of that towering ridge, Williams curved them around to the south-southeast. From here on out they would no longer travel at night and rest out the sun.

Three more days of driving the herd and they struck what the mountain men called the Blue River,* one of the

---

* Today's Gunnison River in southwestern Colorado, what the Mexican traders of that time called the San Xavier River.

tributaries of the mighty Colorado. Finding enough water for their horses was no longer a problem. Nor wood for their night fires. No more would they have to cook their stringy horseflesh over smoky, struggling, greasewood fires.

They had returned to the Shining Mountains.

18

———————— ◆ ————————

"We ain't far now," Bill Williams had declared last night after they went into camp and killed another skinny yearling to last them the next couple of days.

"Robidoux's post?" Titus asked.

The old trapper nodded. "Up the Blue a ways, afore we hit the mouth of the Uncompawgray. Should be there afore sundown tomorrow."

After all they'd endured, that was about the best damned news. Had there been any whiskey in their camp that summer night, there'd been one hell of a collection of drunks sleeping off their revels when the order came to roll out the next morning. As it was, the trappers could only look forward to reaching Robidoux's post, where they were certain to find some Mexican whiskey or sweet fruit brandy, not to mention a few Ute squaws and some greaser gals who just might be convinced to cozy up with a lonely fella gone too long in the desert without some soft and curvaceous companionship.

Early that next afternoon, all fifteen were strung out on both sides of the herd behind Williams, who rode at the head of the ragged column, leading the last of their broodmares.

"Closer I get to whiskey," Jake Corn announced as he eased up beside Titus, "the thirstier I get—"

The two of them jerked at the low rumble of gunfire reverberating from the mesa ahead.

"That was just over the ridge," Bass declared.

Another gunshot echoed.

Far ahead of them Bill Williams was standing in the stirrups, waving his hat, beckoning the men forward.

Titus kicked his horse into a lope with the others as they streamed off the two sides of their herd.

"Bowers, you and Gibbon stay right here at the front of these here horses," Williams ordered in a staccato. "Keep 'em moving—but slow."

"What 'bout you?" Samuel Gibbon asked as three more gunshots rattled in quick succession.

Williams's lips stretched into a thin line of determination. "Rest of us gonna see what all the shooting's for."

"Awright, Bill," John Bowers agreed.

"C'mon, fellas," Williams ordered as he reined around in a tight circle. "Keep your flints sharp and your heads down when we bust outta the trees!"

By the time they had raced no more than another mile up the Blue River toward the Uncompahgre, Bass noticed the thin column of greasy black smoke curling above the leafy treetops. By then, the sporadic gunfire had all but died off.

"That ain't a good sign!" Titus called out to the others, pointing.

Williams and Adair nodded. While they watched, a second, and finally a third thin column of smoke appeared to streak the sky.

Just as the trappers reached the line of trees bordering a small meadow on the south bank of the river, Bill threw up his arm. The rest of them slowed and spread out to either side of their leader, reining to a halt right when three men on foot suddenly burst into view, sprinting on a collision course for the timber where Williams's horsemen suddenly appeared out of the shadows. The trio of frightened men spotted the trappers just about the time the trappers raised their rifles in warning.

"Hold on there!" Titus roared, his horse prancing backward a few steps anxiously.

Bewildered and terrified, the three skidded to a halt, immediately dropping their weapons and throwing up their hands.

Williams reined his horse close to the three and gave every one of them a good eyeing. "Who the hell are you?"

"Two of 'em's Mex." Bass translated what he could of the excited response. All three kept checking over their shoulders as they stood among the trappers, peering back across the meadow. "This other's a Frenchie half-breed."

A few warriors suddenly showed themselves on horseback, breaking out of the trees near the post's stockade. Spotting the trappers back against the trees, the barechested horsemen halted, reining around in circles as they yelped a warning to more of their number. In a moment, more than thirty painted, feathered horsemen belched from the stockade. They poured into the meadow, weaving in and out and around the three separate grass fires raging in the meadow.

All of them beat their chest provocatively and shouted out their boastful challenges to the white men.

"You cipher things the way I do, Titus Bass?" Williams asked.

"Maybeso," Scratch replied gravely. "Looks like them bastards want us to come out and fight."

"These here Robidoux's men?" Williams demanded, indicating the frightened refugees as those distant warriors raced their ponies back and forth across the meadow, working up a second wind in their animals.

Bass nodded, keeping his eye on the Indians growing bolder by the moment. "Figger they skeedaddled afore they lost their hair."

Bill grumbled, "Ask 'em what's the chalk at their post."

From what little Titus was able to recall of the Spanish tongue, he could ask only limited questions, comprehending only portions of the frantic, impassioned jabber they flung at him.

"From what I get, them Injuns is—"

Williams interrupted, "Hold it—did I hear that'un say them are Yutas?"

"Yutas," Bass confided as one of the Mexicans bobbed his head up and down with agreement. But Titus was baffled by this strange turn of events. "Never knowed 'em to take on white men afore."

"Maybe one of these'r parley-voo half-breeds can tell us something," Bill continued, turning to look over his trappers. "Marechal! Listen to this here Frenchie—see what he claims brung all this—"

The raiders instantly wheeled around to stare at the fort the moment they heard high-pitched screams.

At the narrow opening of the double-hung gate appeared more than a handful of women—most of them squaws by their dress, while two were clearly Mexican. A half dozen warriors flushed them screaming and whimpering from the stockade.

"There's your answer, Bill," Titus grumbled. "They come for to get their women back."

Williams wagged his head. "You figger this here raid gotta do with their women?"

"They ain't set fire to the post," Scratch observed.

Jake Corn growled, "Not yet anyways."

"Ain't butchered these here fellas neither," Bass protested, feeling even stronger stirrings of confusion at the Ute attack. "For some reason they let the greasers an' parley-voos run 'stead of shooting 'em."

"There goes your hurraw at Robidoux's, boys!" Williams roared with a cackling laugh. "Them Yutas is taking back their wimmens!"

"An' them two Mex' gals besides?" whined Dick Owens.

"Plain as paint," Bass replied.

"But them Mex' gals ain't theirs to take!" Pete Harris protested.

"Yutas and Mexicans been stealin' women and young'uns back and forth from each other," Titus declared. "Near as long as there's been Mexicans and Yutas in these mountains, I'd lay."

"I say we kill them bucks!" Pete Harris suddenly spoke up. "Get them women back for the fort an' ourselves."

When a few of the other trappers hollered in agreement, Williams and Bass turned to peer at Thompson's old friend together. Titus said, "Your stinger sure must need some dipping in a woman's honeypot in a bad way, Harris!"

"I ain't gonna let no yellow-bellied Yuta scare me off!" Harris boasted.

When Williams shot Titus a sly grin, Bass shrugged and turned to the others, asking, "How's that shine with the rest of you? We gonna lay into them Yuta and run 'em off?"

"Like Harris said," Jack Robinson argued, "them redbellies is taking the women. *Our* women."

"You're all hobble-headed!" Bass snapped. "Them bucks got ever' right to come here an' take back their own women if'n they want."

His neck feathers ruffling, Dick Owens demanded, "You ain't gonna do nothing 'bout it, Bass?"

"Them squaws?" Titus wagged of his head. "My truck with them warriors got more to do with running off white men from their trading post."

"Even if they're no-account greaser and parley-voo?" Pete Harris asked with a big grin plastered on his face.

Titus grinned too. "That's right—even if them Injuns run off Mex and parley-voo too . . . I say we owe them Injuns a li'l lesson in goodly manners."

"An' maybeso we'll get them two greaser gals back for ourselves in the bargain!" Dick Owens cheered lustily.

"We got horses we don't want run off by a pack of these here niggers," Williams reminded harshly. "We come too damn far with 'em awready."

"Bill's right," Scratch agreed. "Let's see what we can

do to run these brownskins off across the river. Maybeso they won't get wind of our herd back yonder."

"Shit," Jack Robinson grumped. "How the hell we gonna hide more'n a thousand goddamned horses?"

Bass turned on the man and looked him squarely in the eye, saying, "I was figuring you was gonna come up with a idee, Jack. Only way you get to roll in the grass with one of the Mexican gals is to take her away from the warriors."

Robinson looked sheepish a moment. "Didn't figger on having to do that."

"Just see you get them two senoreetas back for the traders," Williams ordered. "Far as I can tell, them Yutas ain't kill't or shot up none of Robidoux's parley-voos. So I don't want you hurtin' none of them Yutas."

"Who's coming with me?" Pete Harris asked, his voice rising an octave as his eyes raked over the rest. "You got some hair in you yet, Bass?"

He shook his head. "Nawww. I don't need to hump no Mexican gals no more. So it's up to the rest of you boys to go run off them Injuns and bring them whores back."

"I'm coming!" Dick Owens volunteered.

Around Harris another three fell in with flushed enthusiasm. Harris bellowed like a spiked bull struck with spring fever and led them out of the trees for the fort. As the hell-bent-for-rawhide trappers burst from the timber, the Ute warriors suddenly reined up, appearing to take stock of their situation.

"They're a bit light on the odds, Bill," Titus suggested. "We oughtta show them brownskins the rest of us."

Williams asked, "Hang back near the trees to show 'em there's more of us?"

"That's what I was thinking, Bill."

"C'mon, boys," Williams directed the others as he kneed his pony forward. "Let's spread out and make 'em think there's a hull shitteree of us back here gonna rub 'em out."

The moment the rest of the horsemen came out of the

shadowy timber alongside him and Bill, Bass set up a caterwauling akin to some disembodied spirit streaking back through that crack in the sky to haunt this world. In another two heartbeats the other trappers joined in— coyote yip-yipping, some of them trilling their tongues while others u-looed. A few let fly with a chest-popping screech.

Out in front, Pete Harris and his quartet of trappers took up the call and began to scream for all they were worth as they raced headlong across the narrow meadow for the Ute horsemen.

The sight of those nine trappers emerging from the timber, along with Harris's four chargers, immediately put the warriors into flight. At the fort gates the half dozen Ute then on foot scrambled over one another to reach their ponies and get mounted. Ahead of the trappers, all of the Indians spun out of the meadow, heading for the bank and the river ford.

Into the shallow water the first of them leaped their horses, landing in a spray of water and nearly losing their balance. None of the warriors dared to look back over their shoulders until they had reached the north side of the river.

With the way this meadow ground sloped away toward the crossing, Scratch and those who had hung back with him couldn't really see much of that crossing until the horsemen reached the other side, racing away. But they plainly did hear when Harris and the rest roared with laughter.

Trotting on foot into the ranks of Bill Williams's horsemen, the post employees glanced up at the trappers as if to ask why the Americans were sitting there on their horses when there was a fort to be rescued.

"Awright, you pork eaters," Scratch roared at them with a wave of his long rifle. "C'mon, let's go see what plunder them Injuns run off with."

As late summer crept its way into early autumn, the weather began to cool at the lower elevations—even more so in the high country where the horse thieves drove their herd from sunrise to slap-dark, clambering over one low range after another—plodding slowly up the western slopes until they reached a low saddle, then struggling to keep the eager horses together as they raced down the eastern side of the passes.

This was, after all, country that both Ol' Bill and Scratch knew like the backsights of their guns.

At the tiny trading post, Antoine Robidoux's grateful employees hadn't hesitated in hauling out the clay jugs of *aquardiente,* that powerful, head-thumping concoction brewed down in the Mexican provinces. After all, they had been rescued by a band of dust-caked, desert-scarred beaver trappers. Gone this long drought after the whiskey in Pueblo de los Angeles, all those parched and dusty miles—their gullets were due a hardy scrubbing.

Not only the whiskey, but they were due those two Santa Fe whores they had just rescued from the Ute warriors. In a pair of nearby rooms, the women spent that long, bawdy night on their backs, entertaining an unending string of American suitors. Paying for their pleasure to the tune of a horse for every carnal crack they had at the two whores seemed reasonable enough to the Americans. Why, each man jack of them was rich, rich in horses! What were two, three, even four horses these hungry men would leave behind by the time Bill Williams barked out his marching orders the next morning?

Bass's head hurt worse than ever that sunrise when he squinted into the graying dawn, then stared down at the mud-caked moccasin jabbing him in the ribs. He lay atop a thick mattress, its odor musty from old grass gone to molder, the faint stench of old puke, and more than one dousing in urine. Sometime last night he had managed to drag a blanket over him for warmth.

He found himself lying on the floor of the tiny stable where the post patrons tied up their most valuable animals, not at all sure how he had come to sleep with these horses.

"You ever close your eyes last night, Bill?" he asked, then hacked up the night-gather thick at the back of his throat. Hangovers caused him a little more pain with every year.

"Not once," Williams boasted proudly. "Laid down a time or two—but it weren't to sleep!" He snorted with boyish laughter, then asked, "Why'n't you come get yourself a poke with one of them gals?"

"I'm a married man, Bill," he answered, sitting up and grinding the heels of his hands into both eyes.

"Taking hisself a Injun woman never kept no man from greasing his own wiping stick, Scratch."

Bleary-eyed, he gazed up at Williams. "I don't need to poke no woman bad as that."

"Your woman, she back with her own people?"

"Yep."

Williams watched Scratch stand and dust off the hay from his clothing. "Who's to say she ain't back there right now curled up with one of them Absorkee bucks?"

For an instant he flared with anger, then realized by the look on Bill's face that, in his own way, Williams was just having his fun. "I didn't know you better, maybeso I ought'n bust you atween the eyes for making a crack like that, Solitaire."

Williams winked. "Never settled down my own self, mind you—but, I do know any woman can get lonely."

"I don't figger Waits-by-the-Water for that sort of woman."

"You sure 'bout that?" Bill asked. "After all, you are getting a little long in the tooth, Titus Bass."

Scratch looked his friend in the eye and said, "Maybeso you've never loved a gal like I love this'un, Bill. I'm sure of the woman she is. That's why I'm going home to her and my young'uns soon as we get shet of these Californy horses."

"Damn, if that don't take the circle!" Williams snorted. "Who'd a-reckoned when I'd met you up to the Bayou that you'd ever fill out to be a family man?"

That morning after leaving Robidoux's post, they crossed the Uncompahgre, then stuck with the south side of the Blue, gradually forced to lead their herd farther and farther from the water's edge as the river cut its way through a deep, black canyon. Many days later when the channel split in two, they stayed with the south fork, a river the Ute called the *Tomichi*. The raiders pressed on, climbing to its headwaters, where the horses and men both grew breathless from their struggle into the high country. From that narrow saddle,* they dropped over to the eastern slopes where the raiders got their first glimpse of the narrow, winding ribbon of the upper Arkansas as it was gathering steam in its headlong race to the Mississippi far, far across the plains.

From here on they had only to follow the river out of the mountains.

Thirteen days later Titus caught sight of the low adobe walls raised around a cluster of poor adobe buildings when the raiders crested the top of a low rise. "What the hell are those?" he asked in surprise.

"I'll be go to hell," Williams said in a low voice filled with marvel. "They gone and done it for certain."

"You know who that is down there, Bill?"

He gave Bass a sideways grin and asked, "You ain't been down in this country for a long spell, have you?"

Bass shook his head, his eyes dancing over the mud-and-wattle hovels squatting inside the fort walls and out. Off to one direction a few cattle grazed on grass already smitten brown with autumn's first frost. Two dozen sheep, along with a handful of goats, cropped the gentle slope directly behind the settlement. Even a few chickens pecked at insects near the gate.

"What's this post called?"

"Ain't rightly a trading post," Williams answered. "Leastways, no one man owns it. Only thing I heard it called is the Pueblo. Story goes, Jim Beckwith and a few others come up here from Mexico to get things started."

Titus scratched a louse out of his beard. "Beckwith—the darkie what was a Crow chief?"

"That's him."

Scratch crushed the tiny louse between a thumb- and

---

* Today's Monarch Pass.

fingernail. "Bet these here fellas didn't figger they'd have to go head-on with the Bent boys!"

"I heard they was coming here to do just that."

"If that don't take the circle!" Titus exclaimed. "You s'pose these niggers be interested in some Californy horses?"

The horsemen scattered the chickens and some goats as they started off the hillside more than a half mile from the crude settlement. After rounding the herd back on itself and bringing the weary horses to a halt, the dust-caked weary raiders made camp a good mile up a wide creek from the Pueblo. As they came out of their saddles, Bill guaranteed every man his opportunity to spend time in the settlement that night, or the following day—since they would be laying over before pushing on. Then he assigned a rotation of guards to watch over the herd before he signaled Bass to mount up and accompany him.

"Let's go pay us a visit," Bill suggested. "See who's about."

For the most part, the breeze drifted downhill, carrying with it the settlement's stench. But every now and then as they approached, the wind would momentarily shift—and the odors of human waste, rotting carcasses, not to mention cow and goat dung, would all conspire to slap them in the face. Not that this wasn't exactly how an Indian village stank after several weeks being rooted in the same spot. But then, the tribes always migrated when it came time to move on. From the looks of things, these white squatters had decided to stay put, no matter the stink.

"Ho!" called out a thin figure stepping from the shadow of that bastion erected at the corner of the eight-foot-high adobe wall as the two riders approached in the late-afternoon light.

Williams and Bass reined up. Bill held down his hand, "William S. Williams, Master Trapper."

"Bill Williams hisself," the thin one replied, admiration spread across his face. "I'm Robert Fisher. And who you be?"

"Titus Bass."

"I'll be damned. You're the one what wears the scalp of the nigger took your hair, ain't that it?"

Patting the back of his head, Bass said, "How come you know of me?"

"Partner of mine says he knowed you," Fisher announced.

Scratch's curiosity was pricked, "Who that be?"

"Said he trapped with you some years back," Fisher explained. "Name's Kinkead."

"*Mathew* Kinkead?" he echoed with a sudden surge of sentiment mixed with excitement. "He's your partner?"

"Yep." And Fisher squinted up at Bass, his head twisting round on his neck so he could stare at the back of the horseman's faded bandanna.

"Mathew ain't living down to Taos no more?"

"Not for some time now."

"Kinkead bring anybody with him from Taos? Family?"

"His woman, and they got 'em a daughter—"

"No," he interrupted with a snap, flush with a skin-prickling excitement that made him squirm in his saddle. "I wanna know if Mathew brung any other fellas with him from Taos—*American* fellas?"

Robert Fisher thought mightily on that a moment, as if muscling over a great block of quarried marble in his mind before he answered. "No, I'm sorry. Don't recollect him having no American—"

"Where's Kinkead now?" he demanded impatiently.

The man turned slightly and pointed, "Last I saw of him earlier, Mathew was down by his buffalo pens."

"B-buffler pens?" Williams squeaked, high-pitched and scratchy as a worn fiddle string.

Fisher nodded. "Where he keeps his buffalo calves."

"This I gotta see, Scratch!" Williams roared.

"Saw all them horses you fellers was bringing down out of the hills from a ways back," Fisher stated, stepping up to pat the dirty, sweat-caked neck of Bass's pony. "Less'n you robbed horses from the hull Yuta nation . . . just where the hell you fellas run onto so god-damned many?"

"Californy," Titus declared.

Now it was Fisher's time to sputter. "C-california . . . these Mex horses? All of 'em?"

"We run most of 'em off California ranchos," Williams admitted.

"Some was wild," Bass said proudly. "They joined up on our way east over the mountains."

Bill added, "I figger most of them wild ones made it cross the desert."

"Lookit all of 'em!" Fisher gushed with astonishment, staring at the hillside.

"What you see is less'n half what we took right under their noses," Titus boasted.

"Wait'll the rest of the fellers see this!"

"We're camped up the creek a ways, mile or so," Williams announced, pointing down the slope at the mouth of the nearby Fountain, where the creek flowed into the Arkansas on that broad valley floor. "We'll graze our horses on what grass there is above you on that big flat."

"I'll go fetch up the others," Fisher offered. "Let 'em know you boys come—"

"Don't think you'll have to," Bass said as he spotted more than two dozen figures emerging from the fort gate, headed their way on foot, another ten to fifteen women, children, and a few men clambering out of a handful of buffalo-hide lodges pitched close to the post's adobe walls. "Truth be . . . I think I see ol' Mathew Kinkead's ugly face coming now."

There wasn't a thing that could compare with the strong embrace of an old friend, a companion who had ridden the high country with you, stood at your back time after time against great odds, a man you had trusted with your life.

Scratch gazed at Kinkead's face through damp, misty eyes, his cheeks wet with happiness as they slapped each other on the back and danced, danced, danced.

"Easy now, easy," the large bear of a man huffed as he

lumbered to a stop. "Ain't as y-young as we was back when we could pound each other to a frazzle, Scratch."

"I heard Rosa's here with you," he said, a little breathless too.

The wide, toothy grin drained from Kinkead's face. "Rosa . . . no. She's gone."

"G-gone? Wh-where?"

"Was took quick and merciful two winters after your Crow woman had that girl of your'n. Where's she? You still packing that squaw?"

He nodded only, struck a little numb in remembrance of sweet, round, warm Rosa Kinkead who had helped deliver his first child. "She's . . . an' my young'uns, they're all up to Absorkee. Ain't see'd 'em since early spring." Then Scratch wagged his head. "Can't hardly believe it—not when Fisher said Kinkead was here with his wife and daughter."

"That's Teresita," Kinkead explained. "We got us a daughter too, just like you." He sighed, then said, "How long's it been, my friend?"

"Late spring," Bass answered, "thirty-four." In so many ways—made all the sweeter in staring at his old friend's face—it seemed as if only a season or two had passed them by, instead of more than eight long, intervening years.

What with that sudden, sad news about Kinkead's Rosa, Titus was reluctant to ask . . .

"Mathew," he said quietly, gripping the big man's wrist in his bony claw, "wh-what become of Josiah?"

Quickly, Kinkead's face brightened. "Josiah Paddock, you say?" And he snorted with laughter. "Now there's a nigger made hisself a home in Taos!"

"He—he's still alive?"

"Alive? Damn certain that tall drink of water's still alive," Mathew declared. "Leastways he was the picture of health last time I see'd him early in the summer."

With that flutter of excitement winging through his belly, Titus asked, "You saw him down to Taos?"

"The goods we brung north for our trade room here, some of 'em we bought off Josiah, Scratch."

Titus felt his whole body smiling. "You saying—he's made himself a place as a trader down to Taos, Mathew?"

"Strike me deaf and dumb if he ain't made a damned good trader down at San Fernando." Kinkead laid a big hand on Bass's shoulder. "Just the way you made it possible for him right before you lit out for the mountains. Y-you ain't ever been back down to Taos since you come back from Saint Louis, come back from settling things with Cooper?"*

Scratch shook his head, "No, I ain't been back down there." A surge of pride was sparkling its way through his chest with this grand, grand news about his old friend. "Mathew . . . what of his Flathead woman? And that li'l boy of his, Joshua was his name?"

Kinkead's head rocked back on his massive shoulders as he laughed. "Looks Far Woman talks Mex good as any greaser now! An' Josiah's been keeping her big with child nigh every year. Near as I callate, young Joshua got him least four brothers and sisters!"

Impulsively, Scratch threw his arms around Kinkead again, squeezing mightily in the pure joy brought of good news.

Mathew asked, "That where you're headed? See Josiah down to Taos after all this time?"

He took a step back from the big man to explain. "Your news will have to do for now. We're on the tramp for Bents Fort with some horses to trade."

"I know it'd make the lad truly happy to lay eyes on you again, knowing the way he mourned your going when you pulled up stakes and headed back to the mountains."

"Make me a happy nigger to set my eyes on him again too," he sighed.

Kinkead offered, "If'n you want, I'll ride south with you—"

"Maybe one day soon," Bass interrupted, torn

---

* *One-Eyed Dream*

between two regrets. "But too long I've been gone from my woman, and our young'uns. Too long. It's time I point my nose for Absorkee afore Winter Man blows down on that north country. Tramping south for Taos gonna have to wait for 'nother day, Mathew."

"Truth be," Kinkead admitted, "I didn't much take to the notion of setting foot in the Taos valley again myself, Scratch."

Bass studied the doleful look on his old friend's face for a moment before he asked, "You ain't the kind to have no trouble with the greasers. So why you skee-daddle?"

Kinkead shook his head as he toed the ground beneath a moccasin. "Just ain't the same place it was of a time years ago."

"The Mex?"

"Them, yeah," Kinkead replied. "Them Pueblos too. The Injuns just outta town."

"Josiah and his family—they ain't in danger?"

"Hell no," Mathew said reassuringly. "Them Mex look most favorable on Paddock, most favorable. Why, the lad's a real pillar of that community."

Titus measured the way Kinkead grinned and puffed out his chest appropriately while he spoke those soothing words. It gave his heart no little pride to learn how well his old partner had carved out a life for himself in Taos. Why, of a time many winters ago, Scratch even looked upon Josiah as that younger brother he left behind in Boone County, Kentucky. And, when he owned up to it, there had been those times when, in many ways, he felt as if Paddock could well have been like a son.

Natural to feel as if he could bust his own buttons with pride in what young Paddock had accomplished in the intervening years. Had Titus not convinced Josiah to remain behind in Taos back to thirty-four, no telling what might well have become of the lad: fallen to the Blackfoot when they rode to avenge the death of Rotten Belly or Whistler, even took by smallpox had he been along for that desperate chase to reclaim his family from the Bloods, or killed in his first running skirmish against the Sioux.*

As it was, Josiah would likely die an old man's death now, his gray, hoary head resting on a goose-down pillow as he drew his last breath there in his fine Taos home, surrounded by his children and grandchildren. The lad had stretched Lady Fate's patience as far as any man had the right to do. Any man . . . save for Titus Bass.

If ever there was a man who realized he would never pass over the Great Divide peacefully stretched out on a feather tick, surrounded by weeping loved ones . . . it was Titus Bass. Lady Fate simply didn't hold anything of the sort in the cards for him. No quiet passing would be his legacy.

Scratch swallowed the lump of sentiment clogging his throat and said, "Damn fine to hear Josiah's made a life for hisself. Just the way it 'pears you done right here for yourself too, Mathew."

"Had us a place on up the Arkansas 'bout six miles for almost a year," Kinkead explained. "Started raising buffler calves to sell."

"Buffler calves?" he snorted in disbelief.

"Just like milk cows," Mathew said proudly. "I'd tromp east onto the plains a ways, steal a few li'l red ones from their wet-teat mamas, and drag 'em back here."

"How the hell—"

"Had 'em nurse a milk cow, Scratch," Kinkead explained. "I had me a few good cows took over feeding them li'l calves. And come next spring, Teresita gonna put in her garden again—raise some corn and beans, just like we did upstream. Eat some and sell the rest."

"Who the devil you gonna sell your corn to?"

"Bents allays buy good," Mathew said. "But the reason I moved down here and throwed in with these others is so we could be here for overland travelers."

Bass chuckled lightly. "Now I know you're pulling my

---

* *Ride the Moon Down*

leg, Mathew! Raising yourself buffler calves and selling corn to—what'd you call 'em?"

"They're overland travelers, Scratch. Folks moving up and down the front of the mountains now. Our day's gone, don't you see. It's a differ'nt time awready. Coun-try's changing."

"Travelers? You mean traders—like Vaskiss and Sub-lette. Got 'em that post up on the South Platte—"

"Settler folks, Scratch." And Mathew laid a thick arm across Titus's shoulder as he swept the other arm in a half circle. "We just got the post finished last week, and lookee what's here awready. Damn, if it ain't got the makin's of a real settlement right where we stand. Atween the lot of us, got chickens and cows and goats too, 'long with my buffler calves. Too late of the sea-son to put in the fields now, but come spring we'll be plowing up that meadow there, and turning that'un over there too."

Bass's eyes followed the sweep of Kinkead's arm. Dark-skinned women and children, along with a mess of domesticated animals. Same as it would be down to San Fernando de Taos. Damn near how it was back east at Westport where the Santa Fe traders began their journey to the Mexican settlements. No, this here wasn't like a nomadic village of the Crow or Snake, Ute or Arapaho. What Mathew Kinkead and the others were doing here was putting down roots. Deep and abiding roots.

Here in a country that of a time had known only the hoofbeats and grunts of migrating buffalo, along with the stampede of frightened antelope, not to mention the rut-ted tracks of countless travois, lodge circles, and fire pits, all of which come next rainy season would be washed into oblivion and the prairie would be brand new . . . here Titus Bass looked around him and realized his days were not without number.

Not only had the first of those goddamned sodbusters already crossed the mountains on their way to Oregon country, but here before his very eyes the face of his be-loved mountains was changing. As much as he hated to admit it, Scratch knew there were changes coming to his high and broad and beautiful heartland—changes that made him hurt to his very marrow.

Nothing would ever be the same.

Nothing would ever be good again.

19

———————— ◆ ————————

Puny as it was, that little Fountain Creek—at the mouth of which Kinkead and his four partners erected their Pueblo—just happened to be the Arkansas River's biggest tributary between its source high in the Rockies to a point more than halfway in the river's languid travels across the prairie. Their Pueblo stood at the foot of this wall of mountains, where a man gazed out upon the abrupt and spectacular end to more than a thousand miles of Great Plains.

It was a place far better than most for any five men to raise up their wilderness post.

Back in the spring of that year, 1842, Mathew Kinkead had thrown in with Robert Fisher, George Simpson, Francisco Conn, and Joseph Mantz—unlike Mathew, not one of them a veteran of the mountain fur trade. What did distinguish the four, however, was the fact that none of Kinkead's partners was afraid to hang their asses over the fire. They were the sort who recognized this was not only a land of gigantic risks but a land offering unbelievable riches to those who would seize opportunity by the balls and refuse to let go.

As Titus Bass looked around himself at the Pueblo, appraising the men who had erected this adobe settlement, once again he was struck in the face with the cold reality that his was a bygone era. He belonged to an age already withering like last year's willow, a way of life now struggling to draw in its last breath . . . sucking into its chest that unmistakable final death rattle.

"Damn me if it ain't Titus Bass for sure!" exclaimed the man at Mathew Kinkead's elbow as the two stepped into the firelight late that evening.

He squinted, not sure after all the intervening years, and the darkness, and the toll time took on a man. "Beckwith?"

"In the flesh, you ol' dog!" Jim Beckwith lunged ahead and seized Scratch in his arms.

They pounded one another breathless for a moment, then each took a step back to gaze at one other.

"You was working for Vaskiss and Sublette up on the Platte, last time I heard tell of you," Bass declared.

"I was. Them two had me trading with the Arapahos for robes. Afore they bucked out of the buffler business," Beckwith admitted with a wag of his head. "Bents is too big a outfit for the small-timers to take on in this here country."

"Working up there for Vaskiss and Sublette's outfit, you ever come across a big, tall pilgrim goes by the name of Shadrach Sweete?"

"Shad! Hell if I didn't!" Beckwith cheered. "A square shooter, 'bout as fair as they come when he's dealing with the Injuns."

"So Shad ain't working for 'em no more?"

"Vaskiss gone out of business while back," Beckwith declared. "Ain't no more. When they folded, I headed south to Taos—"

"What become of Shadrach?" Bass interrupted.

"The day Vaskiss pulled out with his wagons and left that fort empty, Shadrach rode off hisself."

Titus leaned in close. "Where to?"

With a shrug of his shoulders, Beckwith answered, "Dunno. Just lit out."

"What direction?"

Beckwith stared at his toes a moment in contemplation before answering, "South by east."

"Heading for Bents Fort?"

"Nawww." Jim sounded definite on that score. "After what they done to run the small outfits off the Platte, Shad didn't wanna have nothing to do with the Bents," Beckwith observed.

"He say what he had in mind afore he took off?"

This time Beckwith half shut his eyes and raised his chin to the sky, as if conjuring up the memory. After a few moments those eyes flew open and his face brightened. "Said he was fixin' to look for the Shiyans. I asked him if'n he was gonna trade with 'em or what, and he just said he needed to scare up some folks to take him in while he figgered out what he was gonna do. Then he rode off and was gone."

Damn, Bass thought as he reflected on it. "That's been some time now, ain't it, Jim? Hope to hell no one's gone and raised that big sprout's hair."

"It's gonna take a passel of niggers to rip off Shad Sweete's topknot!" And the mulatto grinned. "Mathew here tells me you and Bill Williams been out to California for horses."

Titus nodded. "Brung us out a passel of 'em."

"Solitaire tell you 'bout the trip me and him made to California with Peg-Leg?"

"You was with 'em three years ago?"

With a nod Beckwith scratched at his chin whiskers neatly trimmed into a goatee below a bushy horseshoe mustache. "We brung some horses out then. So Peg-Leg was with you fellas this ride too?"

Scratch watched how some of the other raiders at the fire glanced up at him when Beckwith uttered his question. "Peg-Leg and Solitaire . . . they had 'em a agreement on the way back. Ended up splitting the blankets back in Digger country."

With a doleful wag of his head, Beckwith said, "Bound to happen, with them two mule-headed bastards anyway. A outfit can't have two booshways like them. So what'd Peg-Leg do to make hisself a burr under Ol' Bill's saddle blanket?"

"A matter of killing a white man," Scratch declared directly. "So Bill run Peg-Leg off."

"Smith . . . killed one of your men?"

"About come to it," Titus admitted.

"Hell, there's always fights in a outfit like that," Beckwith replied. "Sore feelings, ruffled feathers—"

"If'n it been differ'nt," Titus interrupted, "Solitaire wouldn't had no call to run Peg-Leg off the way he done."

Jim wagged his head, not understanding. "What the hell business Williams got running Peg-Leg off?"

"Already too much bad blood not to," Scratch explained.

"Damn that Bill Williams anyways!" Beckwith grumbled sourly. "He always was a cantankerous ol' bunghole of a bastard. I s'pose he's already told you how he never took to me, and that's the God's truth. Clear on back to the early years, or on that trip out to California neither. Fact is, the two of us just rubbed each other the wrong way right from the start, natural', 'thout even trying hard to work up a lather 'bout me hating him or him hating me."

"I s'pose that's why some folks should never cross trails," Scratch commented.

"You say your outfit come here with Bill—where's that soft-headed son of a bitch now so I'll make certain to steer clear of him?"

"'Round camp somewheres," Titus declared. "You just pushing on through, headed off somewheres, Jim?"

With a playful grin, Beckwith confessed, "I come up from Taos to open a trading house with my partner, fella named Stephen Lee."

"Trading house—here?"

"Yep," the mulatto answered. "We aim to have us a trade room in this here Pueblo. But, hell—I wanna hear what all you been up to in Absaroka. When I found Mathew was bringing out two jugs to have some talk with you fellas 'round a fire, I just natural' invited myself along! Let's sit and wet our tooters."

Kinkead plopped himself down on a smooth-barked cottonwood, setting before him two half-gallon clay jugs of Simeon Turley's pale *aquardiente,* transported north from the Taos valley in carts filled with hay to absorb all shocks. "Say, Scratch—you won't believe what Jim told me just a bit ago."

Bass turned to Beckwith. "Some news from Taos?"

"Might say," Mathew explained. "He got married down to Taos!"

Titus inquired, "That where you come from—Taos?"

"Me and my partner, Lee, yep," Beckwith said. "Brung my new wife up here with us."

"Sure thought you had your fill of wives up there in Absorkee country," Bass snorted with laughter.

"Them was some shinin' times, they was," Beckwith replied while some of the others laughed with him. "But Jim Beckwith's not in the blanket now, so' I took me on just one gal in the proper Mex way—Louisa Sandoval. Come from a fine Taos family."

"You married for serious, eh?" Kinkead asked. "Gone and hitched in the church an' all?"

Beckwith wiped his mouth after a long gulp of liquor, then said, "She's full Mex, Mathew—so you know you gotta marry 'em up right."

Scratch turned to face Kinkead. "What with your new wife, Mathew—how you come to wanna skeedaddle out of Taos?"

"Year ago spring, soon as the snow was melting off the road north, I brung my family up to the Arkansas," the big man declared. "It was time to find me a place didn't have so many Mexicans."

"Winters ago, back when you split the blankets with Jack Hatcher's bunch and give up on the mountains for Rosa an' a feather tick, I never would've wagered you for the sort to *ever* put Taos behind you," Titus confessed.

"True that was—back then. Was a time I figgered I had me a home in Taos for the rest of my days," Kinkead sighed. "But, the last two years or so, the air ain't smelled near as sweet in the San Fernando Valley."

Scratch accepted the jug back from Beckwith. "That ain't nothing new, Mathew. Them Mex was allays squeezing down on us *Americanos* with their laws and taxes anyways. Taking half our beaver when it damn well suited 'em—"

"This was something differ'nt," Kinkead warned stiffly, swiping the back of a hand across his mouth glistening with drops of the potent, opaque liquor.

"Dust it off," Bass demanded as he passed the clay jug on to George Simpson.

Mathew's eyes grew cold. "First off, word drifted in to Taos and Santa Fe that the Texians were coming to invade us."

Elias Kersey rocked forward, his eyes gleaming with intense interest. "Texicans?"

"Texians—used to be Americans. Folks what got their own country east of here," Mathew began. "They call it a republic. Won it away from the Mexican Army a half dozen or so years back. A bunch of Tennessee boys, Kentuckians too—just like me an' you, Titus Bass."

Reuben Purcell waved a bony hand with impatience, asking, "So why the hell was these Texians coming to invade Taos and Santa Fe?"

"We had one report comin' in after 'nother, said they had 'em a big army coming our way," Kinkead explained.

"Why they want Taos when they had 'em their own brand-new republic?" Scratch asked.

Mathew turned sideways and took the jug offered him before saying, "Talk was, them Texians got the high head ever since they throwed the Mexican Army out of their new country, so they got to figgering *all* the land this side of the Rio Grande belonged to them."

Scratch stared at the leaping flames a moment as he grappled in his mind for the location of the Rio Grande del Norte, then realized it flowed west of Taos on its way south.

Jim Beckwith jumped in now, saying, "All the news

we heard had it them Texians was setting a army loose to throw all the Mexicans out of Mexico."

Mathew added, "They was coming to take over the northern part of Mexico for themselves, make it part of their republic."

"But Taos—that's way up in the north of Mexico," Titus offered, his eyes flicking back and forth between Beckwith and Kinkead with growing concern. "What them Texians want with Taos?"

Jim replied, "Take more land from the Mexicans they throwed out, I s'pose."

Nodding, Mathew confirmed, "Ever since that autumn of eighteen and forty, ever' last greaser in northern Mexico had a differ'nt eye when they looked at gringos like me."

"You mean how they treated Americans?" Scratch inquired.

Kinkead said, "Don't you 'member how years ago I become a Mexican my own self so I could marry my Rosa in her church?"

Bass's eyes narrowed. "But Josiah didn't need to—he had him a Flathead woman."

"Josiah Paddock?" Beckwith perked up with sudden interest.

Scratch turned to gaze at the mulatto. "You know Josiah?"

"Me and Stephen Lee—my partner—we bought some of our goods off Paddock," Jim admitted. "He's a fair-handed man."

Scratch took pride in that, saying, "Josiah an' me—we rode together for a time."

Then Mathew continued, "Even though Paddock had a Injun wife, he still become a Mexican citizen so to make things run smoother on his trading business."

"Much as I'd never do such a thing my own self," Titus began, "if a fella lives in Mexico and works with Mexicans, I savvy it makes good sense for Josiah to raise his hand and swear he's gonna be a Mexican too."

"Hold on there, fellas," Jake Corn sputtered through a gulp of whiskey, shaking his head in argument as he glared at Mathew. "Wasn't Kinkead here just saying it didn't make no difference if any American swore to be a Mexican citizen, because every American was still gonna be treated bad the same way by them bean-bellies?"

Mathew nodded emphatically, his eyes gazing into the fire. "Didn't make no differ'nce to the greasers even if we swore to be a Mexican like they wanted us to do. The way the Mexicans was starting to look at us Americans— we knowed we figgered us *all* as spies for them Texians."

"S-spies?" Silas Adair snorted.

"That news of an army coming to the Rio Grande sure did stir up them Mexicans," Kinkead explained. "You know it ain't been that long since them Texians whipped the great Mexican Army—so now when them *Taosenos* hear this story 'bout these Texians marchin' west to take us over too . . . why, ever' last Mexican who ever was my friend turned his face from me."

"You tellin' me greasers black their faces against you?" Scratch bristled.

"Meaning to hurt me?" Kinkead asked. "Lookit me, coon! I'm twice't as big as most any bean-belly in all of Mexico!" Then that merry grin drained from his face, "But . . ."

"But what?" Titus demanded, sensing his own uneasiness stirring.

Mathew sighed, "I do know myself of a fella here or there what had the piss beat out of 'em purty bad."

"Beat on by greasers?" Corn demanded gruffly.

"Yep," Kinkead admitted reluctantly. "An' most of them what's had some trouble like that has already cleared out of the valley."

Titus leaned sideways to lay a hand on Kinkead's shoulder. "You was right to mosey north to the Arkansas. Figgered to find your family a more sleepy stretch of country?"

"Look around, fellas. Beaver's dead," Kinkead complained. "The big companies got their hands around the buffler trade; gonna strangle it to death too. And now the Mexicans don't want Americans comin' anywhere near their country no more. All you gotta do is look around and you'll see this here's the land where a man can make a brand-new start."

Scratch took a long drink. But the whiskey didn't help: he kept growing more fretful. "Afore you pulled up your picket pins and left San Fernando, Mathew—you know of any greasers ever make things hard on Josiah?"

"Nawww, he's a big-boned lad, Scratch. Just like me," Kinkead reminded. "Don't you worry none 'bout Josiah Paddock. You best remember I know the nigger what taught that big lad how to hang on to his hair in these here Shining Mountains. Any man what learns from Titus Bass sure as hell gonna keep a keen eye on his back trail. Ain't no pepper-belly I know of gonna have the *huevos* to go scratching round, makin' trouble for Josiah Paddock!"

Bass handed the jug on to Joseph Manz, then turned back to Kinkead. "You ask the lad if'n he wanted to move north to the Arkansas with you?"

"I did," Kinkead confessed. "But he told me he was staying 'cause he'd come to know them Mexicans and didn't figger 'em to raise no truck with him. 'Sides, Josiah said he had a big stake already made down to Taos, didn't wanna lose if he closed up and walked away from his shop. Said he didn't fear they'd do him no harm—no matter how mean they made it for some others we knowed of."

Bass rocked back and asked, "Them Texians ever show?"

"Not that none of us ever heard. Maybeso it was just cheap talk," Mathew declared, wagging his head with regret. "Damn shame of it, here at our Pueblo we're sitting right where Armijo's *soldados* or them Texians either one could jump us real easy."

"If'n you hear either one's comin'—where's a man like you to go?" Scratch inquired.

Kinkead gazed at him squarely. "Nowhere, Titus. Nowhere. Some men you can push out of one place after 'nother. As for me, I decided folks pushed me off from one place already. I ain't gonna let any nigger push me outta my home again. I figger the Arkansas's my home now, where I plan on livin' out the last of my years."

"Just like Josiah's figgering on lastin' out his years in Taos." Bass worked at calming his fear. "After all this time, I'll wager the lad talks purty good Mexican."

Kinkead roared, "Good as any natural-born pepper-belly!"

When out of the darkness a loud voice suddenly bawled, "To hell with ever' last pepper-belly, I say!"

The men at the fire whirled to find Bill Williams striding up, accompanied by two more of the raiders.

"That whiskey in them jugs?" Williams asked as he stepped right into the corona of warm firelight. "Three of us just been over to see how the herd's grazing—"

His words dropped off in midsentence as Jim Beckwith stood and turned to face his old nemesis.

"How you been, Bill?" the mulatto stated with a flat, dispassionate voice.

The old trapper's face went hard as slate, glaring at Beckwith. "I'll be jiggered, boys. Seein' how this Neegra shows his face to me here sure sours my milk, it does. Never thort he'd have the nerve to stay in the same territory I'm in—"

"Goddamn your eyes!" Jim snarled, muscles tensing along his jaw. "You're the child just dropping right outta the hills. This here's my home!"

"Y-your home, Beckwith?" Williams scoffed. "I say a low-down sack of Digger droppings like you don't deserve no home! Maybeso you best crawl back under some shit-covered rock you come from!"

Of a sudden, Bass reached up and grabbed Beckwith's wrist, stopping the mulatto in his tracks. But he asked his question of Williams, "Bad blood still atween you two, Solitaire?"

Bill's eyes flicked to Titus, then back to the mulatto's face. "Been some, it has. This here mongrel dog of a Neegra allays sided with Peg-Leg on ever'thing that first ride to California." He grinned cruelly, saying, "Wish't Beckwith been along so's I could leave him dry up in the goddamned desert with Peg-Leg."

"That what you done to Smith?" the mulatto demanded, his fists clenching and unclenching. "Leave him in the goddamned desert?"

"We give him plenty of horses to eat," Bass said, releasing Beckwith and standing at the black man's elbow. He took a step backward to place himself almost halfway between the mulatto and the old trapper.

Beckwith's black eyes bore into Scratch. "You was part of this, Titus Bass?"

Before Scratch could answer, Williams grumbled to the others, "What with you boys 'llowing this here p'isen-brained Neegra to make his *home* here with you, our outfit gonna be pulling out come first light." He sniffed the air. "Can't stand this smell of half-dead yellow-bellied dog—"

"You sure mighty big on calling a man bad things when you got all your friends at your side!" Beckwith snarled, his fists flexing as he glanced a hateful glare at Bass.

"Better'n talkin' bad behind a man's back—just what a snake-belly black-ass like you does!" Williams snapped, his right forearm sliding up across his belly, the hard-knuckled, slender fingers coming to rest around that elk-antler knife handle. "Never you had any backbone to say a mean thing to a man's face!"

"You ain't bound to change, are you, Bill?" Beckwith shot back. "Still the same ol' soft-brained idjit you allays was. Still runnin' off at the tongue like a ol' woman—"

"An' you're never gonna be a white man, are you, Neegra?" Williams interrupted, his bony shoulders drawing up threateningly. "No matter how hard Jimmy Beckwith tries to be white—"

The instant Beckwith lunged for him, Williams started to yank his belt knife free of the sheath, but Kinkead snagged that arm just above the elbow.

"No stickers, you sonsabitches!" Bass hollered as he jerked backward on Beckwith's arm, stumbling at the edge of the flames.

The mulatto twisted, wrenching his arm free as the rest of the men at the fire bolted to their feet. Williams whirled around on one foot, surprising Kinkead when he jammed a hickory-hard knee into Mathew's groin and pushed himself free of the big man's hold on him.

"Watchit!" someone cried as Williams lurched between two of the raiders who were attempting to block his way.

Scratch suddenly hopped in front of Beckwith, screaming at Williams, "I'll kill you my own self, you go an' pull your sticker, Solitaire!"

"Best get out of my way, Bass!" Williams shrieked as he lumbered around the side of the fire, traders and raiders dodging out of the fray. "Gonna gut 'im with my bare hands!"

Just as Titus raised his arms out before him and started toward Williams, Beckwith shoved Bass from behind, hurling Scratch aside as the mulatto leaped around him. Landing on his knees, Bass jerked around to find Beckwith yanking his pistol from his belt.

"Goddamn you, Beckwith!" he shouted. "Don't shoot!"

Williams was already under a full head of steam, his neck tucked into his shoulders as he closed on the mulatto.

But instead of pointing his pistol at Williams, Beckwith suddenly whirled the weapon around in his hand, gripping it by the barrel, swinging it backward at the end of his arm before he slashed downward the instant before the old trapper collided with the mulatto. The resounding crack reminded Titus of the dull thud a maul made as it drove an iron wedge into an old hickory stump.

Williams went down like every bone had been ripped from his body.

His heart pounding in his ears, anger at both men rising near the boiling point, Titus got to his hands and knees, crawling back to kneel over Williams.

"He breathing?" Rube Purcell asked as he came up, bent at the waist.

"Yeah, he's alive," Bass grumbled as he stood, not taking his hard glare off the mulatto.

Before any one of them, much less Beckwith himself,

saw it coming—Titus lashed out with the back of his hand, the oak-hard knuckles slashing across the mulatto's mouth.

"You stupid bastard!" Scratch growled menacingly. "You pulled your goddamn pistol, ready to kill a man!"

"By dogs, he was gonna kill me if I didn't lay him out first!" Beckwith protested, then licked at a trickle of blood seeping from the corner of his mouth.

"Maybe he should have kill't you outright," Titus said, a rumble of warning in the back of his throat.

Jim's eyes grew wide with confusion. "You takin' his side, Scratch?"

"I was willing to give yours a listen—till you knocked him in the head," Bass said, tearing his eyes away from Beckwith so he could glance down at Williams. "Maybeso, you'd better go back to your Pueblo now while you got the chance."

"Trouble is," Beckwith admitted, "this ain't finished 'tween him and me—"

"You gone mad with whiskey?" Titus demanded.

That appeared to bring Beckwith up short. "No. No, I ain't so drunk I don't know 'sactly what I'm doing when a—"

"Take him away, Mathew," Bass commanded, wagging his head. "Get Beckwith outta here—*now*."

"I could've killed him. You know I could've," Beckwith pleaded. "But I didn't. Son of a bitch had it comin'."

Kinkead wrapped one of his big arms around the mulatto's shoulders. "C'mon, Jim. Let's g'won back to the Pueblo."

Bass turned away from Beckwith, shaking his head in disappointment.

Kinkead started away, then stopped, still gripping onto Beckwith as he asked his question, "What you gonna do when Bill comes to, Scratch?"

"I ain't got a notion what to do."

"He's gonna be madder'n a spit-on hen," Mathew intoned. "And he'll be hankering to come looking for Jim here. Finish things one way or another. Gonna be messy—"

"I'll do what I can to keep Bill outta your Pueblo to-night, Mathew," Titus vowed. "Then we'll get our horses started away from here at first light."

Titus Bass dug at an itch at the nape of his neck and came away with a louse. Goddamn that Pueblo, he cursed, crushing the louse between a thumb- and fingernail. Then looked again at Ceran St. Vrain. "How many horses did you callate for a blanket?"

"Six," answered the trader.

He laid a hand on the white blanket festooned with narrow red stripes running the entire length of the thick wool fabric, which St. Vrain had unfurled down the long wooden trade counter here at Bents' Fort on the Arkansas. "Sure it weren't *five,* Savery?"

This partner of the two Bent brothers took the reed stem of a clay pipe from his lips and exhaled a white wreath of smoke, smiling. "You know better, mister horse thief. And you ain't no greenhorn pilgrim in this country neither. Yesterday, I sit down with Bill Williams, and I agree to take all I can off your hands . . . six horses a blanket."

"Maybe you oughtta ride east with us, Scratch?" Elias Kersey prodded again as he stepped up to Titus's elbow. "We'll damn sure get better money for 'em back in Missouri."

"True 'nough," Bass replied, brushing his roughened hand across the wool as he stared at the stacks of blankets, the bolts of coarse and fine cloth, those trays of tiny mirrors, beads, tacks, bells, ribbon, iron axes, brass kettles—and on and on.

But his heart was telling him something far different than his head might try to make logic of.

Bass sighed, "Can't think of nothing I want more'n to be home again."

Kersey and those with him could see their enthusiasm for their ride to the Missouri settlements would not convert Titus Bass, so all turned away without another word of advice and stepped back to lean against the wall.

Scratch gazed steadily into St. Vrain's eyes and instructed, "Tell one of your clerks here to go off an' count what blankets you got still in your stores."

"Blankets?"

"Said I wanna know how many blankets you got to trade me."

When St. Vrain had dispatched one of the younger employees from the trade room to the storage rooms, he turned back to return his full attention to Bass. "We met before, I am thinking. Yes?"

"The fort was real young then," Titus replied, struck by the memory of that spring in '34. "Eight summers ago, Savery—when I come here looking to kill one of your robe traders. Name was Cooper."*

"Ah—it was that," and St. Vrain nodded knowingly. "But instead, his cut-nose woman finished him off in our *placita,* our courtyard."

"You 'member me from that?"

"Most I remember you from the old Cheyenne who come to keep you from dying that day."

"He left afore I got pulled outta here on a travois," Scratch said. "You know his name, Savery?"

"He was just another old Injun." St. Vrain shook his head and shrugged. "I seeing him a few times since. But haven't seeing him around the fort any time new."

"Damn, if that red nigger wasn't old way back then," Bass ruminated. "His life was on his fingernails when he somehow brung me back from the dusk of my days."

"Maybeso wasn't your time, eh?" St. Vrain suggested.

Titus reflected, "Maybeso it wasn't after all."

The young clerk rushed back into the room, stuffing a short stub of a pencil over one ear while passing St. Vrain a piece of paper with the other hand.

The trader looked up. "Appears I've got plenty of blankets to trade."

"Awright." Then his eyes danced over the rest of the trade goods. "How many horses for a kettle?"

---

* *One-Eyed Dream*

"Four."

"An' them calicos back in the corner, there?"

"Coarse cloth is one horse for one yard. Them fine bolts is two horses for every yard."

Titus drew his lips up thoughtfully a moment, then eventually said, "Savery—s'pose we see just how close you can come to taking all my California horses off my hands."

Hell if it didn't play out to be a high-plains robbery! But then—when hadn't dealing with a trader in these here mountains always been larceny of the first order? A man accepted the order of things and lived out his days . . . or, he could get out. Head back east, or push on for Oregon country like Meek and Newell had. No sense in gnashing teeth over such a fact of life. Complaining did no good. Them what chose to stay on after the beaver trade died was the ones what figured they might never hold the best cards, much less any winning cards—but they were determined to play out what cards they had been dealt the best they knowed how.

That was the mark of these hardy few who would endure.

No, he'd decided against pushing on with Elias and the others who elected to sell their horses five hundred miles or more east of Bents Fort after more weeks of driving their herd across the great buffalo palace of the plains. "Back east" still held no allure for him.

Instead, such a journey would only delay him getting back to her before winter came shrieking down across the north country. To get back to Absaroka, to search out that first winter campsite of Yellow Belly's band of Crow—Scratch knew he would have to skeedaddle. And to make that march as fast as he needed to, he couldn't be hampered by a herd of wild horses neither.

He hadn't seen her since early spring.

And those two young'uns of theirs had surely grown a foot or more since he had last held them in his arms.

Titus hadn't planned things to work out this way: being gone so long after he had assured her he was leaving only for some spring trapping in the Wind River

Mountains. But that night camped near the Pueblo after they tied up the furious Williams and managed to pour enough whiskey down his gullet to soak him into a stupor so he'd pass out at the fire, Scratch lay in his robes, staring at the belljar clarity of the autumn sky overhead . . . and felt a discernible, painful tug. Something calling him back to her as quickly as a horse's four hooves could carry him north.

His homesickness only deepened as they drove their California horses away from the mouth of Fountain Creek, on down the Arkansas for the mouth of the Picketwire,* where the Bent brothers and St. Vrain had raised their huge adobe fortress squarely on the southern border of U.S. territory, like a gullet-choking gob of reddish-brown mud shoved right into the throat of northern Mexico itself. They found Charles Bent was off down in Taos doing some trading, but brother William and Ceran St. Vrain completed the wrangling with hardheaded Bill Williams to establish a per-head price on the stolen horses once the traders were assured the raiders would bring their herd no closer to the fort than some seven miles.

"We don't want your horses eating up what's left of the season's grass we'll need for our own stock this winter," William Bent explained.

As he had ridden back from the fort with Solitaire and Silas Adair following their negotiations with the traders, Williams told the two how he and Peg-Leg, Thompson, and their bunch had reached Bents Fort with their first herd of stolen horses back in '39 . . . only to discover the traders weren't all that thrilled to take those California animals off their hands. After all those months and miles, after traipsing twice across all that desert—Bill Williams handed over hundreds upon hundreds of horses in return for nothing more than a keg of cheap Mexican whiskey!

---

* What the mountain men called the Purgatory River.

Things hadn't turned out near that bad this go-round with the powerful traders.

As he looked back on the last few months, Scratch could see how he had wagered his life on one more daring, risky venture . . . and somehow slipped through Lady Fate's slim, grasping fingers to end up with more than he would have had to show after a spring and fall season's worth of trapping the high country. Beaver was worth no more than a pittance compared to its high-water heyday. Plews were no longer king. Squaw-tanned buffalo robes ruled the roost now.

So any hivernant who'd had the green rubbed off him would be a durn fool to turn down St. Vrain's calculations on just how many stolen horses it would cost a man for all them shiny trade goods the company had packed up from Mexico in carts, or clear out from St. Louis by wagon train.

Bass had held on to a hundred of the Californians he traded off to a small band of Cheyenne who were camped outside the walls of the fort, down on a bench beside the Arkansas. In exchange he ended up with a dozen of the strongest, hard-mouthed, lean-haunched prairie cayuses he could find among the Cheyenne herd. Twelve would be enough to follow him north to the Wind River country where he had cached his goods last spring. From there he planned on making a short scamper into the land of the Crow to find her and the children.

In less than another day, Bass had his Cheyenne pack animals in tow, ready to march north beneath the burden of more than eighty blankets, along with a bevy of weighty kettles and skillets, not to mention a wooden case bearing a hundred new skinning knives, and several hundredweight of other foofaraw that should damn near make him the king of all Absaroka. Tomorrow he would bid farewell to Solitaire and the other raiders who were now in their third glorious day of a drunken spree.

But for tonight he planned to have himself a doe-see-doe with St. Vrain's Mexican whiskey, and push off at sunrise with a hard-puking, head-thumping hangover. Enough of a mind-numbing hurraw to last him for many,

many seasons to come before he dared again venture out of Crow country—

Then he stopped dead in his tracks, staring through the open doorway into the booshways' dining hall at that wide-hipped, black-faced woman, who wore a bright, multicolored scarf around her neck and a pleated Mexican skirt swirling around her bare black calves. But it wasn't the bosomy Negress who turned and stepped over the doorjamb into the warm, lamp-lit room late that autumn afternoon that held Titus Bass's rapt attention.

It was that pair of small, squirming, pink-tongued puppies she had cradled across her fleshy, brown arms!

20

◆————

"Where the hell you fixin' to go with them dogs, woman?"

That pinned those cracked and scuffed brown boots of hers right to the pounded clay floor. Up and down she gave him a scathing appraisal, then glared straight into his eye.

"Who be askin'?"

"You answer my question first," he demanded with the beginnings of a grin. From the corner of his eye, Titus noticed a thick-armed Negro appear at the open doorway behind the big Negro woman. His shirt was open to the waist, sweat glistening in diamonds at the chest hair. He wore a faded yellow bandanna tied round his head, splotched with damp sweat stains. No matter the man's imposing size, Scratch turned back to argue with the woman the moment she protested.

"Ain't a-gonna answer you, no how," she huffed, and her face grew even harder.

"You work for Savery?"

"I do," and she drew herself up. "So who is you? You work here now?"

"No, I don't," he answered impatiently. "Tell me what you're doing with them dogs—"

"Ain't no business of yours these dogs." Then she progressed another step forward with that armful of squirming puppies.

Feeling emboldened, Bass leaped directly in front of her. Now they stood less than an arm's length apart. "You ain't the cook, are you?"

"Leave me be!" she growled, lunging to the side to start around the trapper.

But he was far lighter, and all the quicker, dodging left to appear in front of her again, blocking her way.

"Who the hell you be, actin' with such bad manners way you are!" she snarled.

Now a new, booming voice announced, "You better tell her just who the hell you are, mister. And what the high most you care where she's headed with them pups."

He glanced as the muscular man eased into the room, slowly volving the edge of a big butcher knife round and round on a flat whetstone he cupped in the other palm. He took his eyes off Bass only momentarily to spit onto the stone, then continued his sharpening.

"Titus Bass," he said in a hurried gush. "I asked if you was the cook, woman?"

"I is," she answered, shifting those wriggling puppies in her arms.

"Wh-what's your name, woman?"

She turned her head nearly around to speak over her shoulder at the man standing in the doorway. "Mr. Dick—you g'won and tell Mr. Titus who I is."

"Charlotte, she's my wife, mister," the man explained. "An' Charlotte be the Bents' cook hereabouts."

Scratch asked, "Charlotte, you wasn't planning on cooking these here dogs, was you?"

A snort of raw laughter broke from her big-toothed mouth while her eyes grew wide and expressive. "Why—I ain't no Shian Injun woman now, Mr. Titus! I ain't never et puppy and I ain't ever *gonna* eat puppy neither. Don't you know I'm the onliest lady in the whole damn Injun country?"

"So them pups is yours, right?"

"These here dogs?" she asked.

"Yes. They yours?"

"They mine 'cause no one else took care of the bitch they come out of," the cook replied.

The man leaned a shoulder against the adobe door-jamb but kept on circling the edge of his knife round and round on that stone. "You want a pup, mister? That why you're asking with such curiosity?"

Pinning his eyes again on the woman's, Scratch continued, "You got more pups, woman?"

"The bitch had her seven of 'em," the cook answered. "Weeks ago now. They been coming off the tit last few days."

"Jehoshaphat!" he exclaimed, his heart leaping. "If that ain't prime doin's!"

"What you got in your head?" she asked, more than a little suspiciously.

"I want them two pups," Bass exploded in a gush.

"There's four others too. I awready give one away," the woman declared. "But, you wanna see them other four too?"

Charlotte didn't have to ask him a second time. Eager, Bass held out his arms and she immediately obliged, passing him one of the thick-furred pups. With the other dog still wrapped in her arm, she turned and led him back through the doorway as her muscular husband stepped aside. Back through the kitchen they wound their way, past small kegs and crates, on through the cool shadows in the pantry, eventually emerging through a low, narrow portal to find himself out in the autumn sun. Nonetheless, he discovered they were still standing inside the fort walls. She paused at one end of an oblong corral, where the black cook immediately stooped over a low, crudely erected pile of brush and firewood meant to serve as a small pen. She set her pup on the ground right in front of the low entrance to a small canvas shelter, where the four other pups burst into view, scrambling into the light around their weary but suspicious mother.

"There they be, Mr. Titus," she said with the most cheerful tone. "Take your pick which one."

When the pup he held suddenly became animated in his arms, all legs and eager yelps, Bass leaned over the firewood fence and returned the pup to his mother and siblings. Some of the other pups hopped right up to give him a good going-over with their noses, sniffing all that was new on his fur.

"I want two," he confessed.

"Two?" And then Charlotte Green chuckled, her fleshy face becoming even rounder in mirth, her big bosom and shoulders quivering with laughter. "That be a double handful of trouble, that's what!"

"So you lemme have two?"

"You can have 'em all if'n you want 'em."

He considered that a moment, then thought of that long ride north. One pup, maybe two at the most—he could handle them. But not a half dozen wild, animated creatures as he marched his laden pack string north to Absaroka.

"Nawww, just two."

"Which'uns you want, mister?"

Pausing a moment more to study them all as they boiled back and forth across their small enclosure—some scratching an ear, others tugging a sibling's long tail as they wrestled, and the rest plopping down in the dirt near the security of their mother's shadow—he quickly decided.

Bending over the fence, he scooped one into his hands, hoisting it aloft to glance between its hind legs. Then he gazed into the little male's face. He approved of the look in the pup's eyes as the dog's tiny pink tongue repeatedly lapped in its attempt to lick Scratch's face.

"This'un likes ye, mister," Charlotte observed.

"Hold 'im for me, would ye?"

Titus moved past her to step round to another side of the enclosure where he held his hand down close to the ground. Three of the remaining five pups immediately came over to sniff his callused, rough hand. But one of the three immediately nuzzled its tiny, cold nose into his palm, rubbing his fingers.

"You too," he said as he scooped up the second pup and inspected its genitals.

"What you got there?" the cook asked. "A li'l girl? You wanna a li'l girl too?"

"Nope. Better for me to take two males, Charlotte."

Again she chuckled with that merry laughter. "I knows! This way, the li'l boy won't be crawlin' on his li'l sister to make more pups, eh?"

"How much I owe you?"

"Nothin'," she answered with a grin.

"I owe you somethin' for these two pups," he pleaded. Then Titus was hit with an inspiration as she shook her head emphatically. "Surely now, you've had your eye on something over to the trade room, woman! Some new beads, or a Mexican scarf. Maybe a bolt of cloth for a new dress—"

"I did see something!" Charlotte exclaimed as her eyes widened like white orbs swelling in a dark firmament.

He gulped, suspicious he might have offered too much. "What can I get for you?"

"I seen some . . ." And she squeezed an earlobe between her finger and thumb as she squinted, leaning close to peer at one of his wire hoops and those tiny small brass beads suspended from it. "Some real purty earbobs."

Relieved, he shifted the dog into one arm and pulled her toward the door. "C'mon with me, Miss Charlotte! We're gonna make us a trade!"

With the two pups in their arms, Titus and Charlotte threaded their way past hunters, trappers, and fort employees lounging in the last of the autumn sun cast against the east side of the inner courtyard, scurrying hip to hip into the trade room where they shuffled around a cluster of Mexicans and half-breeds arguing with one of the traders.

Charlotte began waving her free arm in the air to the clerks at the far end of the counter. "Mr. Goddamn! Ovah heah, Mr. Goddamn!"

Busy over a ledger at the far end of the long counter, Lucas Murray turned to peer over his shoulder as they approached. His face lit up when he realized who had called him out. "Charlotte!"

"You he'p me please, Mr. Goddamn?"

"Help you do what?"

"This here nice man gonna get me some earbobs I took a shine to."

The fort's head trader's eyes trained on the old trapper. "You're Bass—the one took all those blankets off our hands."

He nodded, scratching the pup's neck. "Like she said: I wanna trade for some purty earrings Charlotte's put her eyes on."

Murray leaned across the counter so he could put his lips near Scratch's ear, whispering in delicious confidentiality, "You ain't getting her something in trade for her bedding you. She gonna throttle your wiping stick, that the way of it?"

Titus roared as the trader straightened, stiffening in surprise. "Great Jehoshaphat! She's got that husband of hers—the blacksmith! By the stars, I'm getting her them earrings she took a shine to in trade for these here two puppies!"

Nervously licking his lips in embarrassment, Murray sidestepped over to stand directly in front of the cook, only the narrow counter separating them now. "S'pose you tell me which ones you got in mind, Charlotte."

Bass had to admit they did look good hanging from her ears, what with the way she wore her hair all pulled back and covered with that bright red, blue, and yellow Mexican scarf. As Charlotte was inserting the second earring through the hole in a lobe, Bass turned slightly, noticing the stack of pack baskets woven from oaken slats.

"How much you want for them baskets, Mr. Murray?"

The trader stepped down to the corner and picked one of them up by its single handle. "What you need one'a these for?"

"Two of 'em," he declared. "One for each pup. Here, pass it over and lemme try it."

He handed one of the dogs back to Charlotte, then clutched the remaining pup under one arm before he took the basket and set it on the floor. Then lowered the dog into the basket's wide, oval mouth. Immediately the pup stood up inside, barely able to get its little nose over the top.

"These'll work just fine," Titus commented, taking his hand off the basket where he had been steadying it and the pup both. "How much you trade for two of 'em—and them earrings too?"

Charlotte's infectious, uninhibited laughter split the trading room. Bass turned, watching the pack basket topple over and the puppy come tumbling out. It scrambled onto all fours and was just starting for the door when Titus leaped to grab it. He stood, scratching the pup's ears as it went to licking his neck beneath the graying whiskers.

" 'Bout got away from you, Mr. Titus!" she giggled as the dog in her arms squirmed.

Murray cleared his throat, "You got another two horses, I let you have both of these here baskets and Charlotte's earbobs too."

"Sounds steep to me," Scratch reflected, allowing the pup to gently gnaw on his thumb with its tiny, sharp teeth.

"It ain't steep," Murray replied. "Could cost you more—but the Frenchmen was what used these baskets. So we don't get much call for 'em anymore."

"Two horses?"

The head trader nodded. "Two horses."

"I'll have your horses back here afore you bolt the gate at sundown tonight."

Murray grinned as he turned to step back down the counter to his ledger. "You're one I trust, Bass. Just put them two horses with the others you already brung up to the fort."

"Well, now," Charlotte sighed as she turned toward

Bass, lowering the framed looking glass she had been regarding herself in. "How I look?"

"Handsome as could be," Titus said with a grin. "I declare, if you ain't the most handsome woman this side of the Wind River Mountains!"

They were Injun dogs. Plain and simple.

Their long, wolfish snouts and short, peaked ears marked these mongrels as belonging to a breed much, much closer to their wild cousins than any civilized house or hunting breed preferred by white folks back east.

He could easily believe there might well be some prairie wolf in the pups, what with him getting that brief look at their mother. She was nothing more than a Cheyenne cur . . . that tribe being an extremely nomadic people who had long ago grown attached to those wild canines roaming the fringes of their villages in the prehorse days. From her narrow head and shallow rib cage, the bitch was nothing more than a typical Cheyenne camp dog, homely mongrel that she was.

But the male that had mounted her at the fragrant peak of her last season damn well had some buffalo wolf in him—if not an outright wolf himself. That wild, feral cast to the pups' eyes, the forehead and lean haunches of the two—characteristics that all bespoke an ancient ancestry dating long, long before man and dog ever crossed paths to advance their mutual fortunes.

That first morning marching north, Scratch had them ensconced in their baskets, slung on either side of a gentle, hard-boned mare he figured had to be some eight to ten years old from the condition of her teeth. With a short lead rope he had loosely looped around her neck, he kept the mare close by his knee. Only once did one of the black-eyed pups ever grow fractious enough to clamber his way out of his basket.

Titus watched it out of the corner of his eye: that offhand pup scratching and clawing desperately, pulling himself up with all fours until the dog purchased a hold on the top of the basket with his powerful jaws—pulling the rest of his roly-poly body behind him . . . then *phoosh*—he spilled all the way to the ground. Somehow the gentle mare knew and stopped, jerking back on her lasso Scratch had looped round his left hand.

Suspending his flintlock from the saddle horn using the braided loop he had knotted to the trigger guard, Titus dropped to the ground and stepped around the mare. Now the second pup, the one with those pale, ghost-colored eyes, was yelping—wanting out to play too.

Its darker-haired brother rocked onto its feet, shimmied to dust himself off, then immediately dove under the mare's legs to flee the man just settling to his knees.

"C'mon, you li'l Digger," he said as he stood, slowly moving to the other side of the mare.

Which caused the obstinate pup to scamper in the opposite direction.

Titus stopped, put his hands on his hips, and said in a quiet, clear voice, "So, you don't wanna go north to Absaroka with me—that it?"

He watched how the pup settled to its rear haunches and cocked its head at him—as if trying to understand those sounds the man was making. Behind Titus the other pup kept up a pitiful yowl for its brother.

"It's up to you. If'n you're going, you get over here now so we can be on the tramp. I ain't gonna take you up there to them two young'uns of mine less'n you wanna go with me on your own."

He bent forward slowly, inching toward the pup—which suddenly darted to the other side of the mare again.

"Awright—there'll only be one of you dogs get up there with us for the winter. Damn your li'l black eyes anyway. By mornin' you'll be breakfast for a b'ar!"

Scratch stood, dusting off the knees of his leggings and settling the elkhide coat around him once more as he strode around the mare's head and took up the reins to his saddle horse. When he was settled, Bass loosed his rifle off the round saddle horn and clucked at the mare. "Giddap."

It took no more than three of his heartbeats for the ghost-eyed pup to set up a mournful howl the moment it saw they were leaving its black-eyed brother behind. Scratch turned to gaze over his shoulder at the dog sitting on the prairie, dispassionately watching the string of packhorses pass him by, one by one by one. Eventually he was alone, and the big rumps of those cayuses were passing out of sight in the far trees lining a creekbank.

Yip-yipping, the black-eyed pup suddenly set up its own call—a plaintive cry far different than the mournful howl of its basket-bound brother.

"If'n he don't come—we'll both get over him," Bass assured the grief-stricken, pale-eyed dog.

Then he glanced over his shoulder a third time, spotting the little pup scurrying along the line of packhorses, its short legs churning so furiously that it shot past the string of tall horses, making for the front of the line where the old trapper reined to a halt. After suspending the rifle from the horn again, Scratch eased himself slowly to the ground, turned, and descended to both knees, patting the tops of his thighs.

"C'mon, you li'l Digger! Get on up here!"

The puppy tumbled into his arms, every leg still windmilling as Titus swept it off the ground—whimpering, burying its muzzle beneath Scratch's elbow. He stood with the pup, scratching behind its ears. The way its brother was howling and leaping in its basket, Bass carried the black-eyed one over and let them both lick each other's faces for a long moment before returning the darker one to his basket.

"You gonna stay there now," he chided. "Leastways, till your legs are long enough for you to foller on your own."

He scratched them both atop their bony skulls before remounting. "I sure hope you fellas gonna be as good a dog as ol' Zeke was."

Of a sudden it made his heart small and cold with mourning to remember that gray-haired hound. Loyal to its dying breath . . . killed by the goddamned Blackfoot it was following to protect its family—*

He squeezed his eyes shut against the sting of tears and clucked for the saddle horse, gave the mare's lead rope a tug. Damn, if he wasn't getting more and more human all the time, he reflected as the sun emerged at the far edge of the prairie behind his right shoulder. Older he got, the easier it was for him to hurt, easier for his eyes to seep a little too. Ol' Zeke. Damnation, if he hadn't been about the best dog a man could ever deserve to have as a friend. He blinked and looked up at the rosy-orange clouds strung out in strips across the autumn-blue sky with the sun's rising.

If there was a heaven, and if there was a God . . . then Titus Bass knew the Lord had ol' Zeke at his knee right about then. Up where Zeke was sure to spend all eternity, that faithful dog had to know how Titus Bass's heart still pined for a scarred ol' riverfront mongrel.

Maybeso, one of these two, even both, could one day make as good a dog as Zeke. Him and Zeke—they'd been a pair. Both of them weathered and scarred more than their share. But he'd never heard complaint one out of the dog over their few seasons together. Hell, Zeke had even come along to help him mourn when it came time to grieve alone for Rotten Belly.

He looked over at those two pups, rocking gently side to side as the mare carried them north into the unknown with their new master. Neither one of them made a peep, appearing content as could be in their baskets padded with parts of an old blanket Titus had cut up for them to share. Its thick wool had his smell buried deep within its fibers.

By the time he managed to track down Yellow Belly's village, Scratch was certain the two of them would be imprinted with his smell, the various tones of his voice, the stern reproach when he corrected their behavior, or that gentle feel of his hands as he ruffled their soft fur.

---

* *Ride the Moon Down*

They would no longer be pups just weaned from their mamma. They'd be his dogs.

The day's new sun felt warm on the side of his face. He and the fellas had themselves quite a hurroo last night—all of it wetted down with lots of Mexican whiskey. For some time now Elias Kersey, Jake Corn, and the others had determined they would push on for the Missouri settlements with their share of the horses, no more than another day or two—once they could cure their hangovers. But Scratch wasn't about to wait another day. No matter that his head throbbed more than it had in years, he was starting north.

Like Bass and Williams, about half of the raiders had decided to turn their share of the California horses into mountain currency, getting from St. Vrain and Murray what they could per head, then taking out that credit in trade goods. Oh, there'd been a little good-natured grumbling to be sure, but Solitaire and the rest understood as well as any that the complaining wouldn't do a lick of good.

Out here in this land, on the rolling flats or up into the broken and forbidding high country, freedom meant nothing less than horses to a man. No two ways about it.

But to Titus Bass, his share of those thousands of stolen horses he'd risked his neck to drive out of California were no better than a shackle and thousandweight iron chain hammer welded around his neck. All those animals could make him a veritable rich man for the first time in his life . . . but he wasn't about to push on across the plains to reach the Missouri settlements where he could turn them into a small fortune. With no regret at all, he would once again abandon the notion of growing rich and living out his days in comfort.

Beyond what he could give his family and friends in the way of material goods, this temporal matter of *things* had never been very important to him. Better that a man have family in his arms and friends at his side than live in the finest St. Louis mansion crowded with all the servants, liquor, and rich appointments his money could buy.

Scratch breathed deep of the air still chilly here at sunrise . . . and realized again that he already was one of
the richest men in the whole of all this country west of
the wide Missouri.

It wasn't long before he was thinking back to their last
big hurraw last night—when Williams staggered over, his
stooped shoulders wagging side to side as he lurched to a
drunken halt by Titus there beside their roaring fire.

"I should'a let 'em kill you, Titus Bass," he grumbled,
his face set hard as mountain talus.

"Who?"

"Thompson. Them yellow-livered sonsabitches with
'im. They wanted to gut you so bad . . . I should'a let
'em, goddamn ye!"

Surprised, and made wary with all the alcohol washing
around in his belly, Titus backed a step away from the
man and did his best to set himself for what might come:
a fist, or even the flash of a knife in the fire's light.

His curiosity pricked, Scratch asked, "Why you figger
them low-down bastards should'a kill't me, Bill?"

The old trapper was a while in answering, taking his
stern, half-lidded eyes off Bass to drain his pint cup before glaring again into Scratch's face as he licked at the
droplets suspended like glittering diamonds from the
ends of his shaggy mustache.

"If'n I'd let Thompson an' his bunch do with you how
they wanted . . . then you'd ain't been around a few
nights back when I was fixin' to guttin' that goddamned
Beckwith."

Bass shook his head a minute, his mind confused,
dulled somewhat by the potent liquor. "You want me
dead 'cause I stopped you from getting yourself hurt,
even kill't by Beckwith?"

"That be the sartin truth of it," he slurred. "Damn
your eyes! I'd a-took him for sure, Scratch."

"You was drunk then as you're drunk now," Titus
argued. "Jim'd a hurt you bad, if'n he didn't kill you
outright. I damn sure didn't want that to happen,
Bill . . . for then I'd had to cut Beckwith up my
own self."

Williams attempted to straighten himself and keep from weaving unevenly, blinking his eyes at Bass. Finally he said, "Y-you'd done that for me?"

"Hell, I stood at your back all the way into California, and all the way back out again," Scratch reminded. "And when they was fixing to slit my throat, you didn't look away. Been easy 'nough to do it. But you stood up to 'em, an' Peg-Leg later on too."

"I 'member Peg-Leg." Williams shook his head dolefully. "Dunno where he went bad."

"I figger a man goes bad, like him and Thompson—they're the sort allays was bad. Bad just waiting for a place to happen."

"Damn your soul, Titus Bass." And Williams licked his lips again. "You gone an' 'minded me of why I favor taking to the high lonesome on my lonesome. Being with other coons just too hard sometimes. Finding them what you can count on, that's too damn much work. Better off not havin' to count on no one else but my own self."

"Buy you 'nother drink, Bill?"

Williams gazed down into his cup a long moment, then his watery eyes climbed up to stare into Bass's. "Drinking myself silly—that there's one thing Ol' Solitaire don't cotton to doin' alone."

Other raiders were thumping on brass kettles, clanging iron skillets, or pounding on an old hollowed stump as the rest wheeled and cavorted round the fire. The noise and blur and numbness just like the old times, just like rendezvous. Gone forever now. Like cold mountain water run through a man's fingers . . .

As the night aged, Williams had grown misty-eyed and asked, "We had us our hurraw, Scratch, didn't we?"

"This here?"

"Nawww!" Bill shook his head emphatically. "Riding bold as brass into California and sneering at all them goose-necked greasers. We had us our hurraw showin' them bean-bellies what for and slipping away with all them horse right under their idjit noses. Making it all the way back here 'cross that desert and them Rocky Mountings with what horses could still run with us. That's the hurraw, Titus Bass. By damn . . . if that wasn't a real man's hurraw!"

Scratch's eyes grew misty again too. Suddenly, he was struck with the reality that he would likely never see any of these men again in his life. No telling if Elias and the others would ever come back to the mountains once they reached the settlements with those horses. They'd likely sell every one for a ransom and become rich men overnight. If not rich, at least wealthy enough to damn well do anything rather than come west again in an attempt to scratch out a meager living trapping flat-tails in half-frozen streams, looking over their shoulders for grizzly or Blackfoot either one.

And men like Bill. Likely Williams would be good at his word about running alone and not poke his head in most places where Titus Bass might chance onto him again. So Scratch looked around the fire, at those dancing shadows whirling and spinning and stomping with gusto as they kicked up dust and watered down a long-grown thirst. He was not likely to lay eyes on these fellas ever again.

If for no better reason than Titus Bass couldn't conceive of much that would lure him out of the north country. No matter what an uncertain future might bring his way.

So he had turned to look at old Bill, reading the war map that was Williams's face, knowing his own face read like a war map of scrapes and scraps and battles too—all those times he had managed to slip right through death's fingers . . . not to mention all the suns and the winds, and every last one of the winters that had carved their way onto his face and right on into his soul.

Damn, if the two of them didn't have their epic California adventure to tell their grandchildren! If, that is, any of them lived long enough to bounce grandpups on their knees. They'd always have what they'd shared together.

"Ain't no one gonna ever take our hurraw from us, Bill," he had said to the man seated at his elbow. "No matter neither one of us become the rich men we figgered we was gonna be once we started out for California. No matter we had to fight off Mex soldiers and greasers too, slash our way through them goddamned Diggers and Yutas both just to jab most of these here horses all the way over every one of them mountain passes and down the canyons and valleys so we could reach that Picketwire Creek sitting right over yonder. No matter we hung our asses over the fire an' roasted 'em good, Bill Williams. It still don't make me no never mind we ain't the rich men we thought we was gonna be."

Bill had snorted some mirthless laughter. "Neither one of us ever likely to make ourselves rich by wading up to our balls in icy water to catch them goddamned big flat-tailed rats, Titus Bass."

"Your words are true," he ruminated. "I s'pose after enough seasons out here, them what learns they're allays gonna be poor are the first to skeedaddle back east to what they was . . . while the rest just give up an' head west for Oregon country to try farming."

"What's to become of the rest of us, Scratch?"

"The rest of us?" And Titus paused for some thought before continuing. "Why—niggers like you an' me damn well made peace with being poor a long, long time ago, Bill!"

"What you figger to do with all them horses of your'n so you can stay on bein' a poor nigger like you allays was?" Williams asked.

"Traded most of 'em off—give a few away. Keeping only what I need to get some plunder back to my family," he admitted. "A passel of horses like them'd only slow me down getting north, going back where I belong. An' . . . I don't wanna linger too long striking out for the country I never should've left in the first place."

21

◆

Those rangy, strong-backed horses he traded off a few of Gray Thunder's Cheyenne were a steady lot. Mile after mile, from murky first light until it grew too dark to see much of anything past the saddle horse's muzzle, Titus Bass goaded every one of the creatures north.

The pups seemed to swell and grow each day, steadily filling out, their lanky legs stretching even longer—no great surprise, for they were eating a diet of the fresh game Scratch killed along the way, gnawing at the meaty bones at night while all three of them lay by the fire in those camps he selected so they would be sheltered from the harsh, howling autumn winds and any roving eyes, giving them a few hours respite from the trail.

That first night out from Bents Fort, it suddenly struck him that he was alone again in Arapaho country. Titus had banked the fire and dragged the wood close to his robes so he wouldn't have to slip out into the cold to periodically feed the flames. As he lay there, listening to the dark womb of night surrounding them, Scratch watched first one, then the second pup, tire of chewing slivers of meat from their bones. It wasn't long before their eyes were closed and their tails were curled over their noses.

When he awoke later on, the wind had died some, but it had begun to softly snow, just enough to already collect a scum of flakes on the dogs' fur. After quickly banking more wood on their fire, Bass whistled softly.

Both heads popped up. "C'mere."

He held up the edge of the buffalo robe and patted the blanket beside him. "C'mon, you rascals—get in here."

The black-eyed one was the first to scramble to his feet and prance around the small fire. He settled right against Bass's hip. Then the ghost-eyed pup complied too, settling in against the man's knees. Gently laying the robe back over all three of them, Titus fell asleep quickly—sensing the warmth of those pups seeping into his own old bones.

"I got the feeling we're gonna be the best of friends, you boys an' me," he whispered just before sleep overtook him again.

That next morning, the temperature hovered well below freezing as the pups stirred and poked their noses from under the edge of the snow-crusted buffalo robe.

"G'won, now—go pee."

They stretched and yawned as they emerged into the cold, then stepped away to water the bushes beyond the far side of the fire ring, while Titus shuddered with the stiffening breeze as he laid the last of his wood on the coals. Laying his cheek right above the icy crust of snow, he began blowing to excite the few, fading embers. Finished with his morning business, the dark-eyed one shoved his pointed snout through the two or more inches of snow, searching a moment before scooping up last night's bone. The second pup excavated for his too.

"Already got your breakfast, do you?"

After sprinkling the nearby snow himself, Titus warmed what was left of his coffee from the night before and chewed on some slices of meat he had roasted for supper. It didn't take long before the pups moseyed over, lured by the smell of that flame-kissed meat.

"So now you don't want them bones, eh?"

One at a time, he fed himself and the dogs small bites he trimmed from the slabs of roasted venison until there was no more. Then downed the last of his coffee before pulling on his coat in the gray light, stomping out to take the horses to water.

By the time the pack animals were loaded, Scratch pulled the blanket halves from the two baskets and whistled for the pups. First one, then the other, he set inside their basket and arranged the blanket under and around them both for padding and for warmth.

They marched until midmorning when he stopped briefly to let them pee in the snow and he himself sprayed the bushes. By the middle of the day when they stopped again to rest the horses for the better part of an hour, Scratch unfurled two buffalo robes, one atop the other, and called the pups inside the cocoon with him for a short nap. They pushed on again until midafternoon when he gave the dogs another chance to stretch their legs before enduring a last long stretch that took them right into twilight.

So it went, day after day, as Titus hurried to strike the South Platte. Then late one afternoon, they reached the abandoned adobe walls of Fort Vasquez.

"This here's where I brung my wife and li'l Magpie too—we spent the winter of thirty-five–thirty-six right over yonder in them trees."

Abandoned, and forlorn—how lonely the place seemed now. Then he remembered the Arapaho who caught him trapping in the foothills that early spring of '36. Squeezing the dread from his mind, Scratch decided to stay the night within those quiet, ghostly adobe walls once a witness to far better times. As darkness came down and the wind moaned outside the half-hung gate, he thought of Shad Sweete, how the big man's moccasins had once crossed and recrossed this ground . . . until the fur business went to hell and the traders abandoned their fort. The Bents and American Fur up at Laramie were both able to offer more to the wandering bands for their tanned buffalo robes than any small-time operation ever could hope to offer in trade.

Now Shad had gone off to the blanket with the Cheyenne. Maybe even took him a shine to a squaw, some gal
he couldn't get off his mind or out of his heart. Titus
knew how a man could get himself so lonely for the
touch of a woman, the smell of her too—himself feeling
pretty damn miserable right then and there for missing
his own woman. Month after month of nothing but the
growl of deep voices falling upon his ears—it made him
hunger for to hear her soft, trilling voice at long, long
last. He went to brooding on just how her arms could feel
around him, the fragrance of her hair when she nestled
her head in the crook of his shoulder. A hollow pit
yawned in the middle of him as he remembered the way
her warm mouth crushed his lips so eagerly when she
hungered for him.

And he discovered that he ached to see the little ones
too. Oh, their bright eyes—how Magpie would curl up in
his arms, and the way Flea would tug at his father's one
lone braid. So the old trapper called the pups close,
scratching their ears and rubbing their bellies, thinking
how wonderful a surprise these two dogs would be for
his two children when he returned to Absaroka, long
overdue.

The wind blustered outside those old mud walls,
groaning past the dilapidated gate swinging on the last of
its hinges, a cold wind sighing as it hurtled snow clouds
past the silver face of a quarter-moon overhead. He had
been alone, so very alone before. But never quite this
lonely.

That next morning he left the South Platte to angle
itself off to the northeast as he struck out for the northwest and the base of the foothills that would guide him in
his quest. The sky was lowering, and another storm
would be bearing down on them by nightfall. Better to be
in the lee of the mountains come late afternoon, find a
sheltered draw or ravine where he could protect the
horses and build a fire the wind could not torment.

After dark it began to snow again. He sensed the in-
ward pressure of time. Never having owned a pocket
watch, not a man who was mindful of a calendar either,

Titus nonetheless felt a compression of his soul as the cold knifed its way into the marrow of him. He should have been home by now. Not having the slightest idea where that realization sprang from . . . Scratch nonetheless knew he should have been back to Absaroka by now.

He passed a fitful night, tossing in the robes and blankets with those two leggy pups. The storm moderated by first light as it rolled on east. The exertion made Bass warm as he loaded up the horses, one by one with their Indian pack saddles, then strapped on their bundles and made ready the saddle horse and the pups' baskets. They set off across a new snow that had rubbed the little dogs' furry bellies earlier that morning before he ensconced them in their blankets and baskets for the journey.

His decision was made before the sun appeared behind the thick storm clouds. There would be no trip that would take him to Fort William at the mouth of the Laramie on the North Platte, no trip east from the direct route he had charted in his mind. He didn't have the time for such a luxury. Winter was on its way to the northern plains, and he needed to strike for home as fast as he could push the animals.

In a matter of days he had them skirting around the far end of the Black Hills,* gradually stretching out the daily march even though the number of hours between dawn and dusk was perceptibly shrinking. They could move faster now, cover more ground, the Cheyenne horses hardened to the trail, accustomed to their loads. After all, he knew these hills and bluffs, knew every creek and rivulet as he hurried cross-country, guided by the map long ago burned in his mind.

At last he struck the upper North Platte, and in two more days he put that river at his back—scurrying, scurrying west for Turtle Rock and Devil's Gate, following the Sweetwater in its icy climb into the naked,

---

* What the mountain men called the Laramie Range in southeastern Wyoming; not the Black Hills of today, which rise in extreme northwestern South Dakota.

scrub-covered expanse that would transport a man to the Southern Pass.

But Titus would not be near so patient as to wait for the Sweetwater to make it to the top of the pass before he would turn north. Instead, he struck out across country, praying his memory of the land would not fail him. North by northwest through each shortening day. That first night after abandoning the Sweetwater, he bedded down the weary horses at dark without water. They were too weary to care. The dogs whimpered some, however, tongues lolling—but quieted as soon as he tossed them the raw gut of a skinny antelope buck he had chanced across just before sundown.

Near midmorning the following day, he spotted the telltale brushy border of a creek, that dull gray of leafless branches huddling close to the snowy ground as the watercourse meandered its way across the unbroken white expanse that stretched ever onward toward the harsh blue of the prairie sky. A bone-dry westerly wind prevented the horses from smelling the moisture until they were almost on top of the little creek.

In a matter of moments every one of the animals was lined up, licking at the icy crust, hammering at the discolored slake with their hooves to get down to water . . . what little water still flowed over the pebbled creekbed. The dogs were yowling piteously, clawing at the tops of their baskets by the time he got to the pups and dropped them onto the icy crust of snow. The old, gentle horses were careful for the impetuous puppies as the pair darted between legs and hooves to drink first at one place, then scampered to another, lapping at the skimpy flow.

On his knees after cracking the ice with his tomahawk, Scratch leaned out and lowered his face into the ragged hole. Water so cold it made his back teeth ache clear down to the jawbone. He came up gasping, raking his blanket mitten down his mustache and into his beard, both instantly caked with ice in that freezing wind blustering off the hillsides—

There in the mid-distance, he saw them gathered beneath the hulking, bruised, blue-black clouds. The mountain slopes. They had to be the Wind Rivers. Two days, three at the most, and he would be at the cache. The cache. It was one more milestone to put at his back, each landmark announcing he was drawing closer and closer to home.

The cache. Here he had buried his traps and all the other weighty truck he had not wanted to pack across the desert to California. With Bill Williams's help, he had taken a day to dig that shallow hole before they pushed on south to the appointed rendezvous with the other raiders at both Davy Crockett and Robidoux . . . suddenly it all seemed so long ago. The desert crossing early in the summer, the raids and fighting, then recrossing the desert with all their horses. Striking for the mountains and home. He'd made it east of the Rockies, but he was still far from home.

He let the animals drink and drink. He owed them that much, he decided. Then Bass called the pups to his feet and picked them up, one by one, settling them inside their baskets. For some reason, it struck him just how much they had grown: if they stood on their rear legs, each of the pups could easily leap out of the baskets that weren't holding them much longer. Perhaps by the time they reached the cache and he had his plunder resurrected from that hole in the ground, he could give the pups a try on their own—following the horses north.

Bass mounted, led the pack animals across the narrow creek, and struck for the foot of the mountains.

Late morning of the third day, he recognized the distant landmarks here several leagues south of where the fur companies had held two of their rendezvous. Summer of '30 had been a good one, times were clearly getting better—the mountain men were basking in their glory days. But by July of '38, when the traders and trappers once more gathered in these nearby meadows, dark and ominous shadows had appeared over the mountains. Most of the free men realized the writing was already carved in the wall. The beaver trade was dying. Over the last few years there had gradually been less and less to hurraw about, less to celebrate and revel in, with far less whiskey to kill the pain that came of such a slow, agonizing death.

By sundown a day later, Bass had everything dragged out of the small cache, dividing the square-jawed iron traps and all that extra powder and lead among the baggage he would strap on the packhorses come morning. At twilight Titus celebrated inching that much closer to her and the children.

Here in the lee of the mountains his horses had plenty of grass blown clear by the winds groaning off the eastern slopes of the Wind River Range. Nearby they had a narrow creek, fed by a spring that would keep the creek open most of the winter. Now they were ready to point their noses directly north—following the Wind River into Absaroka itself. He could have done with a little whiskey to toast his efforts this night beside that empty hole in the ground, but Bents Fort coffee would have to do.

That night as he lay in the robes and blankets, scratching the furry ears of those two weary dogs, Bass stared up at the patches of starry sky that appeared through wide gaps in the drifting clouds. For the first night in a long, long time he felt assured that this truly was the same sky she would be looking up at this moment too. No more did months separate them. Now it was only a matter of weeks—days really, or so he wanted to convince himself.

Hopeful the miles would pass beneath him all the quicker for it.

Bad as his joints pained him—especially the stiffness in those hard, raw-knuckled hands, not to mention the afflictions suffered a'times in both his knees and the aggravation that came and went in that left hip—Scratch nonetheless did not tarry at the medicinal oil springs lying north of that old rendezvous site.

Memories were wrenched up just in passing on by the smelly, sulphurous tar pits. In much the same way Titus sensed the ghosts of the past as he stood beneath the lowslung, midday sun resplendent on the bright snow in that meadow where the Popo Agie joined the Wind River.

How many hooves and horses, lodges and lean-tos, trappers and traders had trampled this grassy lowland . . . but those were matters of a bygone time. He whistled the dogs close as he slowly rose to the saddle, grown melancholy with remembrance as he set off again.

Way it seemed, most of his life was already at his back, day by day steadily moving beyond all that he had left behind—friends and fights and freezing streams—realities and recollections that only made the possibilities of what lay ahead that much sweeter.

Titus knew how the pups must feel: for the first time they were allowed their own legs on this northbound journey. He'd realized he would have to check their paws and pads at each stop throughout the days ahead, looking for telltale signs of frostbite from tromping across the patches of ice, stretches of bare, frozen ground, and crusty snowdrifts everywhere they'd turn. Their skinny, wolfish legs would have to grow all the stronger too, what with the endurance that would be required of them if they were to travel with Titus Bass. To have them strike out across the ground on their own seemed the only way to toughen up their pads for this last part of the trail taking them north into the heart of winter. At first they might have only enough bottom to last until the mid-morning halt—but he knew that day by day the pups would harden for both the trail and what new life awaited them in Absaroka.

The dogs were eager to begin their march each morning, but by midday they were tongue-lolling and near done in as they collapsed near his feet the moment he dropped from the saddle. Titus packed them in their baskets most of the afternoon. As one day tumbled onto the next, he found them able to last a little longer. A good thing too, he reflected. Those half-big dogs would soon outgrow the pack baskets he had traded off of Goddamn Murray. They weren't roly-poly puppies anymore. He had burned off their store of baby fat. Mile by mile, they had become lean and hard.

By the time he led them through the Pryor Gap, Titus knew the dogs could survive without him if they had to.

Should something happen to him, they would make it on their own. That gave him peace of mind: knowing that if he were no longer around, the animals wouldn't fall prey their first few days in the wilderness. The pups just might end up having some hair of the bear too, might possess what it took to survive in this raw, wild land.

Once he had started into the Gap, Bass began to train an ever-more-alert eye on the blue horizon, searching for any sign of smoke or dust, something that might foretell of a village in camp or some Crow on the move. Yellow Belly's people could be anywhere in this stretch of country now, he reminded himself. Deep in winter the band might push far south of the Gap, seeking out those protected valleys as the weather intensified its icy fury. But for now, he figured that the village would still be migrating across more open country. Anywhere west from the Bighorn. Pushing on, Titus continued down that river to its junction with the mighty Yellowstone.

From those high southern bluffs he halted to let the horses blow and water while he had himself a look with his brass spyglass. Dragging it from his possibles bag, Scratch snapped open the three long, leather-wrapped sections and began to search the north bank of the Yellowstone, slowly scanning to his right as the Bighorn flowed off to the northeast. Then he inched it around to the south, searching the lower Bighorn valley. Still nothing.

They had to be west of there, he decided. Turning to the left, Titus began to scan the north bank of the Yellowstone for any sign of movement, human or otherwise. Twisting the sections into focus on the horizon, he inched the spyglass across to the southern bank of the wide, icy-blue river. In due time the Yellowstone would ice up for the season.

How desperately he wanted to find them, spot some wispy tower of smoke perhaps, that his eyes strained and grew tired. So tired for the strain in the winter light, from his willing it to be so, that his eyes began to water in the dry cold as the sun sank behind a bank of purple-blue storm clouds. Certain that, by morning, they would have more snow on the ground. For now he could find them shelter somewhere down below.

As he started the horses away, descending through a defile, Scratch decided that was likely what the Crow themselves had done: gone in search of some sheltered valley where they might have more protection from the winter storms sure to roll through with more regularity now.

From firsthand experience, he knew both the river and mountain bands generally spent the early part of the winter out in the open country. But as soon as the storms began to batter the Yellowstone country with some regularity, the Crow migrated to those sheltered valleys in the lee of mountains. True enough, Yellow Belly's bunch could be over east visiting and trading with Tullock at the mouth of the Tongue—but the odds of that were a might slim. They usually put off that sort of journey for the leanest times—late in the winter—after the women had plenty of furs tanned, ready for bartering.

Yonder to the northwest along the Yellowstone lay that country where, he recalled, Bridger's brigade had wintered back in the early part of '37. Titus thought back fondly on that cold time when he was hunkered in among the Crow with his family and decided to pay a visit to see some old friends where the trappers had set up their winter quarters nearby. Ol' Gabe himself, Shad Sweete, big Joe Meek, and others too hadn't been regaling one another with tales of bygone glories for very long at all when some Blackfoot showed up.

"That there weren't no leetle war party, mind you, boys," he said now to the dogs loping near the saddle horse's legs. "It were a hull shitteree of them bad-hearted niggers. Fact be—there was more of them red niggers'n any of us ever laid eyes on!"

Late of a subfreezing winter day those warriors had gathered in force just downriver, clearly intending to wipe out one of the largest contingents of Americans ever to boldly penetrate the southern extreme of that country claimed by the Blackfoot. The sun went down, and the temperature plummeted with it. As darkness closed in around them, the Blackfoot drums began their haunting echoes.

"We could hear 'em beatin' on their parfleche and screaming their war songs," Scratch explained to his canine audience as they continued downslope. "Such noisome sounds could turn a lesser man's heart to water—hour after hour of that goddamned music, just knowing that come morning there was more'n enough Blackfoot to wipe all of us out three or four times over."

Then one of the trappers had shouted for the others to look north into the night sky. The horizon was ablaze with pulsating lights, resplendent with exploding streamers of throbbing color. But downriver a short distance, it appeared those northern lights gradually began to change hue. As the trappers watched, the sky bowed directly over the Blackfoot war camp erupted in a brilliant crimson.

"Damn, if it didn't seem like the heavens themselves was bleeding!" Titus declared dramatically as he related the story to those two dogs.

It had proved to be a long, sleepless, and brutally cold night. And with the gray of dawn, while the ice fog began to swirl and shift, the trappers saw the Blackfoot coming—led by a war chief who had a white robe wrapped about his shoulders.

"We figgered that was it, boys. The last sunrise any of us niggers would ever lay eyes on. But, 'stead of rolling on over us, them Blackfoots squatted right down and had themselves a war council not far from our barricades."

After some spirited debate, the war chief advanced alone to a spot midway between his warriors and the Americans. In sign he explained that the spirits must not be pleased with their plans to attack the trappers. The chief and his headmen had decided that blood-red sky arched over their end of the river valley was nothing less than a bad omen.

"An' them niggers did skeedaddle, just like that!" he clucked, trying his best to snap his fingers within the thick blanket mittens. "Happened, just like I told it—not far yonder there, on the north bank of the Yallerstone."

Come morning, he'd continue west along the Yellow-stone, Titus decided. About the only way to search was to make the sweep and look for sign. Maybe come across some evidence of hunters ranging out from camp. Spot enough smoke to account for a village. Cut some trail sign—

He studied the lowering sky at the western rim of a world shrinking smaller and smaller as his day came to an end. The tops of those far mountains had disappeared beneath a bank of heavy clouds. Snow would be atop them by nightfall. With no possibility of cutting trail sign after the storm.

As his eyes began to scan the countryside immediately ahead for a sheltered nook, he figured the best he could hope for was that in two—maybeso three—days after the storm had waned, the Crow men would again venture out to hunt as the weather faired off. But for the next day or so while the storm left icy remnants of its passage through the countryside . . . both game and hunters would be laying low.

It was nearing twilight when he found a copse of trees big enough to bring all those horses under cover, an open spot in the middle big enough where he would eventually scrape back the crusty snow to build his fire and spread out his bedding. The first item of necessity was to stretch out a long length of one-inch rope between several of the trees surrounding the center of the copse where little of the old snow covered the grass the horses would dig at. By the time he was done bringing the horses into his makeshift rope corral, Titus felt himself breaking a sweat. And his work had hardly begun. Sometimes, everything needed doing at once.

As the dogs scampered off to sniff among the nearby willow while the light continued to fade, Bass tore off his elkhide coat and mittens. The wind was coming up—a sharp, brassy tang announced a hard, dry snow on its way.

Wearing only the buffalo-hide vest for warmth now, he tore at the knots in the hitching ropes with his bare fingers, hoisting the loads from the horses' packs, uncinching the saddles and heaving them outside the rope corral. When the last loads hit the ground, Bass dragged all the baggage he wouldn't need into four piles, then carried the rest toward the base of three cottonwoods that might as well have grown from the same root system, their trunks stood so close. Together the three would make a fine reflector for his fire in the coming storm.

Storm. Fire. Wood.

But first he needed to water the horses—

Titus heard the dogs barking enthusiastically, a different and excited tone from their throats—almost playful. They must have found themselves a porcupine, he thought as he untied two of the horses and led them out of the corral by their halters, heading for the creek less than sixty feet from his shelter.

The dogs persisted in their yipping and howling. If they'd found themselves a porky, or a smelly polecat either one, Titus figured, he would have heard them yelping piteously by now: their eyes and noses stinging with a spray of poison, or their sensitive muzzles punctured by a hundred tiny, sharp needles. Sometimes the only way to learn was the hard way. . . .

He thought about that harsh wilderness reality as he continued to bring the horses, two-by-two, down from the corral to the creekbank where he had knelt and hacked at the thin ice with the tomahawk he carried slung in the back of his belt. He listened, looked about, as each pair of animals drank their fill.

Most folks simply didn't realize that in this sort of country, winter's cold dried a body out even more than the heat of summer. Recognizing that he must do better in such matters, Scratch vowed he would water the horses more often through the days ahead—especially as he taxed them with their long search in the bitterest of northern cold.

From even farther away now he heard the dogs bark . . . then went back to thinking how he had somehow survived while learning things the hard way. No matter what it was that confronted him—he had endured. From what knowledge he had acquired on his fa-

ther's farm in Boone County, Kentucky, to all that he had
absorbed during his journey downriver with Ebenezer
Zane's boatmen. Soaking in what Isaac Washburn had to
teach him before Titus ever ventured to the mountains,
not to mention all the brutal mistakes he made learning
his mountaincraft from Silas Cooper—no matter all those
intervening years, Titus Bass had survived despite the
odds continually pitted against him.

Out here there always had been risks, perils, outright
dangers that would surely chew up lesser men.

So why was it that he was still standing, approaching
his forty-ninth birthday? How had he managed to cheat
death so damned often . . . when other men—those un-
deniably much stronger and those most certainly much
smarter—had fallen prey to this wilderness, succumbed
to the challenges and the dangers this raw land brandished as a weapon against man's intrusion?

When other men were bigger or faster, when that
many more who had come and gone were clearly more
learned of mind—why was it that Titus Bass had outlasted all but the hardy few who remained, steadfast
holdouts like him?

What had singled him out for this honor?

From the echo of their barking, he could tell the dogs
were making their way back. He stood listening to the
dying of the light as the last pair of horses drank their fill.
As the last rays of sun slowly drained behind the nearby
bluffs, his old wounds began to ache with the great and
deep cold that settled in the river valley.

Had he survived merely because he was so vigilant and
wary? Or, quite the contrary—had he survived because
he had ignored the odds and refused to shrink from those
dangers that caused lesser men to cower—taking risks
that spared his life in the end, while other less daring
souls fell to less ordinary circumstances?

The two dogs burst onto the scene, causing the horses
to snort in surprise, perhaps in disgust, at the canines'
playfulness. Titus turned and led those last two horses
back to join the others as the dogs came up, bounding
around him.

"Here. Here, boys," he said as he dropped the lead ropes and patted his knees, calling the dogs. Something on their muzzles, a difference to their noses.

He wrapped an arm around the black-eyed one and held him close for an inspection. "Well, now—lookit you, Digger. What's this?"

Swiping his mitten across the black nose and into the pale fur behind it, Bass grew suspicious.

Biting off his mitten, Bass dropped it at his knee while he licked his first two fingers and used them to wipe at the dog's nose. Then he held the fingertips beneath his nose and smelled. Immediately brought the fingers to his mouth, tasting them lightly with the tip of his tongue.

"Ashes, boys. You had your noses in a fire pit, ain't you?"

He let the darker pup go, snagged his mitten and pulled it on as he stood. Staring off in the direction where the pups had gone to investigate.

Not that the ash could have been warm—sensitive as their noses were, these dogs wouldn't have done that. Even so, had it been as recent as last night's fire pit, still had been a whole day—hunters up and moving off at daylight, clearing out of this country . . .

But, if they had been Crow hunters—why hadn't they just returned to their village after their hunt instead of spending the night out in the cold?

Maybeso it wasn't a Crow fire. Damn, he hated feeling squampshus like this on what had become more and more like home ground after all these years.

Looking around at this place he had chosen, Scratch sighed. He'd build a fire, cook his supper, and heat some coffee. Then take the precaution of building a straw man he would stuff beneath some robes to give the appearance of a man sleeping.

That done and the fire banked, he'd slip off into the dark, back among the cottonwood shadows where he would dig a narrow trench after nightfall. Into that shallow hole he'd lay enough of the glowing coals he could scoop from the fire pit, then sprinkle a thin layer of dirt over them before spreading his sleeping robes atop the trench. That done, he'd sleep warm, hiding back in the dark, laying right where he could keep watch on the fire and campsite through the trees.

Something told him. Maybe it was the fact he hadn't found the Crow village by now. Compounded by the dogs investigating that ash from an old fire.

Then again . . . maybe it was nothing more than that finely tuned edge of discomfort that had saved his life so many, many times before.

22

———— ◆ ————

Damn! He'd dozed off into a sleep too content and restful.

Should have heard them coming.

Bass listened to the night, his eyes straining at the dim corona of firelight that remained through the trees. Nothing moving yet.

Only sounds. The nicker of a horse, soft as a sigh. Then from another direction—this time to his right—the groan of a misplaced moccasin on the icy snow. That meant there was two of 'em. At *least* two anyway.

Already the dogs were alert, trembling in keen anticipation, whimpering low and feral in their throats there at his side, where they lay upon the robes. Before bedding down, Titus had tied them with lengths of rope to a pair of nearby trees, then wrapped bandannas around their jaws to clamp them shut when he inched back into the darkness last night. Oh, he could have tied them up close to the fire and the straw man, but these thieves might well have killed the pups outright. Dogs were noisy in an Indian camp—warning those in the village of all intruders.

This enemy would go right after the pups if Titus had left them tied by the fire.

Better that they were beside him where he could scratch their ears, reassuring them—even whisper to them to hush now that so much depended upon noise, or the absence of it.

While his ears continued to listen for the slightest whisper of telltale sound, he watched the shadows around that copse of trees, that circle of radiant light from the fire he had banked. The glow was fading. A good chunk of time had passed since he slipped back into the shadows to wait out the night. There for a while he had come wide awake with every new sound emanating from the darkness. A restless, wary discontent huddled in the robes laid atop that warm trench of dirt and live coals.

Must've made himself too comfortable, too warm, too secure and lazy. His two pistols jabbing him in the gut hadn't been enough to keep him from sleeping. They were primed and ready for the close work—once the three long guns were emptied. How many would there be?

Then he tried to assure himself there couldn't be that many. If there were—it's for certain the red niggers would have stepped right on into his camp, bold as brass to take his hair. Or, leastwise, to lift that straw man's topknot.

No more'n three of 'em. Maybe four at the most, he convinced himself. No more than four, or these niggers would have been sassier. As it was, the thieves were cautious. And he had long ago learned to be all the more scared of a cautious adversary than to be wary of a boldly overconfident enemy.

As he lay there, trying to work his mind around just how to make his play from the dark, the first of the intruders eased into the outer edge of firelight, just off to his left a little. The warrior moved cautiously, still back in too much of those shadows preventing Titus from determining what the man might be—Blackfoot, Assiniboine, maybe even Crow horse thieves.

At the back of Digger's throat, a low rumble grew. Good thing the wind rustled the leaf-bare branches enough to overwhelm the dog's warning in that moment before Scratch grabbed Digger's muzzle and squeezed it shut. The pup swallowed down the last of its growl.

This Indian had much of his back to Bass as he stepped silently, studying that long form stretched upon the ground, at the far side of the fire from Titus. Then part of the tall shadow moved, and a long weapon appeared in the warrior's hand. A rifle. Maybeso a smoothbore trade gun, short as the barrel was. Its muzzle was being leveled at the straw man wrapped up in those buffalo robes.

It surprised Scratch when the Indian took one of his mittens from that smoothbore and waved it in gesture to the dark. Bass's eyes shifted to the right, watching a second figure emerge from the dark. Out in front of him was a long-barreled weapon—definitely not a fusil. That was a rifle. Likely taken off some white man. Not a weapon bartered in the Indian trade.

Only then did Titus realize his heart was loudly thumping in his chest. He was scared they could hear it too and realize he was behind them in the dark. As the second one took another step into the light, Scratch rocked up on his hip. With a step from the other, he brought out one of the pistols. Each time the Indians moved with a rustle or a shuffle of their own, the old trapper readied himself a little more—shifting the robe out of his way before dragging out that second pistol. If there were two in the light, likely there were others still back in the dark.

Unless they were so cocky that they figured they had jumped a lone white man and he was as good as dead.

The wind suddenly gusted through the nearby brush. With its groaning rise of sound, Scratch whispered sharply to the two bandanna-bound pups, "Shush!"

Bass stood, slowly inching onto his feet, knowing the crackling of his knees and left hip had to be loud enough for the bastards to hear. No longer content to sit, both dogs were on their feet. Titus could tell their neck fur had ruffed.

He waited breathlessly, watching the man to his left start quietly around the fire pit, his smoothbore held low, its muzzle almost on the ground. When he stopped, Scratch froze too. He was just out of the fire's light. Any closer would expose him to the warriors and he would have to wheel to the right to fire at that second intruder. But from where he stood just inside the thick veil of darkness, he could get off both pistols at them without being forced to move for the second shot.

The muzzle of that fusil climbed a little, and the Indian held. It seemed almost as if the son of a bitch hankered to savor this moment when he had the drop on the enemy.

That's when he realized they couldn't be Crow. Once before—not knowing who he was or that he was married into the tribe—Crow warriors had stripped him of horses and left him afoot. If these raiders only wanted his horses, they could have taken them and been gone in the dark.

Chances were damned certain these weren't Crow horse thieves. These were killers. Scalp hunters.

The hair rose at the back of his neck. Blackfoot.

Bug's Boys had killed more good men than he dared to count. Blackfoot took Jack Hatcher. Arapooesh. Whistler. And they killed Strikes In Camp with their pox. Blackfoot kidnapped his woman and daughter—nearly killed Waits-by-the-Water with their slow-dying sickness. No doubt about it: These red bastards had slashed and hacked their way through Titus Bass's life from every which way. And here they were again. Not content to lift his horses, or ride off with all that trading-post plunder . . . the sons of bitches had a hankering to kill him.

Their kind had tried it many times before and failed—

The warrior slowly raised the muzzle until it was less than four feet from the buffalo robe tucked over the clumps of sage and brush he had tied and formed to look like a man—then fired.

Standing near his knees, both dogs jerked, shuddering with the sudden explosion. They pressed themselves against his legs. Titus lowered his arms to momentarily reassure them both by scratching them with the pistols he gripped in both bare hands.

Wincing from the bright muzzle flash, both Indians twisted to the side, covering their eyes with mittens. It was several moments before their eyes adjusted to the dark, when both warriors stepped closer, grumbling at one another. The second warrior brought up his weapon and warily held it on the straw man as the shooter poked the muzzle of his empty smoothbore under the edge of the buffalo robe and flung it back.

The two of them had a moment to stare at the brush tied in several places with leather whangs to form the crude shape of a body, then gaze into one another's faces—before Scratch took those two steps that brought him right to the edge of the firelight.

"Lookin' for me?"

They immediately wheeled on him, utter shock clouding their copper-red faces. The second warrior's long rifle came up as if strapped on a pulley.

"You're dead, you sonsabitches!"

With that first pistol shot, Bass hit the rifleman high in the chest, hurtling the warrior backward a step where he spilled over some of the baggage circling the fire.

Wheeling to his left, Titus found the first shooter lunging to the side. He had flung his smoothbore aside and was scratching at his belt to pull out the tomahawk with its dull, tarnished brass head.

English. French, maybe.

Such a weapon was Blackfoot for sure.

A voice shouted from the dark. Then another from the far right. Shit—there were four of them after all.

Bass ducked backward, retreating out of the light. Kneeling beside one of the old cottonwoods, he laid the empty pistol down on the snow and swapped the other to his right hand. Far, far better with it. He never had been a good two-handed shooter.

There! He spotted that shooter with his 'hawk crouched at the edge of some of the trade goods, what there was of his form illuminated by the fire's light.

Off to his left some of the horses whinnied. Whoever was there, one or more of them, was no longer worried about the white man's horses making any noise. The tomahawk man was hollering. His voice, high and strident. Bass could tell he was afraid, caught by surprise, seeing his friend killed, and now he had to fathom he was pinned down by the white man who was just waiting for him to break into the open.

In the next moment, Scratch realized he needed more than that one pistol in hand. There were at least three of them still out there—each one capable of cutting him down. He whirled about on the balls of his feet, jamming the pistol into his belt and pulling out the larger of the two knives at his back.

Back at his hidden bed, Titus grabbed Ghost's rope in his left hand, sawing the blade against the woven hemp. As the rope came apart in his hand, he reached up and yanked the bandanna off the dog's snout. Close at hand, Digger was lunging at the end of his rope, the length of it snapping taut with so much force it made a dull *pung-pung-pung* sound. He reached the second dog, tearing the bandanna off its muzzle, then made a grab for its restraining rope.

Behind him at the fire, the killers were shouting now. One of them even screaming. Another voice broke into a discordant wail. A death song. *The son of a bitch knows he's gonna die.*

By the time Titus got turned back around and stuffed the knife in its scabbard, he wasn't sure if he was hearing the dogs padding on the snow in the dark or if it was the enemy. He dropped to his knees there at the buffalo robes, flinging back the hides and feeling for the rifles he had exposed. He supposed at least two of them were coming. He could see no movement in the firelight. As many as three. Those two out there in the dark, and now the tomahawk carrier had dived into the shadows, that inky black beyond the reach of the fire's feeble glow.

Weighing what he should do—go in search of them, or wait for them to stumble across him in the dark—Bass listened for the dogs. They would either make a nuisance of themselves in the dark, or they would get themselves killed. Suddenly he felt guilty for releasing them to attack the attackers. They were a threat to the thieves and would likely get—

Then he made himself a promise on their behalf. If he heard a sound from one of the pups or a warrior, Titus vowed he would dash to the sound. He convinced himself that if he reacted quickly enough, the enemy wouldn't have time to kill either of the dogs because they posed a threat.

That was the pale-eyed Ghost's growl. A man suddenly yelped in pain. A dull thud—an instant before Bass started forward in the dark. Then he heard Ghost whimpering in his own pain.

Just as Titus shuffled through the trees at his left, he caught sight of a jumble of shadows at the far edge of the firelight. Ghost had one of them by the calf, his jaws locked tight as the warrior clumsily swung his fusil down on the dog's back again and again, sometimes swinging wild, sometimes connecting. With each noisy thud, Ghost released a groan—but never did release the Indian. It must be excruciating to have those half-grown fangs buried deep into that calf muscle.

From the veil of darkness Digger flew like a blur, striking that same warrior with such force that the Indian spilled over some baggage. As the scalp hunter tried holding off the second dog, Titus kept moving. Before he got to the edge of the light, the tomahawk holder appeared between the trees, his weapon held high as he lunged forward, making for Digger because the big pup had his warrior flattened on the ground, protecting his throat.

At his right hip Titus brought up the rifle on instinct, instantly setting the back trigger before yanking on the front trigger without thinking, much less aiming as he clenched his eyes shut. When he opened them again, he found the tomahawk holder spinning, the upper part of his left arm bleeding. The warrior grumbled as he settled onto the balls of both feet wobbly, then brought the tomahawk back once more as he stumbled to a stop right over Digger.

Scratch dropped the .54 and passed the .50-caliber flinter over to his right side. There was no set trigger on it, Titus reminded himself as his cold, stiffened fingers wrapped themselves around the wrist and trigger guard. He was already close enough to his target that he didn't have to bring the weapon up to his shoulder. Instead, he shot it from his side, bracing the cheekpiece against the bottom of his rib cage.

The ball caught the tomahawk holder low in the face, shattering his lower jaw and driving on out the back of the warrior's head as he cartwheeled backward a step, propelled off his feet to land flat on his back where he slid across the icy, trammeled snow.

Two more of them remained. At least one more out in the darkness, somewhere. He wasn't sure of the voices he heard—not certain of just what he had heard or the tally now as he pitched aside the empty .50 and started for the dogs on those creaky knees of his.

Back and forth the warrior on his back swung his weapon, growling at the dogs that had sunk their teeth into his leg and his forearm.

Dragging the second pistol from his belt, Titus swept in past Ghost, kneeling at the Blackfoot's shoulder to press the pistol's muzzle against the warrior's forehead. That brought an immediate reaction: the Indian ceased his struggles, going cross-eyed as he stared at the muzzle for a moment, his face contorted in pain, before the eyes shifted again, glaring up at Bass's face.

"Git, boys!" he ordered. The dogs did not instantly obey. He could tell they loosened their grips, yet did not fully release the warrior. "I said git! Back off! Back, god-dammit!"

His eyes flicked up quickly, peered around, looking for one or both of the other thieves. Then the warrior moved beneath him—prompting Bass to press so hard with that muzzle he was certain he'd either cave in the bastard's head or shove that head right on into the snow beneath the warrior.

Seizing the man's trade gun in his left hand, Bass

grumbled, "Gimme that, you red son of a black-hearted whore."

He heard its *twung* and whisper, pitching himself to the side without thinking. More a feral reaction than anything approaching a thought process. Damn, if the arrow still didn't rake along the side of his neck as he dove out of the shaft's trajectory. It had been aimed at his chest. The explosion of the bowstring had warned him.

But he had reacted in the wrong direction, diving low as the iron arrowpoint opened up a raw, oozy, throbbing wound along the great muscles where his neck met the shoulder.

Landing on the snow, Titus twisted to look for the arrow, surprised it wasn't embedded in him. A few feet away the warrior on the ground was fighting anew with the dogs. Scratch felt his trade gun pinned beneath his hip as the bowman stepped into the light, holding his weapon at the ready in his left hand, a half dozen arrows clutched in that same hand, arrayed around the center of the bow where they were ready for instant use.

With a *twung* he watched a second iron-tipped shaft hurtle away from the bow. Scratch rolled off the rifle, rocking onto the hip—swinging the smoothbore up and dragging his palm back on the big hammer in a fluid motion. It was already at full cock. Praying there was powder in the pan, he squeezed back on the trigger. The huge frizzen spat a shower of sparks, and the pan spewed a flare of both fire and smoke an instant before the old fusil belched loudly.

As that second arrow flitted past Scratch's shoulder, the bowman was already stumbling backward, his weapon slowly tumbling from his grasp as he stared down at the red blossom in his belly with a blank look crossing his fire-lit copper face—

A fourth warrior shrieked out of the darkness, a club held high overhead, a knife in his left hand. Rushing in under that head of steam, the Blackfoot didn't have time to leap aside when Titus pitched onto his shoulder and held out the empty fusil, tripping the Indian as he stumbled past.

Old as he was, the fear of death nonetheless gave the trapper a little prod at that flickering edge of winter's darkness.

Landing atop that stunned fourth warrior he had just tripped, Titus jammed one knee down on the forearm that held the club while he seized the left wrist and wrenched the Indian's knife from his fingers.

Rocking back on his knees, Scratch brought the long beaver-tail dagger into the air overhead, preparing to hurtle it downward into the man's throat—when he stopped, staring dumbfounded at the Blackfoot's face. And jerked in surprise.

This wasn't a man at all. He was a boy. No more than a youth. A goddamned pony holder! Come to fight like a man with all the life-and-death consequences of manhood. When he was no more than a goddamned pony holder of a boy!

The eyes below him held a fire of such unmitigated hatred, for an instant Bass wondered why he didn't plunge the knife right down into the youth's sneering face itself. Instead Titus brought his right knee up to pin down the boy's left arm as he shifted the knife in his hand so he could grip its blade.

"Digger! Ghost!" he cried sharply. "Off! Off now! Back, goddammit!"

The pups eventually complied, releasing the badly mauled Blackfoot from their jowls.

"Back, I said! Back!"

Both of the dogs began to slink away, their teeth still bared, a low warning that rumbled in their throats as the wounded warrior began to shove himself backward, sliding away from the snarling animals. With one hand the Blackfoot reached out to claw himself along, while his wounded left arm snagged hold of that tomahawk stuffed in the sash wrapped around his blanket capote.

Wrenching his right arm to the left as if cocking it, Scratch flung the arm sideways. The pony holder's dagger caught the warrior in the side of his chest. Instantly dropping the tomahawk, he brought both hands up to grip the dagger's handle, struggling to pull it from his body as he collapsed backward into the snow. His thrashing legs slowly came to a stop and he lay still.

Beneath Titus, the youngster's eyes slowly rolled from the warrior just killed to glare with hatred at the white man no more than a heartbeat before he struggled anew.

With his free right hand, Scratch reached down and tore the stone club from the Blackfoot's grip. He swung it to the side and smacked it along the side of the youngster's head.

All the fight sank out of the Blackfoot.

Waiting a moment to be certain, Scratch finally got to his feet and stared down at the youngster while the two dogs loped up to stand at his side.

"Good, fellas—that's right," he whispered harshly, his eyes scanning the treed circle around them. Listening.

With his own heart pounding loudly in his ears, Scratch finally figured out that if there had been any more of the enemy, the dogs likely wouldn't have been hanging back. They would have been charging into the dark for the enemy. That must have meant he had brought them all down. Including this boy.

"Stay here with this'un," he told the pups as if they would know what he was saying. "Stay."

Both of the pups surprised him when they did stay as he moved off. The dogs stood guard over the unconscious youth as Scratch hurried into the dark, finding the tree where he had tied Ghost, and cut the entire length of rope free. With it, Bass quickly knotted the Blackfoot's hands together, then brought a loop down to wrap more rope around the ankles.

Finally he stood and gazed down at the youngster. The boy would awaken to find himself all trussed up, with a good-sized goose egg on the side of his skull.

"Well, boys," Titus whispered to the pups. "You both was li'l hellions in that scrap—"

The youngster's eyes fluttered, opening half-lidded as the groggy Blackfoot attempted to gaze up at the white man.

Bass dropped to one knee and stared into the youth's face. He began to lower a hand, but the boy jerked his head aside. With his left hand pressed down on the youngster's forehead to hold it in place, Titus brushed snow and ice from the side of the Blackfoot's face.

Then Scratch rocked back on his haunches and dusted off his hand. Staring at the youth, he sighed, "So what in the billy blue hell am I gonna do with you?"

It began snowing just before first light.

There was something significant to this particular quiet that awoke Scratch where he sat propped with his back against a cottonwood. The last thing he could remember was he had been looking at that youngster's face. And now that was the first sight he had when his eyes snapped open with alarm.

Of a sudden every muscle was keenly aware of the overwhelming silence as the snow soughed through the bare branches of the trees. Maybe there were more of them. Titus listened for a long time, weighing what he didn't hear—but when one of the Cheyenne horses nickered in that gentle, contented way of their species, Bass finally let the air out of his chest again.

"You been watching me, ain't you?" Titus asked, more to let the Blackfoot understand he was awake than any attempt at language or hope for an answer.

"This here snow means we ain't goin' nowhere, not till it's passed."

So you just as well settle in till the weather breaks, he thought as he scratched Ghost behind an ear. The dog had its muzzle laid on his thigh.

Easing onto his knees, he crabbed closer to the fire and laid on some more wood. Glancing at what wood he had dragged into camp the night before, Scratch prayed he had enough to last them that day and even into the coming night. With the big, fat flakes coming down the way they were, all too soon it would be next to impossible to find a lot of the small, loose squaw wood. So if he carefully marshaled what he already had, they might just stay warm enough, might not freeze before they could ride out of there and look for the Crow—

"What the hell are you thinking?" he scolded himself under his breath. "Your brains must've gone soft! What the blazes we gonna do 'bout that boy?"

Bass realized he couldn't ride into the Crow camp with this enemy. Soon as his wife's people recognized his dress, the quillwork pattern on his leggings, his hairstyle too, the Crow would drag him to the ground and begin to beat him. They'd inflict a thousand wounds on him, none alone enough to kill the youngster. But as they warmed to their fury, the men would turn the prisoner over to the Crow women. They would be the ones to carefully trim off the Blackfoot's eyelids, ceremoniously castrate him, build a slow, smoky fire on his genitals, then . . . carve off an arm, quite possibly a leg—slowly, slowly, like butchering an antelope or mule deer. Until there was little left that would resemble a human being— nothing more than a scalped head with its eyes poked out positioned atop a slashed, bloody torso—its flailed skin blackened by countless hot embers.

An involuntary shudder washed over him as he brooded on the horror that might await this young enemy at the hands of those women he knew in Yellow Belly's band. Women he knew as mothers and grandmothers, sisters and aunts. Women who were the soul of the Apsaluuke nation. If men were its heart and muscle and bone, then the women were its soul. But . . . times before he had watched those same women grow increasingly more cruel and vindictive as they wrung every drop of retribution and revenge out of a prisoner.

"If'n I let you go, I couldn't give you no weapon," Titus confessed as he settled the buffalo robe back around his shoulders and leaned against the tree again. The two dogs stretched out beside him and yawned.

He was surprised his thoughts had already reached that point: setting the youth free. The Blackfoot might use whatever weapon the white man provided to take his revenge on the white man who had killed three of his companions. Then it struck him: Maybe one of the dead men lying here, or there, was a father. An uncle. Or a brother. Chances were very good that this boy was re-

lated to one of those Scratch had killed last night—if for
no other reason than, for most of the mountain tribes,
this was the way a boy stepped into the world of manhood: invited to ride along as pony holder on a raid conducted by an older relative.

One of these dead men was shepherding this bad-eyed
youngster into adulthood, Titus brooded as he watched
the boy slowly work at the ropes strangling his wrists.
After drifting off a little while, Scratch awoke, thinking
he deserved to know if he was wrong about the boy. Or if
he was right.

"I kill your father here?" he asked as he stood and
started toward the first body.

Kneeling by the dead warrior, Scratch grabbed a handful of the man's hair and yanked up the Blackfoot's head,
pressing the sharp edge of his skinning knife into the skin
of the brow, right at the hairline. All while studying the
youth's reaction.

The boy's eyes filled with even more hate as he redou-
bled his efforts to free his hands from the knotted rope.

"Naw. I don't think this'un's the one." And Titus let
go of the hair, dropping the head onto the crusty snow.

One at a time, he went and knelt at the next two bodies—threatening to scalp them too. While the youngster
did growl in a feral way, Scratch nonetheless figured it
had to be the last one. Especially when he watched how
the youth's eyes widened as he knelt next to that third
corpse.

Rolling the body over so that the youngster could
plainly see the dead man's face, Titus filled his left hand
with hair and pulled the head off the trampled snow. The
instant his scalping knife flashed into view there beside
the low flames, the boy started howling like a pup without its mother. He stopped his knife, then examined the
dead man's face.

"He ain't old 'nough to be your papa. Maybeso your
uncle?" After a long, quiet moment while the fat flakes
fell upon the leafless branches of the cottonwood around
them, Scratch sighed, "But I bet he was your older

brother. He was gonna show you what it took to be a man."

Slowly rising, Bass stuffed the skinning knife back into its scabbard as the look of loathing and fury disappeared from the youth's face. Replacing it was sudden confusion, bewilderment, maybe even a little fear as the boy stared at the white man's every move.

"They was all brave men, son. Just like you was gonna be too."

He shook the coffeepot, heard some liquid sloshing inside it, so he sat the pot at the edge of the low flames.

"Like I said afore: can't cut you loose with no weapon . . . an' I damn well can't let you go 'thout no weapon neither."

That would be certain death. He might as well kill the boy here and now. Not that he hadn't killed youngsters before—but none of that had been in cold blood. Shit, some Crow, Flathead, maybeso someone else, would run this youngster down inside of three days and butcher him.

What the hell was he gonna do with him?

As the dim light swelled into the pewter glow of a snowy dawn, Titus decided that he didn't have to sort it out today. He could wait, thereby giving the right answer time to stew and cook, then bubble to the surface in its own good time. Sometimes weighty matters were best left to the closest deliberation he was known to ever give anything of concern.

He'd think on it now and again while the day passed. Which meant one more day he was forced to put off his search for the Crow of Yellow Belly.

At midmorning when the wind died a little, Titus awoke with a start and clambered to his feet. As soon as the white man made noise, the youngster snapped awake, awkwardly pushing himself back into a sitting position, glaring anew at his enemy.

And that was just how Scratch felt as he stepped around the opposite side of the fire pit, watching the boy's eyes. These Blackfoot had long been his enemy. How many of them had he killed over the seasons?

Maybeso he'd have to scratch at that knotty problem sometime tonight after dark. For now, he bent and grabbed one of the stiffening corpses by the back of the warrior's collar. Raised him up and dragged the dead man out of the copse of trees through the snow that had fallen deep enough to fill most of the hoofprints and moccasin tracks around his camp.

He returned for the second attacker, dropping the contorted body next to the first, downwind and next to a three-foot-high snowdrift. As he stepped back into the trees he watched the youngster's eyes and stopped in his tracks. Something different there now—no longer the unmitigated hatred. Titus wondered if he was a damn fool to think the boy's eyes might be softening, almost pleading with him.

That third body was the boy's blood. Family. Kinfolk. While Titus had given up on his own people, had abandoned his cold and distant parents, his sister and brothers back in Boone County, he had come to possess some strong notion of just what family could mean to a body. Over time, his woman and their young'uns—they had come to be the family he had long wanted to hold close, the family he felt he deserved.

The boy began growling again, a wild, raspy sound at the back of his throat when Bass stopped at the third corpse and bent over to grab hold of the half frozen carcass.

This time Scratch did not turn around in his tracks and trudge out of the trees. Instead, he took the dozen steps that brought him to the youngster's shoulder, where he gently, slowly laid the cold body beside the boy's hip. The youngster's eyes followed the white man as he stepped away to some of his baggage, dusted off some snow with the side of his woolen mitten, then threw back the oiled sheeting and began to unknot a pile of red blankets. More than likely, red would be of special significance.

Dragging the Russian sheeting back over the blankets and trade goods to protect them from the unrelenting snowfall, Bass trudged over to the youngster whose eyes never once left the trapper as he went and came. The black orbs were growing with wonder at what the old man was up to—if not downright consternation—by the time Titus stopped by the corpse, grabbed an edge of the blanket, and unfurled it in the frosty air.

When he had it draped over the body, completely covering the warrior from his greased and feathered topknot to the soles of his buffalo-hide winter moccasins, Bass straightened once more and dusted snow from the knee of his legging.

"I know this'un means something to you," he said as the youngster's eyes eventually climbed to stare into his. "Far as I know, for most of your people—no matter what tribe you be—red's the color for war. No better honor I can give this nigger what tried to kill me than to leave him on his back, facing the sky. And cover 'im with red—head to toe—the color of a warrior's paint."

23

◆

He was relieved when the youngster ate something that next sunrise as the dawn swelled around them.

Throughout the first day, the boy had refused to eat, even turning his head away when Bass offered him a drink of water from a tin cup from time to time while they waited out the snowstorm.

"You get hungry 'nough, thirsty too—I wager you'll let me know."

Bass knelt now, offering him some hot coffee, but the youngster refused it, preferring melted snow in another cup. Then the boy's black eyes landed on the meat Scratch had roasting over the flames as the sky grayed. Carefully carving a long, thin slice from the venison ham that sizzled and popped as it cooked, Titus carried it over to the boy.

Eagerly tilting his chin up, the Blackfoot accepted the offered meat, chewing ravenously as the white man let the long sliver of meat descend between the youth's lips.

"Bet you want more of that."

The youngster's tongue flicked across his greasy mouth while his eyes danced back to that venison haunch broiling over the fire. The boy damn well ate more than half of the whole leg that morning!

With the sun's arrival at the edge of the earth, it was time to bring in the horses one by one. Across their backs he laid the thick wool saddle pads he had traded off Goddamn Murray, then cinched down each of the crude, wooden sawbucks before securing two heavy loads to the saddles, one on each side of the horse. Over the loads he diamond-hitched a drape of oiled sheeting that would protect his trade goods from even the most violent, wind-driven, horizontal rain.

But, he sighed after finishing the knots on the last of the dozen horses, there was little chance for any calamity like frozen rain this day. The sun was emerging bold and brassy in a cloudless blue sky. As far as the eye could see, the whole world was bathed in white, cleansed anew. Damn near as virginal as this land was the day after God made all these fine, fine sculpturings for the few men what lived in such sacred places as these.

Already the glare was growing intense. Here in the shadows of these big cottonwoods the sunlight wasn't near so bad. But out there where he'd be spending the day in the saddle—that intense reflection off the snow would damn well blind him by afternoon. Winter sunlight was even more merciless than summer sun this far north.

His lips were already burnt, cracked and sore as they were. Titus had been breathing hard with the sort of exertion a younger man would've taken in stride. But, Titus Bass was no longer a young man. He was having to admit how his body was tiring of the constant struggle just to do what he had taken for granted a decade ago—much less what he was able to do those seventeen winters ago when he first came to these High Stonies. He couldn't help the hard breathing, or having to take things a bit slower, or being forced to pace himself at every major task that came his way . . . but he could do something about the searing heat of his oozy lips.

Raising the flap on his shooting pouch, Scratch's bare fingers located and pulled out the flat tin made of tar-

nished German silver. Thumbing in the spring-loaded
catch, he flipped back the hinged top before wiping two
fingertips across the hard, milky grease he had rendered
from bear fat early last spring before setting off for the
Wind Rivers: a three-year-old black bear he had killed
down in the breaks of the Bighorn as a change of diet for
him and his family.

As he slowly worked the grease into his inflamed lips,
Titus thought on how human that bear's carcass had
looked hanging there from a sturdy tree branch after he
had skinned it. Damn near spooky. For days after he had
ruminated on nearly every story the Yuta or Snake or
Crow had to tell about their brother, the bear. Human or
not, to have a look at one trussed up and skinned out
sure could give even the most skeptical of men the willies.

Then he sank to one knee beside the fire pit where the
last of the branches had burnt themselves down to glowing, flameless embers. After putting a small dollop of the
bear grease into the palm of his left hand, Scratch
scooped up some of the blackest char he could find at the
side of the pit and crumbled a little of it onto the greasy
palm. Pitching the rest of the blackened wood back into
the pit, Titus used a single fingertip to mix charcoal and
animal fat together until he had a thick, black paste.

Rising, he turned to face the youngster while smearing
a gob of paste across the wrinkled, sagging skin beneath
the one weathered, but good, eye. It would go a long way
in preventing most of the glare he would suffer, since
more than eighty-five percent of the sun's intensity was
reflected off that new, pristine snow they would be crossing in the day's search.

They.

He wasn't completely sure why, but sometime around
twilight the night before, Bass had decided it would be
they today. He couldn't begin to reconcile leaving the boy
behind, all tied up and left to the mercy of the weather, or
critters either one. And if he let the Blackfoot go with a
weapon, chances were the youngster might try to exact
some revenge on Titus. Which meant he'd end up having
to kill the boy. Then again, if Bass let the boy go without

a weapon, what chances would the Blackfoot have to make it back to his own people with no way to provide for himself on the journey? On and on he had argued with himself throughout the day . . . until deciding that his conscience could do nothing but put off making a decision until he had come to a solution he could live with.

A solution the youngster might come to live by.

Kneeling an arm's length from the youngster now, Scratch swiped a greasy gob of the fire-black onto his fingertip, then reached out to smear it beneath the boy's eye. With a menacing growl that reminded Scratch of a cornered dog, the Blackfoot jerked his head aside, his eyes filling with sudden fear.

"Why, you li'l son of a bitch," Bass husked. "I'm doin' this for your own good, dammit."

Again he tried to get the fingertip near the boy's eyes, but the Blackfoot snapped his head side to side. Titus scooted a little closer on his knee. With surprising swiftness he brought up his left hand, pressing the heel of his palm against the boy's forehead, pinning the back of the youngster's head against the tree with all his weight. Try as he might, the Blackfoot could only shriek and snap with his teeth at the hand that proceeded to paint the colored grease beneath both eyes—

Paint. Jehoshaphat! If that weren't likely it!

He released his grip on the youngster's brow and leaned back.

"Lookee here now," and he pointed below his one good eye with that blackened fingertip. "This here's what I'm doin' to you. I ain't painting you up for no mourning or grieving. Don't you see, boy? This ain't no war grieving I'm doing on you—so stop your damned caterwauling!"

A few more times he gestured with that black fingertip, pointing back and forth between his own eye and the youth's eyes until the Blackfoot quit shrieking and the panic drained from the boy's face. Scooting backward a couple of feet, Titus stabbed his bare hands into the snow, scooping up enough that he could use to wash his fingers and that palm. Again and again he rubbed the snow over the greasy, blackened skin until he had scrubbed off about all he could, then swiped his palms down the grease-blackened, bloodstained, stiffened fronts of his leggings.

Titus stood to gaze down at the red blanket. "What you figger me to do with your blood kin?"

When the youngster turned and stared at the shrouded corpse for a long time without returning Bass's gaze, Titus asked, "You don't 'spect me to drag him along with us, now do you? Don't you get that notion in your head—'cause I'd just as soon leave you here with 'im as have to drag his cold carcass with us next few days till we find them Crow.

"Then what?" Scratch continued by asking the big question. Maybe just the rising sound of his voice as he posed the problem made the youth look at him again. "So we take your kinfolk with us when we run onto the Crow. What you expect us to do when those Absorkees find out I'm dragging around a dead Blackfoot? They're gonna chop your relation into some mighty small pieces right afore your eyes—an' you'll go to wailing again."

He sighed, turned slowly around. And found himself studying the copse of trees. There. It wouldn't take long. He could work with a rope, looping it over those two parallel branches—hoist the body up inside its red blanket and tie off the rope. Then he could shinny up that trunk and drag the body onto that pair of branches where he could tie it down in place. A good place for the body to rest, in one of those Bents Fort horse-trading blankets. A red funeral shroud for a warrior.

What in blue hell was he doing? He'd near been killed by these sonsabitches more times'n he had battle scars. So why was he even giving a second thought to burying this red nigger proper right here in the heart of Crow country?

"Shit," he grumbled as he strode over to the cotton-wood where he angrily snapped off a few short limbs no bigger around than one of his fingers.

Quickly he used his camp knife to shave off the bark

from each one, making it smooth, then sharpened the end of each stick until he had a half dozen some eight or ten inches long. Not near as long as lacing pins that locked the two flaps of a lodge over its poles, but long enough for the job at hand.

Dropping the peeled twigs beside the dead warrior, Bass knelt and rolled the stiffened carcass over. Dragging back the red blanket, he studied the young man's face, then peered into the boy's eyes. No reasonable man could deny they were blood kin. Then he gave study to what the warrior carried on his belt. Bass freed the leather strap from the buckle and dragged it loose before he resecured the strap and buckle and laid the belt aside. Not until then did he notice the whistle that hung from a thong around the dead man's neck. At first it had been tucked out of sight in the warrior's armpit.

But by tugging on the thin strap, Titus freed it, dragging the thong over the dead warrior's head. Some six to seven inches long, it was clearly an eagle wingbone carved into a war whistle. Someone, maybe a family member, perhaps even the dead man's lover or wife, had braided red, black, and yellow quills around the middle two thirds of the whistle.

He brought it to his lips, but just as he was about to blow the whistle, Scratch suddenly stopped. Aware that perhaps he shouldn't out of respect for the enemy dead. For a moment, he returned the youngster's quizzical gaze, then scooted over to drop the long leather loop over the boy's head.

"I figger that's rightly your'n, son. Maybeso, he'd wanted you to have it. It and this here belt with his fixin's and knife too."

Bass creaked to his feet, his knees grown stiff on the icy snow. "But I ain't giving you that there belt and knife—not yet I ain't."

He dragged out his own knife and crouched over the dead warrior. Quickly tugging on the four sides of the red blanket, he pulled them together as tight as he could around the corpse. Then hole by hole, he punched the tip of his knife through the flaps of thick wool and inserted

the long, peeled pins that would hold the blanket in place
as a crude funeral shroud.

With two of his short lariats looped over a high
branch above that pair of parallel limbs, and the ends of
both ropes knotted around the frozen corpse—one at the
ankles and one around the shoulders—Scratch went to
fetch his saddle horse. When he had the loose ends of
both lariats secured around the large pommel, Bass
grabbed the reins in one hand, gave the youngster a quick
look, then spoke softly to the roan.

"C'mon—easy, easy now."

As he tugged on the reins, the animal slowly inched
forward, taking the slack out of the ropes, then eased the
body off the ground where it began to swing a little, first
in one direction, then to the other, twisting slowly, slowly
in a half circle from its two ropes.

"That's a good, girl. A li'l more, li'l more now."

He kept the horse moving a step or two at a time until
the warrior had been raised high enough that the body
hung suspended just above the pair of lower branches.

"Stay put," he cooed, patting the steady old roan on
the neck before he turned back to the tree.

There he stripped off his wide belt and the elkhide
coat, then wearing only the buffalo-fur vest in that bitter
cold, Scratch pulled himself off the ground, swinging up
and onto the first low branch. From there he shinnied
himself onto the pair of limbs growing just below the
gently swinging corpse. With his thick buffalo-hide moccasins gripping the two branches, he steadied himself
with one hand locked on that higher limb the ropes were
looped over, then grabbed one of those ropes with his
other bare hand.

"Awright, horse—back now. C'mon back."

He clucked with his tongue too, a sound he was sure
the roan would recognize from their miles and seasons
together. The horse twisted its head around as if to
determine where that noise was coming from, so he repeated it.

Then reassured the roan, "C'mon."

It took two steps back. "That's good. Just a li'l more."

Those coarse one-inch ropes slid through his callused palm as the red shroud eased down upon the two parallel branches. With a little more coaxing the horse inched back three more feet and stopped again; enough that Titus now had sufficient slack to loosen the knots around the ankles and shoulders as he crouched precariously on the limbs above the horse. One at a time he pitched the freed ropes over the branch above him so that they spiraled to the ground below him.

With one final tug on the shroud, he had the Blackfoot's body positioned along the strongest portions of the parallel limbs. Then he dropped to the ground himself to pull on his coat once more before freeing the two ropes from the pommel and stuffing their loops atop one of the packs of trade goods.

Striding over to where the youngster had watched the whole ordeal in utter amazement, Scratch could read a completely new expression on the boy's face.

"I figgered it was what you'd done your own self . . . if'n you'd been freed up to do it." He knelt with a sigh. "Time for us to be movin' for the day."

Stuffing his knife into its scabbard suspended from the wide belt he buckled around the elkhide coat, Scratch worked at the knots tied around the youngster's ankles while the look on the boy's face changed to one of confusion mixed with no little fear.

Titus rocked forward on one knee, locking the other knee down upon the youth's lower legs. "Ain't gonna hurt you."

Still holding the boy down, Titus pulled the rope free of the ankles and wrapped a loose end between the youngster's bound wrists. Now he had a long section of the rope that would serve just like a lariat used on a led horse.

"C'mon. It's time you stood up," he said as he took a step backward, then a second.

Bass gestured with his free hand. "Stand *up*."

Slowly dragging his legs under him, the youth leaned his weight forward onto his bound hands and struggled to rise. But it was immediately clear that the muscles in his legs were cramped from being bound together on the cold ground for so long. Titus stepped around to stand behind the boy, wrapped both of his arms beneath the youth's armpits, and grunted him to his feet.

"Damn, son—if you aren't a big chunk of it," he grumbled as the youth came off the ground shakily.

Standing there at that moment, it surprised Scratch just how tall the youngster was. The top of his black hair reached Bass's eyes. And he felt solid as a hickory stump. Thin, wiry, lean as whipcord to be sure—but solid nonetheless. This was a boy already galloping down the road to manhood, that much was certain.

For a moment the youngster wobbled unsteadily on his legs. Then he gradually got his balance, and Bass slowly released his grip on the Blackfoot.

"You're gonna ride," he explained as he steered the youth toward the horse that had carried the pups in those empty baskets Scratch was taking home as a present to Waits-by-the-Water.

"Take 'er easy," he said as they kept walking, step by step. "Keep them pins under you or you'll spill for certain."

At the horse's side, Scratch gestured that the youngster was to mount. It took no further urging as the boy grabbed a double handful of the horse's mane there at the withers, then sprang onto the narrow back and settled himself. With the boy's rope in one hand, Titus took the horse's lead in the other and led them back to his roan.

Mounting up, he brought the horse around and stopped knee to knee with the youngster. "I figger this can be easy for both of us, or it can be hard on you. You behave yourself and you can ride like a man. You don't behave—why, I'll strap you over that there horse like two elk hindquarters. So it's up to you."

Scratch was just starting to put his heels into his horse's ribs—when he stopped, his eye caught by that whistle hung against the boy's chest. Bass turned a moment to gaze at the body on the limbs, then realized what he had done had one more step before all would be complete.

"You'll wanna blow your kinfolk's whistle, son," he said quietly as he leaned over and grabbed the eagle wingbone, holding it up to the youngster's lips.

The boy stared at him a moment, bewildered. Eventually he opened his mouth, leaned his head forward, and took the end of the whistle between his teeth.

Scratch settled himself in the saddle and nudged his horse forward, turning the roan about as he clucked for the lead horse to follow. The animal that carried Titus Bass's young prisoner started away behind the white man.

And as they inched out of the skeletal shadows of that copse of cottonwoods onto the brilliant, shimmering white beauty of that pristine wilderness illuminated with a newly risen sun, Titus Bass heard the first tentative, eerie . . . and ultimately mournful notes of that eagle-wingbone whistle shriek behind him.

Unmistakably a warrior's song: unearthly notes meant to accompany a fighting man's soul on its lonely journey to that place where all warriors one day were bound to go.

It could have been a lot harder than it was, but for some reason the youngster understood that Titus Bass was just about his only means of staying alive.

That boy could have attempted an escape once, if not a dozen times over the next three days. At the least he could have struggled with the old white man when Bass led him to the pony, or when Titus helped him down from the horse. The youngster could have simply run off into the forest with his hands tied when he had to pee or squat.

But the Blackfoot was old enough to savvy which side his meat was roasted on. While he might hate the white man who had killed his kin or kith, and while he might well be scheming to make an escape of it somewhere down the line—the boy showed he was smart enough not to give the slightest impression that he might flee if given half a chance.

Not for a moment did Scratch think that the youngster wouldn't sink a knife in the white man's heart if he could get his hands on a weapon and was handed the opportunity. Why, it'd be damned foolish for him to believe this half-growed creature had suddenly turned docile. Not no young'un from such a warrior clan as the Blackfoot. Such a man-child was bred, born, whelped, and raised to be a fighter. In the marrow of him, Scratch knew Blackfoot were taught to hate Americans from the time they opened their eyes and sucked in their first breath. Taught to hate Crow too.

So what in the billy blue hell was he doing? Here he was, a white man—the one big argument against his indecision. And he was married to a Crow. Jehoshaphat! If the Blackfoot hated any group longer, hated any group stronger, than Americans—it was the goddamned Crow! A second powerful argument against his good-hearted charity.

Then you went and added the fact that in Yellow Belly's village there were his two young children—half white and half Crow. Lordy! A third and a fourth mark against Titus Bass ever making a friend of the boy. What he needed to do was just turn the Blackfoot loose and ride away. Let the youngster go afoot, even give him some dried meat before he pointed him in the right direction. How had he ever been so foolish to believe that the boy might hold some compassion in his heart for the white man who had killed his blood kin?

Even *if* that white man had gone against his better instincts and put the body of that relative into a tree for a proper burial.

There was no changing what either of them were, and would always be. Enemies.

It was simply the order of things, and no mere mortal of a clay-footed man was going to change it.

For the most part over those next three days, it seemed the youngster rode along with his eyes as good as closed. If they were open at all, they were no more than slits because of the intense sunlight reflecting off that new snow. Especially during the late-afternoon when the sun was setting in the west, far, far in front of them—that's when the glare grew most cruel. It made no matter to Titus if the boy was sleeping as they plodded along, picking their way among and around the snowdrifts, doing his best to stay to the high runs where the snow hadn't piled up so deep or had been blown clear altogether.

It made no difference to the old beaver trapper . . . because the boy never made any trouble for him. The Blackfoot ate when meat was offered him. And he drank when Titus gave him the melted snow in a tin, or provided a cup of weak coffee at their night fires. When Scratch's eyes grew heavy beneath the clear, cold pinpricks of white light shining through the black-velvet drape of winter light, he would crab over to the youngster and check one last time to see that the knots were secure, that those knots on the long lead rope itself were turned toward the wrist so the boy had no chance whatever to work his fingers on them. Then Titus would retuck the old blanket and a buffalo robe around the youngster before he crabbed back to his own sleeping robes once more, dragging the end of the long lead rope to tuck beneath his belt, to wrap a loop around a wrist: the slightest movement of his prisoner would alert the boy's keeper.

Come his rising of a morning, Scratch would find the youngster hadn't budged and had to be awakened. In the end Titus admitted to himself that there was no plotting to escape. That the boy didn't lie awake while the trapper drifted off so he could slip off in the dark with one of the horses, stealing one of those extra guns Bass had plundered off of one dead Indian after another over the seasons.

Right from that moment Scratch had put the body in the tree and placed the dead man's whistle between the youngster's lips, the Blackfoot pony holder hadn't given the slightest hint of struggle or treachery.

So it was that early on the fourth afternoon after the untimely convergence of their fates that Titus Bass spotted a low, thin blanket of fire smoke trapped in the cold sky, a grayish-brown band of it clinging just above the trees . . . and knew it had to be the Crow. If not Yellow Belly's band, then surely they were Crow.

At the top of the rimrock, Scratch brought them to a halt and let the animals blow. He turned in the saddle, looking at the boy, and could see the youngster had noticed the fire smoke too. When those black-cherry eyes shifted to peer into his, Titus could plainly read the fear that was turning to resignation. A look that seemed to say, *I know you've brought me to this camp of my enemies to test my manhood. And I am ready to die.*

It was then that Bass understood what he had to do.

With a sudden sense of urgency, he realized they had little time before the sun would be making its descent.

"C'mon."

He clucked to the horses, his eyes briefly brushing the boy's face, recognizing that the youngster was baffled again. Just when the boy had made peace with the fact that he was being led to torture and eventual slaughter, the white man was turning their little pack train away from the fire smoke and heading down the back side of the rimrocks instead of pushing on for the village that lay ahead in a horseshoe bend of the river.

It took them something more than an hour before Bass felt they had come far enough. They hadn't crossed any pony tracks, so it was clear the Crow hunters weren't yet working this side of the river for game. Here, two ridges beyond the north bank of the Yellowstone, Bass slid from his saddle and hit the snow, breaking through the three-day-old crust and sinking past his ankles.

Immediately he went to the boy's side and motioned that he would help the youngster climb down too. When the Blackfoot stood unsteadily in the deep snow, Scratch pointed to his groin, pantomiming how a man held himself while urinating before he gestured toward the ten-foot-high willows nearby.

"G'won. Be 'bout your business, over there."

The boy stood frozen a moment until Scratch threw down that coil of lead rope he held in a mitten. A bit reluctantly, the youngster turned away to trudge toward the thick brush.

The moment he did, Bass tore his mittens off as he hurried back to one of the war party's ponies, where Titus began to work at the knots holding the blanket and buffalo robe the boy had been using the past few nights—the same blanket and robe Scratch discovered among the raiders' horses the morning after the attack. He took a moment to study the Blackfoot animals—then selected one. As the white man threw the robe and blanket over the back of the strongest pony, the youngster came back to stand, watching the process with no little curiosity.

Understandably, the boy was a little confused too—because this was not the horse he had been riding across Absaroka the last four days. Maybe, Titus figured, the youngster had decided something was about to happen now that it was clear this wasn't just a brief stop to wet down the bushes.

With the bedding secured with a wide strap, Scratch trudged through the deep snow to one of the packhorses, where he lifted a flap of the protective oiled sheeting and freed a pouch of smoked meat. Then pulled out the dead warrior's belt.

Scuffing back through the crusty snow he stopped before the boy and dropped the pouch at the youngster's side. Bass took a moment to inspect the belt, finding a much used whetstone in a leather pouch hung from the belt, an awl in a beaded awl case, along with several small amulets—besides the large knife that swung freely from the thick leather decorated with tarnished tacks of brass.

With a sigh, he finally gazed into the boy's eyes. Then freed the strap from its buckle and placed the belt around the youngster's waist, rebuckling it at the front flaps of the thick winter capote. Taking a step backward, he looked the boy up and down. It was some time before the Blackfoot looked into the white man's face, tearing his eyes from the belt where his bound hands rested, fingertips touching the heads of those brass tacks, brushing those special totems to some sacred power.

Quickly, before he lost the courage and will to go through with his plan, Scratch stepped close once more, his bare hands wrestling with the knots he had secured many days ago, knots he tightened every morning and night. Eventually, the cold, stiff rope relented and allowed him to work it free.

A breath caught in the boy's chest as the ropes fell away and the trapper stepped back again, rapidly looping the lariat in his left hand.

"It's getting late. Late," and he pointed to the sun hanging in that last quadrant of the western sky. "Time you be going." Then he sighed. "I may goddamn well be teched in the head to let you go free, with that there knife of your brother's . . . but I still got 'nough sense not to leave you go with a gun. You'll have to make it with just that there knife."

He bent and retrieved the canvas pouch. Held it out at arm's length to the youngster. "Here. You'll need food afore you ever run 'cross some of your own people. Meat," and he gestured with his right hand, fingers to his mouth as if eating.

The youngster took the pouch.

"G'won. That there horse is your'n now," and he motioned to the Blackfoot pony he had prepared with the makeshift saddle pad. "I'm takin' the rest of them Blackfoot ponies though I don't really need 'em. Hell . . . what good is more horses when I got plenty awready? Likely just give 'em away when I get home to my family," he explained. "Damn, if I ain't seen an' wrangled more horses than I ever wanna see again in the rest of my days, truth be knowed. A damnable breed, these big critters: we come to depend on 'em like no other animule, even them two dogs there. Because of horses I been gone from my woman and young'uns too long. Because of horses I near lost the rest of my hair and my hide too. Californy horses. Shit . . ."

His voice trailed off as he became aware he was chattering, running off at the lip like a nabob. He felt like scolding himself for that attempt to prolong the farewell that must now take its course.

Instead of speaking any further, he reached out with both hands, taking the boy's wrists in them and rubbing, as if to return the circulation to the flesh where the ropes had chafed them raw. Then he turned the youngster around and nudged him over to the pony.

"Get up there. An' go."

The boy swallowed, slowly turned away, and took up the single lead tied to the animal's buffalo-hair headstall. Without hesitation he leaped onto the pony's back. But instead of immediately heeling the horse away in giddy celebration, the youngster sat looking down at the white man.

"G'won. Git. You're burnin' what li'l daylight you got left. G'won back to your own people."

It surprised Scratch when the boy suddenly spoke. Even with those growls, and shrieks, and howls of fury that night of the attack—Titus had never really heard the youngster's voice. Now he was speaking Blackfoot—as foreign as any sound ever would be to fall on Bass's ears. No matter that he did not understand the meaning of the words, he could fathom their import from the tone and tenor of that young voice, from the look on the boy's face, the emotion clearly seen in those eyes.

Even more than the spoken Blackfoot, it surprised the trapper when the youngster eventually put that eagle-wingbone whistle between his lips as he reined the pony away, urging the animal into a gentle lope through the snow as it carried him north from the land of the enemy, back to the land of his people.

It raised the hair at the back of Scratch's neck when the winter wind suddenly shifted, a bitter gust bringing with it the eerie, high-pitched battle cry of that whistle.

And in that moment as the wind blew long strands of his graying hair across his face, a wind so bitterly cold it made his eyes water, Titus Bass came to understand that with the death of one warrior . . . another had been given birth.

24

———————◆———————

He pushed the horses harder now than he ever had on their journey north.

Once Titus had them onto the bottom ground, he goaded the animals into a rolling lope across those last few miles as the setting sun first turned the layers of fire smoke to that dull, washed-out orange of the wood lily, eventually brightening into the same pale pink found in the shooting star that would poke its head out of the snow come early spring. Both dogs managed to match the pace he set, covering the icy ground beside the long-legged horses, their pinkish tongues lolling.

From the top of a low ridge he got his first look at the lodges. Cones discolored to various earth tones of brown, every pair of yawning smoke flaps blackened with un-numbered fires. A few of the lodges even supported by poles so long their shape was that of murky hourglasses plopped down in that narrow, meandering meadow beside the rocky creek he would have to cross before he was home.

Bass sensed his heart catch in his throat to look at what lay before him. The horse herd flooded much of the open ground where the brown cones did not stand in an irregular crescent, their doorways facing the creek. Knots of children engaged in the last games of the day, bundled warmly against the frightening cold, some of them trundling along the stream bank where free water coursed through a narrow channel between two borders of snow-covered ice. Each rounded rock along the shore was covered with a dainty dollop of fresh, white snow, like a scullery maid's white mobcap perched atop her brown hair.

Of a sudden he heard their voices—excited children at play, the rattle of their sticks they raked along the rocks, chasing one another and scraping snow from the stones. Perhaps the older ones had been sent to gather up their younger charges now that night was imminent. Laughter, lots of laughter—

A handful of them stopped their running game and turned to face the ridge. Two pointed in his direction. More of their voices, louder now.

From the trees along the bank appeared more than a dozen riders an instant later. In that silence a moment ago filled only with the laughter of children, now intruded the clatter of pony hooves as the animals lurched off the low cutbank and onto the rocky gravel blanketing the sandbars.

He tore the old coyote-fur cap from his head and stood in the stirrups, waving the cap at the end of his arm. And began to shout, *"Pote Ani! Pote Ani!"*

Four of the riders continued across the ford where the water slowed through a shallow stretch while the rest remained in position on the rocky ground.

"C'mon, boys," he said quietly to the Cheyenne horses. "That's home down there."

After covering some forty yards, Scratch found a wide cut where the ridge had eroded, a cleft that led him and the horses down to the east bank of the creek where that quartet of riders was already waiting on the snowy sandbar.

"These are trading goods from the fort at the mouth of

the Buffalo Tongue River?" asked Three Iron, a younger man, who inched his horse ahead to greet the white man.

"No, old friend." Bass gasped with joy and surprise at seeing a familiar face. "They are presents."

"So many presents?" Stiff Arm asked now as he urged his horse up beside that of Three Iron. "All these ponies are loaded with presents?"

"Yes!" Bass felt exuberant as he dusted off his rusty Crow, unused in so long. "My heart is so glad to be home again."

A quizzical look passed over Three Iron's face as the other two inched their ponies forward. "We . . . every-one thought you dead, *Pote Ani*."

"It has been so long," agreed Stiff Arm.

Bass suddenly felt some of his exuberance oozing as he realized just how long he had been away. "Yes, I have been gone many moons, but, look for yourselves . . . I am not dead."

Three Iron gulped. "Your wife—"

"Waits-by-the-Water?" he interrupted the camp guard. "Does she believe I am dead too?"

With a wag of his head, Three Iron declared, "Like Stiff Arm said, you were gone so long."

Then Stiff Arm himself explained, "And you did not come back."

A sudden cold seized him. "My wife, and chil-dren . . . they—"

Three Iron turned on the bare back of his pony and pointed at the village. "They are camped at the southern end of the crescent, *Pote Ani*. Next to relations."

For a moment he could not get the words out, his mind racing over the vocabulary, struggling to put voice to the question he most feared. Then, "My wife . . . Waits-by-the-Water, she did not give up on me to . . . to m-marry another?"

Stiff Arm shook his head, "No. She did not find a new husband."

"S-so she is mourning?"

This time Three Irons nodded dolefully. "Yes. She has been alone for so long now."

Titus was already jabbing his heels urgently into the ribs of the weary saddle horse as those last few words struck his ears. He yanked on the lead rope to the first packhorse as the whole string clattered onto the stony sandbar and entered the shallow ford. By now, more than fifty people had gathered on the far bank, a third of them children. They and a few camp dogs began to part as his roan came out of the shallow water, the horse's legs dripping in the light that was leaking from the pale, pink western sky. His two dogs bristled warning at the curious curs that slinked too close, then stopped among the snow-covered rocks to give themselves a quick, vigorous shake from neck to tail root before racing to rejoin Bass's horse as it lunged up the low cutbank and angled into the village.

The murmuring accompanied him as he turned among the lodges, sawing the saddle horse left as he hurried toward the southern end of the camp crescent. More and more of the people who had been on their way to the crossing came to a sudden halt, stopping to stare up at him as he led more than fifteen horses right down the main thoroughfare of the village. Some of them called out his name in excitement and relief.

Men who had known him as Rotten Belly's white friend, who remembered him as Whistler's trusted son-in-law, and those warriors who saw Titus Bass as the man who had honored Strikes In Camp with that final battle against the Blackfeet . . . many of them now raised their arms high in salute, some shaking their weapons to pay tribute to a fellow warrior.

And some of those women who recognized him quietly muttered his name. Many put their fingers over their mouths in shock and utter surprise, eyes wide as Mexican conchos.

"Popo!" the child cried.

A few yards ahead he spotted the short figure lumbering toward him across the trampled snow, one arm waving as she shuffled in an ungainly wobble, clearly hampered by the tiny blanketed bundle astride her hip.

"Magpie?" he cried in exuberance, although he was

already sure as he yanked back on the reins. Fifteen yards behind her came a figure, not quite as tall, running to catch up. Titus sang out, "Magpie! It is you!"

"Popo!" she shrieked in excitement.

Titus hit the ground as his daughter crossed those last few steps to reach the horses. The moment he knelt she flung her empty arm around him. Clasping his daughter in a fierce embrace, he felt the tiny body at the very moment the small infant cried out.

Magpie was eight and a half years old now, he thought, surely old enough, responsible enough, to care for someone's child—

Then Flea sprinted up, his copper cheeks red from his dash across the icy snow.

"Flea!" he cried, releasing Magpie so he could crush the boy who would soon be turning six. "Oh, Flea!"

He unwrapped one arm from around the boy and held it out for the tall girl, reminded how long-legged her mother must have been at the same age. Magpie stepped into that embrace he gave both of his children.

"Y-your mother?" he stammered. "Where?"

Flea pointed with his grimy hand at the far lodges, then held the hand up for his father to hold. "Come. I take you."

"No, son," he stood, nudging the boy against his leg. "Here. You will be old enough to serve as a pony boy one day soon. So you must take care of my horses for me."

He looked at the long string, blinked, then looked up at his tall father. "Horses, Popo?"

"Bring them behind me." Bass turned to Magpie and swallowed as he blinked his stinging eyes. Already the tears were beginning to stream down his sun- and windburnt cheeks. "Take me to your mother."

Gazing up at her father in wonder, Magpie laid her head against his side a moment as he enfolded her against his rib cage. She closed her eyes briefly. Then opened them. "We thought you . . . everyone believed . . . Mother knew you did not come back because you were—"

"I am not dead, little one," Titus interrupted and

squeezed her gently against him as they started walking toward the last of the lodges at the end of the camp crescent. "We need to show your mother what you can clearly see for yourself—I am far from being a ghost."

Which suddenly caused him to remember. "Stop a moment." Then he whistled once, and a second time. The dogs appeared among the lodges. "These are yours, my children."

"Your dogs, Popo?" asked Flea as he stopped the saddle horse and sank to one knee, putting out his arms for the darker animal.

"That one is named Digger, son."

"D-digger?" Flea repeated.

"Yes. It is the name of a poor tribe that lives far beyond the reach of the mountains. Out on the desert where little grows but cactus and scorpions, where those people have little to eat but rabbits and crickets."

"Crickets?" Flea repeated. "They eat insects?"

"When they are hungry enough," Titus told his son. "What they love to eat most is a stolen horse!"

The light-colored dog brushed against Magpie's leg as it stopped by its master. "What do you call this other one?" his daughter asked.

"Ghost. Look at his eyes, and you will see his ghost eyes."

"So these dogs followed you all the way back home?" Magpie inquired.

"Yes, I picked them out for you and your brother. They are your dogs now. But come—take me to your mother so she will see that I am not dead—"

His voice dropped off as the realization struck him every bit as cold and hard as an iron maul driving a wedge into a troublesome oak stump. His daughter's long hair was gone. Uneven, shoulder-length tatters rustled in the cold breeze. It had been crudely done, hacked off with a knife as proscribed in mourning rituals. And Magpie's hair wasn't clean at all. Many of the greasy sprigs were still clumped with ashes now that he inspected her.

Titus quickly grabbed Magpie's thin wrist and pushed up the loose blanket sleeve to expose her brown forearm.

A lattice work of old, half-crusted wounds climbed from
wrist to elbow in crude, parallel gashes, most nearly
healed.

"How . . . how long ago did you cut yourself?"

"M-m-many days." Her eyes began to tear as she
slowly slipped her wrist from his hand. She started to step
backward from him when he caught her and went to his
knee.

"Magpie. You did not do wrong. Nothing to be
ashamed of. I am proud of you—because you did this for
me. Mourned me like your mother—"

He bolted to his feet, freeing her arm again. "Take me
to your mother—now."

Inside his belly, his guts felt as if someone had thrown
alum on them, they pinched so bad. Shriveled up like a
hide forgotten or ignored by a hunter, a hide that
wouldn't be salted for tanning.

"Hurry, Magpie," he urged her as they lumbered past
some of those last lodges in the crescent.

After all those miles and months—he suddenly
couldn't cross these last few yards fast enough. Afraid.
Downright terrified at what Waits-by-the-Water believed
had happened to him.

"There, Popo," she said quietly as she came to a stop.

He halted beside her, looked into her face.

Magpie pointed. "There."

Scratch swallowed as he turned to watch Flea come
up, leading the saddle horse. More than two dozen people approached on both sides of his pack string. They
stopped in silence, not uttering a sound as he quickly
licked his parched lips and stepped over to the entrance
of that lodge where a tiny tendril of smoke crept upward
through a gaping, black opening between the smoke
flaps. Already his hands were trembling when he reached
out to rest his rifle against the lodge skins and shoved the
door flap aside.

Ducking inside, he stood, waiting, adjusting his eyes to
the inky darkness. Outside one of the horses snorted, and
he heard the quiet murmuring of voices. Then it grew
quiet enough that he could hear her breathing.

"Waits?"

There was no answer. But as his eyes grew accustomed to the darkness, he was able to locate her in what dim light was radiated by the still-glowing embers in the fire pit. No fire, not even any low flames. Nothing more than a few coals left in that rocky circle.

Bass quickly knelt and found the firewood that she always stacked just to the left of the doorway. If their mother was in severe mourning, then Magpie and Flea would have gone in search of wood, collected water too. His hands felt along several small branches, then turned in a crouch and laid them on the coals. Grabbing his long hair with one hand to hold it out of the ashes, Titus bent low and began to blow on the coals. It took some doing, but after a few moments the dry wood leapt into flame.

Still on his hands and knees, Scratch crabbed around the fire pit toward the rear of the lodge—guided by the rasp of her labored breathing. Waits-by-the-Water lay beneath a buffalo robe, no—two of them lying askew and rumpled where she had crawled beneath them for warmth.

Frightened so much his own breath froze in his chest like a tightened fist, Titus pulled back the robe, finding her heavy winter moccasins. He instantly leaped in the other direction and dragged back the robe from her head. She had her face turned from him as she slept, her labored breathing hard and shallow.

"Waits . . . I've come home."

When he had whispered, Scratch lifted her shoulders, pulled her upper body across his lap, turning her gently so that he could peer into her pox-ravaged face. The eyelids fluttered as he pushed some of the ragged shreds of her once long and beautiful hair from her eyes, her cheeks, the corner of her mouth where the lips were cracked and oozy. She smelled of old fires. Cold ashes. A stale, noxious odor of things dying was strong about her, permeating her hair, smeared on her face and neck.

"Is it really you?" she creaked in a voice so weak it reminded him of the time he almost lost her to that Blackfoot pox. "Not a ghost come to haunt my heart?"

"I am h-here, woman," his voice cracked as the tears began to seep from his eyes anew. "Here, touch my face. Know that I am real."

With one of his hands, he searched under the robe for hers. Finding it, he brought her fingers to his cheek, quickly guided it over his eyes, down his nose, from ear to ear in that graying beard. Then—consumed by his need to know—his fingers inched down her wrist to her forearm . . . feeling the striations of her self-wounding. Long ridges of new scabs intermingled with older scars where the bloody crust had aged and sloughed itself off over time. Reaching down, he gently ran his hand the length of her calf. It wasn't as scarified as her forearm, and the scabs on them were older. No recent slashes.

So he wrapped her in his arms, squeezed her tightly against him, enfolding her as he cried. Rocking, rocking. Crooning to her one of those lullabies he made up and used to hum to their children as he cradled them in his lap—just the way he was holding her at this moment.

And she cried. Waits-by-the-Water reached up to touch his face, fingers brushing his eyelids, feeling his lips as he sang in a whisper. While she sobbed, her chest heaved with great convulsions.

"I was so afraid," she eventually managed to choke the words out. "In the middle of the summer, when you did not come back—I began to worry. We had been together so many summers, I know it is never a good time for your trapping."

Yes, she did know so much of who he was. More than any other person—man or woman—could ever know. His tears began to stream freely now.

"I hoped you would come back from the mountains for to trade with Tullock at his fort," she whispered raspily, quaking against his chest. "But, I worried even more when the weather began to cool, and the leaves began to d—die."

Bass bent his head and pressed his lips against her forehead, tasting the old, rancid ash she had smeared on her flesh. "It was unfair—what I've done to you and the children. I did not realize my journey would take so long."

"I knew you had to be dead because you had never been gone from me, from your family, for so long."

"Never again," he promised.

"Sometime late in the summer, I realized it could not be the trapping that kept you from returning to us," she continued, dragging a hand across her own cheek grown muddy with tears that streaked the ashes rubbed there. "It had to be something more than the trapping—"

"I rode far, very far away to steal horses."

"Alone?"

"I went with old friends . . . and men who were my enemies too. We went to the land of the Mexicans." And he spoke that last word in English.

"Mexicans?" she repeated in his tongue. "You went south to Ta-house to steal horses . . . where Magpie was born?"

"No, to the other land of the Mexicans. Far to the west, by the big water."

"W-was it a pretty land?"

"To some it would be a pretty country," he admitted, lifting her chin with a finger so he could stare into her red, punished eyes. "But, there is nothing so beautiful as this high land of rugged skies, far prairie, and tall mountains."

"Did you bring your Mexican horses with you to Absaroka?"

"No. The ones I brought with me are better than any Mexican horse, because they are older than those we stole. I traded them from the Cheyenne down at Bents Fort."

"I remember you showing me the fort of dirt walls when Magpie was a suckling baby."

"All the rest of those horses I no longer wanted, I traded away for a few goods."

"You are going to be a trader now, like Tullock?"

He finally felt relieved enough now to chuckle a little. "No. I could never be a trader, woman. The goods I brought back are gifts to my family, gifts to your people who watched over you and our children while I was away for so long."

"So you did not steal many Mexican horses?"

This time he laughed louder. "Oh, we took nearly every horse we could find from those Mexicans—and they have many! Let me tell you that my old friends and me started out of the land of the Mexicans with more horses than all of Yellow Belly's village has in its herd, twice as many!"

She stared at him in the firelight with such seriousness, gazing from his good eye to the bad one for some sign of betrayal. "No. There could not be that many horses except . . . except if you raided the land of the Blackfoot to the north—or maybe the Lakota far to the east."

"I tell you the truth," he said with pride. "We took more horses from those Mexicans than ever was taken from them before!"

"I cannot believe the Mexicans had that many you could steal from under their noses without a terrible fight."

"Oh, they were sorely mad at what we had done and sent their fighting men after us—but we pushed them back and started across a great wasteland."

"What is this waste . . . land?"

"Where there is little water, little vegetation, no food for the horses. We lost half of their number before we reached the mountains, crossed over, and started down to the fort."

"So you had only a few by the time you reached the land of the Cheyenne?"

He gripped her shoulders as he explained, "My share was . . ."—and he grappled with finding the Crow term for so great a number—"more than any warrior of your people has ever owned before."

She quickly put her hand over her chapped mouth. "You are making fun with me," she snipped at him.

"It is true. I would not lie to you."

For a long moment she gazed into his face, steadily—as if reading something of import there. "This was a dangerous trip you had."

"No more dangerous than any trip I ever made with you at my side."

She snuggled against his elkhide coat. "The most fearsome trips you ever made were always the ones without me. Because I am not beside you, I know you take chances you would not if I were with you."

Scratch had no rebuttal, because she spoke the truth.

In his silence, she continued, "So, I have decided that—because you always do dangerous things without me along—I simply won't let you go on any more journeys without me."

"I won't argue with you on that," he relented immediately. "Never again will I go anywhere without you and our two children."

She straightened a little and asked, "You saw Magpie? Flea too?"

"Yes, both of them—"

"Did your daughter have the baby with her?"

"Yes," he soothed, remembering that tiny infant Magpie had on her hip. "She held someone's young child in her arms. Carrying it when she came up to embrace me. Whose child is this—who our young daughter would be caring for?"

Waits's eyes narrowed, staring at him strangely a moment, then quietly asked, "Ti-tuzz, did you look at this baby Magpie carried when you rode into camp?"

"I-I did not look at the child, no," he apologized. "More than anything I wanted to hold Magpie and Flea—to assure them I was not dead, then find where your lodge was pitched so I could come hold you. I had no interest in someone else's child—"

"That babe is yours, Ti-tuzz."

His heart skipped a beat, then took off in a gallop. "M-mine?"

"Whose child do you think your daughter would be caring for?"

"I . . . I don't—"

"Your son, Ti-tuzz," she announced. "You have a new son."

"No. It can't be. When I left . . . you weren't . . . I didn't . . . no, it can't be!"

"Do you remember the last time you held me in your arms?"

"That cold dawn when I was leaving on my hunt last spring?"

"Yes," she replied. "There was still snow on the ground."

"I remember, yes."

Laying her hand along his hairy cheek, Waits explained, "I didn't know that morning, but I was already carrying your child, Ti-tuzz. His life was already growing in my belly. I wouldn't know for many days to come—and when I did know for sure, it was later in the spring. I carried this son of yours for many moons, hoping with each new moon that his father would be home before he was born. But—"

"But I was gone too long." Titus felt the stab of pain pierce him as he clutched her tightly again. He had been gone while she went through her woman's time all alone. "You gave birth to him while I wasn't here to hold you, not here to see our child's face, or to hold him while you gained back your strength. I love you for your strength, woman."

Waits-by-the-Water asked, "Did you hear him?"

"The babe?"

"Yes, did you hear him cry?" she asked. "He has the lungs of a little buffalo bull, he is so loud."

Wagging his head, Scratch replied, "No. He did not cry out but once when I squeezed him too tightly when I put my arms around Magpie."

Again she smiled, warming her pocked, ash-streaked face. "You just wait, Ti-tuzz. You will hear that little bull bellow when he is hungry!"

"I will go fetch our children," he said, starting to slip from her embrace.

"It must be dark outside," she said, gazing quickly at the smoke hole. "I don't think I have anything for you to eat here—"

"I have meat." And he bent to kiss her forehead. "You

clean yourself and make ready your pot. I will send Magpie in with our new son and a pouch of yesterday's venison. Then I will take my big son to help me with our Cheyenne horses."

Waits reached out for his bare hand. Grabbing it between both of hers, she brought the hand to her lips, then pressed it against her wet cheek. He sank to one knee and wrapped his free arm around her shoulders.

"I will never leave you again," he vowed. "That is a promise that I will die before I ever break. Believe me when I tell you, I will never leave you, ever again."

Her eyes were sparkling with tears as she peered up at him, releasing his hand.

"Prepare the pot, woman," he reminded as he stood. "There'll be no more starving yourself, for tonight we're going to start putting some meat back on your bones!"

Ducking back through the narrow doorway, he stood in the deepening gloom of that winter evening. All round them the lodges were aglow with a dim, translucent light cast from the fires within. Magpie stood rooted right where she had been. Flea was beside her, the weary horses strung out behind them both.

"My mother—she's seen you are alive?" the girl asked as Scratch appeared.

"Bring my new son to me," his voice croaked as he started toward her.

Magpie held the bundle out to her father. "He doesn't look a thing like Flea. I thought all brothers were supposed to look alike. But this little one, he is nowhere near as ugly as Flea."

Behind her, Flea growled.

"That is just the sort of thing you expect a sister to say about her brother, Flea," Titus confided as he pulled back a flap of that blanket wrapped around the infant.

Beneath the cold starlight, the tiny child looked no different than Magpie had in those days and weeks after she was born, no different than Flea. Not until they began to grow older, a month or two at least, did they begin to take on their individual appearance—differences that became more marked as time went by.

"What do you think, Popo?" Flea asked as he raised himself up on tiptoes to look at his baby brother. "Do you think he is better looking than me?"

"No, you are both handsome Ti-tuzz men," Bass gushed, filled with such overwhelming pride to hold his new son.

"Then," Flea declared, "he must be so much better looking than his big sister!"

She half swung a fist at him as he ducked aside.

"Girl," Titus chided. "You go inside now. And take your little brother with you. He will be hungry soon."

As Magpie folded the infant into her arms, her face went sad momentarily. "My mother has not always had milk for him. She has been too weak at times."

"What did she do to feed your little brother?"

"Sometimes, other women brought milk from a mare," she confessed. "And sometimes . . . I think they brought their own milk. We fed him all we could with a spoon."

Titus wrapped his arms around his daughter and the baby. "You are very strong, a very good sister, Magpie. I promise you that you and Flea will never have to worry about such things again. I will never leave my family, ever again."

"You make good promises," Flea said.

"You know I never make a promise I can't keep."

"You have always kept your word to us, Popo," Magpie said.

"Now, go, daughter! Get your littlest brother inside. Help your mother with the fire, and get some water on to boil. Or keep your brother happy till it is time for him to eat. Now, hurry inside!"

She studied his face. "What are you going to do, Popo?"

"Me? Why, my oldest boy and his father are going to see to these horses. We'll unload all our goods right here beside the lodge, then find a good place for these animals, where they can fill *their* empty bellies."

The boy admitted, "I am very hungry too, Father."

"Do you like venison, Flea?"

"You know I *love* venison!"

"I brought some with me for us to eat tonight," he said as Magpie turned and ducked inside the lodge where Titus caught a glimpse of the flames dancing against the inside walls. Waits had laid on more wood, warming the lodge—just the way things had been in those days before he had strayed all the way to California. "And you, my dear son—you can eat venison till you're ready to pop like a fat tick!"

"Here, Popo," and the boy held up the lead rope for his father.

"No, Flea. You are my oldest son. I count on you more now than I ever did before. You and your sister have shown that you are children to make a father very, very proud. Bring my saddle horse along."

"The others will come with me too?"

"They followed you here to the lodge, didn't they?"

His little head bobbed up and down. "I think they followed because your saddle horse led them all the way back to the land of the Crow."

Titus looped his arm over his son's shoulders and gave him a squeeze as they started away for the snowy meadow. He was filled with such an awesome sense of love for his son, Titus didn't know if he could contain it right then.

"You are a smart boy too. You know the way of horses, eh?"

"I am learning," Flea admitted. "I have paid attention to everything I saw you do with them. And I've watched the other men in the village—when they break horses, or cut them on their privates, or have them mount the mares."

"You have been paying attention."

"Horses. They are something very special to me," the boy expressed. Then he spoke as if sharing something in the strictest confidence. "Sometimes, Father . . . sometimes I think they talk to me in their own language that no one else can understand, or even hear."

Titus stopped as the string of ponies came to a halt around them at the edge of the snowy meadow. "Tomor-

row, Flea—after breakfast, we will come out here together, a father and his son. And you will see which one
of these Cheyenne horses talks to you."

"Chey-Cheyenne horses?"

"Yes."

Flea wagged his head sadly. "If these are Cheyenne
horses, I won't understand what they say to me."

Titus put his fist beneath the boy's chin and chucked it
to the side gently. "If you are a true horseman, Flea—it
doesn't matter what language *you* speak, doesn't matter
what tribe the horses came from. In the seasons and years
yet to come, you will steal horses from many tribes who
do not speak the same language you speak."

"Is this true, Father—that I can understand what these
Cheyenne horses will say, just like I understand Crow
horses?"

Dropping to one knee, Titus gazed directly into his
boy's eyes and said, "If you are the horseman I think you
will grow up to be, my son—then you will understand
every horse."

"So, it really does not matter that these are horses
from far away?"

He stood, tussling the boy's hair. "Tomorrow we see
which one of these horses speaks to you, my son."

"Why are we going to see if one of them—"

"Because"—and Titus turned Flea so the boy could
look up at him in the deepening twilight—"the horse that
speaks to you will be yours to keep, son. It will be your
war pony, Flea."

The child's eyes grew big, his face visibly brightened in
the dim starshine. "Oh, Father—every boy should have a
horse of his own!"

"No, Flea," Titus corrected him with a warm embrace. "Every young *warrior* should have his own
warhorse."

25

———— ◆ ————

Across the next two days he sat in utter amazement at his children—three of them now.

How tall and so like her mother young Magpie had become. Were it not for his daughter's own inner strength and resolve, Titus was certain Waits-by-the-Water could not have made it through her grieving for a husband too late in making his return.

Then there was Flea. For so short a lad, the boy could nonetheless grab a handful of a pony's mane and vault himself onto its back without the slightest exertion. The more he watched his son among their horses, the more certain he became that Flea really did understand the secret talk of their four-legged breed.

And the tiny blanket child—barely weeks old now that winter was fully upon them. Of the three, this boy looked most like his father's side of the family. Sometimes in the way the infant would screw up his nose with a giggle or clench his eyes shut when about to bawl, either expression so reminded Bass of his younger brothers when they were only babes. Back in those days long, long ago before Titus knew there was any other life to covet but what his father's life had been, and his father before him, and his own father before them all.

In those days when Titus had been a child.

Before he put aside childish things and stepped beyond the twenty-mile bonds that imprisoned most men to the ground where they were born and whelped, raised to a life on the soil, and would eventually die having ventured no farther in distance, no further in spirit.

Wanting more than what most men accepted as their lot in life, young Bass had grown old seeking what other men could only dream, having lived what most men never *would* dream.

And in his living out the yearning, Scratch had discovered the mute secrets most men only hungered for late at night after the candles were snuffed and their frontier cabins or stately town mansions fell as quiet as the soft, sleeping breath of their wives and children.

Titus Bass was a man more blessed than any he knew.

Their first night back in one another's arms, Waits showed she understood just how hungry he was for her, perhaps because of her own appetite for him. Long after moonrise when the babe had been fed and the older two were long asleep in their blankets, while the embers burned low with a copperish hue every bit as red as Taos geraniums, Waits-by-the-Water wordlessly sat up in the soft, flickering light and shimmied her deerskin dress over her head. Quickly scrambling back beneath the buffalo robe, her hands raised his breechclout flap and found the belt's buckle. She tore him out of his leggings in two swift tugs.

He wasn't at all surprised to discover how hard his manhood became with nothing more than the delicious anticipation. Yet it virtually leaped when her fingers came exploring its heat. Clearly impatient, Waits rolled over on her side, scooting her hips back against him, then raised a leg and guided him into her moistness. As certain as he was that he would explode then and there, Bass was surprised when she stopped moving the moment he was planted inside her.

"Wait," she whispered in the darkness. "Let this last."

Despite the blood thundering at his ears, Scratch too wanted to savor this delicious joining a few minutes longer before their coupling was over all too quickly. So his hand explored her belly still rounded with the baby's fat, wandering upward to cup and tease that milk-swollen breast. Soon enough his touch had her volving her hips against him, her hunger growing ravenous. He let her work against him while he remained unmoving, until he felt her shudder a second time and—unable to deny this most potent force of nature—he rode out the shock waves of his own release.

Bass did not remember falling asleep, it must have come over him so quickly that first night back in her arms.

"Tell me of the women by the big water," she awoke him with a whisper that next gray morning.

"They are Mexican. You've seen Mexican women."

She propped herself up on an elbow. "Same as the women in Ta-house?"

"Some. There are Indian women, too—slaves and servants in their fields."

"Did you . . . find any of them attractive to you?"

He pulled her against him. "You are the prettiest in my heart."

"Did you lay with any of them?"

Stroking her hair, he assured her, "No matter how pretty a woman might be for that moment of my loneliness—how could I ever consider poor bull when I have prime cow waiting back here for me?"

She squeezed him with understanding. "Did you give your word when you said you wouldn't ever leave again?"

"Meant it down to the marrow of my bone."

When the infant's needs had been seen to, that first morning Waits bathed her pocked and scarred body right there in the lodge by the crackling warmth of the fire, even washed her long-neglected hair with kettles of water Scratch and Magpie hauled up from the half-frozen creek while Flea cradled his little brother. This washing did not take much time, short as her hair was.

After she had brushed it with a porcupine's tail, Waits asked, "Ti-tuzz, will you cut my hair?"

"Cut it? *You* have cut it enough already!"

With two straight fingers pantomiming a knife blade, she mimicked what she had done, saying, "My heart hurt so bad, it did not matter that I did a bad job of it. Please, Ti-tuzz—will you trim it straight as you can?"

So while her hair was still damp, he took up his sharpest knife and began the difficult task of trimming all those ragged, uneven ends so that—while it no longer brushed her shoulders—at the very least it was all of one length.

When he rocked back and sighed, gazing side to side at what he had done, Waits-by-the-Water said, "Magpie, bring me my looking glass."

She peered at her reflection for several moments, first one view, then another, as she studied herself and the job Titus had done to smooth out how she had butchered her locks in thoughtless grief.

"It is so short now," she said as she lowered the looking glass and gazed at him. "I will never let you cut my hair again."

"And neither can you!" he scolded with a grin as the baby began to fuss in poor Flea's lap. "I think he is hungry again."

"Bring him to me, son," Waits asked as she untied the side of her dress, there beneath her arm, to expose one engorged breast. With the infant tucked across her arm and hungrily latching onto the nipple, Waits said, "I think your new son is happy his mother is making more milk."

"How warm it makes my heart to watch him with you, how happy I am for my eyes to look upon my Magpie and my Flea." Bass held out his two arms, and the children slipped beneath them, one at each side.

"As those long summer days of waiting fell behind us, one by one," she began to explain, "I did my best to make peace with that hole in my heart where the fear rested—a hole where spring rains slowly dried at the bottom of a cracked, crusty buffalo wallow . . . this hollow fear that you would never return. And every day as I grew bigger and bigger with this child, the summer grew more hot. By fall I forced myself to admit that you would never return. The saddest part of what I told my heart was you would never see your son. That he would never know his father."

The first tears spilled from the old trapper's brimming eyes as he gazed into her face while she told him the story of her mourning.

"I made so much room in my heart for that grief, doing all I could to fill the gnawing hole you left inside me—that I was unable to believe that it was really you who walked into this lodge last night. Surely, I told myself at first, my heart must be making my eyes see what I hoped they would see more than anything else."

"I . . . I am not a dream," his voice croaked.

"But I was afraid you were—for the longest time—and that when I awoke from my dream it would be another cold morning without you here in our blankets beside me."

"I have given you my promise, woman," he sighed with such sharp hurt for what he had caused, reaching out his rough hand to enfold her slim fingers within it.

"My heart is filled with that promise," she admitted. "No matter where you want to travel, no matter where you want to go, your family will go with you."

"But I don't think I'm going anywhere, woman," he disclosed. "The only place I can think of needing to take you is to Tullock's trading post at the mouth of the Tongue. But we won't go there until the Crow are ready to trade their furs come spring. There are no more rendezvous. No more reason to journey to the Green or the Popo Azia or the Wind River. Those days are long dead."

"You and Tullock are almost the only white men left in the country," Flea commented as he poked the embers with a twig.

He grinned at the boy. "That's just the way we ought to keep it too, son."

"We will stay with this village, Popo?" asked Magpie.

"We're going to live with the Crow, because my family is Crow," he announced the decision he had made last night while he clutched his grieving, disbelieving wife in his arms for the first time in far too many months.

Waits asked, "We will live with Yellow Belly's people?"

"If the Crow have enemies to fight, I will ride into battle with them," Titus answered. "When it comes time to hunt, Flea and I will go in search of game to feed our family. And I will always be at your mother's side each night when the sun falls, to watch our children grow."

She squeezed his hand as the tears spilled down her cheeks, unable to speak until she said, "I think my father, and my brother—they who are no longer with us—both would want me to tell you how proud they were that I married you."

"There was a time when I wasn't so sure how happy it made them that you decided to marry this old white man!" he joked.

"You were with both of them when they died," she reminded. "You had to see . . . had to know how they felt about you—one warrior for another."

Dragging a finger under his runny nose, Titus blinked some of those salty tears away. "You know what the white men call it when one of their kind runs off to live with the Indians?"

She shook her head.

He looked from Waits to Magpie. From her to Flea. And back to Waits-by-the-Water again before answering.

"They call it going to the blanket."

With a grin, she said, "It is a good way to express it, this going to the blanket."

"I do not understand," Flea admitted.

He scratched his chin whiskers a moment, then explained, "I suppose they call it that because one of the most important contacts there has ever been between the white men and the Indians is to trade in blankets. That goes back a long, long time, son. Long before any man now alive."

Flea asked, "So what does this mean, go to the blanket?"

"For a white man to go to the blanket—it means he's

given up on being a white man anymore, given up on living among white folks and their ways ever again. He's going to live in the blanket, with the Indians and their way of life."

Magpie asked, "My father is going to be a Crow?"

"I can never be a Crow," he admitted with a wag of his head. "Not like you and your two brothers are Crow, Magpie. But I will live among Yellow Belly's people as a Crow. I come to the blanket because my wife is Crow. Because my children will always be Crow too. And . . . because there is nothing left for me as a white man."

"This is your home," Waits said as she laid the sleeping infant on the robes beside her and scooted closer to her husband. "This is where we should all stay now that the time of white fur trappers is fading in the past. Now that the mountains are no longer filled with white men, coming and going."

"We'll be just fine, living the Crow way," Scratch told them as he looped his arm around her shoulder. "Going to the blanket, the white folks call it. I won't argue with those white folks who look down on menfolk like me who go to the blanket. Truth be, I'm damn well proud to tell the whole world Titus Bass had gone to the blanket!"

"When can we name your new son in the old way of the Crow?" inquired his wife.

Flea seized on that and asked, "What will you name this little one, Popo?"

"Whoa, son. Hold on there. I haven't had time to think on names for him yet. I only learned of him last night, and you want a name already?"

"He needs a name," Waits agreed. "It is a father's duty to name his children."

"Yes, these two have good names." And he squeezed both of the children against him.

Waits smiled. "So you'll listen to what the Grandfather Above tells you his name is? Now that this child's father has returned home—you must listen intently because the Creator will speak this boy's name to you."

"Yes," Scratch sighed, gazing at the back of the baby's

head as it slept. "I must find the right name for this child who came as a secret I did not know."

"Can we help listen for what to name him, Popo?" Magpie asked.

"No," Titus said gently. "It is my job to hear what the Grandfather Above tells me. I found the right names for you and your brother. So I trust that I will find the right name for this little one."

"When you do," Waits began, "what of a naming ceremony?"

The idea struck him as a good one. "Invite others to come celebrate with us?"

"Yes—we are here among my people, among this child's people," she declared. "We should name him in the traditional way."

"Yes! I agree. With Magpie and Flea—we only had our family. Now we can gather others around us when we announce the little one's name."

She reached over to gently tug on his graying whiskers. "Your wife thinks you should get busy this morning to find out what that name will be."

"Soon enough I will listen."

"Not this morning?" she repeated.

"I have something else to do first," he began with a wide smile, followed by a wink down at his oldest son. "Last night I promised Flea he would have a chance to hear the Cheyenne horses talk to him this morning."

"Will my mother be angry with me?" Flea asked as they neared the end of the meadow where they had picketed the fifteen Cheyenne horses last night.

"Because I came to listen to the horses with you instead of listening for a name to give your little brother?" he asked, patting the boy on the back of the head as they scuffed through the deep snow. "No, son—your mother will be angry at *me*!"

"She will be angry because you are giving me a horse?"

"Yes," Titus answered. "She doesn't think you are old enough to have a horse of your own."

"Maybe she is right." And the child wagged his head.

"Are you saying that because you think she is right? Or, are you saying it so you won't make your mother angry at you?"

He glanced up at his father. "Maybe . . . because . . . sometimes she might be right."

"Every boy your age has misgivings at times," he consoled. "You must expect to have doubts too. Any man who is too sure of everything is a man I am afraid of. Do you understand?"

"I think I do, Father. It is all right to be afraid of some things."

"Yes," Titus answered. "Are you ever afraid of horses?"

"Not much anymore."

"Then I figure it's up to you to decide what you'll do," he said as they came to a halt near the steadiest animal of them all, that old roan saddle horse. "You can deny all that your spirit tells you about yourself just to keep your mother from being angry with you . . . or you can tell your mother that you have this spirit helper inside you that you are going to follow."

"I don't know what she would say to me if I told her that."

"Neither do I, son. But you can't be afraid of displeasing your mother. In the years to come, there will be many times in your life when you have to tear yourself from your mother. More and more as you grow up. You'll even pull yourself away from your father too—so you can be your own person one day, following the call of your own spirit. But that won't happen without some pain for all of us."

"Father, can I tell you when I am afraid?"

Bass squeezed his son against him and kissed the top of his head. "Yes. As long as you let me tell you when *I* am afraid too. Those are the sorts of spirit things a father and a son share between them."

"Will you talk to my little brother this way when he is older like me?"

"When he is ready, he will let me know that it is time for us to talk like this," Titus assured, feeling his heart swell with such pride. "Shush, now—and listen. Let's stand here and see if any of these horses talks to you this morning."

They waited and listened for a long time. Then Bass nudged Flea forward. Together they walked among the animals, slowly, and as quietly as they could upon the icy, trampled snow that squeaked with every step. Of a sudden the boy stopped and turned around to stare back at a claybank gelding.

The horse stood with its rump toward them but had cocked its head around, as if staring at the youngster that just passed him by. Bass held his breath and listened, straining to hear any sound the animal might make, watching carefully to spot any suspect movement by the horse's jaw. But he heard and saw nothing.

"No," Flea suddenly spoke. "But next summer will be my seventh."

It made the hair stand on Bass's arms. His son took two steps away from his father, then stopped, all the closer to the claybank.

"I came looking for a war pony," Flea continued. Then paused as he took another step closer to the gelding that from all appearances continued to study the boy closely.

"I know I am not ready to go to war yet, but my father told me even a pony boy should have a horse of his own."

Somewhat skeptical, a part of Bass wanted to convince himself that Flea was having fun at his expense.

"The bay has the strongest wind?" Flea seemed to repeat. "And the small red is the fastest among you?"

Bass wanted to chuckle. This was a good joke Flea was having on his father—carrying on a conversation with the horse. Now, Titus would readily admit that he did believe different folks possessed different powers, even that his son might possess some special medicine that would allow him to understand the secret language of horses . . . but to carry on a conversation back and forth with this claybank as if Flea was talking to a person?

"Why should I choose you?"

Maybe this joking had gone far enough. Scratch began to reach out to lay his hand on Flea's shoulder when the boy took another step toward the claybank.

"Yes, of course I realize I can hear you, that I can talk to you. But why does that—"

With one more step toward the gelding, Flea stopped all but underneath the claybank's neck, staring up at the pony's eyes. The youngster nodded in the most matter-of-fact manner, then said, "I understand. Since you and I can talk to one another, that does prove you are the horse for me, doesn't it?"

Titus hurried up and put his two hands on his son's shoulders protectively, ready to put a stop to what he clearly did not understand, a situation that was giving him a very eerie sensation.

Flea turned confidently and peered up at his father. "This is the one, Popo. He told me something that makes sense."

"W-what, son?"

"This horse admitted he isn't the strongest horse, or the fastest horse either."

"Then, why have you decided to choose him?"

For the first time, Flea reached up and patted the claybank along the strong jaw. "I choose him because he tells me he is most like you, Father. Not the strongest, nor the fastest. But because he is the smartest."

Over the next few days, Bass spent part of every afternoon outside, basking in the late sun and carving a number of special invitation sticks that had to be ready when the time came for the naming ceremony. Using his smallest skinning knife, Titus carved his own unique patterns on the cottonwood pegs, then meticulously peeled away pieces of the bark to expose the pale inner bark. With a bundle of those sticks carved, he started Magpie coloring the pale patterns for him, using some vermillion powder he dissolved in warm water. He showed her how to dip a fingertip into the horn bowl and rub the part in her hair for decoration—to use the same technique in rubbing the red dye into wood.

On those days when the unpredictable weather permitted, he took Flea hunting with him. Again there were moments Scratch scolded himself for not learning to shoot McAfferty's bow simply because all they ran across were snow-white hares. But eventually, they would happen onto some deer tracks, or even spot a few antelope grazing out on the flats where the wind had blown the old snow clear. The first time he showed Flea just how curious a creature the antelope was, the boy ended up laughing so loud that the few animals bolted away before Scratch could get off a shot. They had to mount up and follow the fleeing animals until the antelope finally stopped again.

Once more, Bass hid their horses in a coulee. "You can come with me, son. But if you laugh at how stupid those antelope are this time—instead of some fresh meat tied over the back of your new horse—I'll take you back to camp tied down the same way!"

"I promise," Flea said, trying hard to wipe the smile from his mouth with his small blanket mitten.

"When I start crawling, you get down on your belly with me," Titus instructed. "There will be no talking from here on."

"All right, Popo."

"Here," and Bass handed the boy his rifle's long wiping stick, to the end of which he had tied a corner of a bright Mexican scarf, a bright yellow cloth covered with a profusion of blue and red flowers. "You know what to do when I tap your shoulder and point?"

"Yes. I'll poke the stick into the snow so the antelope will see the scarf waving in the breeze."

"Good, lad. Their curiosity will work against their suspicious natures and bring them to us so that we can pick one of them for our supper."

The boy's face got serious. "No laughing at those stupid animals though."

He laid a mitten on his son's shoulder. "Just make sure that one day in your life, you don't become like the antelope and are fooled into being so curious you blunder into your own death."

They emerged over the side of the coulee where the ravine grew shallow, staying on their bellies as they crawled a few yards onto the prairie. Bass stopped and put out his hand to touch his son's arm. Flea nodded as he reached forward the full length of his arm and jammed the ramrod into the crusty snow. Now they had only to wait while that Mexican scarf rippling in the wind worked its magic to lure the unwary antelope into range.

As a doe moved closer, Titus dragged the hammer back to full cock as quietly as the lock would allow. She was clearly nervous, pacing anxiously side to side several yards at a time—never coming directly toward the hunters—but her eyes always watching that scarf nonetheless. As wary as she tried to be, her curiosity was soon to be her undoing. Then at sixty yards, it appeared she wasn't going to come any closer.

Titus glanced up at the scarf, measuring the strength of the breeze and its direction. Laying his cheek against the rifle, he snugged the weapon into the curve of his shoulder. Squeezing back on the rear set trigger, he moved his bare finger forward in the trigger guard to wait there like a summer's whisper while he got the sight picture he wanted on her front flank. She turned, still nervous . . . so he repositioned the front blade.

Then squeezed.

That .54-caliber Derringer roared—old workhorse that it was. He knew this rifle, knew where it would shoot and where to hold, as steady as any man was with a firearm.

Flea was up and running across the snow as Bass clambered to his knees, then brought his legs under him. He stood reloading there and then while the boy reached the antelope and danced around it.

"Let me dress it! Let me do it this time!" Flea cried as his father approached.

"You can help," Titus offered, glad for his son's enthusiasm as he came to a stop beside the antelope doe, "but you must learn what is most important, son."

"What?"

Holding the blade, Titus handed his knife to his son. "Remember that your empty hand must always know what the hand with the knife is doing."

They knelt together, and Scratch grabbed a fore- and rear leg on one side, easing the doe onto her back. He stretched out her neck, then cupped his hand around his son's hand as they lowered the knife to make that first incision from throat to groin.

"Feel it in your hand, in your arm and shoulder too," he instructed. "Don't stab the point too deep, or you'll make a mess of her insides and it will spoil the meat."

As they gently worked their way down the chest, Titus gradually took some of the pressure off his son's hand, allowing Flea to do more and more of that first carving by himself.

"You must always be careful not to cut off your hand, Flea," he reminded with a grin, his son nestled there within his arms as they worked in tandem. "Unless you want to be a one-handed horseman when you grow up!"

This antelope was a most welcome change to the deer they had harvested in the shady bottoms or that elk cow they had spotted in the hillside timber. A different taste altogether. It warmed his heart to see how eagerly Magpie and Flea ate and ate, until they were stuffed at every meal—knowing how little the children might have had to eat while he was away chasing not the mountain beaver but California horses. And each time he gazed at their greasy, smiling faces, watching them gnaw every morsel from the bones, he silently renewed his vow never again to leave his family behind.

It happened that a name was spoken to him.

At sunrise the next morning Titus bundled the children against the bright, sunny cold, pulling fur hats down over their ears to protect them from the frigid winds and the sprinkling hoarfrosts. As Waits nursed the infant, Magpie and Flea stood before their father.

"I want my son to carry these sticks in his mittens," Scratch instructed, then handed the carved and painted cottonwood pegs to Flea. "And at each lodge, you will give one to your sister so that she can make the invitation."

"I ask them to come?" Magpie inquired.

Waits answered now, "To our lodge. At sundown this day. For supper and a naming."

"Do you understand, children?" Titus asked them.

Both nodded their heads. Then Magpie answered for both of them. "We are ready to do this for our little brother."

Scratch sank to one knee and gathered them both in his arms tightly. He released them and arose, saying, "Go then. And when you are done, hurry back. We have much, so much to do."

After the two had shoved the door cover back in place over the opening, Waits-by-the-Water sighed, "You have decided upon a name?"

He chuckled, then said, "Dear mother of my children—we couldn't have a naming ceremony for the boy if the Grandfather hadn't already told me his name!"

At the appointed time late that afternoon the first guests arrived to scratch at the door pole.

"Is my white brother receiving dinner guests?" Turns Plenty asked.

Titus shoved the door flap aside, saying, "Come in, come in. I'm sorry you had to ask. Please, take a seat of honor as our first guest."

As Turns Plenty eased around the left side of the fire in the path the sun takes across the sky, Scratch set his hand on his son's shoulder and said, "Quickly now, put on your coats, children. I want you both to wait outside to welcome our guests. Magpie, you greet them, and Flea— you pull the door flap open for them to enter."

The eager children quickly dressed for the cold and dived outside into the last of the sun's light.

Singly or in pairs, the respected men of the tribe, as

well as those who had long ago befriended Titus Bass, all appeared at their door. When the last had arrived, Scratch called his children inside to join those who encircled the cheery fire, so many they formed two rings. Warm as it was in the lodge, the men quickly shed their coats before they were offered what tin plates Waits-by-the-Water owned, along with lap-size sheets of scraped buffalo parfleche. On these the guests were invited to take their choice from chunks of the boiled or roasted elk speared from the steamy kettles and pulled from those roasting sticks positioned around the fire pit.

With supper done and everyone licking the grease from their fingers and lips, the coffee was ready to pour. At their father's signal, Magpie and Flea began passing out the shiny, new tin cups Titus had traded off Lucas Murray at Bents Fort.

"The cup my children give each one of you now belongs to you," Bass explained. "It is just the beginning of the gifts from my family to you—in return for honoring us with your presence while we announce the Grandfather's name for our new son."

With grunts and murmurs of agreeable good humor, the guests held out their new cups as Titus and Waits each transcribed half the circle with their steamy coffeepots. Many of the men clinked their empty cups together merrily, holding their gifts aloft to salute respect for their generous host.

When he finally filled his own cup and set the pot down at the edge of the fire pit, Scratch retook his spot beside the oldest among them and said, "Real Bird, will you honor us with a prayer over your pipe before we begin this ceremony?"

From his beautiful blanket pouch, this ancient warrior and mentor to Rotten Belly and many chiefs took his pipe stem, the bowl, and a large tobacco pouch made from the scrotum of an elk bull. Though many, many winters had turned his hair completely silver, Real Bird nonetheless still possessed a strong "elk medicine" unlike anything his people had ever known. He was a physician and healer, as well as being a diviner who could see into the days ahead and know what would come to pass.

With his pipe loaded, Real Bird held it before him and offered his prayer, face gazing upward through the wide, black hole where fire smoke rose in twisting spirals into the dark, winter sky. When the old one put the stem to his lips, Scratch picked up a small coal with a pair of iron tongs and placed it atop the tamped tobacco. After the diviner's prayer, the pipe came next to the child's father, Titus Bass, then continued on to the left until it reached the doorway, where it was passed back to the second row of guests so that its path continued back to Real Bird. Next it went hand-to-hand along the right side of the lodge, as each visitor offered his own extended prayer of blessing before drawing in his own six puffs of smoke that sent the prayer to the four cardinal directions, and to mother earth and father sky.

Once the pipe was back in Real Bird's hands, the old shaman emptied the black dollop and separated bowl from stem. Then he called the mother forward with the infant.

"Give the child to its father," Real Bird instructed.

Titus took the boy into his arms as Waits turned away and took her seat behind the second row of chiefs and headmen, near her two children who were watching in rapt attention from the shadows that leaped and danced upon the dew liner and lodge cover.

"Take the dressings from him," the old shaman said.

Resting the bundle in his lap, Scratch pulled the blanket aside, then loosened the knots tied in the calico that was wrapped around the boy's genitals to contain his elimination. Titus carefully wiped the child's bottom with dried moss, then held the infant aloft upon his two hands. Hoisted upward there in the fire's light, the youngster lay higher than any of them, suspended between the oldest of the band and the Grandfather Above.

"Father of this child—what is the name the Creator has chosen for the boy?" asked Real Bird in a reedy voice.

Tears glistened in his eyes and Bass found his throat

clogged when he first tried to speak. "I-I have learned his name is *Iische*."

"Jackrabbit?" Real Bird repeated as Waits-by-the-Water silently put her hand over her mouth, her eyes welling up.

"Yes."

Around them many of the guests grunted or nodded to one another to signify their approval.

Turns Plenty announced, "It is a good name for a boy-child."

"His legs are always busy," Titus explained, "as if he wants to be let down from our arms so he can jump around."

"Soon enough he will be," Real Bird prophesied, then chuckled some as he raised his arm and placed his wrinkled, withered hand on the boy's chest where Bass held the child aloft. "*Iische* . . . I name you by all that is holy to our people. You are loved not only by your father and mother, but your sister and brother. And you will always know the love of all your people."

Several of the others openly and loudly offered their praise.

Then Real Bird continued, "You come from the finest of blood, *Iische*. In your veins flows the blood of your mother—and through her comes the blood of warrior chiefs: Arapooesh, Whistler . . . and Strikes In Camp."

By now Titus was starting to tremble, not from holding the tiny infant aloft, but from the emotion threatening to overwhelm him as he considered Real Bird's wise and moving words.

"And in your veins too flows the blood of your father," the wrinkled shaman continued. "A man who was not born a warrior, nor born a friend of the Crow . . . but a man of honor who has become a warrior and many times proved himself a protector of our people. *Iische*, with your sister and brother you have a great honor to uphold. Your mother has proved she is the bravest of the brave, and your father is our unquestioned friend."

Many in the lodge muttered all the louder now in their approval of the old shaman's words.

"Our enemies are your father's enemies," Real Bird continued. "Our friends are his friends. And his children . . . are our children. If ever death should claim your father, children—then know that there are a half a hundred of us who will step forward to raise you as he would himself do."

Tears were streaming unchecked down Scratch's face and dampening his beard as he peered across the lodge to find Waits-by-the-Water's eyes glistening as she repeatedly swiped fingers across her own wet cheeks.

"*Iische*—may you grow as strong and true and every bit as straight as the Creator intended for you when he sent you to these parents He alone chose to give you, parents who would teach you, protect you, love you," Real Bird prayed. "Jackrabbit—little Crow warrior!"

With those special words, the entire lodge roared with one concerted response, "*Heya!*"

Bass folded the naked child back against him once more, so overwhelmed with a gush of emotion. "Come over here, children," he called and gestured to Magpie and Flea.

They squeezed behind the second row of warriors to reach a small place made for them now right behind their father.

"It is time for the gifts now," he instructed as they sat, his voice still unsteady, clogged with sentiment. "Do you remember those stacks of blankets we dragged up just outside the door this afternoon?"

"Yes, Popo," Flea answered with an eager nod.

"As our guests leave our home, give them each a blanket as a token of our love, our esteem for them honoring us with their presence here tonight."

As the first of the leaders and headmen began to stand in the crowded lodge and pulled on their fur coats or blanket capotes, Magpie and Flea threaded their way through the guests to dive outside to make ready their final part in the ceremonies. And when the crowd had thinned enough, Waits-by-the-Water got to her feet and moved over to sit beside her husband near Real Bird.

By now Titus was struggling with the last knot to retie

the calico wrap around the squirming infant—all arms and legs in constant motion.

"Here, woman of my heart," Scratch said, his face beaming with pride and love as he pulled the small blanket back over his son and handed the child to her.

"*Iische*," she repeated. "It is a very good name for him!"

"You see these strong legs of his? How they kick when he wants to go find you!" Titus cried with joy. "Your little jackrabbit—I think he is very hungry again!"

26

◆

That winter the cottonwoods boomed with the bone-jarring cold . . . but the worst was yet to come.

For the next three winters a deep, unrelenting cold was visited upon the north country, keeping the men close to their lodge fires, yearning for spring when they could return to stealing horses, raising plunder, and squandering the finest seasons of their young lives.

Far too cold that no tribe did much raiding until the weather finally warmed weeks after the equinox. Altogether, it was a string of four winters unlike any the Crow had ever known—four years when the tribe wrapped itself in a growing sense of invincibility and security that come each winter, no thoughts of danger or guarded wariness need trouble all of Absaroka.

But through each spring, summer, and into the early autumn before that first freeze . . . it was a celebration of the old life. Throughout the land those few men who could remember a time before the coming of the whites were growing long in tooth and dim of eye, their shoulders stooped with age and their infirmities, eyes rheumy with their years, their exploits, their memories a great and glorious day now gone on the winds.

That first of those next four winters was a time that was like no other Bass had experienced among the Crow. And he knew that come a day soon no man alive would ever remember the halcyon days before beaver pelts and buffalo robes changed everything in the northern mountains forever.

When he had first come among the Absaroka long ago, Titus was as an outsider—wintering with the three thieves who posed as partners. Although befriended by Bird In Ground, the young Apsaluuke with a powerful man/woman medicine, Bass had remained an outsider until he returned to the Crow alone. Eventually he took a Crow woman in the manner of the country, and she birthed their half-breed children. Yet, despite how much his old friend Arapooesh had hoped for the acceptance of his white friend, the band was reluctant to treat him as one of their own. Even after he stood beside his woman in the promising ceremony, or went to avenge the Blackfoot bringing the pox south of the Yellowstone, or when he named his third child in the old manner of things . . . he still could not shake that sense of aloneness, of standing apart from his wife's people.

No, it was not until that next spring after the naming when he did not make ready his horses, did not load burdens upon them, and did not depart for weeks, even moons, on end in that way of a white man. Instead, he stayed. Most of the Crow expected him to pick up and be gone one of those bright spring days, but he stayed. Word among them rumored of the promise he had made to his wife and their children.

"He has come to the blanket," someone said. "Now he wants to be one of us."

"Perhaps," others agreed guardedly, "but—we all remember the stories of the Medicine Calf* and how he

---

* Jim Beckwith—adopted by the Crow, he lived among them for many years, took several wives, and fathered many children before he grew

took to the blanket, only to forsake us when it suited him."

"This one is not like Medicine Calf," another would say assuredly. "Medicine Calf was lured and seduced back to the land of the white men. But the gray-bearded coyote, Waits-by-the-Water's man . . . he left nothing behind there in the land of the white men. He claims no family, no friends back there. He knows no other home but this."

Titus Bass stayed on, season after season—while other white men had always come and gone, like footloose transients come only in search of the furs before they were gone again. Now the beaver trade had breathed its last—a final, wheezing death rattle all could hear rumble with its final gasp. No more did the Crow happen upon any trapping parties, much less the huge brigades that used to winter anywhere from the big bend of the Yellowstone east to the Bighorn, perhaps as far as the Tongue. The only whites they chanced to see now were a trader and his engages who sat out the seasons in their tiny post at the mouth of one river or another on the Yellowstone.

Rumors floated into Absaroka of traders far to the south, said to have built their posts somewhere on the lower Green River where, so the Snake and Bannock tribes told Crow hunting parties, Big Throat Bridger had stacked up log walls and begun housekeeping with his Indian family and a few white partners.

But up in this country, the era of the white man was behind them now. The only white face any of them ever saw outside of that of the post trader's was an aging, wind- and sun-ravaged face that Titus Bass had dragged around with him for seasons beyond count. He had stayed. Because they saw he did not leave in the way of all other white men, the Crow gradually came to accept him as part of their lives. With every season he became more like them: his children growing up among theirs, hunting with their men, joining with the other old war-

weary of the diversion and abandoned his families and adopted people.

riors to counsel those young men gathering in war parties or preparing to set off on raids into foreign lands. He and old fighters like him always stayed behind to guard Absaroka, to protect the camp, if need be to put their lives between the enemy and their women and children.

While the young men rode far and wide carrying forth the glory of the Crow, it was always the old warriors who stood as the last great fortress of Absaroka—arrayed like a bulwark there against the many Blackfoot to the north, the Cheyenne on the south, and those Lakota who were migrating out of the east. The old men knew what the land of the Crow had always been . . . and they stood ready to defend what they prayed Absaroka always would be. So Titus Bass stayed.

How often in those circles of the seasons did he look back on those glorious days following the naming ceremony!

With the help of his children, each cold morning Scratch loaded up one of the packhorses with two great bundles of goods and walked through the camp. At the poorest of lodges the three of them would stop and he would ask what that family could most use—a new, thick blanket, perhaps? Or maybe a kettle? Some cloth for a new dress or to wrap up a young child?

"A man who holds too tightly to his riches," Titus reminded his children during their daily ritual, "he will forever stay a poor man in the eyes of others. But a man who lets his riches flow from his fingers—"

"He," Magpie finished his oft-repeated admonition, "is a man who is rich beyond compare in the eyes of his people."

"To give away his wealth," young Flea repeated his father's moral, "is what marks a man truly blessed by the Creator Above."

So a brass kettle went to some, an iron skillet to others, and those new blankets to shelter one from the brutal cold that had visited itself upon the north country. And there were earrings, rolls of brass wire, and domed tacks for decoration he put in the hands of many of Yellow Belly's band. A rainbow of colorful ribbon, tiny waxed packets of vermillion, not to mention a myriad of other small tools, decorations, and sewing goods he pulled from his packs like a peddlar as he and the children inched their way through camp for the next four days. Something for every lodge, especially those families who needed the most. This sharing of riches was a lesson like no other he could teach his children.

What joy it was to return to the lodge when they were done with their day—finding it warmed by a merry fire, the babe asleep, its tummy filled, and Waits-by-the-Water busy at supper, or working her colored quills onto some strip of soft antelope hide, or sewing up a new pair of moccasins for one of the children. More times than not, their feet outgrew old moccasins before those moccasins wore out.

After nearly a moon at this site, the crier brought word that they would move in two days. Time to pack up, make ready with what they owned, repair old travois hitches. The grass was gone, the firewood too. Besides, the camp had begun to stink with the offal and refuse of those hundreds.

Less than a dozen slow miles away, the camp chiefs had already decided upon a new site nestled in the lee of a hill. While the spot did not possess any meadows near as free of snow as the last camp, Yellow Belly's people did find plenty of wood, and some open water where a spring fed a nearby creek even though most every other stream was frozen from bank to bank.

For days at a time throughout the long and horrid winters, the Crow were imprisoned in camp, if not in their lodges, unwilling to brave the terrible winds and brutal temperatures brought with each new storm. But the weather always moderated, the sun reappeared, and the first, resolute hunting parties embarked in search of what game would be out to feed with the passing of the storms.

It didn't take long for him to realize that life was growing easier than he could ever remember it having been. Almost from the time he ran away from the homestead and put Boone County at his back, Titus Bass had made a living from the muscles in his back and the sweat of his brow. But it wasn't brawn that allowed him to endure. Some might well claim he had survived more by virtue of his wits than by his wisdom—so be it. Whether it was toting up bales and baggage at riverport towns on the Ohio or the Mississippi, or sweating over anvil and forge in St. Louis, even unto immersing himself up to the balls in high-country streams little more than liquid ice for months at a time—nearly every function of his life over the past twenty-some winters out here in the mountains had aged his body that much quicker than it would have aged had he stayed back in those peaceful, predictable settlements.

In adapting to life with the Crow he lulled himself into peaceful rhythms that most suited a man who had celebrated half a hundred birthdays. Last out the long winters, do some hunting, maybe run a daytime trapline come each spring if he took a notion to and a stretch of country looked promising, help others break and breed the horses all summer through, then pay a visit to the trader downriver when autumn turned the cottonwood to gold . . .

"Well I'll be jigged—you're a white fella," exclaimed the man stepping from the open gate of his log post, peering up at Titus Bass before he glanced over those warriors and women, children and old people, all arrayed across the prairie behind Scratch. "From a ways back, you looked about as Injun as the rest of them you brought with you."

"Guilty there," Titus answered with a smile. He held down his hand to the man. "Name's Bass."

"Murray," he replied with a real burr to the *r*'s.

"Met a fella same name as you down to Bents Fort last fall. You related?"

"Don't have any relations in the country," Murray admitted.

"Mite s'prised to see a man's built anything here on the river," Titus said as the last of the Crow came up noisily and started to dismount in the meadow nearby.

"If'n it don't make you no nevermind, this bunch'll make camp here for the night."

"Where you bound downriver?" Murray inquired.

"Tullock's post near the mouth of the Tongue."

"Tullock is no longer there," Murray explained. "Last I heard he's nowhere to be found on the upper river. Don't know where he's gone."

"Don't say?" Bass replied with a little suspicion.

"And his old post, Van Buren, is no longer there. We burned it last autumn."

That struck him as downright criminal. "Why the devil you burn Tullock's post for?"

"Under orders to, by Culbertson, company factor up at Fort Union. A year ago May he sent ten of us upriver with Charles Larpenteur in charge, ordered to close down Van Buren and build this post." Murray held out both arms expansively to indicate the compact log stockade enclosing the post that stood no more than one hundred feet square. A handful of stone chimneys constructed of river rock poked their blackened heads above the eight-foot walls.

Bass cleared his dusty, parched throat. "So this here's American Fur?"

"And me as well. I've been the trader for more'n nine months here already," Murray admitted. "Larpenteur was called back to Union last November—so it's just me and four engages."

Titus finally swung to the ground as his wife and children came out of their saddles. "So Tullock and Van Buren ain't no more."

"No, sir. You know Tullock long?"

"Me and him go back some. What'd you name this place?"

"Larpenteur named it for our chief factor."

"Fort Culbertson?"

"No. We've blessed it with our factor's first name," Murray declared. "You're standing at the walls of Fort Alexander."

Over the next few days the visiting Crow went about their business with the powerful company that had brought an end to both the beaver business and the mountain rendezvous, the economic giant who had crushed a glorious way of life in its mighty fist. It surprised Titus to discover he was still sore having to deal with American Fur again, but he reminded himself he'd done it before. What few furs he had managed to trap the previous spring did garner some shiny geegaws for the children, a few yards of wool cloth for Waits, and that much-needed powder and bar lead. Their trading done with Murray at this new Yellowstone post, Yellow Belly's band turned about on the fifth morning and started upriver once more.

That second winter began early and proved to be even harder than the last. Spring was long in coming. Because the weather had made them prisoners, few of the Crow had many furs to trade on their next journey down the Yellowstone to Fort Alexander.

"Murray here?" Titus asked the figure stepping from the gate as he and two dozen of the Crow men dismounted in advance of the village.

At first the solidly built man did not acknowledge his question; instead, he shaded his eyes that early autumn day and noted the dust haze rising over the hundreds of Crow who were steering their herds into the expansive meadow filled with grass already cured by the first frost.

"No, Murray doesn't work here no more," the stranger replied as his eyes finally came back to look upon Bass.

After another full round of seasons spent listening to nothing but the Crow tongue, Scratch's ear picked up a strong Scottish accent, all that much heartier than Murray's brogue. "You in charge?"

"No. The factor's named Kipp."

"He here?"

"Inside. Come with me," the man offered, then he gestured at the Crow men. "Three of them at a time, only."

Scratch hit the ground and rubbed his aching knees. With the advent of every year he resented that pain brought of being in the saddle a little more. Holding out his hand, he said, "I'm Titus Bass."

"Robert Meldrum," the man answered, brushing a thick shock of sandy brown hair from his eyes. "You live with this band I see."

"With my wife, young'uns too."

Meldrum surprised Scratch when he turned to face the throngs of Crow men and suddenly began speaking loudly, in a respectable Crow. "Your chiefs must decide who among you will be the first to come inside and smoke before trading. We'll set the prices, then the trading can begin in earnest after sunrise tomorrow."

As the headmen gathered to discuss who would accompany the trader into the fort, Bass grabbed the white man's elbow. "You speak good Crow, Meldrum."

"Had some practice," the trader replied.

"Figgered you for a Scotchman, from the sound of your words."

"I'm Scots, that's for sure," Meldrum admitted with a characteristic burr. "Born on the moors in the second year of the century. Came to Kentucky with me parents."

"You've been out here for some time," Titus observed.

"Came west with Ashley's trading caravan in twenty-seven. Didn't go back with the other clerks after rendezvous."

"Twenty-seven . . ." And he pondered the roll of sites. "I recollect that'un was held over at the bottom of Sweet Lake."*

"Still some small affairs back then," Meldrum declared as he kept his gray eyes pinned on the Crows' deliberations. "But they got bigger."

"An' noisier too," Scratch said. "So how come you speak such good Crow?"

"Married one. It helps."

"Damn if it don't. Haven't got me no idee how a fella gets along with a Injun gal if he don't know her tongue!"

"Most fellows, they have no intentions of sticking around long enough to learn to speak their woman's language."

---

* Present-day Bear Lake, in northeastern Utah; *Buffalo Palace*.

That evening Scratch and his family were invited to sit for supper with the post's factor, James Kipp. Even more so than Robert Meldrum, this man was clearly educated; not the usual sort who had worked his way up through the ranks on muscle.

"I heard your name afore—from a ol' friend of mine works downriver at Fort Union," Titus explained as they were introduced.

"Who was that?"

"Levi Gamble. Maybeso you know 'im."

"He was a good man, a steadfast employee in his day."

"In h-his day?" Titus echoed. "He ain't working at the fort no more?"

"Last word I had, Gamble took to drinking, hard too," Kipp disclosed. "Seems he lost his wife when she was burned terribly, a lodge fire as I recall. She lingered awhile, pitifully—then died in his arms."

"Damn," Scratch muttered under his breath, his eyes flicking quickly to glance at his woman.

"I was told Levi never got over her painful death. Immediately took to drink. On this last stay of mine at Fort Union, I heard he'd died of consumption . . . although I think he succumbed to a powerful combination of too much alcohol and his just plain giving up after the death of his wife."

"This news about Levi come recent?"

"Yes. Seems I'm newly come here from Fort Union myself," Kipp explained with a generous smile. His well-wrinkled face crinkled warmly. "It's been no more than two weeks since the last supply steamboat came upriver and dropped me off with the year's goods."

"In less'n a year—this place awready had three booshways," Scratch commented.

"It's a fact of the business," Kipp explained with a shrug of his shoulders. "I myself have been shuttled around from post to post since I came upriver."

"Where you born and raised back east?"

"Born in Canada," Kipp disclosed. "Eighty-eight. That makes me fifty-six years old now."

Scratch folded fingers down as he calculated. "So you're six years older'n me. An' that's some, Mr. Kipp. Out here I don't run across many fellas what can say they're older'n me."

"Spent a lot of time among the Mandans when I first ascended the Missouri. Learned their language, could even write it too, while I was in the employ of the Columbia Fur Company."

"Can't say I ever heard of 'em."

Kipp grinned. "They're no more, Mr. Bass. Long, long time ago, they merged with American Fur—which made John Jacob Astor all the bigger."

"You stayed on, I take it."

The factor nodded. "They liked the cut of my timbers, so the bosses gave me the job of building Fort Floyd."

"Ain't heard of that'un neither. Where's it stand?"

Kipp poured more coffee into Waits-by-the-Water's cup as he answered, "You've been there: mouth of the Yellowstone. Never was known as Fort Floyd for long. It's been called Fort Union almost from the first day."

"Then I have been there," Scratch confessed. "Years back, when the Deschamps family was near done in."*

"A most awful blood feud between those families," Kipp clucked, then settled back atop a crate with his glass of port. "After building that post, the company partners thought well enough of James Kipp to put me in charge of raising Fort Clark back among my Mandan friends."

"When was that?"

"Thirty-one," Kipp answered. "A profitable year for the company."

"Aye—them was shinin' times. Each year beaver just kept getting better'n better too," Bass said with a wistful smile. "You s'pose beaver's bound to rise, Mr. Kipp?"

The trader wagged his head. "The sun has set on the beaver trade, my good man. But I must say that—in those years when beaver was king—I met some interesting people while downriver at Fort Clark," Kipp explained.

---

* *Ride the Moon Down*

"One of the most remarkable was an American artist named Catlin, George Catlin. He was at the post, painting the Mandans left and right. The following winter, thirty-three and thirty-four, a German prince—Maximilian—came upriver on a sportsman's holiday. He brought with him a wonderful artist who became a fast friend of mine. Karl Bodmer was his name."

"I met a artist fella my own self once, years back at a ronnyvoo it was," Titus chimed in. "Named Alfred Miller. You met him?"

"Can't say as I have."

"Miller come west with a Scotchman—a rich fella named William Drummond Stewart. That Scotchman even brung ol' Jim Bridger a suit of armor one summer!"

"Yes, I've heard of Stewart," Kipp disclosed.

"You was at Fort Clark till you come here?"

The trader shook his head. "Once my employers had their Mandan post running smoothly, I was dispatched into Blackfoot country, where I built Fort Piegan at the mouth of the Marias."

"Damn, if you ain't the fort-buildingest fella I ever met," Bass enthused. "Time was, there wasn't a post in this north country . . . and now the Injuns can durn well pick where they wanna go, north or south, to trade off their robes. Beaver ain't wuth a tinker's damn no more. Just robes. Life's changed, Mr. Kipp. Life's changed a hull bunch up here in the north country."

"I detect a strong note of resignation, Mr. Bass. If not a deep regret."

With a slight nod, Titus sighed, "Some long winter nights, I sit with my woman and young'uns by the lodge fire, thinking back on how things use to was. But the beaver are near gone most places I go, and they damn well ain't wuth the time to scrape 'em no more anyhow. 'Sides, no fur companies like your'n ever gonna hire trappers no more—you just trade all your furs off the Injuns."

"That, yes—but we also barter with a few of the last trappers—men like yourself who are still working the mountain streams." Kipp scratched at his bare jowl thoughtfully, then said, "It won't ever be the same again, my friend. God knows things won't ever be the same again."

"Missionaries been trampin' through my mountains," Scratch grumbled, feeling very possessive and protective of his shrinking world. "Bringing their white women. For now they're just passing through on their way to Oregon country . . . but one of these days, I know in my gut they're gonna stop and settle down right here in the mountains. Gonna ruin what life we got left."

"The Jesuits have dispatched one of their own, a Father De Smet, to make contact with the northwestern tribes," Kipp announced. "I met him at Fort Union two years ago when he came through."

"What's a Jesuit?"

"Of course, I couldn't expect you to know that it's a Catholic order of priests—"

Scratch howled with alarm, "The Papists are sending their missionaries out here too!"

"De Smet told me he attended the last rendezvous ever held, on his way to the Flathead in the summer of forty. Later that fall, he came downriver to Fort Clark, where I made his acquaintance."

Titus wagged his head. "Even when things are changing all around me," he declared, "I wanna believe things don't have to change for me. Not for me and these Crow I'm running with."

"What do you think of Mr. Meldrum here?" Kipp asked, indicating the post trader seated down the table.

"He seems to be a likeable kind." And Bass winked at Meldrum. "Any man what speaks Crow good as he does and marries hisself into the tribe can't be a bad sort, now can he?"

"Some of his wife's people watched Robert blacksmithing," Kipp declared. "So the Crow call him Round Iron."

"That's another reason for me to like Meldrum," Bass admitted. "Back in Saint Louie I sweated over an anvil and bellows for a few years afore I come out to the mountains."

"You were apprenticed in your youth?" Meldrum asked.

"Nawww—was awready growed—a good trade for a man to learn," Titus recalled with a sigh. "Meldrum ain't the first trader your company's sent to Crow country to get married so all the tribe's furs come to him."

Kipp's eyes flashed to Meldrum for a moment before he asked, "You're referring to the mulatto Beckwith?"

"He's a humbug if ever there was one!" Meldrum growled menacingly.

"That's probably the nicest thing Robert could say about the mulatto," Kipp replied. "While Beckwith might have been on the company payroll, he never was a company man."

"Not only is he totally without any abilities as an honest businessman, but—he's a scoundrel of the first order!" Meldrum roared his disapproval. "Cheated whoever got within reach or was in his way: the Crow, the company, his factors—"

"Last time I see'd Jim Beckwith, was two year ago," Titus confided. "He and a few other Americans built themselves a small trading post on the Arkansas."

"Near the Bent brothers' fort?" Meldrum inquired.

"Upriver a good ways, closer to the mountains."

Meldrum snarled, "I say, let that southern country have him so the thieving bastard won't ever show his lying face up here again."

"Far as I know he's settling in down there, for a fact," Titus told them. "Got him a Mex wife, even opened up a li'l trade store too."

"Is he even aware that some of the Crow mean to kill him if he ever returns to this country?" Meldrum disclosed.

That shocked Titus. "W-what for?"

"They think he betrayed them by living with them for so long, then suddenly leaving them to return to civilization," Kipp explained.

"That's right," Meldrum added. "A few—not all, mind you—but some of the harshest warriors and headmen would love to get their hands on him, Mr. Bass.

Believe me, I married into the same band Beckwith ruined with his shameless scams. There's no affection for him among the Crow people now."

"Damn shame," Scratch brooded, thinking how Bill Williams appeared to hate Beckwith with this very same fury. "I knowed Jim Beckwith for almost as long as I been out here in the mountains. Shame to see what haps to a fella when he turns his back on them what was once his friends."

Many were the times since that autumn journey to Fort Alexander when Titus reflected on how circumstances changed the folks around him—when he didn't consider he was any different. Not from that first winter with the Yuta,* and not from the time of his first contact with these Crow . . . Scratch looked back to weigh the possibility that he might have treated anyone less than the way he wanted to be treated himself. If there ever had been a code among men out here in the mountains, that was its evenhanded preamble.

But as the fates undermined the economic structure of their lives, Scratch had watched the long-held code splinter. No longer could a white man count on the help of another without question. White men stole not only from white men—just as the big fur companies did day in and day out—but desperate white men had taken to stealing from their red allies.

That whole unspoken code of honor lay in shambles by the time Scratch had followed Bill Williams and Peg-Leg Smith west to California. It was clear that the new watchword was now: *every man for himself.* No more camaraderie. No longer any sense of that fraternal brotherhood he had experienced in the heady heyday of the beaver trade.

As Yellow Belly's band turned around on the Yellowstone and started up the Bighorn in the last autumn moon, something struck him for the first time. While a right-thinking man knew he never could recapture what

---

* The Ute tribe; *Buffalo Palace.*

had been . . . Scratch held out the possibility that, at the very least, he might well revisit old memories. And while his most glorious days were behind him now, he decided a man was due a chance to relive those seasons through reminiscence with old friends.

Not once that following winter did he ever give any serious thought to heading back east to find Hames Kingsbury or any of Ebenezer Zane's other Kentucky riverboatmen.* Those who hadn't suffered a violent death in the intervening thirty-five winters surely weren't the sort of men who left any traces of their whereabouts, from New Orleans at the mouth of the Mississippi all the way north to the upper waters of the Ohio River.

Then too, no man could argue there was any need of hunting down the three who had stolen a fortune in furs from him back when he first came to the mountains. More than ten years ago he stumbled across Bud Tuttle, who had become a Santa Fe trader, then hunted Billy Hooks all the way to dockside in St. Louis, finding that poor demented soul was dying fast from the venereal disease eating away at his brain. But the sweetest revenge came when Scratch watched Silas Cooper die with his own eyes.†

And there was no sense in trying to turn back the calendar in hoping to run down his old partner Jack Hatcher. Any reunion they might have shared had been snuffed out by a Blackfoot bullet in Pierre's Hole. Not to mention how Asa McAfferty had gripped fate itself by the throat and strangled the life out of it high in a snowy bowl at the end of a long manhunt.††

But there had been a man who had stood at his shoulder through one skirmish and ordeal after another, a man who had lived through some of the last glory days of Titus Bass. And he was still alive . . . at least according to Mathew Kinkead's claim. How long ago was it? Back

---

* *Dance on the Wind*
† *One-Eyed Dream*
†† *Carry the Wind*

in the fall of '42, that's when Kinkead declared the man was doing well for himself.

"Yes," Waits-by-the-Water said with a smile as harsh winds gusted a new snow outside their lodge, "I remember your friend, Josiah Paddock. Do you remember that you believed I loved him?"

"I was pretty stupid back then."

"You were all I wanted, Ti-tuzz."

"I can still remember what a fool love can make of a man."

"Love did not make you a fool," she corrected. "It was jealousy. Blind jealousy.* After all these winters, is your heart telling you that it must apologize to me again for thinking I did not love you?"

He gently touched her hand with his callused fingers that morning as they sat by the fire with their children. "Every day with you is like a new beginning. I am thankful for each morning like this when I awake and you are with me."

She leaned against him, her cheek resting against his chest. "When you were away—and I believed you were gone forever—every day was a torment I could never describe to you. So I know your words are strong when you tell me how thankful you are to be here with me. I am grateful for every day, season, and year we have shared since you returned to me—not once, but twice."

Then she gazed into his eyes. "You don't need to bring up old memories and mistakes to make me grateful for this time we have in our lives."

Touching her cheek, he admitted, "I asked if you remembered Josiah for a reason. You remember his wife—Looks Far Woman? Their little son, Joshua, too?"

"I remember them, and the mud lodge where we stayed in Ta-house," she said.

"Rosa is gone," Scratch confided. "And Mateo Kinkead has married another."

---

* *BorderLords*

"I hope she will make him as happy as Rosa made him when they were together in Ta-house—"

"Do you want to go?"

Waits's brow furrowed as she looked him squarely in the eye. "Go . . . where?"

"Taos."

Her eyes grew wide, and she immediately laid fingers over her lips in that Indian way of preventing her soul from escaping in unabashed wonder. She turned slightly, looking at Flea, at Magpie who held little Jackrabbit in her lap, as the three of them chewed on some dried chokecherries the children had collected last summer.

"It is so long a journey—we will take the children with us?"

He grinned, and said, "I've promised I wouldn't go anywhere without my family!"

"T-to Ta-house?" she repeated.

"What is this Ta-house?" Magpie asked before Titus could answer his wife.

Waits turned to her daughter, saying, "Far, far, far to the south—farther away than I had ever gone before, or have been ever since—is a land where a people live in mud lodges, eat food that is hot on your tongue, and talk much different than the Americans where your father comes from."

"This is the place our father wants to go?" Flea asked as he cupped some chokecherries in his hand for his three-year-old brother, Jackrabbit.

"It will be a grand adventure!" Waits cried, enthused. "It has been . . ."—and she counted on her fingers—"twelve summers since we left that place with our baby daughter!"

For Magpie, the enthusiasm was clearly contagious. "Do we start soon?"

Titus shook his head. "The snow is too deep and the cold would make such travel too dangerous—for a fourth winter in a row. To start out now might well kill us all. No, we won't leave until late this summer when the buffalo are migrating south once more."

"Ta-house." Flea tried out the word, then turned to his

father. "Popo, what will you find in this faraway place that makes you want to go back after so many summers?"

Scratch thought, then said, "Old times, and old glories, my son. But mostly . . . I want to find an old friend."

27

◆

The family traveled as light as they dared when they set off on their march south out of Absaroka. Down the Bighorn at the Wind River, they entered the land of the Shoshone. From the Wind they continued up a tributary until it elbowed its way directly toward the saddle of the Southern Pass, lying to the west. In less than a morning's march from there, they struck the Sweetwater, following that river east.

For the first time in all his years in the mountain West, Scratch spotted long grooves cut upon the land, a corduroy of iron-tired tracks—more of them than all the carts in a trader's caravan would carve while plodding their way to a rendezvous encampment.

"What is this?" Waits asked him as he stood afoot, gazing first to the eastern horizon, then turned to stare as those scars followed the landscape rising toward the Southern Pass. "These are not the marks made by travois?"

"The white man's boxes you have seen teams of horses pull into summer rendezvous many years ago."

She gently wagged her head. "There must be many of them going across the mountains."

Bass laid his arm around her shoulder and snugged her against his side. "I hope that's where they all keep right on going. Hope they don't ever stop. I don't really care how many of them want to cross the mountains . . . just as long as they push on through."

"These people, the ones who made these tracks," Waits-by-the-Water said with a small, unsure voice, "they aren't like you and the other fur hunters?"

"No, they are no way like us," he answered grimly.

Titus remembered all that he had run away from back there in Boone County, on that farm outside the tiny crossroads of Rabbit Hash. "The folks who leave marks like this on the land are the sort of folks who will cut through the ground with huge knives, to plant their crops and make them grow. Folks who come in their wagon trains aren't like me at all because when they stop somewhere . . . they mean to stay put."

"Then they are not like my people either."

He grinned at her. "They sure as hell ain't."

"Are you, Ti-tuzz?" she asked, surprising him. "Are you like my people?"

Scratch realized he must answer her truthfully. "No, I'm not like your people either. Not like white folks, and I'm not like Indians. Figured out I wasn't much good at being white—but, trouble is . . . I'll never be an Indian in my heart."

"You are a man in between," she put it succinctly.

For a long moment he stared deeply into her eyes. "Perhaps I am just that, Waits. A man in between. Not a white man, and not an Indian either. So it pains me even more deeply to think of what's coming."

"Tell me, Ti-tuzz. What do you see coming out there, on the far horizon?"

He gazed into her eyes with such sadness, such despair in realizing his time had come and was all but gone. The evidence of it lay in those scars beneath his feet. "The white people, there are too many of them. They keep growing like the blades of grass in the spring—spreading everywhere. And where they go, they push out who was there before. It will not be good when they reach Absaroka."

"Perhaps we will be old or long dead by then," she said with hope in her voice.

Scratch looked at his three youngsters a moment as they tossed rocks at a fleeing jackrabbit. "I pray the children will be very old, perhaps long dead too, by the time this land is swallowed up by whites."

"Perhaps wiser men could prove me wrong," Waits said as she stepped against him, resting her cheek against his chest, "but I don't think the future can be changed now."

A deep pain stabbed through him. "You're right. What's to come, will come . . . and one man like me can never stop it."

She explained, "Surely the buffalo will be wise enough to stay far, far away from these travelers. So let the white people go on to where the sun sets, and we'll stay away from this sunset road, like the buffalo."

Sunset road. Titus thought it was a heart-wrenching and accurate description of this trail stretching from the eastern edge of the frontier all the way to Oregon country. A fitting name for the trail if for no other reason than he realized the sun was already setting on this raw and wild land. A way of life was ending as the sun set on an era, eons of living and dying in utter freedom. The glory days were over for men like him. All that life had been out here in these mountains was preparing to take its one last breath. Standing here now, gazing at the corduroy of tracks extending off to both horizons like the mourning scars on a woman's arms and legs after she lost her man, Scratch knew he could hear the death rattle warning as it rumbled deep in the hollow breast of these mountains.

"Yes, maybe we can avoid them—but only for a time," he consented. "I'm afraid that where their kind goes, they bring the sunset with them. For now they may just pass on through, but they have still poisoned every inch of ground they touch."

She stepped around in front of him again, staring up at his face to say, "We'll go higher than these white people will ever dare to venture. We can take our children and the life we still have farther and farther back into the mountains—where these white settlers will be afraid to live."

He pulled her against him. "It doesn't matter how many miles I get away from them—because it's the simple fact that they are in our country. Look at these marks on the ground. It means their kind has already come to *my* mountains. Think of how you would feel if another tribe came and squatted down right beside a Crow camp. It won't work, ever. Those who are coming will ruin what I came out here for."

"I can't ever remember seeing you so sad, Ti-tuzz."

"Maybe . . . because . . . I'm sorely afraid that what I came to get for myself, I went and ruined just by opening the door for these others to waltz right on through," he tried to explain his disappointment, that bitter despair at what he believed he had done to bring about the downfall of his own kind. "I fear that what I came for is no more—and will never be again—because I pointed the way for the kind of folks who should never have come out here to destroy what once was."

Two days later, after they made their late-afternoon camp in the shade of some rocky cliffs, Scratch led his wife and their children on a short walk into that narrow maw the Sweetwater had carved out of solid stone, a place where the river's flow was so restricted that it boiled and foamed in angry fury every spring—a landmark the mountain man had given the most appropriate name: Devil's Gate.

"I do not understand this expression," Waits declared.

Bass did his best to translate, "When a person does nothing but wrong—the sort of wrong that constantly hurts other people—we call what that person does *evil*. And the creature who does the most evil in our world is called the devil."

"Is this devil here in this place?" Magpie asked.

"No," Titus answered, feeling as if he should never have attempted an explanation. "But the water rushes so fast it can cause a lot of trouble for men in bullboats."

Waits lifted young Jackrabbit onto her hip. "So this is the doorway you spoke of, where the white fur traders must pass to take their pelts to the land of the east?"

"Yes."

Flea stepped over, surprising his father with a perceptive question, "Why don't the white men beach their bullboats back there behind us where the stream is quiet, then carry their furs around the canyon so they won't spill into the water?"

"What you say makes a lot of sense," Titus declared. "But there are times when men will do something that does not make as much sense, when they attempt something for the challenge or the danger of doing it."

"Why?" Magpie asked.

"Perhaps it is something for young men to understand," he began. "Why young Crow warriors make bravery runs at their enemy, why they go out alone to challenge the wilderness in search of a vision."

From the way she looked at him, Titus got the feeling she was a little suspicious of his answer.

Then Magpie said, "Tell me, Popo—you never did anything that didn't make sense."

He ruminated on that a moment, gazing at the relatively low water in the river at this late season of the year. Then he explained, "I remember there were times in my own life that by doing something dangerous I felt that much more alive."

"Maybe this is the reason we are on this journey to Ta-house, Ti-tuzz?" Waits asked as she slipped her hand through the crook of his elbow when she stepped beside him.

"You know better than that," he protested. "I would never take you on a dangerous journey."

"No, not the danger," she replied. "But you have needed something to make you feel more alive, I think."

Squeezing her gently against him, he asked, "Why do I need that?"

"Because, husband—your spirit has been yearning to free itself from the fences of Absaroka."

"You do understand what a fence is?"

She nodded. "As you explained, the white man's fence keeps animals inside, where they can't wander away."

So he snorted, "But Absaroka has no fences!"

"Are you sure, husband?"

Her certainty gave him pause. "Perhaps . . . I gave you the impression I needed to travel again, as we did in the long-ago days."

"One long year of living with my people, one year of not leaving our village—that was easy for you," she said with a grin as she looked up at him. "The second year was harder for you, but nothing you could not do because you loved me, loved our children."

"And remember, I made a promise."

"That promise is why you forced yourself to stay through a third year, husband," she said. "But soon you were staring at a fourth winter of being a layabout in Crow country."

"A layabout, am I?"

"All the older men are," she explained. "It is what warriors do after they have spent many summers as young men riding off to steal horses or bring home enemy scalps."

"An old man like me can't be a warrior still?"

"Come along, let's go back to camp so I can cook supper for our family," she prodded, slowly turning him by the arm to start out of the canyon. "I understand that this journey to Ta-house is something your spirit needs now. Besides, it is something we can share with our children."

"Especially Magpie," he said as he looped an arm around his daughter's shoulder and pulled her against his other side. "To show her where she was born that spring she became our first child."

Something his spirit desperately needed, she had said.

Titus pondered that into the following day when they made camp in the lee of Turtle Rock.* Its massive surface already bore the scratchings of numerous fur trappers as they inscribed their names and a date of passing this important landmark on the route to the Southern Pass. But what astounded Titus was the great number of names carved into the rock's surface—names he did not recognize, accompanied by dates that saddened him all the more. A lot of time had passed, and with it more and more settlers punched their way right through the heart of what had once been an inviolable wilderness where only a few intrepid, daring souls dared walk.

As Magpie and Flea scrambled up the side of the immense rock, anxious to view the entire valley from its top, Titus traced some of the scratchings with his finger, a little baffled by just how much time had slipped by.

The last of the holdouts had gathered for their final, miserable rendezvous over on the Green in July of 1840. The following summer Fraeb's hunting party was jumped by half-a-thousand Sioux and Cheyenne over on the Little Snake. So that made it 1841. All right, his mind hadn't totally turned to horse apples.

And after wintering in Absaroka, the next spring he was trapping the fringes of the Wind River Range when he chanced upon Bill Williams and they began their epic trek for California and the land of Mexican horses. That would have been '42.

In so many ways, that whole journey felt like it was no more recent than ancient history: returning to Bents Fort, trading his horses for blankets and kettles, beads, powder, and puppies too.

He turned to glance at the two dogs, fully grown long ago, watching them race back and forth at the foot of the rock, howling and yipping at the children scrambling up the rock above them when the dogs weren't able to make the ascent. It struck him now—the dogs had grown. For

---

* Today's Independence Rock in central Wyoming.

some reason, time had seemed to stand still once he made it back to Absaroka with those Cheyenne horses laden with trade goods. Maybe it felt the same for the Crow people who could not remember a time before the white man came.

Beyond that winter he returned to Absaroka, Scratch could mark time's passage with his annual trips to visit other white men. Tullock and Van Buren were no more—the man had flown to unknown parts, and his post at the mouth of the Tongue had been burned to the ground. But the Crow had stumbled across a company trader named Murray who ran a new post called Fort Alexander. Would have been the fall of '43.

Titus settled in the shade, leaning against the smooth rock, tracking his mind over the dimming back trails the way a man might turn around in the saddle to assure himself nothing was sneaking up on him. The next time he visited the post, Murray was gone and a Scotsman named Meldrum was there—yet he was only a little booshway to a fella named Kipp who the company kept busy building one fort after another. Autumn, '44.

See there? He knew he could piece these things together, sure enough. And now—the next year when he returned with the village for some trading, Meldrum was minding the post himself while Kipp was away, gone downriver to Fort Union on some company business. That tallied his mental calendar up to '45.

1845. So it must have been in the autumn of that year when he decided on taking his family south once the summer hunt was out of the way and they had jerked a lot of meat.

Waits-by-the-Water had left her lodge in the care of her sister-in-law, who had remarried, becoming a second wife to her own sister's husband. With the older warrior, Bright Wings had someone to care for, someone to provide for her and the children. And Waits's mother, Crane, had someone to watch over her as she grew infirm too. It did not make much sense to drag their lodgepoles behind them all the way to the land of the Mexicans, so they had decided to travel light. If they encountered a thunderstorm, an odd occurrence late of a summer, they could find shelter, making do with their blankets and hides until the weather passed. He'd have them safely in Taos before the first snows.

Days later they crossed the Sweetwater, just upstream from where it poured into the North Platte. From there they followed the Platte south as it collected the water from untold streams and creeks on its tumble down from the high country.

"This is a land I have never seen," Waits commented several days later as they left the broken terrain below and began their ascent of timbered slopes. "Has it been so long that I don't remember our trip north from Taos after Magpie was born?"

He reassured her, "You're right—you've never been here before."

"You are taking us by a different route?"

"Yes," he answered. "We're going by a new path." He glanced at the two children, who rode on either side of their five packhorses. "I thought it safer for us to stay in the mountains as much as possible since we are going through unknown country."

"But you know the way?"

"I think I remember how to get us from here to South Park through the high country," he declared.

"And from there we aren't far from Ta-house," she added. "So why do you want to travel in the mountains when it is harder for our horses and takes more time?"

So the older children would not hear, he quietly explained, "These mountains are no longer the same country I once knew."

Her brow furrowed and she asked, "But—the mountains, they do not change."

"No," he whispered, "but the people in them do. Once I only had to worry about Arapaho who traveled through these high mountain valleys searching for plunder. But, years ago—you will remember the Sioux who attacked us when we were on our way to the Vermillion Creek post?"*

Waits nodded, and her eyes flicked back to their children. "I agree. We are safer in the mountains."

"Out there on the plains, where we traveled north from Taos more than ten summers ago, many tribes follow the migrations of the buffalo, north and south, moving along the base of the mountains. Not only Arapaho—but I fear the Sioux and Cheyenne have come to join them too. Where the buffalo graze at this time of the year, so too are the hunters who are working hard to kill enough meat to get their people through the winter."

With a sigh, Waits nodded. "It is good I married a man so cautious!"

Camped in the heart of North Park six days later, for the first time Bass told her of Fawn, the Ute widow who took him in his first winter in the mountains.†

"I never knew you were partial to the Ute women," she said, not raising her eyes from the child's moccasin she was repairing.

"She was fair to me, not asking me to stay when it came time to go," Bass explained. "For that I am thankful. If she hadn't let me go the next spring . . . I never would have made it to Absaroka, where my eyes first saw you."

"And when your eyes finally did see me?"

He snorted with laughter, "Then I was no good for any other woman! I had to have you and no other!"

High upon the southern slopes of that high mountain valley the mountain man called Park Kyack or Buffalo Park, he stopped them near the middle of the following day to give their horses a breather. From there he pointed out where the Ute village had stood.

"Flea, Magpie—I want you both to hold up all your fingers for me," he instructed.

They glanced at one another, then looked in wonder at

---

* Fort Davy Crockett; *Ride the Moon Down.*
† *Buffalo Palace*

their mother a moment before they turned back to their father and did as he had asked.

"There. I want the two of you and your mother to look at all those fingers on your four hands," he said. "Two-times-ten of your fingers. One finger for each year it has been since I first came to the mountains. Two-times-ten winters now since my first winter here, spent among the Ute."

Their eyes looked over the twenty brown fingers they held up, spread apart, then gazed down at that grassy park below them. An elk bugled at that moment. Its singular sound always made the hair stand on the back of his neck.

"Two-times-ten," Waits repeated the number. "That is a long time for a man to take risks with his life."

"I don't have to take chances anymore," he said. "Now that I have everything I ever wanted, I've learned I should never take risks again."

Crossing the divide they dropped into Middle Park, another, but smaller, mountain valley. All around them now the elk were bugling, the cows herding up for the rut and the bulls beginning to spar as the grasses dried a little faster now and the morning breeze carried a stiff chill with the sun's rising.

As they climbed across the high saddle that carried them from the south end of Middle Park, the sky lowered with a harsh, metallic urgency. They plodded through a swirling storm the rest of that day, camped, then awoke to the same storm. On through that day they pushed, then most of a third before he could finally start them down into the northern reaches of that southernmost of the mountain *parcs,* known to the mountain trapper by its ancient French name—Bayou Salade.

"Does this ground look familiar?" he asked his wife when they halted and dismounted just past midmorning the following day.

She looked high on either side of them, studying the ever-rising tumble of snow-covered slopes that climbed into the belly of the gray clouds. "I have been here before?"

"Not this spot,"* he replied. "But you've been in this valley."

She peered down the narrow vale running north to south. Then she looked at him again. "This is where you killed the men who attacked Looks Far Woman."† Waits-by-the-Water turned and gazed into the valley once more, and shuddered with the memory. "And this is where all four of us had to slay the others who came after us when you killed the first warriors."

"That was a long, long time ago," he said, watching her eyes glance at Magpie. "Yes, when those events took place, you already carried our daughter in your belly."

She turned in her prairie saddle to look at him, rubbing a mitten across the hot tears that had spilled down her cheeks. "I don't want to spend a lot of time in this place, Ti-tuzz. The memories are bad. Please—take us through as much of this valley as you can before it grows too dark to ride."

Till the end of that shrinking day, and on through the next, Scratch pushed the children and their animals alike—from that first gray stain of predawn until the last moments before the arrival of slap-dark, putting behind them every mile they could—sensing his wife's growing anxiety to be gone from this place of an undeniable horror.

Halting at midday only to water the animals and climb down from the saddle to stomp circulation back into their legs, Bass's family doggedly pressed on as the winds blew stronger and the snows fell deeper upon those slopes above them. The farther south they marched, the more an old nostalgia rose in him like the buttercream that floated to the surface of the steamy milk he had just coaxed from his father's cows back in Rabbit Hash. With each new day, he felt as if he knew how it was to be a mule with the scent of a home stall strong in its nostrils.

As the days continued to shorten, he found himself

---

* Today's Kenosha Pass in Colorado.
† *One-Eyed Dream*

growing all the more restless and increasingly impatient at their night fires, where he began to talk more and more of the Taos valley, more and more of the spicy food and heady liquor and that strong native tobacco—not to mention how he described the raucous, risky recollections of his adventures in that dangerous Mexican village. He tucked the blankets and robes over their three children, who slept together to hold the dropping temperatures at bay, then crawled in beside his wife. Waits snuggled tightly against him.

"I have grown a little afraid of something, husband," she whispered.

He combed her hair between his fingertips and soothed, "That was more than ten long winters ago. You don't need to fear the Arapaho now."

"It isn't them I am afraid of," she explained, wagging her head against his chest. "Ever since that day when we looked at all the tracks made in the grass by the white man's little houses, I started to wonder about something."

"If not the Arapaho, what makes you frightened?"

"I saw how you looked at those white-man tracks going off to the far horizon in both directions. Ever since, I've been scared that you no longer feel you belong in Absaroka."

He saw how much worry was etched on her face. "Why would you think that?"

"The spring when Magpie was born, and we were going to leave Ta-house—you told me it was time for us to return north to the mountains because they knew our names. To return home to the land of my people."

"Yes, the mountains are our home—"

"But, Ti-tuzz," she interrupted, "I fear going to Ta-house means your heart has changed."

"Changed?"

"I think you will want to make Ta-house our home now," she confessed. "Because you have grown tired of Absaroka in the last few winters."

He took a few minutes to consider his answer, then said, "If you think back to that time we spent in Taos ten years ago, I think you will remember one thing is clear: That land ain't for me. In the same way, I could no more go back to Saint Louis with all the crush of folks and their judging eyes. No, I wouldn't dare sink down roots in Saint Louis, or in Taos, neither. Too many folks for my liking. Besides, the life people in those places hold dear is a life that turns my heart hard and cold."

"You are sure? You don't want us to live in this Ta-house?"

He chuckled, looking down at her eyes. "No. It's a fine place to visit every ten years or so, but it isn't for the likes of me, woman."

"But—if your heart isn't at home in Ta-house, are you sure it's at home in Absaroka?"

"The only thing I am certain of anymore is that my home is with you and the children," he admitted, clutching her tightly against him. "Where you are, that is my home."

Her voice quivered when she asked, "Do you mean to say that your home is not in Absaroka?"

"No," he admitted. "I don't really know for sure where my home is anymore. This country is changing, and the old ways have been yanked out from under me. I fear I'm not a man who can easily change. All that I once believed in has been battered and wounded and shredded in recent years."

"What you call your code?"

"Yes. It's a different time. Now folks are lying. Friends stealing from friends. Men saying one thing to me when they damn well don't ever mean to stand by their word. And all them newcomers too—black-robed priests and hard-nosed missionaries, prissied-up white gals and their whiny ways . . . why, this is just no longer a country where a man can count on his friends if little else. What's wrong is . . . I'm afraid I've gone and outlasted my days."

"You are not old, Ti-tuzz," she pleaded with him. "You have many, many winters yet."

"It's not just how many winters I have left to live. The trouble is, I may be nowhere near ready to die, but my days are already in the past," he admitted, overcome by a flood of memories. Sadly, he confessed, "There's bigger, even more terrible changes coming for this land, and I'm sure I won't know where I belong when they come."

After marching out of the bottom of Bayou Salade, Scratch pointed out to his family the beginnings of the mountain range that stretched far into the haze on the southern horizon.

"Children," he haled them as they stopped to let the animals blow. "Among the white men long, long ago there once was a very holy man. This holy man was betrayed by his friends and nailed in a tree to die. Long ago when the Mexicans first looked upon these mountains at sunset, they noticed how the snows were painted with a red glow. Because of that color, they gave a name to the mountains—*Sangre de Cristos*," he spoke the three words in Spanish. "That's Mexican talk meaning the blood of the one who was betrayed by his friends, the blood of that holy man, shed while he was dying."

"They think the holy man's blood is still on those mountains?" Flea asked.

"Only because the peaks are colored red like blood at sunset," he explained.

Then Titus pointed down at the narrow northern reaches of the valley below them, showing the children where the valley eventually widened its funnel into a fertile, verdant floor carpeted with autumn-crisp grass crunchy beneath the icy remnants of a recent snow.

"And down there, you see that river on the far side of the valley?"

"Is that called the blood river?" Magpie inquired.

"No," her father said. "It is called the grand river of the north."

"Why do they call it that—when we have come so far south?" Flea contradicted.

"This is pretty far north to the Mexicans," Bass told them. "Once we are in this valley—we know we are in Mexico."

Flea shaded his eyes and studied the land below them. "I can't see the village of the Mexicans."

Titus snorted with a grin. "We still have a few days to go, son. We probably won't see a Mexican anywhere this far north."

"If they won't come here to protect their country the way Crow warriors protect Absaroka, then this land should not belong to a people too lazy or cowardly to protect it."

"That may be, son. The land where we stand might still well be the land of the mountaineer like me, and the Indian like you. The Mexicans talk big and puff out their chests—but they've never had the manhood to come north to confront this country on its own terms like the Americans always have."

"How many days now, Popo?" Magpie asked.

"Less than a handful. The worst of the ride is over." Then he sniffed the cold air deep into his lungs and turned to gaze at Waits-by-the-Water, his eyes growing big as Mexican conchos. "Glorree, woman! Why, I swear I can smell tortillas frying and beans boiling already!"

Two short winter days later Scratch caught sight of his first herd of wild horses racing along a low ridge not far ahead on their left. Not one of the creatures exhibited the least concern about the humans plodding through their territory. In fact, the wild horses loped along their line of march for several hours with an easy nonchalance, as if intending to discover where these strangers were headed and what they were all about. The farther south they pushed, the more of those mustangs they encountered crisscrossing their trail day after day.

"What tribe lets their horses run free?" young Flea eventually asked his father.

"They are wild horses," he explained. "About as wild as any creature you'll find out here, son. Almost as wild as you!"

"If I were a little older," Flea announced, "I would like to steal these horses and take them back to my people."

Bass grinned. "Just the way your father went to California to steal Mexican horses. Truth is, Flea—the land of the Mexicans, here or in California—is a horse thief's paradise."

"I would steal many, many horses to give away to my people," Flea boasted.

"You make me proud," Scratch responded. "To truly be a rich man—"

"A warrior must give away all that he does not need for himself," Flea completed his father's moral.

Bass pounded the boy on the top of the thigh with gratification. "One day soon you will be the richest man in the eyes of all your people!"

28

◆

As they rode south along the Rio Grande del Norte, Magpie and Flea remarked with growing frequency at their wonder at just how the changing face of this country differed from what lay to the north in their homeland.

Indeed, this region of the Southwest, where the Rocky Mountains gradually began to trickle out, was nothing less than a land of extremes. While the warming temperatures of each spring would give birth to richly flowered valleys, at the same time tall mountaintops rose well above the desert floor, still mantled with snow. Lush, green meadows blanketed the foothills all the way down to sun-baked desert wastes speckled with ocotillo and barrel cactus, mesquite and paloverde trees, as well as the meandering black of lava fields that served as a reminder of an even more ancient time.

For millennia without count, this had been the land of the lizard and horned toad, the rattlesnake, tarantula, and the scorpion, but this was also a country where a man found cottonwood and willow bordering the infrequent gypsum-tainted streams where that warm "gyp" water was likely to give the unacclimated stranger a paralyzing bout of bowel distress.

The plains of this vast, yawning Rio Grande River valley stretched upward toward the purple bulk of timbered foothills, from there up to the burnt-umber red of serrated mountainsides dotted with the ever-emerald-green of fragrant piñon and second-growth cedar. Every sunrise, Titus Bass would be the first out of the robes to gaze around their camp, finding the red, naked ridges glaring back at him like a swollen, inflamed wound. But by the time the sun was rising behind those heights and they were putting to the trail, the children would find that same red vista already brushed with a hazy blue. Then late of the afternoon, the skies finally turned a deep purple as the sun tumbled to its rest.

For much of the last few weeks, Titus Bass had threaded his family and their nine animals through this high land of brilliant color and startling contrast, following the Rio Grande almost due south. But early one afternoon, they stopped to rest and water the stock near the mouth of a narrow creek that spilled out of the hills to the east, mingling its frigid snowmelt with the Rio Grande.

After drinking his fill at the bank, Scratch got back to his feet and swiped a hand over his mouth and beard before pulling on the blanket mitten once more. "This stream is called the Little Fernandez."

"Another Mexican name I don't understand," Magpie commented.

Her father grinned and slapped her rump as he stepped around her to reach his horse. "The more Mexican names there are to hills and creeks, the closer we are to Taos, little girl!"

He remounted and took up the lead to the first packhorse. "This stream is where we turn east. The village isn't far now."

Hours later the sun had sunk to the last quadrant of its trip across the sky. For suspended moments the Sangre de Cristos took on that vivid crimson hue so familiar to travelers in the Southwest. Far over their heads, the remnants of an early winter storm was exhausting itself among the high peaks and granite escarpments. But down here along the Fernandez no more than a few gentle flakes swirled on those breezes crossing the valley floor.

"Will we sleep in Ta-house tonight?" Waits-by-the-Water asked.

He could tell she was weary already, the children too. It had been an exhausting journey for them all: the longest Waits had taken in more than ten winters—unquestionably the longest their children had ever endured. Far better for them to reach Taos and the doorstep of old friends when they were all fresh.

"We'll ride on a little farther. Find a place to make camp. We can wait to ride into the village till morning."

It had snowed overnight, but no more than a dusting of light flakes that would shake right off of their buffalo robes when he prodded the young ones from their communal bed where Jackrabbit lay sleeping between the two older children.

Titus had found it hard to sleep himself, despite how weary he had become from unloading the horses, or helping the children drag in wood for their fire and water from the creek for his wife. What had brung him satisfaction was that throughout all their preparations in making camp, little Jackrabbit was at his older brother's side. It made Scratch proud, even though he felt a sense of regret that neither of his younger brothers had ever bonded themselves to him in this way. Scratch turned and rolled through the night, hopeless at finding comfort for the aching hip, no matter how much of the blanket he shoved beneath it.

Eventually he had slipped quietly from her side and left the warm robes to stoke the fire before dragging the dented coffeepot to the edge of the coals where he could reheat the remains of last night's brew.

He had always liked this time of day the best. As good as eventide was with its varied textures and hues of light, these moments when night had grown exhausted and was prepared to give way to day . . . such were the most dramatic moments of the day. There Titus sat, sipping at his coffee this last morning on the trail, staring into the dancing flames when he was not studying the eastern sky, harkening back on fond memories of those squeaky boots and the way Josiah had cinched up that worn leather belt around those store-bought canvas britches threatening to fall off his skinny hips. How testy the lad had been in those first days as they gradually came to know one another, day by day, mile by mile on that early-summer crossing from the Wind River Mountains to Pierre's Hole.

Lo, the times he had grown disgusted with Paddock, ready to ride off on his own, leaving the boy behind—or just as soon let Josiah stomp off by himself with no more than a call of good riddance . . . Titus was grateful for every moment they had shared. As much as Paddock might have needed a hivernant to take him under his wing and teach him the way of the mountains, Titus Bass had needed a companion—needed a friend—all the more. They had been there for one another, at the very moment when one had to give what the other needed most.

Titus stared up at the sky a long time, dazzled at the countless stars in this early-winter sky—and realized once again he could not deny the presence of something far greater than himself at work in the lives of man.

He had crossed paths with Josiah Paddock at a crucial juncture in both their lives. That following winter Titus had returned to the Crow with Josiah, at just the moment when a young woman was ready to take herself a husband. Not to mention how the Grandfather Above had blessed him and Waits with these three beautiful children who amazed and stunned their father without fail every day.

With all the people, the trials and the joys that he had encountered in his own inconsequential life . . . Bass knew he could never deny the hand of the Creator in all that had transpired. While most young men more often than not saw their lives in terms of their own accomplishments—the older Titus got, the more easily he could admit that the crucial turnings in his life had been guided by another's hand.

It was clear as sun that, for some reason he did not fully understand, he had been granted redemption more times than a man might have the right to expect.

"Morning is coming soon." Her soft voice surprised him at his back. "We can finally reach Ta-house, to see our old friends again."

He peered at her over his shoulder and smiled. "Yes. Finally, after a long, long time."

"You did not sleep well: restless to have the journey done?"

This woman never ceased to amaze him—how perceptive she could be at times. "Once the journey itself was enough to hold my heart. But—I am growing old. As my allotted days grow fewer and fewer, I have come to think my travels need to have some purpose. When a man realizes he has less and less days ahead of him, every single one of those days becomes all the richer in meaning."

Scooting over behind him where she could wrap her arms around Titus and lay her cheek against that notch between his shoulder blades, Waits-by-the-Water said, "You and I will grow old together, watching our children become men and women. We will see our grandchildren born, hold them in our arms and prop them on our knees to tell them marvelous stories of a bygone time."

He felt tears sting his eyes as he cradled her arms across his chest. "I pray it will be so, woman. I only pray it will be so."

When a graying light finally swelled along the horizon, Scratch left her at the fire and went to the nearby rope corral. Two-by-two he led the horses to the creekbank where they drank their fill, then he picketed them on a patch of short-grass until he was ready to pack them one at a time for the last miles of their long journey to Taos.

Jackrabbit was already awake, cuddling with his mother, when Titus returned to the fire. Scratch put his finger to his lip, then knelt by the other two children and gently rubbed their heads, speaking low. Eventually all three sat in their blankets, chewing on cold meat left over from last night's supper as Bass set off to bring in the first of the packhorses. Each one stood patiently as he strapped on its saddle, loading it with their camp equipment, then returned the animal to the grass so it could continue grazing until all were prepared for the trail, when he could string them together with long leads of hemp rope.

This matter of the lead rope was something different that morning. For most of their journey south, he had let them follow on their own, giving each trail-savvy animal its own head. But now that they would be nearing a concentration of strange men and even stranger beasts—squawking chickens and bleating goats, not to mention noisy brass bells and tin horns the Mexican herders used—the long lead rope was a precaution against the trail veterans becoming startled and bolting.

The sun had risen, making its trek low across the southern horizon, where it hung at midsky when he stopped them late that morning. "Children—look."

He watched their faces for a long moment, studying their eyes now that they were seeing this valley for the first time. Off in the distance at the far side of the valley lay Los Ranchos de Taos, a small village. But what truly caught the eye was the large maze of low buildings nestled beneath a shroud of grayish fire smoke, a far, far larger community. With that new dusting of snow and those whitewashed adobe walls—most every object reflecting the brilliant winter light—it was difficult for his tired old eye to discern that cluster of huts, hovels, shops, and—then suddenly he made out the cathedral's tall bell towers. Even more impressive after this absence of more than ten years.

"That big village, it's Taos," he announced, a dry lump suddenly clogging his throat. "W-we come to Taos."

Titus watched their eyes grow as they raked over the scene before them. Against all the white of that new snow, he spotted an orderly line of horsemen just then appear from the cluster of huts and houses, no more than a couple dozen of them emerging on their left, riding two-by-two down that road that would lead a man to Santa Fe. A small flag popped and quivered in the winter breeze above one of the front riders. *Soldados*, he thought, his hackles going up. After all these years, Bass thought he was done with Mexican soldiers.

Little chance any of them would recognize him after all this time, he thought warily. Nor would any of these *soldados* remember his face from far younger days when he had done his fair share to raise hell and shove a chunk right under it. But just to be sure he pulled up the furry collar on his coat and tugged the coyote-fur cap down to his eyebrows.

He squinted at the short column now in the bright, reflected glare of the sun as the horsemen loped closer and closer. Scratch held up his arm and instructed his loved ones to halt with him a safe distance back as the soldiers approached.

The packhorses were clattering to a halt beneath a thick wreath of their gauzy breath smoke when Titus suddenly stared at that snapping flag—completely dumbfounded. Why, if he didn't know better . . . damn, if there weren't red and white stripes. And that broad field of blue dusted with four rows comprised of twenty-seven gilt stars. He had seen such flags, the last one many years ago above the wide double gate of Bents Fort. These soldiers, were they countrymen?

"Americans!" he cried out loud as the leaders came within hailing distance.

Now he could see these wool-wrapped horsemen weren't Mexican at all—they had American faces and dark blue American uniforms, leather belts strapped across their shoulders, gaudy red sashes tied around their winter coats. Emblazoned on the arms of those blue wool coats were gaudy stripes of gold.

"American soldiers," he repeated, but this time in all but a whisper as the first of them streamed past.

The eyes of every dragoon turned momentarily to regard Scratch's strange procession, even though the soldiers' heads never moved. All of them stiffly facing front as they headed south for Santa Fe—

From the village came the surprising peal of a solitary bell, its first loud clang drifting across the snow and sage, piñon and cedar. After it rang twice, a second bell joined in with a faint chorus. Back and forth the two iron bells clanged in concert for a half dozen heartbeats, then faded into the sunny midday light as silence replaced their joyous, jarring song.

"W-what was that, Popo?" Magpie asked, her voice a bit tremulous in fear.

Bass saw the surprise and apprehension in Flea's eyes too. He grinned to show them there was no reason to fear. "Among the Mexicans—sometimes the Americans too—they have a place where they listen to their holy men. It's called . . ." and he searched for a Crow word to call those buildings. There was none. He had to speak that one word in English. "In my language it's called a *church*."

"That sound is a ch-herch?" Magpie did her best to mimic the word.

"No, the sound is a pair of big bells," he explained. "You have small bells of your own. I have bought them for you children ever since you were babies."

"Bells?" Jackrabbit repeated.

"Yes," Titus said, turning to him. "But these are big bells, son." He held out his arms wide. "Big, *big* bells."

"They make that much noise?" Flea inquired.

"Giant bells, up there in those two tall . . ." and he was stumped for a second time, searching for how to describe a steeple or tower. Instead, he explained, "The white man builds a tall house for his holy men. And at the top of each tall house is a bell. This Taos *church* has two bells, one in each of its two tall houses. One bell for each. The Mexicans in this village ring those bells at dawn. Again at midday. And a last time at dusk."

"Must be midday," Waits suggested.

"The beautiful lady is right," he responded with a wide grin, a shiver of anticipation shooting up his spine. "Come on. Let's go find Josiah Paddock."

As they set off, he led them onto the road the dragoons had taken in the opposite direction.

Waits-by-the-Water came up to his side, riding knee by knee. She said, "I wonder how many children Josiah has given his wife."

Looking at her with an evil grin, Titus asked, "I haven't given you enough with these three already?"

Waits returned his gaze from beneath those thick lashes. "Perhaps there are more babies for us to have, you handsome American."

He winked at her as they reached the western fringes of San Fernando de Taos. Into the mouth of a narrow street their horses clattered over the frozen, rutted ground compressed between two rows of low-roofed mud buildings, their fading, whitewashed walls like prairie skulls pocked with narrow wood-doored nose rectangles and empty eye sockets of tiny, lightless windows. Snarling at every inquisitive dog, Ghost and Digger drove off the Mexican curs with their tails between hind legs. These new arrivals reined this way and that around every crude, wooden-wheeled *carreta* shoved empty and forlorn up against its owner's house, or rumbling noisily behind a burro pulling it from the center square.

Titus drank deep of the air—light and dry—as only winters in the Rocky Mountains could be, filled with the sharp tang of another snow soon to follow on the heels of last night's. On that air his nose recognized the fragrance of burning piñon and the heady perfume of cedar—each clear and distinct in the cold that brought a rose to their burnished cheeks.

As his heart rose to his throat in anticipation, he suddenly found himself worried—brooding that something could surely go wrong. Josiah might have pulled up stakes and lit out. Why didn't he think of that before? After all, it had been four years since Mathew Kinkead described just how successful Paddock had become. . . .

Don't fret, he scolded himself as they approached the *placita*.

The end of the street they were on disgorged them onto the crowded town square where their animals clattered to a halt in the midst of adults and children, burros and dogs, *carretas* and a blanket of wispy smoke from many open fires . . . and lots of discordant noise. Such deafening noise. Braying mules, women yelling at their children, boys and girls crying or laughing or screaming at the top of their lungs. The only thing anywhere like it was the racket of a Crow village setting out on the tramp. Right behind Titus, his three children stared incredulously at this strange and raucous scene.

An empty cart stood nearby, resting at the corner of an adjacent street, its stubby double-tree plowing up a pair of short furrows in the frozen, snow-crusted earth. He tapped Waits on the forearm and pointed at the *carreta*.

"We'll tie up the horses over there," Bass explained. "Then go looking for some word of Josiah."

Minutes later she was walking behind him, clutching Jackrabbit's tiny hand, while Magpie and Flea both held on to their father's hands as they melded into the bustling cacophony of the market square, where Indians from the nearby pueblo rubbed shoulders with straw-hatted peons, farm laborers, and house servants too. In this rigid society built upon a strict adherence to separation of the classes, the wealthy landowners and their bold, leather-clad vaqueros strutted and preened like nobility, parting those of lower stations as they moved from vendor to vendor.

In those first moments as he struggled to take it all in at once, Scratch saw how the dark eyes of the Mexicans or blanketed Pueblo Indians were trained their way . . . how quickly those hostile stares turned away as the strangers ebbing and flowing around his family went back to what had occupied them before they had noticed the newcomers in their midst.

Stopping at the center of the square, Titus turned round and round again, gazing upon it all, a riptide of memories battering him suddenly: a journey here with Hatcher's outfit and their pursuit of Comanche raiders, recollections of that tiny booth Bill Williams set up to sell off his extra trade goods, memorable visits here with Asa McAfferty . . . and that fateful visit to Taos thirteen winters gone now.

His gaze was drawn to his daughter, perhaps seeing

her with new eyes in this moment—recognizing how tall she had grown, how much older she appeared now that he realized she stood on the verge of womanhood.

Suddenly Bass reached out and grabbed the arm of an older man with a kind, furrowed face—clearly a poor *pelado*.

"*Señor*, do you know Josiah Paddock?" he asked in the Spanish he had not used in more than four summers.

With frightened eyes the man glanced down at his elbow. Titus let him go. "Paddock?" he repeated the name with his Mexican flare.

"*Si*," Scratch replied, sweeping his arm in a half circle around the market square. "*Dónde esta* Josiah Paddock?"

This time the old man's face softened, and he took hold of Bass's elbow, turning him a quarter circle, leading the American trapper two steps toward that side of the square.

"There—that is the store of Josiah Paddock, *señor*."

"A st-store?"

"*Si*," the man replied, then gave the Indian woman and their children a quick, cursory glance. "Josiah Paddock. *Americano*—like you."

A handful of dark-skinned Indians from the pueblo moved past, slowing to give Bass and his family a brusque appraisal, then hurried into the narrow mouth of a street that took them out of the square and into a maze of lanes and courtyards.

When Titus turned to speak to the old man, he found the *pelado* already stepping into the crowd. "*Gracias, gracias!*"

"What did he tell you?" Magpie inquired.

Grinning at his wife, Titus said, "He has a store! Josiah has a store now."

"Which one?"

"There—that one!" And he started them toward the western side of the square.

"It is his alone?"

"Just look! It's plain he's done very, very well," Scratch said, proud enough to bust his buttons.

Arrayed above the brick-red clay tiles of that porch running the entire width of the building was a wooden sign, its paint beginning to show years of sun and weathering. The four of them stopped out in the sun with Titus as he translated its words to them.

"Paddock's Emporium," he said in English before explaining in Crow. Scratch pointed to those two large words at the very top of the sign. Then below it, he read, "Trade goods, notions, general merchandise of all description."

Right below those bold English words, he spotted smaller letters that had to comprise Mexican words. "Perhaps Josiah gets more of his business from American traders than from these Taos Mexicans."

"Will he be here?" Waits asked, tugging on his elbow as she stepped onto the low porch spread beneath the wide tile awning.

"Let's see for ourselves," he replied, following her between a knot of shoppers and those stacks of barrels and crates cluttering the crowded porch.

They stepped through the open doorway, when he was immediately struck by the heady perfume of cedar burning in the two small mud fireplaces, each in its corner at the back of the store. His eyes raked over each person, then suddenly he recognized her across the counters and displays. Oh, how the years had changed the young Flathead woman who fell in love with Josiah back in Pierre's Hole so many summers ago now.

As he stood there with his family crowding to a stop around him, Looks Far Woman happened to glance up and he caught her eye. She stared blankly a moment—then her eyes widened like a wild horse's on the run.

He instantly put a finger to his lips, signaling her not to call out. With a hand clamped over her mouth to keep from screaming in excitement and surprise, Looks Far Woman nodded eagerly. Then Titus put both his arms up in a gesture, as if to ask, "Where is he?"

She grinned as she pointed to the far corner where three vaqueros huddled around a taller man, whose long hair spilled to his shoulders. Paddock's back was to him.

"Wait right here, children," he whispered to them before he took three steps to the center of the store, where he stood in the open.

"I heard tell of a goddamned lazy, no-account, pork-eatin' son of a bitch from Saint Louie claims he's proprietor of this here mercantile!" Bass roared.

As his voice boomed, it instantly silenced every voice in the shop, every patron riveted in place—all wheeling suddenly to stare at him in a mixture of confusion and outright fear. All . . . save for that tall, broad-shouldered American.

Scratch waited for his old friend to turn around so he could have a good long look at the man, to measure the passage of time on Josiah's face. It had been more than twelve years now, after all . . . but Paddock stood frozen in place, his back still to Titus.

Near Josiah's elbow a tall, thin youngster appeared around the end of a wooden shelf holding bolts of cloth. His eyes narrowed menacingly on the gray-headed fur trapper dressed in buckskins. "You know what's good for you, mister," the young man warned, "you'll back right on out of here before my pa walks over there to toss you out on your ear!"

"Joshua?" Titus asked in little more than a whisper, inspecting the boy up and down in utter disbelief. "Is that really you? Damn, but I used to hold you when you was a squawlin' li'l bear cub—"

The boy grabbed his father's arm, saying, "Who is this, Pa?"

Baffled that Josiah hadn't turned around immediately, Scratch stared again at the back of Paddock's head while more of the Mexican customers backed away from the shopkeeper. Titus was just opening his mouth to speak—

The very instant Paddock growled, "Seems I can place that voice now . . . though it's been years. Sounds to me like it belongs to a boneheaded, dog-ugly, side-talking, beaver-loving idjit who never had the good sense to come in out of a winter blizzard."

Slowly Paddock turned around, his eyes already misting. "Appears I'm that son of a bitch you're looking for."

His voice was clearly growing raspy with emotion as he found it hard to speak. "I'm proprietor of this mercantile for no other reason than what that dog-ugly, big-hearted bonehead done for me so many, many years ago!"

They collided in the middle of the store, crashing bone to bone with a resounding crack as the taller, more muscular Paddock threw his arms around the shorter, thinner man, rearing backward as he swept Titus into his arms—hopping and dancing around and around.

Looks Far Woman was already moving, flushing down the backside of the long counter, her arms waving convulsively in the air, braids flying and tears streaming down her cheeks as she squealed in delight. Waits-by-the-Water herself streamed down the front of the counter that separated them, blubbering nonsense at this long-overdue reunion.

Near the center of the store Magpie stood dumbfounded, gripping one brother's hand in her right, the youngest's hand in her left, as all three stared in rapt amazement at the noisy, confusing scene unfolding before them. In the next few moments a group of youngsters came to join the tall adolescent who stood almost as tall as his father. Both groups of children alternately glared at one another, then looked at their backslapping fathers, and over to their weeping, blubbering mothers, before they glared warily at one another again.

"I feared you was dead!" Josiah exclaimed breathlessly while he came to a halt with Bass at the end of his arms.

"Me? How many times was it I had to tell you I ain't near good enough to go to heaven—an' the devil don't want me around neither!" Scratch cried, laying his gnarled hand along Paddock's bare cheek. "Damn, if you ain't a sight after all these years, Josiah."

"Twelve! Can you believe it's been twelve years, old man?"

Turning slightly, Titus waved an arm across the store. "Just lookit what you done for yourself."

"What we've done," Josiah argued as he waved Looks Far over.

"You're still as pretty as the day I first laid eyes on you in Pierre's Hole!" Scratch declared as he pulled the Flathead woman into his arms and promptly squeezed the breath out of her. "You've done a fine thing, Looks Far—sticking by this wuthless polecat's side through the last dozen winters!"

"It came hard at first," she said in mock seriousness, but good English, then winked at Titus. "All the early years, settling in a new life, around new people and a new tongue too . . . but,"—and she took a step backward to loop an arm inside Josiah's elbow—"my husband always kept me big with child, so I couldn't leave!"

"Child?" Waits echoed in English, recognizing that word from her husband's language.

"We have five now," Looks Far disclosed. Her face went sad momentarily when she said, "We lost one before I grow too big in my belly . . . and another was stillborn. But all told, we had four healthy children come to join Joshua."

"Joshua." Titus repeated the boy's name, turning to look eye to eye with the tall youngster. "It can't really be you."

"Come over here, son," Paddock prodded his first-born. "I want you to shake hands with this old friend of ours."

Joshua stepped away from the cluster of his brothers and sisters, stretching out his long arm with that big hand as he asked, "It really true what you said, mister: You knew me when I was a baby?"

"I was the one what taught you to quit squawling one night when you was scared of the stars."

"S-scared of the stars," Joshua scoffed as he shot a warning glance at his siblings.

"I remember that now, son," Paddock said, looping his long arm across the youngster's shoulders. "The night of falling stars, and you wouldn't stop bawling for your mother or me, so this man poured water on your head till you shut right up."

"He poured water on your head?" one of the young boys repeated with a smirk.

Titus glanced at the boy and said, "It's a ol' Injun trick. They can't have babies crying and squawking to alert any enemies, so they teach all their young'uns not to cry out. Ever' time they make a noise, them babies get water poured on their heads so the young'uns learn to hush real quick."

Turning to his father, that young boy gushed, "He really did pour water on Joshua's head, Pa?"

"Come on over here, Ezekiel," Paddock said to the youngster smirking at Joshua.

"So you're named Ezekiel?" Scratch asked, dropping to one knee. "How old are you, son?"

He glanced up at his father. Josiah nodded. Ezekiel looked squarely at the stranger and held out his hand. "I'm nine years old, sir."

"Sir? Sir? Why, will you listen to that?" Bass cried. "This boy's got better manners than his ol' man ever did! Ezekiel, remind me to tell you some evening the story how your father come to run across me in the mountains. He wasn't at all the sort to practice a lick of good manners back in them days. Well, now—I'm mighty pleased to meet you, Ezekiel. Do folks call you Ezekiel?"

The boy cleared his throat and declared, "Only my parents, sir. My mother and father. All my friends call me Zeke."

"Zeke, is it?" Titus rose to his feet and looked at Josiah. "You gone and named your boy after my dog?"

"A dog?" Ezekiel squeaked in disbelief.

"They named Ezekiel after a dog!" squealed Zeke's older sister as she started giggling.

"No, son," Josiah assured with a chuckle. "I always been partial to that name. It's a good name, a strong name too. That's why we gave it to you."

Then Scratch explained, "I had a dog named Zeke back when your father an' me was runnin' the mountains, I want you to know."

"Ol' Zeke," Paddock said wistfully. "I remember that gray mutt now. Rescued him from a waterfront dogfight in Saint Louis, didn't you? Then we brung him west, all the way to the mountains with us that spring."

"Damn, if we didn't," Titus said softly, the memory stabbing him of a sudden after all these years.

"Where is ol' Zeke? He lope down to Taos with you, Scratch?"

Swiping a gnarled finger beneath his nose, Bass cleared his throat and said, "Zeke's . . . he's gone, Josiah. Been some years now. B-blackfoot kill't him sometime back."

Waits-by-the-Water stepped up to her husband's side to explain, "The dog, follow Blackfoot. Blackfoot come took me, me and Magpie too. Dog go follow Blackfoot."

Josiah shook his head, not able to understand, so Bass explained, "Those black-hearted sonsabitches come an' stole my wife and my li'l daughter one winter. I didn't know it, but Zeke took off ahead of me, followin' that war party, hanging on their back trail till they shot 'im with a arrow. Damn poor way for that critter to die . . . suffering like he done."

"You caught 'em, didn't you?" Josiah asked. "I know you made 'em pay for what they done to your family. To Zeke."

"Damn right, I made 'em all pay, Josiah. You know I ain't the kind to leave no nigger standin' when I got my dander up."

Paddock laid a hand on Bass's shoulder. "He was a damn good dog to the end, Scratch. Just the way we knowed he'd be afore we put Saint Louis behind us. I always figured he'd lay his life down for you or yours one day."

Titus swiped a tear that had spilled from one eye and said, "He was a damn fine dog. Better a dog'n I ever deserved, I'll tell you."

Paddock turned to Ezekiel and explained, "So if you want to think you were named after a brave and big-hearted, ol' gray dog named Zeke—then so be it, son. Because that was one special damned dog."

Wiping another tear away in remembrance of the old cur, Scratch agreed, "That's right. Zeke's a fine, fine name for a young man like yourself."

Ezekiel grinned, looking up at his father. "Don't you

see? You just give me 'nother reason why you and mother gotta call me Zeke instead of Ezekiel."

"All right, Zeke it is," and Josiah tousled his young son's hair.

Of a sudden Titus remembered a dark face from the shadowy past. His eyes widening as he wheeled on Josiah, he asked, "Where's that Neegra we brung here to Taos with us? The one we saved from the Pawnee—"

"Isaiah Bass?" Josiah spoke the name. "You recollect how he took your name the day you rode north outta Taos?"

"Isaiah Bass," he repeated that name softly. "Claimed he was gonna work with you setting up your shop here."

"Isaiah did just that," Josiah explained. "Stayed on for a couple years, anyway—afore he come to me one day, asking to take his leave."

"His leave? Goin' where? For to do what?"

"Lighting out for Fort Hall with some traders hauling goods up north. For the first time since we brought him to Taos in thirty-four, Isaiah told me how bad he wanted to find a place where folks weren't so mean to him, like the Mexicans had been."

"These greasers made it hard on Isaiah, him bein' a Neegra?"

Paddock nodded. "So I outfitted him and sent the man off with them traders," Josiah declared. "Last I've seen of him."

"Damn shame these greasers run him off with their ways. Isaiah was a good man." Scratch cleared his throat, blinked, and said, "So . . . tell us who these other young'uns are, Josiah—them standing back there with such good manners."

Paddock went on to introduce his oldest daughter, Naomi, who he explained was some eleven and a half years old; then his youngest daughter, Charity, who was seven and a half years old; and finally, while Looks Far stepped away to take care of a customer, Josiah introduced their youngest.

"Come up here, boy," he asked. Positioning the short youngster right in front of his legs, Josiah announced,

"This here's Titus Mordecai Paddock. He'll soon be four years—"

"T-titus Mordecai Paddock?" Scratch echoed.

"Yes," Josiah answered quietly. "I give him Mordecai for a middle name because he was the fella—"

"I know," Scratch interrupted. "The fella what you came to the mountains with. The one died on you that first winter."

"Mordecai was the one helped me get to the mountains," Paddock explained, gently patting the small child on the tops of his shoulders.

Scratch beamed. "An' Titus? How come you give 'im my name?"

The boy twisted slightly, gazing up intently at his father who towered above him. "You named me after this old man, Pa?"

"Yes. You were named after the most important man in my life, son. I expect you always to remember that. This here's the man who saw to it I lived through lots of things that would've killed lesser men."

Josiah sank to one knee and gathered his four-year-old in both arms. "Truth is, Titus—if it hadn't been for this old man here . . . I'd never been alive to raise you."

29

◆

They completed introductions all around, both sets of
children standoffishly sizing up their counterparts as all
youngsters are prone to do. Then Looks Far called her
eldest over to her, unknotting the string of a canvas
apron around Joshua's waist.

"You take our old friends to the house. Move your
tick and Ezekiel's too—get them out of your room and
into Naomi's to give our guests a place to sleep."

"Yes, mother."

"We're all going to sleep together in our room?" Charity whined in that way of a child feeling put out.

"If I did my ciphering correct, there's only going to be
five children in that one room, Charity," Josiah scolded.
"But there's going to be a whole family in Joshua's room
for a while."

Scratch blurted, "We don't mean to put you out—"

"Damn! You ain't putting us out!" Paddock exclaimed. "How I've yearned to lay eyes on you, so many
times in the last twelve years . . . but feared you was
dead."

Bass snorted with a little laughter. "It weren't for no

lack of trying by some red niggers, and a few white bastards too!"

"He curse that way all the time, Father?" Naomi asked.

"I'm sorry, Josiah," Titus apologized sheepishly. "Forgot myself around the children. Most times with my own pups I'm speaking Crow so they don't understand no American cussin'."

"You young'uns wanna know how to cuss at someone you don't like?" Josiah asked his children. "You pay real close attention to this here old man, youngsters. He's the cham-peen who's gonna teach you to do it right!"

"Go on now, Joshua," Looks Far nudged with a big grin. "Take these friends to our place and get them settled. They must be tired from their long journey."

Scratch admired how well she spoke English after all these years of practice. "Looks Far—I'll wager you're pretty good at talkin' Mexican too."

She smiled even bigger in that round face of hers and answered, "I get lots of practice with both. We hardly ever use any Flathead at all down here." She winked at Titus.

"You talk good 'Merican," Waits-by-the-Water agreed in her own halting English she rarely used.

Joshua quickly kissed his mother on the cheek, then asked, "How long will you be?"

"We always close up at sundown," Josiah explained to his son. Then turned to Titus, saying, "Looks Far is usually the first to head for home. She gets a fire and supper started before I lock things up here."

"We'll be pleased to light a fire and heat up some victuals for your family," Titus volunteered as they started toward the door. He halted at the doorjamb and marveled at Joshua. "This big lad of a boy can show us where everything is. Damn, if he ain't gonna be a big chunk of it, just like you was, Josiah."

"Glory, glory, glory," Josiah whispered as he stopped in the open doorway and pulled Scratch into another fierce embrace, refusing to let go right off. "Never, never, never did I think I'd ever see you again, old friend."

"Don't you remember what I said that spring morning when we gave our fare-thee-wells?" Bass prodded.

Paddock nodded. "I can recall it like it was just last week—I think about it so often. You was sitting on your horse, everything loaded up to go, with the sun just breaking over the Sangres . . . an' you told me, 'This ain't the last you've heard of Titus Bass!'"

"Ain't I allays kept my word to you, Josiah?" Titus backed away a step so he could gaze into Paddock's glistening eyes. "I wasn't 'bout to go for my final ride across that big belt in the blue 'thout seeing Josiah Paddock again."

"How long can you stay in Taos?" Looks Far asked as she joined them at the door.

"It's winter out there," Bass declared, nodding toward the square. "I recollect we were fixin' to spend us a winter here in Taos long time ago. This time I reckoned on finding ourselves a place to hole up till spring comes round again."

"A place to hole up?" Paddock repeated, his voice rising. "You're damn well gonna hole up with *us* till spring!"

"Only if'n you lemme work off what I'll owe you for putting us up," Titus offered.

"No man as old and skinny as you—not to mention ornery too—could ever work enough to pay for his keep!" Josiah roared and slapped Titus on the back. "Now take your family on to our house and relax till we get home to start swapping stories of the ol' days!"

"C'mon, Waits," Titus said, stepping onto the low wooden porch that fronted the village square. Directly across from the Paddocks' shop stood the Catholic cathedral with its pair of bell towers. "I gotta have some time to cogitate on this so I can come up with a few stories 'bout Josiah to tell his young'uns."

"Nothing you can say to these children of mine are they gonna believe from you anyway!" Paddock snorted with laughter.

"By the by," Bass said of a sudden, halting at the foot of the porch and heeling around to look at Josiah. "Just remembered I wanted to ask you 'bout something we saw a while back when we was coming into town: there was this bunch of soldiers heading down the Santa Fe cutoff. At first, I see'd 'em from a distance and thought they was *soldados*. . . ."

"But they weren't Mexicans, were they, Scratch?" Josiah asked knowingly, the merry light of humor gone from his eyes.

Titus wagged his head. "Strange to see them horsemen riding along under a flag the likes of what they'd fly back in the United States."

"You're right. What you saw was an American flag."

That confirmation surprised him, almost as much as seeing those American dragoons. "So how come them soldier fellers is out here?" Bass inquired. "That government back in the States hammered out some agreement with these here Mexicans now so they can have American soldiers ride up and down the Santy Fee Trail atween the settlements and here? I reckon it's a good idee for them soldiers to protect all the traders hauling goods down here to Mexican territory, what with running mules and gold back up to Missouri. Soldiers to guard all that money on the trail, I'll bet."

The big-toothed, ready smile had drained from Paddock's face. "I s'pose you didn't know a thing 'bout any of it when you headed down here."

"Nothing 'bout what?"

"I just figgered you'd come down east of the mountains," Josiah declared. "Maybe hear word of it when you come through the Pueblo or Hardscrabble. Maybeso even stop at Bents Fort—"

"We didn't come down east of the mountains," Bass explained, mystified and uneasy at this sudden turn in Paddock's mood. "Figgered it was safer going through the parks."

"So there was no way you could know 'bout the American soldiers."

"Know *what* 'bout 'em, Josiah?"

Paddock cleared his throat. "Taos ain't Mexico no more, Scratch."

"Ain't . . . M-mexico no more?" He glanced around the square, shocked and baffled. It looked the same. Mostly Mexicans, a generous sprinkling of Indians in from the nearby pueblo. But only a small scattering of pale-skinned folks who were clearly American—foreigners standing out every bit as much as a kernel of corn would if it was laid atop a bowl filled with black peppercorns. "Can't believe it—"

"Army from the States marched through here last summer," Josiah declared. "Drove off the Mexican Army without a fight, throwed out the Mexican government. We've got us an American governor now—Charles Bent."

"The hell you say!" Bass said, struggling to absorb it all. "Not that weasel Armijo now? Your governor's one of them Bent brothers?"

"Right. He's in charge of things now . . . him and a few troops General Kearny left down at Santa Fe when he went marching off to seize California from the Mexicans. Charlie Bent's family stays up here in Taos—so he comes up from the territorial capital in Santa Fe to see 'em couple times a month."

Scratch peered across the square, then turned back to gaze at Josiah. "I'll be go to hell right here and et for the devil's tater if that ain't some news guaranteed to take the shine off a new brass kettle. You . . . you ain't pulling on my leg, are you, Josiah?"

Paddock shook his head, his face all seriousness. "It's the honest-to-God truth, Titus. Taos is U.S. territory now."

Taos, Santa Fe . . . all the rest of it too. Country he'd slipped into and out of, ever watchful for Mexican patrols who enforced the laws, seizing a man's beaver pelts to collect their heavy taxes. Country where he had always been an interloper, nothing more than a pale-faced visitor in a foreign land. And now this all belonged to the United States of America? There really was something tangible to celebrate this holiday season!

While the Mexicans' preparations for the approaching

Nativity was nothing new to Waits-by-the-Water, all of the decorations and traditional practices were strange and curious to Magpie, Flea, and Jackrabbit too. In those last few days before the Catholic population celebrated the birth of their Savior, the priests conducted a procession every morning, then again every afternoon. Children sang as they paraded through town, marching for the square and the cathedral, carrying boughs of piñon or cedar, some hoisting platforms where carved and painted effigies of the holy family sat in plain view of the throngs who crowded the *placita*. It reminded Scratch's children of the Crows' annual tobacco celebration, or the revelry at the return of a victorious war party.

How Titus loved to stand on the porch of Paddock's store and witness the grand parade twice a day with his youngsters. Too, how he took so much fun and satisfaction in secretly buying the three of them and Waits little presents, sneaking into the shop's back room to wrap up those gifts with colored paper Looks Far provided, tying them up with twine. But after all the building anticipation, the special day came and went so quickly—a day when the shops remained closed and the Paddocks slipped from the house early to attend an early mass.

"It's helped me some," Josiah admitted later that morning when his family returned to have breakfast and open their presents. "Not that I understand much of what the priests say in the masses—hell, I've learned Flathead and Mexican too, but the tongue them priests use I can't savvy at all."

"It helped being a Catholic like all of them, eh?" Bass asked. "Mathew Kinkead told me you'd taken the vows."

"There's some Americans in the village—a few anyway—say they don't plan on sticking around down here for long anyway," Paddock explained. "Just make some money and be gone back to the States. As for the rest of us, we've made a home here and plan on raising our families in Taos. I hope the Mexicans and them Pueblos look at us different now that we made ourselves a part of this place."

"Besides, with having a Injun wife and half-breed young'uns," Bass agreed, "you ought'n fit right in."

Paddock grinned as Looks Far brought them steaming cups of Mexican cocoa. "My family's home is here now. Mexico wasn't bad to me for them years after you left. But now that this here is American territory—it suits me just fine. There was a few tense times when General Kearny pulled out for California, but things simmered down all right. We'll just give it time and life'll go right back to the way things were before the army marched in and throwed the Mexican government out."

Six days later Looks Far Woman came home early in the afternoon, with Joshua and Naomi in tow, the three of them carrying long garlands they had constructed of gay paper flowers tied to thick strands of brown baling twine. In the main parlor of their small home, Looks Far and Waits-by-the-Water helped the youngsters hang the garlands while baking fragrant treats for the celebration planned for that night and into the following day.

"Just what are you having your friends come over to hurraw about?" Titus asked Looks Far.

She stood clutching one of the garlands for Joshua, who was up on a chair, hanging the strand in long loops over nails he had just hammered into the adobe bricks near the low roofbeams. Looks Far stared at him as if Bass had lost his mind. "Josiah wants everything to be right for you, Titus."

"For me? Why all this fuss for me?"

Now she squinted her eyes at him as if he'd lost his mind. "Why—Josiah, he invited many of our American friends to come here—to help celebrate your birthday with us!"

"M-my birthday? I'll be damned," he exclaimed.

Looks Far glanced at Waits, finding the Crow woman smiling with great approval. Then she said to the old trapper, "You forgot your own birthday?"

"Can't 'member the last time I took special notice of that day, no," he answered.

From his perch on the chair, Joshua asked, "How old you gonna be, sir?"

"Well, now," he delayed thoughtfully, staring at the floor, a bit baffled as to just where to start. Then he looked at Looks Far to inquire, "What year this gonna be—when it turns a new one at midnight?"

"Why . . . it will be 1847, Titus."

"So lemme see," he sighed, sinking onto the floor and holding his palms up, so he could begin counting.

Scratch had gone through folding down all his fingers twice when Looks Far came over to kneel before him.

"You want us to count the years for you?"

He beamed up at her, extremely grateful. "I'd be real 'bliged."

"Joshua, come over here and help Mr. Bass figure out how old he'll be tonight."

Clambering down from the chair, the youth grabbed a thick hunk of chalk and a small slate board from a wide, wood shelf, then settled on the floor right in front of Titus and crossed his legs, mirroring the trapper. "All right. It's gonna be 1847 at midnight tonight," Joshua began, writing down those numbers on the slate. Then he looked up at the old man. "When were you born, Mr. Bass?"

"I told you afore, Joshua—I want you to call me Titus."

"Yes, sir, Titus."

Scratch cleared his throat. "I was born on the first day of 1794."

Joshua noticeably rocked back in astonishment. "That's a long time ago, Mr., er . . . Titus."

"1794 *was* a long, long time ago—no argeement on that."

Then he cocked his head to the side to watch how Joshua scratched out that year right below the first four numbers. After a line was drawn beneath them both, the youngster went to ciphering, arriving at one new number at a time—but, to Scratch's surprise, Joshua held up his slate when he had only two numbers written below the line.

"You'll turn fifty-three tonight."

He swallowed at the mere weight of that figure. Then

looked up at those gathered near, everyone staring directly at him as if waiting for him to react to the news. "Hell. I can't ever 'member knowing a soul near as old as that. 'Cept for my grandpap, I durn well may be older'n anyone I ever knowed!"

Just past sundown they began to show up at the door—single men, and those with families too. They slipped off their heavy woolen coats, mufflers, and scarves, disposing of them and their winter caps in the corner of a small bedroom at the back of the house. Soon there were enough people crowded in the front parlor that some of the guests began to trickle over into other rooms of the Paddock residence.

"*Hola*, Sheriff!" Josiah called out to the man just coming in the door with his wife, a small boy, and a chilling gust of cold. Paddock grabbed Titus and Waits by their elbows as he had done several times before, escorting the two of them to greet every new guest.

Looks Far embraced the man, then helped him off with his coat before shuffling away for the kitchen once more, chatting with the sheriff's wife as the two of them threaded their way through the gathering with the young child in tow.

"Josiah!" the new arrival cheered, holding out his hand. "Thanks for inviting me."

"Sheriff, I'd like you to meet my old, and dear friend— Titus Bass," Paddock started the introductions.

"I'm Stephen Lee," the sheriff declared. "And Josiah here's told me a lot about your days together. Heard tell of you my own self more'n a time or two."

That name sounded familiar, then he found the peg to hang it on as they shook hands. "Wasn't you hooked up with Jim Beckwith for a time?"

"Threw in together to do some trading up at the Pueblo a few years back," Lee explained. "Things didn't turn out the way I figured they would so I sold out to Beckwith and come back down here."

"So you was out here some time before giving the Pueblo a try?"

"I trapped more'n my share," Lee admitted. "Ran

with outfits working out of Taos afore I moved up to the Arkansas with Beckwith. After I sold out to Beckwith it seemed the natural thing to do was get on back down here to San Fernando. You see, close to twenty years ago when I first come to the village, I'd spotted a purty gal I just couldn't take my eyes off. Ever since we was married, I been putting down some roots."

Titus squeezed Waits against him and said, "Women have the knack of doing that to a man if you're not careful!"

"You come in for the winter?" Lee asked as Josiah stepped back up with a clay cup for the sheriff.

"From the looks of it, we're here till the weather fairs off enough, maybe come March," Scratch explained. "Then we're on the tramp for home."

"Where's home?"

"My wife's Crow," he said. "It's her home."

"From the sound you just gave it, Crow country may not be your home."

Titus thought a moment before he replied, "Just about anywhere there ain't a village or settlement or town is my home, Sheriff."

"Please call me Stephen."

"All right," he agreed. "Ain't you used to folks calling you sheriff by now?"

"Haven't been county sheriff but a few months really," Lee confessed. "Kearny came through late last summer—and turned everything on its head around here. Jesus, can you believe this is American territory now, Josiah? No American fur hunter is gonna have to swear allegiance to Mexico, not ever again."

"Damn good thing too, Sheriff Lee!" Tom Tobin cried as he stepped up to the group, hoisting his clay cup over his head.

"A toast to America's newest territory!" John Albert cheered as he joined them.

All round the room, guests stopped in the middle of their conversations to hold up their cups and glasses, some calling out "here, here," while others huzzahed lustily and the cups clinked, good wishes being shared.

"There's my daughter an' her husband," Lee said as a young couple came out of the kitchen. "I'll speak at you boys a li'l later."

Paddock bent to whisper at Bass's ear. "Stephen's daughter there—Maria—she's named after her mother: Maria Luz Tafoya, a prominent Taos family. Li'l Maria got married herself couple of years ago."

For a moment Scratch studied the pretty girl across the room as her father approached and they hugged. Bass said, "Two years ago? Jehoshaphat! She don't look much older'n Magpie is right now, Josiah!"

"She was old enough by Mexican custom," Paddock disclosed. "She's sixteen now."

"You're telling me her father an' mother give her away when she was *fourteen*?" he asked incredulously.

With a nod, Josiah said, "The Mexicans marry 'em off awful young down here. But she married a good American boy. Came out here from Missouri with his folks not long before they married. Name's Joseph Pley."

"I can see I better keep an eye on my daughter till it comes time to get outta here an' back to Crow country!" Scratch commented as Paddock drained his cup.

"Simeon!" Josiah shouted across the room, holding up the empty clay cup. "You'd better open up that next case of your lightning before all these tongues dry out and won't wag anymore!"

"Turley's here?" Tom Tobin asked.

"Hell, yes! I asked all the foreigners our Mexican friends hate so badly to come tonight!" Paddock replied.

Albert pointed out two men at the middle of the room. "An' we all ain't 'Mericans here—there's two Frenchies the Mex boys seem to hate just as much as they hate us."

"Antoine LeBlanc works for Turley," Paddock explained. "And the other's Jean-Baptiste Charlefoux. He's the one there with his Mexican wife and their daughter. She's a pretty girl, just turned seven."

A loud pounding thundered on the plank door. Josiah tore it open and immediately backed inside as a pair of men stepped into the house. Suspended between them was a huge brass kettle. Both called out to the crowd, asking the guests to step aside and clear a path as they slowly made their way to the kitchen.

"What you have there, Asa?" asked Charles Town when he came up to raise the kettle's brass lid.

"What the hell you think it is?" the older man growled.

Bending at the waist, Town sniffed beneath the lid, drinking in the fragrance. "Your famous New Mexican eggnog!"

Another cheer went up in the room.

"You didn't shut down your cantina for the rest of the night, did you, Asa?" Tom Tobin inquired.

"Got some help minding the bar for me till I get back," replied the tavern keeper as they pushed on for the kitchen with their eggnog. "Already got sign of being a busy hurraw."

"That's Asa Estes," Josiah explained as he slipped up to Bass's elbow once more. "Owns a watering hole not far from here. A good man—Missouri bred. Been out here for several years now, and does he make a nog that'll pin your ears back to your ass if'n you aren't careful!"

"Just look at you, Josiah Paddock," Bass said proudly, beaming once more at his old friend.

The younger man grinned. "What you mean by that, ol' man?"

"Why, here you got Simeon Turley who makes some damned fine lightning, I must say. And you got this fella Asa Estes comes by your shindig with his famous eggnog," Scratch explained. "It's plain to see that you're a man who has some fine friends. Friends who sure as hell hold you in high regard, son."

Laying his long, muscular arm over the shorter man's shoulder, Josiah spoke close to Bass's ear. "If there's one man—one *friend*—who taught me the real value of friendship, who taught me that my family and my friends were my true wealth in life . . . then you are that man, Titus Bass."

He looked up at Paddock, his own eyes clouding with

sentiment. "Damn, if you don't know how to make a man proud."

"Cornelio, c'mon over here and meet a friend of mine from way, way up north," Josiah called out.

A thin-boned, dark-skinned Mexican stepped over, and Scratch recognized him for the man who had helped Asa Estes carry the kettle into the house.

"This here's a good friend of mine, Cornelio Vigil," Josiah announced. "And this is Titus Bass."

Scratch held out his hand and said, "Good to meet any friend of Josiah's, Señor Vigil."

"Please to call me Cornelio," the man replied. "We are friends now too."

They shook as Paddock went on to explain, "Cornelio was appointed as our district attorney by General Kearny."

"Sounds like you got handed a tough job," Bass commented. "Bet it keeps you busy nowadays, bringing justice down on all them folks gonna cause trouble for the new American officials?"

Vigil grinned slightly. "Some of my people still haven't made the adjustment, Señor Bass. To their way of thinking, if they can stir up enough trouble, they can throw the Americans out."

"Throw Americans out?" Titus echoed. "Josiah, how can any of these Mexicans down here think they got 'em a better life under Armijo and his government than they got under the Americans?"

"Truth is," Paddock began, his voice growing quiet and confidential, "Governor Bent's folks heard tell of a plot to stir up some big trouble—a well-planned revolt of Indians and Mexicans too."

Vigil nodded. "Earlier in the month, Señor Bass."

Titus asked, "What come of it?"

The new district attorney answered, "Soon as word leaked out that Bent was coming to arrest them, the two ringleaders vamoosed. Rumor says both of them scampered south into Mexico for safer territory, fast as their horses could carry them."

"So news has it the governor's relieved he was able to

cut the head off that rebellious snake before it had the chance to bite anyone and hurt some innocent folks," Josiah declared.

"From all that Stephen and I hear from our informers around town, everything has settled down in the last two weeks," Vigil explained. "With both of those revolt ring-leaders long gone from these parts, life here in Taos has gone back to being just the way it always has been: peaceful and sleepy."

"Did Charles Beaubien come up from Santa Fe for New Year's?" Josiah asked Vigil.

"No, he stayed down at the capital," Cornelio answered. "I think he really savors playing judge more than he should."

"Beaubien's an old Frenchie trapper," Paddock explained to Titus. "Appointed by Kearny to serve as one of the three judges on the Santa Fe court. His teenage son is right over there—"

Bass let Josiah turn him slightly as Paddock pointed out the handsome young man. His eyes immediately widened and his nostrils flared. Angrily he asked, "You mean that parley-voo spooning my Magpie over there in the corner?"

"That's him. Narciso Beaubien," Josiah replied. "He's a good lad. Seems to have a fine eye for a pretty girl too."

Titus could feel the heat climbing from his neck into his beard. "I figger that good lad needs to know he better damn well stay away from my li'l girl—"

"Hol' on, Scratch," Paddock warned as he snagged hold of Titus's arm, stopping the trapper in place. "Lemme go and tell him myself. We're both fathers—you an' me—but it might be better if I do this for you. That way it won't embarrass Magpie in front of anyone."

Scratch was surprised at how quickly he had been ready to boil. Never before had he seen any young man give his daughter a second look. But as he gazed at her now, he realized for the very first time that she really did appear far older than her twelve and a half years. She was already blooming into quite a beautiful woman . . . just like her mother.

"Awright," Titus relented. "You just tell that boy her papa's gonna gut him with the backside of a rusty file if I ever catch him sniffing round her anymore," Bass demanded in a growl. "Go remind 'im she's only twelve years old."

"Hol' on, hol' on," Paddock soothed, patting both of his open palms against Scratch's chest. "Maybe them talking is all innocent and nothing to fret over, Scratch. Sometimes you got a real quick temper."

"Me?" he grumbled, his eyes locked on the pair of youngsters flirting across the room. "A quick temper?"

"Seems I remember a winter—long time ago, after we brung back McAfferty's hair—in a instant you convinced yourself Waits had wronged you and I was the one who betrayed you with her."

Slowly his eyes came back to Josiah's now, and blinked self-consciously with deep regret. "I . . . I never should've figured either of you'd go and wrong me. I allays been sorry—"

"I don't expect another apology, Scratch. I only want you to hol' on a minute and let me go over there 'stead of you," Paddock offered again. "I'll take care of this quiet."

He watched Josiah turn away, threading his way through the crowd to reach the two youngsters. It was but a matter of moments before Magpie's eyes suddenly flicked in his direction and locked on her father's angry glare across the room. She quickly averted her gaze and stared down at the clay floor, just before the young man turned his head to look over Paddock's shoulder, studying the room a moment before he located the gray-headed trapper who was glaring a hole into him like a hot poker.

The young man protectively glanced at Magpie, then stared down at the exact same spot she was studying between their toes. Josiah put a hand on the girl's shoulder a moment, then she stepped around his elbow and started along the edge of the room, making for the kitchen. With Magpie on her way, Paddock looped his left arm over the young man's shoulders and they turned together, inching into the crowd toward that spot where Bass and Vigil stood watching it all.

"Narciso, I want you to meet Magpie's father, Titus Bass," Josiah introduced.

Beaubien self-consciously held up a hand between them. "My apologies, Mr. Bass. I had no intention of giving anyone the wrong impression, especially your daughter. I was not . . . I didn't know she was so young, sir. I apologize profusely. I hope you can understand just how pretty a girl she is—and understand that she looks much older. I'm extremely chagrined at my mistake—"

"Sha . . . sha?"

"I'm very, very embarrassed, sir," Beaubien admitted.

"You talk like you've got a helluva lot more education than most every man in this room, son," Titus declared.

"I've been east, to the States, at college, Mr. Bass. I clearly should have known better. I meant no trouble to you or to Magpie. When I arrived, I quickly realized she was one of the few guests of my own age here—so I naturally went over to introduce myself and engage her in conversation. I thought it would be polite to welcome her to the Taos valley—"

"You apologized enough, son," Scratch interrupted with a sigh. "I'm sure my daughter enjoyed your flattery."

"I meant no harm by talking to her—"

"No offense taken," Bass replied. "Now that I understand." He looked at Josiah. "The Mex folks, don't they have a custom of chaperons?"

Paddock's face brightened. "They surely do, Scratch."

Titus turned back to the young man. "If you wish to talk to my daughter, please do it when her mama's around—like in the kitchen there, with the both of 'em together."

"Oh, no, sir—she's too . . . far too young for me to consider courting," Beaubien explained. "I'd have to wait three or four years until I would court your daughter."

"You'll have to ride a long, long ways to do that in three or four years, young fella," Titus stated.

Beaubien said, "I don't understand, sir. Don't you plan on making Taos your new home now that this territory belongs to America?"

With a wag of his head, Titus declared, "No. Soon as winter's done, I'll be taking my family back where we belong."

In that heavy silence, Beaubien nervously presented his hand to Bass again. "It was a pleasure to meet you, sir. I'm sorry for the misunderstanding with your daughter."

Scratch watched the young man shoulder his way into the crowd, headed for another part of the house.

Grabbing Titus's upper arm, Josiah said, "All that just made me remember something I should have told you before you rode off from Taos years ago."

"What's that?"

Paddock confessed, "When I look back on our years together, I remember you showing me how I was angry at *every*thing and *every*body. What you taught me was I could trust someone again, ol' man. If I hadn't learned to trust—truth is, I'd been dead inside of a few weeks of when I run onto you."

"You was a hardy lad," Bass said, feeling a bit self-conscious himself. "Chances were, you'd made your way without me—"

"No," Josiah interrupted in protest, leaning his face close. "Don't you see what I owe you, ol' man? If you hadn't helped me sort through all that drove me from Saint Louis, if you hadn't taken me back there with you to face up to what I'd done—likely I wouldn't be standing here today . . . wouldn't have the life I do for my family."

Patting the younger man on that spot where his neck met the muscular shoulder, Titus said quietly, "Maybeso, in your own way, Josiah—you helped save my life too."

30

───────────◆───────────

Neither one of the two men proved good at concealing the worry hewed on their faces as Scratch stepped through the door of Josiah's shop.

"Troubles?" Titus asked the moment he joined Paddock and Stephen Louis Lee.

Josiah began, "Naw, nothing really—"

"Listen, son," Bass interrupted impatiently. "You and me didn't spend all those seasons together for me not to read what's on your face, so g'won and spill it."

"Really, Mr. Bass—it's nothing to concern yourself with," Lee apologized.

"Beggin' your pardon, Sheriff—but if it's something sticks in Josiah Paddock's craw . . . it damn well is my business. Two of us go back a long way—"

"All right, Scratch," Paddock whispered. "Let's go find us a spot in the back to talk. I don't want to do nothing to upset Looks Far. So don't either of you go looking like you just ate some bad apples."

"Hell, Josiah—you're the one got the hangdog face," Bass whispered as they started toward the curtain behind one end of the long plank counter.

Paddock made sure they were out of earshot from the partition before he grimaced at the sheriff and asked in a whisper, "The Pueblos are making tough noises?"

Lee nodded his head. "I heard something the Injuns didn't think I was s'pose to hear early this morning. Last few days they've had some bad sorts out there, fellas rousing 'em up."

"But that ain't nothing new," Josiah replied.

"For the first time they've put a day on it," Lee admitted. "A night when they're gonna raise hell."

For the first time Titus spoke up, "What you mean—raise hell, Sheriff?"

Lee looked at him. "Talk is—those plans Bent broke up last month is on again."

Scratch shook his head. "I thought you fellas told me the leaders of their little rebellion awready skeedaddled off to Mexico."

"They did," Paddock answered, glum.

Bass looked at him. "Then they sneaked back to the Pueblo?"

"No," Lee said. "Word I got is some new leaders gonna lead the attack."

"Attack?" Bass echoed. "Attack what? March down to Santa Fee and have 'em a fight with those dragoons?"

"These are bad Mexicans and even badder Pueblos," Josiah admitted sourly. "But they're savvy enough not to do something stupid, Scratch. This bunch ain't about to march down to Santa Fe and tangle with Colonel Price's soldiers."

For a long, still moment, Titus looked at Paddock, then Lee, then back to Paddock again. "So, if these niggers gonna attack . . . what they fixin' to attack?"

"Taos," Lee confessed.

Bass snorted, "But there ain't no army here for 'em to fight. What the hell these niggers thinking of . . ." And his heart skipped a beat as it struck him cold in the pit of his belly. "Oh, shit."

Josiah could tell that it had suddenly registered on the old trapper's face. "This bunch of butchers aren't the sort to wanna have nothing like a fair, stand-up fight of it."

Lee agreed, "These Mex and Pueblos are nothing more'n dirty fighters. Downright backstabbers. I figure they're planning to make it a massacre."

"When the bastards come after Americans," Titus declared, "we'll be ready for 'em."

"With your own eyes, Scratch," Josiah argued, "you've seen there ain't but a few of us Americans in Taos."

"Those niggers gonna butcher anyone who ain't Mexican or Injun," Lee snarled. "What I hear says they even got their blood up to kill half-breeds: Mex or Injun, don't make 'em any difference."

Titus looked long and steady at Paddock. Then he said, "Bein' half-breed don't count for nothing with 'em, eh?"

Paddock wagged his head. "We seen this coming for some time now, ol' friend. So trust me when we're telling you, these murderers gonna butcher my half-breed children right after they slit my throat."

Scratch could feel the bitter gall rising at the back of his throat, turning his heart sour and mean. "Any nigger makes war on women and children—they're no better'n animals." He turned to Lee and asked, "So, Sheriff, you here to spread the word to Americans?"

"Came here to talk with Josiah. I want his help figuring out how not to alert the bastards that we know what's coming, or when," Lee responded.

"When?" Paddock asked.

"Tonight," the sheriff disclosed with foreboding. "Tomorrow morning by the latest. They was just waiting for Bent to get in from Santa Fe."

Josiah asked in a whisper, "Charles back? In all this snow?"

"Got home near noon," Lee explained. "Took 'im four days up from Santa Fe, deep as it is out there."

"You tell the governor, Stephen?" Josiah demanded.

"Tried to. You know how Charles is. He says he's married to a good Mexican family. Says his children are part Mexican. And when he's done saying all that—

Charles tells me he's always been good to folks in these parts—"

"In other words, the governor doesn't believe there's any real danger to him or his family," Paddock interrupted him.

With a doleful wag of his head, Lee said, "He didn't figure there was anything to worry about since he scared off the other ringleaders last month. Says all that's going on now is a lot of loud and angry talk."

"So what you figger us to do?" Titus asked, his wary senses tingling.

"I think it best we get on through this day till sundown when we close up shop, real normal," Josiah explained. "We try to light out before, any time in the day, we're bound to attract attention."

"They'll know where you're going," Lee added. "So they'll come track you down."

"I'll give 'em a chance to track *me* down, I will for certain," Bass growled.

"Don't you see?" Paddock asked, seizing Bass's forearm in his hand. "There's hundreds of 'em all together. It won't be nothing like a fair fight, Scratch. Like nothing you and me ever fought our way out of."

"By the stars, there's more'n a thousand souls living in that Injun Pueblo a couple miles from here," Lee stated. "A thousand of the niggers!"

Titus swallowed. "So sneaking off is our only hope?"

Paddock looked at Lee. "You think folks oughtta head north?"

The sheriff nodded. "Maybe hole up at Turley's till someone can get word down to Santa Fe and Price can march his dragoons up here."

"Even then, them soldiers still gonna be outnumbered ten to one," Josiah groaned.

"Maybe the most we can hope is they'll scare the shit outta the bastards," the sheriff said.

Paddock quickly stepped to the low, narrow, back door that opened onto an alleyway. He cracked it slightly, peered out for a moment, then shut it again quietly. "Don't have long till sundown, fellas. I think we better start working on getting things ready to head out come dark. Where do you want us to meet up with you, Stephen?"

Lee wagged his head stoically. "I ain't going with you, Josiah."

"I know Maria ain't in no danger," Paddock begged, "but what about li'l John?"

Titus agreed, "He's a half-breed."

"So he's marked for death," Josiah argued. "If your wife doesn't wanna come, then at least get the boy to safety."

"He won't go without his mama. So I'll bring the two of 'em over to your place just after dark," Lee promised as he stepped to the back door.

"And you?" Josiah prodded. "What you aim to do, one man against a bloodthirsty mob?"

"I'm gonna make sure every American, parley-voo, and foreign-born gets word that they better make tracks outta town tonight . . . or they won't see another sunrise," the sheriff declared solemnly.

"Spread the word. You'll still have time to come leave with us," Paddock begged.

Lee stared at the ground a long moment, then his eyes leveled on Josiah's when he said, "I figure if there's gonna be trouble in my town, I oughtta be here to do all I can to put out the fire."

"But it doesn't make sense for you to stick your neck out if you don't have to—"

Stephen Louis Lee interrupted his friend with a gesture of futility while he said, "That's what a sheriff does, Josiah. He's s'posed to protect others."

Their courtship had been nothing less than a whirlwind romance. She, a beautiful young widow related to several prominent, well-established families in the Taos valley. And he the eldest of two American brothers who had carved out a financial empire for themselves here in the Southwest.

Maria Ignacia Jamarilla Bent smiled as their three chil-

dren embraced their father and kissed his cheek before
they retired that evening of January 19, 1847. Her life
with Charles—her sweet Carlos—was idyllic. The only
thing that could possibly have been better was if he
hadn't been appointed governor of New Mexico by the
American general who had marched through Taos and
Santa Fe last August on his way to conquer California for
the Americans. Over the last few months, her husband's
work kept him in Santa Fe for extended periods. So these
visits to Taos were a rare treat—even more unusual that
her husband had surprised her by returning home that
afternoon, a Tuesday.

"I finished what had to be done," Charles had explained when he came bolting through the door at the
noon hour, "and I set the rest of it aside, Ignacia."

It's what he called her—not by her first name but by
the one he believed was most different, a name all the
more beautiful for it.

"Four days to get here," he had gasped at the door,
forty-seven years old, so still somewhat breathless as he
dragged his long wool coat off his arms and shook the ice
frozen to it. "Four days instead of two—the snow was so
deep, so deep."

Ignacia stared at him in sympathy, seeing how he was
soaked through, clear to the waist. His hair had gone
completely gray in the last two years, along with those
deep, dark, liver-colored bags under his eyes, both con-
spired to make him look so much older, all the more
weary and trodden. They had embraced in the entryway,
she so short of breath at his sudden, surprise arrival,
while the children and their two house servants fluttered
around them, everyone chattering and cooing at once.
Even Ignacia's young sister, Josefa—who was Kit Carson's intended—and Ignacia's teenaged daughter,
Rumalda—who had given her promise to Tom Boggs, another American—both swept into the room to welcome
home the patriarch.

"How long can you stay?" Ignacia asked in her English that grew better every day.

"Till Sunday after mass," he vowed, then kissed her on

the cheek and sank to one knee so he could hug the clamoring children.

She had him until after the Lord's supper on Sunday, Ignacia had thought as she watched the joy register on everyone's faces that her Carlos was home. How she loved him for relenting on his own personal views and accompanied her to mass whenever he was in Taos—even though Charles loathed the powerful Martinez family. Especially its patriarch: Padre Antonio Martinez.

This most influential religious, political, and social leader in the valley hated both Charles and his brother, William, as well as their partner, Ceran St. Vrain. For years now Padre Martinez had utilized every ounce of the power and pull at his command to thwart the Bents' increasing foothold in New Mexico. The padre had been at the very heart of a climate that fostered discrimination against, if not outright hatred for, the American traders and businessmen in northern New Mexico. Through exorbitant taxes and tariffs, as well as protesting every purchase of huge tracts of public land north of the valley, Martinez and his cronies had made enemies of these three most powerful foreigners.

But now a new era had just dawned on New Mexico. No longer in charge were those venal Mexican officials so susceptible to bribery and graft. No more would the church officials wield such control over the government. Now all political affairs were in the hands of the American army and its appointees. From here on out Padre Martinez would have to content himself with attempting to manipulate things from offstage.

So while the ousting of the Mexican government from New Mexico had been cause for great celebration in the Bent household, Ignacia fully understood that the takeover only served to antagonize Martinez's anti-American faction with even more hatred and loathing.

She and her Carlos had enjoyed more than eleven years together already, steadfastly weathering the troubles they encountered with her being a daughter of Mexico, and he a son of an upstart, expansionist America. But now the vexing, difficult times were all behind them. The future looked more promising and rosy than it had in a long time.

While her husband's brother had married into the Cheyenne tribe to cement an alliance with his wife's people, Charles had married her to forge an uneasy alliance with the people of northern New Mexico. So it was not altogether unexpected that she learned of the angry grumbling of some *Taosenos* against her husband told to Ignacia by her servants on those days they shopped in the local market. Still, she continued to believe that—given enough time—her people would come to see that all things were for the better now that the Americans were in charge of New Mexico. Especially now that her husband could prove to all those doubters just how incorruptible, fair, and benevolent a leader he could be . . . despite all the unmitigated hatred still festering just beneath the calm surface of everyday life here in Taos.

Late that evening she was once again ready to believe him when he attempted to convince her that she had nothing to fear, despite the nerve-racking noise outside on the streets as small, noisy, arrogant mobs roamed the darkened village. Terrified to the soles of her feet when they heard the first gunshots, Ignacia flew to his side, huddled against him there beside the fire.

She sat quivering in his arms as he told her, "They're just blowing off some steam. I didn't want to tell you . . ."

"Tell me what?" she demanded, frightened and angry both.

"Coming up the road from Santa Fe this afternoon, we'd reached the edge of town," he related, "when we found ourselves suddenly surrounded by a pack of those Indians from the Pueblo."

Ignacia immediately put both hands over her ears, as if to block out the sounds of terror outside their courtyard, even to shut out his own description of a narrow scrape with danger.

Gently Charles pulled her hands from her ears as he continued. "They demanded I have Sheriff Lee release their friends who had been jailed for petty offenses—like theft. Though they shouted and threatened, I managed to convince them that the law must take its course, that this matter would be handled through the courts as things were handled with American justice."

"And they let you go?"

He nodded. "While we kept talking to the Indian leaders, I started my group away from them very slowly, making our way through the crowd. Perhaps they did not know what to do except growl at us, making threats and bloody vows as we finally reached town."

More gunfire echoed outside now. She whimpered, "Oh, Carlos—"

"You must not fear. There really is no cause to worry," he consoled. "They could have taken me this afternoon if they had wanted me. The noises you hear out there are all bluster and bombast—nothing more than a defeated people blowing off steam at their conquerors—"

A knock came at the front window. She nearly jumped out of her skin.

Charles told her to stay put as he got up to investigate. But she disobeyed and followed him to the door where Charles cracked it open, whispering to the visitor hanging back in the shadows, who dared not show himself.

"You must take your family and flee at once, Governor!"

"Flee?" Charles challenged. "A governor does not *flee*! Matters aren't so serious for me to be seen escaping into the night."

"*Sí! Vaya pronto!* Things are getting more ugly every moment," the disembodied voice warned. "For the sake of your family, for the sake of Mexicans like me who believe in you—go now before it is too late! *En el nombre de Dios!*"

Then she heard the fading rustle of footsteps as someone scurried across the gravel and hurled themselves over the side wall so they would not be seen dropping into the narrow street at the front of the house.

When he had bolted the door, she pressed herself against him, wanting to cry, to beg and plead with him to take the family and go for his sake.

"*Ya viene!*" she sobbed. "Now it's coming!'

But he stroked her hair and convinced her of what she was truly desperate to believe: that there was no real threat of danger. These were her people, this was her town—and he had married her. Their children were Mexican. Nothing would happen to them. Ignacia wiped the tears from her cheeks, saying she would look in on the three children, then say good night to her sister and niece.

"I don't want to stay up late tonight," Charles said to her as she came back into the parlor minutes later.

Ignacia stopped behind his chair, wrapping her arms across his chest, and laid her cheek on the top of his head. "I imagine you are weary from the ordeal of your four-day journey."

He kissed the palms of both of her hands, then said, "It's not for want of sleep that I want to drag you off to bed, Ignacia."

She stared down at his upturned face, into his tired eyes. Charles pulled her mouth down against his. She trembled when his fingers lightly brushed her breasts as he slowly inched both hands upward to grip her shoulders.

"Bring a candle," he said huskily as he got to his feet there by the hearth.

With a furtive glance she could see how readily he had been aroused. It pleased her no end to realize that after all these years and their three children, she still had this immediate effect on him. What power she alone held over the governor of New Mexico.

How she enjoyed giving herself over to him when he closed the door to their bedchamber behind them and she set the candle on the stand beside their tall, Mexican-style canopy bed. It took but a moment for her to realize how hungry he made her for him as he worked at those tiny buttons and ties binding her inside multiple layers of winter clothing. Why, he had her skin so heated with delicious anticipation that the muslin sheets chilled Ignacia . . . at least until her Carlos made her forget all about the cold bedding he dragged over the two of them the moment he slid on top of her naked, trembling body.

Hard and insistent and every bit as hungry as she had prayed he would be.

She awoke slowly, groggily, sometime long after they had both fallen asleep; he tucked against her back like a nesting of spoons. The noises outside the house were liquid—thick like syrup—not quite distinct: loud voices, shrill and angry, unearthly screams and bloody oaths, along with the clatter of wood and the jangle of iron hardware—

That first thunderous slap of something solid against the bolted front door brought her fully awake. Charles was already rolling away from her, leaping off the bed, lunging around in the dim candlelight flutting against the wall from that single wick now awash in its own small puddle of opaque liquid.

"Get your gown, Ignacia!" he ordered, his tone so harsh it frightened her.

"G-gown?"

"Go to the children," he demanded as he found his britches on the floor near her side of the bed. "Gather them and take them to the pantry door."

She hated to leave the bed now that it was warmed to their bodies—

"Ignacia! Move, now!"

Swinging her legs off the bed, she bent forward and scooped up her dressing gown, dragging it off the cold, clay floor that was covered here and there by small rugs of Navajo or Pueblo wool.

"W-where are you going?" she asked as he pulled his shirt over his head and dragged the braces over his shoulders.

That terrifying clamor grew more insistent at the front door: eerie, screeching voices and that thumping that seemed to fill the whole house.

He grabbed her by the shoulders and yanked her upright beside the bed. "I fear something evil is afoot, Ignacia."

Then he embraced her roughly, passionately crushing her mouth with his, and finally stared into her eyes to say, "Now do as I told you—get the children and the others to the back door, and when I have gone to the front of the house—flee out to the alley as fast as you can get everyone to safety."

"S-safety?"

His jaw went rigid, muscles flexing. "Get our family to the church," he said with a flat and hollow voice. "Take sanctuary there."

"No! No!" she screamed, throwing her head from side to side. "I'm not leaving here without you!"

He shook her, then promptly seized the two loose ends of the cloth belt that hung from the waist of her dressing gown. He tied it in a knot, then gave it an extra jerk to hold it securely over her naked flesh.

"If you have ever wanted to show me how much you love me," Charles began, "if you have ever wanted to show how much you love our children . . . do this for me now, Ignacia. Do this without question."

"Father, what is going on?"

It was Alfred's voice on the other side of their bed-chamber door.

"Get your sisters and meet your mother in the pantry, Alfred!"

"Father?" the boy pleaded. "What do they want?"

Charles was at the door, yanking it open to suddenly stare down at his ten-year-old son. "They want me, Alfred. Now help your mother get your sisters to the pantry as I've ordered!"

"Charles!"

It was Rumalda, still an adolescent. At her shoulder stood Josefa. Ignacia prayed that moment Carson and Boggs could be there to protect them at this moment of danger.

"Ladies, please," Charles begged, "help me with Ignacia and the children. Get yourselves to the church, to safety—"

"No, no, no," Ignacia mumbled when Charles pulled her against him, pressed her cheek against his neck, her nose buried in that filthy shirt that smelled of horses and sweat, of trail grime, fire and tobacco smoke. Most of all, it smelled of him, just the way he had smelled last night when he had smothered her with his body—seizing her with all of his being.

"I love you, Ignacia." Charles choked out the words. "I always will."

Then he was cruelly turning her around, shoving her into Alfred's arms. Josefa and Rumalda came forward in their bare feet to each take one of Ignacia's arms. Beyond them, she saw Estefina and Teresina standing with the two female servants, one old and one almost as young as her children. They all had their sleeping caps on and dressing gowns hastily pulled over their shoulders.

"Go together—now, hurry!" Charles ordered in a loud voice as a splintering racket suddenly reverberated from the front parlor.

They had broken through the door! Voices shrieked just down the hallway.

"Do not make a sound!" he screamed above the tumult as the crowd surged into the parlor. "In God's name, *run for your lives!*"

That last glance she took over her husband's shoulder was to see the shadows bobbing on the parlor wall just a matter of yards down the narrow hallway. So many shadows that she could not begin to count the intruders who had violated their home.

Then she gazed at her Carlos's face even while Alfred dragged her into the darkness, toward the rear of the house, all of them scurrying like frightened animals for that door that held the only chance of escape.

Upon reaching the far end of the hall, she struggled to have a last look upon her Carlos, ducking her head this way and that over young Alfred's head. She watched her husband step into the firelit shadows of the parlor, shouting boldly at the intruders—throwing up his hands and screaming back at those who had invaded the sanctity of their home, those who had sullied this beautiful sanctuary she shared with her husband and their children.

At the very same moment Alfred pulled her around the darkened corner toward the rear pantry, Ignacia watched more than a dozen pairs of hands and arms and a multitude of angry faces take form out of the dim, flickering firelight, all those fingers like buzzard claws as they seized her Carlos and dragged him into the shadows with them.

She started to scream—

But her sister's hand immediately clamped over Ignacia's mouth.

"Mother!" Alfred whispered harshly to her. "Hush! Not a word! Remember what father told us!"

Yes—she thought—I will remember what your father told me.

I love you, Ignacia. I always will.

If any of the Pueblo Indians hated their American conquerors, it was Tomas.

This violent, foul-humored miscreant had eagerly joined the plot when the three Mexican ringleaders— Archuleta, Duran, and Ortiz—had vowed they would throw off the American yoke, or die trying. But when that trio's plans were discovered and the Mexicans fled for Chihuahua, Tomas alone did all he could to keep alive the embers of revolt.

Then Big Nigger showed up at the Pueblo, come home to see his wife. The huge, brooding Indian immediately stepped forward to join Tomas's call for death to all foreigners. Tomas thought that was ironic, seeing how Big Nigger was a foreigner himself. Yes, an Indian—but not born of this land. Many years ago he had come to northern New Mexico with an American trapping party.

But none of that mattered now that he and Big Nigger, along with at least two dozen more Pueblos, had confronted their most despised enemy that afternoon on the outskirts of town. After the American governor had slipped through their mob, Tomas and Big Nigger rallied hundreds to follow them into Taos, intending to free their compatriots who were rotting in the Americans' jail.

The *Americano* called Lee—he was the man who had imprisoned Tomas's friends from the Pueblo.

Well after dark when the mob noisily burst into the jail

brandishing guns, butcher knives, and torches, they caught the surprised sheriff scrambling off his cot in his longhandles. Several of the Indians grabbed the sheriff and dragged him to Tomas's feet.

"Set our friends free!" Tomas demanded.

"No," Lee said in English.

Even Tomas could understand that, what little of the enemy's language he understood. He slapped Lee across the mouth, which spurred a loud chorus from the crowd pressing in around them, eager to watch how Tomas would open the cell doors. Tomas glanced at Big Nigger for approval. The Delaware nodded slightly.

"Open the cages, gringo!" Tomas growled before he slammed a bony fist into the middle of Lee's face.

Blood spurted from the sheriff's nose, oozing freely over his mouth and bare chin. It took a moment for Lee's eyes to focus again.

The American licked the warm blood from his lower lip, then centered his gaze on Tomas. "No."

Tomas slammed his fist into the sheriff's face again, then again, and another time too. With each blow he watched how Lee's head snapped back, then lolled forward until he could open his eyes—likely fighting unconsciousness every time.

"Stop! Stop this, I say!"

Tomas wheeled at the sound of the voice crying out in Spanish—wondering why one of the Mexican conspirators was demanding a halt to this torture. The crowd surrounding Tomas was grumbling with ugly intent as they rolled this way and that.

"You lawless scum!" the voice ridiculed the mob.

More shrieks from Tomas's rebels as the thin Mexican shoved his way toward the steps of the jail where Tomas gripped the front of Lee's bloody longhandles in his fists.

"By all that's holy!" Cornelio Vigil growled as he came to a halt four feet away. "Not one of you are worthy to stand before a man of God!"

"So, it is you, Vigil! Friend to the American tormentors!" Tomas shrieked when he recognized the Mexican official.

"*Malditos usted!* I'll kill you with my bare hands," the prefect vowed. "Free that man and go back to your Pueblo. Break this up now and I'll deal with you tomorrow—"

Suddenly two of the Indians leaped forward, seizing Vigil's arms.

"Let me go, you snakes! Let me go!" the prefect ordered his manhandlers. "You should tremble to even lay a hand on me!"

With a strident laugh, Tomas screamed, "We aren't your inferiors now, Prefect!"

Two more large Indians squatted at the Mexican's knees and hoisted the struggling Vigil completely into the air. The prefect scuffled, flailing his arms and bellowing what he planned to do about this unthinkable act of rebellion by his inferiors. He reminded them he was their better, from a noble class—a group of people who sought to help the Americans because it was good for business.

But this was the moment it fell to both the poor of the Pueblo and Taos itself to reclaim New Mexico for its native peoples.

"Scoundrels and scum!" Vigil screamed at them as four of the mob dragged him off the steps at the front of the jail and into the center of the street. "Disperse now or your lives will be forfeit!"

Tomas released the groggy sheriff for the moment. He could come back for Lee in a few minutes. For now he followed the four through the surging crowd. "What do you think of your poor peons now, Vigil?"

"*En el nombre de Dios*, you'll hang for this!" the prefect shouted.

"No—you'll hang!"

"If you'd fight me fairly like a man," Vigil was shrieking, spittle crusted at the corners of his mouth, "I'd show your kind for the cowards you are—rebel scum!"

"Kill him!" Tomas suddenly yelled.

In less than a heartbeat the four keepers dropped the prefect onto the icy street before the throng collapsed over Vigil. Tomas heard the Mexican screaming in agony, watched the dozen or more arms rise and fall, the machetes and scythes, hoes and butcher knives rising after each descent, more and more blood glistening on and dripping from their blades.

Suddenly a disembodied arm was brandished overhead. Then a lower leg, with pieces of Vigil's boot still dangling from a nearly severed foot. Tomas was just about to shove his way into the mob when a dark, round object was hurtled into the sky by one of the murderers. It sailed down into the crowd, but was caught and immediately tossed into the air again. Up and down the spinning object ascended into the flickering torchlight as Tomas slowly recognized it for what it was.

Vigil's patrician head—a look of horror frozen forever on his features.

After more than a dozen short flights into the air, Tomas retrieved the head from the trampled, snowy, bloody ground and ordered the others back. From the hands of one of those nearby he wrenched a long, iron-headed pike he now shoved into the base of the severed neck. Tomas hoisted his grotesque battle trophy aloft.

Those wide, anguish-filled eyes, and that gaping mouth twisted in anger . . . Vigil would trouble them no longer. Never again would the Mexican look down his long, patrician nose at them. At long last the prefect had gotten what he deserved for bedding down so comfortably with the conquerors. Now his mob would do to the other foreigners what they had done to Cornelio Vigil.

Next to die—would be Sheriff Lee.

But as Tomas wheeled about, brandishing his first victim's head above the mob on that long pike, the rebel leader realized the porch was bare. All of Lee's guards had poured into the street as soon as the fun began with Vigil.

"Lee!" Tomas roared the American's name in English. All around him the crowd fell to a murmur.

"Lee!" he shrieked again, fury growing.

Those in the mob were turning this way, then that—

frantically searching for the sheriff, who should have been their next victim.

"Find the American!" Tomas bellowed with the screech of a wounded animal. "Lee—we are coming for you!"

31

◆

"There he goes!"

When that shrill warning caught him from behind, Stephen Louis Lee quickly glanced over his shoulder, finding the dark clot of the bloodthirsty mob gazing up at him as he scrambled onto the flat roof of the shop next door to his jailhouse. The muddy, trampled, snowy ground beneath the angry Indians and Mexicans vibrated and pulsated with the flickering light of their crude torches.

They had spotted him.

Thank God his family was already on its way to safety with Paddock and Bass.

But where he could go from here, Lee did not know. By now his stockings were soaked, his feet half frozen, colder than they'd ever been since that first winter he endured trapping in the mountains. Like two cakes of ice they were now as he had heaved himself onto a window ledge, teetered there to reach up and grab the hollowed-out top of a high wall where the shop owner would plant geraniums come spring—and once he stood upon that wall, Lee hoisted himself onto the second-story roof.

Perhaps he could dash across the crusted, icy snow to

the back of the roof in time to jump off the edge, down onto a neighboring one-story building, and from there he could leap into the alleyway—find himself a horse or a mule and race out of town. Once in the desert it would be dark and he might stand a chance of them not finding him.

The bastards! The bloody, ungrateful bastards. Red niggers, brown niggers—they were no different. Crying to get things back to the way they were when they thought their peoples were on top of the heap! Stupid *pelados!* They were never on top!

Only Governor Armijo and Padre Martinez were at the top echelon of the social pecking order . . . not these poor sonsabitches. They were a simple, simple lot. Easily stirred up by the likes of Martinez. Damn his Catholic balls anyway! This bloody coup had Martinez's prints all over it!

Lee knew nothing would ever convince him that the venal, corrupt padre hadn't cooked up this little plot to kill all the Americans who had removed that godless Christian friar from his cozy seat of power.

Angry shouts and bloody cries echoed from the snowy streets below him as the mob flowed around the line of shops on both ends of the square. Those poor, downtrodden bastards had no idea they were merely pawns in Martinez's plot to put him back on the confessional throne.

Huffing to the edge of the adobe roof, the sheriff stared down at the one-story building below him. Before he could think of why he shouldn't jump, Lee flung himself off the edge and went sprawling on the crusty snow, sliding uncontrollably for the edge of the flat-topped building. Twisting, he flopped himself onto his belly the instant his legs went out from under him and he went down: grabbing, clawing for anything that would hold him . . . but he kept right on oozing for the edge.

The fury in their voices grew in volume, echoing, reverberating, slamming off every *placita* wall. He heard his name again, and again. And again still. With nothing to stop his slide at the end of the roof he spilled on over, landing in the snowy alley on his hip and shoulder. Both joints cried out with cold stabs of sudden, sharp agony. Lee knew he had torn himself up something bad, if not broken something outright.

Shakily pushing himself onto his hands he looked left, then right, unable to spot an animal. But he did see the flickering lights of their torches illuminating the walls at both ends of the alley. If he could crawl behind those crates, they might not find him and rush on by.

Their shrill cries, and how they all took up his name like a curse, grew louder and louder still—the sound of their shrieking bouncing off the adobe walls, thundering upon him like the reverberations from a canon.

Suddenly one of them seized his ankle, pulling him from the crates.

Lee twisted, lunging in an attempt to hold on to the side of a huge box, hoping his fingers would find something to break with his bare hands so he had anything for a weapon. He was screaming at them in Mexican now as they dragged him out into the fluttering light of their hissing torches. Smoke steamed up from every one. Angry vapor whispered up like gauze from the face of every last one of the Indians and Mexicans as they closed around him.

"Lee!"

He felt the first knife go in slow. Lee winced, immediately angry at himself for showing them any pain. He would not show his murderers any of that.

"Lee!" they cursed again.

Suddenly his shoulder burned where before it had been nothing but bone-numbing cold. Twisting to look at the wound . . . he saw that his arm was gone—cleaved off clean, right at the shoulder.

"Lee!" the shrieks came louder, right at his ear.

His eyes climbed up to the man who had taken off the arm as the bastard held it aloft and shook it over the crowd, splattering many with warm blood, each spurt of crimson steamy on this subfreezing night.

A leg burned.

Gazing down he could see them hacking crudely at his

left thigh—cutting him into pieces while he still lived. These goddamned Mexicans and their Pueblo henchmen—Martinez's Catholic goons . . . heathens who didn't even have the Christian decency to kill a man before they chopped him to pieces.

Lee was gurgling, trying to catch his breath—then realized they had slashed his windpipe. It wouldn't be long now. The burning. The cold. The pain. None of it any stronger than the anger he felt for every last one of them. But even his hate for these butchers would soon be over.

Blood gushed from the side of his mouth as he tried to hoist his head up and look down at what was left of his body. Both arms gone and one of the legs ripped off already. And while two of them sawed away at his last leg, another had his manhood gathered in his dirty brown hand, preparing to hack off his penis and scrotum with that butcher knife. The bastard looked up and found Lee staring at him in half-lidded pain.

Then the brown-skinned son of a bitch started drawing the knife back and forth, slowly—to make long work of it.

"Lee!"

Something about that voice he recognized. Despite the fog of his pain and the blindness of his hatred, the sheriff looked up, and blinked, locating the face of Tomas—the Indian who was leader of this gang of cowardly cutthroat scum.

Then Stephen Louis Lee could not hold his head up any longer. He knew that last sudden breath he had taken was already done and no more would he ever suck another ounce of air. His head spilled back, praying his family was safe out there in the darkness with that old trapper now.

Lee couldn't remember his name. Funny. But it really didn't matter because something told him that old friend of Paddock's would get them all through on the other side of this.

Oh, how he wanted to laugh right in the mob's faces . . . as he thought on how his old friends, trappers all, would avenge his death. On how Price's dragoons

would gallop up from Santa Fe and execute the ringleaders by firing squad—Padre Martinez and all the rest.
No . . . all the rest like this Tomas, they would hang at
the end of an oiled rope.

To see these butchers dangling there for long minutes
while they slowly strangled, kicking, kicking and shit in
their pants.

I'll see you in hell, Tomas—Lee thought, his eyes glazing in death. One day soon, you an' me gonna settle this
in hell.

They called him Big Nigger.

That wasn't the name given him by the men of his
Delaware tribe far away to the east. But it was what he
was called by those hardened white frontiersmen whose
trapping expeditions he had joined after he came here to
the Southwest. They used to joke that he really wasn't a
redskinned Delaware Indian. Truth was, his flesh did
have the look of glossy char, the appearance of a burnished ebony. And he was big. The Delaware trapper
stood nearly a foot taller than most men of the day, his
long bones riveted with bulky straps of muscle that made
his stygian skin shimmer when he walked.

Big and black, and imposingly scary too—they called
him Big Nigger.

Years ago, more than a handful now, Jim Swanock
had brought Big Nigger and some other members of the
Delaware tribe west, more than a handful now. Some
reports stated Big Nigger had reached the mountains not
long before the beaver trade died. Others claimed that no
trace of him existed in the West before 1842. No matter
what any of them believed—Big Nigger was one of those
faceless, nameless breed who walked out of the eastern
woodlands and slipped unseen into a shadowy life among
the recesses of the Rocky Mountains.

That is until old chief Jim Swanock engaged his band
of twelve hunters to accompany John C. Fremont on his
infamous third expedition to California in 1845. Big Nigger went along, just for the diversion of it. Then he was

back in the southern Rockies by the following June of '46, for the traders' records show he bartered away a few furs at Hardscrabble and the Pueblo. But he didn't follow the Arkansas on out to Bents Fort. Around the time of the expedition with Fremont, Big Nigger had come to hate the Bents and everything they stood for: money and power, white dominance over the region, and more money and power.

Only a few of the traders up at Greenhorn or Hardscrabble, sometimes at the Pueblo, ever saw Big Nigger after Fremont's expedition to California. Likely they were the only ones who knew that he had a woman tucked away down in the Pueblo outside Taos—a half-wild, purebred she-cat of an Indian who had just borne him a son early in the fall of '46. Though Big Nigger came and went, disappearing for weeks at a time among the mountains, he nonetheless always returned to his wife and her people at the Pueblo—spending ever more time in those six- and seven-story mud fortresses after Kearny's army marched through northern New Mexico, bringing American rule and driving out the former Mexican and Catholic despots.

His wife's people had been here so long, far longer than the Mexicans, here even before the coming of the Spanish. Their adobe pueblo had been their sanctuary in this valley far back into the time the Apache conducted their annual raids from the west, when the Comanche raided twice a year from the east.

Now the American dogs believed they could just dance right on through and upset centuries of tradition and custom, overnight. Especially when they didn't leave but a token number of their dragoons—and those were all more than seventy miles away in Santa Fe!

Back in the Taos Pueblo late last autumn for the birth of his son, Big Nigger listened to lots of angry talk bubbling to the surface. In and out of the old mud fortress slipped disgruntled Mexicans keen on casting out their new overseers. If there was any time to do it, a moment to wrest control back from the Americans while Kearny's army was consumed with conquering faraway California, this was the time to strike.

"But to assure our victory over the Americans," Big Nigger explained to those ringleaders planning the revolt, "you must chop off the head of the beast."

"The head?"

As he had gazed around the dimly lit adobe room, Big Nigger's eyes narrowed into the slits of a copperhead. "We must kill Governor Bent."

"Bent is down in Santa Fe," protested Tomas, one of those who had taken up the rebellion's cause once their Mexican leaders had fled south months ago. "He has some soldiers around him down there, far out of reach."

Big Nigger had smiled cruelly, seeing this as a beautiful opportunity not only to strike a blow for his wife's people but to rid himself of one of the great American oppressors with the same bold stroke. "He married a Mexican. A Taos family. Surely the governor comes home to visit his wife and children."

"Yes, he does!"

"Then we lay our preparations, have everything ready for a time Bent returns to visit Taos," Big Nigger coached them. "And when he does, we strike!"

"Kill the Americans!" the room roared.

"Kill all of them!" Big Nigger led them in the oath. "Man, woman, and child! Not one left breathing!"

Like a ram blindly leading his pack to the slaughter, Bent had returned to Taos for an unexpected visit.

The breathless runner had carried that electrifying news from town early that afternoon. The Pueblo was instantly abuzz with preparations. Men came and went. Arms were gathered—such as they were—knives and pikes, axes and a few old fusils too. They would not need many firearms, Big Nigger realized. They had the strength of hundreds . . . while the Americans, while the foreigners, while all their wives and children polluted with the strangers' blood, were pitifully few in number.

The killing they had to do would not be conducted at the long-distance range of a rifle. Nor even the short distance of a belt pistol. No, this revolution Big Nigger would lead them on would be one of close-up, face-to-face killing. An occasion to see the fear in the white man's eyes as his heart turned to water and he pissed all over himself knowing he was about to die like a cowardly pig. It was the finest sort of killing, this done face-to-face.

To be able to cut a man to pieces, bit by bit by bit, a little at a time while your enemy was still alive.

If Big Nigger had learned anything from his Delaware people back in the eastern woodlands, it was how to make exquisite torture of dispatching a captured enemy. Suspend a live victim upside down over a low fire and cook his brains until steam spurted from his ears. Or cut a small incision just below a victim's navel, reach in with your fingers, and pull out a section of the man's small intestine so you could nail it to a tree—then force your enemy to walk round and round that tree, slowly, agonizingly, dragging more and more gut from his belly with every tortured step until he died in his tracks.

What would he do now to his enemy, this Governor Bent?

A little while ago Big Nigger had watched how the Indians and Mexicans had hacked their first victim into pieces right in front of the American jailhouse. They let the sheriff escape—so the mob went looking for him. By the time they hunted down the American, Tomas's mob had worked themselves into even more of a fury. But now the Indians appeared to take much enjoyment in seeing just how long they could keep the sheriff alive while they carved off a little more of the white bastard with every slice of their machetes.

By the time they were finished with him in the alley, the mob had grown too big. Some splintered here, others there, different crowds streaming off behind one leader or another in search of an American's shop to plunder, or an American's house to raid, seeking to murder the inhabitants—men, women, and children too.

But those who stayed behind with Big Nigger were the ones who knew the Delaware had big game in his sights. The biggest in the whole damned territory.

He led them to the walls surrounding the Bent house.

And they hoisted two men over the top of the adobe barrier, dropping to the ground inside the courtyard where they hurried over to drag the huge log from its hasps inside the gate. The pair had barely dragged the hewn timber through its iron sockets when Big Nigger threw his shoulder against one side of the double gate and flung his way into the darkened courtyard.

Screaming, shrieking, crying for blood, more than thirty of the Indians clambered on top of the house with their planting tools and began to hack a hole in the roof. Big Nigger grinned wolfishly. This was just like digging into a burrow to yank a cowering prairie dog from its den.

Using the large, squared cottonwood log from the gate, a dozen of them battered at the door to their enemy's house. Finally a single wide panel shattered and they could peer inside. He saw shadows flickering at the mouth of a hallway. Voices, both angry and afraid too, echoing down that blackened hall.

Some Mexicans stepped up beside him, elbowing close with their muskets. He inched backward, wary that they knew little of their firearms while the attackers shoved the gun barrels through the gaping splinters of the door and fired.

"I hit him!" one of them cried.

Furious, Big Nigger seized the Mexican by the neck and flung him backward like a rawhide doll. "No one kills the governor—no one but *me!*"

He peered inside, spotted Bent leaning on the mantel, clutching a bloodied hand to his wounded face in the fire's reflection. Suddenly at the Delaware's shoulder stood a Pueblo warrior he knew by sight only—a skillful hunter.

"I'll wound him bad enough he can't run away with his family," the bowman vowed, bringing his short weapon up and pulling the string back to his cheek.

While Big Nigger watched through the splintered door, the first arrow pierced Bent's cheek. As the governor snapped it in two and ripped it from his face, another arrow struck him high in the chest. He staggered, his knees becoming watery.

Now Big Nigger was furious.

"Enough!" he screamed, propelling the bowman aside so roughly he took three others with him when he sailed backward against the mob. "Bring that ram up here! Knock this door down!"

Stupid fool that he was, Bent was attempting to run away—staggering from the parlor as the remaining sections of the front door shattered into splinters and the mob streamed through the portal. The American was shuffling toward the hallway, raking at the arrow in his chest like a drunkard, mumbling incoherently.

With his left hand Big Nigger snatched a torch from one of the Mexicans and stalked after the wounded man the way a hunter would follow the blood spilled by his wounded prey. Far down at the end of the hallway he heard frightened talk, muffled voices—then a shriek as Bent must have come into view of them. Sobbing women, several of them, Big Nigger thought as he penetrated the shadowy veil of that hallway.

Now that his men had the back door blocked, he turned right into the blackened hall and saw them— the women and children. Strange thing was, one of the women was already half through the wall. She was reaching back into the hall, her arms held out for a child the others were passing to her. Big Nigger stood rooted to that spot a moment more when the women spotted him and screamed in terror, shoving the children through the hole they had made in the wall. A fireplace poker and a large pewter serving spoon lay at their feet on the floor. He admired their fortitude in digging through that wall by scraping out the mud seal around the adobe bricks with their simple tools and fingers too.

"Charles!" one of them cried, the woman who was halfway through the hole.

The rest started backing away as Big Nigger slowly advanced, his torch hissing in the darkened, narrow confines of that hall. There could be no escape. His enraged mob of Pueblos and *Taosenos* had the entire block surrounded. No one was escaping anywhere. Especially the wounded head of the beast.

"Run, Rumalda! Oh, run!" another woman shouted to the one in the wall as she and another seized hold of the governor, dragging him toward the hole.

As the two women attempted to push the man through, the one already in the hole used what little strength she possessed to pull the stocky American into the opening of their makeshift portal. Bent was trying to speak—nothing any of them could understand, every word of it garbled and nonsensical. Even for Big Nigger, who understood enough English to know that Bent was already out of his head and dying.

But not, the Delaware vowed, before he could get his hands on the governor.

With more than two dozen of the Indians pressing up behind their tall leader, Big Nigger watched Bent do something very strange. With his sticky, bloody fingers, the American fumbled in his vest pocket and pulled out a crumpled sheet of paper. The governor held it up, his lips quivering, his hand trembling as he appeared to implore his enemy to take it.

That made the Delaware hate him all the more. With the muzzle of his pistol, Big Nigger knocked the hand and that crumpled paper aside.

It seemed that tiny act of violence on his part spurred three of the Indians to shove their way past Big Nigger and rush to the hole in the wall. They seized Bent from the arms of the woman and dragged the American back into the hallway. One of them held Bent up by his leather braces, then flung the governor against the wall, where he collapsed onto the clay floor.

As that lone woman disappeared into the darkness on the far side of the wall, one of the Pueblos unstrung his bow and hurled the bow aside as he crouched over the American. Bent was groggy, mumbling nonsense as the Indian positioned the governor's head just so—as only a warrior could do—then deftly used his narrow, twisted rawhide bowstring to slash the scalp from the white man's head.

Watching the horrid scene were those children hiding in the folds of the women's dresses. One of them was shrieking, her whole body shaking as she collapsed to her knees. Arms held out, she was begging. That much was clear to Big Nigger. She was pleading for Bent's life, for their lives.

"You fools!" he thundered at the Indians suddenly.

The three of them atop Bent immediately froze, gazing up at their leader in confusion and utter fear.

"Don't you see, you senseless fools?" he roared as he lunged over the scalper and slapped the man hard enough that he collided with the far wall when he flew off the American's body.

"What are you doing?" one of the trio demanded.

Big Nigger swung his torch inches from the man's nose, making the Indian shrink in terror, the sleeve on his greasy wool coat brushed with embers he frantically patted until they were smothered.

"You've killed him now," Big Nigger snarled. "We should have kept him alive."

"Alive?" one of the Mexicans demanded.

Big Nigger recognized the man—a surly one. He was one of the head priest's lieutenants. One of the handful of Mexican couriers who was often seen riding back and forth between the pueblo and Padre Martinez's church in this last two weeks, carrying plans and instructions. Big Nigger shook his torch at the Mexican.

The man leaped back a step, his face registering sudden fear.

The Delaware shook the torch at the Mexican again, backing him farther still until the man was forced to stop against the crowd packed into the hallway.

"Alive is what I said," the Delaware repeated. "We'll kill him when *I* say we kill him. We could have kept him as a valuable hostage until it was time for him to take his last breath."

Turning to look over his shoulder, Big Nigger saw that Bent's chest moved only with shallow respirations. Good thing too. After all, the Delaware wanted to be the one to kill the governor himself.

So now his gaze moved to the women and children cowering at the end of the hall.

"Put them all in a room that has no wall to the outside," he ordered.

Some of his trusted comrades crowded past him in the narrow corridor and seized their captives, dragging them into one of the small bedchambers as the women wailed and the children screeched. The door was closed on them.

"Two of you, stay right here," Big Nigger ordered, glancing at the hole at the bottom of the wall. "See they don't escape."

"Why let them live?" a voice asked.

He stopped, standing right over the governor's body, and told that mob packed in the hall, "We could have kept him from dying until I was ready to kill him. He would have been some use to us. Now we have to keep the others alive until we know if it is better for us that they live, or that they die."

He knelt by the governor, noticed how Bent's hand twitched. The bastard somehow clung to life. These stupid Pueblos had ruined his plans, Big Nigger thought, when he had wanted to keep the head of the family alive. But now Bent was anything but head of his family—

That was it!

"Bring him and follow me!" Big Nigger roared at the swarms of men who stood sweating in bloodlust, packed elbow to elbow in that crowded hall. He shoved back through them to reach the front parlor.

On his heels came the scalper. Once into that front room, the Indian found a small board and some brass tacks. As they waited for the governor's body, Big Nigger watched the bowman stretch the American's pliable, bloody scalp on that board, tacking it down in place as a battle trophy.

Though it was a struggle, a pair of the Pueblos finally dragged the heavy American out of the crowded hall and over to their leader. The others inched back to give Big Nigger room as the pair dropped the wounded white man onto his face at the Delaware's moccasins. Someone edged out of the crowd and grabbed Bent's ear, yanking on it to expose the fleshy neck. Such a pretty, white neck.

"We must cut the head off this American beast!" Big Nigger shouted at them in their Pueblo tongue. Some translated it into Spanish for the enraged Mexicans among them.

"With the head cut from it—a body will wither and die!" the Delaware exhorted them.

"You cut the head?" someone yelled.

They had blood in their eye, and the taste of it already sweet on their tongues. Their knives were ready. He could see they would mutilate this American beyond recognition within a matter of heartbeats . . . just as soon as he gave them permission.

"Yes! Cut it!" the crowd bellowed. "Cut the head from this beast!"

Handing the torch to one of the Mexicans, Big Nigger took a huge knife from the man. Then knelt and seized a handful of what stark, white hair remained at the back of Bent's neck. Pulling the head to the side, he gazed at the flabby white skin on the neck.

Bent's eyes fluttered. The lips moved slightly in the flickering torchlight.

But not one sound of protest came from them as the Delaware began to slice, inch by inch, all the way through the neck until the body dropped away and he was left holding the head at the end of his arm.

"Go! Find the others!" he shrieked at them, shaking the American's head at them, splattering blood and gore on those closest to the scene.

The first of the mob turned for the open doorway as he roared his commands one last time.

"No man. No woman. And no child," he growled like a beast with the scent of a kill strong in its nostrils. "Leave not one of them alive!"

32

◆

There was no doubt in Scratch's mind that his children weren't suffering much at all as they crouched among the piñon and sage at the bottom of this narrow cleft in the valley floor several miles north of San Fernandez de Taos. But he did worry about Josiah's offspring.

While Magpie, Flea, and even Jackrabbit had grown up enduring weather far, far colder than this—and knew how to keep themselves warm out in the open—Titus wasn't sure if Paddock's town-raised young'uns could last out a subfreezing night. If it indeed took them all this night to creep and stop, creep and stop, until they reached Simeon Turley's whiskey mill at Arroyo Hondo. Once they could reach the sanctuary of those stone buildings, Bass felt confident they could hold out until soldiers marched up from Santa Fe . . . or enough iron-forged mountain men came riding south from the Arkansas to drive back the brownskins who had let the wolf out to howl.

But there was little chance in hell of either, he realized as the hours dragged past. Slim chance of someone sneaking out of Taos to gallop south to reach the dragoons in the territorial capital. Even less of a chance that a lone man might brave those hundreds of miles of frozen winter wilderness between this Taos valley and those faraway American settlements on the Arkansas. And if by some miraculous turn of fate some brave soul managed to do the unthinkable, just how many Americans could he round up for the ride back to Taos? Nowhere near enough to even up the odds when it came down to wading into those hundreds of Pueblos and *pelados*.

But he didn't breathe a whisper of his doubts. Looks Far Woman and her children were relying on Josiah. And once more Paddock was relying on Bass. Scratch wasn't about to let any of them down by telling them the brutal truth. Part of protecting those he loved might well lie in protecting them from the truth.

"We been in worse fixes, Josiah," he whispered in the dark as they lay stretched out on their bellies, watching that long strip of horizon where the pale, icy-blue horizon met the black underbelly of the night sky.

Paddock's teeth chattered. They'd been moving and stopping for most of the night. Every time they heard a suspicious sound, or spotted something out of place, or even when some hunch Scratch felt made him wary—they had gone into hiding while the two fathers lay flat on the high prairie and scanned the country in all directions for enemies.

Earlier that afternoon, Titus had hurried Waits-by-the-Water back to the house, where they warned Looks Far and began making preparations to leave the village after dark. Young Joshua stayed behind at the store with his father to make everything appear as normal as they could. They planned to show up after the shop was closed at sunset. In the meantime, Looks Far kept her children busy by bringing in wood for the three fires and readying food they would need for the coming ordeal.

Waits helped all the children prepare some extra clothing for their journey into the snowy countryside once night had fallen. About the time Stephen Lee's wife, Maria, and their son, John, showed up, Scratch went out to see to the animals. Back in the small pasture behind the house, Scratch began to drive the Cheyenne horses toward the corral. Josiah's mules and horses followed the obedient and steady Indian ponies into the pole corral. Titus quickly counted noses—and riders. There would be twelve of them needing a mount when they slipped out of Taos. Twelve horses, what with Flea riding with either his mother or father, and young John Lee riding double too. That meant that he needed to find the best three Paddock owned. No, four—three for riding, and a fourth for packing what they would need in the way of blankets, extra clothing, and food for what could be days in the foothills of the Sangre de Cristos at Turley's Arroyo Hondo.

It would be days, and long nights too, holing up at Turley's mill before any force strong enough arrived to put down the rebellion and bring peace to this sleepy Mexican town. There he went again—thinking of Taos as a Mexican town. It was American now . . . and that heartless, cowardly mob out to kill American women and children were little more than outlaws deserving of nothing so good as a quick death.

The sky still had a faint glow to it when Josiah brought his eldest home from the square. Everyone found a place in the parlor where the women served their supper of beans mixed with peppers, some boiled mutton, and large chunks of rich, black bread.

"Eat your fill, children," Josiah reminded them, one and all. "Gonna be some time before we have our next hot meal."

Time and again the two men stepped outside together, walking to the corral where Titus had put a bridle or halter on every one of the horses and that mule he chose to carry their supplies. When the moment to escape arrived, all he, Josiah, and young Joshua had to do was to throw the thick *tirutas*, the very best wool saddle blankets woven of Navajo wool, and saddles on the animals' backs.

"Good chance it'll never make a difference," Titus had explained there in the darkness while the horses grew restless in their pole corral. "But you're American—we're American. Maybeso some of the bastards are keeping an eye on this place, laying plans to jump us. So I didn't want them niggers to see we had our horses saddled and ready to ride."

Josiah had squeezed Bass's arm in a sign of appreciation from long ago. "That's just the sort of thinking has kept the rest of your hair locked on your thick skull, ol' man. All these years I been down here . . . they made me less than watchful. I ain't near so careful as I used to be when I was riding with you."

When slap-dark finally arrived and the sky turned utterly black but for a dusting of stars, they decided the time had come.

"We gotta be miles from here afore moonrise," Bass reminded them as he stepped inside the warm kitchen. "Magpie, you help your mother," he instructed her in English. "Bank all the fires good and hot. Lots of smoke from all three. Now scoot."

Then he stood at the rear door with Josiah as Paddock buckled the wide belt around his wool coat and stuffed the two pistols at his waist.

"I'm going to point 'em off due north," Titus reminded his old partner. He pointed up high at the bright stars in the Seven Sisters. "I'll have every one ride for the North Star, Josiah. You'll be waiting under that North Star for 'em."

Paddock nodded grimly as Looks Far came up with his old Henry mountain rifle and shooting pouch. Josiah looped the strap over his shoulder, then took the long, fullstock flintlock in his mittens. After running his hand down the dark, curly-maple wood, Josiah looked up at Bass.

"I remember when we got this for me."

"Pierre's Hole," Bass replied.

"It's been so damn long," Paddock sighed. "I hope I remember how to shoot it."

"I'm praying you won't have to, Josiah," Bass declared. "But if you do—I ain't got a doubt that it'li all come back to you real quick."

Josiah bent to kiss and embrace his wife. Then he was out the door and into the darkness. Scratch listened to the quiet of that winter night as the horse's hooves faded on the hard, icy snow blanket. Then saddling another horse, he returned to the house and walked the first of the children into the corral, to see them mounted and on their way. Josiah's oldest girl would be the first to follow her father.

"Naomi," he whispered after he had hoisted the eleven-year-old into the saddle. "You ride good?"

"Yes, Mr. Bass."

"That's a good girl," he said quietly. Then pointed into the sky. "You see them seven stars?"

"The Big Dipper?"

"Yes. You see that bright one?"

"The North Star—yes. It's so dark tonight, I see it real good."

"Ride for it, Naomi. Don't stop for nothing. Your father's out there underneath that star, waiting to gather you all up again."

"Yes, sir." And she tightened her wool mittens around the reins.

"And Naomi—if'n you spot more'n one rider comin' in your direction, it ain't your father."

"Sir?"

"You see two or more horsemen comin' at you, I want you to kick the devil out of this Injun pony, you understand?"

"K-kick him?"

"You damn betcha. You just holler at him an' keep kicking him till he's running with you for that North Star."

"Y-y-yes, sir."

"And, girl"—he felt his throat clogging—"if you gotta run away from some of those folks mean to harm you—don't you dare let this horse slow down for nothing till you reach your father."

She swallowed hard and bobbed her head in the starlit darkness. He blinked back some tears while he squeezed her wrist and said, "Now's the time, Naomi. Go find your father under the North Star."

One by one by one, he had seen them away. And one

at a time Josiah had found them out there in the darkness lit by nothing but those stars and hope's faint light. The three women rode out near the end, each mother holding her youngest behind her like a fat tick clinging to a cow in the season of the rut. Then Joshua followed them.

As Bass waited, counting out the minutes, he stoked the three fireplaces one last time, banking the wood to assure a long burn. He lit candles and two more lamps. All the more reason the cowardly niggers would think the house was still occupied. Then it was time to bring the pack mule out of the low shed, saddle up his horse, and head into the night.

That trip to the end of the Seven Sisters felt as if it took forever. Longer than any night's ride he could remember.

"They all get here?" he asked as Josiah and Joshua appeared out of the dark more than an hour later.

"Yes. All come in fine," Paddock said with relief. "I was getting worried about you. Figured when you took so long getting here, that they'd awready come to the house. So, me and Joshua—we was fixing to come back and help."

"Damn you, Josiah Paddock!" he growled as they reached the other horses and the people on foot among the brush. "Don't you ever come back for me."

"But, I figured—"

"You get yourself and this fine boy both killed . . . what happens to our women, to their young'uns?" he demanded sharply. "What the hell then, Josiah?"

Only by nudging his horse up close could he see the shame written on Paddock's face. Scratch sensed a sudden stab of regret. He squeezed down on Josiah's wrist. "Ol' friend, didn't mean to bite down so hard on you. I should've remembered it's been a long time since you've had to reckon on looking after such things as this."

Paddock's eyes glistened. "I'm glad you're here to do the thinking for both of us."

"C'mon, Joshua," Titus said as he turned to the youngster, "the three of us gotta hide these women and

young'uns while your father an' me go have us a look at
our back trail."

"How many of 'em are there?" Paddock whispered.

Bass squinted, not sure. What with the darkness, the
way those hissing torches flickered in the cold wind,
spewing and spitting with each rising gust, their dancing
light reflecting off the wind-crusted snow to create those
weaving, bobbing shadows as the mob marched across
the frozen prairie on foot . . . he could only guess how
many were in that brazen, gutless mob.

"More'n a hundred," he sighed with futility. "Hundred twenty. Maybe even more."

He heard the air go out of Josiah beside him on the
prairie. Scratch rolled onto his hip and gazed at the sky
there above the mountaintops to gauge how long they
had before sunup.

Paddock whispered, "I was counting on us reaching
Turley's."

Titus nodded without taking his eyes off the distant
flicker of torchlight as the mob neared the far reaches of
Arroyo Hondo where Simeon Turley operated his mill
and made a powerful whiskey. "I know. We could've
held up there till help come."

"Simeon's always got folks there who could've
helped," Josiah explained, desperation creeping into his
voice. "Hired men, sometimes fellas pushing through."

Even in the dark it was plain to see a few dark figures
emerge from Turley's tall two-story stone building to hurriedly pull their horses and mules inside the structure.

Titus whispered, "Likely whoever's down there heard
the niggers comin' too."

"How we gonna get our people in there before that
mob starts their attack?"

Bass looked at Paddock a moment, then confessed,
"We ain't, Josiah. Those fellas down there with Turley
right now, no matter how many there are of 'em—they
ain't got a chance again' all them Injuns and Mex *pelados*. If'n we was in there right now—an' I knowed how

many was comin'—I'd be finding a way for our women and children to get the hell out."

"You figger those men are doomed?"

"Good as," Scratch answered, watching the front rank of torches start off the prairie, slithering like a many-scaled snake down the narrow, slanting road that took a horseman into the arroyo. But these weren't horsemen. They were rabble, a mob come on foot. Which meant Bass maintained a small advantage in moving his people all the faster on horseback. Especially over the next hour or two while the murdering niggers were consumed with destroying Turley's mill and butchering the men inside. Now was the time to flee.

"North, Josiah."

"You know how hard it is to walk away from fellas who are my friends?" Paddock asked.

"We don't go now, find us a place to hide out up in the foothills at the north end of the valley . . . then you won't be doing what's right by your family."

"All right," Josiah relented with a heavy sound to it as he shoved himself back from the icy edge of the arroyo.

The first gunfire reverberated off the rocks on the far side of the ravine. Screams and oaths immediately erupted from the mob as they scattered and took cover. Some of the Pueblos and Mexicans returned fire on the stone house, lead balls splatting against the rocks.

"Those boys'll keep them niggers busy some," Bass grumbled as he rocked onto his knees, then stood. "Teach that bunch of *pelados* to keep their heads down too."

"Thought you said Turley and the rest didn't stand a chance. You change your mind?"

Titus said glumly, "No. Only a matter of time afore more'n a hundred of the brownskins overrun 'em."

It had been eight days of hiding, more than a week filled with constant fear that they would be discovered. One thing for a man to be on the run himself; something entirely different when that man had women and little ones to protect.

In the dark of that first night they had struck north along the east bank of the Rio Grande del Norte. At the third small stream cutting its way out of the Sangre de Cristo range, he and Titus turned them east, into the foothills where they could find more vegetation, which meant more cover come sunup, and maybe the chance of game when their food ran out.

Back then Josiah Paddock didn't know how long they were going to have to hold on. At least the weather moderated. No snow since that night before the rebellion. By the afternoon of their first day in hiding, Scratch was clearly growing about as tight as a rawhide bowstring while the hours dragged by.

"I ain't gonna make it hiding out like this," Bass said in a whisper when he and Josiah had moved off from the families.

"You got a better idea where we can go?"

"No," Titus said. "So I was thinking: I'll go for help alone."

He asked the old trapper, "You figure me to watch over the rest?"

"The women need you, sure as hell the children need you too," Scratch explained. "No sense in two of us getting ourselves killed if the bastards are out there."

If the years they spent together had taught Josiah anything, it was that he wasn't going to talk Titus Bass out of something once the man put his mind to it. Resolved to staying behind, Paddock said, "Where you heading?"

"North," Bass replied. "Ride for the Arkansas."

"Settlements there?"

"See how many men I can bring back." Then he sighed. "Won't be anywhere near enough to fight them niggers. But maybe we can figger out a way to get back at 'em for the killing they've done till the army comes up from Santy Fee."

"We'll make sure you got food for the trip."

"No," and Bass shook his head. "Leave the food for the young'uns. I'll make do on my own." Then he gazed into Josiah's eyes steadily. "Let's use what light we got left to make our people comfortable as can be back in those rocks, Josiah. I'll be off come dark."

For the next seven days Josiah took his son Joshua out to search for game trails, keeping their eyes open for the movement of men. Second morning into their ordeal, they spotted two columns of black smoke far, far to the south along the endless white horizon. But they heard nothing, saw nothing up at this end of the valley, so could only believe that the rebels were mopping up ranchos south of Taos instead of marching north toward the Arkansas—that longtime boundary with the United States.

Time to time, Josiah brooded on how long they were going to have to endure the wilderness like this. Moving camp a mile or more each day, collecting wood, bringing water in, seeing to everyone's needs in addition to hunting while their town food slowly gave out.

You've done this before, he reminded himself. Time was, Titus Bass taught you to be pretty damned good at it too.

Still, he wished the old trapper hadn't gone. It was one thing to have Scratch there to lean on out here with the waiting and the wilderness. It was something altogether different to have no one but himself to rely upon.

"This the way you used to live, Pa?" Joshua asked one afternoon as they sat watching a band of two dozen horsemen riding north up the valley past the rocks where the two of them hid themselves.

"For a time, yes."

"When I was young?"

He gazed at his son. "When you were a baby, Joshua." Then Paddock stared at those disappearing horsemen again. "Till I figured out I didn't want to tempt fate any longer. Not fair of me to put your mother and you in danger any longer."

"So that's why we come to Taos?"

"Like your mother's told you children: We was already down here for a visit. So you might just say we *stayed* in Taos."

It was some time before Joshua spoke again, his throat

raspy and raw with the cold, high, dry air. "Pa, you ever regret not going with Mr. Bass when he rode off?"

"Someone had to stay with all you children and the women—"

"No, Pa," Joshua interrupted. "When Mr. Bass left you behind in Taos. You ever regret not going with him?"

He gazed into his boy's eyes and knew he could not speak anything but the complete truth. "There were times I missed him, missed the wandering, missed all the not caring. At times my missing that life got so bad it was like a cold stone lay in my belly . . . sometimes I wanted to be with him so bad it brought tears to my eyes, Joshua."

"But you stayed." And Joshua laid his head against his father's shoulder.

"Yes," Paddock finally admitted, his throat sour with sentiment. "I stayed for your mother—so she'd never have to fear for her life again. And I stayed for you, hoping you'd have a chance to grow up to grab what you wanted from life. Stayed for the rest of your brothers and sisters too as the years went by."

Joshua asked, "Sometimes a man makes the decisions he does for the people he loves?"

"Not just sometimes, Joshua," he replied quietly. "All through his days."

"I love you, Pa."

Josiah laid the rifle down against his bent knee and wrapped a second arm around his eldest. "I love you too, son."

That band of cutthroats they had spotted had to be heading north to hit the Ponil and Vermijo ranches that belonged to Bent, St. Vrain & Company, Paddock figured later that night when he sat crouched by their small fire. Gone to run off all the stock. Maybe even run over to attack the little settlement on Rio Colorado. Every now and then a few Americans took up winter residence there. The Mexican and Pueblo rebels ride through there, the trappers would be hash in no time.

By the seventh day, Paddock could read the worry graying the face of Waits-by-the-Water. After dark that night Josiah squatted next to her by the fire as she cradled a sleeping Jackrabbit in her lap.

"He'll be back," Paddock told her quietly, hoping he wouldn't disturb the others, who were asleep in their blankets.

"If Grandfather Above . . . he let Ti-tuzz," she struggled with the English words, "yes—he come back to us."

"We just have to wait," Josiah tried his best to soothe.

"Yes. Ti-tuzz come back. He promise."

Josiah wasn't sure, but from the look in her eyes, Waits was concealing some deep pain, something more than just the worry, the longing to have him back.

After some moments, he assured her, "What that ol' man says he'll do, you can believe he'll do it."

The next two days in hiding crawled past. Then Josiah spotted more black figures snaking across the snow at the north end of the valley.

"I see them, Father," Joshua breathed beside him. "Raiders?"

"Probably the same bunch we saw riding off up north to hit those ranchos," he growled.

They watched as the dark forms slowly drew closer and closer. From the way the horsemen rode with no formation to their march, Josiah was even more certain these were Mexican and Pueblo raiders returning to Taos from their hit-and-run attacks. But something nagged at him because the group looked smaller, less formidable, than it had when the raiders passed by three days earlier. The closer those horsemen got to his perch, the more Josiah thought the raiders were a ragged, motley bunch.

Of a sudden, something pricked his distant memories about one of those horsemen who rode at the vanguard of the group. The way the man sat a horse, maybe the appearance of that coat he wore, and the fur cap upon his head. Altogether, they caused a tug at a distant, but indelible, memory.

"I ain't for certain, Joshua," he said quietly, not even daring his own heart to leap with hope, "but I think Mr. Bass has come back to us."

33

◆

Sure he promised her he'd never again go anywhere without her and the children . . . but this was a horse of an entirely different color—a situation reeking with far too much danger to even entertain any thoughts of taking them along with him. There was no question that he could travel faster, with far less sleep, and not have to concern himself near so much with food, if he didn't have his family along.

Those first miles, those first hours, all through the first three days, Scratch was constantly reminding himself how good a thing it was that he had gone for help alone. Easier to cross a snowy country barren of much timber and cover when he was by himself. To take along a whole cavvyard of folks and animals could only draw the wrong sort of attention. Not only those rebel Mex and their Pueblo henchmen, but Cheyenne or Comanche hunters too. If some warriors caught him out on his own, chances were Scratch could make a good run for it, or stand off a small hunting party by his lonesome. But, with a woman and young'uns along . . . it just made all the calculations real messy.

In those first hours of darkness after he tore himself away from Waits-by-the-Water, Titus kept dwelling on the expression on of her face as he did his best to explain why he was leaving without her after he had given her his vow. It made him feel all the worse that she hadn't ranted and stomped in anger. When she accepted his decision, taking his measure with those red-rimmed eyes he feared were ready to pool, it made him feel downright hollow and guilty.

"This ain't like the horse stealing in California," he tried his best to make her understand as twilight's cloak sank in around them. "Back then, you didn't know where I was going."

"This is different?"

"Different, yes. Now you know where I'm going and why."

"Doesn't make being apart from you any easier."

He had sighed, "Just remember I'm doing it for you and the children. And for those wives and mothers and children who got butchered back there in Taos."

"We could make it with you," she whispered so the children would not hear her plea. "Better than waiting for these enemies to find us in the foothills. Better to keep moving than to die here."

"It is dangerous everywhere," he had argued, pulling her against him. "But far more danger waits out there on this journey north. I simply don't know where the enemy is, how far they've roamed, or if they are searching for anyone who might've fled the valley."

"I will wait," she sighed against his chest in resignation. "Again."

Kissing the top of her head, Bass whispered, "This time, don't mourn me before you know I'm dead."

He nudged her chin up with a finger, gazing into her eyes. She reluctantly smiled.

"No, I won't cut my hair, or scar my flesh, this time if you are late."

He promised her, "This time . . . I won't be late."

No matter what became of his ride to the Pueblo on the Arkansas, or even downriver to that mud-walled fortress at the mouth of the Picketwire, he vowed he wouldn't make any of them wait very long there in the shadow of the Sangre de Cristos.

That first night his horse made good time beneath the guiding stars. For many of those early hours, he kept his mind busy trying to sort out how far it was to the river, to where Americans clustered at the edge of what had been Mexican territory—before the army came and claimed it for the United States, before that army left again and Mexican feelings grew raw and angry at their new overseers. Had to be more than a hundred miles, easily. Probably closer to one hundred fifty.

But, he told himself too, they had already covered a little distance out of Taos. Every little bit he put behind him was that much less he had to endure.

Because of where he found himself at dawn the first morning, Scratch led his horse into the foothills. The going was rougher, a lot slower to be sure, but up on the slopes he could keep on moving instead of hiding out the day as a man would have to down below on the valley floor. Across the hillsides there was simply more cover. And he had a better view of things for miles around too. If he kept his eyes moving, and stopped to let the horse blow every now and again, he could keep on moving and not be forced to wait out the brief hours of daylight. He had to keep going. Everyone he loved was counting on him to get through.

Hour by hour, the journey began to take its toll: his horse began to grow weary. Already the snow lay deep on the western slopes of the Sangre de Cristos, and it continued to snow from time to time throughout that second day and into that second night. Then late in the morning of the third day, not long after he had rested the horse near a narrow stream fed by a small spring, the bone-weary horse stumbled, pitching him free as it went hind flanks over withers.

Landing hard on the icy snow and skidding among the sage, he had the air knocked out of his lungs. Bass lay there in the cold several moments, waiting for the sparks of bright, hot light to clear from his eyes. Slowly he sat up and brushed the snow from his hair, off the side of his face—so shockingly cold on his bare skin. Titus rolled off his aching hip and started crabbing toward his rifle and the fur cap—

Then froze on all fours, watching the horse scramble up from the sage and stunted piñon. Onto three legs, the fourth dangling like a marionette's limb. Clearly broken just below the joint, flopping as the horse righted itself, then shuddered in pain.

He angrily swept up the cap and jammed it down on his head, his gut already churning as he cursed his damnable luck. Then Titus scolded himself for that stupid selfishness as he read the fear, the outright pain, evident in the horse's eyes. Good, steady Cheyenne pony. Not some young, wild thing. Not any green Mexican horse. Instead, an animal bred for these mountains and high plains . . .

And it had carried him this far. As far as it was going to take him.

For what felt like a long time, he stood there with his arm wrapped under the pony's neck, patting its strong muscles that frequently quaked with shudders of pain. He whispered to it softly, words strung together with little meaning, nothing more than their soothing sound as his eyes warily raked the valley below them. Bass found nothing moving but some antelope and a few whitetail deer.

He scanned the snowy slopes above him, and hoped the gunshot would not carry. It would be better to use his knife . . . but that way only seemed to prolong the agony. This animal deserved better. It had carried him north from the land of the Arkansas and the Cheyenne, crossed and recrossed the land of the Crow in the intervening years—hunting, trapping, and always migrating. This pony deserved to die quickly, deserved to be put down with mercy.

It took only a matter of minutes to untie the buffalo robe and his few fixings from behind the saddle, dropping them onto a patch of scrub piñon so they rested out of the snow. After pulling the pistol from his belt, Scratch had to use his pan brush to clean out the dusting of icy flakes clotted around the pan and frizzen before he recharged the pan with powder. Then stepped back over to the wide-eyed pony, patted its neck one last time.

"Thank you," he whispered as he set the broad muzzle of the .54-caliber pistol just below the ear and pulled the trigger before he gave himself any more time to think about what he was doing.

Shuddering violently, the animal weaved for a flicker of a moment, then collapsed heavily to the ground.

"Thank you," he repeated as he turned away from the head, quickly reloaded, then stuffed the pistol in his belt.

Over his shoulder he laid the wide, rawhide strap that was lashed around both ends of the roll of buffalo robe. Then picked up the long rifle. And continued north. On foot.

Folks were counting on him to see this through.

There were many times in those first hours after leaving the Cheyenne pony's carcass that he regretted not carving some meat from one of its lean haunches. He had survived on horsemeat before. Wasn't near so bad, a man got hungry enough.

With every step as he waded through snow that billowed around his knees—placing each moccasin ahead of him, then sinking forward until the foot contacted the ground, dragging the trailing foot out of the deep snow, across the icy crust, to plunge it ahead—step after step, he doggedly marched north. And with every hour, every mile, every exhausting breath, he used up more and more of his slim reserves of energy.

Oh, there were times he believed he could not take another step—when he gave himself a chance to blow, resting against a large clump of scrub pine, squatting there as he chewed on his dried meat, licking at the snow to wash it down before he forced himself to get back onto his feet and continue on. One time he awakened, scared to death because he hadn't remembered falling asleep. Confused and disoriented as he blinked at the dim globe of the sun half hidden behind a thick streamer of clouds . . . desperately trying to remember where the sun had been when he stopped for a few bites of stringy meat.

Try as he did, Titus couldn't remember.

He felt the tears of frustration start to well up in his eyes as he shoved himself back onto his feet. And he pressed on, more determined than ever that he could cover as much ground on two legs as the pony could on four. Determined that he could do this without sleep. He had done it before when he was younger, back in those days when he and McAfferty slipped through the gauntlet of Apache country without much sleep. He had done it before. Bass told himself he could do it again.

When the young doe crossed his path the next afternoon, stopping suddenly no more than thirty yards ahead, Scratch did not resist. He brought her down with a quick snap shot, then lunged across the snowy terrain to watch that one big brown eye start to glaze as he laid his rifle across her flanks, wrenched out his knife, and made that first long incision from throat to pelvis. The warm, steamy entrails spilled out upon the blood-tinged snow.

Tearing his blanket mittens from his hands, Titus stuffed his cold, rigid fingers into the warmth of that pile of steaming guts, held his face close to the entrails, letting his stiff, rawhided face sense the blessed caress of the dead animal's last warmth. When he opened his eyes again, he shoved back the sleeves on his capote and buckskin shirt, then dug for the liver. He cut it loose, dragged it out, slippery and steamy, cradling it a moment in both trembling, blood-soaked hands as he considered its meaning to him. Then Titus ravenously sank his teeth into its juicy heat.

One bite, then a second, and a third he tore from the raw meat—then suddenly turned his head aside as his cramped, revolted stomach violently flung itself upward, rejecting the hot, raw, bloody meat after being empty of most everything for much of the past two days. Dumbly, he stared down at the hot, yellow-tinged bloody flesh he had vomited into the snow.

Maybe he could take the liver along . . . oh, how he

didn't want to abandon the meat. Ounce for ounce, in his weakened condition, the liver was the one part of the doe that would offer him the most energy. Yes, he could wrap it up in a small skin bag, eat it raw, suck its juices and blood, sometime later after his stomach had grown reaccustomed to food.

After swabbing some cold snow across his face and beard, greedily licking and sucking the blood-tinged flakes from his fingers, Scratch dragged the skinning knife back and forth, peeling the hide away from a rear haunch. When enough of the red, raw meat was exposed, he stabbed the tip of the knife into the thick muscles and carved himself out a double handful of warm flesh.

With it laid atop the pile of gut, he went back to peeling more of the green elastic hide from the muscle. When he had a patch big enough, Titus trimmed it free and stretched it on the ground. Then he cut an inch-wide, three-foot-long strip of green hide. Laying both the liver and the haunch roast in the middle of his crude square of hide, he gathered up the edges and lashed it closed with the strip. This he tied securely to his buffalo robe.

But before he stood again, he cut himself a long, thin strip of meat from that sundered haunch. Finally back on his feet, with his load settled across his shoulders and the rifle back in hand, Titus brought the raw, lean meat to his mouth and began to suck. Slowly at first, aiming to let his stomach grow accustomed to the warm blood and juices.

Assured his belly wouldn't revolt, he stumbled away from the carcass and pushed on.

Just past sunrise the next morning he smelled woodsmoke on the wind. From the top of a knoll where he bellied to the skyline, Titus spotted the tiny cluster of mud-and-wattle huts, a collection of dogs and outdoor ovens in the crude shape of mud beehives—and realized it had to be a Mexican settlement. From the adobe chimneys rose thin streamers of breakfast fires. How taunting, how seductive, that alluring fragrance of woodsmoke.

Would these people know of what had happened down in Taos? Were any of these *pelados* in revolt against the Americans too?

He argued with himself, wanting to shout down his empty, protesting belly, telling it to stop arguing with him . . . then finally scooted back away from the skyline and plodded down the backside of the slope. Titus lumbered miles out of his way, staying behind a low range of hills, avoiding that tiny settlement* and its Mexican inhabitants.

That day had dawned clear and cloudless, cruelly bright as the light bounced off the snow. He stopped to drag his mittens off while he caught his breath. Then poured a little powder from his horn into his left palm. He spit into the powder and mixed it up with a fingertip, swabbing that finger in a crude crescent below his right eye. He washed off the black goo in the snow, pulled the mittens over his hands, and pushed on.

But by midday the intensity of the sun had grown so cruel as its light reflected off the seamless, pristine white landscape that the powder painted beneath his eye was no longer effective. Dropping his buffalo robe to the snow, leaning his rifle across its bulk, he settled onto his haunches and dug into his wool possibles pouch, sewn from pieces of an old white blanket. While his leather shooting pouch hung at his right side, this second bag hung at his left, where it contained a second fire-starting set, extra tools and strips of rawhide whang, an extra bullet mold, and some cast balls. As well as two spare bandannas. Black and silk, and huge, he had bartered them off St. Louis traders summers long ago when supplies were still hauled out to rendezvous on the Wind, the Popo Agie, and the Green.

For a long time he stared down at the bandanna he pulled out of the pouch, feeling its texture with his fingers. Silk. *Damn worm makes silk that put us beaver men out of work. Drove us out of a life.*

Finally he dragged out his skinning knife and picked a few stray deer hair from the guard where they were

---

* The short-lived Greenhorn settlement, on Greenhorn Creek in present-day Colorado.

frozen in a thin layer of frozen, crusty blood. Scraping them off with his fingernail, Titus next cut the bandanna in half, diagonally, from one corner to another, and stuffed the section he didn't need back in his possibles pouch. Then he trimmed off a four-inch-wide strip at the widest part of the bandanna and put the small, remaining triangle of black cloth into the pouch, securing the wide flap with its huge button made from the rosette found at the base of an elk antler.

He brought the long ends of the strip together, found the middle, then laid it across his knee. Measuring out the width of two fingers from that middle, he stabbed a crude slit some three inches long. Four finger widths from the end of that slit, he started to cut another slit—then he remembered it didn't matter. It had been many years since he needed a slit for his left eye. Titus trimmed the cloth away so that he had one narrow gap no more than a half-inch wide.

Resting his knife atop his thigh, Scratch held the bandanna up to his eyes and positioned it. Looking left, then right. Ought to work fine. Quickly stuffing his knife back into its scabbard, Titus dragged off the coyote cap, then tied the long ends of the mask at the back of his head, knotting it atop the knot holding the bandanna around his entire skull, covering that patch of bare bone. He shifted the mask, stretching the silk cloth over his brow, satisfied he could see well enough through the narrow slit, then pulled his coyote cap back onto his head.

Standing, he gazed out onto the brilliant expanse of white wilderness and spotted the far range of hills. Even with the brilliant glare, his heart leaped because he knew those hills. At their foot he would find the Pueblo. Friends. Americans. Old comrades and compatriots who would rally their forces and ride back south to retake Taos from the butchers and murderers and fiends who had made war on not just government officials and soldiers—but on private citizens . . . on helpless women and children too.

Friends were gathered there inside the Pueblo on the Arkansas.

As the sun sank, the pain in his eye gradually lessened. He stopped to blow and pull the mask down from his eyes. It only took a man one time to suffer from snowblindness to teach him that he would do just about anything so he'd never suffer the pain and helplessness again. Like gritty, liquid sand trapped beneath the eyelid—grains that would not wash away with all the tears his burning, inflamed eyes produced. Damned slow to heal too. Days it took.

But he had managed to prevent it that day, first with the powder goo, and then with the sun mask. He had made it through that cloudless, sunny day without growing blind—forced to wait out more days before he could see well enough to move on.

With the black scarf hung around his neck, Scratch had trudged on into the waning of the light. Hopeful at first, it was long after twilight when he accepted that there wasn't much chance for a moonrise that would shed enough light to brighten his way across the uneven ground.

With every dozen steps, a feeling grew inside him that he should have already reached the Arkansas. Time and again, Bass halted to catch his wind, staring with that one good eye to the west. Hoping to discern some blackened landmark rising against the pale evening sky.

He stumbled on beneath a bright dusting of stars that nonetheless failed to shed any of their light on the snowy land he crossed. At times he stopped and scooped up a handful of snow to give his parched mouth a little moisture. Dry and harsh was every breath of air in this high, arid country.

He was gasping when he imagined he heard a dog bark. Then a second dog answered that first with its own low, throaty warning.

The hair at the back of his neck bristled. Could be an Indian camp. Cheyenne or Arapaho down here in this country, he warned himself.

But at the brow of the next rise he stopped and stared, thinking he could make out the neatly organized rows of some dingy gray wall tents, interspersed with a few darker huts partially constructed from logs at the bottom of the slope. He could smell woodsmoke now. And hear dogs raising a clatter.

This wasn't any Indian camp. That much was for sure. Maybe he'd stumbled onto the army's winter quarters up here near the Arkansas. Some of the soldiers Kearny had left behind to protect the nearby settlements at Bents Fort and the Pueblo.

Running onto these dragoons would be so much the better.

He reached the first of the tents before a dog slinked up to growl, daring to get close enough to sniff this strange creature that skulked out of the darkness. Swinging the rifle, he laid the narrow butt alongside the dog's head with a resounding crack. It whimpered and bellied off with a pitiful whine, its tail tucked between its legs.

"Who goes there?" a voice suddenly called out from the darkness.

"Y-you a s-soldier?" Bass stammered with a dry tongue and an unused voice box.

A form loomed out of the night, taking shape from behind one of the tents. There were rustles of other movement farther behind the man.

"Soldier?" the man said as he inched closer. "I ain't no soldier, mister. S'pose you tell me who you are?"

"You're American, ain'cha?" Titus asked. "You t-talk like American."

The man snorted as a dozen others hurried up to join him, each of them carrying some sort of firearm. " 'Course we're American. What the devil are you?"

"I w-was . . . American," he admitted. "Of a time . . . long, long ago. Born back to Kentucky. Seems so far away now. So many years too . . . years since I was American."

The thirteen of them had him all but surrounded now, jostling close, shoulder to shoulder, as each of the strangers strained to make him out in the dimmest of light thrown off by those stars overhead.

"Where you come walking in from?" one of them asked.

"Taos. South. There's been bad trouble," he rasped. "Americans killed. Injuns and Mex greasers. Been killing Americans."

"Taos—that's more'n hundred fifty miles off!" another voice exclaimed.

"I come for help," he admitted. "Was making for the Pueblo. Got friends there can help me. Don't know how I got off my track and run across your camp."

"The Pueblo?" the first, familiar, voice echoed. "You just missed it, off over there. We ain't camped far from the Pueblo."

"Gloree," he sighed as his breath came easier. "Thort at first I was in a army camp. Dragoons come to take Mexico away from the Mexicans."

"Army? No, we ain't nothin' but the army of God," a new voice spoke up as some of the other men parted for the newcomer.

"Army of G-God?" he repeated, baffled completely.

"We're the Saints," someone declared. "Church of Jesus Christ of Latter-Day Saints."

"S-saints?" he repeated in a whisper, his head almost dizzy with confusion.

Weakened, thirsty, hungrier than he had been in many a winter . . . Bass almost doubted he was still standing.

Saints?

Oh, sweet Jehoshaphat! Was this how it was to die?

Maybeso he was really lying half dead and delirious, out of his mind, somewhere on that journey north! Maybe this was part of the horrible dream that came with dying.

Saints, they came and helped a man get done with the living.

Maybe he was so close to death that he just dreamed this cluttered collection of tents and log huts, these dogs barking and this group of Americans. Maybe all his weary, hungry brain could do was to paint this strange, foreign picture while he was passing through the frightening veil into death.

Saints?

"That's right. Saints," another voice affirmed. "Some folks call us Mormons—"

"This poor man doesn't need a theological lesson now, Hyram," a new and unfamiliar voice boomed from the dark.

The crowd parted for the huge bulk of him as he stepped into the breech.

"Said he was looking for the Pueblo," one of those closest explained. "Says he's got friends over there."

"You've got friends here too," the big man assured. "And we'll see you get yourself over to the Pueblo." He turned his bulk toward the others in that dark starshine and bellowed, "Oran, go fetch your springless wagon and hitch up a team. I want you to carry this stranger to his people at the Pueblo."

Dumbfounded, Bass stood there staring, still not sure this was real, that he was on the Arkansas, that the Pueblo was even close at hand.

Then the wide, pan-faced man with the shovel jaw turned back to Titus and studied him up and down intently before he said, "It's now up to the might of our hands that we'll see this man helped upon his way . . . for it was by the grace of God alone that this stranger has stumbled out of the wilderness and into our hands . . . alive."

34

◆————————

Looking back on his life, many were the times when Scratch knew there was no other reason for him shinnying out of danger by the skin of his teeth but for the mighty hand of something larger than himself. With his delivery from the winter wilderness, he couldn't help but think that he was being told something.

Now the hard part would be trying to find out just what he was being told.

At that dark, early-morning hour, men from that overland-bound camp of Mormons carried Titus Bass back to the Pueblo. With more dogs barking alarm, they banged on the open gate, throwing their voices into the empty *placita*, finally arousing the first of the post's inhabitants to appear at a darkened doorway.

"But they've got the army down there!" exclaimed Robert Fisher the moment the wagon driver announced he'd brought in a survivor who had stumbled in with news from Taos that the Mexicans and Indians were butchering all the Americans they could get their hands on.

"Has this man been drinking?" Fisher asked, refusing

to believe what few details the Mormons had already learned from the lips of the old mountain man.

Then the trader hobbled from the *placita*, a capote wrapped over his faded longhandles, hurrying to the wagon where he finally laid eyes on the messenger. And stared a moment.

"You 'member me, don't you, Fisher?"

Suddenly, the trader's face brightened with recognition. His face went gray with worry, knowing this was no drunken prank. "Met you years ago. You're Mathew's old friend."

"I . . . I come to tell of some turrible news—"

"Kinkead!" Fisher interrupted as he wheeled about and screamed through the open gate. "Kinkead! Manz! Get up, everyone! Get up!"

One last time the trader glanced at the old trapper as Scratch started scooting off the end of the springless wagon; then Fisher bolted away, shouting, "There ain't an American left alive in Taos!"

Within seconds the other traders, their wives and children, hangers-on and passers-through, were staggering into the darkened courtyard. Bleary-eyed and mumbling as they shared the shocking news brought by the men from Mormon Town, the crowd inched close as Mathew Kinkead lunged up to confirm what his trading partner had already learned from the man who had just appeared out of the winter wilderness.

"Josiah? His family?"

"They was safe in the hills when I left 'em few days back."

"What you figger we oughtta do, Scratch?"

Titus wagged his head, looking around at those worried faces in the dark, suddenly aware of just how fruitless his journey here might have been—

"Grab that Mexican!" a voice suddenly cried out.

There was a brief, fierce scuffle as traders and trappers and freeloaders scampered after a pair of Mexicans who were attempting to slink out the gate unnoticed. Both were immediately pitched to the ground and pummeled until Francisco Conn and Joseph Manz put a stop to the beating. Fisher and another man dragged a third Mexican out from behind a stack of firewood. All three stood shoulder to shoulder in their homespun *jerga,* pleading in Spanish to the Mexican wives of the Pueblo traders, cowering as the Americans argued in loud, strident voices over just what to do with their prisoners.

"Lock 'em in the fur hold," Kinkead ordered. "But first off see there ain't nothing in there for 'em to get their hands on. Them greasers can rot in there till we know what's become of Taos."

Men scattered this way and that, lamps were lit, and Americans returned with rope to tie up their prisoners, ankles and wrists, before they hobbled away with their handlers to the tiniest hovel in the Pueblo.

It wasn't long before Titus himself was under a roof, using a brass ladle to slurp water from an *olla,* a tall clay water jug, and watching as strips of last night's meat was laid on a plate before him. Meanwhile others rolled up their *colchónes,* those thin mattresses stuffed with hay, stacking them against the wall. Split wood was laid on the coals in the small trading room's open-faced oven, quickly driving the chill from the place while more and more men—traders, trappers, and Mormons too—crowded in hip to hip to hear the details of the bloody rebellion.

Mathew asked, "Beckwith's old partner?"

Scratch swallowed that bite of dried meat. "Sheriff Lee?"

Kinkead nodded. "He had a Mexican wife. A daughter, and a young son."

"We brung his wife out. The boy too," Scratch explained. Then he wagged his head. "Don't know about the daughter."

"She was married to an American," Mathew groaned.

"Lee didn't say nothin' 'bout her. Only asked us to get his wife and boy out."

George Simpson surmised, "Maybe they weren't in town when the trouble brewed."

"Lee join up with you and Paddock later on?" Kinkead asked.

" 'Less he got away north after I started for the Arkansas," Titus declared, "I don't figger he slipped outta Taos with his hair."

"Lee," one of the nameless men whispered the sheriff's name in the silence of that room filled only with the quiet sounds of breathing and the crackling fire.

"They've gotta pay," another man growled.

A new voice vowed defiantly, "We'll make 'em pay."

"There ain't 'nough of you to whip them niggers," Scratch grumbled, hauling them all up short.

"We gotta do something," Mathew said.

"What 'bout Turley?" Fisher asked.

Bass dug at his cheek whiskers with a dirty fingernail still crusted with a dark crescent of the doe's blood. "Last I saw of the Arroyo Hondo, the greasers and them Pueblo niggers was shootin' up his place. 'Less any of Turley's men got out right when they was jumped, I don't figger they stood a chance again' so many."

Joseph Manz moaned, "Turley too!"

One of the faces stabbed forward into the firelight as the stranger said, "Leastways, the governor hisself was down to Santa Fe. When he hears what they done to his half-breed young'uns, he'll be riding right out front of them dragoons!"

"That's right!" a new voice cheered. "Governor Bent will see ever' last one of them niggers hang for what they done!"

"Charles Bent was in Taos," Bass told them.

The crowded room fell to an awestruck hush.

"Ch-charlie Bent too?"

"Don't know for certain," Titus declared. "But that was the plan Sheriff Lee heard tell of. The greasers was waitin' till the governor was back in Taos afore they let the wolf out to howl."

The quiet was oppressive again, for the longest time. So quiet, Bass could hear one of the Mexicans calling out from the tiny fur room on the far side of the quadrangle, begging for his life, whimpering and sobbing, while one of the other prisoners cursed his cowardice.

"Someone's gotta ride down the river and tell William 'bout his brother," Kinkead said softly.

Pounding his fist on the table, surprising them all, Manz said, "Maybe there's enough fellas down there!"

"Damn right! They can meet us on the trail," Kinkead replied.

"None of you realize what you're goin' up against," Titus declared. "There ain't 'nough of you here, not near 'nough down there at the Picketwire. Shit!" he exploded with exasperation, slinging his arm to the side, sweeping the half-empty pewter plate from the table where it clattered into a corner by the adobe fireplace. Hushing them all.

Bass let his head collapse into his hands, miserable. "I never should've left 'em. Why in hell did I ever think comin' up here was gonna do any good?"

Kinkead had his arm across his old friend's shoulder. "I'm going, Scratch. My wife's got family down there. I owe it to her to find out what's happened."

"You'll get yourself kill't," Scratch said as he raised his head and looked around the room. "All of you. Go ride in there and that mob of angry niggers cut you into pieces with their farm tools."

Kinkead angrily seized the front of Bass's buckskin shirt in one fist. "What the hell you come to tell us this news of killing in Taos if we wasn't supposed to do nothing 'bout it?"

Bass locked his gnarled hand around Mathew's wrist and gently tugged it from his shirt. "Only thing you can do, is be down there—waitin'—when them soldiers come marching up from Santy Fee."

Kinkead spread his big bear paw of a hand on Titus's cheek, apologizing with his eyes for exploding. Scratch smiled, saying quietly, " 'S'all right, Mathew. I know just how you feel when you ain't sure how the hell to do right by your family. When you don't know which way to turn."

In the end, they decided to hurry down for the valley of the San Fernandez . . . where they'd wait in the hills for more of their number to ride down from Bents Fort.

All of these frontiersmen and traders vowed to keep watch south of the village for the expected approach of the army.

With a young courier bundled against the frightening temperatures and carrying a satchel of dried meat to sustain him on his way, word was dispatched to William Bent and Ceran St. Vrain downriver at their adobe fortress. Then efforts turned to preparing for their own march south into the land of the rebellion.

"The Mormons ain't coming," Fisher explained to those in the *placita* when he returned two hours later as the horses were being saddled. "Their leaders say they hardly have 'nough men left after the rest marched off to fight with Kearny in California."

"We'll do what we can with what we got," Kinkead vowed grimly.

At sunup they moved out for the valley of San Fernandez de Taos.

And by the late afternoon of the third day, halting only to rest the horses for a few of those darkest hours each night, that pitifully small posse from the Pueblo was within striking distance of the Mexican settlements, when Bass spotted two riders coming down the slope of the foothills. When one of the horsemen tore off his hat and began to wave it at the end of his arm, Scratch was no longer unsure.

"That Paddock?" asked Kinkead.

"An' I bet that's Joshua with 'im. The boy's growed into a fine lad."

Mathew reached over and clamped his mitten on Titus's forearm. "That means your family's safe, Scratch. They're all safe."

Bass turned to gaze at Kinkead. Knowing how Mathew had suffered through the loss of a wife. His own eyes began to brim so much he had to blink hot tears away to see clearly as those two distant horsemen kicked their animals into a lope, hooves spewing up high, cascading rooster tails of snow as they hurried down the slope toward the motley party of rescuers.

"I ain't never coming back to Mexico, Mathew,"

Scratch vowed, gazing beyond those two distant riders, searching the foothills where his family was hiding. "I ain't never setting a foot down here again."

Both of those mongrel Indian dogs yipped and howled at his return, jumping and leaping around the feet of his horse until Scratch finally vaulted out of the saddle and caught all three of his children in his arms at once.

Oh, how good they felt against him, especially the way little Flea placed his tiny hands on his father's cheeks and said in uncertain English, "I know you come back, Popo. I know you come."

That's when Scratch's eye climbed over the small child's head, finding his wife patiently waiting, wrapped in her blanket, tears streaming down her soot-smudged cheeks. He stood among his children, then lunged toward her, enfolding his wife in his arms. Both of them breathless at this reunion.

"I always knew I'd make it back to you," he declared in a whisper.

Her cheek against his neck, Waits-by-the-Water said, "I always knew you would make it back to me. But . . . the days and nights—they don't grow any easier without you here."

Around them now the trappers, frontiersmen, and traders from the Pueblo were dismounting noisily. That big bear, Mathew Kinkead, wrapped up the Paddock children two at a time in his fierce embrace before he came over to kneel in front of the three youngsters he did not know.

He said, "You must belong to Titus Bass."

"Ti-Tuzz, yes," Magpie repeated in her father's unfamiliar tongue.

As Scratch and Waits stepped up, Mathew ripped off his mitten and took the girl's small hand in his big paw, caressing it. "What is your name?"

She started to speak it in Crow, then stopped and said it in English.

"Magpie," Kinkead repeated. "That's a pretty name

for such a pretty young lady. Do you know you were born in my house?"*

"You are Mateo?" she asked haltingly, her eyes flicking to her parents.

"Yes. I am Mateo Kinkead."

"I am Magpie," she said again in English, with more certainty now. "Born in Mateo's lodge, in Ta-house."

Kinkead stood, resting a hand on Flea's shoulder. His eyes touched Bass's. A lone tear slipped from one eye. "I remember that night . . . a long time ago, Magpie. In a time and a Taos long, long ago."

Behind the hills far across the valley the sun was easing its way down on the hills with winter's aching quickness.

Titus turned and stepped over to Paddock, putting his arm around his old friend's shoulder. "You have 'nough meat here to feed all these new mouths tonight?"

"I think so," Josiah answered. "Joshua's become a pretty good shot over the last few days."

"Just like his pa," Titus said. "You give a lad a chance, and he'll show you the man he's made of, Josiah."

That night at their fire Scratch told again of his journey north on horseback and on foot until he stumbled onto Mormon Town in the dark and was delivered to the Pueblo. And once the youngest of the children were tucked away in their blankets and robes and fast asleep, the men gathered at a nearby fire, where they began to talk in low tones of just what the next days and weeks might bring.

"We waited this long," Josiah cheered those men who had marched down from the Arkansas. "We can wait till more help gets here from Bents Fort, and those soldiers come up from Santa Fe afore we make any moves to take on them butchers."

"Then we're gonna give back hurt for hurt," Mathew vowed.

Paddock turned to Titus, reaching out to slap a hand on the old trapper's knee. "There may not be much left of

---

One-Eyed Dream

our house when we get back to it—but you're welcome under our roof till spring gets here."

"Spring's a long, long ways off, Josiah," Scratch said, patting the back of Paddock's hand before he stood. "I'm laying my head down for to sleep now. Come morning, I'll be off hunting meat for the camp."

That next, short winter's day went all the more quickly with the men coming and going—a few daring to ride off to the south with Kinkead, while most spread out into the hills in search of game. Each time a hunter dropped a deer, he returned to camp, warming himself by the fire before he ventured out again to continue his hunt.

Having his family around him once more, lying beside his wife in the stillness of the night, Scratch knew . . . even before Paddock, Kinkead, and the others began making their plans for retaking Taos once the army arrived. Scratch knew.

"They should'a been up here by now," one of the men grumbled.

"Maybe them soldiers already have," Kinkead ventured. "And they found out there's more'n they can fight by themselves."

Bass nodded. "You 'member what we saw at Turley's, Josiah?"

"I do."

Scratch looked at a few of those around the fire. "That mob of angry niggers outnumbered this bunch by more'n ten to one—"

"With our guns, each of us is worth more'n ten of them greasers any day!" one of the Pueblo men interrupted sharply.

Leaning toward the man, Titus said, "But Paddock will tell you same as me: That big mob we see'd at Turley's was only part of 'em. Josiah, tell these fellas how many of them Injuns live in the Pueblo."

"Likely there's more than a thousand," Paddock confirmed dolefully. "But there's no real telling. No one in Taos ever counted. Could be a lot more."

"An' ever' one's got his blood up because they've had it easy so far, tearin' Americans apart, piece by piece,"

Titus warned as he noticed Waits-by-the-Water sliding down inside their robes at a fire nearby. "You ain't takin' Taos back easy. Not even if Savary brings down a hull shitteree of riflemen from his fort to join up with all of them dragoons coming up from Santa Fe."

"We can do it, Scratch," Josiah prodded.

Titus stood, hankering for bed and a stretch of uninterrupted sleep . . . ready for it all to be behind him. "Maybe you can, Josiah. But—this ain't my fight. It's yours."

The stunned silence followed him as he inched toward the next fire where his wife and children lay curled up in their bedding. By the time he pulled the blankets up to his neck, and Waits nestled her head in the crook of his shoulder—he knew the murmured whispers involved him.

"He'll feel differ'nt come morning," one of the voices said.

Another confided, "Come tomorrow, he'll be better."

Titus Bass slipped out of the robes well before first light. He'd always had trouble sleeping the night before a long journey was to begin.

He was cinching the pack saddle on the last Cheyenne horse, tightening it down on the saddle pad, when he felt the hand laid upon his shoulder. Scratch turned, peering up into the ruddy face.

"I got the feeling this will likely be the last time I ever see you, Titus Bass," the younger man said with difficulty.

Scratch finished looping the cinch strap, then turned to Paddock. "Man was never meant to know what's in store for 'im, Josiah."

"But you and I both know," Paddock declared. "After you went off to your robes last night, Mathew told me just what you'd said to him when you spotted me and Joshua riding down off the hills. Said you wasn't ever coming back here again."

He sighed. "I'd be lying to you if I said I was."

"You're leaving without joining in the fight to get Taos back?"

"Like I tol't you last night—it ain't my fight, Josiah. For all the good days and happy nights I spent in Taos . . . there's 'nough dark memories that the bad comes out weighin' all the more'n good when you hang 'em in the balance. I think it's time I paid attention."

"Paid attention," Paddock sighed. "Like I did when I figured the time had come for me to quit the mountains."

"You get to hear Lady Fate cacklin' at your back only so long afore she slips up behin't you and sinks a knife atween your shoulder blades."

"Taos is all I've got now, Scratch—"

"You don't owe no man no apology for wanting to go back into that village and clean up the mess been made of the life you made for yourself, Josiah," he declared. "Least of all me. I'll be the last man to say how 'nother man should live, where he should draw the line an' make his stand."

"What you think of me has always mattered, ol' man."

Scratch smiled, feeling how that tugged at his heart. "How you thought of me allays meant the world to me too."

"There ain't a chance in hell of talkin' you outta leaving this morning, is there?"

He stared up at Paddock's face, really noticing for the first time how deeply the wrinkles and lines had carved his old friend's face with character. "No, Josiah."

"Then," Josiah said quietly, glancing at the ground while he dragged the back of his hand under his nose, "I suppose you best tell me what I can do to help you get ready for the trail."

Bass laid his hand on Paddock's shoulder. "Afore we load up these here packhorses, what say the two of us mosey back to the fire an' have us a last cup of coffee together, Josiah."

As much as the two old friends kept themselves busy with tying up bundles of baggage and seeing that youngsters ate their breakfast and that bedding was brushed free of snow, then lashed onto one of the three remaining Cheyenne packhorses, there was a weighty tension that grew all the more palpable as the minutes galloped past, one by one, drawing them both closer and closer to the moment of that final farewell.

Finally . . . with the sun's hidden radiance beginning to turn the snowy valley to a pale, blood-kissed pink, the men and women and children circled around those riders who stood beside their eight Cheyenne horses.

"You two'll take good care of one another," Scratch said as he finished hugging Mathew Kinkead.

The hulking giant of a man had tears in his eyes. "We done it afore, Scratch. Josiah and me can do it again."

"Take care of that new family of your'n, Mathew," Titus asked. "They deserve to have you make it back home."

Kinkead swiped some fingers beneath both eyes as he took a step backward. "I know my own self just how it feels to lose someone so special—like my Rosa. I ain't ever gonna make my family go through nothing like that on account of me."

"Maybe you'll sashay up north someday?"

Mathew shrugged. "You never know which way the winds'll blow a man, Titus Bass. When I first come west, never figgered I'd ever quit the mountains. Never figgered I'd raise buffler calves either. Hell, never thought I'd be a trader on the Arkansas . . . so who knows now where I might end up."

"Till then, Mathew Kinkead," Titus snorted away some tears, "you watch your back trail."

The big man started to speak again, but couldn't—so he quickly turned on his heel, spearing his way through the group of frontiersmen who stood as witness to this painful parting.

"There'll always be a place at my table, a dry spot under my roof, for your family, Scratch," Josiah said as he stepped up to Bass's saddle horse.

Titus glanced a moment at how Looks Far and Waits hugged and sobbed, reluctant to let go now that they had again been through so much together. Then he explained, "If there's anything I can count on, it's you, Josiah Paddock. Still, if you're ever to lay eyes on me again, it won't be in no settlement or village or town—be it Mexican or American." He began to choke with emotion, "Goddamn the settlements: they'll likely be the death of me."

Paddock tried futilely to laugh a little as he said, "I remember how the last time you left Taos, you told me, 'Damn the settlements while there's still buffler in the mountains.' "

"I'd sooner die, Josiah—than have anything to do with where folks gather up elbow to elbow, side by side by side. There'll be no Saint Louis, no Oregon, no Pueblo, an' no Taos for this here child. Not for what days I still got left me. Where folks plop down right next to one another . . . there's bound to be trouble raise its head, just sure as that sun's coming to light this day."

Paddock confessed, "Last night I laid there thinking— how in so many ways, I wished it were years ago now, Scratch. An' we was back in the mountains. Living and laughing—"

"Much as I wish it could be so, Josiah . . . that was a time just ain't ever gonna be again. There's forts on the Arkansas an' the South Platte. I've see'd where emigrants been cutting wagon ruts all the way from Westport landing clear out to Oregon country. An' I'm afraid when they got that territory all crowded up out there, them settlers gonna come washing back here to fill in what country they passed through on their way to Oregon."

"With all that's changing around you," Paddock admitted, "Titus Bass isn't a man much ready to change."

Scratch shook his head. "A man either figures he can live all crowded up with folks—with trouble a constant shadow lurking just outside his door . . . or he sets his sights on taking those he loves off away from the shove and clutter of so many others."

"Listen, Scratch," Josiah said with a sudden breathlessness, "I haven't talked about this with Looks Far, but maybe you should take her and our children north with you." He blurted it out in a gush. "They'll be safer with you than they'll be in these hills while we got some bloody work left to do before Taos is safe for women and children again—"

"No, Josiah," he interrupted, clamping both hands on the taller man's shoulder. "What's your family gonna do 'thout you—their husband and father?"

Bass watched the worry darken Paddock's eyes, recognized the pain there, and sensed the stab of guilt anew for that time years ago when he had abandoned his own loved ones to steal some California horses.

"You're all the family they have, Josiah. There is no other kin for any of 'em to turn to down here. If they come with me, and you never find us in Crow country, they'll never know for the rest of their days what really become of you. I learned firsthand that's no way to leave things be with the ones you love."

"Every now and then"—and Paddock wagged his head—"it gets real hard for me to know what to do."

"Right or wrong, Josiah—live or die, you keep your family by your side. Now that you're gonna make Taos safe for families again, you keep Looks Far and all your young'uns close . . . that way they can hug you if you drive back all them Mex and Pueblo murderers. Or, they can hold you in their arms if you're terrible wounded. They can even bury you proper if your time's been called. But one way or the other, Josiah—your family deserves to know."

"You'd never be happy anywhere but that north country," Paddock said after he embraced Bass again. "Back in your mountains."

"That's why I'm takin' my family home."

"Sometime last night," Josiah said, "I thought on just what you should name the land where it is you belong."

"What you figger I should call it?"

Paddock blinked, and said, "The used-to-be-country."

Scratch repeated the words in a soft whisper. "Used-to-be-country."

Then he sighed and signaled his children to mount up. Titus cupped his two hands together and hoisted young Jackrabbit onto the buffalo-hide pad draped over the wide back of a gentle horse.

"Flea," Bass instructed in Crow, turning to his older boy, "you take your little brother and start these three packhorses down to the valley. Rest of us should catch up to you by the time you turn north. Follow the tracks. They're plain enough. You'll do just fine with your horse medicine."

The ten-year-old beamed with pride, sitting up all the straighter on his claybank gelding as he slapped the rump of his little brother's horse and jerked on the lead rope strung back to the pack animals. Flea called over his shoulder, "See you down the trail, Popo."

Magpie and Waits-by-the-Water sat atop their ponies as the clatter of hooves faded and things grew very still, all but for the crackle of the morning fires, and that cold winter breeze sighing through the sage and cedar.

Dragging his sleeve beneath his runny nose, Scratch climbed slowly into the saddle. Sensing how his bones were getting old. This cold hurt more and more every winter. And damn, if he couldn't point out to you every last one of the bullet, knife, and arrow wounds he had suffered since setting his heart on a home in those high and terrible places among the Rocky Mountains. This journey north in the middle of winter had all the makings of a tough one for the old man and his family.

But at least he had his nose pointed for home.

"My used-to-be-country," he quietly repeated what Josiah had called those northern mountains while he put the Cheyenne horse into motion down the slope. "Sounds to me like it's just the sort of place for a used-to-be-man."

ABOUT THE AUTHOR

TERRY C. JOHNSTON was born the first day of 1947 on the plains of Kansas, and has lived all his life in the American West. His first novel, *Carry the Wind*, won the Medicine Pipe Bearer's Award from the Western Writers of America, and his subsequent books, among them *Dance on the Wind, Cry of the Hawk*, and *Long Winter Gone*, have appeared on bestseller lists throughout the country. He lives and writes in Big Sky country near Billings, Montana.

Each year Terry and wife, Vanette, publish their annual "WinterSong" newsletter. Twice every summer they take readers on one-week tours of the rendezvous sites of the early Rocky Mountain Fur Trade, and to the battle sites of the Indian Wars.

Those wanting to write to the author, those requesting the annual "WinterSong" newsletter, or those desiring information on taking part in the author's summer historical tours can write to him at:

Terry C. Johnston
P. O. Box 50594
Billings, MT 59105

Or, you can find his website at:

http://www.imt.net/~tjohnston/

and can e-mail him at:

tjohnston@imt.net

TERRY C. JOHNSTON

Ask for these books at your local bookstore or use this page to order.

Please send me the books I have checked above. I am enclosing $____(add $2.50 to cover postage and handling). Send check or money order, no cash or C.O.D.'s, please.

Name _____

Address _____

City/State/Zip _____

Send order to: Bantam Books, Dept. TJ, 2451 S. Wolf Rd., Des Plaines, IL 60018
Allow four to six weeks for delivery.
Prices and availability subject to change without notice.   TJ 6/00